The Method Actors

Shoemaker & Hoard   *Washington, D.C.*

The Method Actors

· A NOVEL ·

Carl Shuker

The author would like to thank the following publishers for permission to reprint material from:
The Historian's Craft, by Marc Bloch (Manchester University, 1953); *Shakespeare: The Invention of the
Human*, by Harold Bloom (Riverhead Books, 1999); "China Girl" Written by Iggy Pop and David
Bowie © 1977 James Osterberg Music (BMI) / Administered by BUG EMI Music Publishing /
Jones Music America (PRS). All Rights Reserved. Used by Permission. "Wake Me Up Before You
Go Go" and "Careless Whisper" by Wham! Published by Warner/Chappell Music Inc.

This novel was completed with the assistance of a grant from Creative New Zealand.

Library of Congress Cataloging-in-Publication Data
Shuker, R. Carl, 1974–
The method actors : a novel / R. Carl Shuker.
p. cm.
ISBN 1-59376-065-5 (alk. paper)
1. Missing persons—Fiction. 2. Military historians—Fiction.
3. Brothers and sisters—Fiction. 4. Japan—Historiography—Fiction.
5. World War, 1939-1945—Historiography—Fiction. 6. New York (N.Y.)—Fiction.
7. Tokyo (Japan)—Fiction. 8. New Zealand—Fiction. I. Title.
PR9639.4.S56M48 2005
823'.92—dc22
2004025463

Book design by Mark McGarry
Set in Dante

Printed in the United States of America

Shoemaker [SH] Hoard
A Division of Avalon Publishing Group, Inc.
Distributed by Publishers Group West

10 9 8 7 6 5 4 3 2 1

To

Ryan Skelton   *Anna Smaill*   *Melissa Boehman*

Contents

At that time there was no general term or special term used for the acts that had been committed.

—Itaro Ishii on the witness stand

The Method Actors

Prologue
Going Down the Rabbit-Hole

The young historian sits at his desk high above Tokyo on the day he disappears.

It's Christmas, and Shinjuku is a ghost town, the population of the city gone to parts unknown, or, as is traditional for a J Christmas dinner, to a KFC. The young man is of a nationality not halfway decipherable; perhaps part Japanese judging by his eyes, his thick and short black hair shaved hard back, and his waxen skin: the color and depth of wax melted, cooled and clouded. Who could say for sure, but he's young, and in this air-conditioned hotel room high in the Shinjuku Prince he sits at a desk piled with primary sources, lost in thought, and he is tapping his forehead at the hairline with a small piece of a sword. He is wearing, in this bitter Japanese winter, just jeans and a gray marl T-shirt, from a Shimokitazawa military surplus store, with a single word—BUNDESWEHR—capitalized across the chest.

He checks his watch.

And then, as if perhaps surprised to find how much time really has passed, he checks the room around him: it's still large, beige and empty but for a gigantic mirror leaned beside the kitchen door, and this explosion of static activity where he sits. Empty, and listen for the hiss and buzz of quality aircon, that sounds like a whispered *businessbusinessbusiness*. He turns back to his desk, and after a moment lapses again into thought; taps his forehead; scratches at his hairline with the *kissaki,* the flat expanse of steel on the flanks of the very tip of the broken sword.

What's on his desk?

Old photographs of crisply moustached military men, letters from embassies, pieces of Imperial Army insignia, an empty Smirnoff vodka bottle. The crimped and drooping tentacles of power and internet connections. An empty plastic baggie with crumbs of something blue inside. A picture of Marilyn Monroe, a Larry Burrows photograph of a GI waist-deep in a river with a rocket launcher on his shoulder, stacks of papers, records of the dead from competing sources, maps of mass burial sites, three volumes—on the desk; more are stacked on the floor—of Northcroft's Tokyo War Crimes Trial transcript, lifted from the unculled collection of three hundred and seventy-seven volumes at the University of Canterbury in Christchurch. Moldering in the Stack, these books are the originals, from one of only eleven sets in the world. And thus they must be stolen. And papers of survivors' testimonial are arrayed before him as if too well thumbed; like the playing cards of a strewn pack, hinting at his suspended game of atrocity solitaire.

His eyes move down the list of the eleven judges on the wall over his desk, and he scratches at his forehead with the sword. He's waiting for something. He checks his watch, then by way of passing time turns over the first page—a new arrival, a new translation—and begins to read aloud in a firm clear voice, pristinely free of emphasis and accent, tinged even, maybe, with a tang of the sardonically amused:

"'Under Mufu Mountain, Command is encamped. I can hear, distinctly, three sounds. The first is the General coughing. Abed and tubercular, he coughs with a painful, hacking sound. How violent the disease must be to a frame so small as his. The second is something between a sense and a sound. Not too far off, the mighty Yangtze, in flood, awesome miles wide, sprawls through the plains. From my tent alongside his I can see nothing but darkness to the North, but to see that river once is to imprint it like a flash upon your eye, a score across your heart. Somehow even darkened miles distant I see and hear that river.'

"'The third sound carries no such ambiguity or sentimentality.'

"'To the West the sky is orange with fires. Gunfire crackles through the air—thin and clear and never-ending. They are already mopping up at Nanking while I tent next to the Commander-in-Chief, the sickly victor, hacking in his cot.'

"'A sergeant says he hears the pillage is awful and wonderful. He tells me of rumors, Prince Asaka's 16th slaughtering them like pigs.'

"'I have listened in silence to the commanders, who report to the General an orderly invasion; restraint; running water already restored.'

"'I work on my translations. I write poems about the things I see and the way I feel, and wait.'

"'I am furious at my posting; eager to see the vanquished city and find out for myself.'

"From diary entry for December fourteen, 1937, of Lieutenant-Colonel Yamagata Daisuke of the Central China Expeditionary Forces, Japanese Imperial Army, under General Matsui Iwane. As translated by Ko Ishikawa at Keio University, Tokyo, at the behest of Michael James Edwards. Misaddressed and finally arrived yesterday. Too late to make a difference."

He places the translation on the pile, stares a little while at an exposed piece of desk, an odd brown geometrically obscure shape left there, bare—a trapdoor through the confluence of all this paper. Then he picks up a yellow pencil and begins to sketch intently and impatiently on the wood, and as he draws it becomes apparent that the shape being drawn is in fact upon the wood and not any of these piled papers for a very good reason: the outline, eyes and ridged contours of the muzzle of a horse; the shadows of the nostrils like a skull's velvet dark and empty eyes and the grain of the mane and the shine of the hair, all suggested by the depths and distortions in the mahogany.

He adds a final touch: a unicorn's horn on the horse's gnarled brow; though the horn is odd: not conic as would be expected but the merest suggestion of a curve, and narrow, too; fine to the point of resembling a blade. He shades in a rippled wave down its length. It seems to approximate the ripple left by the swordmaker's hammer down the real blade he holds in his other hand. Then in the mahogany flames appear, and the student of history turns a page.

"'Lined up by the river at the docks by Li Gang's warehouse, just west of the city,'" he reads in the same cool, accentless voice. "'I estimate there were a thousand of us. The Japanese men smoked cigarettes and erected machine gun tripods. The shoemaker kept clutching at my elbow, I remember. I remember that, and how he scratched at himself in fear when I shook him off. It was a moment of pure aloneness. One thousand alone Chinese men, standing at the edge. We could hear screams, and suspected what was happening in the city. To our daughters, to our women. This was the second day proper—they hadn't calmed their frenzies; these executions were messy and brisk. There was no order. My friends were screaming. The machine gunners had clean uniforms; they'd just arrived. I'd seen children tied with signal corps telephone wire. Threaded through their bodies. Terrible things. I was shot in the hip and fell into the river with the rest. Miles down I climbed onto the bank. I distinctly remember trying to decide how to drag my useless legs up the bank; where to put my hands. Atop the bodies that lined the bank, the soggy moist bodies, or between them, where my hands would surely sink into the mud and bring me face to face with someone I might recognize.'

"From speech read by Zhang Lao, seventy-seven, at Nanking Memorial Museum, China, at the Nanking Commemoration Conference, six slash fifteen slash ninety-seven. Recorded and translated by Michael James Edwards."

His eyes squint, and he scratches at his skull with the sword. Written under the burning horse, now: *And how we do love helpless things and glory doomed to failure!—and so what it is to eat of that which all and only ever eats.*

And under this: *call Dad.*

He turns another page.

"'Yes, I remember actually this botanist from New York who was researching of all things some freakish Chinese corn only found in the Nanking area that was delivering massive yields, huge per-acre poundages, and was more than likely a useful cash crop in Illinois or Iowa or some such. But the botanist told me that in his opinion the average Chinese was dirty and hysterical but passionate; versus the average Japanese, who was clean and disciplined but completely lacking any individual spark or flair of any kind. He had a theory that a Sino-Japanese hybrid would be an Asian he could respect. He was a xenophobe and a bigot, and I told him so. I remember him saying, somehow quite slyly, "Yes, John, but I am xenophobic and bigoted *for a reason.*"'

"'I got out of Nanking just in time, in November, and I didn't hear the stories of what was supposed to have gone on afterwards for months. And what I took away with me personally were three things.'

"'One was a memory I have of a Chinese doctor—a friend of a zoologist friend of mine, Hamish Macintyre—a Chinese doctor having a fit in the faculty common room at Nanking University, getting very worked up, and waving his arms around, saying there'd been some terrible massacre on the way to Mufu, and that worse, much worse was to come. Screeching rape and scorched earth. And I remember us all sitting around very naïve and bemused.'

"'The second was a telegram the faculty received from the Japanese Embassy after Hamish made some polite, probably quite badly translated enquiries, suggesting nicely that if we felt uneasy in the city we were welcome to leave by boat and that we would go unmolested. We believed them and we were right to, because, of course, this was before the USS *Panay* was sunk and before our government did little or nothing about it.'

"'The other thing I took away was a long, loathsome depression, and the conviction—if you'll allow me to wax lyrical a moment—that when oil is poured into water, anything else in the mix just sits at one edge or another.'

"Excerpt of interview with John Henry Barnes, eighty-one. Interview as conducted in Twin Falls, Idaho, by Michael James Edwards, zero four slash eleven slash ninety-nine. Barnes died four weeks subsequent to our interview. None of the others mentioned in his interview are living, now, either."

As he finishes the last line aloud, from the very tip of his long, narrow, un-Japanese nose falls a drop of blood that spatters on the text with an audible dry tap. Closing his eyes for a moment, and then opening them slowly again. Soon another spatters there and together they begin to spread and obscure the words.

He watches the fallen drops touch each other tenderly, a test, as if he is waiting, as if these drops will change; change again. He removes the sword from his forehead. Outside the Prince Hotel a bitter wind roars muffledly like a dull and blundering static, obscuring the sizzle of the air-con for seconds at a time. A spider, a surprise, skitters certainly across the pages, and at the tiny garish Rorschach of spattered blood on the text it stops. And waits.

He stares at it. And after that he disappears for the last time.

I

Green Rooms

Yasu
September 2000

The young mycologist's name is Yasu, short for Yasuhiko.

His grandfather was born in Tokyo, fifteen hundred miles from China, on the same day that tubercular General Matsui Iwane of the Japanese Imperial Army had, on horseback, formally entered the Mountain Gate of Nanking, the city curled into the banks of the Yangtze, to find the streets of the old capital he had conquered from an army cot, feverish and coughing blood, streets he had conquered *in absentia,* filled with cheering soldiers and completely emptied of corpses, equipment, civilian blood and rapists' ejaculate. The birthmarks of atrocity lasered clean from his infant campaign for China.

Yasu's grandfather was born that day, December 17, 1937, but Yasu is unaware of the coincidence. And if someone had ever tried to explain the significance of the date to him, tried to explicate the weight of the events, to fathom his ignorance, to extract some emotive response, he would probably have shrugged. He would have nodded, wondered vaguely if this meant he was guilty of something furthest from his mind, again.

He knew about the events of the subsequent six weeks and eight years only from the weight given to silence; the reverence afforded ghosts. Spun-off associations: faded glory, decline, the beginnings of ends, corruption. A baffling miasma of the expectation of guilt for something unreal, the need to demonstrate it, the need to keep it hidden; a miasma darkened further by the need to never let it solidify into the thing, guilt, itself. When he thought of Japan and the war, he felt confused pride. The pride of impact; of force and righteous potency now waned. When he thought of China he felt a four-thousand-year-old waiting, a dark thing looming blindly, yet hunched, muscular in Asia, crouched in a deeply shadowed hole.

He felt confused, so at twenty-five, a scientist, isolated, ostracized, he did not entertain thoughts of war much at all.

He lives alone now, in his parents' apartment out in steamy, concrete Saitama, twenty minutes by train from metropolitan Tokyo. He is alone, orphaned and dishonored in the community, expelled from a doctorate at Saitama University on suspicion of drug offenses. What this means mostly to Yasu, the most visible and felt aspect of his exile day to day, is that he no longer gets service in the restaurants his father took him to as a child. The mamas in the sushi store, the yakitori shop, the ramen store, don't smile or tousle his hair now. They look away when he passes them standing outside their stores, sweeping the dirt from the road with their brooms made of bundled twigs. He buys his cigarettes, the same brand as his father's, from a vending machine instead of from the old woman at the tobacconist's. He eats at Jonathan's, or Denny's. ¥290 gyudon from Yoshinoya. And takeout from Burger King, McDonald's, Mos Burger. Bento boxes, instant ramen and cans of six percent by volume grape Chu-Hai from the 7-11 or the Familymart.

He doesn't grow his mushrooms in a laboratory, for research, anymore. He grows them in his bedroom in his dead parents' apartment where the jars of their ashes once sat on the blacked-out windowsill; he has converted the bedroom into a large terrarium. He grows them now for love.

And foreigners' money.

Yasu is always disturbed at seven o'clock, from Monday to Saturday, by the sounds of the family who live in the apartment above him getting ready for the day. There is only one child now, a boy of five, who goes to the elementary school on the next block, a mother and a father who works in Tokyo. A little girl of ten has been missing, presumed abducted, for just on three months.

Sometimes at night he sees the father from the upstairs apartment, returning home late from drinking, with his tie undone, staggering up the road from the last train. He curses anonymous bosses, or his own helplessness, maybe; shouts out, *"Baka!"*—idiot!—*"Bakayaro,"* to the thick, wet night. Vomits, sometimes, into the gutter. Yasu has no air-conditioning and his living room is very hot, but he always goes quickly inside and plays a little Gameboy, smoking furiously, or chews some lukewarm Burger King for a while. Once the man gets inside—an echoing, metallic trawl up the iron steps in back—and the low voices above him merge into shouts and the crying of the lonely little boy, Yasu goes back outside.

He is considerate. He is shy. He is pariah, and knows it.

At seven o'clock this morning in September, it is too hot to sleep in Saitama. The humidity meter on the wall beside the airlock to Yasu's converted bedroom is reading the same as outside: 95%. 95% is perfect.

But the heat—his thermometer, on the wall alongside the humidity meter, is reading in the high nineties, nearly forty degrees Celsius—this, for a shroom, means rapid thermal death.

Yasu sometimes sees the drunk father because, late at night or early in the morning, like today, in summertime when he can't sleep, before he checks his converted bedroom, Yasu rises from his futon and goes outside to water his own—dead—father's bonsai.

The tiny apartment is still in his father's name, though he died five years ago, when Yasu was nineteen and studying undergraduate plant biology at his first university, Rikkyo, in Ikebukuro in Tokyo.

Yasu remembers his father mostly only from Sundays, his one day off in a seventy-hour working week.

On a Sunday, sitting hunched on a stool in the path, holding pliers, a thin man winding wire through the roots of a new tree.

The cancer is already in him, and he peers down his nose at the azalea, through the strong, lower portion of his bifocals and the drifting smoke of a Mild Seven. Quietly, to the tree, and to young Yasu cross-legged beside him on the path, his father says, "Tight is tight for now and a long time, Yasu." A small silence. "Too tight is forever broken."

There are two small rooms in the apartment, with a tiny kitchen and an even tinier bathroom. As close as he is to the station, a five-minute brisk walk, the apartment is typical in Saitama for two fairly well-off people, even spacious. The living room where Yasu now sleeps and eats has sliding doors that open onto a tiny veranda. His old bedroom is off to the left of the living room. There are no actual doors inside the house, so in the bedroom's narrow doorway a large makeshift polythene airlock hangs like a plastic-wrapped corpse, stuffed and taped into the frame. The house has tatami matting in the living room and did once in the bedroom, but tatami in a humid summer is a greenhouse for bacteria and all kinds of invasive fungi, and he has torn it up.

The kitchen is at the rear of the apartment, a thin strip of linoleum

made even thinner by the stacks of fat comics and softporn *Splash!* magazines, and the heaps of rubbish, the cup noodle bowls and greasy convenience store trays swarming with tiny Saitama flies, the Burger King bags,
Mild Seven cigarette packets, the Chu-Hai cans and used tissues, the disposable hashi littered over the landscape of trash like the strewn, stripped trees
of a flash flood. The rubbish is heaped against the wall opposite the sink
and the bathroom door and is settling like a fragrant, moist pile of leaves.
The kitchen's small refrigerator has long ago been moved into the bedroom and a slightly less densely packed square of rubbish, in the far corner
of the kitchen by the almost-blocked back door, reveals its previous home.

All because Yasu doesn't cook, and isn't quite sure which day trash is
taken away.

There is little left of his parents' presence in the living room, either. In
the corner a 20-inch Sony Trinitron sits on a Sony HiFi video that sits in
turn on a Nakamichi amplifier, a double MD player and a DVD. The
speakers have thick cables that cost over ¥15,000 a yard. There is a brand
new titanium Macintosh G-4 Powerbook, closed and charging. There are
CD-ROMs, CDs, DVDs and MDs, hundreds of them, stacked on the TV
and the tatami all around the tower of equipment. There are piles of
videotapes, *Beautiful Woman's Fan, Schoolgirl Rape!, Mortal Kombat: Annihi-
lation,* all seven seasons of *Melrose Place.* In the opposite corner by the
kitchen doorway a mound of clothes blocks access to the wardrobe door,
where a ripped poster of Mariah Carey in a tiny Santa suit hangs, dog-
eared at one corner. Littered over the rest of the floor, a bare few feet of
tattered tatami, are magazines, four brimming ashtrays, an embossed
Zippo, a bottle of illegal internet Zoloft, some expensive hardback mycological texts under a book titled in Japanese *Speak Perfect Conversational
English in Four Weeks.* There are two or three old spore syringes, an old
microscope, a Playstation, a deck of American pornographic playing
cards, a scalpel. When he tries to sleep in the summer, Yasu moves it all
just enough to unroll his futon, and in the morning—or the afternoon,
whenever he wakes up—rolls the futon up and lets all the ephemera of
someone unused to money gather around him again, sitting cross-legged,
sweating, in the center of the tiny room.

Outside the house the disorder has a different bent.

From the living room's tiny veranda out to the street, and the concertina gate that is beginning to rust and stick, there is a narrow path that
runs between waist-high concrete block walls.

The path is squares of concrete surrounded by loose stones, once regularly raked smooth and carefully weeded by his father, now patched green and brown, pocked and heaped by shuffling feet. And lining each side of the path is bamboo shelving, tied at the vertices with twine. The shelving built by his father before he was born, and although the thick bamboo is now dark brown and frayed, and the twine knots caked with the ashy black sediment of Saitama air, the racks for Yasu's father's bonsai are rock-solid.

All down the shelves, lining the thin path where his father sat, on two levels, on both sides, almost forty plants, Yasu's father's bonsai decay.

The leaves of the slender maples, the last potting his father ever did, a clump of nine, have grown thick and unruly. The largest maple in particular is a graveyard of ambition. From two branches, lines of dirty string with tiny, empty nooses dangle limply. The stones that once hung there to drag the limbs down have long since fallen free, lost now in the chaos of the path. The branches have grown proudly on their way, absorbing the weightless yokes in bark.

The dangling strings are as dirty and hairy as the peeling raffia wrapped around the branches of a tiny Chinese elm, bandages to heal the wounds of an overheavy pruning. And a lone bonsai jack, shaped like a capital G, tied to the elm's trunk to correct an unsightly lean, or to foster an elegant one, has rusted solid. The job finished long ago, it hangs loosely in its harness, both incongruous and peaceful, like rusting military equipment abandoned in a jungle.

An ochre moss has crept inexorably up the double trunks of a miniature maidenhair, intercepting the tree's moisture, and the drying powdery soil has shrunk away from the sides of the tray. The maidenhair leans inappropriately now, held only by its roots wired through the tray to the bamboo.

There are weeds growing in the ancient azalea's tray, and the spring blooms that once frothed brilliant pink under his father's steady hands are now always sporadic and uneven, brown with disease.

A cascading juniper has had to be turned to prevent it from crowding the path.

In the fifth hot, wet summer since his death, all his father's carefully engineered distortions are steadily either righting or perpetuating themselves.

And so here's Yasu, plump, twenty-five, walking down the path in shorts, sandals, YALE T-shirt and glasses. At seven o'clock in the morning in September's still-soupy summer heat, woken by the voices and clatter of breakfast from above, knowing the strange French boy is coming today, Michael-san's friend—and knowing he will have to decide if he will hand over the terrible new blue unnamed and miraculous mushroom to take away for Michael-san—and so this might be it, in the summer, when you never can really feel success, this is forever the unfortunate timing of achievement—and he is watering his father's rabid bonsai with the special bonsai watering can (with holes so small the spray is just the merest mist), watering the bonsai and, occasionally, his own face.

And nouveau riche Yasu finds himself thickly fascinated at the ruin of his father's labors. Somehow unwilling to lift a hand to stop or slow it, the decay, and sometimes even finding himself bent double over the slanted trunk of a windswept black pine that has begun perceptibly to straighten, examining the tortured, writhing effect in the very tips of the branches, wiping the can's spray from his glasses with the back of his hand and peering closely, trying to locate the exact spot on the twisted trunk's rough bark where the tiny pine had begun to adjust itself to freedom.

Catherine
March 2001

Nedan dake. Just the price.

This is the last Japanese phrase I learned in Japan. I used it half an hour ago, here on the plane, on the runway at Narita, pointing at the duty-free Gucci in the inflight magazine. But when she answered, the J-looking flight attendant had a Canadian accent.

"You'll find all the prices in the back, ma'am."

Outside the window I'm watching the city fall away. We took off at eight and it is getting very dark very quickly and from this height the expressways are long seams of light through the crumpled fabric of the outer suburbs east of Tokyo, Chiba, maybe almost Ibaraki. The coastline is suddenly revealed. It's hard for me to process the speed at which we are leaving the country. The coast is a wandering ragged crack dividing the land, which is sprinkled with light to the very edges, and the ocean: black and midnight and dense. I press the service button on the arm of the chair by my thigh and the older Japanese man in the seat next to me, already trying to sleep, flinches. He has nice glasses and has drawn the airline blanket up to his chin. He has good skin, tan and creamy, a weird shine in his cheeks. He flinches again. I can tell it's because he's dreaming. Michael told me after the only night in his rooms at the Shinjuku Prince I refused to have sex with him that I flinched and muttered and convulsed all night. He used the word "convulsed." As in, "You convulsed all night."

I never told Michael I know he sweats in his sleep. I did not tell him that there have been nights I have reached out to touch him on the huge bed, thinking him fast asleep, his breathing regular and heavy, no dreaming airless shallow gasps, his face smooth and unworried, lips still and open. He sleeps flat on his back, perfectly still, like a corpse, his arms at his sides, hands resting in his groin, like a child: a dead child, hands in its lap. I did not tell him that there have been nights I have reached out and touched his chest and recoiled from the heat of his skin, the bitter intensity of it, a boiling jug's spray. I did not tell him that in the middle of the night in his rooms at the hotel that he kept at 75°F summer and winter I have peeled the sheet back and seen patches of wet, dark enough to be visible in the darkness of the bedroom, and that he would not move, lie there still as a lean, tan corpse disinterred, beads of sweat across his chest, dotted around the tiny key on the thin silver chain he never removes, pooling in the separations of his stomach muscles, running in glinting streaks down his ribs.

It was another thing we did not talk about.

I order a glass of chardonnay from a different flight attendant, and wait for it to arrive. It will be my fifth for the day but only my second on this flight. You use the phrase *nedan dake* when you are buying something or selling something, or more precisely, when you are thinking of selling something but you want to know how much it is worth, or thinking of buying something and you want to know how much it will cost. *Ne* pronounced "nay"; *dan* pronounced broadly, "dahn"; *dake:* "dah-kay," with an equal stress on each syllable: "nay-dan-dah-kay." Just the price.

I have my first essay to write for the Phoenix correspondence course, I remember. I consider reaching down for the blueberry Miu Miu handbag, the nicest thing I own, the bag he bought me, to find out the question, but my chardonnay arrives, and I don't. I am twenty-four. It is March. The question is on Shakespeare's *Twelfth Night*. Michael had the book and the course sent to me. As a gift; with a card inside the book. In a box with no return address, postmarked Wellington. I have my laptop in the overhead compartment. I could start work on it now. I have gone to the limit on my American Express for this trip that no one, not even my husband, knows about. Since my father's death this presents no serious problem. I am giggling. The Japanese man is flinching. I may be doing a stupid, stupid thing. When you only want to know the *price*. It's even possible he may not be there, where I am going, and if I know anything, he certainly won't be *waiting*.

In the small rectangular window the shielded light above me is catching my reflection's hair, but nothing of her face. What I see of her is blond wavy hair to the graywhite shoulders of a Chanel suit. The suit is creamblue in sunlight and I feel old inside it, but I always wear a suit when I fly. Her face is a darkness filled with stars, and I lean back so the light catches her nose, her cheekbones and lips. But her eyes look like black hollows to me and I feel stupid and too drunk so I lean closer to the window and shut out the light with my hands.

And I see that down at ground level we have crossed the coastline, revealed only by the fact of: no more lights. Into a pure, near-abstract blackness, maybe thirty, maybe sixty miles up the coast from Tokyo Bay a peninsula looks to me like a ghostly, semiformed finger made of shifting lights, hooked and gnarled, pointing blindly into the Pacific and the way we are going. Somehow angry, the lights moving in it, blind, semiformed creatures, real or imagined, moving behind it, as if in a dream, words coming to me: *oishii,* Bruno Magli, Anna Molinari, Consuelo Castiglioni designing at Marni, pearls from Paspaley, a lyric he lilted to me: "Lotta lost motherfuckers, stuck on what they gonna be." Do you love me. We're going into night, the hours we jettison will fall like scales through time zones and clouds, and though he injures me my light is something none but him will ever see.

I am a rose.

I was not really aware that the relationship with Michael had really ended when I went home for Christmas, almost three months ago. It's all over now, and to make any sense of it all you have to go back from so many directions. I was home for two weeks, till just before Christmas.

This is my memory of my mother's first words to me in the airport garage at JFK.

I have to load my luggage in the back of the Audi myself while she waits behind the wheel. She starts the engine as I close the trunk. I get in the passenger seat, close the door, sigh.

"Hi."

She says nothing. Traffic this night is atrocious and whole lanes into Manhattan are closed down by snow and accidents. My mother has avoided the Fifty-ninth Street Bridge on reports from WINS. We're headed for the Upper West Side, Columbia and Mom's apartment in Morningside Heights. But it doesn't matter anyway because we slow to a crawl over Hell's Gate and finally come to a complete halt, trapped in a jam in no-man's-land on the Triborough Bridge, right above where the Harlem joins the East. My mother stares out her window down through the whirling snow at the black mass of the converging rivers, the streaks of traffic trapped all down the FDR. And the news is the East Side is a mess, an overturned semitrailer spilling dry goods all over First Ave, two tollbooths knocked out due to construction. I pick through my handbag, jet-lagged, so tired after the nineteen-hour flight, Narita–Hawaii, Hawaii–LAX, LAX–JFK, I feel like there's glass dust in my eyeballs, lead in my belly. I find some lipstick, flip down the sunvisor. My mother sighs, works the stick through each gear. She's wearing only jeans and a parka, no glasses. She checks the mirror, turns to me and looks at my hair, my coat, the bag, the suit, my shoes, back up to my hair. I ignore this, stare up into the mirror on the visor, try not to look at my eyes that are bloodshot and bagged. It's even enough, I make a kiss, close the visor, return the lipstick to the Miu Miu, ignore my mother's stare. She eventually turns back to the snow blowing between us and the taillights smearing across the windscreen. She checks the rearview mirror again, works the gears again, sighs, subsides into the upholstery. And then she says, "You look like an anorexic."

After my winter vacation I flew straight back to Japan. I took the N'EX from Narita airport into Tokyo, a ninety-minute trip, and I arrive in Shinjuku at eleven o'clock and from a bank of phones by a Doutor coffee shop call Yu first at the apartment in Daikanyama, then at his office at Rikkyo U. where he's still working, and I lie, tell him that I'm still out at the airport, customs trouble with some handmade cigars I bought for him from some expensive cigar shop in TriBeCa, that I won't make the last N'EX into Tokyo let alone the subways, and that I have to stay in a hotel out here.

("Oh, really? Uh-huh. That's fine," he says. Long silence. "I mean, were they . . . confiscated?" It takes him a little while to locate the word. He uses the special toneless tone of someone using a second language, who's not sure they've said the right thing, and knows you know what the right thing is. The voice suddenly emptying any human warmth or inflection, just the trained interrogative lilt at the end, even now, with me, after two years of marriage; this is one of the reasons I sleep around on him: his voice. It's enough for me to fake a tantrum: "So that's all that matters? I'm jet-lagged, Yu. I'm exhausted. New York's freezing, Tokyo's freezing, the whole fucking planet is cold, yes I got the cigars, and I'm staying out here tonight," etc, etc. I make him glad to leave me alone.)

(Yu will only find out that this time I'm gone forever when he gets home from Rikkyo—always so late—and finds the box I left him on the bed in the apartment. It contains a letter, some photographs, the Anne Klein II crucifix he bought me from Marui and a copy of a biography of Anna May Wong.)

I choose the South exit from Shinjuku station because I can use escalators all the way. And I take a taxi to the Prince even though it's only maybe a couple of minutes to walk, maybe two hundred yards away, the driver has to confirm the destination, the fare doesn't even pass flagfall.

Outside the hotel leafless trees in concrete tubes are whipped against the plate glass by the merciless wind coming down the street. I have come to realize that wind is far colder than snow ever is. Snow muffles, suspends. Wind chills. The staff here still treat me like a stranger even though I know some of their faces better than my brother's. They collect my luggage and call me "Mahm."

I take the elevator to the penthouse suites, tired enough and angry enough to not be afraid or even excited. I walk down the corridor and straight in the open door—Michael's rooms, actually his father's, are the only ones on this floor—and Michael is in boxer shorts, sitting at the desk, working. I don't take my shoes off, because there is no *genkan* or space to leave them anywhere, and hotels like these are so Western it both feels wrong and doesn't seem appropriate. The room is ridiculously huge and neat and totally undecorated apart from the gigantic gilt-framed mirror leaned beside the kitchen door. Through the doors into the bedroom I see a suit laid out on the white queen-size bed, and beside it is a pile of money, ten-thousand-yen notes scattered messily over the duvet. On a 40-inch TV a videotape of a close-up on blue flames is paused. He looks up as I drop the handbag on the coffee table, and I shrug and stalk over to the huge leather sofa. He turns in his chair to follow me.

"Tough trip."

"Don't even bother," I mutter.

"You should have called first," he says. "Where have you been? I could have got you some of those little coffee jellies."

"I called you from New York. A few times." I try to make it sound casual, unconcerned. I try to not think of my name materializing on a tiny screen, his hand casually dropping a beeping phone on a bed.

"Even 3-G phones couldn't reach me where I was," he says.

"You're a drama queen," I say.

"We were method actors," he says. "To know you've gotta feel. To feel you gotta do. What if you could steal imaginations, Cathy? That's what I ask myself, every-morning-I-wake-up."

His sarcasm is horrible, and disbelievingly, shaking my head, I whisper, "Oh fuck you, Michael," but then he's grinning, and I can never help but smile when he does, and his back is long and tan and lean and curving as he turns back to the desk, and I notice more fresh scars on his left upper arm, bright, thin red slits, days-old scars down the muscle, and his hair is very black and shaved very short, and slowly at first, picking through the old books and pages and the digital videotapes spread around a half-empty bottle of Smirnoff, the bottle of Dolce & Gabbana and a piece of a sword on the desk in front of him, speaking as if to himself, his beautiful back to me, he tells me this:

"So, Simon's back in Japan. We were invited to the New Zealand Embassy closing party a week ago. You know about that don't you. Closing the embassies, here and Dubai. They're moving the consul and some of the staff into, quote, rental accommodations. I mean, Dubai's not a bad call. They run out of oil in less than twenty years and they're going to try and survive on tourism. But selling up prime Tomigaya real estate. It's *Tomigaya* for Christ sake. Shibuya-ku. Even though the market hasn't been this depressed in two decades it's still *desirable*. To finance student loan recovery, quote, *strategies* in London. And the scuttling of a few destroyers. Getting ready for the third world. We're a joke here. A sinking—fucking— ship. Everyone knows it, no one talks about it. *I* don't care. Drinking fucking Lindauer. Falling—the fuck—*off.* They wanted the ballroom at the Park Hyatt and it would've been appropriate. It's like Shanghai in the 30's, apocalypse looming, rumors flying. But anyway, they couldn't afford it. So they fly over the Food and Beverage Manager for the fucking Sheraton, and he brings over these crates of Lindauer and smoked salmon and kiwifruit and they have the party in the embassy itself. Think plastic-covered furniture. Think jet-lagged Polynesian waiting staff. Think bins of shredded documents in the bathrooms. Feel the general air of trepidation. My father was invited and refused to go. It's just embarrassing. They're even selling paintings. Anyhow, I'm standing with Simon and the consul and this Indian sushi chef he's found."

He's flicking through pages on the desk. I'm lying back on the long sofa now, and the ceilings in Michael's rooms at the Prince are beige and smooth and relentless. I place the back of my hand over my eyes, relax into the leather. His accent is becoming increasingly northeastern sometimes, New Hampshire, Maine, the thick r's, the rusty, almost lisping sibilants.

"Simon's father is setting up a Japanese food restaurant chain—that's how he refers to it: *Japanese food,* I mean it's not like there's an overwhelming passion or like *drive* in the guy to like make tempura or anything remotely specific, it's there on this prospectus he's just produced: *Japanese Food*—but anyway, Simon's going to manage a branch somewhere in the world, so he's got a place here, his father's got him an apartment in Omotesando, for only like a couple of *months,* quote, researching. This is Omote*sando.* We're talking monthly rental figures with so many zeroes you think you've *bought* an apartment. But anyway, this drunk woman, a PA or embassy secretary, who knows, one of the redundancies anyway, being sent home, comes over to Simon and me, and she's worked in the embassy for maybe eight years and still can't tell he's a Chinese, and she mumbles in just *pig* Japanese, fucking awful flat vowels, 'Oooh, se ga *oki.*' The consul immediately goes to get her another drink. Simon says, 'Oh, thank you. I'm Simon,' in this fat Californian accent. 'And what's your name?' Jesus. 'Se ga ooki.' 'You are large.' It's all she can manage to like elicit after eight years here."

I look out from under my hand and he's scratching notes on a page now, reciting this, like he's reading a part for a play. I love his passion; I love the way he hides it carefully behind the flat anger, the sarcasm he thinks I never get.

"Why . . . are you telling me this Michael?" I say, and I start to laugh.

"And I tell her, get this—"—he's laughing too, now—"*Spend your check wisely baby,* because you're never gonna work in the diplomatic service again, and she knows Dad, she knows who I am, and *learn the fucking language too,* I like, hiss in her ear—"—we're both cracking up now, I'm shaking, too tired by far—"What you're *fumbling* for is *se ga takai,* you are *tall,* which also means you are high, and we will be very soon, I tell her, and you'll find it also means *you are expensive,* and you better be*lieve* it, I say, just like this,"—he pauses, turned in his seat now and looking right at me and when he's laughing he's the most beautiful thing I've ever seen, his eyes bright and fierce, and I'm not laughing now, there's a wetness between my legs that is making me very still, watching his face, the thin slits on his arm, and then down to his stomach, and his long, lean legs—"He *is* expensive."

I stare at him. I don't want to move, I want to be *reminded* how horny I am, how only he can make me feel. "This all sounds a little more like something Simon would tell me," I can tell him coolly. "What are you getting at, Michael?" He looks back at me.

"Anyway, what I'm getting at, Cathy, is that Simon has this apartment in Omotesando. Western-style, multiple rooms, veined marble floors, three to four bathrooms. Even a fish tank. You can probably stay there. The desk's got his keitai number."

Briefly, the burrs and nuances disappear from his accent, his voice seeming to relax into something placeless, international. The beige in this room is colorless and overwhelming.

"Catherine, this is Man. Man, Catherine," he says.

"Hi." The voice comes from the bathroom door. I turn my head, and the girl's Japanese and standing in the doorway and might have been for a long time and she's maybe sixteen and half my height. Her hair's short and black as his. She's gorgeous, but like different species can be gorgeous. She's wearing a negligee. I'm rising slowly, a standing ovation for his scene. My vision's a blur, they are dark shapes at the edges.

It's so *contrived,* I'm thinking. It's ...*cruel?*

"Oh. She's pretty," I hear the girl say as I collect my bag.

In the elevator I lean on the close door kanji until an alarm goes off. I take off my panties and put them in the Miu Miu. Down in the lobby I find a bathroom and try to apply more lipstick but it's a mess and then I'm out in the lobby and the bare trees outside the Prince are whipping and scratching the plate glass and I send the concierge for my luggage and go outside and wave to a taxi and then I stand in the wind for what feels like a long time ignoring the open door of the taxi and then I come back inside and reserve a single room on the third floor and charge it on Yu's Visa and once inside I take off all my clothes and I squat in the gigantic shower where everything is chrome and turn the water on full and hot and wash myself so long I hurt. Then I dry myself off and I go back into the bedroom and I turn the heat up and I sit curled up in a beige velvet armchair for a long time before eventually I do fall asleep, naked on the armchair, fetus-style. This was how it really ended, in Japan, three months ago.

I wake from a dream, woozy and disoriented, sweating, somewhere over the Pacific.

It's getting near dawn. This is just a feeling, because the slide on my window is still down. There are no flight attendants in sight and the galley lights are off. The Japanese is still asleep, his glasses askew, the flexible wings of the seat's headrest supporting his head. The lights in the plane are down, and red LEDs in the floor of the aisle are on to indicate the way to the bathrooms. The movie screen is two rows ahead of me, in the middle aisle, and it, too, is off. The curtains that divide Business and Economy are closed. In Business every passenger but me is asleep. It occurs to me how they engineer this downtime on overnight flights, how they feed us drinks, snacks, dinner. And an hour later, when we are stuffed and drunk and lethargic, they shut the lights down and disappear. I fold my tray up from the arm of the seat and there's an inset circle in the plastic to support a glass. Next to it is a brown ring of spilled coffee. But I don't remember drinking coffee. I fold the tray back down and it squeaks; but the Japanese doesn't stir. I pull out the inflight magazine and flick to the Gucci again. The pricelist in the back tells me that it is AUS$255. Dolce & Gabbana for men is AUS$55 or $125. I hate flying Australian airlines. Yen to U.S. is fine. Everything else I have to do second-order: Yen–U.S.–Australian. I fear losing large sums in the conversion.

I adjust the moneybelt; it's hot against my stomach and the thin leather strap is biting into my hips. In the semidarkness I undo my seatbelt, lift the moneybelt out from under my skirt and unzip it.

I count the money. The ten-thousand-yen notes are moist and soft from the sweat of my dream. I count the money twice.

I remember the dream almost perfectly.

I am somewhere in Roppongi, near the Almond Café and my old clubs. But instead of the usual crowds of tourists and GIs and clubbers there are scenes of poverty, madness, alcoholism. Black men, African touts and pimps from the clubs, in rags worn like togas, with wide, staring eyes. Rows and rows of high-rises. Everywhere burned-out cars on blocks, overgrown grass on the sidewalks, store doorways filled with trash. I arrive well-dressed, on some kind of business. I am in my mother's Range Rover from New York, which she sold after my father died. I leave the car unlocked, and between two buildings I walk down a bare earth path made by hundreds of feet, surrounded by weeds yards high, loomed over by the gray towers of the high-rises. There is the feeling of danger, but urgent business. I walk the path for some time but can't seem to find what I'm looking for, so I turn back. When I get back to the Range Rover there are two black women and a black man sitting inside, from Light, or Flood, Nigerian touts from one of the clubs, maybe the man is even that Senegalese who caused Michael and me to meet. They are all dressed in good suits. They have the exaggerated blankness and silence of guilty children caught in an act. I say, this is my car. Get out of my car, now. The woman behind the wheel, avoiding my eyes, as if I won't see her act if she doesn't see me see, tries to start the engine. I lean in the window to pull her hand from the ignition. I'm somehow unperturbed that the steering wheel is on the right, J style. But the woman in the passenger seat releases the handbrake and the car begins to roll backward. They are all the while silent, intent, desperate. I twist the wheel in her hands, running beside the car, leaning in the high Range Rover window. It turns in a semicircle and hits a wall. The rear corner caves in.

The Tokyo Metropolitan police and my lawyer from New York eventually come. My lawyer tells me the car is someone else's, that these three have a legal claim to my car and, he tells me, my apartment. He looks at me slightly incredulous, disappointed that I could be so childish, not understand such simple things, not understand how clearly I was the guilty one here.

The dream warps. I'm walking on a vast, sloping grassy meadow, beautiful and flowered, in brilliant sunlight. It seems familiar to me. I'm carrying a radiocontrol handset. Ahead of me is the little car I'm controlling. I am guiding it over the meadow, across the grass, yards ahead of me. The only obstacles I must negotiate are small intricate piles of makizushi, stacked Western style in clumsy pyramids. The police, more lawyers, touts from the clubs, hundreds of people are running after the car now, not me, unaware or ignoring that I control it.

The dream warps again. At the foot of the meadow I'm standing beside a doorway in a great glass wall that stretches up out of sight. No more sushi; no more cars. Beyond the wall of glass the woods begin, thick and cool and inviting. The crowds of people are all around me, shouting angrily about my responsibility. Then Michael appears, striding confidently through the hot sun and the crowd, the people parting respectfully for him. He steps up to me and embraces me and I embrace him back, but in my ear I listen to him whisper, kindly, *"Don't look back,"* and down my cheek I feel that he has the nose of a witch, too-long, crooked, warts, tapering early to a pencil-thinness, gnarled and bent and pointing like the finger of lights in the ocean.

And then I wake up, sweating into my money.

I rifle through my bag for my toothbrush and deodorant, and I find the first assignment for the Phoenix class. I leave it on my seat for when I return. There is a lot of legroom in Business, enough for me to step past the sleeping Japanese without disturbing him. I follow the LEDs up the aisle to the forward bathrooms. It's the first time I have stood in five or six hours of flying and I'm unsteady and my legs feel swollen and heavy. I have to hold on to the headrests of the sleeping for support. There are four bathrooms in the alcove, for the maybe thirty passengers in Business.

The doors to the bathrooms fold in leaves, and the alcove is covered in warning stickers. A stick figure smoking a cigarette with a line through him; a smoldering butt with a line through it. On the door there is an open padlock and a closed padlock. There is a mother holding a child on a changing table; a suitcase in the aisle outlawed; a seated stick figure denied. Inside the tiny room an undrained sink is warned against and liquid soap is indicated. There are no words anywhere, only symbols.

I use the bathroom; wash my face and pat it dry with a paper towel. I brush my teeth and apply some deodorant.

The hum of the airplane feels like it is inside me.

Back in my seat I finally read the Phoenix correspondence course's question on *Twelfth Night*.

"Shakespeare, with *Hamlet,* arrives at an impasse still operative in the high comedy of *Twelfth Night,* where Hamlet's inheritor is Feste."

—Harold Bloom, *Shakespeare: The Invention of the Human*

Discuss Feste in terms of his truancy—presence and absence—in the diegesis both before and during the action of *Twelfth Night.* (A starting point might be Maria's quote in Act 1 Sc. 5: "My lady will hang thee for thy absence." Where was Feste? Why? What happened to him? Who was he and what role does he play in the action of *Twelfth Night?* How and what does Feste inherit from Hamlet?)

5000 wds
Due 5/30/01

I'm crying by the time I finish it.

I push my window's slide up. It is getting near dawn. The window is divided: sea and sky. Out at the horizon there are smudged bars of orange. Above them the sky is white fading into cornflower, then cobalt, then midnight blue. Then there is pitch blackness and a single star. The ocean's blackness is more than half the window's contents, bulging at the horizon into the hints of dawn. The orange is strong and deep like old blood on a bedsheet and near-silhouettes of tufts of cumulus cloud are some forgotten film's towers, far out at the end of my vision of the world.

It is strange for me to think that this high up and this enclosed there is no weather, no brutal winds, no muffling snow. Only light and dark. Things are clearer, cleaner, more detached and less real up here. My thoughts seem to move in me like rain-filled clouds; visible to me; separate, heavy, lumbering things. I check my watch. It's 4:03 a.m. Tokyo time, Monday, March 10. I am supposed to arrive in Sydney in three hours and board a connecting flight to Wellington less than two hours later.

I wonder if there is enough of me to make this trip and wonder when it was that I became no longer sure. When he made me a mystery to myself.

My heart feels unsteady; too fast, or too big.

At 4:15 the staff stir and lights in the galley come on.

I never had a chance to ask him about the fresh scars. What happened while I was away. What made him disappear, and what made him feel he had to push me away just before I went. I never had a chance to tell him I can forgive anything because I have done wrong. The worst things in the world according to what I believe.

At 4:18 the movie screen flickers grayly, and a graphic shimmers and consolidates into the South Pacific and our progress. A thick red line begins at Tokyo, Japan a baby at the breast of the Asian continent, and crosses the ocean; at its end, a plane graphic the size of Taiwan.

At 4:30 the captain announces breakfast.

And finally a pinkorange flare, the sun bursts at the horizon, and at this height it's too bright to look at, too intense to resist.

Andrew
Four Days Before Christmas 2000

I'm outside the back of the Bolton St. house with a tumbler of antique Courvoisier brandy and a stogey in one hand, talking to my drug dealer on the cell phone in the other. It's seven o'clock and dinner begins in half an hour and I can hear Elise screaming either at one of the help or Hüsker Dü, up in the house above me; possibly in one of the lounges; possibly the dining. The lower storey of the family house is lit up ludicrously, really a travesty. There are bunches of colored lights pinned all around the ancient cedar architraves, synthetic aerosol snow stencils of stylized Christmas trees sprayed over the hundred-year-old windows of each room. A real Christmas tree, of truly awesome proportions, is visible through the lounge window, propped against the fireplace.

Or rather, I'm *not* talking to my drug dealer because the blasted drug dealer *is not picking up.* I'm pacing past the drained swimming pool, empty since Michael and Meredith moved out, surreptitiously smoking the cigarette. The ring tone is buzzing meaninglessly in my ear, and I cross the lawn, sticking close to the walls of the cellar so I won't be seen from the windows. I sip a little more of the brandy and follow the lawn around to the side of the house. What I am doing would qualify as *sneaking.* At the end of the lawn I turn up the stone path that climbs through the conifers on the south, cold side of the house to the back door porch. But in the lights through the trees I see the damn security guards are watching my lurching progress through the foliage and I curse and turn back, suck quickly on what's left of the cigarette and try to flick it away into the garden without spilling my drink, but of course the drink sloshes and I sidestep quickly and lift the glass up like a toast to the house to save the tuxedo.

I'm checking for glints of liquid on the fabric in the lounge's borrowed light when at last the tone ceases and the bastard picks up.

"Good evening," a flat, dry, *female* voice announces.

I stride back toward the empty pool quickly.

"Never," I say quietly, "confuse the map with the territory."

"What is the map?" she asks.

"Temple, structure, artifice."

"What, then, is the territory?"

"The human heart," I answer.

"A," the voice says, "lovely to hear from you so soon."

"I absolutely *must* borrow a car this evening," I say, and I'm possibly flirting, just a little, with this anonymous voice.

She ponders this, possibly checking some horrendously packed and encrypted schedule of deliveries that could implicate most of the city's legal community.

"Which car would you like, A?"

"Ah, the Citroën, always the Citroën."

"It's a little late, A. I'll have to check with my husband."

"Of course, I understand," I say, but she's gone.

A long silence follows. It has never been a woman before. What does this mean? Possibly just a lot of business tonight. I place my drink carefully on the deck and pat down the tuxedo's pockets for another stogey, watching the windows for signs of life.

The voice returns.

"How long do you need the car for, A?"

Excellent. *Relief.* "Just one hour, if that's convenient and so forth."

"And you need it when?"

"ASAP."

"I'll be around as soon as I can."

"Excellent. I'll leave your nom de guerre at the door," I sign off, droll, but she's unappreciative and hangs up without answering.

I drop the phone in my pocket, and momentarily purposeless I stare up at the huge bulk of the family house, the dark upper storey, the garishly decorated lower. At the width of the lit windows, and the mottles and distortions in the aging glass where the molecules have surrendered to gravity over almost one hundred years. A fact I suppose not widely known: glass shifts over time; is prey to gravity.

And then I'm staring down into the empty swimming pool, at the leaves strewn over the tile and the Perspex of the underwater lights, and at a thin, colorless scarf wound into the drain in the far, deepest corner. And the tarnished chrome ladder bolted to the wall of the pool above the drain is glinting dully in the Christmas lights, like a petrified abseiler, frozen in chromium terror, clinging to a rockface, trapped between decisions.

And after a little while I suppose I finish my drink because when I look down it's empty too.

We're gathered around the great mahogany dining table at the end of dinner, a little after half-past eight. The turkey was acceptable, if a little dry, the cranberry sauce fabulous, the vegetables expendable. We have a rule at Christmas dinners, even pre-Christmas childless Christmas dinners like this one, that dates from when Michael was born: no shop talk. So far the conversation has been limited to football, Robert's plans to attempt a solo round-the-world yacht trip, the state of the Augusta course for the Masters this year, the imprisonment of a Tiger Woods impersonator for cheque fraud (an imploring and resigned look from Elise prevents me from remarking on the absurdity of sentencing the poor boy to consecutive terms totaling *two hundred years*), upholstery, house conversion, conservatories, who has new houses, who has new holiday houses, who wants new holiday houses, where they want them, Capri, the Amalfi coast, Montego Bay, Round Hill (Henry offered this: "Noël Coward, Grace Kelly and Groucho Marx all holidayed there. It has a fabulous pedigree, you've got to admit." The wondrous Patrise responded: "Groucho Marx's wife was thirteen. He used to call her 'the greatest walking aphrodisiac.'" This received some muted laughter. My whisper: "Patrise. *Patrise*. Hair is *fabulous*." I received a smile).

The dining room is lit dimly by the massive chandelier above the table, the rheostat turned down by Elise to, quote, *generate a mood*. Over the table the Limoges china littered with the remains of dinner is also illuminated by four candles. The table is as big as a competition snooker table and covered in a plain white linen tablecloth. The carpet in here is thick burgundy shag and the huge mirror in the elaborate gold frame on the west wall only reflects the maroon opposite and from where I'm sitting just looks like a framed piece of wall. The cabinets beside the hallway door are huge and mahogany too, and closed. The curtains behind me are open so we can see the lights of the city as we eat.

I am at the head of the table, of course, with my back to the windows. I have changed my suit. It's summertime; it's hot; none of the other men are wearing tuxes; so fuck it, Elise, is what I say. I'm on safari, my Donna Karan khaki linen suit, a finely pin-striped cotton shirt and a plain black silk tie. I look like Jeremy Irons.

I lean toward Patrise, who is sitting to my right, and lightly rest my hand on her thigh.

"Do you think I look like Jeremy Irons? I'm on safari. Patrise."

"*Andrew*," she says, and removes my hand. "You're drunk. And anyway, you look more like Alain Delon in *Plein Soleil* than Jeremy Irons, darling. You should get some nice white moccasins to go with that suit."

"I could wear some espadrilles. I do have some Brazilian espadrilles. For sailing. Not exactly safety footwear though. If I'm going hunting, Patrise."

Patrise is Henry Harrington's wife and is simply delicious. Let me try and capture this: Think thirty-fivish. Think blinding white double-breasted Ralph Lauren suit with six large gold maritime buttons. Think no visible blouse under the suit *whatsoever* and thus: Gold Coast tan unimpeded. Think a hanging men's gold Rolex. Think gold hooped earrings. Think blond hair tied in a loose ponytail. Think bluegray eyes as Mediterranean as her tan. Think of her leaning back, I would hesitate to say *slumped*, in the dining chair, dangling a champagne flute between legs that are spread just *brashly*.

But next to Patrise is Jan, Orson's wife, who is wearing a dull charcoal Gucci suit that is not impressing me in the slightest. She is arguing past a silent and brooding Orson with Elise, my wife, opposite me at the other end of the table. Next to Elise is Henry, and next to Henry is Robert, Blythe's husband, and next to Robert is Blythe, and next to Blythe is me. Blythe is wearing a strapless navy woolen bodice and green silk trousers with a miniature gold belt the width of a bracelet, all by Ralph Lauren. Our end of the table is ignoring Elise and Jan.

"I look like Jeremy Irons," I say loudly.

"Don't be so hard on yourself," Patrise coos to me. "You're far better-looking than Jeremy Irons."

My wife interrupts her conversation with Jan, who is a dentist, long enough to say, "No one likes to be told the same thing twice, Andrew."

"On safari," I reiterate for her benefit. "Hunting... quail? But perhaps I shouldn't have shared."

"You're being a boor, Andrew. Have another Courvy for God's sake," Patrise says, smirking at me.

"Patrise, o *rara avis*, let me make it very clear that this is not just any Courvoisier. I've got hold of one of the better Courvies. 'There are many you know,' as Nixon once said. But if you insist, I shall." I stand, only a little unsteadily. "Who needs drinks then? Orson? Another Jack?"

Orson is slouched and possibly asleep between Jan and Elise, who are leaned forward and talking politely over his lap.

He surfaces briefly. "Hmmm? Yes, actually make it a triple, Andrew, if you don't mind." Orson is a plastic surgeon in private practice, with whom I wouldn't trust my pedicure let alone my face, and has set Jan up in the same building as him to treat the only part of the body he supposedly can't renovate: teeth.

"*I* don't mind." I am slurring but we're all fairly drunk here, even the women, and I guarantee that I *will smoke inside* before the evening is out.

"Henry. Drink? I *demand* you order a drink from me," I say. Henry is a judge, too, district however, so we like to spar. And I adore his wife. He may be thirty-bloody-something and born a decade after me, but his taste in evening wear is *godawful* tonight: a small-lapelled Country Road pinstripe woolen suit with an open black shirt beneath exposing a tan comparable with Patrise's, and that I suppose is meant to be vaguely *Oriental,* the lapels I mean, but with the pinstripes the overall effect is more *punitive.* I slam my hands down on the table. "*Henry.* Answer me."

"Another chardonnay, Andrew, while you're up and about," he says.

"Another chardonnay? Oh, I'm up and about alright," I'm muttering to myself. "I'm on safari. Preparing to leave the compound, to brave the wilds and hunt, to slaughter beasts, *wildebeests,* in fact, yes, and feed the starving tribe. Blah blah blah."

"Nixon's guiding metaphor was tension. A holding-in, a clinging-on," Robert is saying to his wife. I do and always will detest marriages that involve serious conversations.

"Robert. Drink," I rasp.

"I would characterize Nixon as a self-aggrandizing fatalist," Henry offers. Chump.

"I would characterize *myself* as a self-aggrandizing fatalist," I hiss. "And you are not luring me into this."

"You'll find I'm right," Robert says. "Andrew agrees. This is the subtext to all he's ever written about him. Nixon was all about a gathering-toward. Control, preparation, eventualities, contingencies. Rule through readiness. The man was constantly primed. I mean, has anyone considered Watergate as a metaphor? A linguistic pun? You know the famous pose, Nixon all tension, leaning from the hip and the neck, shoulders hunched, arms outstretched, fingers in V's. I see Nixon straining at the dike with too many holes and not enough fingers."

"An ulcer factory," Patrise offers from beside me.

"Exactly," Robert says. "I see Watergate as, well, not to put too fine a point on it, inevitable overflow." He looks up toward me. "And I'll have a GT, multiple rocks, Andrew, many thanks."

"Not at all. Not at all. To hunt is to solve," I'm droning to myself, anyone that might be listening. "To leave behind these bleatings of the ignorant, and bravely penetrate the heart of the beast of mystery with the keen blade of intellect, tear out and consume that heart and thus absorb its wisdom. Yes, Patrise?"

"Yes, Andrew. You're a genius and a delight. But I want champagne this instant."

"No one demands in this house, Patrise," I tell her, "but you."

"Oh Andy." Even drunk, I love it when she calls me Andy. I lean over, plant a kiss at her hairline.

"Please leave her alone and fetch *drinks,* Andrew," Elise says sharply from the end of the table.

"And you of course, light of my life, fire of my loins. Drinks are *imminent.* Blythe? What can I get you? If I could ask you two to pause for *one second.*"

But Blythe is off too. What I loathe about Blythe and Robert is they argue like strangers. No givens, no codes. Married for fourteen years and this is Blythe's offering:

"Alright. On your terms then I would oppose Nixon with Kennedy."

"Oh, now *that's* an original construction," I mutter, not quite successfully to myself.

"And Clinton," Patrise adds.

"*And* Clinton, then, as a generosity. The cup that brimmeth over. More is more. A generous President. A *loving* President."

"For God's sake, you're not even *arguing*. You're liberally mixing your fluid metaphors, but you *agree*," I say. And, *Fools*, I mentally add.

"Clinton as loving President," Robert says. "You said, um, a mouthful there. Cigars anyone?"

"Not inside, Robert," Elise says.

Patrise sniggers.

"You're *crude*, Robert," Blythe says.

"*Oily* Cameroon wrappers."

"The cup that brimmeth all *over* the place," Patrise says.

"*Stop* it."

"Smooth on the *draw*, but plenty of *kick*."

"And *hand*-wrapped. Do *you* smoke in your office Andrew?" Patrise again.

"I *smoke* wherever—and with *whomever*—I please," I say.

"Good for you."

"Andrew? A bourbon, Andrew. If I'm going to try and cope with all this crudeness," Blythe sighs.

"Certainly, Blythe. Is that everyone then? I can't even remember. I'm a little smashed."

"What about Bush then?" Robert says.

"Bush won that election by more than anyone knows or wants to admit, and he's the real boor, by the way, Patrise," I say.

"*Stolid* is the word I'd use for Bush," Patrise says.

"Stolid and dependably stupid," Robert says.

Blythe, obviously content we're back to politics, ejaculates: "He's *evil*. The way he holds the tip of his tongue between his lips. Uh." She shudders.

"Whose—drink—haven't—I—got," I'm asking.

"Don't you have a maid, Andrew? Why don't you utilize the help?" Henry finally chimes in from the other end of the table.

"Henry. You're awake then?" I say.

"Sorry old man," he sneers. "Fell asleep waiting for drinks."

"It wouldn't be the first time you've fallen asleep on the job, *old man*, or so I've heard," I reply. "And the thing is, if I call the maid in, she'll open the door and Hüsker Dü will eat you alive."

"Hüsker Dü is *gorgeous*," Patrise says.

"I thought he was Meredith's dog," Blythe says. "Isn't he pining?"

"Why don't we have some music?" Robert says, rocking back on his chair. "You've got some Brubeck on vinyl, haven't you Andrew? *Take Five?* Or Thelonious Monk?"

"Where *is* Meredith?" Patrise asks me.

"God. I must have a drink," I say. "Meredith has gone back to Japan. But who knows. *We* don't know. She's no doubt spending her allowance on travel and hot baths and cocaine. And *horse tranquilizers.*"

"Oh, *Andrew.*" Elise has heard me. I sit back down, finally.

A silence comes down over the table.

No one says anything.

Blythe looks at her lap. What for? An answer? A *question?*

Robert lets his chair settle, then clears his throat. Henry doesn't move.

Jan looks from me, over a still-sleeping Orson, to Elise. Elise adjusts a fork on the plate in front of her.

"What about Michael then?" Patrise asks.

"Michael is in Asia," Elise says. "He is traveling in Asia. I'm afraid that's all we know."

No one says anything.

"Roaming the fields of Cathay," I mutter. "Giving or getting tattoos. Who knows."

"Andrew." Elise.

A long silence.

"That's just the thing with children, isn't it. You have to be prepared for that possibility, that when they leave and go searching, they might not ever come back," Elise says.

"It's a load of bullshit," I say.

"Why don't I go and get the drinks in," Robert says.

"I'll help," says Blythe, and they both stand.

"Children leave," Elise says. "That's what they should do. They're your conscience, don't you think? Or they should be."

"I remember a thing that really tripped Michael up was some case of a war surgeon in a POW camp, forced to resuscitate one of his countrymen in the midst of a torture, presumably for more torture to be inflicted to extract more information. That's the last one I remember him telling me about. He never had the stomach for it, that's all. And yet he persisted. That's the only question of *conscience,* here."

"Who would?" Elise says. "Have the stomach for it."

I'm looking for something to break. Blythe and Robert are gathering the glasses.

Patrise puts her hand on my shoulder.

Another long silence.

"Who's got a stogey for me," I say.

Surprise. Henry slides a packet of Benson & Hedges down the table to me. I pull one out of the pack and light up off a candle. I suck in hard, and breathe out twin plumes of smoke from my nostrils, inhale again sharply.

"A Courvy," I say. "With water. Not from the tap. Triple Jack Daniels on the rocks, a chardonnay, a gin and tonic, make it Tanqueray, multiple rocks, champagne for Patrise, open another bottle if it's finished, bourbon for Blythe, a vodka and cranberry for my wife and an ashtray, and don't let the fucking dog in here while you're at it."

"*Con la pancia,* Andrew," Orson stirs and mutters from the other end of the table. "Belly is full."

"Oh *Orson,*" Jan says.

"Yes, alright," I say. "Alright. Tonight I shall be Alain Delon. Excellent. Fine, then."

It's a little after ten, I suppose, and out in the foyer at the foot of the main staircase, where and when we say our good-byes, because dinner has *wound up.*

Hüsker Dü is barking loudly somewhere deep in the house and *Sketches of Spain,* clanking, blaring sad, discordant trumpet and maracas, and . . . *sleigh bells,* coming from the lounge and the brandy fumes and the oily carrots are making me feel a little queasy, together with the little dance I did by the fireplace, which seemed to have been some kind of cue for everyone to stand, finish off drinks, direct murmurs to Elise, gather handbags, purses, keys, *whatever.*

I'm standing in the corner of the foyer, leaning against the frame of the massive oak and leadlight door that opens out onto the porch and the cobbled path up to the driveway.

The guests are filing past Elise, adjusting clothes and bags, and she is hugging each in turn, kissing cheeks, whispering the usual phrases, "Thanks so much," "Have a great holiday," "A *very* merry Christmas," *etc. etc.*

The door is being held open by one of the security guards, a giant Polynesian who is studiously avoiding my staring.

"Quis custodiet ipsos custodes," I mutter loudly, directing this at the guard.

"Andrew, you're swaying, my man." It's Robert, through the gauntlet.

"Robert."

"Thanks so much. Had a great time," he says.

Staring at his chin, I say, "Merely his miss, old man, merely his miss."

He laughs loudly, a little worriedly. Blythe appears.

"Thank you, Andrew. Have a wonderful Christmas." She leans in and kisses my cheek.

"Mmmm," I murmur, nodding, but then they're both quickly gone from my line of sight.

"Thanks ever so, Andy. Christmas at the Edwards'. Always a pleasure. I'll see you at the track, then," Orson says, appearing, suddenly.

"Orson, Jesus, of *course*, ever so, you know I will, sir," I say.

"Alright, then," he says, a little confused.

"I will then," I say.

"Bye-bye, Andrew, look after yourself," Jan says quickly.

"Yes, yes," I mutter. "I'm fine, supergood," and then they're gone, out of my vision.

And Patrise appears, a blur of blond, white and gold, a flurry of emotions I should feel. I push myself off the doorframe and hug her. She hugs me back. "I'm very sorry if I'm . . . a little drunk then, Patrise," I'm saying into her ear. "Please forgive me if I'm a little drunk."

And, a little sadly, Patrise is saying into my ear, "It's alright, Andrew. It's alright. They'll be back," and patting me gently, and I feel suddenly as if I could maybe cry and I don't want to spoil this moment by saying . . . *who?* so I'm saying, "Of course, I know that, it's just, you know, Christmas . . ."

I feel her hug relax and I let her go. She takes my hands and kisses me lightly on both cheeks and says, "Take a holiday, Andy. Go water-skiing or something. Relax a little."

"I know, I know," I'm muttering, "Got to work less and so forth . . ." and there's a tap on my shoulder and it's Henry.

"Good god, man," I say. "Christ." I gather myself. "I congratulate you on the lapels. A brave departure."

"Andrew," he's saying. He's holding something out to me. "I know this is a little difficult, I mean especially uh, right now."

"Oh Christ, get it out," I sigh. "I have to vomit."

He laughs sharply, and visibly relaxes.

"Look," he says, and I can tell he's looking hard at me, something in the tilt of his head, a slight lean, maybe this is something serious. "I'm doing a little business with a Chinese I've heard you may be aware of."

"Land conveyancing?"

"In a manner of speaking, yes, actually."

"Typical. The ubiquitous golf courses and access roads," I'm muttering, but he cuts me off. Patrise is standing very close to him.

"Listen, Andrew. He's very serious, very connected." I make an effort to look Henry in the eye. "Hong Kong," he says earnestly to me. "L.A., Tokyo, New York. Mostly real estate, but recently, restaurants. You've heard of the Chang Group." It's not a question and it's dawning on me Henry really might be serious. I look down to what he's holding and it's a business card.

"Yes," I say.

"Thomas Chang is his name. Here's his information." He tucks the card into my breast pocket. "He has a son, too, Andrew. He manages one of Thomas's restaurants in Long Beach, or maybe West Hollywood. I don't know which. And I don't know if you're aware of this, but this boy was at school with Michael. Here in Wellington. All I'm saying is, if you really want to find him, and I'm not saying you necessarily do, maybe Thomas or his son can . . . you know . . . help."

Henry, whom I've previously regarded as a lightweight, is taking on something of a new density.

"Thomas and I go further back than you can possibly know, Henry. His son has slept under this roof more times than I can count," I say. "And Michael can look after himself, as far as I'm concerned. He's currently cut off. I let him use the suite in Tokyo simply because I cannot expend the energy required to retrieve the damn keys. God only knows where the boy is now." I'm almost singing this, plucking syllabic emphases out of thin air to approximate some kind of passionate resignation. "He cut himself off, so in return we do the same. At twenty-four, boys are all Iago. Chock-full of motiveless malignity."

"Oh. Well. He's not a racialist, is he? I remember his short haircut." Ha! Just a little perturbed that I know Thomas, the *obscurant.*

"He is an historian. An acclaimed and gifted young historian. And the moor is within, Henry," I say, sneering at him. "The moor is within."

"Well, I'll leave it in your capable hands, Andrew. Good night. Thanks for dinner," he trails off.

"Thanks, Andrew," Patrise says, and she smiles and they turn and walk slowly together, the speed of the blessed and the damned, out on the porch, up the path, away.

I turn back from the doorway. Elise glares at me.

"What?" I say.

She just looks at me.

"Where is Hüsker Dü?" I say.

"In the kitchen, Andrew."

"What's the major problem then? *Elise?*"

"I'm going to bed," she says, turning away.

"Take some Panadol, for God's sake," I say to her back. "And calm down."

"Fuck you," she whispers.

"Fuck *you*," I whisper.

Desperate for a cigarette now, I sway down the hallway to the downstairs office. I rifle through the old desk, even checking the damn safe. There's nothing, anywhere. I collapse back in the leather chair, defeated.

And the phone is ringing.

I stare at it, at the light blinking, listen to the digital burble for three rings before it occurs to me Elise may answer. I snatch it up.

"Hello?" I answer.

There's a buzzing and crackling.

"Hello? Who is it?"

"...forty-nine there," I catch, the voice, male, pixilated and distorted, it sounds cellular, outside the borders of the phone's reach, a cheap satellite.

"Hello?" I say again.

There's a silence, some buzzing and pops. Some static follows and a hard clatter.

"Who is it?" a male voice says.

"This is the Edwards residence," I say. "Who is this?"

There's a long pause. Then a laugh.

"Hi," the voice says. "Dad."

"Michael," I say, my voice dropping and serious. "Michael?"

I hear a loud bang and laughter, followed by more static.

"Michael? Is that you son?"

There are other voices, distorted in the background, like a foreign language, both male and female, somehow robotic.

Suddenly his voice comes back.

"Anata wa, piero des. Papa. The grossness, gross, grossity, Mount Grossglockner," the voice says.

"Michael?" I say.

"I...have wanted to say so many things," the voice says.

"What's wrong son? Where are you?" I say.

"But...now...I'm scared...of those many things."

In the voice's background a silence comes down and the line clears suddenly.

"And...oh...so *many*...flings."

"Mike?"

"I took my chance...made my choice...chose...forgotten...Chinese ...hills...to roam." He's reciting this, bored, mechanically, like he regrets it already. This may not be him; it sounds like his voice, but deepening, more angry than I've ever heard him speak before.

"In search of...understanding...bewitchment...self...knowledge... and new form..."

"Michael..."

"And...in the dark...I wandered so far...I...cannot...find a...way ...home..."

"Don't be stupid," I say. "You're drunk. Where are you? Tell me now."

"Merry Christmas, Dad," he says, and laughs. "I'm home. At the Prince. It's been more than twelve, Dad. Others come and go. I've lost some of them."

"Some of who? Where is Meredith, Michael? Is she with you? I let her go and look for you, son. What about Simon Chang?"

"I've really lost them...I don't know...This time I don't know if I'm gonna come back again. It's..."—his voice breaking now—"It's...Dad?"

"*Yes,* Mike."

"I'm sorry. I'm really sorry."

The line crackles, there's shrill laughter in the background, abruptly cut off, and it falls dead.

Uselessly, to a hiss, I whisper, "What for, son? What for?"

There is no answer.

"Michael?"

Outside the back of the house, I'm sitting in the driveway at the edge of the garden with the bottle of Courvoisier, two-thirds empty, smoking a

stale Marlboro I found in a crumpled pack in Meredith's desk. The security, the cook and the maid have been sent home and the drive is empty of
cars. The Milky Way is a blurred sprawl of stars over the sky, Crux directly
above, Alpha and Beta Centauri point to Scorpius, inverted, long and
winding, Antares the eye a baleful, sour, orange pinprick glow. The driveway is black bitumen and winds down from the private road to the
garages and the cobbled path leading to the porch and the main rear
entrance to the house. It is easy to see the stars because the lights in the
house are all off, including the Christmas lights. I've been waiting out here
for twenty minutes. My dealer has never before been so late. On a stone
globe in the garden a splay-footed cherub with angel wings slumps, hands
in its androgyne lap, neck bowed, dead, tired, scolded or shy; another
gaudy Elisesque decoration. The garden lights—there are more than
thirty—are a foot high and shaded in green steel like table lamps. In the
one closest to me, the one that's illuminating the cherub, a daddy longlegs
has discovered a web from the shade to the stem, and is unsteadily negotiating a route to the center of the citadel. I'm thinking of a celebratory dinner held in honor of my first, ill-omened nomination for the circuit in
1989. Silver trays of salmon canapés, puff pastry with goat cheese, bottles
of chilled Krüg. The Millet I bought for myself and the family to commemorate the occasion. The *heirloom*. Sitting at the landing at the top of
the main stairs, overlooking the lobby, on the burgundy carpet in a tiny
black tuxedo, Michael, eleven years old, black hair shining, an untouched
plate of toast and asparagus and a crystal tumbler of raspberry cordial sitting by his folded knee. Watching the string quartet on the landing playing
the expected Bach arrangement, *Air on a G String*. Entranced, staring at the
instruments, the spruce and maple of the cello all aglow like caramel fire
in the lobby's chandelier. Staying there the duration of the dinner, staring
at the young violinist's small sad face as she played solos, a twelve-year-old
Japanese prodigy, her hair black as his; she was hired through the caterers:
hired by Elise.

And Michael, fallen asleep with the light on, three years old, his tiny
body made the giant bedroom, the double bed, obscene. *I Can Fly*, collapsed on his chest, he'd fallen asleep reading it, what dreams did he have,
at three? Elise bought the book for him when she saw a photo of two-year-
old Caroline Kennedy clutching it, staring up, and smiling, at Jacqueline in
Givenchy. *I Can Fly*, spine worn to the thread, collapsed on his tiny chest,
the span of my hand, ribcage like a rose, sleeping, sleeping.

People say of the daddy longlegs, it's one of the most poisonous arachnids in this, a country of a few lethal animals. That the fangs are so fine they cannot penetrate human skin. What I know: it's a myth. What I also know: they don't produce silk. This one's caught in someone else's web.

The card between my legs on the bitumen of my driveway is familiar to me, and reads simply,

Thomas Chang

Chang Group

Hong Kong   Tokyo   London   Los Angeles   New York
A phone number.

My drugs eventually arrive, pull up in a silver BMW 325i with a woman, maybe the one from the phone, maybe not, but she's no more than twenty, has long blond hair. I leave the card on the driveway, lean in the window, kiss her on the lips, her tongue touches mine, the vial is passed, one gram, one hour, the taste of flavorless lipstick, the touch of her tongue, the stars turn, all things shine, she wishes me good night, a merry Christmas, an empty driveway, a drained swimming pool, I look again for the spider but it's too late, there are too many lights, too many choices, too many second chances, no excuses, my last words to Michael— they were meant in jest—*you failed the test.*

March 2001

Catherine Barnes
Tut. 1B
Journal Question One
William Shakespeare's *Twelfth Night*
5000 words
Due May 30, 2001

Twelfth Night is about love, nation, and mistaken and assumed identity.

William Shakespeare's *Twelfth Night* is about love, nation, and mistaken and assumed identity.

Sebastian and Viola, the main characters of William Shakespeare's *Twelfth Night,* escape a shipwreck and are washed up on the shores of the land of Illyria. Each thinks the other is dead, so they start their lives again in this new land. But everything in Illyria is really really

73 words
4927 to go
78 words
4922 to go

Including title page,
89 words
4911 to go

1989

And you know, a particular photo can get taken for as many and more different reasons as there are people in that photo, despite the fact that even if you maybe asked each single person in that photo, their answer could be the same.

One of the framed photos on the wall of Andrew Edward Edwards' office is ostensibly he and his family, in the American Embassy office of the chargé d'affaires in 1989. Andrew's extracurricular monograph—"Nixon and the Minor Nations: The Harassed Envoy in the Pancake Makeup Makes For the Mirror Cities"—in *The U.S. Colonial Review* had led to a publication offer from Little, Brown for an as-yet-unwritten book and the *Lady of the Strachy* Ribbon for Services to U.S.–Commonwealth Relations from the American Embassy. The family stands in an uncomfortable semi-ellipse; Andrew at the center, beside the chargé d'affaires, Elise on his other side. Meredith stands by Elise, smiling, but one shoulder a little raised revealing her discomfort with a blue, cream-frilled evening gown

that, with her height, makes her older than her eleven years. On her slim
chest is a small badge that reads *"Minke Whaling = Ocean's Lobotomy."* The
office is all gaudy cochineal carpet and three-quarter rosewood paneling, a
giant mahogany desk behind the crescent of four figures in formal dress,
one not so. Andrew's hands are clasped at the hem of his jacket; and his
expression is neither here nor there, which is revealing enough in itself.
Elise, a head shorter than the chargé d'affaires, is inclined a little away
from him, toward Meredith and her raised shoulder. Elise looks, with her
shortish, slicked-back black hair, her slim, almost hipless figure, too young
to have mothered these children who seem to maybe have her hair—and
in Meredith, her waxen skin—but little else Japanese. Elise's dark purple
skirt and jacket are darker against the white of the office's windows, and
she has a small handbag in her hands. She and Andrew stand the same for
formal photos, but their physical disparity means they never seem as if
they do. The chargé d'affaires is smiling merrily, his chestnut fringe a
floppy cowlick over his left glasses' lens, and his right hand is slightly lifted,
the elbow just crook'd, as if he had noticed some amusing problem with
the camera—a lens cap, maybe—just as the photo was snapped. Michael is
thirteen and to Andrew's left. His black hair is long, down over his ears; his
jeans tight and crumpled, his black wool jacket unzipped. He's sneering,
because although to Meredith this photo is a mundane chore and embarrassing, gross egotism next to which she feels just an ugly prop; and
though to Elise a chore also, but a duty, an obligation, and (perhaps she
supposes sarcastically to herself) a story for dinners, too; and although the
photo is to Andrew a timely record of timely recognition (High Court
nominations quietly beginning again in eighteen months), Michael's
ungracious reading of the photo is that Andrew is well aware of the similarities in the composition, distribution of the photo's constituents, and
choice of shoot, to one of his—Andrew's, of course—favorite historical
milieux, and photos: John Paul Vann's family at the White House in 1972,
receiving for him the posthumous Congressional Medal of Honor from
Nixon. So Michael's sneer is not really at the sense of some sordid, hypocritical and amoral farce being acted out, as per Vann's pacifist son Jesse's
in 1972 (Nixon's five o'clock shadow bristles through the pancake makeup
for the television cameras), but at the imitation, or the unwillingness to
resist the appearance of imitation, or perhaps—to be charitable to the
sneering thirteen-year-old—the coincidence. Either way, though he was
wrong about the contrivance (all those photos tend to look alike: the

sparsely furnished official offices; the carefully neutral civil servants, veterans of a thousand such shoots; the austere and dignified soldiers; the uncomfortable families), he felt he knew too much about his father too young to ever show much respect for his chosen profession or the small and infrequent public recognitions that were attached to it, even if his father was, at this point, largely blameless with regard to things Michael had come to understand then were already really and truly and almost overwhelmingly starting to become his obsession.

Simon
September 2000

So I'm in the shuttle heading from the southern extension into Terminal 2 of Narita airport and the shuttle is packed with people, tourists, almost all of them Americans and assuming I'm not, these bigots on some kind of company tour because they're all wearing suits, and earlier as we boarded the shuttle I clearly heard one slightly younger dude say, "The spring business is . . ."—falter—". . . bouncing," and I had to turn away to the window to keep from totally losing it, and so now I can see the bright lights of the control tower, floating over the endless runway, and all down Terminal 2 the tails of 747s rise up, immense, the logos of Aeroflot, Lufthansa, Air France, Cathay Pacific, THAI, Virgin Atlantic, JAL, ANA, Air India, Swiss-Air, arrayed the length of the massive terminal, the dimpled metal of the aircraft shimmering and blue in the heat and the floodlights, and the ripple of the exhausts rising from engines makes landing lights shimmer like orange stars, and the logos on the tails are just eclipsing one another, but as the shuttle draws closer and closer to Terminal 2 they're slowly beginning to merge into the solitary crane of the nearest JAL 747 as my perspective shifts.

Beside me is a guy who's obviously not with this group of businessmen, he's older, he's Japanese and dressed casually, jeans, a V-neck sweater. He's staring out at the jets too.

Then he says, bizarrely, in a thick South Carolina drawl, "You know, fifty years ago this airport was all farmland and Imperial estates. A horse ranch that was here before the Tokugawa shoguns. It was so beautiful they used to call it the Barbizon of Japan. Thousand-year-old cherry trees. The farmers filled them full of five-inch nails to stop the chainsaws." He sniggers. "The old women threw bags of human feces at the riot police. The police were just kids. Sons of farmers from around here. They were baffled. Old women throwing shit at them."

He turns and looks at me closely and realizes something.

"Oh, excuse me. Do you speak English, son?" he says.

I turn back to the window, as the shuttle slides into Terminal 2. The flight was long but I slept well. I'm feeling pretty perky. I pull my keitai out of my pocket—a sorely neglected item for the last twelve months that I have been in LA—and the batteries are still good, and my father's people have obviously done their job with my various debts over here, because although the No Signal kanji appears from LCD gray as we enter the huge building, its appearance now is implying its absence just a couple seconds ago.

"Dude, I get the distinct impression you think I've never been here before," I say, staring down at the screen of my old Tu-Ka phone. "But I am back in business."

At the restaurant in Long Beach one month ago the decorators had almost finished. A young black electrician was working in the kitchens but it was late in the day and all the new furniture was covered in drop cloths and stacked against the walls. The polished pine floors were done and dry and the signwriters had completed the kanji on the windows: *Shinsekai:* New World. The most important thing is to get the name up first, my father would later tell me. There were ten-liter tubs of paint and pieces of crumpled sandpaper, stepladders and toolboxes. The LA branch is supposed to be the flagship of my father's new restaurant chain, the first of the initial ten he will open all over the world.

The electrician had let me in, and I had flirted with him a little, and he had flirted back, but when my father's BMW pulled up the electrician went back to work and I sat down on a paint-splattered stool by the desk for the maître d', a desk made from a Harley Davidson, to wait for my father, and the "talk" we "need to have."

In a dark suit out of the violet LA twilight, a slight Chinese in glasses with a truly awful combover, he unlocks the double doors, closes and locks them without acknowledging me, and strolls into the restaurant. He inspects the floors, wanders over to the stacks of furniture and lifts a corner of a drop cloth, glances over at the kitchen.

"Hello?" I say. "I think you missed me."

He shows no sign of hearing me and disappears into the men's room. When he reappears, he's smoking a cigarette. He walks slowly toward me over the broad expanse of polished pine clouded by sawdust, stops directly in front of me.

"Um, I have people I need to meet—" I start, but I'm cut off when he clicks his tongue, an old signal.

I stare at the floor between my feet and fumble in my pockets for cigarettes, finding one, lighting one. He stays there in front of me for a long, long time, then turns and strolls into the very center of the dusty floor of his new restaurant. I take a long drag, glance up, see that he's staring up at the panels in the ceiling.

Exhale, and it begins.

"So. How are your college studies at the USC going for you." To the ceiling, no intonation.

Another drag, I lean my head sideways, the impression of reflection, exhale hard to the windows. A cracking sound from the kitchen, I just know the black boy is going to hear this whole thing.

"Um, I guess it's a bummer actually, but I know I can . . . you know . . . pull things together . . . in time . . ."

I trail off.

"In time . . . for . . . what?" Very quietly.

"For like, finals. I assumed that was what you were getting at."

"Please don't . . . lie to me, Simon," my father whispers upward. It is so bad when he whispers.

"I'm not . . . *lying,*" I mumble.

"What are you doing, then."

"I'm . . ." I start giggling, I hate it, really fast and breathy, I can hear myself, at the floor, "I'm dis*torting* the facts maybe a little, Dad, but I'm not really . . . *lying.*"

He doesn't respond to this. A glimmer of light, I'm encouraged to go on. "Like, by the time finals start I'll be, you know, totally . . . prepared, I bet."

He sucks lightly on his cigarette, washes the smoke in his mouth, his cheek muscles contract, and he puffs out a perfect smoke ring.

"So then. Now you are not at college anymore, Simon," he says.

I look up. "What?"

"I don't think you are so excited about your studies, so enrollment is canceled."

"What do you mean. Canceled?"

"Nulled and voided. Stopped."

"You . . . can't do that."

Another clatter from the kitchen.

"I have done that."

"You . . . fucker," I whisper to the floor. Incredulous, but then, "I don't give a shit. I don't care. It bores me anyway."

"Don't whine, Simon," my father says, and he walks slowly over the vast floor of the restaurant toward the men's toilets again. He turns, and smiles. "This is what is going to happen with your life, my son," he says, very gently, from across the dining room of his new restaurant. "You are going to go back to Japan and work for me."

The Chinese are taking over Japanese food, and I suppose I am meant to help.

I'm deep inside Terminal 2. Immigration is an air-conditioned cavern blanketed in mauve airport carpet, the ceilings hundreds of feet up. At the far end a series of more than thirty kiosks are manned by young Japanese Immigration officials, both sexes, one relentless expression of barely masked bored hostility. There are two long, wide queues winding through a chemical symbol maze of silver pillars and nylon tape.

I am in Foreigners, and we are moving way slower than Japanese Nationals. Directly in front of me, an ancient Chinese woman with only one arm is keeping a yard of the mauve carpet between herself and the more than thirty members of the Uruguay National Karate Team ahead of her, a noisy crowd of all different skin colors and ages, all different sizes of white tracksuits. Some of the karate team are very young, and growing restless. Some game is being played, they're bumping into each other, grabbing each other's hands. One little girl has her arms inside her jacket, imitating the old Chinese woman, shimmying side to side to make the empty sleeves fly around her. And a few of them are ducking under the tape and ducking through the weaving queue in front, through nationalities I can place at a glance: five Nigerians in robes and red fezzes; the New Zealand boys in the Nike Air caps, the sandals, the shorts and the shock-

ingly white, hairy legs; a German couple arguing, the woman jabbing her
finger urgently at a landing pass; two huge Sudanese in matching black
and silver Adidas full-length tracksuits guffawing deeply at something; the
American businessmen who got ahead of me at the metal detectors; a
Malay family nearer the front; some Koreans, French, Australians, Taiwanese, Vietnamese; maybe a hundred foreigners in all, queuing for Immigration in a winding mass.

I feel like dying from nicotine withdrawal and the queue is moving at
the speed of proton decay and I can feel things happening out there, while
I'm stuck in Narita on stolen farmland, stuck in this queue, things I'm
missing, fifty miles away in the city, things that might have happened,
things that will. I can feel people I know and people I don't know moving
through floods of shining black hair in Shinjuku and Shibuya, fat tourists
staring over with glazed, semidesperate eyes at a lit-up Marlboro billboard
the size of a house by Fuji Bank. Me, Michael and Ko and Jacques, my
French "acquaintance," and tall silent Catherine, a married "friend" of
Michael's, buying five ¥15,000 bottles of red wine in an underground Italian restaurant from sheer boredom and Jacques guzzling it from the bottle
to freak out the waiters, and in the dim light the waiters thinking I'm
Japanese, looking at me imploringly for help. I can feel the Koshukaido
Avenue bridge outside the Shinjuku South exit flexing and shaking with
trucks, thousands bursting at the seams of the sidewalks, the Don't Walk
icon holding them fast. The concrete of the bridge is broken by corrugated metal seams, the slack for concrete to expand in the summer heat,
and the gray turned indigo in the streetlamps for me, twelve months ago.

I can feel things that happened and are happening without me,
strangers buying the wicked and totally legal Japanese mushrooms from
the allegedly silent boys at the allegedly brilliant and reasonably priced
Heaven On Earth and staying out all night tripping for ¥5000 a gram or
like US$50. I can feel lost time, backlit violet kanji on a dark building like
scars: "What does it mean," I asked someone. "Adult Entertainment,"
someone different answered. A long Christmas dinner at the cavernous
Buddha Trickbar in Shibuya, a giant gold Buddha—at least twenty or
thirty feet tall—in lotus beside our table. Doing coke in the bathrooms and
dropping the shrooms casually in the restaurant with our lemon sours and
tofu. Who was there? Jacques, for sure. Was Michael? Then Catherine,
surely. And the J boy, Ko? Meredith. Brigit and some other Canadians, and
the Australian ex–smack addict. Maybe Anton was there, maybe not. Ariel

was, I know. A blurred train ride, a mad old J guy on the train, losing clothes, someone demanding karaoke. Cum shining on cheap vinyl, on a hand, beer—was there blood? The memory, if it is one, is hazy—on a floor, a naked tattooed back, a tiger, foreigners getting touchy-feely in different booths as we passed, leaving, marauding through the endless beige corridors of Echo Karaoke in Ikebukuro. Things that are happening, things that might have happened and things that still might, merging together. The decay of sarcasm. Bored foreigners in endless parties, one izakaya after another, lying to each other about their countries, the Japanese-English girl whose name I forgot—Chantelle? Sian?—idly explaining the phrase "Cheers, mate," to nodding black Dwayne from New York—a forty-three-year-old guy who worked for a shelter in Brooklyn teaching homeless black kids for free, now teaching English to a director of Sumitomo Insurance for ¥15,000 an hour—the English girl telling Dwayne, totally deadpan, "In England, when we're really lazy, we say, 'cheesemai.'" Me, spraying lemon sour over the table, losing it, hissing, "Oh, *bullshit*," Dwayne roaring with laughter, but still not quite sure what he'd learned, a haunted look in his eyes, and her, surprised, a shy grin, pleased to be caught in her lie, and a handjob later that night in the toilets of White in Harajuku, a favor for knowingness, a gratuity.

And I can feel Ariel, kneeling in an apartment in Roppongi, her curly ponytail impossibly perfect, her eyes neon aquablue, lips like soft silver on coffeemilk skin, leaning over some J boy's coppery cock, tickling his balls, smiling serenely, whispering, "Can you say carrotstick? No? Can you say raisins?" the clouds floating above her as blue and strange as her eyes.

I lived in Tokyo for eight months. It moved quickly, and now there is a disassociated quality to it all, like a dream in which I can't remember myself as a character, like a movie with no sound. I tried, soon after I returned, just once, to explain the feeling to someone back in LA, and they said, "You can be whoever you want to be. Is that it. Or was it the drugs." "It's like, everything you learn outside Tokyo is useless in Tokyo. Everything you learn in Tokyo is useless outside Tokyo," I answered. Was this true? What does it even mean? "What about the language?" they said to me, sceptical of my confusion. "It's just another big city, man."

I was twenty-one. Although my face is Chinese, and apart from the two years of high school in New Zealand, I have lived in LA all my life. Tokyo is the only Asia I have ever known. It won't be the same. It can't be the same. All those I knew will have gone.

"Come on come on come on," I'm muttering.

The queue shuffles forward, just barely.

The old one-armed Chinese woman bends, picks up a bag made of woven string and places it a few inches ahead of her. She takes a single step forward, so the bag is at her right foot, keeping a strict three feet of mauve carpet between herself and the last member of the Uruguay National Karate Team, a stocky white tracksuit, a blond bob, an older woman. The word "Manager" is written in peeling fabric letters across the polyester of her shoulder blades, and when she turns to see who the armless little girl is looking at while she sways from side to side, side to side, flapping her empty sleeves, the manager has achingly blue eyes, whose coldness and complete lack of interest in me quickly and harshly remind me in turn of Ariel; concrete; lights you can taste; the feeling of being in Tokyo that has no name; the imperative of this place: if you can't keep up, stay the fuck at home.

I am a Chinese boy standing behind the manager of a karate team from Uruguay, in a queue full of strangers, wearing a pale blue British RAF T-shirt and expensive Swiss army trousers—in the pockets of which are my passport, a passbook for a new Tokyo-Mitsubishi bank account, a year-old and therefore ancient Tu-Ka keitai, a map to an apartment rented by my father that seems to me to have the exact street address of Dolce & Gabbana in Omotesando, a sticky piece of BlackJack nicotine gum—and the coldness and implacability of her eyes tells me this:

Freedom.

Now I am back.

Heaven On Earth
Shibuya 2000

Lit violet on bare concrete, arrayed in the store are books: *Psychedelic Experiments, Hemp 4 Victory, Dope Mania*. A video: *Tantra—Art of Conservational Living*. A poster of the season six cast of *Melrose Place*. Candles shaped like mushrooms, mushroom-shaped lava lamps. Skulls, ashtrays, bongs, pipes made from American .50-caliber bullet shells. Mona Lisa stickers, dope leaf stickers, incongruous Phish and Allman Brothers albums; incense, papers, Zippos with a thousand embossed designs. A postcard on the door that reads, *Russian Ladies For eating, dating or marriage.* Cases of bottles and boxes: St. John's Wort, Dexatrim, Xenical, ExLax, Biogen GH, Renova, Celebrex, Aricept, Melatonin, Chromium Picolate, Kinerase, Diflucan, even Prozac, a newcomer to Japan, sometimes packaged blandly as Fluoxetine Hydrochloride. Salvia divinorum extract 12, Phentermine, Viagra. Foreigners moving through the violet light, humphing in delighted surprise. Because of mushrooms. Baggies of dried shrooms by the hundreds, filling up the glass display cases, pinned behind glass to the walls like butterflies. In their bags they are shriveled and demure behind labels that read *Psilocybe* this, *Psilocybe* that. Disingenuous disclaimers that read, *Mushrooms are specimens only.* Mushrooms bagged by the gram: one, three and five. Pinned in neat lines, scaling over one another to fit as many in as possible. Hanging in display cases; piled in display cases. Two silent boys behind the concrete counter, say nothing to no one, not even each other. Foreigners moving through the violet light, planning trips inside this trip; second-order insular adventures to cope with this one they've already begun. Flipping through the bags with the fingers of a DJ, planning a night at home with a loved one, watching them shrink before their eyes in their tiny four-mat rooms.

They say Tokyo makes you live in your mind—hallucinogens make perfect sense.

Yasu

July 1995

And then, from above, a tiny voice. High, and husky.

"You are alone all the time."

The morning after a five point oh earthquake that he feared shook the terrarium badly, five years ago, one year into exile, Yasu was outside hanging T-shirts to dry.

"You are alone. All the time," said the small voice from above.

Yasu looked up over the washing line to see ten small fingers curled through the aluminum struts of the upstairs apartment's balcony, a miniature nose in sunlight.

"Why aren't you at school," Yasu said, through a clothes peg in his teeth.

The little girl opened a hand on a strut, flexed it, and closed it. The way children test their bodies when they concentrate.

"I'm not allowed to talk to you," she said.

"You should be in school," Yasu said, and removed the peg from his mouth, rigged up the corner of a gray marl T-shirt. The T-shirt read KEEP BACK 200 FT.

"I'm not at school because I'm sick," the girl said. "But you don't ever go anywhere and you're not sick." Then, confidence growing at her own boldness, "You stay inside all the time and sometimes you come out but only at night and you never go anywhere apart from the convenience store." Pause. "And your house is dirty." Smaller pause. "I'm not allowed to talk to you."

As he pegged out his washing, a rare, once-a-week occurrence, Yasu was wondering if the earthquake had dislodged the drip trays in any of the small stand-alone terraria. If drips had fallen on the budding caps. Or even worse, trays had come loose inside the terraria and crushed the fragile fruit, some of them at the pinning stage, rising from the fluffy mycelium-covered substrate fine as needles in baby's hair.

The earthquake.

When it is possible that months and years of work have been destroyed, at a single stroke, Yasu feels that putting off a damage assessment is understandable.

Some kind of internal evaluation happens first, among those very dedicated. Some private inventory of commitment and laziness; the task factored with time against love; devotion versus loneliness; boredom and destiny. A scale is built: one arm loaded with sacrifice, Heaven On Earth's money, faith, the romance and wonder of the work. Offset by inertia, useless solitude, arbitrariness, the randomness of fate, the eyes of his professor at the hearing. Which wins, which is the more weighty. Does he really care, or did everything simply fall down this way. Does he feel it and so must do it; or does he do it and feeling is consequence, the side effect of a labor persevered with only out of familiarity, the absence of options. Why go on. Because he loves. Or because he merely does. Choice or hazard; strength or momentum. How is he to know, so far down the line, if the line is not in fact the skewed carve of a blade trained only by the grain of the wood?

And if it really is the former, his life defined by the choices he has made, how much of himself does he really give? If he really cares, why all that wasted time, why all those half-measures. Why the drunk nights when he could have been studying. Why that cheaper desiccant. How much of him is really gone now, should his work be destroyed? Is it the utter end if nothing is left.

Or could it be even worse. If he has in fact given all there was to give, but the destruction is not quite total. If he is forced to murder healthy-looking, possibly radically original specimens that have been compromised; beautiful but useless pieces of self; those quiet funerals of the flushing toilet.

What would it really feel like, would it break his heart, to have to start from the very beginning, yet again.

"I wonder who it is that says you're not allowed," Yasu said. He heard the unsteadiness in his voice. He leaned down to the washing basket.

"Papa says."

Yasu nodded slowly to himself, and lifted up a bright yellow T-shirt that read MTHRFCKR in black letters.

"I wonder why he says you are not allowed to talk to me," he murmured, and placed a peg between his teeth.

The little girl hesitated.

"Because . . . no one else does," she said.

"What do you think of that reason?" Yasu said to his T-shirt.

The little girl waited, thinking. She sensed she was being made fun of.

"And because . . . you're . . . a . . . drug dealer," she whispered.

Yasu slowly lifted his head to look at her.

She stared down at him, watched his eyes, waiting for a reaction to this. Her daring.

Quickly the tension was unbearable, and she ducked out of sight.

But Yasu did not hear the sliding door close.

He took the peg from his teeth and dropped it back in the basket. A little plastic clatter to tell her, not gone yet. The air was so thick and still the sound seemed suspended, insoluble. A plastic gurgle, a sac of sound in oil. Yasu was weary. Tense, headachy in the humidity. He hadn't slept after the last aftershock. Still not wanting to go inside yet. Maybe it was all okay. How terrible was it to begin again. There would be disappointment, and anger. There was enough money to support a few months of preparation. All the sterilizing, another total fumigation maybe. But so tired. New supplies. Expensive, yes and very. So much work. So much time. Weeks for sterilizing. Months for mycelia and fruiting. They won't like it. They might be angry. If they won't pay.

He sighed, shakily.

"Hey. Little girl."

No answer.

"I know you're up there. Hey."

A scratching sound.

"Hey. Little girl. Do you like to eat mushrooms?"

A silence, and then, an answer, very quietly. "Maybe." Her voice came through the struts, but her head did not appear.

"What kinds of mushrooms do you like?"

Silence.

"I bet you like shiitake. And hatsudake."

No answer.

"What about matsutake. I bet you like the matsutake in tea with lemon juice."

"I had little matsutake in miso soup at Tomozushi sushi store once." Her head appeared above him.

"Those would be just baby mushrooms. How did you like them?"

"They're yummy. They're cute." Giggles. "They...sometimes they look like little willies. They look like willies, cut off and floating in brown soup. Papa calls them 'the take,' instead of matsutake, so Mama won't laugh at him."

"Do you know where mushrooms come from?"

"They come from a spore."

"Good. Good girl. Do you know what mycelium is?"

"And...and..." Pause. "No."

"The spore is put on a thing that has nutrients. We call it a substrate. You can use sawdust logs. Or brown rice flour and water. In the wild it would be decayed leaves. But in the lab if it's clean and sterile and nutritious and everything is perfect, what we call a mycelium will grow. All from that little shapeless flake."

Yasu sighed, and sat down on the edge of the veranda with the last T-shirt in his lap.

"If everything is perfect, it will be pure white. If it's uncontaminated. Pure white. And fluffy. Like..."

"Like a toy."

"Yes. Yes. It's very soft and very beautiful and if it's healthy it grows all over the substrate. Then, when the time is right, and everything is just perfect for that mycelium, everything sterile and the correct and stable temperature and humidity is maintained for the right amount of time, fruiting will occur. Mushrooms will grow. At first they will be tiny, like little pins. When they first appear it's called pinning. And then they will thicken. Grow firm and strong. A bulge will begin to form at the tops of the pins, and soon a split will appear under the bulge."

"I'm too hot. It's too hot out here."

"Traces of the rupture remain as the volva on the stems. Like a tatty, ripped collar. Then the caps expand and flare open in slow motion. Like umbrellas, bursting on the street in a monsoon. Imagine the street filled with people when a monsoon starts. All those colors, reflected in the rain in the street. Bursting open. Like butterflies from cocoons."

"It's going to rain."

"Mushrooms are a thing completely different from people and plants."

"There was a big earthquake last night."

"They have gills. They have colors. They come in more shapes than flowers. You touch them, you feel them and they don't feel like anything else in this world. Skin finer than a young peach. Flesh softer than the orchid's bowl."

"It was a really big one. Mushrooms are boring."

"I love them," Yasu said quietly. "Yes, I do."

He stood up.

"I love earthquakes," said the little girl. "And . . . and . . . rain. You're a drug dealer, all alone."

She disappeared.

The sliding door slammed shut.

Before he went inside, Yasu checked the skies.

Clouds were crawling in, clouds that had traveled from Mongolia, over the endless mountains of Northwest China, over the plains and the Yangtze delta, clouds that had rained into the Japan Sea, and risen again in the heat to stifle the valleys of Nagano. Now spreading across the skies of Saitama, colonizing the deep blue that was black seen through ozone. Spreading relentlessly, like the tendrils of hyphae of a thickening mycelium; the beginnings of a new and strange life, a foundation: an invasion of fluffy white mold, or an army, of the new and the pure, from spore inoculated into a land, a sky, a substrate. And, at last, fruit: empire, storm, a tiny perfect mushroom. Not made but conjured. There are three Kingdoms by one way of thinking, Yasu learned in high school. Plant, Animal, Fungi. A mushroom is not a is not a. It comes and is made from the clouds that flood a sky. But clouds never take that crystal step unless you say it is water, snow, ice. A glacier, a berg.

The whirling white so insubstantial makes this tiny thing so real.

Heart beating hard, with strength gathered at last, Yasu pegged the final T-shirt's corner as the rain clouds massed above him.

He opened his own sliding door, stepped gingerly over one of the fanned stacks of CDs.

The girl's feet above rumbled across the ceiling or was it thunder.

He pulled down his shorts and his boxers in one bundle, and stripped off his FBI T-shirt.

He checked the humidity meter.

96% and rising.

Temperature:

93°F.

Naked, he untaped the left side of the airlock.

"Oh, no," he whispered.

Before stepping into the dimness of the ex-bedroom, in the wash of cool wet air and in the borrowed light from the living room and the open refrigerator's lamp he saw what the earthquake had done.

The land's ripple had toppled from the windowsill the twin tall urns of his parents' remains.

Toppled, and smashed.

Across his workbench pieces of porcelain and the ashes of his mother and father had poured and mixed, a gray, rough dust over the jars, the flasks, the Bunsen burner and the petri dishes. Some of the dishes were used, lying open, and the ash was darker on the moist agar. And onto containers cracked from the impact, holding the substrates made from rice flour and water, prepared days before, sterilized and ready for inoculation with spore. The ash covered everything, contaminating everything. The test tubes, the syringes, the bottle of sterilizing alcohol. Coating the shade of the UV lamp, heaped on four small glass terraria, spread on his notebooks, his records of growth. A fine dark mist over the new series of slides at the edge of the bench by the best microscope. Spilling over from the table onto the floor and into the trays of Chinese organic cornflour substrate arranged underneath, the free-growth experiments.

And fat black flakes hanging in the spiderweb between the workbench's leg and the wall, the web of Izanami, the huge spider he let stay, who survived fumigation, she earned respect, a pet.

Catherine
March 2001

High above the Pacific Ocean, the airplane peels through the darkened sky.

Below, the clouds spread out like sheets of moonlit snow. Finely puckered, like untouched ice cream, tufts drawn up by the seal of the container's lifted cap. An updraught far off at the horizon makes a winding-sheet of furling clouds.

Inside the airplane, seat 2A, a young blond woman's hair is bright and deep, as are the shadows of her nose and cheekbones under the tight glare of a reading lamp. The airplane's sound around her is like a roaring river deep inside rock. Passengers sleep. The Japanese man beside her is fully encased in an airline blanket; his shoes precisely tucked under the retracted footrest like cutlery. Down the aisle, two or three other reading lamps light up bald spots, shine on the fine oil of scalps. No attendants roam the aisles, or move to pick up one small fallen pillow, smeared in pink patches by the floor's red LEDs.

She stirs. She had fallen asleep over her laptop. The woman's gray suit is only a little rumpled with all these hours of flight. She has brushed the fabric taut several times in the bathrooms, on this long trip, to smooth out the creases before they fix. The suit's stomach and bust is lit grayly by the screen of the slim black laptop, alight in her lap. She is traveling to another new country after living in Japan for more than two years. She sits up a little straighter, and starts typing silently, in short sporadic bursts, stabbing at it with some difficulty, as if the keys are displaying wrong characters, betraying her will.

The progress is rough, with large pauses between efforts. Sometimes she lifts a hand and turns the pages of a paperback, nestled on the other books in the crook between her left thigh and the armrest.

She types, and turns pages.

She sighs.

She squints down at the screen, forehead lined in concentration.

As her fingers move, the letters that appear begin to clot up the borrowed glare on her smoothed suit with complexities, begin to fill the white void with spidery black ivy.

Gradually the rhythm settles, and the cushioned keys make muffled padding sounds like kittens' feet on hardwood floors.

Catherine Barnes
Tut. 1B
Journal Question One
William Shakespeare's *Twelfth Night*
5000 words
Due May 30, 2001

Twelfth Night is about love, nation, and mistaken and assumed identity.

Shakespeare's *Twelfth Night* is about the relationship between love and nation, complicated by

William Shakespeare's

made more complicated by identity mistaken or assumed
that is mistaken or assumed
or both

William Shakespeare's *Twelfth Night* is about the relationship between love and nation and mistaken and assumed identities. A brother and a sister, Sebastian and Viola, come separately to the beaches of the bewilderingly strange land of Illyria after their ship sinks off its shore. Both think the other has been killed in the wreck, so they each try to start new lives in this, a strange new land. But in the new land the world they find is pervasively filled with a spirit of revelry and hedonism and self-indulgence. This is echoed in the title: *Twelfth Night.*

Twelfth Night is the Feast of the Epiphany, the last night of Christian Christmas festivities.

Orsino, the Duke of the land of Illyria, sits around and listens to music and says beautiful things about love, but he seems to be indulging his sadness at his unrequited love.

For example, he says

He likes to talk about his feelings and his hurt and voice his theories about love, and love that is not returned. He loves to listen to music that reminds him of his sadness. This makes it feel really real so it's a kind of happiness or revelry in feeling in love when it's not returned. I don't think he knows what sadness really is.

The spirit of revelry that exists in Illyria is contagious, too. Because after the shipwreck when Viola has only been in the land a little while and has said only a few

has said just twelve lines,

that include talking about her own brother dying, she mentions that she has heard the Duke Orsino is a bachelor. Already she is thinking about sex because here in this new land there are no rules for her. She has no family and no nationality. She feels free, with no responsibilities, only opportunity.

Olivia, who(m?) Orsino loves, but who she is very cruel in return to, is a bit of a moper too. Olivia is mourning her brother who died seven years ago but this often seems like just an excuse to put off Orsino (sometimes/perhaps). And later, the Fool says she is a fool to mope.

For example,

It has been seven years. You could say she is "reveling" in her misery, wallowing in her sadness in the same way as Orsino wallows in his. "There is no cuckold but calamity" Feste says. This means you cannot be true to sadness forever. That you betray sadness, or the terrible thing that makes you sad. You could say that Shakespeare is saying these two characters in this new land are pleasure seekers too; (or:) that they are hedonists of sadness. You could say a lot of things but the things they say about their sadness are beautiful and sound very sincere. Olivia's cousin Sir Toby and his friend Sir Andrew Aguecheek are always drinking wine and dancing. They tell jokes and enjoy life. They trick Malvolio with Maria and the Fool. This is revelry, too. But later, at the end of William Shakespeare's *Twelfth Night,* bad things happen to them both. So the title seems to say that the end of the festivities in Illyria are growing near and people have to pay

But this question is about the Fool, so as the above characters are obviously not important I will deal with them no further.

I will deal with them later.

The Fool only appears in scene five, Act One, and the first thing that is said to him, by Maria, is "My lady will hang thee for thy absence."

Since the Fool, Feste, is the subject of this essay, on William Shakespeare's *Twelfth Night,* I will now discuss him in terms of his absence before the play's action and then I will discuss his role in the actual action of the play and in relation to the other main characters in the world of revelry which is as what I will call a moral chorus, or blind justice

806 words incl. title page

4194 to go

814 words

4186 to go

819 _____

The airplane thrums and roars in the hollow of space, the sound muffled by sky and metal. An off-sound, a no-sound. The roar of a heart between beats, the hum of violent thoughts in a giant silent crowd. The light thrown on the woman's chest is silver and brighter now. Her finger moves over the obsidian pad, the half-pear of the flesh of her palm furrowed, whitened slightly, against the laptop's edge. The glint of a fine gold watchstrap.

See her: the fabric of her suitsleeve: cream, blue, gray, what is it now, in the glare of the screen.

She spell-checks.

Yasu
February 2000

It is almost completely silent in the terrarium.

Silent, cool and damp. The only light comes from the lamp inside the small doorless refrigerator, a faint gray from the blacked-out window and a ghostly, mottled haze through the triple-layered polythene airlock. Inside the terrarium the airlock is less strange than it appears in the living room, because the room's walls and ceiling are covered in polythene. The polythene sheets are glued to the walls at intervals and taped at the seams and corners and against the ceiling. Because of the regularity of their spacing, the room resembles a padded room for violents in an old asylum, the glue like the buttons in crisp plastic pillows. The polythene is beaded with condensation. Occasionally droplets fall from the ceiling and spatter on the floor. The sounds are dead and echoless and only very occasional because, like the drip trays in the fruiting terraria, the polythene ceiling is glued at an acute angle to the ceiling. Most of the condensed moisture runs east, down the wall to a plastic gutter, and into a bowl in the corner that must be emptied every forty-eight hours. The liquid from the bowl has a tinge of salt from his body.

Yasu, sitting cross-legged and naked in the center of the room.

The refrigerator's lamp makes deep shadows in the folds of fat at his hips and belly. It shines in his glasses, across the pages of the thick book in his lap and in the glass of flasks, beakers, the small terraria on the bench. In the dim light, large trays of substrate are visible under the bench, uncovered, the experiments in free growth using the bedroom as a macro-terrarium. It is too dark to see if there are any mushrooms fruiting, let alone if they are contaminant-free. It is dark, cool and moist. Very quiet.

In the corner by the airlock, a shelf system the height of a man holds several more terraria, maybe twenty acrylic polyhedra, inside which rice cakes the size of saucers, covered in blinding white mycelium, some fruiting, some not, rest on wire mesh. Like the draped ceiling, the drip trays above them send the condensation east. Yasu has many routines, many rules of practice that meet only spiritual needs. Each terrarium has its own miniature homemade humidifier alongside it on the shelving, humming faithfully, sending cool, moist air inside the boxes. Two full-size industrial Panasonic humidifiers are next to the shelving system and their hum merges with the smaller hums and becomes background, a feel of busy silence. The humidifiers took the terrarium up to 94% humidity and down to 83°F. Yasu moved in the refrigerator, removed the door and shaved off two degrees while picking up a single, vital percent.

At last count, including the free trays under the bench, Yasu had ninety-three cakes in different stages of fruiting and forty-one steadily colonizing with mycelium. Yasu sees himself as neither amateur nor professional. He likes the sound of "semi-industrial." The maintenance of a project this size is a full-time job. To keep a steady supply of full-grown mushrooms he needs to have fungi at every stage of growth. Five years ago, the incident he refers to as My Own Private Kobe shut down sales for five months before a new crop of saleable quality was ready. Every piece of equipment to sterilize, every piece of polythene to replace, a total fumigation, new rice cakes to be mixed and heat-treated, the waiting, the watering, the endless maintenance, the inexplicable survival of Izanami throughout the entire process. Then, after weeks of waiting, monitoring of the wispy white hyphae for patches of color in the white, came the ecstatic days of the arrival of pins, and heart-in-throat inspections of the fragile, miniature blooms for any discoloration, the telltale bruises of purple and blue. He cannot afford to relax. Alien fungi in the shrooms and weeks later in a club in Tokyo someone will collapse, spinal cord clenching, blood and froth and pieces of his mushrooms on their lips.

Some of these are foreigners. He knows he would be found.

Today the bonsai are watered, the cakes are checked, the bowl emptied, the temperature and humidity correct and stable, Yasu is showered, exfoliated with pumice, and now sitting, moist too, in the peaceful dim, surrounded by silent life, his keitai mute at his feet, reading to his children from the *Kojiki*, the *Record of Ancient Matters*.

Yasu has reached Chapter 3 in Book One. The seven generations of the age of gods have appeared from the primordial chaos, including Izanami and Izanagi. He begins to read, at first in a whisper, until he grows accustomed to the sound of his voice, and then a little more loudly.

"At this time the heavenly deities, all with one command, said to the two deities Izanagi and Izanami, 'Complete and solidify this drifting land.' Giving them the Heavenly Jeweled Spear, they entrusted the mission to them. Thereupon, the two deities stood on the Heavenly Floating Bridge and, lowering the jeweled spear, stirred with it. They stirred the brine with a churning-churning sound."

Yasu murmurs in the hum and the dim, "*Koworo koworo, koworo koworo*," swaying back and forth, as he reads.

"And when they lifted up the spear again, the brine dripping down from the tip of the spear piled up, and became an island. This was the island Onogoro."

He pauses.

"Descending from the heavens to this island, they erected a heavenly pillar and a spacious palace. At this time Izanagi asked Izanami, saying, 'How is your body formed?'

"She replied, saying, 'My body, formed though it be formed, has one place which is formed insufficiently.'

"Then Izanagi said, 'My body, formed though it be formed, has one place which is formed to excess. Therefore, I would like to take that place in my body which is formed to excess and insert it into that place in your body which is formed insufficiently, and thus give birth to the land. How would this be?'

"Izanami replied, saying, 'That will be good.'

"Then Izanagi said, 'Then let us, you and me, walk in a circle around this heavenly pillar and meet and have conjugal intercourse.'"

Yasu arches his back, rolling his shoulders to stretch. A boy his age, less accustomed to solitude, might have sniggered. Yasu does not snigger anymore.

"After thus agreeing, Izanagi then said, 'You walk around from the right, and I will walk around from the left and meet you.' After having agreed to this they circled around; then Izanami said first, 'Oh, how good a lad!' Afterward, Izanagi said, 'Oh, how good a maiden!' After each had finished speaking, Izanagi said to his spouse, 'It is not proper that the woman speak first.' Nevertheless, they commenced procreation and gave birth to a leech-child. They placed this child into a boat made of reeds and floated it away. Next, they gave birth to the island of Apa. This also is not reckoned as one of their children."

Yasu lowers the thick, hardbound book, which once belonged to his father. He peers under the workbench, waiting for his eyes to adapt to the dark. He cannot see her web, or her. He closes his eyes.

"Izanami. Izanami," he whispers. The humidifiers hum and sputter faintly. "Did you hear that. Don't talk before I do. All the babies will be leech-children. I'll have to flush them away."

Izanami does not answer.

Yasu opens his eyes and holds the book up into the light. He flicks forward a couple of pages. He summarizes, for his own, more than the terrarium's, benefit.

"Izanagi and Izanami repeat the marriage ritual correctly. They give birth to many islands. Then they give birth to many deities, like the deities of the seas and the rivers, the winds and the trees and the mountains and the plains. At last Izanami gives birth to the fire deity and her genitals are burned and she gets sick. In her vomit are gods. In her feces are gods and in her urine are gods. She dies from the birth, and goes to the land of Yomi." Yasu lifts his head, the light playing on his glasses, and says to the darkened underside of the bench: "In death there are all these kinds of life."

He begins again from Chapter 8. The father kills the child who killed his mother in the act of being born.

"'Alas, I have given my beloved spouse in exchange for a mere child!' Izanagi cried.

"Then Izanagi unsheathed the sword ten hands long which he was wearing at his side and cut off the head of his child, the fire-deity. Hereupon the blood adhering to the tip of the sword gushed forth onto the massed rocks, bringing three deities into existence. Next the blood adhering to the sword-guard of the sword also gushed forth onto the massed rocks, bringing three more deities into existence. Next, the blood collected at the hilt of the sword dripped through his fingers, bringing two more deities into existence. These are the eight deities born by the sword.

"Some say this is the myth of sword-tempering," Yasu murmurs. He has read the Kojiki so many times he knows these favorite sections by heart. Dialogue in the Kojiki is often punctuated with exclamation marks and when he reads the dialogue aloud, though his voice remains a dull, flat monotone, the voice he hears in his head is exultant, strong, convinced. A freshly tempered sword could be completely sterile, it occurs to him. He flicks pages slowly.

"At this time, Izanagi, wishing to meet again his spouse Izanami, went after her to the land of Yomi. When she came forth out of the door of the hall to greet him, Izanagi said, 'Oh, my beloved spouse, the lands which you and I were making have not yet been completed, you must come back!'

"Then Izanami replied, saying, 'How I regret that you did not come sooner. I have eaten at the hearth of Yomi. But, oh my beloved husband, how awesome it is that you have entered here! Therefore I will go and discuss for a while with the gods of Yomi my desire to return. Pray do not look upon me!'

"Thus saying, she went back into the hall, but her absence was so long that he could no longer wait. Thereupon he broke off one of the large end-teeth of the comb he was wearing in his left hair-bunch, lit it as one fire, and entered in to see.

"At this time, maggots were squirming and roaring in the corpse of Izanami."

Yasu pauses here, one of his favorite moments.

"And in her body were all the thunder deities."

Outside, as Yasu summarizes Izanagi's fear, his flight from Yomi and the pursuit of the hags sent by shamed Izanami, it is growing dark. It is February in Saitama, and this means early nightfall and bitterly cold winds. Inside the terrarium it is a steady 81°F, and the growing darkness outside throws a greater emphasis on the red and blue displays of the humidifiers, the tiny glare of the lamp inside the refrigerator, the sparkles and glints in the glassware. It's maybe five o'clock, and the children from the apartment above are not home yet. It is very quiet in the spaces between Yasu's reading. He sometimes spends whole days in here, especially in summer. Yasu's mother and father both contracted cancer within months of one another and were placed in separate hospitals in Yokohama. Prodigious Yasu was studying undergrad biology under a special dispensation from the grad school of Chemistry at Rikkyo (née St. Paul's) University in Ikebukuro, and coming up to final exams. Their deaths were not protracted, and his enduring memory of the last days was their mutual, separate insistences; their telephoned refusals to see him or distract him, right to the end.

Placing the urns of ashes in the terrarium had been his tribute. It had also been a kind of claim on their attention. Yasu is a scientist who has been a long time alone. His understanding of souls has developed its own private structure. Part-Shintoist, part-scientist and part-Buddhist, with a somewhat baffling graft of American Episcopal Christianity at Rikkyo. This was where the early work in plant biology, the long commutes and his parents' deaths prepped him for the endless hours required of a doctorate in advanced Plant Morphogenesis closer to home—the smaller, newer, less prestigious Saitama University—and the isolation, the total commitment, the distrust of boundaries in research that led to a couple of months of yet more prodigal status and finally the scandal and his disgrace. Thrown out and upon his own devices for five long years, he still feels himself a complicated kind of failure, and he has developed strong beliefs in soul–body indivisibility, even post-cremation. But keeping his parents' ashes instead of having them buried was a matter not really of religion, but of love, and acceptance, and the cleansing of guilt, and therefore very private. Forlornly, guiltily fumigating the terrarium, cleaning and sterilizing every single piece of equipment, vacuuming, heat-treating, even scouring the walls and floors with industrial bleach in a polythene pantsuit, have not, though, removed his parents from what was his bedroom. Though for his mushrooms he made the decision to evict, purge utterly, clean house, fumigate, and that in some ways he broke his own heart for the thing he does—his work—he doesn't know that some of their remains do in fact still linger in the free-growth trays under the bench he moved briefly outside then straight back in, completely overlooking the influence of his mama and papa, pervasive even post-mortem, post-cremation, post-revelation.

"Hereupon, Izanagi said, 'I have been to a most unpleasant land, a horrible unclean land. Therefore I shall purify myself.' Arriving at the plain Apaki-para by the river-mouth of Tatibana in Pimuka in Tukusi, he purified and exorcised himself. When he flung down his clothing various deities came into existence. He dived into the river. When he washed his left eye, there came into existence a deity named Amaterasu. Next, when he washed his right eye, there came into existence a deity named Tukuyomi. Next, when he washed his nose, there came into existence a deity named Susa-no-wo. These were his last children. To Amaterasu, he said, 'You shall rule the sun.' To Tukuyomi, he said, 'You shall rule the realms of the night.' To Susa-no-wo, he said, 'You shall rule the ocean.'"

Yasu is suddenly startled.

His keitai is shuddering violently on the floor in pulses, the screen lit puce-red.

He stares about the room, at the flashes of red, the harsh glints on the polythene, the shimmering, jagged shadows of his equipment cast distorted onto the walls.

The keitai describes a small, shivering circle on the floor at his feet. Yasu lowers the *Kojiki* to his lap. Still watching the walls, he reaches slowly down with his right hand and tries to locate the phone using his hand's pulsing shadows. The vibrating phone makes a droning, almost human, moaning sound. His hand begins to follow the expanding circle the phone is tracing, in slow motion, like a blinded person checking for a heated element on a stovetop. Seconds before the tenth ring finishes and his answering service begins, in one motion Yasu lowers his hand, takes the phone smoothly and presses TALK with his index finger.

As he lifts it to his ear, the side of his face is lit red and his glasses sparkle.

It is his first phone call in weeks.

"Yes," he says.

"Hey. Is this Tanabe Yasuhiko?" the voice says.

"Yes."

"Hey, man. What's happening. It's Suzuki Manabu. From Heaven On Earth."

"Oh. Yes," Yasu says in the darkness.

"Hey. Long time no see, man. It's been like, six months."

A small silent space.

"That is almost correct," Yasu says.

"Uh-huh."

The voice pauses.

"So," it says. "Right. A long time."

Yasu doesn't help.

"Hey. Well, are you still, like . . . growing, man? We had a lot of feedback on your old stuff. And we've had a lot of, uh, well, a *lot* of requests for more. And a few warnings, too." Laughing is audible, somewhere in the background. "But uh, we usually take that as, you know, a pretty good sign. Of like, potency. And you know, some of our customers are firsttimers. And foreigners."

"Yes," Yasu says. There is no interpretable change of tone.

"So. Man, we haven't seen you in such a long time. What's happening? I've been meaning to catch up."

The caller waits for an answer.

There is none.

"Are you still growing, man? Your stuff is the best, you know that. The percentages are like nothing on this earth, man. We had to cut doses by two-thirds and up the price. You know we branded yours separately, don't you? I mean, so what I'm getting at, I guess, is that I'm wondering if we can like help you go ahead and foist some more of that crazy shit on the world through, well like through our little shop. Yeah."

Yasu doesn't reply. The boy's voice is gravel in his ear, the sound of any language an intrusion in this room. He is wondering if the red of the display would be visible through his cheek if he opened his mouth. He doesn't want to tie up the line. There are other calls he is expecting. He will check his cheeks in the darkened bathroom mirror when the call is over.

The caller, failing to get a response, tries a different tack.

"Right. But anyhow, hey, and so we found another Grade A continuity error in *Melrose Place*, man! Fifth season. Episode twenty. It's a really good one. Jake thinks Alison doesn't want to have his baby. He freaks. He trashes D&D. He goes to see his ex-girlfriend in Sutter's Creek, the mother of his son. He gets real angry and kicks in her fence. You know this one? It's a subtle one, man. Really . . . subtle. You may not have picked it up. He fixes her fence. So at the beginning of uh, episode . . . twenty, he's getting ready to leave . . . and he's sitting on his motorbike, and they recap everything . . . his ex-girlfriend keeps calling him 'rigid,' it's great, man . . . 'You can be so . . . rigid,' she keeps saying . . . yeah, and but, so, she says, 'Thought you might want another cup of coffee. It's a long way back to Los Angeles,' because he's going back to, like, pregnant Alison, you know, with her incompetent cervix, and he says, 'Sure,' and so she gives him the cup of coffee and he's sitting on his bike drinking the coffee . . . and the son comes out and the ex goes inside . . . do you know this one, man? I bet you don't. It's a subtle one. And Jake and his kid talk . . . for a long time . . . about father–son stuff . . . and then . . . they stop, and the kid runs inside . . . and Jake drives away. And then but . . . the cup . . . the coffee cup disappears. It disappears, man. He doesn't bend down and put it on the ground. He doesn't put it in his pocket. The cup just completely disappears from the dialectic. Massive, Grade A continuity error. What do you think?"

Yasu can see the episode clearly in his head. Jake is astride the big bike, rear wheel against the curb, his hands cupped in his lap. Colleen jogging inside to find the son's gym shoes. The estranged David, maybe ten years old, standing, talking with Jake. He can see the subtitles, see the line breaks. He can hear the dialogue, the English only ten percent understood, the rest blurring.

So you're done running away, huh?

Yeah, I guess I am.

You know, I knew who you were when you showed up. Mom never said any-thing, but . . . I just knew.

You did, huh.

Yeah. Hey, remember that time we talked about getting pissed off at stuff? I used to get really angry at you, cos you weren't around.

Yeah, I'm sorry about that. You know, things were kind of complicated. And by the time I did get to meet you, your dad was gonna adopt you. So I had to let you go.

I know. I'm not mad at you anymore. I already have a dad. I used to wonder about you. Like where you were. Did you care about me at all?

I care.

Yeah. Hey, I'm glad you came. I like talking to you. It means a lot to me.

Me too. You're a good kid.

Exeunt.

Yasu sees Jake kick-starting the big motorcycle. The smooth accelera-tion out into the road and off into the distance. And the son running inside the house to his mother, he's happy, so mature for his age, the acceptance of both adopted and biological fathers, but content with his choice, the "father who was there" is always the best, but stay in touch, he's running lankily inside, legs long and crooked like a foal, late for school, hands clasped in front of him.

"Are you there?" the caller says. "Like hello?"

"It's a B," Yasu says.

"What?"

"It's a Grade B. It's episode twenty-one of season five, and it's a B. First aired seventeenth of February, 1997. Your error stems from the counting of the earlier double episode, "Great Sex-pectations," Parts One and Two, as a single episode. It was a double episode because Part Two was Melrose's one hundred and fiftieth episode. If you count it as one episode you make a mistake. You eliminate the reason for the double episode's existence."

"Oh. Right."

"When David runs inside he is carrying the coffee cup that Jake had in his hands during the conversation. It is difficult to see, because his back is turned, but we are afforded a glimpse. We can assume the cup changed hands outside of shot. It doesn't constitute a Grade A violation. It's a B: an uncomfortable but explicable transition in the characters' relationship to the mise-en-scène. It's a B."

"Oh."

"Hey, I'm glad you called," Yasu says in English. "I like talking to you. It means a lot to me. You're a good kid."

"What, man?"

Yasu presses END.

He puts the keitai down on the floor and claps the *Kojiki* shut in his naked lap.

A scattering of wayward spore, no bigger than motes of dust, flakes of life, trapped in Chapter 12 of Book One, are puffed out. In the updraught from the closed book they shoot invisibly straight up. As Yasu puts the book aside and uncurls his legs and prepares to stiffly stand, they waft gently down, one tracing his forehead like his mother's fingertip, catching unnoticed in the lashes of his left eye. He blinks as he crouches beside the workbench to see if Izanami is still in there, after all his one-sided conversations, and the spore falls free. It drifts down the inside of the thick left lens of his glasses and floats slowly and lazily out on the draught of his breath, sideways and down through the moist air, and settles at last, joining the others on the tray of moist substrate at the very rear of the trays under the bench, in the darkest, coolest spot, directly beneath the place where pregnant Izanami's web stretches up and away from the wooden leg of the workbench.

James
1999

For me, summer in this city is days of waiting for my flight to Japan, days of waiting to leave New Zealand, days of hot nor-west winds. I get headaches and my skin itches. My eyes always hurt and I have to wear my glasses and I don't eat and I drink too much. The heat makes smoking unpleasant but I do it more anyway. My flat is almost empty. My flatmates have already gone. There is too much dust and no TV and no stereo and I can never sleep; just drink late and remember things as if I am dying.

It is near the ends of things, just days before I am due to leave the country forever. The people I know are divided only into those who are leaving and those who are staying. Time is unmarked, unpunctuated by any routine. There are only stupid farewell parties, my increasingly pathetic phone calls to my bank—sometimes pleading, sometimes deliberately stilted and vague, like I don't understand my obligations, the size of my overdraft, so many figures it's simply surreal to me now—and the loneliness of enrollment week when you live in a university town and you're neither in nor out, the flat cleanouts and garage sales, and an Orientation emphatically (and for the first time, not as a matter of taste) nothing to do with me.

I am sleeping in my brother's sleeping bag on the floor in my empty flat, my room bright all night from streetlights that hiss and flicker outside my now curtainless windows.

There are words printed on the boxes that are stacked in the corner of my room, beside the phone on the floor that is still connected and for which I will foot the bill: *Pringles 10 x 200g. Skittles 10 x 20pcs. Marlboro. Dunhill. Peter Stuyvesant. Benson and Hedges.*

These boxes contain the only things left of my life here: clothes I want to keep; clothes I want to throw away.

So it's the end of summer, and I am leaving soon.

I saw Michael again for the first time in two years when I was walking home from the Dux Deluxe. Even though they have jobs Daz and Chelsea invited me to another farewell party, parties that are dragging out now interminably. We sat outside at a rocking plastic table and I paid for a pitcher to share and smiled when Daz made another of the toasts.

"Here's to all our futures." He really holds up glasses and toasts. He's hard to resist sometimes.

"I'll just have iced water, I think," Chelsea said.

Thank god, I thought.

"You're not drinking," Daz said.

"Daz, I'm on antibiotics," she said.

Chelsea only says his name when I'm around. This is one of those incredible things about couples you suddenly just know.

"But that's no reason not to drink though is it?" He looked at me. I shrugged, and sighed, tried to smile.

"Oh alright," she sighed, and we laughed (*I* laughed) and poured her a drink.

And by midnight and closing Chelsea was vomiting under the table and Daz was leaning over her feebly patting her back, whispering into her hair, and when we tried to carry her to a taxi Daz staggered and lost his grip under her armpits, her shirt ripped, pulled up, showing her bra as her head bumped on the ground and I thought this is now way too . . . but what? She did it: bumped and moaned and whispered secret Gaelic words, she moaned them incoherently, and I did not believe, I said I don't care, I am glad to be leaving this, this doesn't matter now, I am glad to be going, and I gave them twenty dollars for the taxi, left them sprawled in the back seat, mumbling love and complaint, and I walked home up Victoria Street alone.

And it was then, the moment, as I walked past the Carlton two-four, that I saw the boy in the expensive ragged khaki shirt being served at the counter. And though I didn't know it was him straightaway, I stopped. Because I'm susceptible to all kinds of things, especially repetition.

As I waited he paid and smiled and then he came out the automatic doors and he was walking toward me past petrol pumps and air pumps and bent men doing difficult things under fluorescent lights, a package of tobacco in his hand and his long stride and I just knew it was him so suddenly, and he'd gotten so thin and so pale and his black hair was so short and some people you see and just know there's something special, his pants ripped and stained but somehow clean, a different kind of clean than my own clothes ever achieve, and I felt I was falling down to something when he smiled and it's one of those smiles, a smile that makes decisions, and he came upon me suddenly, too close, and said, or whispered really,

"James."

"Michael," I said, and then he was hugging me and his smell was all around me, alcohol and sweat and smoke and cologne, and some smells go deep and I dropped my keys and left them there on the footpath as I hugged him back.

Halfway through my second year, when my father was sick in Christchurch Public Hospital and I had finished my midyears, I took a bus to Picton alone, crossed Cook Strait by ferry on my student loan, all to visit him at his parents' house in Wellington. This was before anything had happened, two and a half years ago, when we were friends. We would drink together at his flat then and sometimes he would try to explain things to me, once, "nada." ("Nada," he would say, leaning over, smiling at me, smelling of tobacco and beer. "Nothingness. Absence. Just think about it for a moment." "I'm trying, Michael," I would say, smiling back at him, and I was, then.)

He would get agitated. He would rave, drunk, drawing diagrams illegible to me he claimed visually demonstrated postmodernism does not exist. He would lecture me about literature.

"The tradition here is ruined by this just constant parochial lyricism, actual *kinds* as opposed to *degrees* of sentimentality, the perpetual obsessions with memory and loss and fucking *hills,* and lately these annoying middle-class varsity graduate girls whining in first person about how hard love is and how shitty and weak men are," he would tell me, staring intently at me with bloodshot eyes.

"But Michael, you don't even read novels," I would gently tell him.

"Who does?" he would mutter. "Poetry's quicker," and he would stand up, pace the room, play *Pathétique* andante on the untuned piano, finish his drink and spend half an hour in the bathroom painting his face camouflage.

I knew his address in Wellington and took a taxi from the ferry terminal. Somewhere near the Botanical Gardens, backed by trees and bush and hills, his father's—a judge's—house was huge and old. No one was home, and I could hear Hüsker Dü, his sister's German shepherd, barking deep inside the house, and I waited on their veranda for five hours, watching their pool and smoking cigarettes.

He never arrived, no one did, and I came back to this city and never told him about my trip, never told him I had seen his house.

Walking in long, easy strides toward me, a blue fifty-gram pack of Drum in his hand, so tall, his clothes hanging off him, darkness around his eyes, a brilliant smile, his hair shaved so short but still thick and black, he says it, my name, coming toward me, my name is all it takes.

"James."

"Michael," I say back to him before he hugs me.

Can a thing be a memory if it just happened.

Is a memory more or less powerful if it is just days old.

Does distance make something more a memory or less.

These are the questions that preoccupy me as I piece together a life, waiting, in this place.

And then, three days after I saw him, it was the phone call from Elisabeth, one of Michael's ex-girlfriends.

"Hello?"

"James. Hello."

"Elisabeth."

"When are you leaving."

"Soon. A few days."

"Well. Michael called me."

"Did he."

"He said he'd seen you. And that he wants to see you again before you go. *You,* of course."

"What did he say."

"He wants you to bring him a cap. *My* drugs, but he wants *you* to bring it. It's just typical of him. I suppose you've been seeing him a lot."

"It was the first time in two years, Elisabeth. What did he say."

"He asked me if I was still dealing. And what you were doing. It's like, Hi. Are you still dealing. What's James doing. Haven't seen him since he disappeared and the fucking second thing he asks me about is you."

"What does he want."

"He wants you to bring him a cap of oil. *My* oil, if you can believe that shit."

"Did he sound alright?"

No answer.

"Elisabeth?"

"I don't know. I can't tell now."

So now I had to buy a fifty-dollar cap for Michael with my last New Zealand cash. All I would have left would be traveler's cheques in US dollars. A mystery, because I know he could get hash from Simon, his itinerant Chinese-American homestay. On the phone Elisabeth gave me her address, and a code number for her gate, some faux-secure peach stucco Bealey Ave gated apartment with a lap pool and security cameras, told me to come around and pick up the cap, anytime would be fine.

She was nice to me, surprisingly, because I suppose she still loves him, even now.

I never told him I had seen his house, but I did tell him my father was sick.

After he returned from wherever he had been (he never told me; I never asked) we were drinking beer in the living room of his place here, listening to Tom Waits on his stereo. Michael lived alone in a house in Saint Albans then, and he did something at the university that drove him mad, but I never found out what, exactly. If he was in the country, he was always home, and I would arrive in the evenings, find him reading, and we would walk to the bottlestore together and buy two riggers of beer each (Canterbury Draught, Southern Draught; although his father was a judge and he'd been seen around in a sports car, I suspected it was Simon's and he always bought cheap alcohol, draught beer to drink at home).

The staff at the bottlestore knew him by name. I later learned he babysat—actually *babysat*—for the manager's wife. When we got back we would sit and drink together and he would try to read Faulkner, sometimes muttering—hissing almost—*"Yes,"*—but never to me. As he read I would listen to Tom croaking and watch the sunstripes on his mattress shift and move, the shapes of smoke from his rollies dissolving into a haze that filled the room. I would pretend I was reading, too, and wonder why he smoked tobacco from a pouch when he had a passport so thick with staples and stamps.

Sometimes, later, if we got really drunk, he would run around the room, climbing over the sofa and onto his tiny rocking desk, jumping on the mattress and bouncing up and down, his eyes wild, laughing madly, actually cackling, throwing pillows and books at me to make me—his words—"less becalmed." He would invent impromptu raps and name his furniture after famous crusaders like Walter the Penniless. His mother was Japanese, though it was hard to see it in him other than his skin, which was waxen, and the darkness of his hair and eyes. I'd heard his father had a "significant number" of shares in Ciba-Geigy.

"I'm a mountebank and you're my zany!" he would shout at me and make me race him to the two-four for snacks and more tobacco. I was nineteen, and all I knew was he was younger.

The afternoon I told him I was drunker than him for once and he'd been watching me, just sipping at his drinks. I kept changing the music in the middle of songs, trying to piss him off. It only made him smile.

Later, I lay on his couch with my eyes closed against the headspins and whispered it.

"My father is sick."

He didn't say anything, but I heard the springs in the armchair creak and light footsteps coming across the floor. He sat on the arm of the sofa. He stroked my hair and neither of us said anything for a long time.

Finally, I said, "I think he's dying."

"It's divine," Michael whispered in the dark above me. There was a long silence. "If you don't feel anything, that's divine too."

I remember the only night he slept at my house, later, after it first began.

I remember him asking me to be quiet so he could listen to a Spiritualized song. I remember not being able to concentrate on anything when he was in my room.

I remember standing naked in front of the stereo in my room at three in the morning, looking for a CD in the dim green light of the stereo's clock.

The bed creaks behind me and out of nowhere cool fingers run up the inside of my thigh. The smell of his aftershave, and cigarette smoke. His palm cups my balls, and I jolt and shudder like I've been electrocuted.

I remember it was like that after we first began. The more we were together and the more we slept together, the more sex we had, the more he only made sounds to me. Never words; just sounds.

As we lay together in utter darkness, when he was asleep or dozing or beginning to wake, he would make soft grunts, tiny sounds without shape, beginning or ending. Vocalizations and nothing more.

I remember thinking they were the most beautiful sounds.

Walking toward me, long lean legs in loose ripped cargo pants, a face at once open and closed, eyes intense, unwavering, his hair shaved so short but still thick, densely black. Before he speaks I see him like this: painfully young, his corrupt pout revealing some different kind of age, walking toward me, choosing me. Out of the bitter bright fluorescent lights of the two-four and into the street in a loose khaki shirt, *Juan* written on a patch at the breast pocket, fifty grams of the only tobacco he ever smoked in his hand.

He says, "James," like he knows who that is. I drop my lighter, of course, a metallic clatter as I hug him back. I smell him, feel his stubble on my cheek, feel his stomach against mine, warm, hard and unashamed. Feeling almost sure I'd let him do anything to me.

Just ask. Just ask.

"What are you doing?" you ask.

I am walking up Papanui Road, past the gaudy glass temple of the Pavilions Hotel, in a Christchurch summer days before I leave the country for good. I am spending too many days alone, like I'm weaning myself off people. I am no longer speaking with my mother, who resents me leaving her now, and sends me notices of career opportunities in places as absurd as New Plymouth. I am masturbating— sometimes what I would term "frantically"—in the shower and in bed, on a daily basis. Sometimes just to get to sleep; sometimes just to forestall anything like lone- liness coming upon me unawares. Horniness is only loneliness and I don't need anything so irrefutable as an erection to tell me what I am.

What am I doing? I am walking with you beside me, and you are one of the few who are taller than me. I'm remembering eating complimentary oysters in the half shell at Pedro's with you, complimentary because somehow you knew the chef, the way you always know people. I'm remembering you dancing with the owner of the Greek ouzerie, a blond, older woman, maybe forty, my jealousy, some Greek wine with pine resin, retsina, and marinated feta, my refusal of your hand, my decision not to join you. I'm remembering you standing over your desk with your shirt off, daydreaming, your fingers running across a page.

What am I doing?

"I'm getting ready to leave."

"Flame on. You're gone. I think it's fantastic, James," you say. "You're strong."

"Yup," I say. "It's fab." You're looking at me when I say this, and you laugh. We pass St. Margaret's in darkness and silence until I say, "Well. What are *you* doing?"

And, "Feeling like a cigarette, actually," is how you reply.

You sit on a conduit box and take from your pockets what you sometimes called your "makings." You used to refer to John Steinbeck as "Johnny Steinbeck" like you'd shared a loaded okie truck together. In your hands you have fresh yellow ZigZags and a new bag of filtertips. You squeeze a filter through the hole the bag once hung from and tuck it in your lips. You take pinches of fresh soft tobacco, line them up in the tent of a paper. You massage them into shape. I'm remembering fucking you, you reaching back, guiding me into you, the way your body seemed to settle and relax as I first entered you, like books on an unfilled shelf aligning as the last volume is returned. I'm remembering the moles on your pale skin, fine hair at the small of your back, the arch of your spine. I'm remembering your bowed head, your asshole contracting around me like the first fingers of a fist, and your cool hand reaching back for my thigh, whispering, slow down, slow down.

The place it ended two years ago was, of course, his house.

The reason it ended was a thing impossible to define, or express. An insoluble math problem that complicated the air in the house to a point it was difficult to breathe. It seemed as if structures kept me away from him: equations, symbols, diversions, tangents of feeling, an obscure calculus of things unsaid and things misrepresented.

The day it ended I had this feeling: to reach out and try to manipulate these variables—to rearrange the events and the memories, to reenact the transactions, find a loophole, locate a solution—was not a task I was equipped for. There were codes I didn't understand, things I knew I could never feel, and I was sick and angry and baffled—frustrated and disappointed by how easily baffled I seemed to be.

The way it ended it seemed there were attachments on my body, a subtle mechanics that connected us and held us apart as I paced and smoked, as he sat in his armchair and waited. Struts and stringencies, flexing, adjusting, compensating as I moved; allowing me so much freedom and no more. What made me angry was that I did not know what these enigmas kept me from: at no point was I resisted, at no point checked, and I knew only that the cage knew more than I.

And what made me most angry was the suspicion I held that he knew all this, knew all about me. That he was possibly cruel. That he felt the arcane machinery of past and present, our memories, our wills, and that he accepted the fact he could take or leave me. That it was complex and inevitable, even beautiful to him. That he would sit there sadly, a pale blue Yves St. Laurent shirt open to soft pale nipples, and wait for me to realize the only conclusion there was, the one he knew, and that he would wait for me to leave, "storm out," uselessly slamming the door. That he would sit there after I left and test the air, as antennae probed presence and absence, as wings folded gently, the circuits of whatever tenuous thing holding us together falling quiet. That he would sit there and feel these things, observe them coolly, taste them dispassionately.

And that he would then quietly reach for one of the books stacked in piles around his armchair and against the walls, for one of the young girl novelists he'd started reading: Chidgey, Kassabova, Quigley, Perkins, McDowell; and that he'd finish one in a couple of hours, testing his feelings against representation; thinking about lyricism; wondering about levels of mimicry, creation and distortion, memory and loss, loss incurred in the will to enforce narrative where there is none.

That he would read till he grew bored, like he did with me.

I leave him. Leave Michael at the corner of Papanui and Saint Albans, outside the Methodist church. He's going deeper into Merivale, to a different house. ("I've moved," he told me, "to Merivale where everyone is healthy.")

To say good-bye he flicks his cigarette away half-smoked. He hugs me again, but I am already half-gone. He kisses my cheek but I am turning. Onto the road, empty.

"James," I hear him say, and turn back.

"What."

"You seem like you've got . . . hard."

"I'm leaving. That's all there is to it."

"You aren't dying. It's not like dying."

"I don't want to talk about it," I say. I am on the street, backing away from him. Something occurs to me.

"Where did you disappear to, Michael?" I ask him. "Where did you go?"

"Where is never as important as why."

"It was two years." I want to ask things of him, which is wanting to know him, and I don't want to want anything from him anymore. "Forget it."

Turning and turning, down deep into Saint Albans where he used to walk at night, where the houses bore his stares. Dimmer, deeper orange than the glares of Papanui and something is said to my back. Keep on walking, remember a lyric or a line, stare at the concrete or hold your head high, it makes no difference; you're doing the right thing or the wrong thing, it's all memory you can ponder on a plane, an unpassable exam, a stain like a birthmark. Is it more powerful now. Am I stronger because of this. Is the memory recorded wrong—distorted; revised.

Just walk away.

Down the very center of the empty street. Near where Albany meets Saint Albans there are boys, maybe ten of them, maybe twenty years of age. They have shaven heads and rugby jerseys. They are on this road in the orange glare, throwing around a white cube of polystyrene for a ball, the cube molting fragments like static on the asphalt. They are drinking cans of Budweiser. They are smoking cigarettes and noting your approach. Some on the footpath, some on the road. You are not registered with more than a glance, but there is a preparation, a palpable shift in posture and pose. A voice quiets; another raises. Timing becomes an issue; the self-consciousness of these so suspicious.

You're passing between two. A cigarette is flicked to the ground spraying sparks at your feet. You're passing two more, and you're in the thick now.

What do you feel as you pass: nothing, not even triumph.

You're ready when their surrogate ball thumps pathetically on your back.

You don't react, keep walking. The voice comes from the footpath, the accent broad as the moment, the question the same one:
"Don't you wanna play our game?"
It's easy not to answer. To answer risks everything, and you're past.

Leaving Michael, leaving the country, on board the plane, after the fasten seat belts sign dims, as the g forces ease, as we rise over Christchurch, me, becalmed, leaving a becalmed city, the first thing I want to do is masturbate.

And in the tiny toilet cubicle, after I come over the toilet bowl and it's sick black hole, a line of cum hangs from the lips of my cock, a perfect elongated tear, swaying limply as I lean and breathe.

I squeeze my cock one last time and it falls. The milky white stretch of jelly flops and spatters on the plastic of the toilet bowl with an audible sound.

I sway above it. It glistens weakly. I press the tiny black flush button and the toilet roars and sucks and howls and the sperm, with the shit and urine of thousands of strangers, is purged and sprayed uselessly over the country I am leaving.

I wait for the first rush of his cap; the cap of oil I bought from Elisabeth with my last native cash; the cap I never gave him, the cap I kept for myself, the cap I dropped in the toilets at the airport.

I wait for that first rush to come on as I disappear into Asia.

Drew
June 1999

Why Japan?
Moths.
Moths, fluttering above your head in the darkness, as you lie in your bed the last night before you leave and can think only about your failure.
This is the sound of the reason why.
Fluttering, dry, invisible moths. The big ones; near your ears and your eyes. A scraping on a scale so small you cannot comprehend. Your head

coming apart because despite your best efforts there are things you cannot change by immersion in extremes. A going-away party where your own behavior is what you'd characterize as "pure abandon." A drunken night with your friends, and their spouses (new or soon to be; all the Toowoomba boys—and the way they drink is now literally "a few quiets" where that once used to be code for "a lot of louds"—sitting with their girls, appalled at your antics, mentally thanking their gods or congratulating themselves that they are no longer anything like you, that they "have lives") and you, falling away inside yourself as you see the looks on their faces, as you swill the gin back, fall over the coffee table, find yourself outside at three a.m. smashing the windows of your flat's garage with a ski pole, while they watch and then quietly inform you they're going home now, and good luck in Japan and all that.

You pant, the ski pole dangles, shards of glass glint on the lawn.

Someone saying, "Drew, we're leaving now," two or three times before you finally mutter "well bye then" and finish the job, which takes you another twenty minutes.

And you don't move on to the house, which is lucky because that's more than your bond's worth.

And then a day and a night. Final packing, hungover (a gin hangover: dry mouth all day, no sleep, but then again, no nausea), and trying to sleep, great, dusty gray moths fluttering in your empty room, in your empty head, you were in a sleeping bag with no pillow on coarse carpet, the streetlight shone through a window with no curtains, you're twenty-two, you told someone sometime during that party that you refuse to trade your madness for purpose and it sounded cool at the time, you flew Brisbane to Sydney the next morning alone, stayed the night in a cheap hotel arranged by JAL, you met a guy called James from New Zealand the JET people told you to meet at Sydney airport the day after for the nine-hour to Narita, you're meeting the JET people by the Arrivals Board in Narita in three hours, you'll be in Tokyo in four, you'll be drinking with the orientation people then tomorrow you're going somewhere to live you know you can't even pronounce.

Life is all laid on for you in a place you've never been, you're swaying in a tiny white cubicle over a vast black ocean, you owe AUS$5000 on your credit card, you haven't touched a vein in more than six months and the tracks are starting to really heal and you haven't even thought of her name in three days.

What's the sound of failure?
Great gray moths, fluttering in the darkness.
That's why Japan.

Yasu
September 2000

"Good morning!" in loud, exuberant, poorly accented Japanese. *Ohayo gozaimasu!* The same stern, positive greeting Professor Maeda once gave every morning in the labs at Rikkyo.

Yasu jumps, cringes, inwardly and out. Almost drops the watering can.

He hears, in English: "Hey! Hey. Sorry, sorry for fright, man. I am ear." A laugh. "I am ear for gear, man. I am early today, sorry."

Yasu checks the street nervously. Children hold hands, walk in lines. One salaryman, sweating already, hurrying to the train. No one watching.

"Wait," Yasu says. "Where is Michael-san?"

"That," the French boy says, "seem to be a big mystery to all of us."

"Please, please," Yasu says, gesturing. "To the inside."

Two hundred miles away, unbeknownst to her oldish friends in this city, Meredith Julia Edwards' plane touches down at Narita airport on the first day of a three-month tourist visa that will expire on the seventeenth of December.

She's come looking for her brother.

All through a million miles of airspace a million people remain in transit between time zones and nations and nationalities but it would not be overstating the facts to say that as of mid-September 2000, in Tokyo—like a diamond that reflects and refracts all it centers and gathers toward itself, that breaks up and reconstructs inside and around itself; recolored, refaced, renamed, remade—in distorted forms and shifting reflections *everyone and everything is here.*

II

The Empty Stage

September 2000

Wash my soul. Wash my soul, say the song, whispring, to me.

Topless bar. Topless bar, I whispr, 2 you. Mmm mm. Com inside. You so fat, you so white and sweating. Yeah I sweatin 2, but I use 2 it, I use 2 long long summas. With you you look scard. White an all sof. Com in, com in, we no gon bite you. We eat you fuckin hole yeah. HAHAHAHAHA. Im jus fuckin w U. Com on com on. I seen u walkin up an down lookin 4 a place. Look aroun you at the street. You see what you need out there o no ono no. Cos you gotta go inside, deep inside to find that place you looking for. U gotta choos. Choos my plase, bes plase, down here. Bes price bes service bes poon on tha face o tha place. We got all down in here 4 you. Yeah I see yoo look at that street layin out there. So black like it oil. Bakin in tha heat. Come on in and we make evrything all right for u yeah. Don't wan stay out here all hot night no fun w these place these lil bitches all down corner down there. They all diseese an bad shit for you. I tell you come inside. Com inside where it cool, we make you shining drinks and you float away from you. Where I from hot like this many time. I know too hot 4 you. For me it is OK all time OK. No aircon in my partment and there are six o us now with Shan com from home. Shan tryin hook a arbeit sellin Champion for Hiro w the poor dum niggas up in Bukuro now. But s no good 4 him. Arbeit is partime work that don get u no visa. He got no visa so no good so he need real job soon. I no you white boys come in on tourist visa, piece soft tit 4 you white boys 4 90 days. Me an Rox an Jan and Handsome and Corbin and now Shan we close to trouble now. The amnesty finish, no fuckin way I go to amnesty right? Waddayoo think. NO fuckin way. Go to amnesty like lying on cardboard box in Ueno Park. Yoo wait to be swept up. Made stand in line, get your cardboard take away an put in a big stack an stand in lines, all those smellin mothafuckas. AN you get hit you try an run. You get nocked down. Standin with these guys. So too much sun them skin turn like wood. Shinin shinin eyes like they know something. Like they on to something real big. Snot all hangin down in they whiskers an shinin eyes like amnesty is no lie. He wakin up in a new place nex morning so far from where he born he don even know the diffrence. Dum mofuckas just look for a dry place. For a bathroom you know. Dirty mothafuckas don need no visa. Cos they home where ever they are even they don recognize.

Mofuckas don need no visa. Me an Rox an Jan and Handsome an Corb an now SHan we diffrent.

I see you lookin ova down them little girls down there?

She Umi, she Tomomi. She all diseesed now you just go on you get all sweaty an more. She Miyoko. You look like you can have. True. Many this all for you. Many this made for you. Many all this you can have.

But you lookin over there and you see them girls waitin roun down under tha Almond Café, thos perty girls evrybodys lookin at, cos all tha boys wan fuck them an all tha lil girls wanna be like them. An I tell you this white boy w yor sweat and yor all big and soft and yor bllue genes an yo nice shrts an yo slick hairs an all tha nots o money. They way out your leg. I no they hooked up an I no who watchin thm an I know wat happen to any one who try recruiting for a little arbeit off those girls that off limits even GIs. They all namegirls. She Cathy. W tha blon hair. She use to work here, in my club. Bak when she new to tha city. Now she big news. Boys like tha blonds. She Yumiko. She Amelie. She down there Man. Man news too. She a evil sprit say. No all the big people. You no touchin her 2nite boy. She lil coal angel mongs all white angels. Mos beautiful thing like a snake. She big trouble 4 lil girl cos she all connected. She play violin yoo no that? Say she a gnius, sing yoo 2 asleep yoo neva wake from. Talkin 2 her start get u witched. But yoo no trouble enyhow cos yoo all fat an sweaty, fresh off tha boat, don think I don no that. You no trouble man, cos you no organising any more then nex drnk. Thats good for yoo cos I seen wat happen hear 2 y's guys organising trouble. I seen wat happen 2 y's guys down hear think they no, thing they gotshit down. I seen wat happen to like the Russian y's guy trouble-man SLobosomthing. Las year. Russian mobs y's guy. Nise suits, big an white an sof like U 2. He come in town open club and then restaurant and then salsa dansing club an he big news. Then he start recruiting new girls. Take Korean and Chinese and Taiwanese girls an so many girls out schools mak evrybody happy. Put lil schoolgirls in lil rooms he rent an take out o them pay. Four in room, sleepin 2gether lik poor lil kittens all woun up in one tiny lil room. But soon he gets figgure out little ones from the schools wear out realquick. That they go for reasons. You don't want reasons. Reasons is problems. You want like me. Not ugly like me HA. You want me in heart. Willing an Abel. You hear a song you come down explain all about me. Willing an Abel. You wan a girl that is ready. All that is that matters. Russian SLobosomthing go lookin for Abel girls an start smellin in wrong places. He askin roun otha people girls. J girls. Englsh girls. Namegirls. Amelie. Yumiko. Man an Sonoko o no. Start layin cardboard in Ueno Park HA HA HA. He get packed up. Wake up in tar pit in Kanazawa no arms no legs. An the mofuckas. They so thorugh. He got twelve rgular girls an they all gone to. One nite. All poor little girls go to grave. Cut out they insides leave them all on floors o the lil rooms Slobo rents for his girls w them own money. Bodies all gone jus insides left behind mix togetha so police don know how many girls. All thru tatami mats. No way to clean that out tatami. Worse than anything that inside stuff. It smell like shit and bad black badness and it just all brown and red like nothin from a girl. Bad business. Police roun. NewsTV. No sof white boys. SLobo gon, no-one try recruiting those girls again. Tellin yoo. Listen. Cmon lil white puppy. Hop in my arms. I stronger than yoo dream and yo dreams don know what I got. Hol yoo like a baby. Yoo going down a place where yoo lose evrything and what save you only first thing I takin from you. Fore yoo lose say yo blue eyes. No amnesty down here for those lil girls. Nothing waitn but enless pain. Visa fo place men cut up lil girls lik fish. Say no. Say ono. Go home fat white. Go home. I got no visa. Go home. Shan got no visa, dum mofucka. I got nothin. I got time heer. I got paid. SHan wife at home. I got no wife. SHan need visa. SHan need money, for famly. I got no famly. Shan gettin desprate. He talkin in he sleep now he hear floods at home. Dreamn o floods in th village shinin like a new visa. But he young. I old. Wash my soul, was my soul, sayin song, whispring to me. COme nside. COm ensde

JET
August 1999

The three JETs stand lightly clothed on the busy street corner in Shibuya on a Tuesday night. It's too hot and they're a little drunk. They've left the post-orientation dinner at a tiny pub in a place called Roppongi that's become rapidly far too claustrophobic, what with the sitting on the floor, the tiny tables, the low roof, the JET vets trading meaningless jokes involving Japanese words that could be names, could be places, or could be just dishes on the menu but mean just as little either way (and all using the letter J either as an adjective or a noun, they're never quite sure).

Two boys and a girl.

They've walked for twenty-some minutes now, alongside a seething black expressway into the hills of Shibuya, the couple trailing behind Drew and his map.

Drew says, "Let's get some vending machine beer, boys and girls. And drink it out on the bloody street. You know why? Because—"

"Did you hear what that really really black guy whispered to me?" says Sam. "Way back there?"

"—we *can*."

"He said, *Topless bar, topless bar.* But he like, whispered it in my ear."

"No way, mate. No way I'm going in one of those places. They rip you off wholesale," Drew says. "Once you go in those places, they can take you for everything you've got. Even foreigners. There's no laws to stop them just saying your beer costs forty thousand yen. Tell them to fuck off and you'll get your arms broken. It's true. Wait till we're drunker."

"God it's hot," says Sam.

"We've got eighteen hours, boys and girls," says Drew. "Of piss, and *poontang.*"

"I want to go home," Brigit says.

It's said the thing with being a JET is everything is all laid on.

That the thing with being a JET is you can come to Japan and not only do you get a shiny new visa, you get a very well-paid job, and a pretty decent apartment.

And also your plane tickets get organized for you, and you get maps, wads of informative unevenly photocopied material on Japanese customs, food, geography and climate, a two-day orientation of sorts in Tokyo with JETs from participating countries (mostly Australians, English, North Americans, Canadians, New Zealanders) that after the absurdly pompous contract signings is mostly hard and expensive drinking with wasted-looking older JET liaisons all referring to their chopsticks as hashi and trading jaded, incomprehensible witticisms in tiny Japanese pubs you soon find out are called izakayas, plus tickets to your posting, detailed instructions on which trains to take and how to take them, detailed and vehement warnings about getting off your shinkansen in the fifteen seconds the doors stay open lest you overshoot your stop by two hours and between two and four hundred miles. And that you get a polite Japanese teacher to meet you at the station of your new town, an orientation in earnest broken English of your new town ("I amu Mista Suzuki," "zat isu shurine," "zat isu yo locaru Sebun-Erebun conbeniencu"), a drive to your new apartment, often completely furnished with futons and TV and aircon and computer so you can either cry yourself to sleep or lie awake all night staring at your first Japanese cockroach on the wall in your new town in relative but alien comfort before you start work in a job that you'll soon find out doesn't matter a jot that you have no desire for or even remotely applicable experience at, *the very next day.*

But on the other hand, "all laid on" apparently also means your visa, your job and your apartment are inextricably linked. Quit or get fired from your job (really quite hard to do, unless you break your contract or the law in a fairly drastic way, like try to import Ecstasy or molest your students— simple laziness or incompetence usually doesn't quite qualify) and your visa automatically expires. Quit or get fired from your job and your accommodation "expires," too.

And the other thing: your visa is valid for two days before you get to your job and your contract begins. Then it's valid for the year of your contract with the school. And then, unless you've negotiated an extension via the immensely convoluted bureaucratic channels you'd swear were designed to *discourage* you, your visa expires a couple of days after your contract.

And that's it. If you haven't signed on for another year and you decide not to make your flight out, you're an overstayer, and you better either stay out of sight or take your chances with amnesty.

So it's one way into Japan.

But unfortunately, and with that sinking feeling you get when you realize you might have really missed out on something just through your own lack of cojones, when you see Tokyo, and you see the freedom most foreigners enjoy in Tokyo in your first few days in the city, or more likely when you reflect on what you saw once your mind-numbing routine of "teaching" "English" to little kids by standing in the corner occasionally muttering "No, my name pronounce is 'Smith'" to be greeted with complete bewilderment or embarrassed laughter (every day) starts to tell, you'll realize JET is not Japan. JET is JET. A well-padded cage that, should you decide is not for you, you've also decided to leave the country.

Sam is a U of Manitoba School of Journalism graduate who sometimes likes to exclaim in muddled German when he becomes excited in conversation, and his girlfriend Brigit is a week late and a U of Manitoba Faculty of Fine Arts Photography major who loves to photograph neon: abstractly, close-up. They have been living together for eighteen months, twelve in their last year at school, six largely unemployed, planning and waiting for JET's summer intake. Drew is a commerce graduate from Brisbane or really Toowoomba with a fledgling obsession for olive skin, narrow hips, shining black hair and shy averted eyes. He also has a credit card bill amounting to five thousand Australian dollars after a spring postgrad diploma in fledgling heroin addiction. He's big, but not as big as he once was, and clean, now.

Sam and Brigit made it very clear to their JET liaison at the Winnipeg information sessions—a smiling, immensely fat man their age, a JET vet of three years who pulled at the waistline of his shirt when he laughed, because when he laughs, he moves, and cotton touching the parts of you that move will always remind you that they're moving—they made it very clear that they were very much prepared to be posted in different high schools, and that separate apartments, even, were acceptable. The fat young man laughed and said, "Sure, fellas," and showed them how to write their preferences for place on their application forms, how to list under Questions 20 and 21 their reasons why, their commitment to each other, their love, their plans for their future in Japan together.

That night, after hours of hard silence, wrapped up together, but apart, in a huge feather comforter against the chill ("Fahkink Vinterpeg," Sam shouts, first thing in the morning, in winter, in Winnipeg. It's something, the very-early-morning swearing, that Brigit had to get used to; she has learned to if not love, then at least see this as a sign of spirit), they at last made their decision, together. If they did get posted to different schools, if they were given separate apartments, the plan would be this: the money was good enough and the JET-subsidized rents cheap enough that they could leave one of the apartments mostly empty, and live together in the other. Without having to inform JET, or their respective schools, if it came to that. This would be their secret, in Japan. Which apartment, they would decide when they saw what was offered. The bigger one, of course. The nicest one, in the best location, with the best shops, handiest to the station with the most lines. If the two apartments were close enough, they could even use one as an office. "Or a darkroom," whispered Brigit. "It could be so cool." "Yes," said Sam. "Ve vill make it verk." "Jawohl," said Brigit, and they had hard, good sex, and were not scared, or worried, together.

The next day they signed their application forms and in a few weeks were interviewed and in a few more weeks informed they had been accepted—placement pending—for the August intake. They went about selling off old stuff, planning their packing, halfheartedly learning Japanese phrases (Brigit would haltingly order a drink with "Ano, nama biiru hitotsu, onegai shimasu"; Sam would growl in Deutsch delight, "Sehr *gut*, Fraülein!"), getting physicals and visa photos, opening fresh new email addresses to replace old spam-stuffed ones (where their JET predecessors' warning emails sat unopened), moving into Brigit's parents' basement from their apartment (where their notifications of placement location arrived and laid on the chill hallway floor, unopened, too), and saying good-bye to Winnipeg friends who had begun to make their choices among babies, careers or more (and more) school.

And they felt free.

This morning, their first day, in Tokyo station, in August, in 95°F heat and 80% humidity at nine a.m. underground, surrounded by their hand luggage and the hand luggage of seemingly hundreds of other JETs, they learned from a strangely sweatless three-year JET veteran, an intensely thin woman with a clipboard and a permanent sneer that said the three years had been *lonely*, that Sam had been posted to a senior high school in Sapporo City in Hokkaido; and that Brigit had been posted to a junior high school in Fukui City, Fukui Prefecture, Honshu.

Different apartments; different schools; different cities; different prefectures; *different islands*.

They are to leave and part tomorrow.

Drew and Brigit both have cameras, but Brigit isn't taking photos.

It's late now, almost eleven, and in the streets of Shibuya the crowds are thinning out. All three of them have cans of Sapporo from a beer vending machine. They stare around themselves at the narrow shops, the swathes of neon, the stalls jammed in next to each other, some so narrow a person could lean against one wall and touch the other with an outstretched hand. Only a few shops are open at this time, so the chaos seems broken by the dead patches of corrugated garage doors, pitted and billed with peeling signs in kanji. They walk down a gently sloping street littered with cigarette butts, paper cups and burger wrappings, lined by shoe stores, HMV, McDonald's, Wendy's, record stores, jewelry stores, ramen stores, Burger King, Yoshinoya, game arcades six stories high, still howling and clinking, a few kids squatting outside smoking cigarettes, boys laughing shrilly, faces lit blue and orange by their keitais as they read their skymail. They've been drinking steadily for almost six hours and with the heat their faces are sheened with alcoholic sweat and the strange oil that the air and the humidity wring from pores.

When they look up, the sky is a blackgray pinprick static cushion, too dense, bulging and somehow particulate, or pixellate: millions of points of shades of gray. The sky looks plump, like fine, dark sand recently fluffed, or a dusty charcoal mould. It looks pregnant with something and appears to them in shapes delineated by the tall thin buildings: huge dusty ideograms as foreign as the kanji. Now they see an L of sky, but inverted. Now, as they pass a crossroads, a huge, monolithic K with an extra, broken arm dangling from the K's back. Now, on the street that slopes to Starbucks and the station, a long but flawed girder of an I sprouting extra stalks pruned close along its length; all studded with orange blooms of streetlamps, like a gigantic rune relieved in ruins, overgrown with marigolds.

Everywhere they hear the far-off hum and rattle and wash of motors.

They keep drinking, buy three more cans apiece from another machine, and stash them in Drew's backpack. Alcohol vending machines close at eleven; another piece of advice from JET.

"How would you describe this place," murmurs Sam.

"America's deformed little cyberbaby," Brigit says. Sam looks up at the flatness of her voice.

"It doesn't matter," Drew says. "What it can give you is what matters. What you want. What you can get."

"What time . . ." Sam mutters. Then, "I forgot. When's your . . . train."

"My train," Brigit says. "It's not a train. It's a . . . bus."

Drew looks at them both, then turns and wanders away, over toward a shop window.

"I leave at ten in the morning. From . . ." He thinks. "Shunjuku?"

"You're first then. I leave at twelve."

"We...have to...oh, man," Sam says.

Brigit examines his shoulders, and his neck. She doesn't look at his face. "We have to just go. That's all. There's no other choice."

"We...They tricked us. They...they all but lied, Bridge." His tone is accusing. "We could complain. We could go to the embassy."

"How do we find the embassy? Who can we complain to. It's...not going to happen like that. We don't know enough. We have to do what's arranged. They could cancel the visas."

"We can..."

"We don't have enough money, Sam. We can't do anything now."

"Do you want to go away then? So it's okay then?"

"What we want doesn't matter here, now."

Sam turns and looks down the street. He watches Drew staring into a blackened shop window. Then straightening, peering down the hill at something. A few doors up from them a garage door rattles closed; another shop shutting up.

"I don't care about anything then," Sam says. "None of it will be any good."

"We'll have holidays. We can travel and visit."

"We're on different *islands*. We'll have to take trains...and...*ferries* and things. Why are you being so...I don't know...so very pragmatic about this. No, it's...actually it's more like completely fatalistic, Brigit."

"Sam." She's staring away down the hill. "We're in a place we can't afford to be anything else."

Sam looks up, to her face, surprised and hurt. But she's staring past him.

"Drew's waving at us."

Sam doesn't say anything.

"Come on."

She walks off down the hill and, in a moment, he follows.

At the foot of the hill the narrow street abruptly widens and meets a large intersection. Four other streets fan out from this hub, and opposite is Tobu department store and the Hachiko exit of Shibuya station. Though on this particular street there are few people, the crowds gathered at the islands of sidewalk waiting to cross are dense and clogged. Floodlights throw ovals of light up the huge thighs of two GAP models on a billboard. The unmoving crowds seem to shift and blur in a pulsing, irregular light from something they can't see.

At the bottom of the street, Drew is standing in the gutter, leaning over a small cluttered desk with chrome legs, perched on the edge of the sidewalk. The desktop is sloped like a shrunken lectern. It has a small lamp and is slanted toward Drew. He is peering down at the lectern like an immensely tall lecturer examining his distant notes, the lamp lighting up his crotch like the floodlights do the GAP models. Opposite him, in shadow behind the lamp, a young Japanese boy with shoulder-length hair points, bored, at something on the desk. His hand becomes a white spot for a moment, then recedes.

Brigit walks down the hill and pauses behind Drew. Sam stands out in the street and stares across to Hachiko, at all the cut-and-pasted buildings like the stacked shoeboxes of an immense foster family.

On the desk, pinned in neat rows, are more than fifty miniature plastic bags of shriveled brownish objects.

Each bag is individually labeled. Drew is staring down, examining the labels closely.

"What's this?" Brigit says.

"LBMs," he mutters.

"Uh-huh."

"Little Brown Mushrooms. *Legal* little brown mushrooms."

Brigit leans down beside him. Each bag is ziplock, and as small as a bag for a collectable coin. Inside, the mushrooms are more a fawn-gray than brown, and thoroughly desiccated. The texture is something like velvet worn to a near-shine. The tiny caps are elongated, puckered and pointed; the stems crooked and crushed-looking. They look unappetizing, juiceless and banal, like the dried corpses of the most childishly drawn generic mushroom shape.

On each small white label a string of kanji, a weight in grams, and on one in maybe every four a biological name written in rude penciled English.

"They can sell them on the street?"

"It certainly looks like it, doesn't it."

Drew is absorbed. The Japanese boy opposite him is smoking, bored. He points down at one of the bags and mutters something noncommittal.

"How much?" Drew looks up. This is the most serious Brigit has seen him in the twelve hours they've been thrown together.

The boy thinks. Drags on his cigarette.

Breathes out smoke, and through the clouds huskily says, "Sebun-sowzanden."

"Seven?" Drew says, incredulous.

"Uhn." The boy nods with the sound, the nasal barely voiced; the Japanese assent.

"One gram?"

Brigit laughs and Sam looks over at them.

"Uh. Won guramu," the boy nods. Brigit looks at the boy's long, clean hair, dyed brown with messy silver streaks. Black eyes in an unnaturally tan face, a nose ring, yellow teeth. And a black T-shirt that reads HIP LOCK! IT'S CHEERFUL GIRL MONSTER!

There's something pleased on her face.

"One gram. It's robbery. And they're bloody *legal*."

"I still feel kind of... criminal though."

Sam stands beside her.

"You're doing these tonight then, eh," he says.

"Maybe."

"Before you... The night... before we leave."

"*May*-be," Brigit says. The *may* drawn out; the high *be* not a question but near a taunt.

"What the hell is wrong with you Brigit?"

"Nothing is wrong. This is Japan, Sam." She laughs. "Sam, Japan. Jap Sam. A man. Marzipan jam, Sam."

He looks from her to the desk, then back to her. She leans down closer to the display. He looks out to the street and grits his teeth.

"That's like a hundred and twenty bucks. Aussie," Drew says. "Fuck!"

It sounds harsh and ugly to Sam, like a deep squawk. *Faahk.*

"We can't afford that, Brigit."

"One?" Drew says to the boy, tapping his chest, then holding up a finger.

The boy nods, bored. Sense of too many fingers, too many times.

"Uh. Won guramu, you."

"Fa-*ahk.*"

"Don't do it, don't do it," a voice whispers faux-dramatically behind them.

It's a tall foreign boy with short black hair in a white singlet. Sam can't place the accent. It's placeless. Brigit glances up, sees the black diagonal stripe of a bag strap across the singlet. That's a wifebeater, she thinks, the English name for a singlet.

Drew ignores the foreigner and points to a different bag.

"Seeksowzanden."

"Fahk."

"Australian, Canadian, Canadian. He knows you're JET. He's screwing you." The boy steps up on the curb, leans over and points at a bag and says something in Japanese.

The Japanese boy swats his finger away and hisses a rapid sentence.

The boy laughs, relents.

"I'd walk away. He speaks English, you know."

The Japanese boy steps out from behind the desk as if to push him.

"Come on, Manabu, give them a break," he says, and smiles at the boy.

Drew and Brigit and Sam stare at the exchange.

The Japanese boy turns back to them, his bored mask gone, then to the new boy.

"Everyone, go out," he snaps. "Closed. Closing."

The boy laughs, and says, "Come with me. I'll hook you up."

At the corner of an alleyway, Drew a little reluctant and a little suspicious but in massive debt, Sam hanging back and Brigit taking charge, the boy sells them three single-gram baggies of mushrooms he produces from his satchel, for just a thousand yen each. His baggies are unmarked, the mushrooms as unassuming as the others.

"They're very good. I know the guy who grows them. He's almost a genius," the boy says. "He's the Mao of shrooms."

"Right," Drew says. "Uh-huh."

He gives Brigit a business card with no business on it.

"Mao-shrooms," she says. "I get it. You have long fingers. Michael Edwards."

"Before I go," he says, "can I ask you some simple little questions? Tell me one thing you know about this place."

"It's hot," says Drew.

"Why?" Sam says.

"Just for my own . . . research purposes," he says.

"We're here to learn about it," Brigit says. "You can't know a country unless you live there for a time."

"Experience is important."

"Yes."

"Who are you?" Sam says.

"It feels . . . it feels like a lonely place," Brigit says.

"How it feels is important."

"Of course."

"One thing, then."

"Okay. It's . . . incredibly vast. And dense. But everything feels . . . used. Too looked-at."

"What about you," the boy says to Sam.

"What research?" Sam says. "Who are you?"

"Come on. Just one thing. Indulge me."

"I don't in*dulge* drug dealers. You're just trying to make fun of us."

"Sa-am," Brigit says.

"Just tell him something," Drew says. "This is a good deal."

"Alright then. I know quite a bit about the monument made by the family of a war criminal with Japanese clay and mud from China. It's of Kannon. The Buddhist god of compassion. It's at Atami, to commemorate the Sino-Japanese war dead."

"*Lonely Planet*, page 201. 'Excursions.'"

"Fuck you."

The boy laughs. "I made that addition. It was . . . fiercely resisted, I think the term would be. And heavily edited."

"Hey, no, I've got a real one," Drew says. "The Japanese make sashimi out of blowfish. Pufferfish. It's called fugu. And like two hundred people die every year from eating it. Some of it's poisonous. They're the only people in the world that eat it. I wanna try it man. I'm ready."

"They cook it, too. The u is sometimes almost silent, so it sounds a little like 'foog.' Or 'hoog.' There's a fugu store up there," the boy says, pointing up the street. "If you want to see."

"How did you know we were JETs? How did you know where we're from?" Sam says.

The boy dabs his finger at each one of them in turn, as if he's counting. "It's written all over your faces. I can read it."

Before he turns and leaves, he says, "It's written all over your eyes."

The three JETs stand at the end of the alleyway in Shibuya on their first night in Japan, examining the little baggies in their hands. It's grown even more humid, the air hot and close, wet as sticky milk. An odor rises up through manhole lids in the black, greasy, litter-strewn street: a yellow diarrheal smell like sulphur. All three of them are sweating heavily. Their faces glisten in the orange streetlamps and soaking T-shirts hang taut and darkly on the slopes and bumps of young shoulders. Another rattle sounds close by; another shop shuts up. It's hard to draw breath. Drew smokes, but hasn't lit a cigarette since the air-conditioned bar in Roppongi. To smoke in this air seems absurd.

"I'm doing mine now," he says abruptly. "I'm gonna do the shrooms now. Fuck it."

Brigit laughs. "Fuck it, *maan*," she says. "But my beer is flat."

"You guys are ridiculous," Sam says. "These could be dangerous. Poisonous. God knows."

"You're going to have a great time in Japan, mate," Drew says. "I can just tell." He reaches into his backpack and pulls out one, then, dramatically, two, then three cans of Sapporo.

"But they're warm already," he says, and looks at Brigit.

She looks at him, then at Sam, then back to Drew, and a helpless grin takes shape, like an amused groan. Like she's remembering something left behind, and leaving it there.

Drew is nodding, grinning too. He throws a can to Sam.

He catches it. "Guys," he says, and breaks off, looking at their grins, starting to smile too. "No way."

"Way," Brigit says. "Oh, *way*."

Drew whoops suddenly, punches the air with the baggie in his hand. "We're gonna get hi-*igh*," he shouts.

"Let's do it," Brigit says.

They squat quickly down on the curb at the corner of the alleyway. They open their beers, suck the froth that bursts out, wincing, making noises at the warmth. Drew is suddenly very businesslike. "Everything is legal," he mutters, fumbling with the baggie. "Street beer, mushies. There are no rules." Brigit watches Drew for clues, and imitating him, pours the contents of the little baggie into her palm. "There are no rules at all." In her hand are three whole shriveled mushrooms, one cap and three stalks surrounded by dust and fragments. She picks through them, looks up at Drew. He puts a whole mushroom in his mouth, and staring first at her, then Sam, chews quickly, exaggeratedly, making sticky clicking noises.

Through a mouthful, trying to grin, he mumbles, "Remember to masticate the head hard and fast, Brigit," and snorts.

"Jesus," Sam says, and delicately puts a piece of cap in his mouth. He blinks and puffs his cheeks. "They taste . . . they taste like *dirt*."

Brigit imitates Drew, and squatting, facing each other, faces working, jaws clicking, teeth sometimes bared and sipping beer to chase the taste that's more like very lightly perfumed cardboard, the two eat their bagfuls quickly, finishing obsessively, holding the bags up to the streetlamps, flicking them with their fingertips, licking their palms.

Sam is still eating. "Oh my god they're dis*gust*ing," he splutters.

"Don't you *dare* spit it out, don't you *dare*," Drew shouts.

"God, he's right," Brigit says, grimacing, shuddering at the aftertaste. "Ooh, God, Drew, they're really *awful.*"

"No," Drew says. "They're beautiful. Say it with me. They taste beautiful."

"They taste beautiful."

"Jesus, God," Sam says.

"It doesn't work."

"I can't eat these, I can't."

"Give them here then, mate," Drew says. "I'll eat them."

"I'll eat them, too," Brigit says.

"Good on ya," Drew says. "Gimme."

He snatches the bag from Sam.

"Take them. They're foul."

"Me me," Brigit says.

Drew pours the remains of the third baggie into his hand, divides the pile, hands her half. They both chew, shuddering, laughing, drinking more beer, Sam shaking his head in disgust.

When all the bags are empty, they leave them lying on the street by their empty cans like burst balloons.

And these streets where they weren't raised is where they walk, waiting for the drugs to come on. It's a different kind of tourism now: they seem to stare at the stores and the tall thin buildings with an expectant childlike energy, waiting for them to change. What was a weary trudge has become a light quick step, of a specific mission, a pleasant appointment. They turn corners without dissent or debate. They pass a line of immense, mirrored escalators, emptily turning—four down and four up—into a giant blue neon-lined chamber. It's ignored, or glanced sharply into then away. Their eyes are bright and alert.

Deeper into endless asphalt Shibuya hills; loomed over, darkened. Sam looks back only once, briefly.

Brigit says, "I need to find a convenience store. Some gum for the taste."

Drew just nods. They continue up the hill.

"Segafredo," he reads from a sign. "What about a drink. Will that do?"

"I need gum."

"Chewing will help."

Something has changed between them, even Sam. Like now they hold a shared secret; like now they hold three corners of a laden table.

Segafredo is a two-storied cafe, all red and black tile; plastic furniture outside. It's mostly filled with Japanese, but a lot of foreigners, too, especially later in the evenings. Upstairs is nonsmoking. They stop outside, in front of a table of four young foreigners, all different races.

Drew asks a dark, curly-haired girl.

"Do you speak English?"

There's a young white girl with long black hair and a Chinese boy, and a tall pale boy with shaved hair.

It's him that answers. "Very well thank you, yes."

"Is there a convenience store round here?"

He turns in his seat and points up the hill. "Go go go," he says. "Then left then left. Hill. Right. Comme ça."

The Chinese boy laughs at him. "Oh 'very well, thank you.' Asshole, Jacques."

Brigit's staring inside the cafe.

"What," Sam says.

"That looks like," she says, and laughs abruptly.

The four at the table look at her. "Don't," the Chinese boy says. "Don't say it."

"That's Stephen Dorff," Brigit says, incredulous.

"Holy shit," Drew says. "It is."

He's sitting at a table just inside the doors of Segafredo, ignoring a Japanese girl.

"Don't say anything," the dark girl says. "He gets pissed."

"It's not," Sam says. "Is it?"

"Wow," Drew says, beginning to laugh. "Oh wow. Japan."

At the table the Chinese boy is sneering at them.

"Come on," Sam says. "It's not. Let's go."

He takes Brigit by the arm and pulls her with him.

"That's so cool," Drew says.

"Assholes," the Chinese boy says loudly as they leave.

For Brigit, suddenly, out on the street, speaking suddenly and silently to herself at the onset of the low dosage, her own voice inside the feeling feeds her this:

what are you really doing here a tiny nauseaworm is asking, turning in its own heat and feces. what do you really want now coiling around the fetus in her womb. do you think he's a strong boy shaking scales off in her arms. how pretty am I the worm is asking pretty enough to stay and stay alone forever ever in the oilyquiet heat?

"Um," Brigit says.

"Come on," Sam says. "Let's go. Come *on*, Brigit."

"Oh. I feel a little sick, Sam," she says. "I feel a little nauseous."

"Oh shit," Drew says, beside them, laughing. "Oh shit that's the first sign. You're gonna be tripping soon mate. Get ready."

"I need... something. I need gum."

"Are you okay?" Sam says.

"I feel funny, Sam," she says. "I feel funny."

They walk up to the end of the street and turn left at the corner, Brigit following Drew, Sam beside her. The crowds are thick but thinning as the first night in Japan wears on.

Drew glances back past them down the hill, an amused and wearied grin as he sees Brigit's pale face, and then a little twist as a tiny Japanese girl shrieks with laughter right beside him, and quickly in a voice, recognizably his own but utterly accentless, as the shrooms start to come on, he finds he's telling himself:

the deserts near Toowoomba were rolling hills like these for you but why does that come to you now when the real question is do you want to eat them to make you wet or why? what's enough for you are you enough for one who knows you really anymore that's the really simple little question with spines. watch the flanks of thighs go walking it's you who are wet and silver inside and they are dry and you should know this feeling this bitter sticky sickness but at home it's a dry heat man a dry heat you know is what makes and made your world and it used to be the awful twilight lie down in awful twilight when the day dies there was nothing left and you wanted to be cool and warm at the same time but that can never be and everytime the thing can never be is

really it was always money money money and so many days and ways of sad-
ness and aloneness till you do it again with a hand on a thigh and a sigh and
then wet and cool and warm and dry and a line of light is blackness bursting
from a hole so familiar but and then like now always always always made you
new and weak and that is all that is good

"Ha!" Drew says. "It's funny."

He gets no answer.

"They're different aren't they," he says to himself.

His voice is utterly sad.

"That's the thing with shrooms. They're always, always quite different."

Past the corner young Japanese girls in smocks are carrying in the
boxes of Don Quixote products stacked outside the doors.

A jingle plays, a high girl chorus, "Don Don Don, Don Quix-o-te-e."

Outside the big store is a circle of park benches round a grizzled black
old tree. They pass it by; a biker astride a huge Yamaha spurs the engine,
makes it howl and murmur.

Brigit jumps at the sound, looks back once toward it.

Sam quickens his step and walks up beside her.

"Are you alright? Do you feel okay? Brigit?"

"Yes," she says sharply, then softer, "Yeah. Yes. Hold my hand." She
reaches for his hand and holds it tightly, and they walk along the crest of
the hill together, behind Drew, who's rubbing the crook of his left arm
absently, kneading the dip at the end of a bicep.

They walk the length of the block, then turn and follow Drew up a steep
side street. Sam glances up to Brigit's face every few steps because she's
frighteningly pale, her eyes wide and staring. Her right hand in his is very
dry and is sporadically clutching hard, then soft, relaxed, then pumping his
fingers together like she's fighting something painful. Drew is half the steep
little block ahead of them and is pausing, checking across the street.

Sam sees the bright pink and yellow and blue of an AM/PM convenience store ahead, layered back into the ground floor of a squat concrete
building like a cave. There are kids outside, mostly Japanese but also foreigners, and they form the ragged end of a queue to the club that's further
up the hill. Another squat, lopsided-seeming building, the hill forming
a violent angle with the last stair of a well that's crammed with people
waiting.

"Here we go, Bridge," Sam says gently. "We'll get some water here, too."

"I don't want to go in," Brigit says. "I can't go in, Sam."

"Don't worry," he says, and smiles. "I vill get evrysing ve need, Fraülein. Der Deutsche-mark matters not, ja?"

He's close, still holding her hand, speaking quietly, lightly. She's staring eyes wide up the hill, to the queue, and the store. When she turns her head to him and smiles quickly her eyes don't light on his at all.

"Wait here," he says. "Don't move. I'll be back."

He glances down the street and jogs across, through the loose clusters of kids.

Brigit sits shakily on the milky plastic cube of a PARKING sign. She looks for Drew up the street, but the queue is spreading like a spilled thick-shake across the black little street and down the hill. He's lost in it, and the sound of the music from the club is a ferocious thumping.

"Drew," she says quietly. And looks up at the sound of her own voice. "Sam?"

wormausea wind and lick and furl asks what is this ve haf here zen? mocking him no he's strong don't say that stronger than me because I falter now I falter I don't know if it's better to go to fukuimiguchihonsho so cruel the words in this place and isn't this when you should be kind? but there's decisions to be made and simple little questions have no place when there are decisions to be made don't you don't you mock him evrysing ve need he said the fucking idiot no don't you say that don't the worm turns the worm turns around the little thing that's purple and sad inside her little lie her little secret her stupid stupid little flight no no not sad inside her god no don't let it know and have wise and sad and violet eyes open inside her let it be cool and sleepy there for simple little questions have no answers here is it your heart? is it your heart? is it your heart?

Brigit gasps a little, and stands up unsteadily, one hand on the PARK-ING sign for balance. She breathes out sharply, strongly pale; her eyes are wide and her mouth is a violent frown. The look is like feigned or exagger-ated confusion. Wild confusion; almost horror. As if she had seen some-thing terrible. She stares up the street, across to the AM/PM. She can't see Sam inside. There are too many people to look through.

She staggers once on her way up the street and into the crowd.

At the crest of the hill that she begins to climb the narrow street forks. In the tiny block formed by the splaying streets there is a building, which at its widest point is no wider than two people arms outstretched, and at its narrowest—where it meets the forked roads directly; there are no sidewalks here—there is a small violent concrete slope. A driveway, going underground into the heart of the hill. A miniature basement garage— Drew had ducked down to look inside as he passed beside the building: at the level of his feet there was the inverted armadillo-shell of the garage-door opener attached to the garage's roof, just four feet away; he could almost reach inside and touch it—for a miniature-seeming office building that, when he dizzily raised his head, he found was more than twenty stories high.

The hills of Shibuya are mined and crusted; the buildings like a porcupine's spines with follicles diving deep beneath. All the surfaces are deceptions; every one is true.

Even deeper beneath, the subway thrums.

Over the crest of the hill, the right-hand fork of the road soon meets a major highway. Taxi after taxi shines past; nearing midnight now, and the trains will be stopping soon. There are few other kinds of vehicle on the road. The median strip is a box hedge; the sidewalks cater for only two abreast. There are handrails for busy days. Lining the streets of this area are mostly business premises; anonymous stone and glass lobbies. From the street they're little more than alcoves poured with tile, elevator doors and ashtrays clinging to the walls. Gold kanji glittering in the streetlamps hangs in the air, sprinkled on the windows; their dark distorted doubles lurk on the walls inside. Nothing stirs but dust and cigarette butts and coffee cups, dancing in sluggish eddies, clattering in the grained marble corners of entranceways. Inches away, inside the thick plate glass that's coated with the air's sediment until it's cleaned early tomorrow morning, huge paintings, Hirsts and Onicas and Savilles and Lyes, hang on the lobby walls under the shadow kanji, great darkened slabs of beautiful money.

Another taxi purrs past, coasting away down the hill toward the 109 Building and Hachiko. The winds that trouble the buildings' occupants in the day when the men head out for lunch—whipping trench coats so hard against legs they shuffle like girls in kimono; bursting umbrellas, puncturing them with an audible sound like a gunshot; tearing sunglasses right off—are made by the buildings themselves. In Shinjuku, the Yasuda Kasai-Kaijo Building flares from the fifteenth floor down to disrupt the power of these gusts as they funnel around the skyscrapers. In monsoon season, when the winds come, there is the salaryman with his ruined stalk of plastic and aluminum dangling, his suit sopping, hairpiece askew, shaking his fist at the new elements.

But Shibuya isn't conducive to the new wind. The hills dip and trick it. The hills break it down into tiny frantic squads, quarrelling in corners, turning on one another, reduced to feeble little dervishes like these, scrapping over litter.

So it stays humid.

And in the deep and wet and humid air Drew is down the sidewalk standing outside a restaurant that's not open.

It's not open but the window is dimly lit. His soaked T-shirt and his awestruck face are lit to a silver sheen by a small light inside. The window is narrow, and only the height of Drew. It is blackened glossily from the sidewalk to his waist; an aquarium fills the rest. He's staring into it. The fugu store.

Above it all, the surge and tide and swell of emotion, is the overriding command he gives himself, a cry:

remember this.

First there's the calm shock: fugu do not look like blowfish or pufferfish at all. They are quite reassuringly fishlike. They are bluegray and silverspotted in the tank. Two hand-spans long. More like cartoonish snub-nosed cod; not ominous, spiked or worrying. The outside of the tank is stained with a green and white sediment, blurred to streaks of smeared gray where a half-hearted dishcloth has lazily wiped. Once, twice. The floor of the tank is painted aqua with large darker blue spots; faux-deco ocean, on top of which the oxygen supply is a rusting metal box the size of a pencil case. It bubbles calmly from a corrugated pipe. The back of the tank is a faded poster of a white plate turned yellow with age, with bite-sized pieces of opaque, cooked fugu resting by a single sprig of parsley.

Before their future, the fugu float, lit from above by two miniature fluorescent tubes.

Drew stands, staring, stunned.

Beneath the lights one floats on its side; eyes like drops of mercury unblinking; it gasps at the surface. The eyes and lips have crimson linings, rawlooking. It gasps in beats as regular as the bubbling of the oxygen. Open, shut, open shut, breathe, don't breathe, breathe.

Beneath it, four float free in the center of the tank.

The fugu in the center of the tank have fins that are torn and blistered, white and soft from lack of use, weeping ragged holes like pieces bitten out. They sweep slowly through the murky water, pass each other, bump, and push weakly. Their lips are red and tatters hang from them.

Another bumps its head softly in a glassed corner. There are sores around its eyes.

Through the middle of the tank two filaments of transparent material drift. Sometimes the fish float past them, cause them to trace lazy lines along their flanks. The fugu in the corner bumps its soft white snout against the glass and gasps. The lost soul at the surface floats on its side, near death.

Drew stands and stares, his T-shirt adhering moistly to his stomach, lit silverblue by the light of the tank.

The words and remonstrances have given way and he sees only floods.

"Oh my God," he whispers, without a trace of an accent.

"What's that smell?" Sam says suddenly beside him in thick Canadian. Then, "Look at them. They think they're in some ancient sea. They're actually in a box."

Drew flinches, slowly.

"Makes me want to puke. Where's Brigit?" Holding gum and a bottle of VOLVIC water.

"I..." Drew whispers, "don't...*know*...you..."

Later, they'd find her in a glassed doorway, crying, sobbing. Sam would go to Hokkaido alone and in two months move a Japanese secretary into his apartment. He would learn to speak slowly and clearly, and never fake a German accent. Brigit would bleed the next day and never go to Fukui. In Tokyo she would get a new visa and a new job and a new last name through a friend of Michael Edwards, and move into an apartment in Shimokitazawa with Drew, whose taste for heroin had gone with his Australian accent, and who started to get really thin and found work and visa sponsorship writing for *Tokyo Classified* and who would also swear, once, in hushed, accentless tones to a nodding Michael and to Brigit, that the kitchenhand he glimpsed behind the tank was carrying a sword.

Publishing History
(A Work-in-Progress)

I. Article entitled "Shibboleth: Rye/Ergot Poisoning and the Nanking Massacre: The Untold Story of the Other Great Salem Witch-hunt," as published in *The New Republic*. Dec. 17, 1994; Vol. 211. Pgs. 20–57. Also published prior in *Hagiohistoriographica: Studies in Postmodern Historiography, Festival Essay Edition, Part III: On Revisionism*, 29 (1994): 39–66, as "A Modest Proposal."

II. Article entitled "In re. *In re. Yamashita:* Crimes Against Peace and the Chain of Command: A Precedent for the Soldier Who Serves a Living God," as published in *Journal of the International Law Association* CXXVIII, 5, 12 October 1994. Pgs. 113–147.

III. Essay entitled "Guile, Metaphor, and Persuasion in the Imperial Rescripts of Hirohito," in *Difference and Distinction: Theories of Tolerance in Meiji and Post-Meiji Japan,* ed. Cornelius Wang and Johannes Bartez (New York: Cameron and Shuttlefield, 1996), 305–329.

IV. Multimedia exhibition: "Son et Lumière: Media Atrocity after Dien Bien Phu." An installation featuring pre-Communist traditional T'ai folktales performed in cartoon, "Yankees Go Home"–style, mostly leering, clownish foreigners and serious, muscular peasant farmers, accompanied by newsreel and print reporting of the siege at Dien Bien Phu and ultimate rout of the French. Followed by a detailed examination of all "R&R"–type activities sanctioned for French troops. Film, print, slides, newsreel, pamphlets, graffiti, cartoons, radio transcripts, postcards, comic books, chapbooks, tattoos. Exhibited twice: 1992, at Wellington Boys' High School, Wellington, New Zealand, and 1993, at the City Art Gallery, Wellington, New Zealand. Currently in storage.

IV.a. Short film including a series of interviews with selected US war photographers. DV. 8 mins., entitled "What Right Have You To Keep Me From Committing Suicide? Standing Too Tall: War Photography and the Guilt of the Noncombatant." Exhibited as part of "Son et Lumière."

V. Essay entitled "The Soul Unmoored: Japanese POW Involvement in the Japanese Anti-War Alliance in Communist Yan'an: The Opportunism of the Acculturated Mind, or, The First Brainwash Isn't Necessarily the Deepest," as published in *Journal of Sino-Japanese Conflict,* Vol. 5, No. 4, November 1994. Pgs. 11–42.

VI. A monograph apparently positing Hamlet of Shakespeare's *Hamlet* as the putative Prince in Machiavelli's *The Prince,* with Horatio of *Hamlet* as Machiavelli himself, tragically composing (in Italian) *The Prince* as ode to his dead Prince in the diegesis post-Hamlet-mortem of *Hamlet,* the play. Entitled *"The Prince* and the Prince: Horatio and Niccolò," and narrated in the first person, a typical extract, comprising a putative "Hamlet" monologue reported by "Nicoloratio," the retired Danish-Italian statesman and vassal of the long-dead prince, who during the composition of *The Prince* receives a visit from the ghost of the raving dissatisfied Dane, appears below:

> Is the difference between the starving and the hungry a matter of kind or degree? If kind, then is a shift in moral ground implied? If degree, then are not the *starving* greater latently, more *powerful,* than those who merely *want*? Is desire a disposition of power? And if then I starve starvation, feed it full of itself and thus eat that which only eats, will it not then know surfeit and expire in a black blink of logic? This at least would be *action.* The true sickening fall is to indulge. The bleakest of all nights is that of the day's satiation.
> And thus...
>   What? I am not a fanatic—I am merely becoming in myself a weapon of my thought. Bringing all that has made me to bear. Oh, to *do;* oh, to *be.* To starve emotion for the sake of something greater, is this not the test of all things great, momentous and pure? Starve love for justice; no limitations. An international law that might cross border and time zone and epoch and yes—be futuroretroactive. A man with a definition of himself so strong he becomes a metaphor for the state to ingest. A man to be model and chide for a tardy and childish god. What less was the Nazarene, or anyone who offered us a higher realm? What less am I, now? Yes I was given much, and much was asked of me, and I am grateful for both. *Yet it is not enough.*
>   *I starve, I starve.*

A second extract, narrated by Nicoloratio as an attempt to sketch the Prince's character, manifests a near-unreadable expressionistic density:

> The matter of his mind he came to view as an empire of knowledge that was an hallucination, less or more; that perhaps had an informed

history and omenic precedents none of which were utterly disprovable and which showed hints together of a final shining form—and but yet did not insist upon it!—with ripple effects from which origins could be traced to a hundred different sites and dispersed permutations of circumstance. Knowledge was a fluke concatenation of fact and statistic, instinct and educated inference, compiled and presented as evidence to his own merciless, insatiable and juridical consciousness that *everyone is guilty.*

And thus no one could be culpable.

He hoped not to see history's treatment of his history; he hoped to, for once, be done with something and become like the prism of his work: empty, pure form, a referent-free metaphor, a *yoga,* a way, free of particularity of time, goal and circumstance, a pure pursuit. Some part of him knew this desire was historical in form, too, and he grew sick of his own head; the firmamental curve of his own vanity that suggested stars but was only a reflection of stars he knew were inside him.

Despite, or perhaps because of, its often Nietzschean tone and streak of Puritanism, this part-historical, part-confessional and part-Shakespearean commentary met with some consternation upon publication in the London periodical *Excogitation* (Vol. 17, No. 13, Sept. 1997), but subsequently, translated into Italian and published in the Neapolitan periodical *Gracchus,* it seemed to find a home with the more esoterically minded Italian historical community and won Edwards the *Premio Inganni* for Shakespeare scholarship in 1998, the first piece in translation ever to do so.

VII. Essay entitled "She Smells of Fire: On Martyrdom and the Christian Peasant." A long essay on the "exact religious equations" computed in the minds of neophyte Japanese peasants executed by their feudal lords in the persecution following the expulsion of Portuguese and Spanish missionaries in 17th C. Kyushu—special emphasis placed on later rural corruption of Jesuit dogma to suit particular trying circumstances in the absence of religious guidance was taken as a metaphor for culture shock. Published in *Culture Shock: Perspectives,* ed. W. Reader and V. Rastos (New York: Routledge Kegan Paul, 1997). Part of an intense flurry of scholarship seeming to diverge from a prior focus on pre–World War II Sino-Japanese relations that was near-exclusive.

VIII. Book review of *Japanese For Everyone, 2nd Ed.* entitled "Actually, English For Everyone." New Zealand *Listener,* September 1998.

IX. Article entitled merely "Temparogens," as published only on the
website www.highlife.org.cn, sometime in late 1999. A long piece on the
history of organic and synthesized hallucinogens and their use in covert
military and national security operations. Veers sharply from historical
mode into a discussion of first-person testimonies of severe breakdowns
and reconstructions in experience of time after organic hallucinogen use.
Takes a line from Nietzsche ("*This* is your eternal life") as segue into tem-
parogen-affected time as a constantly available resource—all lived time
being available to a subject at once, seeming to envelop him/her in a
series of currents characterized as "the gyre," through which the subject
may step into different currents of his/her own life. The Time-As-Mael-
strom image becomes somewhat more abstract and difficult when the
gyre is characterized as both "feeding itself, and feeding on itself," in a
kind of Escher-like paradox, positing time as lived in loops, self-perpetuat-
ing, infinitely repeating and infinitely available, and is taken yet further
when the hypothesized "radical temparogen" is posited as rupturing this
concentric integrity, allowing the subject's time to float free amongst
other subjects' times, and other "Time" in a more overarching sense, generally. Last few paragraphs approach impenetrability in terms of (Adorno-
esque) confrontationally labyrinthine sentence constructions and obscure
LeFebvre-influenced spatial metaphors.

X. *METHOD ACTING.* Lost; last; a short film only referred to in a
putative curriculum vitae emailed as an attachment to Tsuji Ken in application for the position of senior foreign film archivist at major Tokyo-
based publishing house Kodansha, March 2000, described therein as "a
kind of guerilla film," wherein "confrontational interviews" were conducted with civilians on the streets of Tokyo, Shanghai and Nanjing, on
the subject of "historical and moral impulse-buying," intercut
chiaroscuro-style with grainy, sometimes uninterpretable and apparently
source- and subject-contentious film and still footage of wartime
(pre–World War II; circa the Japanese invasion of China—apparently a
sharp and emphatic return to this subject matter) executions, burnings,
mass grave disinterment, river dredgings and, ultimately, grotesque military surgical procedures. The piece was informed by a kind of Brechtian
insurgency: interviews were apparently conducted by young non-Asian
residents of the cities mentioned above, who, during the course of the
interview, are "replaced and found generally to be replaceable." The film
was apparently only webcast simultaneously with the interviews con-

ducted; an aesthetic ensuring its own oblivion, and concurrent both with a scepticism of the word, and the piece's commentary on an *"enfantin* cultural relationship with history as *gomi"*—the Japanese word for—and amongst more typical Western understandings of the word: discarded bicycles, laptops, TVs, fridges, microwaves and assorted furniture (a weekly replenished resource often plundered by Japan-resident gaijin for free household goods)—trash.

N.B. The entry in the curriculum vitae did not specify *whose* or perhaps *which culture's* relationship to history was, in this context, *enfantin*.

Jacques
December 12, 2000

Jacques has been up since half past five to catch an early train out to Saitama and Mr. Y, which is not such a bad ride because the trains heading out of Tokyo are way less crowded than those coming in at that time; no need for the Japan Rail boys in their military-style or really naval-style black uniforms with sailor-type lanyards at the shoulders and peaked caps with thin brims like shiny, black fingernail parings and just as plastic-looking as their flat shoes because Japan Rail is an ex-government-owned company and the money's just not really there to fit out these early-morning herders in the same way as the Tobu or Seibu conductors and ticket vendors with their fawn and orange uniforms as beautifully cut and luxuriously tailored and just as military as Mishima's own private army's privately designed and tailored uniforms briefly were, but no, no need for the part-sailor, part-Gestapo-uniformed boys on the outbound side of the Saikyo line stations, which was where he stood at six in the morning and watched them on the other, inbound side, pushing, or even heaving, the last few inbound commuters inside, tucking in hands and briefcases and stray coattails, to let the doors close, pushing with their white-gloved hands, either for that military look designed to spill over into corporate discipline or simply to protect them from actually having to touch the suits and overcoats—because it is winter, and the fashion this winter is no longer the gray or charcoal or black overcoat, this winter the fashion is firmly entrenched as the trench coat, in regulation fawn slash tobacco slash sepia, and the only real differences between the coats are their cut; whether they're belted or not; buttoned or un-;—of the men—because it's mostly men, the "office ladies" make up maybe three or four to each carriage that can carry sometimes close to a hundred—who jam themselves into the Saikyo line trains (*Saitama*, into *Tokyo*, equals *Saikyo*) heading for the business districts in Shinjuku, Shibuya, Ebisu, every morning six or seven days a week, in winter the windows steamed solid marble by their collective heat.

So the ride out was fine; he had a seat, and he held his ungloved hands down between his knees to warm them on the updraught of dry heat from the vents that line the undersides of the seats in JR trains. Beside him on the seat he had more than enough room to leave Michael's gift: Tim O'Brien's *Going After Cacciato,* creased and plump from reading, a bookmark protruding millimeters from the end. Posters hung from the roof low enough to brush high Western hair. Advertising J-Phone keitais; *SPLASH!* magazine; The Yen Shop, a legal loan shark company with 20% interest rates and Yakuza connections if you don't pay; NoDo, a spray for sore throats; and pictures of Fuji and shinkansen, JR skiing packages to Nagano, the JR slogan, "TRAING," not striking him as weird after so long in the city. But coming back in, there'd been a suicide near Jujo so the Saikyo went down, a thirty-minute delay at Akabane, long messages in Japanese over the public address. By the time he came back into Tokyo it was getting near 11:30 a.m. and the rush had slackened off so he got a seat in, too, but by now he had gotten plenty warm, and the underseat heating just made the backs of his thighs burn, so he spent the last part of the thirty-minute trip back into Shinjuku standing, hanging off a plastic ring on a leather strap to keep his balance.

And now out of the station into brilliant morning sunshine and the bustle of winter Shinjuku, he walks into a sea of fawn trenchcoating interspersed only very occasionally by a brown or black remnant from last year; the air chill and alive and smelling violetwhite with exhaust fumes.

Jacques, in a sea of trench coats, staring up at the huge TV by Studio Alta, tying the ends of his scarf in a soft knot, shifting the knot round to the nape of his neck.

He wends his way through the crowds, Princeward.

When Jacques is sad he likes to get high and ride trains all day. So that's what he's going to do today. In the pockets of his own, white, three-button and three-quarter Ermenegildo Zegna coat are a lighter, a baggie of gear, four baggies of dried shrooms from Saitama and an old-skool roll of rolling paper, gummed along one edge, with which he can roll a joint of any absurd length he likes. In the elevator ride up to the penthouse he doesn't stare long at the digital display counting up to the abbreviation, "PH." Instead he stares at the crevice between the dimpled metal doors, and just quietly waits for the elevator to slow and make the surge in his stomach like cresting a steep hill.

He'd met Michael at Mr. Y's place, and he had been pretty quiet there. Michael was getting his own gear from Y, which was different from what Jacques got. M apparently never does the shrooms but needs them for some experimental academic research, for which he's internationally renowned. But Jacques doesn't care because he—Jacques—certainly does do them. Michael suggested a competition, a test. They'd split at Omiya and Jacques would take the Saikyo back in and Michael the Keihin–Tohoku, the two lines like the splayed legs of a man balanced on the ball of the Yamanote loop, and they would see who got to the Prince first. Then they'd get high and Jacques would hang around a little bit and then he'd go and ride trains for the rest of the day, with a bag of gear in his pocket for when he came down. A good option would be the monorail out to Haneda airport. Because it went somewhere and came straight back, and because it leaned into corners and ran over water and freeways, and as the sun goes down there's nothing more beautiful than the golden light in the petrol rainbows, ragged mirrors on the canals. He didn't know the little competition would be the last words he ever spoke with Michael.

The elevator hisses to a halt. He uses the small circular key on his keyring and the doors slide open. The early-morning sun floods the long beige corridor through the security glass of the fire exit at the very end. He strides down carpet turned white by the sun. Halfway down the corridor, the door to the penthouse is open. No one in the living room, but papers scattered over the carpet round the desk. Some empty glasses on the coffee table. A single photograph lying on the carpet that he's seen many times before: Michael's father and his family receiving an award from the chargé d'affaires in their home country years ago. The TV screen dead and reflecting a rhombus of the sunlight, broken and distorted, across the tan leather couch.

"Hey," he says loudly. "Michael? The fuck are you?"

He listens, baffled.

There is only one noise.

A faint humming, from the kitchen. From behind the kitchen's always-closed door.

He leans against the door, presses his ear to the wood. As he listens, the hum subsides, and five long, regularly spaced beeps follow.

He opens the door slowly.

On the bench by the refrigerator, the microwave finishes its cycle.

He walks over and leans down to the window. The internal light flicks off before he can ascertain the contents.

He pulls the handle's latch and opens the door.

The light returns, and inside the plastic of a baggie is steamed like the windows of a commuter train, sucked tight to the contours of a small, still visibly violent-blue mushroom, the condensation sizzling. The adhesive label on the plastic has blackened partially, but in purple writing he can still read "AT ME."

What a joke. He must have missed him only by a couple of minutes.

Meredith
October 2000

The usual trajectory is they come to Tokyo looking for other selves, and only later do they begin to look for other people, whom they'll somehow magically find those other selves within.

Meredith Edwards is back in Tokyo, twenty-two, and sitting in the West Shinjuku Starbucks, opposite Takashimaya department store.

She's sitting on a tall vinyl stool at the window. She has a large date scone and a grandé cappuccino in a mug. The window faces onto Microsoft Promenade, a wide, pink-tiled walkway lined with overmanicured gardens that lie between the chasm of the tracks entering Shinjuku station and the pillars of the Microsoft Building and others. The Promenade marks the edge of skyscrapered West Shinjuku.

It's hot but not unbearable outside and it's a little after five. The foot traffic is beginning to become intense and relentlessly one-way, and Starbucks is filling up quickly.

The clues as they stack up so far are what's in the penthouse, and that's not much. There are four rooms, and in the living room is a desk covered with paper and paraphernalia. Stacks of books on and around it. Pieces of paper tacked to the wall above it. And there is nothing else that is not hotel property, in that huge room. Couches, a television, the open fireplace, a smoky glass coffee table. A great mirror propped between two doors. In the bedroom, the sterility continues. The hints of his presence are books in the closet, two shirts and a suit. In the bathroom the slate floor is cool, the mirror is huge and subtly lit, the benches are marble, the bath is free-standing and the only toiletries are the hotel's own. In the kitchen the tile is as beige as the carpet and walls, the benches long, the sink empty and bright. The cupboards are filled with white plates and bowls, wine glasses and tumblers. There is a microwave and an oven; both SMEG. Nothing is particular; nothing has been used; everything is clean beyond familiarity.

Since she's been here, she's been doing a lot of walking. To get back a sense of the place. She's found Kinokuniya Bookstore again, and an internet cafe. She's regained a sense of the relationship between certain key landmarks, certain narrow streets. She's connected up Marui and Isetan; Tsutaya, Virgin and HMV. She's been all the way up and all the way down thirteen floors of Takashimaya department store's escalators, counting Louis Vuitton bags passing her, as many as floors, alone but for thousands of Japanese.

Her days have been strange since arriving back. She's seen no one, and made no effort to find who might still be here. She's organized all the old elements of her other life in Tokyo that might still apply now. She's bought an MD player, signed up a twelve-month contract for a bilingual keitai. She's joined a video store. It's like she's staying a little longer than a tourist visa allows.

And the idea that someone in this world can really disappear is somehow terribly not troubling.

Why is she here? Because one month ago in Wellington it had been like this:

"Meredith Edwards. Leave a message."

"Merdy, this is your father. Please call us as soon as possible. It concerns the family."

* * *

"Edwards residence. Andrew Edwards speaking."

"Daddy."

"Meredith, my dear. I just left a message on your cellular phone."

"I know. I star sixty-nined you."

"Sorry?"

"I star sixty-nined you, Daddy."

"..."

"..."

"Don't ever do that again, Meredith."

"..."

"Perhaps I'll call back and we can start afresh."

"Daddy."

"..."

"Daddy?"

"..."

"Jesus."

* * *

"Hello?"

"Meredith, my dear."

"How are you."

"Fine, fine. As busy as usual."

"Busy."

"Yes, yes. Actually, some very interesting research I'm doing right now is taking up all my spare time. On the first post–Cultural Revolution visit by an American president to China. Nixon in '72. Kissinger crossing the border from Pakistan incognito to prepare the ground. The man was so excited he only took one shirt. Subsequently mortified when the only shirt he could borrow and wound up getting photographed wearing, to commemorate the 'diplomatic revolution' as he called it, was a): several sizes too big, and b): made in Taiwan. Endearing character, Doctor Kissinger. Very funny."

"Uh-huh."

"And the ridiculous détente this ridiculous country has reached with the States post-ANZUS means the Embassy won't allow me access to their photo archives but *will* renew my access to the Tokyo apartment. And they've offered me quite a hefty research grant into the bargain. It's all as droll and contradictory as ever. But an amusing sideline, nonetheless."

"Michael used to call this country a sinking ship."

"Did he now."

". . ."

"So."

"So."

"Have you . . . Well."

". . ."

"Well, I *am* glad you're still using this cellular I secured for you, Meredith."

"Oh, Daddy. Don't."

"No, no. I'm not implying anything more sinister than my own happiness at having the ability to contact you when the need arises."

". . ."

"Given the absence of permanent abode, and so forth."

". . ."

"So you will tell me where you are, please. Now."

"I'm *here*, Daddy. In Wellington."

"Oh. Good. Good. I'm here at Bolton St. Where are you?"

"I'm staying at a friend's."

"A friend's. A trustworthy friend's."

"A trustworthy friend's. Yes, Dad. And I don't have a job yet and I'm not going back to university and I don't know what I'm going to do 'with my life.' So let's just take *that* as 'given.'"

"You know, to me, Meredith, defensiveness implies weakness. Lack of confidence in one's own position manifests in the attempt to preempt challenges to that position."

". . ."

"To wait, listen calmly, ride out bluster and strike in the calm that follows seems to me to be the hallmark of strength."

"What do you want, Dad."

"Well. Given some recent information that's come to light. With regard to Michael. And, given your current, less than liquid situation—"

"What information?"

". . ."

". . ."

"Please never interrupt me when I'm speaking, Meredith."

"I'm not counsel, Dad."

"Nevertheless, you are my daughter, and though not currently under my roof, you remain under my wing, financially speaking. So I feel a modicum of respect and deference is due on merely the pecuniary grounds, don't you?"

"..."

"I'm sorry, dear. I don't mean to... Well, anyway, the information that's come to light is that Michael has, since in Japan, what with the free accommodation, I suppose, and the constant flow of my cash into his bank account—"

"Daddy."

"The fact is, Merdy, Michael has had a fairly absurd student loan for a fairly absurd length of time. And he has recently paid it off. In a single lump sum. In yen, in fact. The Inland Revenue wound up forwarding the change to me."

"But... wasn't it... huge?"

"Relatively speaking, 'absurd' is the term I prefer."

"Wow."

"Indeed."

"..."

"..."

"So, I suppose... you'll be... wanting me to do the same, won't you."

"Now, now. Elise and I have been discussing this in depth, and there are many more factors than the financial in play here."

"Like you discuss things in depth with Mum. And what factors."

"There is the absence of communication between me. And your brother."

"..."

"And Elise."

"..."

"Let me clarify that. I mean, there is the absence of communication between your brother, and me, and Elise. Between Michael, and Elise and I. To consider, I mean."

"Okay, Daddy. I understand."

"Quite. Well. We are, in the light of this abrupt liquidity, a little, perhaps not so much concerned, as *intrigued*, with regard to his activities in Japan."

"When did you last hear from him?"

"It was a postcard. From Hangzhou. In China. Eighteen months ago."

"Jesus."

"Quite. But you mustn't worry. Though the phone doesn't get answered, Daisuke, the Prince manager, tells me he has been using the

Tokyo suite intermittently up until just weeks ago. So we are working under the assumption he is in Japan, now."

"So you're suggesting I go back."

"We're not reacting in a knee-jerk fashion, first. What we're suggesting, Merdy, is that if you . . . You seemed to enjoy your brief sojourn there last year, so what we're suggesting, Elise and I, is that if you were interested in returning to Japan on a tourist visa, and . . . perhaps looking for gainful employment and so forth, and, while there, bringing us up to speed on your brother's whereabouts and peregrinations and perhaps even the methods by which he gained the wherewithal to dispose of his loan in such a radical and extravagant fashion—"

"Daddy?"

"If you were inclined to do this, Elise and I have resolved to both finance your flights, allow access to the Prince suite, or provide finance for alternative accommodations should Michael still be there and the concept of sharing be far beyond the two of you. And keep up your allowance."

" . . . "

"Meredith?"

"'Keep up.'"

"Come again?"

"'Keep up,' my allowance."

"Correct."

"So what you're actually saying is if I don't go and find a job and look for Michael you'll cut me off."

"Meredith, that is merely a particularly harsh spin placed upon words that, when assessed with clarity and balance, you will see are more than fair and equitable to us both, all things considered."

" . . . "

" . . . "

"What does Mum say?"

"She's a little sad at you leaving the country, but behind me one hundred percent."

"What's it like, being a judge, Dad? What's it like to choose words so you're invisible inside them? How do you feel when you make yourself invisible to me?"

"Don't use an angle on someone whose business it is to study angles, Meredith. That is my advice to you, and I mean it with love. So, yes or no."

" . . . "

"Yes or no, Meredith, my dear."

And it's funny, because she remembers a comparable situation with what feels like loss, though of what she can't frame the thought, nearly ten years ago, the first time she left home and the country.

An airport scene, nearly ten years ago:

In the middle of the Departures Lounge, look, here are twenty or more girls who are all between thirteen and fifteen.

This is a high school trip but they're not wearing school uniforms. It's apparent they're part of a sporting team: all but one of the girls is slim and tall; all but one is wearing some permutation of trackpants, tearaways, hoodies, new Nikes, Reeboks, ASICS. They stand in a loose and shifting segment of a sine wave; everyone faces someone. The girls are all talking, and at first the talk is nervous and meandering, shifting topic and trailing off as eyes flick to catch each new set of prospective passengers and each missing team member the sliding doors admit. The doors' glass is tinted, and the sunlight of early, early morning at Wellington airport seems to be eclipsed by thin but sharply defined clouds casting shadows over the rectangle of bright then dull extra-mauve airport carpet created by the doors and the sun that at its terminal edge is filled with the bright and silver trainers of the girls, and the sandals of the only girl not dressed as if for the bench (she's bigger, sunglasses, and the coach's daughter, whose life they knew was touched in complex, terrible but sometimes sweet ways by this team) and the rough mix of hairless white (male or female) legs and charcoal gray legs of those parents who work on Saturdays (but at the kinds of jobs that allow absences for such things as a child's first parentless flight), the parents who at the distance that implies a kind of amazement surround the sine of rapidly conversing girls, whose nervousness and interest in the airport are soon forgotten as the whole team is accounted for and whose staccato conversing shifts to other topics like shin splints and Air Gel or whose nervousness is expressed in the enthusiasm shown for that bag or Meredith's brother's handsome friend, and what it's like is that the curve's frequency of oscillation is upped and the amplitude increases, the curve grown more and more self-absorbed till the group of girls admits no parents, no outside intrusion to their talk.

Andrew Edwards' brief yet polite conversation with the father of the point guard has subsided. He pans across the girls, past Michael grinning at Meredith on the other side of him to point guard Sr., an expression on his face Elise—née Honda—his wife might remember as the barely reigned pleasure of a problem solved, an upper percentile penetrated: his face has a stillness, with a half-smile just emerging, and an alertness in his eyes that what it is, is: seeing this whole bizarre and selfless ritual clearly, newly, with a kind of shock and near-violent sense of privilege.

He's realizing again these things are given the father of a daughter; he's realizing again he is the father of a daughter.

Andrew waits quietly till he knows Meredith knows that he is waiting (a brief lull in her conversation, she looks around Departures, "at all the people," to herself, though they both know she's making this quick check that he really is still there, fourteen-year-old butterflies in her tummy with heavy wings).

As her gaze passes over, around, leaps nonchalantly past him, he speaks, in that confidential tone used by intimates through crowds, that though everyone in between hears they really somehow don't.

His chin slightly lifted, head tilted (if Elise had been there, she could have fallen back in love or at least in total trust with the openness on his face, the softness and that hint of a dare in the single word he directs to his dark daughter, who knows something is coming without really even catching his eye).

"Excited?"

Meredith's pause is evidence enough of respect, that's the really subtle part of the play that shows the truth behind what follows.

She rolls her eyes, literally snorts.

"No, Dad," she says. "Not at all." And she turns mock-despairingly to Michael for corroboration of this embarrassment.

She feels but does not see Andrew's tiny settling. She neither feels nor sees his heart burst a tiny seam at the magnificence of this absurd moment when the daughter is sarcastic to her father on the day she leaves to play basketball in San Francisco.

Later, something changed.

After she left Tokyo and returned home, the emails from friends and acquaintances she had made were sporadic, sparse and dried up quickly. It wasn't a matter for regret or recrimination. She felt how the worlds were discordant, how even fun was frantic here. Their emails were short because there was too much for them to explain; to distill and convey.

They seemed breathless, bored at the idea of trying to convey their lives. All she got were jokes, or the most mammoth events in their lives.

Jacques: NY tomorrow. Job interview Goldman Sachs NY. Wish luck! PS End of yr sale at Marui. PS. best new banana name: Jules Watanabe PS. Miss you somewhat rotten

Catherine: Hallo Meredith! Been to Kyoto w Yu. Was beautiful. My dad died. Not going home for funeral though. Tokyo is aaagh. Am very sad. I haven't seen your brother in a while. I am not sure he wants to talk to me and I guess he's always fairly busy. How's being home again?

Nothing from Simon, but that was to be expected.

Things move too quickly to record. It was too fragmented. Each fragment too dense, overloaded with information. She knew people in the city developed different techniques for dealing with it—for putting the pieces together or for living with them apart. Some came to Tokyo looking for other selves; some simply became other selves. Some practiced yoga, some danced, some drank, some became hypochondriacs, some shopped rabidly, some filmed the city, some wrote about the city, some lived deeply inside their obsessions: sports, food, film, jazz, hard- and software, pool, wine, sex, salsa, chess, tango. Her lack of a guiding obsession so somehow banal and harmless and sweetly coherent made Meredith feel semiformed, lacking, even bitter, when she was last here. There was no complete reason to be here, and she didn't find—or even fall into—any good reason to stay.

Her first time she had stayed in a low-budget gaijin house in Jujo. She was out of high school and it was a time when freedom from family had to mean freedom from an entire country. And was more important than comfort.

The gaijin house was two floors, eight rooms, and ten nationalities. It was isolation, together. A stairway with steps twice as high as they were deep, seeming to betray some fundamental ergonomic axiom. Doors with a peculiar symmetry: they all ended an inch above the ground, and they all rose to only an inch below her head. A notice board above the payphone with thumbtacked messages in English, French, German,

Japanese, Arabic.

And an alarming message left by the landlord—the worrying Shin Takahashi—for the previous troublesome tenant, found inside the wardrobe of her room:

Mr. Benny Souza-Leite

To: Souza-Leite

This Is second WARNING!
I know you've picked up and read my first Warning, but later you took it to the post office to send it back to me, leaving your fingerprints on it. I warned you "NOT to cross the threshold of this Jujo House" which you have nothing to do with any more.
Of your repeated vandalism and your rude painting, the POLICE will look for you one of these days.
    S. Takahashi

And the bizarre and ever-changing kitchen smells.

She was introduced to kimchi'i, and huge Purity crackers from Newfoundland, floury and thick as toast, dipped in chunky Saskatchewan chili. Oranges posted from Virginia. Udon made by a gypsy from Liverpool. And last of all, flaking, beautiful, crisp and fawn chou à la crème, remainders brought home by her next-door neighbor, the tall and pale French boy who worked in a restaurant and always left the House kitchen when the foreigners argued in the tiny, steamy room.

Framed on the wall in that little kitchen, the glass greasy with the fumes of a thousand different meals cooked in a thousand different ways by people from all over the world, dated 12 June 1963 and unsigned: a small, carefully written and largely ignored animadversion.

Japan is a riddle, yes. But what gall to assume its composition—by millions of individuals, thousands of years and hundreds of nations—is for *your* amusement.

She remembered how her dreams changed, in her four point five tatami mat room in that gaijin house with no aircon, windows on two walls and curtains thick only as dishcloth. Forever either too cold or too hot, her dreams seemed to pare strongly down to the last one of home. She could not know if this was the only dream she had, or the only one she remembered. Or if it was the only one she remembered simply because the rest were about Tokyo, and how does the dream of Tokyo differ from the reality? Who was qualified to answer?

In her one dream of home all she heard was, faint and slowly rising, her mother's voice calling her to wake: "Merdy. Merdy. Merdy. Merdy Merdy Merdy Merdy Merdy..."

And she always woke, angry, irritable, feeling she was late for something vital, but still angry to have been reminded. She woke, and sometimes blurted, loudly, to the eerie room with its thin curtains and frosted glass, tatami filled with the dust of so many different nations, *"What? Jesus."* And even if she woke up alone, or, as soon became the case, with Jacques, she still felt guilty that in her one dream of home, rather than roll, sleepy, and smile, or mutter "Hmmm?" she would say this first, harsh thing to her mother.

So the way the city affects memory becomes attractive.

Family, school, friends at home. Politics at home, music, art, food, fashion all get replaced by all that meets here.

Painfully and absurdly at first. A New Jersey girl who moved in had broken down crying on her first day. Trying to buy bottled water, and price seemed a guarantee of quality, she had chosen an immense flask of vodka.

But the accidents got shared, and they made new lives out of a communal pool of information. She learned that at a certain level this pool expands so rapidly the flood bursts the banks of an individual psyche; the concept of choice becomes overwhelming and, to manifest personality, obsession becomes something almost vital.

Here, time is different. She left, knowing that this feeling might be dangerous, that there should be longer-term considerations, that there were futures to be negotiated. But being back, now, there is something delicious in the letting go. In the acceptance that all found here may be just as valid as the rest you've ever known, and that it may not be wrong to let yourself fall into something so much bigger than yourself.

But she's suddenly worried. More than worried.

She has a *Tokyo Classified* from Tower Records. It's Friday night in Metropolitan Tokyo and certain familiar ways of feeling are starting to reassert themselves. Despite the fact there is a curious pleasure in the fact she has a quest, a mystery, at last an obsession given her on a plate, a straw in the flood and a direction, however vague, to swim, she is suddenly really troubled about being back.

And the primary reason Meredith is troubled, so suddenly, after only being in the city for three weeks, after finding the suite at the Prince empty, filled with Michael's "materials" but empty of him, and so hers to use as she wants (no more Jujo, dirty kitchens and banged heads on doorframes), after checking her Visa card and finding her allowance intact, after basically finding she has everything she needs for the city, 90-day tourist visa, cash, Tsutaya video membership, new MD player, keitai with nearly instant if cryptic responses from Jacques, and even Simon, by skymail, the reason she is suddenly hit hard and finding herself inexorably drawn to the eight pages of *Personals* in the *Tokyo Classified* instead of *Concerts* or *Travel* or *Eating Out* or *Looking Good* or *After Dark* is that the steadily darkening evening has made the windows of Starbucks begin to reflect those inside, and because she is sitting on a stool at the bar that lines the long window, and can see all that goes on behind and around her, can see the queues for coffee and muffins inside reflected against the stream of humanity flooding down the Promenade toward Shinjuku station outside, the J girl sitting beside her doing her makeup in a fliptop mirror the size of an octavo novel, and the J boy on the left changing the film in his camera, his friend just beyond him staring at him incredulously that he still has a camera that uses celluloid, and occasionally checking his hair in the windows, can see, too, reflected against the steady seethe of the crowd the staff of Starbucks, working hard not to appear harried, though they are, and the twenty or thirty people that are waiting for seats, queued against the wall behind her, flattening themselves against it to let others pass, a single foreign boy at the round table in the corner made of glass left of her, a table designed to seat four, but because he's foreign no one is asking him to move or share or even to let them have one of the seats he isn't using, and who is sipping a thick green grandé spirulina and is so obviously fresh off the boat it makes Meredith cringe, all sweat and redrimmed wide-open eyes and a kind of blasted interest, a shattered watching, and who had stared at her when she sat down like she had elephantiasis or something and who she can see is eyeing her on and off and is maybe slowly becoming aware that he might be committing some kind of awful faux pas by hogging a table with four seats as the queues for seats here in Starbucks start to extend out the doors beside him, and the reason Meredith is suddenly brought low, hit so hard, after the thrill, after the

string of epiphanies, suddenly really questioning the wisdom of coming
back to Japan, really questioning her own motives, the actual value of the
things she really came back for, all this anonymity, the disconnection, the
freedom, and the potential, is because she's nibbling a piece of Starbucks
date scone on a Friday night in Shinjuku, and facing the window that looks
out on floods of salarymen heading to the station that only provide a
flicker, a steady ripple in the reflection of herself, with the date scone in
right hand—left in her reflection—black headphones and long black hair
actually making a kind of shimmering gash in the reflection in the window and the Starbucks lighting, long black hair and black headphones and
black holes for eyes full of marching suited men, scone held in her right or
her left but she can only assume from her reflection that she is nibbling the
Starbucks scone because her actual mouth and the scone and any evidence
of actual eating is blocked, obscured, hidden by the flat pale expanse of
her left or her right hand, corrugated with shadow, held at an angle, like a
soldier paused halfway to a salute, hand covering her mouth, J girl style,
because if you're a J girl *it's impolite for your mouth to be seen while you eat,*
and Meredith is holding her hand like this, covering her mouth as she
chews, and her hand has done this without any kind of premeditation or
conscious decision, she's just absorbed this mannerism like a fact, like a
street name, she's sitting in Starbucks, she's only been back three weeks,
she's found another thing the city can do, and she's instantly depressed,
lonely, almost horrified, and wanting to be made more so by the pages and
pages of bravado and self-flattery and sometimes occasional actual bravery
("Persian male, 36, seeks honest and serious female for his last relationship
hopefully leading to marriage. No hatful mail please. Email rajkol@
hotmail.com") that's even worse than the really awful, jaded advertisements (Meredith sighs, because the Persian's right below "Part-man, part–
love machine, English gentleman executive, thirties, working in Tokyo
with wife in London, would like to experience erotic and steamy liaisons
with young and lithe Shibuya beauties. Email shavedsack@yahoo.com")
and the Persian's missing "e" somehow really and truly brings home the
deep acidic loneliness in the foreigners of Tokyo, the city full of lonely
people, and she's sitting, foreign, holding her left/right hand in front of
her mouth, chewing a dry Starbucks scone, not even being watched anymore by the baffled boy in the corner whose table is now completely surrounded—some of the standing Japanese even forced to lean right over it
to clear a passage for others to the bathrooms—with her hand hovering in

front of her face to prevent no one but her rippling self in reflection and inside her reflection the panels of suits of the right-hand sides of thousands of passing men from seeing her mouth while she eats.

Simon
September 2000

So I'm back, in Shibuya, and the twilights of early mornings and the twilights of early evenings are totally the most terrible times to meet anyone at the Hachiko exit from Shibuya station. Sunday afternoons can be totally just as bad. Unless you know Shibuya, unless you have a keitai, or unless you have a rendezvous—the dog statue, the tourists' metal map, the phoneboxes or the police koban—it's gonna be a problem. Right now it's a little after six, Friday night, I'm fresh off the boat, a seventy-minute trip to Shinjuku by N'EX, five to Shibuya, and I'm standing just outside the ticket gates. I'm leaning against the wall of the station waiting for Jacques, between the police koban and the gates, and above me is a giant GAP billboard with two foreign girls in floral and the script reads, "That's Autumn Dream."

The sun has left a faint lemon haze in the purplish gray smog up the street between the neon signs of Marui and Tower Records, and I had forgotten what this was like. I may be jet-lagged. I may be tired. I may have been lazy in LA but I had forgotten this feeling.

It's a corner of concrete, the size of a baseball diamond. It's a place where thousands and thousands of Japanese wait to leave. To cross the road into the spokes of the wheel of Shibuya, winding up through the hills. People are crowded from the edge of the street back to where I'm standing like the starters of a marathon and opposite them thousands coming down the streets are waiting to cross against them. The people waiting at Hachiko are boxed in on three sides, waiting for the lights to change, the flood of buses, taxis, cars, trucks and motorbikes to subside, so they can cross and the crowds from the hills of Shibuya can come down and together they can flood the intersection.

People are clustered together tightly at the street's edge and only a little less so the closer you get to the station. There are thousands and thousands, on this corner alone.

Opposite, on the Tsutaya building, a TV four or five stories high is play-ing a Microsoft advertisement and in the dimming twilight the TV is light-ing up the faces of the crowds in flickers, shining on a thousand heads of black hair. The air is thick and hot, radiating up from the concrete, and the traffic is roaring and the advertisement has changed to a video for the new Hitomi single and while I have been waiting here for Jacques to arrive I have seen a homeless man dragged past me by two uniformed Tobu department store staff to the police koban, protesting mildly, flapping his hands, some fluid leaking out of his pants, leaving a trail of wet on the concrete all the way back to Tobu, but it's so hot and there are so many people the fluid has already mostly evaporated or been tramped inside Shibuya station.

I'm smoking a cigarette, a Seven Stars, and drinking a can of Sapporo, but my hand that's holding the cigarette is still shaking.

And there are foreigners, Europeans, scattered through the crowd. There are groups by the Hachiko dog statue but in the crowds waiting to cross it's easy to spot them, a head taller than all the J around them and I can still pick their time in-country in seconds. The tourists are always sweating, either panicked or dazed. They sometimes try and feign famil-iarity. I see a tall American, his head freakishly perched above the masses of black hair around him, pink jowls, some kind of puckered, crimson burn on his cheek and ear, white, wispy hair, sweat glinting in the TV's lights. He's in deep, waiting for the lights to turn. He keeps looking up at the lights and the TV, squinting across the crossing, trying to be a tourist, then quickly down to his feet. When the crowd shifts, he lifts his hands to steady himself like he's on a boat. He twists and stares around him.

The fresh off the boat are always like this. In a way they are more true to who they are in this country than someone who knows how to handle the crowds. They move jerkily, and watch their feet like they can't control them. They stupidly look for gaps, and push people to get through. They check their friends and family every few seconds like they might be kid-napped. They look like they're having trouble breathing. They make body contact, put their hands roughly on the J when they lose their balance, making them flinch, and blink in polite disgust. There is the constant air of the hunted around them, the smell of fear. They don't speak the language and I can watch them for hours because the way I look means I am anony-mous to them, another dirty Asian among the clean Asians.

I'm back, and it's come back to me straightaway. How to go with a flow. How to look where I want to go, not at my feet. How to take small, steady steps. How to make gaps in the crowd with a hand, slicing through, something between an apology and a push. I let the crowd decide my speed. These are the things I learned here. This is how you have to be.

The twilight's dissolving and what neon isn't on is flicking on all through Shibuya, walls of kanji, and my keitai vibrates in my pocket for the second time since I arrived.

The skymail reads, "IMA DOKO." Old skycode, pig Japanese: "Where now?"

I type in "BY ZA KOBAN."

And then from beside me, dropping out of the crush, there's a hand on my stomach and a French accent intact if not worse, whispering in my ear, "Hey, hey, Simon. Meaning is sensation. Enlightenment is illusion."

"Hello Jacques," I smile. "I'm back."

It never really gets dark here but it's become as dark as it ever does as I follow Jacques past Tsutaya and Starbucks and up toward HMV through the early evening crowds. The sky is the color of dust and the crowds are mostly young, our age and younger at this time, the salarymen still working, the schoolkids at home. Older people don't come to Shibuya because they think they're too old to come to Shibuya. Another way the city works. There are couples and groups of young guys and girls hanging out. We pass one of the Israeli girls selling jewelry out of long flat suitcases, opened and sitting on trestles, the insides lined with black velvet and watches, rings, bracelets, leather bands, a droning generator at her feet powering tiny spotlights. There's a group of sweating Brazilians outside the Yoshinoya, and they're standing around sharing cigarettes and looking aggressive and kind of bewildered over the street at four young girls in massive platforms squatting on the corner looking at their keitais. As I'm staring at them staring I bump into a girl who's wearing a tiny pink T-shirt saying FACILE: TASTY CHARACTER IS OUR BASIC CRITERION and eating a crêpe and she pokes her tongue out at me.

The geography is coming back. The record stores in this part of town, two Recofans, the Discwave, HMV. The department stores, Seibu, Parco, Loft, Marui Young and Marui City. Restaurants, Kirin Beer City, Pronto, the mostly cheaper places. Ahead of me Jacques is weaving confidently through the crowd and I keep my eye on his shaven head, his thin neck, the collars of a loose white shirt.

On a billboard outside a tiny shop:

SAIGON INVASION TEESHATS
¥2000

MUKDEN—MARCO POLO – NANKING INCIDENT—TET OFFEN-
SIVE—HANOI P.O.W. – K.I.A.—M.I.A.—SUNK OF THE PANAY—MY
LAI—MANCHURIAN   INCIDENT—STRIKE-NORTH—STRIKE-
SOUTH

4 for ¥10,000

Outside the steps up to HMV Jacques stops and looks around past me over the crowds. Without looking at me he says, "Hey. You want to go eat something?"

"Yeah, sure," I say.

"What do you want to go eat?" He smiles.

"Let's do Segafredo," I say, and I smile back at him. "I haven't been to Segafredo in a year, man."

"Mm, mm. Segafredo then," Jacques says, and immediately looks away over the crowds. "Segafredo, Segafredo, Segafredo," he mutters. Then he looks back at me, a surprised expression on his face, and he says, "You look so handsome, Simon. I shall buy you dinner for you, handsome boy."

Sitting downstairs in smoking at a table next to a table of six older Italian guys and a solitary little J girl. All the Italians seem to have long hair and dark suits, and they keep looking over at us. I'm eating a chicken panini, the first food I've had since the flight. Jacques isn't eating and we're both drinking bottles of Heineken. On the other side of us is a young Japanese couple chain-smoking Marlboro Lights, drinking iced water mixed with gum syrup for sweetness.

Jacques is fidgeting, eying the waiters, and the Italians who are talking in loud voices and waving their hands.

He turns to me.

"New English idiom, man. Check it out. 'From whoa to go,' man. Hey? What do you think."

"I think it's go to whoa, man. You've inverted it," I say.

He looks over at the specials board.

"Go to whoa? Are you sure about that, man, because I've been using this new phrase all of the time."

"Yeah," I say. "I think whoa means stop."

He sips on his Heineken and thinks about this.

"But I don't understand what's wrong with stop to go, big guy," he says.

"Uh, because," I falter a little, trying to remember what this idiom is actually used for. "Because, like, people don't . . . use it . . . like that."

"I don't understand it, man," Jacques says, peeling at the label on the Heineken, looking over to the doors.

"But, I guess . . . you could," I say, and I don't want to disappoint him, plus I honestly can't remember what this phrase is even for, if I've actually ever used it. "Stop to go. Go to stop. Um, it's . . . I guess either is okay."

"Either is okay then."

"I think so, man. I'm really not sure."

"That's cool. Uh-huh." He sighs. "How is the panini, man. Lots of memories for you here I guess, huh?" He doesn't wait for an answer, checking out the Italians who are getting louder next to us. One of them has a whistle. "Stop to go, go to stop."

One of the Italian guys at the table, with long black hair in a ponytail, leans over to the Japanese girl and says something close to her ear. She turns and looks at Jacques, and then at me, and then back to Jacques. Jacques puts down his Heineken. She turns back to the Italian guy, and I clearly hear her say, "Baka."

Jacques hears this, splutters, hisses really low and fast at the Italian guy, "Ptits cris. Vatu faire crosser," and starts getting up and the Italians all get up too and there's like six of them and I'm taking Jacques' arm and stepping past the table, grabbing our beers awkwardly in my left hand, and Jacques shouts back over his shoulder, trying to shake my grip, "Par ta mère! Mother*fucker*," and we leave Segafredo to thick Italian laughter and the Japanese couple staring at us over the table littered with gum syrup containers.

It's very hot and the streets are still full of people on the move, so many they have divided into lanes, the left side moving down toward Hachiko, the right deeper into the city. We're standing drinking street beers outside

Don Quixote, a couple of shops up from Segafredo. The Don Quixote in Shibuya is smaller than the branch in Shinjuku, but anyone who knows knows it's better. It has only three floors compared to five in Shinjuku, but the range of food and alcohol is wider and the layout is less confusing. In Shinjuku the Don is a maze that straddles two buildings whose floors don't match up, and the stacks of boxes and racks of products wind through staircases and landings, heaped on flimsy wooden steps built quickly to change levels, to ease transitions. At the Don you can have anything, buy anything, and I remember searching the Shinjuku branch trying to locate the food and beverage department. I had run out of money. Because of the prolonged absence of communication from me my father had cut off the allowance, so I couldn't afford an apartment let alone a hotel. I was moving into some shitty gaijin house in Mejiro for my last months in Tokyo and needed cheap food. I was getting ready to leave for good, so everything had to be temporary, cheap, smaller than usual. I found the foreigner's house on the net: a tiny room with a shared bathroom and kitchen, for sixty thousand yen a month.

Lost in the maze of products in the Shinjuku Don for more than half an hour and so I asked the first foreigner I saw, a tall pale boy with short hair leaning over a case of fake Seiko watches, where the food department was. He looked up, stared away, squinting his pale eyes, and finally said, "Man, I think I am lost too."

This was how I met Jacques, and how you meet any foreigners in Tokyo. They all go to the same places.

I hadn't known about the Shibuya Don until Jacques told me. He drew me a map, directions from Hachiko, landmarking Segafredo (which was how I found that, too) to a large X marked "Donkey Otay."

I took a guess that French boys don't like it pointed out when they've made a mistake, and took him back to my tiny room.

There's a ravaged old tree coated black with exhaust fumes in a circle of park benches and trashcans outside the Shibuya Don and often biker kids hang out there, smoking, getting drunk on the cheap Don alcohol. There's already one young boy lying back under the tree in the dirt and grass, comatose, his girlfriend sitting next to him in black and red leather, idly patting his chest and talking with five or six other girls, standing around, also in leather, with mohawks and spiked hairdos.

The endless tape of the Don song plays: *Don Don Don, Don Quix-ote-e.*

Jacques and I are drinking large red cans of Asahi Super Dry and smoking my Seven Stars. We're standing under the tree, watching people, the endless flow passing outside the Don on a Friday night.

"I've remembered how to deal with the crowds," I say. "Treat the J like ghosts and you move through them just fine. I pretend they're not there. They part for me. It's not like LA. People are polite."

"Uh-huh," Jacques says, not really listening.

"So," I say. "What's happening? What're people doing? Are you still doing photography for *Tokyo Classified*?"

"On and off, you know," he says, watching the girls in the leather. "Sometimes yes. Sometimes no. Drew gives me work there. But for the money. Mostly I am living on my savings, doing video now. For myself."

"What's Brigit doing?"

"Brigit is breaking up with Drew, I think."

"Is she still in PR? Like organizing... events, or whatever?"

"Maybe, man. Or modeling. I'm not sure." He takes a big drink of the beer.

"How about Catherine? Is she still hostessing? Or dancing or stripping or whatever she does."

"Catherine has found a very big apartment in Daikanyama. With Yu. And I think so. One of these you say." He sighs.

"And Meredith?"

He laughs at this. "Meredith is..." He makes a swimming movement with his hand. "In and out, man. She is out then in. She is back. I have a skymail to which I have returned."

"No shit? She's come back?"

"Yes. I guess so. I got the skymail from her on my old phone, so this means the same country. So, yes."

"Are you like, going to..."

"We are like going to nothing man," Jacques snaps. "Sometimes in the past we have made love and sometimes we didn't. Now she seems to come and go. She is like the moon."

I take a sip of the Asahi. It's already warm. Jacques is practically daring me with this and I'm not falling for it. Meredith was just a little hanger-on to Michael and me back when my father exiled me to New Zealand. It was flattering for a while, but not a very long while. She even followed us here, though Michael had already taken off somewhere else again. Fucking her was a fatal mistake, and to this day I do not know if Michael ever found out I did it.

The girl sitting under the tree has found a spider in the wasted, carcinogenic grass. She is playing with it in her hands above her sleeping boyfriend's cheek, making it scuttle from one palm to the other. Her hands shift like scales, like she's juggling something terribly fragile in slow motion over his slack, open lips.

"Have you seen Ariel, much, then, Jacques," I say, and return the dare.

He turns and makes a mouthing movement with his hand.

"Man, you are all questions, questions, questions. You've been away a long time. Things have changed. You don't know what's happening."

"That's why I'm asking," I say. "Cool down."

"For an instance, you know what happened last week?"

"What?"

He doesn't answer.

"What, man?"

"Alright, I'll tell you the story. In all the newspapers. At Shin-Okubo station, one stop from Shinjuku. On the Yamanote line."

"I know Shin-Okubo, Jacques."

"Okay. Yamanote line trains run every three or four minutes. It's about nine p.m. Four policemen have been out drinking at an izakaya somewhere and now they're going home to their wives. They are standing on the station platform, which is six yards wide by two hundred fifty yards long, waiting for the train. They are quite drunk and playing around. Imagine it. They are hanging off each other, arms wrapped around each other, carrying cans of beer from vending machines. Where I come from, if you act drunk this way you are only pretending to be drunk. Slurring your voice strongly, hanging off your friend like a woman. But this is the way the Japanese do it. This is how they male bond. So they are singing and hugging and bonding. They are standing eighty yards from the end of the platform the train will arrive at. I remember all the figures I get from the newspaper. And one of the policemen is hanging off his friend. Very drunk. Then his arm slides off his friend and he loses his balance and falls sideways, down to the ground and then he rolls off the platform and down onto the tracks. This is a fall the height of a person, an adult. He lands on the tracks. He is stunned and dazed and winded and very drunk. The tracks are rough, slippery. Did I say it had been raining? He is looking at the under of the platform. All those cigarette butts and empty cans and cigarette packets and gum wrappers, pushed aside by the wind of the train. How different it would be to look at the station from down there. The train is coming from the next station up, which is Takadanobaba. They come every three or four minutes, you know that. He is lying there dazed from the fall. On the platform his friends quickly move, as soon as he falls, to help. They jump down from the platform, difficult to get footing on the tracks. Under the tracks is Okubo Avenue. So not gravel, but iron plates, around the tracks. Nowhere to escape to, because the tracks are on a bridge. The train is coming now. They are drunk, but adrenaline, you know? They are trying to lift their friend, who is dazed, maybe unconscious. Shoes too slippery to hold on to warm, wet iron. They can't lift him. And then a Chinese boy, a student, twenty-six years old. He jumps down to help. The train is coming. The driver blasts the horn. It's a frightening sound, louder than you can believe. To lift a man over your head. He is heavy. Your arms shaking when you hold a heavy thing that high."

He pauses in his story. He checks the end of his cigarette, and flicks it away. Jacques looks tired suddenly.

"So what happened man?" I say. I grin. "You tell a good story."

"Of course, together they throw the fallen policeman up onto the platform and the train comes slowing and hissing and howling but still too fast and it hits and kills the Chinese boy and the three policemen down on the tracks."

"That's . . . too bad. So what . . . would be . . . the point."

He sighs deeply. "I don't know what's the point. That's my problem. It seems important. Does it seem important? I want to know the morality of that story. I heard it and I thought of you. In the story in the newspaper they said, 'Chinese student, Chinese student,' over and over. These were the most important things about this boy. This was all we knew about him. Chinese student, aged 26. They . . . I think they hate to think a Chinese could be this way. Be so selfless. It made me think of you. I can't stop thinking about it. That's all."

"You mean moral."

"What?"

"You want to know the moral of the story. Not the morality."

"What's the difference?"

"You got some facts. You want a point."

"I want to know a point then."

"The point, Jacques, is that to die like that, being drunk could either really suck, or be like, the best way."

He shakes his head, and looks out over the busy street. "You are something else, Simon. You appall me."

"I know, man," I say. "I'm a monster. But what's the point of this like, bland concern? All I'm saying is that their world exists, and our world exists. It's like what I said before. Pretend they're ghosts, you get along here just fine. Stay out of J affairs. People say, oh, to understand the culture, you've got to understand the people. That's purely sentimental. They don't want us here. It's that simple. We are not wanted. Once you get over that fact, you can enjoy the place."

"I see their world, but what is our world? I think treating others like ghosts that you run a fast risk of ending a ghost too. And if you think this place is like this why are you back then, man? Why did you come back?" He's still staring out over the street.

"Cool down," I say. I laugh. "I'm back. I have a job. I'm working for my father, I've got a place to live in Omotesando. I'm kickin it, man. A one-year visa. And like, yen in pocket. We can have some fun. And our world is leisure, dude. Lee-du-damn-*jour.* Somebody's gotta do it."

I hear the girls squealing with laughter.

"Uh-huh," Jacques says, and sneers.

"So is White still open?"

"Yeah."

"How about Blue?"

"Yeah. It's open."

"Are you still hanging with Michael?"

He snorts. "Uh, *un grand guignol.*" He finishes his beer, and spits down at his feet. He throws the beer can into the trash. Then he looks up at me.

In winter, he was so pale I could see the veins in his temples through the skin, faint, purplish blue smears. In summer he tans the color of milky iced coffee, and the veins only appear when he's pissed or agitated. He's looking in my eyes as I'm watching the veins in his forehead. As he watches my eyes Jacques may be thinking I'm trying to figure out his feelings. Or he may be thinking I'm staring at him in affection. He may be unsure if it's empathy, or distraction. But it has the same effect.

He calms, the veins disappear. His face softens.

"Hey, hey. I am sorry. The fucking city, you know."

"I know," I say.

"Soon summer will be over."

"Soon summer will be over. You like winter the best," I say.

"Let's go see Michael then," he says. "Let's go see Michael." He leans over, kisses my cheek. "I am glad you're back. It makes me feel many different things, that's all."

"Well, alright then," I say. "Hey, Jacques. Still like bananas?"

"You're a banana too, man. But you went rotten."

"Hey, man. I'm Alfredo Ono."

"Okay. It sound like a recipe, but okay. Philippe Watanabe, then."

"Helmut Wang."

"Guy Hayakawa."

"Seamus Suzuki."

He laughs, finally. "Kick ass," Jacques says.

"Ace. Let's go get some shrooms or something," I say.

As we walk past the sooty, ruined tree and into the millions and millions of people, Jacques takes my hand and I let him.

The J girls have left, and the comatose boy is still lying there in the dirt, totally out of it, mouth wide open.

I wonder about the spider, if the girl could do such a thing.

Back in Japan, easing transitions. The sky's the color of dust.

But of course we never make it to Michael's on my first night back.

Jacques tells me Michael still has rooms his father—a judge—pays for at the Shinjuku Prince, but we start making out in the street on the way back to Hachiko and the subway is so much closer so we take the Hanzomon line just one stop to Omotesando, holding hands, sometimes kissing on the train. We walk through the streets trying to find the new apartment, but it takes too long, and we get lost, and I spend my first night back in Japan with Jacques, in a ¥15,000-per-night love hotel somewhere between Aoyama and Roppongi, a christening of my father's new bank account.

For what it's worth: he never makes me wear a condom and never makes things too demanding.

Meredith
November 2000

Another Friday night low has been pushed south a little, by a Saturday morning shoulder, olive, alive and perfect beside her, folded into her brother's whipped white sheets at the Prince.

It's early morning, maybe six o'clock, and despite the constant temperature and the lifeless air of the hotel room, Meredith can feel and sense the dawn. She's lying naked, a little on one flank, looking with lazy, rested eyes over the olive shoulder and the mess of black and brown hair on the other pristine pillow, to the nightstand. It feels good to be in clean sheets and a wide bed, a cool smooth-skinned boy sleeping within reach. Meredith feels herself and whole again after the sex. She feels like a simple thing, like she's flowing and draped like stretched linen, relaxed in the big bed under a single sheet.

After too long alone in that room, she had chosen a Roppongi club at near-random, the boy too. He was with three J friends at a nearby table. She sat alone with gin and tonic and picked him up, easy as that. A smile through their conversation that he returns; and returns again from the bar, he's maybe eighteen, and she smiles again and then, she pats her table. He sits and here they are. The pat a gesture of scorn for eight pages weekly of *Classifieds,* all the loneliness and all the male endowment. Just so simple. She had felt it without knowing it. Just be honest.

The conversation was just a game, too. For once there was so little frustration; she knew and he seemed to. They spent ten minutes just teaching each other to pronounce their names; ordered one more drink each and then outside and cooling Shibuya air hurried matters; Meredith waved down a taxi and he followed. A pure thing; a sweet and smooth and dirty thing.

She had walked to the vast clean ensuite in borrowed digital light to use the bathroom, and on the way back to bed, removing her earrings, shuffling feet delicious in the warm wool carpet, she dropped one. She crouched, and stroked with two slow circling palms, the carpet a lunar Braille. Around where she had been standing. Back toward the ensuite door. Around, under the nightstand. Along under the edge of the bed. Right under the bed. Fingertips of one hand touched hard-grained wood. Further, a warm, oiled cylinder. Further, a long metal fillet, a blade. And back again, puzzled. A curving, fingerwidth bracket; inside it, a smooth crescent.

She still slept for four hours, hand on the Japanese boy's hip, over the length of it. Something about Japan. There was strangeness in too many directions to be alarmed or even intrigued by everything. It was too tiring. Until she woke, alert.

There are images, episodes of her brother that play in the presence of suggestion, in the dark of his empty rooms and the stacks of papers and books, loose photos, insignia. They play as she lies a little sideways, knowing she will roll over this boy when he wakes and take him in her hand. It is easier to think with this boy that guarantees something beside her. To see his blink and smile close-up.

There is Michael's back at the bedroom door in the Bolton Street house in Wellington as he peeked at their father's sway in the hall. The bedroom's ceiling flickered in the big television's light. The smell of dope, she sat on the floor, back to the bed's side; coming up through the carpet the noise of the party with the Attorney General downstairs. She is maybe twelve so he is fourteen. They watched *The Poseidon Adventure,* eating chef's home-popped corn, drinking stolen half-empty bottles of Montana chardonnay. They got stoned together and used the cordless phone to eavesdrop Grossness' late-night calls. Learned the code for their own cocaine but didn't call for years before they plucked up courage. Jumped drunkenly on beds to *Bitches Brew* and always spilled the popcorn. Found husks and kernels in corners into their twenties, stale and coated in dust.

Her father at the door, eyes red and hunted: "How are the little cruelties, then."

In unison: "Fine."

The way in Japan you can miss nicknames you may have hated, wind up giving out unsigned confessions, telling near-strangers your shame. Trying to remind yourself one little part of who you once were, no matter how painful, or how outgrown. The way you can miss the backlog of tease that is one file of life.

The *Family Ties* thing had started with her and spread to Michael. They watched the last season as children. "Alex," for him never stuck; there was the Michael J. Fox connection, ditto with the prodigious elder brother, but there was no mileage in it, no second-order salt, no barb to make it catch. Andrew's nickname, The Grossness, Grossity or just Gross, came from the actor who played Steven Keaton, the father: Michael Gross. Elise was just Elise was her mother, but her name had been the coincidence, the adhesive that made the others stick, and the origin of Meredith's own nickname, which, beginning at primary school, but winding up in all sorts of places now, was Bax, or Baxter. After Meredith Baxter-Birney, the actor who played Elise. A distortion that stuck and warped further. They came and went: Backslash, Backstroke, Backstreets, Beeswax, Backscratch, and Simon's all-time faves, Bitchslap and Backdoor with and without Deliveries.

The boy shifts in his sleep. He grunts softly, inhales; and out in a long tired sigh.

Meredith reaches out and holds her flattened hand an inch from his spine. Then under the sheet she runs it down, flinching back when she touches his skin. She traces an aura down to the small of his back and round a flexed buttock cheek. If you were found in circumstances like these you would go straight to prison. The laws are draconian and the jails dungeons; or rumored to be. Foreigners busted for drug possession, coke or hash, Special K, even marijuana, just disappear. Sometimes immediately deported, sometimes straight to jail. Either way they are often never heard from again. There are Amnesty International petitions for drug-busted foreigners swallowed up by the system; families all over the world desperately taking second mortgages and Japanese at night school. If you're found with something like *that*.

She is twenty-two and doesn't know anyone in Japan any more than four years older or younger than her. Of the people she knows in Japan she has slept with the two she knows best. She doesn't know the language. She doesn't know where the Embassy or her older brother is. She is alone. She's been here eight weeks. She is fighting a wave of panic, the feeling of unreality, disconnection, so many faces of absence. She palms the boy's cheek and it's firm and handsized; cool and certain on her palm, then deeply warm. Her fingers tuck in the cleft between the cheeks and he stirs for real this time.

He rolls slowly, languidly over; a khaki blur on white in the dim. She lets her hand ride with the movement over onto his hipbone. Her fingertips snarl in sparse crinkly hair. He's looking at her and his eyes are black and he blinks once. This sign, this prediction and she is quickly wet, her left leg shifting almost involuntarily until her knee meets his thigh.

"Mmm," she murmurs, deep in her throat.

"Mm," he replies.

She feels his abdomen muscles tense and his hand touches hers at his hip. Then brushing through the hair of her forearm and dipping under to her open thigh's inside but moving too quickly upward and she shifts and stops him.

"*Wait,*" in a whisper. Then, softer, "Wait." She takes his hand back down to her knee, places it carefully. Her hand runs up his arm and back to the edges of his pubic hair. "Just wait."

His hand stays still on her knee.

Her eyes closed now, from beside her she hears a soft, throaty question.

"Daijobu?"

A pause.

She whispers, "My dad used to come in and ask us, 'How are the little cruelties, then.' We'd always answer, 'Fine.' Fine."

Reassured by her voice, the hand moves on her knee's inside.

"My first time was at a memorial service," Meredith whispers in the dark. "Yup. It was for a judge who sat at the Tokyo War Crimes Tribunal, and I was fifteen. My . . . father made the whole family go. It was kind of a big thing. There were people from all over the world. Indians, Americans, Canadians, Australians, Indonesians, Chinese. Relatives of the counsel and the other judges on the bench. There was champagne and canapés and white trestle tables with umbrellas on the grass. There was a dais and a string quartet. I had to wear a Balenciaga. My mother loaned it to me. I was tall. I was fifteen and I really . . ."—a breath—". . . *really* really didn't want to go."

She's taken his cock in her hand and it is full and hard, hanging over his stomach. His hand is on the inside of her thigh, dry and steady, cupping the muscle. His breathing is a little faster, and she talks to the ceiling with her eyes closed.

"The Prime Minister was even there for a while. We went in a hired Mercedes and I had to wear a proper dress. I hated it. Michael had promised to turn up. There were speeches about this judge fishing in the lakes at Hakone between depositions. How long the trial lasted. His contribution to justice in Asia. About his criminal neglect in local histories. His name was Harvey Northcroft, I remember that. There were jokes about the Russian judge who couldn't speak English or Japanese, and didn't know what was going on. How they gave him his own channel on the translation equipment and the Chinese complained. And the American lead prosecutor who was an alcoholic. The absences. The length of the thing. Polite laughter. I was so bored. Grossness was drinking and getting loud. It never . . . really occurred to me it might be uncomfortable for Mum."

Her breath catches a little as his hand reaches her crotch and his fingers move through the hair. She spreads her legs a little wider to let him and he ripples his fingers well, she feels the wetness spread around herself, cool in the creases of her thighs. She sighs softly, pleased, and removes her hand from his cock, licks her palm and fingers slowly, returns it, begins to stroke him, peaks rising and falling slowly in the white sheet, gray in the strange light.

"He arrived with Michael. In a Trans-Am his father bought for him here. He went to school . . . with Michael. And they were both high. Wearing these matching Commes Des Garçons tuxedos. That I know for a fact Simon bought . . . in Japan. They were standing at the bar. Drinking red wine from the bottle, and smoking, and heckling . . . people . . . you know, bowties . . . all undone. But Simon mostly kind of watched. I didn't know him really at all . . . then." She has drawn her feet up, lying flat on her back now, and he's moving his fingertips along the lips of her cunt. She lets go of his cock with her right hand, licks her left palm and reaches down and takes him again. She runs her right hand over her breasts on the way to her neck as she whispers, her breath less steady.

"He was Chinese American. From LA. Michael introduced us. But they'd talk about him . . . at school. We used to call them . . . S and M. He was . . . good-looking. They were high and drunk. On Dad's coke. He was . . . gorgeous, really."

"Turanji ahm," the boy whispers. Meredith rolls her hips and pushes down, his fingers inside her. She grunts softly.

"My brother went up and took the microphone . . . and accused that dead judge of condemning an innocent man . . . one of the Generals . . . they hung . . . a Buddhist . . . called him a scapegoat . . . a sick man . . . about a massacre . . . he kept shouting names . . . dates . . . Chinese cities . . . Mike was . . . wasted on the Bordeaux . . ."

She lifts her left foot and hooks it between his thighs, spreading his legs apart.

"When they made him come down . . . I left with Simon. . . . And we smoked a joint in his car . . . and drank more . . . I loved the way he talked . . . his accent . . . we listened to . . . Psychedelic Furs in the Trans-Am . . . he was older . . . handsome . . . it felt . . . right . . . like . . . a drama . . . it wasn't . . . traumatic . . . and I asked him . . . if I could trust him . . . and I remember . . . he said . . . 'You can decide . . . for yourself' . . ."

She's masturbating him faster, her hand sometimes slipping off. Shaking and hot flush on her chest and cheeks and the boy's thumb at her clitoris a little too hard so she reaches down, to calm him, show him, feels his breath and a grunt in her hair, her hand catches in a fold of fabric.

Paused there for a second as she begins to feel it really coming on, the sworn statement, to feel real here, to hear and not hear her own voice telling another, but a second's doubt, of who she's telling or why, what it can even mean, to confess this, and who it should be to and who decides, and how it should be done, sudden doubts through her mind she'd done this to dispel, but in the smoothness of his cock and in his fingers she feels something older and quicker, maybe true anonymity in those two hands and she makes the decision, lets it be, tell it hard or don't tell it at all.

She pulls the sheet off roughly and tensed, neck bent, ripples in her stomach as she looks down to their hands, his cock in her moving fist and his hand and her hand in her thighs she grunts, "And...I fucked...him in ...his car...and I bled...on the damn dress," and lets it all go and falls back and comes and comes around his fingers, feeling his cock throbbing and warm pour on her fist and forgets him, feels only the pulse and flow outside of them; the hot rise inside and around.

And though she doesn't hear it, when the air conditioning comes on, the temperature finally alters in here, and the tiny tick beneath her is old steel cooling; the lock of a bayonet.

Simon
October 2000

So I sleep in the one room of this new apartment that has tatami, and my dreams are filled with the raw, strawlike smell of it, rising up through the futons. Sleeping in Japan is never restful; my dreams get so dense, and the humid tension of Tokyo never lets me completely relax. Sometime late in the night, early in the morning, the phone rings and the fax chugs and chatters for what feels like so long I think I actually go back to sleep, waking again only when it finishes. I finally chose this room to sleep in because I don't like sitting on tatami—fear of bugs—and I can use it solely as a bedroom, leave my futons out all day, carpet the room with them.

The apartment I'll admit is lavish compared with most I've known and must be costing my father the earth. It's not Dolce & Gabbana, but it is two blocks off Omotesando-dori, has three different-sized rooms none more than four mats big, one bathroom and an ensuite with marble floors, no oven but a Black & Decker dishdryer, a gigantic aquarium built into the wall with a functional, bubbling oxygenator but no fish, and the VP of

Marketing for AGF Foods lives in the apartment next door.

I think my keitai rings, too, sometime in the night, and throughout it all I doze more than sleep, like in summer when it's impossible to even breathe without aircon. The fridge hums and subsides, and when I wake again I stare dazed up at the remote control for the aircon that is dangling above my face, the front door clicking closed, it's getting light and I'm relieved I can spread out over both futons, naked, flat on my stomach, glad he's gone, the tatami odor rising all around me. I half-dream that I'm swimming in tea, cool and antiseptic all around me, light and palely green.

The television has an alarm, and a bilingual on-screen menu, so it's this that wakes me properly when it comes on at ten. The hazy feeling of never quite leaving consciousness all night makes it easy to make resolutions, and mine is this: I will not sleep with him again. I promise myself this, guiltily because it is hard here, in this world, to believe your own private resolutions really count for anything. Somehow, guilt and resignation seem totally in tune with this city; compromise and whim the appropriate responses. I lie here, feeling totally weary like I'd played the first hard game of tennis of the season yesterday, though all we did was spend the day out in Shibuya and Harajuku clothes shopping. That these—compromise, whim, a certain kind of resigned, pleasurable corruptedness—are the appropriate responses maybe seems like a bad thing, a problem, but what I know is this: moral aversion is just culture shock, and to not tune in to a place—breathe it in with the air—is to decide very quickly to leave or be suffocated.

I stare at the TV, nestled in the bookshelf over the fax, which is piled with wads of paper.

I suddenly realize I recognize the show that's on, that it's still playing on whatever channel this is—NHK, maybe—after a year. And I start to watch, first with the pleasure of strange-shaped memories of Japan, of who I was then, a year ago, watching this show in a shitty gaijin house, in Jacques' shitty gaijin house, in Michael's hotel even. Then I start to watch with a kind of pleasure that's somehow similar to that of this morning's resolution. Something slightly queasy and real like a lie or a bruise.

It's a semidocumentary that follows the apprenticeships of young guys into a like guest sous-chef position in various different J restaurants. The music, the voice-over and the narrative arc of the show are always the same; it's the restaurant, food and characters, the background to this arc, that are different every week.

A chubby guy, thirty-one (all I can read of the kanji flashing across is his age in brackets), starting work in a ramen store somewhere in Tokyo. The voice-over is a deep, ominous-sounding male Japanese, the muzak blary and melodramatic. They have cameras in the bedroom of his apartment and the apprentice rises before dawn. He is shown eating breakfast, with his wife, cross-legged at a low table. She's nursing their child, and the guy kisses them both before he leaves, and is followed riding a typical big black J bike through typical dark and narrow J streets. When he arrives at the restaurant, the boss berates him in a good-humored way out on the street. The boss is older and thin, and his quiet, violent little questions get sharp nods and a meek, muttered, "hai," from the apprentice. Kitchenhands hose down the street outside the store, and the apprentice moves to get out of the way without turning away from the boss. It's still dark.

Next he's preparing stock for the ramen; chopping onions and leeks and daikon and dropping stripped chicken carcasses in a gigantic vat. In the background of this obviously contrived soap two-shot, rising into focus, the boss does books at a table, too badass to even look up. In spotless white, young kitchenhands clean and move deftly past as only good J waiters move, just the very subtle movements in the hips that show they're avoiding the apprentice.

Flash to the apprentice cooking noodles. He has a long-handled shallow sieve that he dips into another giant vat of boiling water, the man's face red and streaming with sweat as he lifts the sieve, knocks water from the noodles, flips them once like a pancake, then pours them out into bowls. Of course, when one noodle slides from the side of the sieve back out into the vat the rest follow in a steaming ivory clump, and we see the boss kick the apprentice hard in the ass for the first time. He then goes and kicks him a second time as he reaches for a towel to wipe his face. The apprentice jerks and stops whatever he's doing when he gets kicked, baffled at being kicked, and so makes things worse for himself by not concentrating on the noodles. The chef stalks off in disgust and we're left in a close-up: the apprentice's hands shaking.

As dawn comes and the restaurant gets ready to open for business, the apprentice has bowls of steaming ramen broth lined up along the bar. The boss watches from close beside him as he pours a clump of noodles into each bowl, trying so hard not to splash the broth. The boss points, and hisses, disgusted and incredulous at the apprentice. As the first customers begin arriving, kitchenhands shimmy by the two, their hands laden with bowls, out into the restaurant. The boss slaps the apprentice on the back of the head hard enough to knock his hat off. As he bends to pick it up he's kicked again in the ass. The apprentice gets his hat and stands and turns back to the ramen. The boss kicks him hard in the ass again, for emphasis. The music soars and the narration drops away in deference to the fact that the climax to the show has been reached, as it's reached every week (afterward, for the last fifth of the show, it's all about his growing competence and the grudging acceptance of the boss—the climactic breaking of the apprentice actually brings boredom), the moment we've all been waiting for arrives, and after the appropriately tender push-in to the man weeping in the alley behind the restaurant and the tantalizing close-up—his fat, red cheeks, sweat and tears streaming, snot running from his nose, as he punches himself in the chest with a closed fist—there is a commercial break.

Brad Pitt in *Seven*-esque salaryman shirt (I think he wore Armani in *Seven*) and black tie, in an office high in a skyscraper. No one's around, it looks like a lunch break. He leans back from his computer, spins in his chair. Then, with a certain kind of sneaky look in his eye, he rises and sidles across the office to a vending machine. He slams the button hard, and lifts a can of Georgia Café Au Lait to his lips. He leans on the window, looks out over Tokyo. He takes another sip; rolls up his sleeves. Next thing, he's shadowboxing around the office, punching the air, weaving between desks. The music is J rock, brash and flashy, really eighties. A montage of sparring shots follow, Brad dipping and punching. Then he pauses, takes another sip, sits back down at his computer. Though we never see any Japanese enter the office, you get the feeling lunchtime is over.

Brad shifts his chair closer to the desk, turns back to his computer with a sly smile. He's got a secret.

10:13 a.m. now, says the light on the fax, and I drag the top pages into bed with me, and read them in the thin, ungreen light coming through the thin ungreen curtains in this, a country or a city in which I have never yet encountered curtains that do their job properly.

FROM: CHANG GROUP CENTURY CITY
PHONE NO.: 03-3954-4162
OCT. 9 2000 01:33AM P1

To Simon Chang,

Hello, how are you back in Tokyo? How is the apartment? I have not
seen it, and hope so that everything is fine there. Are you glad to be in
Japan again? I hope so, and that you are settled. I have received a telephone call from Andrew Edwards in New Zealand who you remember.
He is perturbed at the whereabouts of Michael and asks if you are
making his acquaintance there again. Are you? Please let me know if
this is so. Andrew's daughter is now in Tokyo also, and he tells me she
is keeping her eyes out for him. Please help her, and thus Mr. Edwards
and thus me. Shinsekai Long Beach opening was now ten days ago. We
were happy with a small ceremony and a few special guests. We make
our first appearance in the Michelin this month. The chef's name is
Mastika. He is a Malaysian who has studied in Aizu, in Japan and has
suggested that you make contact with potential top-line staff in Tokyo
who are non-Japanese, with a view of offering work. He thinks non-
Japanese working in Tokyo are more flexible and open to new ideas,
and grateful for a relaxed working environment and competitive US
dollars wage rates. If you know or come to meet with potential top-line
staff, please show them the prospectus attached with its contact details.

Further, below is restaurants for the next week. I have attached
the maps, too.

Remember that I am interested in detail.

Oct. 18: So-an 5-17-11 Hiro-o, Shibuya-ku

Oct. 19: Torigin 5-5-7 Ginza, Chuo-ku

Oct. 20: Aoyuzu B1F Daikoku Bldg, 1-8-14 Ebisu, Shibuya-ku

Oct. 21: Shinjuku UN Misuzu Bldg 1F, 7-8-3 Nishi-Shinjuku

Oct. 22: Gonpachi 1-13-11 Nishi-Azabu, Minato-ku

Oct: 23: Nobu Tokyo, 6-10-17 Minami-Aoyama, Minato-ku (Look for
stylist differences from LA, Simon. Remember, I am interested in
detail.)

This is not a demanding schedule.

Your mother sends her love and best wishes, and hopes you are
content to use a sento because of the lack of a bath. Please keep in
contact, I look forward to hearing your thoughts and ideas.

Remember that Tokyo is the most expensive town on the world, so you should be careful with the money I am sending. I do not mean that you should be a skinflint or miserly—in particular, despite the Tokyo custom, I will ask that you tip generously at all restaurants you visit—but be careful. Fifteen percent is the figure I recommend.

Don't be perturbed at your lack of experience, give it your biggest shot, and you have our faith. Remember who you are and why you are there.

How are you spending your days?

Your father,
Thomas.

The maps and copies of the pages of the prospectus are lying in a crumpled wad on top and behind the fax. The paper shiny and crookedly copied, the black and white images faded and unconvincing.

I stare at the fax from bed for a long while.

"In a daze, man," I whisper. "I spend them in a daze."

Late in the morning, walking through the empty rooms of my new apartment naked, staring into the empty aquarium, making plans for Muji furniture and making these resolutions, the first again, more sure this time:

I will not end up sleeping with Jacques again.

I will not sleep with any Westerners at all.

And because I'm strong enough to not rely on Western company, because I have a real job, because I have a great apartment, because I am in Tokyo for at least a year and am now basically set up, I can therefore go about becoming someone better here. And for this I need a new keitai (in my first week here someone told me a keitai in Tokyo will revolutionize your social life, and they weren't wrong), and I need friends and I need contacts. I need to get back in with Anton, and Michael, and I need to carefully wean off, then back on, this time just as a "friend," Jacques. I have been here almost five weeks. How have I been spending my daze?

So it's Shinjuku, and to hell with saving money, and I'm hanging out, digging the scene because I like the people and I like the lights.

I'm sitting in a line of J boys and girls on a pink tiled step on Microsoft

Promenade, opposite Starbucks, and far off, over the tracks, the hunched mass of Takashimaya. It's getting dark and the crowds of salarymen heading toward the South exit of the station are thinning out, and it's still kind of hot and gassy and the indigo streetlamps are on as are the red aircraft warning lights at the horizon of skyscrapers ringing the Shinjuku station tracks and the promenade like an amphitheatre. Like a J guy after a hard day I have a couple of Asahi Dry's from the Lawson under Takashimaya and a Gap bag with a belt and a couple of T-shirts and a yellow plastic Tower Records bag inside which the CD of *Vanishing Point* has been wrapped twice because J packaging is nothing if not thorough.

From where I sit, the place I first kissed Ariel relatively sober, turning 3600 from hard left, these are the words I can see, in English, or in roman letters, at least:

Armani
www.yahoo.co.jp
GAP—That's Autumn Dream
Good Day Good Time
Lumine 2
JR
South Exit
Marlboro
STRBCKS CFFE
Takashimaya Department Store
Pesce D'oro
Casio
Microsoft
Emporio

This is basically one-third of the signage displayed to me. Though the model I wanted only cost one yen, trying to buy a new keitai took almost an hour before I finally walked out, because the contract was totally in kanji. I waited, sitting on a stool in Bic Camera Ikebukuro, for them to find an assistant who spoke English, and when he arrived it turned out he'd lived in San Francisco for a year and had kick-ass American English but a totally crappy job here with Bic and was embarrassed and pissed off and resentful and made me wait so long I walked out.

I keep seeing flashbulbs going off down the walkways, this side and over the tracks under Takashimaya, like half a mile away. There are couples sitting on the park benches over there, kissing, or staring out over the tracks through the Perspex walls under the department store. The trees this side are chained to the ground against the winds of the microclimates; on the other side they're encased in Perspex tubes. I even bought the same beer I bought that night, and I remember that she had bought apple Chu-Hai, three 500-ml cans, and that I knew this was a good sign.

What did she look like?

Like nothing I'd ever seen, let alone touched, before. Make sense of this: she's ostensibly Canadian, but her mother is apparently half-Filipina, half-Jamaican. Her father is German and she was raised in Montreal and has a couple of passports. She is, I think, twenty-four. She is shorter than me. I had only one photo of her at home; although I took hundreds in Japan (not just of her, maybe hardly any—I'd be too shy to ask) I never knew enough J to get them developed, and in the final mad weeks of leaving—ruthless packing, throwing stuff out in the gomi, weighing suitcases and throwing more stuff out in the gomi, paranoidly burning papers like an ambassador after a coup d'état, giving stuff away to other foreigners in the gaijin house at Mejiro, to the middle-aged English couple, the Singaporean video producer, the German who never came out of her room, the strange quiet J girl named Yuriko who always apologized for using the bathroom and who must have done who knows what shameful thing for her family to let her wind up in a gaijin house—somewhere in this I lost all real records of being here. Seven rolls of film. And when I received that photo, posted to me by Michael in an envelope that contained nothing else but a Post-it note with a message in purple ink that read, "Thought you might want this," and I saw her face again, even after a couple of months, and school, a new and totally different life, it didn't matter. The feeling was absolute, and clean. Like falling and liking it; like leaning too far and seeing great things just at the moment you overcommit and are gone. And the funny thing was, the aspects of her face I most adored weren't in that photo. Her eyes are closed, and she leans back, pouting for the camera, at a farewell party for someone I barely knew in some air-conditioned izakaya near Yurakucho, sitting at a table with her arm linked in Anton's, next to Jacques, Michael, Catherine, Dale, Brigit, two Australian girls I don't remember, and four enormous pitchers of beer. And because of the air-con, you also cannot see the delicate shine of the sweet oil that came from her skin in the Japanese summer, that night we spent drinking and making out right here where I'm sitting, the oil that even with the humidity and pollution ran sweet and thin as cologne.

Hazel; aqua; green; seablue; I don't know. Is it that I can't remember, or is it that her eyes are too unearthly; impossible to describe? Her skin then: for some reason, not just color, I will always compare her with iced coffee, with whipped cream and vanilla ice cream, and only ever caster sugar, because it dissolves the best and most completely. The girl who called me sugar, and I could *taste* it. Split skirts that revealed coffeecream-colored legs to the thigh, and would leave me speechless, my breath shallow as an asthmatic. The colors of her hair, her skin, her eyes, a sly grin she had; I felt a kind of real yearning for the sun in her body, a kind of tan poise that said somewhere else she'd been all about sea and summer and sky. The night she dumped me, the night of that photograph, she wore one of her split skirts and sat close beside me at the table in the Yurakucho izakaya, the first time she'd ever done so in public. The fact we were secretive made me love it more; not just that I wanted her, but that no one knew this was happening, a secret affair that seemed to me to implicate half the world. She told me about a guy at her work she'd blown off, who'd taken it badly, and said something cruel about her legs, right to her face. (I made instant lifelong resolutions to never badmouth any girl, no matter how harsh the rejection, ever again—though her legs were perfect, she bruised her knees when she drank and danced—she danced crazily, all pelvic thrusts and ass, but this turned me on even more, the bruises, the abandon.) She told me she'd thought of me, nice things I'd said about her legs, the night at Michael's, the first time.

"The guy was just a cocksucker," I said. "Man, a cock*sucker.*"

She sipped her drink and listened to me, and seemed to think about something for a while, sadly, and then she whispered to the table, like she was lost in thought of something else, in this husky flat whisper that was more sexy for its total un-self-consciousness, the sense of a total lack of an audience, of a potential listener, of me:

"I'm a cocksucker."

And I think I died, there; fainted away, and no one there at this party of maybe twenty people knew what had happened or would between us, and under the table I put my shaking hand on her cool, smooth thigh, high up, inside the split of her skirt (maybe slightly bruised, I couldn't know, but the thought was almost too much for me). She took a mouthful of her beer, and so did I, and I desperately fought for something to say.

Finally, I said, "Oh, hopefully," and knew then exactly what kind of a fool I could sound like and always could be, and that anything she ever gave me I would take but never truly deserve.

Where I sit now is the place we sat for our first real date, a week after we had had sex, this one time, the first, on the bedroom balcony at Michael's. It's almost totally night now, and I'm halfway through this second Asahi, and something about Shinjuku, I guess, or something about me makes these things get equated: wilted flowers in the beds under the streetlamps, petals coated in powder from the air, and the dresses she chose in summer. Stained skies, and her mad curly hair, eight shades of brown. The way the Koshukaido Avenue bridge ripples with trucks and the dark tiredness around her eyes. Indigo concrete under the Armani billboard and a sweet oil from her skin that was so unbearably soft and smooth and coffee-colored I wanted to eat her, bite chunks out of her cheeks, consume her. The chained trees opposite me, underlit and beautifully artificial-looking though they're not, and the way she muttered, with a T, "Foolhearty foreigners." The taste of Japanese beer and the odor of exhaust, and the feel of the curled roots of her hair, scratchy, tight and strong against my skin, my cheek, the palm of my hand. The foreign boy in the corner of the crowded Starbucks, and the foreign girl in headphones at the window, and the way she laughed out loud at some old bald white guys in the Microsoft Building, where we used the toilets near the Kinko's and stole an ornamental potplant. The rattle and knock of all the trains that pass through Shinjuku, and the way she walked toward me on this pink tile, coming back from a second trip to the Microsoft toilets, her hips in that split skirt, the tight violet shirt close to her belly, suggesting her breasts, somehow faintly communicating with me, my hard-on in my jeans, long and hot down the inside of my thigh, then and now, as I lean forward and adjust myself and sip my beer and draw on my cigarette clumsily because my hand is literally shaking, and the way I got up, hard-on and all, off this same tiled step a year ago, and walked toward her, dizzy and absolutely ready for anything, willing for anything, confident after what had happened on the balcony, and making out here on the step, the way she sauntered toward me, unearthly eyes locked on mine until the very last moment in the dying everything-violet light when she sidestepped, like, basically, I'd expected nothing less.

It's deeper into night.

I've finished my beers, and dumped the cans in the bin outside Starbucks, and crossed the tracks to Takashimaya. Along the walkway, tongue-

and-groove timber, trees in Perspex between park benches that face out the head-high Perspex walls onto the Shinjuku tracks. Halfway down the escalator to ground level I'm gripped by the irresistible lonely drunken drive to call her, just call her up and say, "What's up, I'm back." I'm gripped by the sudden feeling she's in Shinjuku too, or at least Shibuya, Harajuku, somewhere close. Like a longing, but not stupid, because foreigners all go to the same places. Is this still true? I'll say, "Hey, I'll buy you dinner," or just, "Have dinner with me," and she'll be lonely, like us all, willing, miss things about me, miss things I said about her legs that I'll willingly, feelingly repeat. Just, "Have dinner with me," and it will be quiet and romantic somewhere, and she'll be relieved, tired of preparing meals for herself, maybe even thrilled someone from our old group is back, some flash of an innocent past when we were all discovering each other, and no one had left yet. And especially, slyly thrilled that it's me. And we'll eat something Italian, shrimp and pasta, take the last train to the new apartment, and she will stroll through it, get excited by the size, the location, and I'll be casual about it, laid back, we'll watch movies and drink wine and stay in bed in aircon cool and the smell of fresh tatami for two entire days.

I flick through the directory on my keitai going down the escalator, through the names I entered more than a year ago, one follows another with numbers like barcodes underneath, keitais and home phones and faxes and businesses, Ariel1, Ariel2, Anton, Brigit, Dale, Graham, Hiromi, Hitomi (I can't remember which was which, what either even looked like), Home, HomeWork, Jacques, Ko, Meredith, Michadl, misspelt, Ariel1 and Ariel2 again, names of people scattered wherever, a list that defined a transitory time, that fixes the subjects of lost photos and blurred memories in a way that hits me harder for its familiarity, and especially in the familiarity of this situation, halfway down an escalator, looking at my keitai and a list of people I would otherwise define by who I slept with and their nationality; this, the simplest rendering of my history here, a piece of work so stark and yet so personal it means something only to me.

But I'm drunk and this is too important to be done drunk and besides, I reach the bottom of the escalator.

I stare at the skateboarders out in front of a hiking store in the alley that runs from Meiji-dori under the Koshukaido, back to the Gap and Tower, but more particularly I stare at another guy who's staring at the skateboarders, or actually at his keitai and then the skateboarders, bewildered, but kind of smiling, a young guy in an expensive-looking gray four-button summerweight suit, with a fat purple tie, standing by a pillar, and this guy's been injured, horrifically, somehow. He has a gigantic white neck brace and an eye-patch, one arm in a sling, the hand—his left—swathed in new white bandage as fat as an ice hockey glove. He looks at his keitai, then over at the skateboarders, then back to his keitai. He nods, and laughs, bemused, dumped, fired, bankrupt, bereaved, semi-stunned at something I will never, ever know.

He watches the skateboarders for a while. Then he limps off.

I turn back to the escalator and it's so late it's frozen.

"Hello?" With noise.

"Um, so where are you?" I say.

An old joke, that Jacques would never get and always answer truthfully (which drove me nuts). First words of any J keitai call you ever overhear seem to be place-names. (Shot of a salaryman, answering his phone: "Hai." Pause. Listens. Looks around. "Ano,"—thinking—"Shinjuku." Shot of me, sneering.)

(Of course, this may have something to do with the fact that place-names are mostly the only J words I know.)

"Simon. Simon?" Anton shouts. "Where are you?"

"I'm back, man. I'm back," I say.

He whoops in my ear so loud I have to hold the phone away.

"Man, it's so great I almost crapped myself!" he shouts, and with his voice I can see him again really vividly on some interchangeable platform at some Yamanote line station, immense, in a big black suit, shining white shaved-bald head and scar and goofy Raybans, towering above the crowd, gleaming with stressed, excited sweat, shouting into his phone. I can see him here again only because I am here. But for some reason, I see him in a neck brace, too, a sling, a single bandaged finger as big as his keitai, an eye-patch.

"Dude, are you okay?" I say.

"Man, this station is crazy," he says.

"Seriously, where are you."

"Ikebukuro. I work here now. Oh man, sexy yay chicks surround me like flies. Behind my shades I have a migratory eye."

"What work, man? You do work?" I'm competing with a J voice warning people to stand back, a million voices, the static rush of a train.

"I'm a partner now. We have a proper company. I and E. CBCs. Ph.D."

"You what?"

"Import–Export. This is my business code now, man. You'll love it. We're importing Cock and Balls Condoms from home. Edible and Western-sized. Pubic Hair Dye in twelve shades. Everything you can think of. We're called 'Ran no Rabu.' It means 'Dutch Love.'"

"Jesus," I say. "And I think you mean roaming eye, by the way. Like, I think flounder have migratory eyes."

"I think it means that, anyhow. It's supposed to. Where are you, Simon?"

"Ha ha."

"Serious."

"Anton, can you still get drugs? Can you still get coke?"

"Oh, Simon. Michael and Jacques have their own private mycologist on retainer, too. Life is good."

"What's a mycologist?"

"Whoa, hold on. Oh shit."

"What?"

"Oh shit, wait. Oh man."

"What, man. Jesus. Are you okay?"

"I just stepped on a yay girl. Oh man, she's crying."

"Anton."

"She has only sandals. I stepped on her toe."

"Shall I call you back."

"Yeah man, we'll hook up. I'm so stupid, man. Oh God. She's crying."

"Sure," I say. "Sure, Anton. Hey, you're okay, right? You're not like, hurt or anything?"

He's hung up. I hang up too, and wish I'd called her, instead.

I'm exhausted. And starving.

Thinking of fresh tatami, pale green. Someplace cool.

Sleep.

Anton
Winter 2000

In winter, Anton does Kabukicho, the red-light district of Shinjuku, on his company's money. He wears a suit and no matter what the cold, never a hat of any kind on his bald brash white head. He walks with his hands in his pockets, big legs a little tenderly knock-kneed, long, square-ended boots scuffed from the trains, though he's stood on more toes than he likes to remember. Bent from the hip like he has a heavy head, elbows not out but on their way, no tie, no hat in the freezing winds, Anton goes walking the narrow streets looking for a J girl who'll have sex with a bald scarred white man.

He doesn't ever wear hats because any hat has a double effect on his old injury. The first is bearable: it's the itching of the crumpled wound where it knit together. With the heat and contact of a beanie or even a cap there starts a deep ferocious irritation in the innermost seam of that knit flesh, down where no fingernail can reach, where the flesh seems still shocked and humbled; tentative, stretched and stunned and craving integrity. It itches in a fiery fine line like a fault, and if he lets it, it gets so bad he wants to peel that violated scalp apart again, for better pain than that unceasing pinscratch, flashbulb-flashing back to those weeks in a hard bed, a feeling like hot flies brewing in a round maggoty patch on the very crest of his head, a leathery yarmulke of his own skin sizzling in his hospital dreams.

So that's bad enough, but half that inflammation is memory. The second sensation that's slower to come on is not borne up or away by description. That feeling for Anton is just that:

that. Even this is inside. Nothing's worse; nothing helps to compare. Nothing reveals it or resembles it, and it in turn reveals and resembles nothing. It happens when his scalp gets warm enough—warm enough and deep, to the bone: neither summer nor central heating will make it happen because it's a proximate effect and it takes wool or cotton. Or Sonja's hand that once, one night: *that* descends or ascends, solidifies or forms like a cloud, drills for foundations, locks itself home with brass dynabolts in the concrete of his fractured skull and takes him physically back to 1995 and the year it happened. Shake your head and it won't go. The idea is like heresy, and unforgiven. Bathing in cold water or even icy water; icepacks, acupuncture, marijuana. Even whacking up intravenous cooked-up morphine only seems to move that thing a little higher in the air.

He'll never touch it when it feels this way. He lays on a stripped bed with his eyes lightly closed, naked, no pillows. For hours, he thinks of things and people and places with an intensity of recollection, color and shape that painless Anton never could match. Times like this he feels not sorry but sad for himself. And he doesn't touch it even lightly because he fears and feels so vividly that a fontanel is gone, or worse yet is gone soft, paper-thin and hot but yet holding on to that iron pain like a seer.

So Anton goes hatless, big man in freezing cold Kabukicho, to keep his head the same temperature as the city. Looking for prostitutes who are generally warmer-clothed than he, not out of any nostalgia or particular sexual need, but from the odd sense of self he derives from the calm averted-eye rejections of girls who will not sleep with foreigners. When the money changes hands with the girl who finally will—the Korean or the Chinese or the Taiwanese, generally—Anton's moment is over, because where everything seems accepted rejection is a titillation. Here is the jail of what's happened to his arousal and here is the jail where he waits for his hurt. If he finds a girl, he'll ask her to clean him with a heated towel when they finish, and often see a movie afterward, right there in Kabukicho, go home to the apartment in Shinagawa and tell Sonja he'd seen two. The first and only time they'd fallen asleep together with her cool Russian hand idly laid across the rupture, he'd woken in the iron dark and heard the decorative bamboo's muted clack outside and burped a spurt of black bile on the futon sheets from pain. From then on she treated that part of him with the reverence of a stunned lover holding her hand an inch from what has stunned her, like a blessing.

He was eighteen and living in Amsterdam when it happened. Moving on the fringes of some loose and dodgy crews, hash rats who knew a few pimps and had some aspirations toward cash and organization, some puta- tive gangbangers too few in number to call themselves a gang. He knows now—and kind of good-humoredly did so then—that the guys he hung with were perennial losers, not really even half-waiting for a break. Young men with no education or legitimate prospects and no real flair for the underground, squatting in one-roomed unfurnished apartments and roaming through the last Amsterdamian summer Anton had.

He was one of them too, but he was young and new and not quite trusted, or at least not much respected, but this was okay with him because he didn't much respect them back; this loose group with a loose figurehead in an older guy, a Serb named Serge who was rotund in a hard, threatening way, and black and curly-haired, with a coarse woolly goatee the size of a fist, and sideburns, who wore beads and different kinds of woven jerkin over pristine white Hanes beefy-tees. Anton had gone to visit Serge the day he was struck on the head, at his tiny fourth-floor one-

room apartment somewhere in Oudezijdsvoorburgwal in the heart of a
summer as hot and wet as those of Tokyo. Bjorn was Serge's hanger-on
and fan—"little Bjorn," to his disgust always the one to puke first when
they had Sessions. Anton had knocked at the door and watched the light
behind the eyehole dim and little Bjorn with a mohawk opened the door,
checked Serge behind him and it was then Anton had seen the girl they
stole.

The room was radically unfurnished and smelled of mildewed laundry
and piss and with a void of weeks to follow he will always remember
every detail. Stripped wood floors unvarnished, white fibreboard walls
scuffed and pierced with picture hooks all over, from which yellow plastic
twine had been strung all through the room like a cat's cradle. It was wet
and stinky and there were damp black towels of every size conceivable
hanging from the twine and the girl's head and a man as big as Anton had
to bend double to get inside.

Serge sat cross-legged on a stained bare single mattress that took up
half the floor, spooning yogurt slowly from a pottle. She squatted in the
corner where the mattress was jammed. Not tall and a little chubby, hugging thick legs wrapped in a denim skirt pulled tight down to her ankles.
That, and the ringletted ends of deep brown curly hair resting on her
knees was all Anton could see, because Serge and Bjorn had draped a
damp black towel over her head.

"Sit," Serge had said, with a white tongueful of yogurt.

Anton sat. Lying on the mattress behind Serge and just in front of her
denim hidden feet was the long shape of a rifle wrapped in chamois cloth.
Bjorn in his mohawk stepped over him onto the dirty mattress and sat by
Serge so Anton faced between them the stolen towel-draped girl behind.

Serge wiped the tin lid of his yogurt with his index finger. He licked the
finger and showed the wet pad to Anton.

"You shouldn't stay, Ant."

A transistor radio in the rooms next door was playing some crazed DJ.

"What did you do," said Anton.

Under the wet towel she'd stirred at the new voice, and Bjorn turned
around to check, and the back of his head was a pincushion of razed
coarse black follicles.

"We got her off the road," Serge said. "Is all."

"So you just grabbed her," Anton said. He watched as the hands
unclasped and lifted from her shins very slowly, all her fingers splayed.

"It was so easy," Bjorn said. "But fruit: *every*where. She was on a fruit stall. We didn't get any of the fruit."

"Yes, I would have liked some feijoas," Serge said. "Feijoas in the freezer for half an hour. Yum."

"You don't have a freezer," Anton said. "You don't have anything but black towels."

Reaching blindly out but closing auspiciously on the chamois-wrapped barrel of the rifle, and starting to rise from her squat, head leaned forward like a sad Madonna, the damp black towel hung like a veil, fringed with the crimped ringlets of her hair.

"You know it stinks in here," he said.

"Go then," Bjorn said with a sneer. "Why did you come? You don't really care."

Serge sniffed.

"I don't really care," Anton agreed.

"The next thing is a freezer," Serge said. "I've decided."

"So what are all these towels for," Anton said, and he had watched as the black veil rose slowly and behind a second veil of a hanging wet black handtowel, and the rifle in her hands rising too.

"Grabbed her by the hair," said Bjorn. His voice softened. "Pulled her over the nectarines. And nectarines went *every*where."

"Very professional," said Serge. "Very, very bad."

"Well," said Anton brightly. "So your search wasn't fruitless then."

Serge stared at him.

"And I guess you've done this before and I guess you're fairly cool with all that's entailed and everything you need to do."

His voice was getting louder and more cheerful.

"But you kind of chose a pretty tubby-looking girl when you could've gotten anything you wanted, man. A dumb chubby farm girl, that's what she looks like to me. Ha ha, of all the choices you could have made, it's kind of funny that you'd find, like, your stolen fruit's gone off—"

Bjorn had watched his mouth moving and speaking with a sincere contempt like he could see it being damaged; Serge with a speculative increasingly amused assessment, and Anton had not watched as the draped shape rose and silently rose.

"Ha ha ha, you guys, you're just so cool. You just make me laugh, you really do. So, so cool—"

And when she had brought the raised rifle blindly down, the chamois had slid from the wooden stock right to the trigger guard, and it was the trigger guard that snagged on one of the washing lines above them and so it was that the rifle slid directly across them, sideways and over, popping picture hooks from the wall in sawdust puffs. And so it was for Anton and not Serge or Bjorn, then, a gift, an absurdity, an act akin to a final banzai. It was a mistake he took upon himself gladly without knowing why, the heavy oiled wooden stock first, and Anton will always remember the sensation, how that impact was freezing and glittering.

Comes down.

A jolt in his neck there but not especially, a bitter compromise of spine at the nape, too—that heavy thing she'd hefted—but really, really, truly, at the actual point it struck, on the very crown of his then-haired head, the flash of freezing more than anything else of it he recalls: drops of white freezingness, foreign glitter, fell down his face like she'd hacked into a Sapporo ice sculpture with an axe. Cold fingertips touched his cheek a second and were gone and going inside, icy whitenesses found his eyes and burrowed inward to explode up and out that hole like a trauma orgasm. The whitest strongest vision was given unto him and so cold of snow bursting upward out of his head like flakes of a cottoncold bloom that drifts and dies and goes down and in again, and the freezing tracks left upon his cheeks were trails left by snails made of ice, his tears.

"I think something is wrong with my head," he thinks he remembers he said and woke up (he was told) six days later in intensive care and he never saw Serge or Bjorn or that girl again—though of course there was no way he could possibly have recognized or described her, anyway.

Some damaged people like this come to Japan.

Meredith
October 2000

Seasons change quickly in Tokyo and Meredith wound up buying clothes before she bought the camera. She left the hotel in jeans and trainers and a suede jacket in late morning, not to avoid rush hour; late morning is just when she woke up. Her first stop was a hiking store opposite Takashimaya department store. She bought a puffy black North Face jacket, a polypropylene bandanna and tan Timberlands. She changed into the boots in the store and carried her jacket and her old trainers through Shinjuku in new bags. Crowds move quicker in the streets in late fall and no one lingered to watch the giant Tower TV at the steps to the station. Trucks rumbled above her on the Koshukaido Avenue bridge and her toes were cold in the stiff new boots.

She browsed in the secondhand electronics stores across from the Gap; cameras by Sony, Nikon, Panasonic, Mitsubishi; still cameras, Polaroid, digital video, VHS, super 8, Beta; prices ranging wildly.

The older clerk, who had called out, "Welcome!" when she entered, had watched her, and she felt his attention, growing steadily more and more irritated. As she halfheartedly stared into a case of Sony digital video cameras, the clerk glided in beside her, inclining his head as he unlocked the case and slid it open.

"Please," he said in Japanese, and gestured to the open display. Meredith gritted her teeth and picked a camera up at random. The clerk saw the muscles contracting in her jaw and stepped back a little, keeping the English he had summoned to himself. Meredith turned the camera in her hands, monitoring the clerk who stood near in case he was needed. It was too early for politeness; far too cold and early for interactions. She put the camera back, muttered, "Arigato," one of the maybe twenty Japanese words she knew, and left quickly.

She eventually chose the camera by choosing the biggest electronics store between the Gap and the Prince: the eight-storey Yodobashi Camera. She showed a clerk the digital videotape she had taken from Michael's desk in the hotel room and shrugged her shoulders, looking around the store. From the range the clerk showed her she pointed at a ¥250,000 Sony and muttered, "This."

"This?" the clerk asked, indicating the camera.

"Yes. Excuse me," Meredith said.

At the counter when she came to pay, a different clerk asked her, "Do you have a Yodobashi Camera point card?"

Meredith waited. The clerk seemed to be waiting for a reply.

"Yes. Excuse me," she said.

The clerk waited for the card, looking down at the counter.

Meredith began to flush, confused. She looked around for help, then back to the clerk.

The clerk looked up. "Uh, the card, please. For your points," he said.

Meredith, face hot and red. "Yes. Excuse me."

"Uh, do you . . . have a point card?" The clerk said again, the first phrase he used, something he repeated countless times in a day. Meredith looked at him, and then down at the counter.

"Yes," she tried again to the Formica.

In the queue behind her the talking had stopped. She opened her wallet and began counting out money, breathing through her teeth. The clerk, a boy maybe seventeen, had begun to blush, too. She held a wad of ¥10,000 notes over the counter to him. He hesitated, looked at the money, bewildered, and up at Meredith's blushing, angry face, and quickly back to the money.

"Uh, do you have a . . . point card . . ." he began again.

"Please," Meredith said, her voice shaking, in English.

Behind him, the supervisor at the other counter excused himself from a customer, swiveled on his chair and murmured, "Don't worry about it, Tanaka." He looked up at Meredith and nodded his head.

"Please," he said in English, too.

Meredith nodded back, and smiled a painful, forced smile, her jaws aching from clenching her teeth. At last the boy took her money, gave her the change.

Another wait as her camera was wrapped, wanting to disappear utterly, out of here, out of Tokyo, out of herself.

"Please thank you sorry please hey one thousand yen this excuse me, excuse me, excuse me," Meredith said to the clerk and turned and left.

Outside on the sidewalk, bags of shopping by her new boots, sweat in her armpits, adrenaline silvery all through her, Meredith lit a Marlboro and drew deeply, working her jaw. She doesn't want to tell herself what to do anymore. Sometimes she just wants to be told what to do. By someone who simply says, "Okay."

Her first time out in a week and she had used all her Japanese apart from good morning and one to ten.

On the way back to the hotel Meredith went quickly into Tsutaya video. She rented three tapes of *X-Files,* staring the clerk down, embarrassing him into silence, into finishing her transaction as quickly as he could.

The beige of the Prince lobby, the shining vanilla tile, the huge sandstone sculpture of a wave, calmed her. The concierge greeted her, called her "Mahm." He spoke English, and took her room service order for a bottle of chardonnay and a bowl of popcorn at half past two effortlessly in his stride.

In the long ride up in the elevator with her shopping Meredith sighed heavily three times. Once remembering the secondhand store clerk. Once remembering the Yodobashi store clerk. And once for the fact that the day was over as far as Japan was concerned, that this was how bad it felt and she hadn't even been on the trains.

The doors opened and she left the elevator and walked, distracted, down the long beige hallway, the chiseled grip of the new boots catching at the carpet. She stared at the toes of the boots, the tan a camouflage clash. She was halfway down the hallway when she looked up, startled. She could hear laughter. There were voices coming from behind a door. There were doors in the hallway; maybe eight or ten. She could hear voices laughing. She stopped, turned, looked back down the hall to the elevators. She heard an American girl's voice from behind a door say, "I wouldn't call it a cancellation." A male laugh followed this. Then the girl said, "It's not as if this is an outright no."

There were only two doors and no one else on Penthouse. Meredith had left the elevator on the wrong floor.

Bewildered, she looked up and down the corridor. She had been in the elevator alone. And no one had been waiting on this floor. Could she have pressed the wrong button? PH for penthouse at the very top.

Boots sticking in the wool, Meredith headed back down the hallway.

When she remembers something she finds embarrassing, Meredith almost always makes some kind of noise. She sighs heavily, or whistles part of a song. Hums, or mutters, sometimes. "Je-sus." She was not even aware she acknowledged her tiny failure to herself, let alone why. As she waited for the elevator to return to this floor, what it turns out was the twenty-seventh, and stared up at the digital display flicking over, eyes hunted and red-rimmed at two thirty-five, holding the boxed camera, she hummed and nodded her head to andante *Girl From Ipanema*.

She can sometimes accidentally spend entire days here by herself, without speaking a complete English sentence to anyone.

When she was still two years from finishing high school the adulation and attention that had surrounded Michael fell off, and she began to feel it transferred to herself. It was not due to any particular diminishing of his abilities or any sudden flowering of hers; it was simply because he seemed to abruptly lose interest in all measurable forms of achievement. While his long absences from high school—including legendary drug-fueled road-trips around the country with Simon and several rumored flights over-seas—became chronic, and his Bursary grades dropped to merely high B's in externally assessed subjects and in those internally assessed to E's and occasionally sometimes actual F's, Meredith quietly took his place in her family's hopes. She saw this; the decline in conversations involving his name, the silences following any use of it. And the interrogations he had borne the brunt of beginning to focus upon her.

At the dinner table at the Wellington house in 1993, so she was fifteen, he seventeen. Exams started in late November; it was October. School Certificate for her and Bursary for him. Grossness had arranged admission to the exclusive Knox Hall in Otago for Michael. Meredith and Michael knew, but had to pretend surprise when notification came.

The pretense of surprise was the real lesson Grossness wanted taught.

Dinner table silent but for china clinks and chewing, the hiss and gur-gle as the old man blew on his bisque.

In the usual way he circumlocuted.

"Where will *you* go to university, I wonder, Merdy." Said to his steam-ing spoon.

She looked across the table at Michael, who winked at her, and undid the top button on his shirt.

"Hot in here," Michael said. "Steaming."

"Don't take your clothes off, darling," Elise said. "Open a window if you're uncomfortable."

"I'm still wondering about your plans, Merdy."

"I haven't really . . . I'm just thinking about School Certificate. My exams."

"Less time spent on the phone and more spent planning the future might be an apt suggestion. Have you thought which city, perhaps, as a way in to the question."

"It depends on what I get for School C. What I do next year. Next year's more important, for what I decide to do. I can't decide until I know how I do." The defensive monotone, she could hear it in her voice. Michael's foot under the table nudged hers, and she kicked it back.

"Sometimes I think the way to approach your future is not as a set of obstacles to be negotiated, letting those obstacles determine and delimit your route, but as a journey toward a goal, in which impediments are merely challenges to the maintenance of your focus."

Michael spluttered, spat soup into his bowl.

"The challenge makes your determination stronger."

"*Andrew*," Elise said, and laughed once, a quick puff of air, sucked back before it could escape.

"Um, this . . . bisque . . . is bitching," Michael muttered, staring into his bowl. Meredith giggled, then tried to compose a straight face. She turned to Grossness and his face was lined and serious, turning from each member of the family to the next.

"Merdy," Andrew said. "Your brother's language perhaps reflects the fact that he has decided to let his education slip; allowing reputation to precede him as he makes his way through life. Allowing prior achievements, rumor and influence to smooth his path."

"Daddy, don't," she said.

"Indeed, when we are the master of many things at age sixteen we feel we must surely remain master of all things throughout life, without work, without struggle. How sad we become at eighteen when suddenly we find ourselves relying on others to secure places we thought ours by right."

"*Wow*. Is there a whole lot of Tabasco in this, Mum," Michael said, staring down into his soup, stirring it slowly with the handle of his spoon, his shirt undone halfway down his chest now. "No way bisque should have this . . ."

He kicked her foot again and she kicked it back again.

"This *flair*. This *vim*, this *verve*."

"Oh, you're flattering me, darling," Elise said. "I think. It should be subtle and creamy, really, shouldn't it."

"And well, seventeen, actually, Dad. If the 'we' you're talking about is actually in fact me. And not, you know, you, or anything."

"The subject will not move on to the bisque until I say so, Elise," Andrew said. "Merdy, we only want to know where you plan to go to university. It's a fair question. It's a subject you should be pondering. Perhaps just an indication of island. Or nation-state."

"Christ," Meredith muttered. "Do you have to always be sarcastic."

"Christ now, is it. Your brother teaches you well. Perhaps if you believed in the man I'd have a little more reaction to this."

Michael was humming, "I love to go a-wandering, along a mountain track." Elise staring down at Andrew, sipping her wine, head tilted in tipsy resignation.

"Just *say* it," Michael said, leaning down now, bumping his forehead lightly on the rim of his soup bowl. "You madman, just say it."

"I'm sorry?" Andrew leaned back in his chair to finally train his stare on his son.

"*Say—it.*"

"Say what?"

"What do you want me to do? Why do you want these games in your house for Christ's sake?"

"Ah, Merdy's source confirmed. Your academic writing style is coming along then."

"Oh, *don't,*" Meredith said.

"Do you want a speech? Do you want me to kowtow? What if I told you I don't care?" Michael had leaned back in his chair too. Meredith was almost crying. Elise's hand was shaking as she poured more wine.

"Don't care about what, Michael?" Andrew said, dry and quietly. "You have me at a loss."

"Ah, I've decided I'm not going to university," Michael said, looking across at Meredith. "Ah, I've decided to become a firewhirler. I'm going to juggle."

"Really."

"You are *nuts.*"

"Michael," Elise said.

"For Christ's sake, I am not going to thank you for something I not only didn't ask for, but don't even want. It's just bullying. You're bullying me down there."

"What *are* you referring to."

There was a pause as Michael growled at the ceiling, infuriated.

"I *know* you got me into Knox, you mad old badger."

Another pause followed.

"Ah, Michael," Andrew said at last, satisfied. He leaned forward again and picked up his spoon, dipped it into the cool seam of the soup. "Ah, my son. You see? You failed the test."

Michael watched her across the table. He let a little grin buckle his cheeks a moment, then suppressed it and turned back to his bisque, suddenly seeming very calm.

Then, part of her resented him standing in the way; resented how he must see himself to come to her defense, no matter how obliquely. Now, or even when he seemingly began to really slip, she simply respected him.

Meredith grew sceptical of her own achievement in the way, she thought, he had become about his far earlier. Because he'd done it first, because she was sure he grew sceptical about how high he'd risen so quickly, because he was older, and she was young and had watched him and trusted him for a long time, she felt not just justified but almost obliged to act, if not be, so sceptical herself.

The first hint for her, just sixteen, that Michael's absences from high school might have been out of something a little more complex than simple disillusionment or dissolution came right out of the blue. Letters addressed to him suddenly began to arrive at the Wellington house shortly afterward, the end of 1994 (he would have been eighteen), and continued to do so for months to come. Envelopes with the letterheads of Harvard, Beijing and Keio Universities; three independent historical journals, some fungi periodicals, Reuters, APA, Bloomberg, *Time* magazine. A phone call announcing an award from the East Anglia Asian Historical Society that Andrew had to decline on behalf. Meredith could remember him explaining to the kitchen telephone, one hand clenching and unclenching on the bench's edge: "No, no. I'm sorry. No. We don't know where he is. No. No idea. Yes. I'm sure it was. Uh-huh. He has in fact retired from the national education system at *secondary* level, you're aware of that? Uh-huh. No, I'm assuming that we're—and I might add I find myself sometimes actually approaching the stage where I'm in fact *contriving*—not to know in the near future either." Slamming the phone down. And sending her to her room at two o'clock on a Saturday afternoon for running too noisily on the stairs on Friday.

And with the officially marked mail, a series of otherwise unmarked plain manila envelopes, with Asian postage (who knew where), addressed to "The Author of, 'Shibboleth: Rye/Ergot Poisoning and the Nanking Massacre: The Untold Story of the Other Great Salem Witch-hunt: A Modest Proposal.'"

One clearly containing the shell of a bullet.

January 1996

15 January 1996
Jonathan B. Haberman, M.D., Ph.D.
Managing Editor
Cambridge Journal of International Mycological Studies
Dean
Cambridge University
Depts of Botany; Biology; Microbiology
Michael Edwards
c/o Thomas Chang
Apt. 1 Nezu Bldg.
14-12-21 Minami-Aoyama
Minato-ku
Tokyo 144-0031
Japan

Dear Sir:
Re: The article entitled "Shibboleth: Rye/Ergot Poisoning and the
Nanking Massacre: The Untold Story of the Other Great Salem Witch-
hunt," as published in *The New Republic* Vol. 211. Pgs. 20–57.

I thought it advisable to correspond with you on the matter of some
factual discrepancies in the *New Republic* article mentioned above. First of
all, however, I would like to commend you on such perspicacity with
regard to the impact of mycological phenomena on historical events and
their recording and transmission!

Few historians of my acquaintance have traced the impact of the
anamorphic effects of naturally occurring empathohallucinogenic fungi
on both the perception of, interpretation of, and emotive responses to
phenomena—"real" and "imagined"—of the ordinary people who subsequently become the witnesses and lapidaries (I wish to imply the oral traditions here, also) of human history. Despite the lack of experts in this
field, and despite a general climate of scepticism with regard to hallucinogenics and the imagination, hallucinogenics and history, hallucinogenics
and what—in the late sixties before Leary and Alpert's inexcusable neglect
led to the inevitable criminalization of LSD and the closing-off of that
rich back-alley to the imagination—what we used to confidently and
unembarrassedly refer to as *the soul,* yes, despite this faddish cynicism and

spiritual timidity masquerading as intellectual rigor, the interest aroused by this piece is well on its way to becoming what one might humbly call "widespread." From tenured colleagues in America I have heard with no small satisfaction of three Ivy League universities; a couple Almost-Ivy; Keio, and the Imperial in Tokyo; and Beijing (not to mention several lesser schools) who are in the process of introducing the article as required reading in no fewer than two separate disciplines: graduate history and microbiology. Perhaps the future of mycology in a new interdisciplinary approach to understandings of our sense of historical events will be firmed by your piece. I can only sincerely hope so.

The piece, you may be disappointed to hear me report, has not been received well in certain translations. Some alarmingly vituperative, violent and often fairly grammatically suspect reviews from several Chinese historians have wended their way to my desk. I hope, for your sake, there is no Chinese equivalent of the *fatwa*. They are very protective of their historical narratives, but understandably so, I feel. However, I am told that the ancient and extremely learned Chinese mycological community and a sizable contingent of the Japanese academic community are giving your work a very warm and admiring (if somewhat bemused) reception.

My championing of the article has received some resistance from certain scholars who no doubt feel challenged, if not a little threatened, by the directions your conclusions appear to lead. I will decline to mention their names or institutions here, and apostrophise only that cowardice and vanity in high-level scholarship are endemic, and often fatal for budding careers.

I have also been perturbed by some seemingly absurd rumors that you, the author of this piece, are currently in fact a senior high school student! Could this be true, Mr. Edwards? My sincere and heartfelt apologies if I have been misled. I mean only to imply not that the piece is or could be interpreted as in any way amateurish—strongly the opposite—but only that if you are in actuality producing this kind of material at such a young age, I hope you are receiving such expert and qualified tutelage as is commensurate with your abilities, and that I eagerly look forward to reading much more such original, muscular and provocative scholarship as your experience grows. If your age is not so tender, please disregard my—in that light—somewhat patronising comments on tutelage; but certainly do not disregard my eagerness to examine your future scholarly productions on this subject.

However, despite the piece's obvious merits, and with the hovering yet

insubstantial specter of your possible age and inexperience, I do feel it my
duty to bring to your attention some minor points of mycological and historical significance with regard to ergot poisoning and China in the period
and location in question.

1. Other instances of ergot poisoning.

You of course cite the Salem witch-hunts. The phenomenon of citizens who found themselves at the prey of seasonal epidemics of burning
flesh, visitations by devils, snakes writhing in their bellies, fiends in relentless pursuit, rape, sodomy, intense and unbearable cramping of muscles,
limbs seeming (and, with certain ergot strains, literally) to fall off, has
been largely superceded historically by the citizens' response to these
events. I use the term "events," as opposed to "hallucinations," after your
fashion. Some citizens' limbs indeed fell off; some felt them to fall off.
Simply because there exist people who did not experience or observe the
things "felt" does not mean the things are in any way less real—simply
that Western rationalism superstitiously will not make a place for them in
privileged discourse. As a new century approaches, and an holistic scholarship becomes once again a little more possible in the Academy, I can per-
mit myself on paper to side with the American DeLillo and say proudly
that dreams are real.

Therefore—no longer dreams. What difference is there between a
dream influenced by your supper as much as your experience, and an hallucination influenced by an organically occurring fungus? Agency is all,
and the world, the "real," can suddenly be a much vaster, more mysterious, more *possible,* place. Once you transcend the idea that your experience constitutes the truth, then realism is what you decide is real; the
direction you choose to look. Every culture is a novel. It has to manufacture morals, revolutionise them, violate them for interest in the third
quarter. Choice is turning cultures into novels; national passions into
curios. We are all witnesses. There is the magic intrinsic to humanity in
the disparity of our testimonies.

Re-institute the dream! I always cry. Re-privilege the individual and the
events occurring only in his mind *because that is the only place anything ever
occurs.*

I'm deadly serious.

So, the people of Salem attributed their ailments to spells cast by individuals, "witches," unfortunate souls with deformities, or unconventional
beliefs. You make clear that discordant nationality, here, was certainly an

example of a "deformity" sufficient to get your arms torn off by horses and chains. (Was this what you meant by "shibboleth"?) Thus, the Salemites brutally burned, tortured and drowned individuals they felt responsible for the pains and visions that always seemed to come the winter after a particularly cool and wet spring. Little did they know that the source of the visions was in fact their dinner. The fungus, *Claviceps purpurea,* busily growing its devilish, lumpy and hallucinogenic sclerotia in their crops of rye, corn and wheat; enabled by the narrow climatic window of moist, cool spring conditions that creates the necessary environment for *C. purpurea* just a few times every century. The poor Salemites stored their ergot-laced grain away, and hard upon the winter broaching of their caches, the visions and sensations began. Thus botanists and meteorologists have been able to link these special weather conditions to the periods prior to more than thirty recorded instances of witch trials in the seventeenth century.

I turn now to an additional, recent historical instance of ergot poisoning, occurring circa 1959 in the small town of Pont l'Esprit-Saint in southern France, in an obscure but nevertheless very interesting mycological text by T. J. McCrumb, the traveling mycologist and social historian. In *The Fungal Hypothesis: Reenvisaging the Historical,* McCrumb reports that after citizens of Pont l'Esprit-Saint began to experience the above-mentioned and other more violent and hideous phenomena—such as Basque separatists invading homes and lopping off limbs, claiming ancestral ownership; fatal, unfounded belief in the ability to fly; complete and partial paralysis; spontaneous abortion; the ubiquitous sensation of insects tiptoeing across the skin, whether ants, scorpions, wasps or spiders, which said fearsome araneation, I might add, has been consistently reported in documented ergot poisonings ever since the infamous "St. Anthony's Fire" was misnamed for the church where the Viennese were *cured* of their burning limbs—after all this, with ample reason, the town and region were in an uproar. Multiple "suicides" were reported, as citizens tried to escape or embrace the things they perceived occurring by immolating themselves to delouse, jumping from windows in dreams of muscular wings smelling of snow, or hurling themselves bodily into freezing rivers to put out fires of the mind. Eventually, the visitations subsided of their own accord, and post-hysteria the link was made by some intrepid municipal scholars to the town baker, one Maurice—*pistor infamis*—Maillot's dough. Opinion as to whether the "poisoning" was due to ergot of the grain for Maillot's bread or to some unspecified insecticide is still divided, but poor M.M.'s business suffered badly, and his suicide by self-immolation within his own bakery's gigantic oven was apparently in no way ergot-related.

On to

2. Moisture levels.

Rains in the Nanking area were recorded as from 10 to 15 mm a week in the spring preceding the "massacre" in question; i.e. that of March–May 1937. This is the time when the *Claviceps purpurea*—that by your analysis would have been ground into the meal and subsequently find itself in storage and moving virulently in the food chain the following winter, the so-called six weeks of terror of Nanking—would have been germinating. However, 10 to 15 mm per week and prevailing temperatures of twenty to twenty-five degrees Centigrade are not conducive to germination of the strain of *C. purpurea* you claim. That amount of rain in and above the Yangtze basin would have been insufficient to generate the soil saturation levels necessary to support germination and growth of the poisonous resting structure: the potent sclerotium, which grows in the shape of that fleshy flange on a rooster's leg, hence the French sobriquet: *ergot;* or spur.

And, penultimately,

3. Rye

As you correctly point out, many more grains are suitable as hosts for ergot than is conventionally accepted. Barley, wheat, oats and rye, of course. Corn, as known by North Americans, *Zea mays,* is also, given the correct conditions, susceptible to certain Asian strains of ergot.

You claim that as compared to the large numbers of Chinese witnesses who testified to the massacre and the huge numbers of dead, injured and violated, only an extremely tiny number of Japanese soldiers reported such a massacre in the years after the war. You claim this was due to the fact that only certain small communities in Japan (those residing in mountainous Kyushu, especially, where conditions and topography were and are inimical to the cultivation of rice, these areas sempiternally altered by the presence of Jesuit and Franciscan missionaries and the Dutch and English merchants residing there sporadically in the so-called Christian Century of 1543 on), that only small communities in these areas habitually grew and ate corn at this time, and thus only those communities' sons, as soldiers, could or would have eaten the corn of Nanking—which was, of course, a staple of the Chinese diet in the lowlands straddling the Yangtze.

Thus, your statistical breakdown of the percentage of Imperial Army soldiers in the Ninth, Eighteenth and supposedly notoriously brutal Sixteenth Divisions who would have been conscripted from these districts does, I acknowledge, correspond with the small number of soldiers who have come forth with stories, and support the essay's overarching thesis that the "Rape of Nanking" never happened—or, at least, with regard to my stance on the status of the "real" as is so often opposed with the hallucinated: "Happened"—and was in fact the product of corn/ergot hallucination. The Chinese all ate the corn. But only a few of the Japanese soldiers would have. Thus, the Chinese claim a massacre, while a mere handful of Japanese do likewise.

However, the statistics you provide, though supportive, do not trace the actual hometowns of the penitent, or the eating habits of their families. If the individual soldiers who made confessions are not directly linked to corn-eating regions, these figures should at best be used as *obiter*, and footnoted as such. Otherwise, you leave yourself wide open to the sophistry of a certain minority of disgruntled and bitter academics who prey on good work like vultures at an elephant's carcass, and you should take special care not to leave those giant ears of yours unprotected.

I understand a background trace on all the soldiers who spoke out is impractical for the purposes of a single research paper, and possibly increasingly impossible due to deaths, persistent right-wing intimidation, the passing of time and men's fungible memories. One can only sigh at such rigor's impracticality.

But my point here being that perhaps you should change the title of your essay.

To *"Corn/Ergot &c.,"* instead of "Rye," I mean.

I am at this moment experiencing something of a dizzy spell.

And finally,

4. Dissent

Mr. Edwards, one brave young Japanese historian, a Master Ko Ishikawa, has gone as far as to say the entire essay is a cynical twisting of what he earnestly persists in referring to as the "truth"; he calls it a "test" of the "elasticity" of history!

In a heartbreakingly poorly written and/or translated monograph in the obscure Malaysian periodical *Malay History* (only a single malnourished issue ever struggled weakly from the press, apparently), the fellow claims impassionedly that the events you trace to ergot poisoning and mass-hallucination were,

"One such as Japanese youngsters are tricked and bullied from knowing from in the schooling, that there terror might not touch them deeply in the mind and force all love and care for Japan and even for any nation for all and good time." (*sic*)

He is referring here to the issue of gaps and/or distortions of historical events in those Japanese school textbooks; the politicised controversies of the 1980's. He unfortunately uses the term "historical events," with some inattention to the terms and subtleties of the article. He also claims he was compelled to publish offshore and only in the short-lived *MH* out of consideration for his family (with regard to certain overtures of violence made by some burly right-wingers in his parents' small Nagano neighbourhood), and partially due to the fact he is, apparently, merely fourteen years of age. I am reminded of seventeen-year-old Otoya Yamaguchi, the right-wing youth who assassinated Socialist Party leader Inejiro Asanuma in 1960. The political conscience is alive and earnestly kicking in Japan's youth, it would seem, and so vehement as to lead to acts of this kidney, and indeed, Otoya's subsequent prison suicide.

A further interesting point: you cite the abortifacient alkaloid decocted by boiling the ergot sclerotia, the method widely used in Victorian times for inducing labour in parturient women, as the real physical source of the low childbirth rates subsequent to the "Rape of Nanking." You make the connection between the visions seen and the abortive side-effects that followed the ergot poisoning as the source, distorted by ergot hallucination and paranoia-induced "bad trips," of the tales of soldiers attacking pregnant women on the streets of Nanking and forcibly removing unborn children from the womb.

The young Japanese fellow takes issue with your claim, and yelps from the page:

"These and all the more horrors are baleful and say no to life, but even if many China's women too say, 'No, such things did not happen,' it is from the shame. For this new article to say, 'it is all just the terrible ergot poisoning, that makes the people see things that are not there,' is another very bad thing, in deed." (very *sic*)

This one poorly educated pup aside (though, interestingly, what motive could this lad have at such an age for perpetuating such a damning version of Japanese history?) the responses in many Japanese history journals have been quite universally laudatory and panegyrical indeed.

One example from *Mainichi Shinri*, Jan. 3, 1996:

"This new historian is truly a 'new historian.' Combining a penetrative knowledge of the intrigues of Japanese and Chinese politics of the period with a deep understanding of the impact of the imaginations of nations on the recording of history, wrapped up in a commonsensical yet radical and terrifyingly compelling thesis: *that nothing really happened at Nanking* as claimed by a bloodthirsty media, Mr. Edwards begs us and all nations to review the ways in which guilt gains its own momentum over time, and lies beget lies. Seminal."

This by Hiroyuki Matsudaira, as translated by Professor J. Matsumoto, who was visiting here at Cambridge, and alerted my attention to this article. Matsudaira's take on "stories" composed from a nation's own collective imagination supports your thesis, in that the Chinese hallucinations would perforce be composed of what is already known to them. Here he mentions the reports of decapitation, castration, slicing off of women's breasts, the carving and roasting of organs, live burials, slicing of children in thirds and fourths, impaling of children tossed into the air on bayonets. He asserts the historical precedents for this behavior in China, and denies any such precedents in Japanese narratives. Matsudaira asserts *there are traditional methods* for the killing of Chinese children: that the Chinese are *re-imagining their own brutality.* I am prompted to return to the *Malay History*'s inaugural and solus issue, where the aforementioned young Japanese historian says, in a rare moment of tip-top translation: "Truth is not facts, or words; these are merely the weapons of politics. Truth is experience."

To sign off, sir, I wish to append a recommendation that you seek out kindred spirit R. Gordon Wasson's highly regarded yet widely neglected works (*Mushrooms, Russia and History* and *Persephone's Quest*) on fungi and the human imagination. I do see you have taken the step Wasson did not, and extended their influence to *all of human history.* Indeed we have now proved that psilocybin, the humble fungal derivative from the "magic" mushroom *Psilocybe cubensis*, is chemically almost equivalent to human *serotonin*, i.e. a naturally occurring external facilitation of human *pride*, of *self-esteem.* What implications did our little helper have for the quality of life in cultures who habitually and ritually used *P. cubensis*? For their art? For their relationship with their *God*? The connection between fungi and spirituality over the ages is extant and troubling, in that the decline in the privileging of both as an essential part of human existence in the West has led so inexorably to this hollowing out of modern postindustrial life, this decline in imagination, this narrowing, and graying of the potentially brilliant rainbow of the human experience: culinary; imaginative; spiritual; physical; temporal.

To sum up, your paper makes it clear that histories are inextricable from those who recorded them, and the natural world that surrounded those who recorded them. That the hallucination of the historic event is, over time, no less real than the "real" historic event. That the relationship of the present to both is similarly aesthetic; differing only in terms of text. There is the merely written word, the document, the primary source that demands and then, reified, contains our reverence and our fidelity while remaining fundamentally a contingent linguistic construct. I detect a kind of Foucauldian *frisson:* that the true rebellion is unseeable, because it is not permitted by power. All we may see and know is what is permitted to be seen and known. Therefore we must *learn to see what is not there.*

But, Mr. Edwards, in your metaphysics I sometimes wonder if I do not also detect the merest hint of an irony, a satirical glimmer?

There are those who are capable of being physically hurt by ideas; there are those to whom history deals shocks to the body. The trauma of a lived horror is felt, by some, in a guilty midbrain, perpetually ashamed of not only its temerity but the ailment itself, which it cannot escape. And also fears to escape. The end of empathy is that it takes over like a virus. The self-mutilator, the anorexic, the child, the teenage girl with her sewing scissors and scarred thighs, the slim man with his loneliness and his ryvita. The gift, the curse, the pure new individual strange self. The touchstone, in whom all the factors that meet to make the worst history possible are gathered and recognised for what they are. They are catalysts, firestarters. Dotted through the culture these figures arise, burn bright in the arts, and disappear. Consumed by guilt, self-medication, self-loathing. Or consumed by the evil they seem so utterly compelled to examine.

If your essay is right, and if you are honest, what is left for us now is no more than a series of what we might in effect call "historical novels," more or less "imagined," "projected," or "propagandised." The historic is left as nothing more than what Nietzsche in *The Birth of Tragedy* saw as those latter Greek tragedians' understanding of all that *lived* experience could ever truly be: nothing more or less than an aesthetic event.

In an instant, thousands of lives become merely a chum of clues spread by some great amoral fisherman/historian/artist to lure the mindless marlin of the public; and the massacre is puzzle, is game, is *fun.*

I wish to add yet further, that *if you are wrong*—if you lie, if you satire, if you are an ironist who seeks advancement, if those Chinese are nobly fighting for *the* truth, washed away by Mao, MacArthur, Confucian virtue, Cold War political posturing, and you—then God help you getting to sleep at night, my friend, because the spirits of those raped and murdered will kneel at your bedside, whispering their secrets all night long.

Without further allusion to your age, I am,

Yours,
Jonathan B. Haberman

Simon
October 19, 2000

So guidebooks say twelve million people live in the twenty-three wards of metro Tokyo. And that by working day this increases to twenty-four million. This gives some idea, but not really, of the state of the trains heading out at around eight-thirty on a Friday night. And you factor in after-work drinks and it becomes clear both how lucky and aggressive I was to get a seat for the forty-minute trip on the Chuo out to Hachioji, and why I'm wearing sunglasses although it's pitch black outside.

Because it's Friday night, the usual silent misery of Tokyo trains is lightened and there's even conversation, and drunk salarymen semi-shouting in each other's ears, polite even when they're wasted, or very drunk salarymen swinging weak-kneed from tethers, drifting in and out of sleep. The standing are meshed in hard with the seated; bent knees alternating with straight; little sighed arrangements come to over whose shoe fits where; minute accommodations reluctantly made for someone's broken arm.

I caught the Chuo at Shinjuku, which was beyond berserk, and the technique I used was this: queue in the painted lines that funnel you to one side of where the train doors will open, and then, though it causes trouble, trips people up, gets your feet stood on and your bag crushed, shrink away from the doors, opt out of the queue as it surges in. Maybe three trains and twenty minutes pass this way, until you can take a place near as possible to the front. And though the Chuo has uplifted thousands

from Marunouchi and Otemachi and Yotsuya and Yoyogi, a major percentage are going to disembark at Shinjuku, transferring to the Yamanote or
the Keio or the Saikyo or the Sobu or the Seibu or any of the subways, so
if you've got the balls to fight the tide the moment the doors open, sidling
through the mutters and sucked teeth—I have; the balls, I mean—and if
you put your faith in the end seat hard left inside the door—which is really
the only seat you've got any kind of shot at—and if you're quick and
impolite and merciless—if you've adapted to the city—and if you're just
lucky, you can get a seat. And then, like most of the seated J, you can
maybe fall asleep as the Chuo heads out elevated in the darkness of the
Tokyo commuter barracks, the dormitories, apartment blocks and 7-11's
and pachinko parlors and Ito Yokados and dying bankrupt Daieis—*urbur-
bia*—while the windows shudder and roar behind your slowly nodding
head as the empty inbounds pass you by.

My skymail went something like this: *Hello, am back in town, dinner? ima
doko? Friday night?*

Ariel's skymail, an hour later (I wasn't really waiting): *Sounds good
sugar, Friday, have work so 9:30, Hachioji east exit?*

My reply: *Yup.*

Subtract vowels; capitalize.

When she says sugar, you can *taste* it.

Lights play through the people, thinning as we get further inland, and
behind my sunglasses it's easy to stare at individuals, or pieces of individuals, as the pleasant voidish numbness of traing—a JR phrase—the most palpable social contract foreigners sign here—leaves you silent and mid-doze.
It's a semi-alert numbness, a prickly passive pose that's adopted from those
around you, and can scare you, in the city, when you find yourself inside it.
But in a way, though, I know that it's easier to be as blank and bereft as the
faces here, to think only about or not really think about but simply look at
this girl diagonally opposite me in really gigantic tan leather platforms, cork
heels down and toes up, fishnet stockings on thighs the width of my wrist,
applying lipstick in a mirror, her fingers nailed like claws, her hair a sixties
bob and a brown and spangled-silver skirt and a tiny maroon T-shirt that
reads WELCOME NEW MACHINE! than it is to try and plan something,

think of something to say, imagine a scenario and prepare for it, wonder what might exactly be on the cards, exactly what a dinner date *she suggested* for half past nine might mean when we both know the Chuo stops just after midnight, just exactly how far either way such a piece of evidence could go. It's easier to look slyly sideways and feel nothing for the old, frail rich guy in a black cashmere sweater (in October) reading a novel and tapping a fan on his knee to a rhythm in the kanji, his skin the caramel color of care, silver hair precisely combed—a man who smells of Chanel and money. He's sitting right next to me. He coughs against something rising he can't seem to fight, his narrow chest shaken and he squares his shoulders against it, lifts a tissue—the cough moves in him again, and I feel maybe a little guilty—and he sighs. Under the cashmere his body is shrunken and wasted, and he sighs again. He lifts the tissue gently to his nostril, coughs again.

He turns the page.

And standing right in front of me—it's these things make you really realize this stuff about complicit numbness, and what you give up too easily—a semi-Brazilian girl with skin just like Ariel's in a strip above her jeans, cream, tobacco, honey, caramel, smooth, a down of hair, a proud, non-J belly above faded blue jeans with bright silver buttons on the outside of the fly, her belly button clean and petite and puckered inside and basically right in front of my nose. And she reaches down and adjusts her belt just once, eyes outside the window or on her own reflection, it's hard to tell, and lights move across her as she sways gently with the swing of the train, the surge and roll and judder that makes my erection strangely numb and distant, yet hard to bear. And the lights play across all of those who stand in here, a line above the seated staring out the windows, staring over me, lights playing across their clothes and pieces of their bodies, my heart beating way too fast as we pull into Musashi-Koganei, twenty-one minutes from Hachioji and Ariel. The lights flicker and disappear in fluorescent glare, and her stomach does too.

She must live here; the province of the train that is detail.

What can you do to deal?

Put your glasses and your headphones on, turn the volume up and, frozen, numb—it's just aircon—obey the decisions of the bass.

A hot wind, all around the raised ramparts of the platform outside the department store. The station is inside, deep beneath the Ito Yokado.

Beneath me, taxis are gathering, parking in lines. A dead straight highway disappears into the distance, north or south or somewhere in between, I can't tell. But perpendicular to the tracks of the Chuo. There is a busker with a Gibson who looks thirteen and no one else around and mauve tile on this platform as far as I can see. The buildings that line the highway seem both massive and miniature at the same time. I'm smoking, waiting, leaning on a curved chrome bar that surrounds a huge tacky aluminum sculpture of a woman holding a baby above her head, a baby that has its arms outspread like wings; rivets on their bodies leak rust on the milky metal like bleeding freckles. I have more than ¥60,000 on me in cash, and I've been standing here for ten or twenty minutes but three cigarettes, anyhow.

There's a moment when nervousness just widens into dread.

The taxis move out from under me, orange and black and quiet, disappear down the wide, surreally straight highway. What's here: the Ito Yokado department store, McDonald's, Nova, two Marui department stores, a gigantic billboard for Salem cigarettes, another Takashimaya. The endlessness; the weirdness of so few people. The recession. The blackest of all black skies—in the summer you come to know the sky through the night as a gas. My cigarette butts leak cinders onto the tile at my feet, and I think (I *think*) Anton was pleased to hear from me. A bus coming this way passes a taxi and disappears under me. Anton is importing sex toys. Is he going to start talking like a manager now? Do sex toy import–export companies have corporate codes and generic vocabularies? Will he use the word "product" in every second sentence? Will the subject of his business bring on a seriousness so exaggerated and sincere it will be like a disease of the brain, and I won't be able to mention it unless he does first, and then in such a circumspect way, deferring respectfully to his knowledge, so sensitive to his willingness to discuss that I can only ease my utter boredom by congratulating myself that I am a "good listener"? Never be sarcastic or joke about it, because they for damn sure won't. The best businessmen I've ever known (and by that I mean the richest) have been colleagues of my father's, and they were loud, opinionated and always had a finely tuned sense of the ridiculous. Cock and balls condoms are cock and balls condoms I'm sure Anton knows. Pubic hair dye is only "product" in a certain sense of the word. He can still get drugs. I still believe in Anton; he's only twenty-five. Men who obey corporate codes always seem like earnest aliens to me. In this way I do respect my father. He at least is totally up-front or something about this chain and his role in it. At the very least, my father still knows the meanings and uses of indirection, sarcasm and cruelty.

I am starving, a kind of freezing ache in my neck from all this nicotine. The blackest of all black skies, out here in Hachioji.

It takes maybe thirty seconds of staring at the pristine white Yankees cap coming up those steps to realize who's wearing it. I walk toward her and she looks up and smiles, and then we kind of turn and walk together back wherever she came from and the silence though it doesn't last seems to set some kind of tone.

Not much is said on the bus ride, but she tells me to take the only available seat while she stands, and she drops ¥100 coins in the machine for me and she seems to know the driver. Whether it's nerves turned to hunger or too many cigarettes, this strange place that's just like another rearrangement of certain elements of Japan, there's a total bleakness cloaked all over this; the heat and silence in the bus, her jeans and T-shirt in the aisle a seat ahead of me. The effort to try and extract motivation from exactly how close she's standing is so far beyond me she might be kanji. Beautiful, close, "Adult Entertainment," an utter cipher in such a depth that translation brings only more riddles, a deeper fall toward a center that's one of too many, a darkened maze out here in Hachioji. There's a movement in me and outside of me in this dark bus and I am terrified.

"You look good," she says, as we walk from the stop to her apartment. She has a frank way of looking me up and down that I kind of both love and worry about. "Very nice."

"I think I could really really use a drink," I say.

"Mmm-hmm," she answers, and we walk together for a while, and I reach for a cigarette and light it and I've had too many and throw it away.

We turn a corner into a narrow street, under a convex mirror that's there to give drivers a warped suggestion of what's to come.

"Are we gonna eat?" I say.

She's pleased at this. "I've . . . prepared victuals."

I smile at her. She takes my hand and mine is cold and hers is warm.

"You're cool," I say. "It's cool to see you."

She doesn't reply, and looks ahead and doesn't let go my hand and I never know, with her, the right thing to say.

After a while she murmurs, shaking her head just slightly, "What a fuckin situation," as we reach another corner.

7-11: we buy bags of alcohol: cans of grape and apple and lychee Chu-Hai, screw-cap red Delica Maison and Mon Frère (she sneers when I place it on the counter—mutters, "tin can wine"). And cashews and corn chips and Skittle Sours and Mike popcorn and bottles of VOLVIC water. I suggest we get some Ben and Jerry's or Häagen-Dazs for dessert and she says anyway, we can come back, and then that she's getting fat, anyway, and I say, *that's* crap, but too loud, and wish I'd said it nicer. The attendant knows her and is shy, and we buy ice, too, and cigarettes, Indian Spirits for her, Mild Sevens for me, and some minidiscs and a Doraemon on a leash for her keitai, just because it's there, on the counter, and easy and we're rich and it feels good just to take it, make it hers, or even ours.

"Plass oh dahm," Ariel says in the doorway to her apartment.

It's the second floor of a small four-storeyed block that's not quite pre-fab-seeming but more like during-fab: all aluminum and half-assed stucco, squat and over-boxy and kind of half-finished. Every line is straight: the stories piled on top of one another so flatly, like an earthquake has collapsed the distinctions. This, another gaijin phenomenon you read in each other's faces: the only apartment you're ever pleasantly surprised by is your own.

She's opened a door like a meat locker's, riveted and metal, and I'm unlacing my trainers in the genkan, and, "Plass oh dahm," she says, and places her hand on my bent shoulder.

"Um," I say to my shoe, too aware that this is first contact, first nearly real flirt, and just a little bewildered, "I . . . didn't catch that?"

"Make way for the ladies."

She steps past me, and heels off her sandals without turning, and I watch her pad through the darkened kitchen into deeper dark beyond.

"Right."

Her kitchen is the size of a motorcycle. There seem like a hundred different horizontal surfaces in here, shelves, things on shelves that are more shelves, possibilities jammed with spice and keys, tomatoes and flaking garlic in a wooden soapdish; there's a phone handset with no cradle and a 250-ml Hello Kitty Coke can filled with pens, a dishrack filled with pots suspended above the sink, two Pizza-La box spines tucked like books in a space between cabinets.

There's something wary and tense in the way she's said this. Sometimes visiting someone else's 1K (1 room, a kitchen) is more intimate than kissing. It looks like six mats large, possibly parquet past the kitchen. I can't tell because she's moving in darkness, leaving off the light. It's suffo-catingly hot in here; with the door closed behind me the only light dim through a gap in the thin curtains and security glass, a streetlamp out there past the veranda.

"So how much do you pay for this," I say.

"Shut the fuck *up*," she says, and laughs, a silhouette sliding the veranda door shut.

"No, no. I like it. I'm wondering, that's all. It should be cheaper out here."

"Not all daddies are CEOs," she says. "Not all of us slamdunk with a stepladder."

"Hey," I say. "Not all daddies are career diplomats either. It's not a con-test."

"Not anymore," she says.

I'm standing in socks in the kitchen holding shopping and don't know where to go. The room's still dark and she's moving around in it, adjusting things, moving something large that could be a futon, the scrape of a supermarket bag, the flutter, clatter and hum as the aircon comes on.

"What does that mean?"

"Anyhow," she says, "you're right. Cash just falls from the sky here. Money falls from the sky."

"Can I come in now?"

"Wait. I'm tidying. I didn't tidy."

"What about the recession, though. It's supposed to be bad."

"Foreigners just sit on the edge of it, and catch the cash as it falls in."

"Ariel—"

"What."

"Hey, I can't say anything about your place and I'm not saying anything about your place because for the main reason that I can't even see."

She's quiet for a minute, then the shuffling, the clinks resume. There's a refrigerator now, I see, just at the end of the little kitchen, and when she opens it and reaches inside, the light beyond the door shows a foot of par-quet bare and dustless, and what might be photographs on the wall; a postcard, a maple leaf, a World Cup promotion.

"Shall I bring the drinks in?"

"One second. *Damn.*"

She's crouched down in the center of the room, a dark shape in a white cap.

Then she stands, triple-clicks the string of the center lamp above her, and the dimmed light flickers tentatively and there, revealed, she's standing looking down in the middle of a demure six-mat parquet room, with a folded futon for a couch, TV and tiny stereo in a cabinet, fridge and a tiny bookshelf by the kitchen, more photos on the walls, and arrayed around her feet are a dozen or more plates of J food, a floor-level banquet: pickles and sushi and sealed pots of soup, mounds of shredded white daikon artfully arranged beside two tiny pottery bowls of wasabi, a cube of tofu with flaked bonito and onion—spring—sprinkled on top, two pairs of hashi on blocks, plates all sizes and shapes on the parquet, the largest a rectangular sashimi platter of red maguro, tako, white rubbery ika, salmon, pink scalded ebi, tamago, hamachi and even some store-bought yellow uni in battleship wrap, maybe frozen but finely veined in black like the good stuff, all on a plate as big as a VCR.

"Ta-dah," she says.

"Oh man," I say.

She's immediately embarrassed and bustling, and looks away from me at her work, steps carefully outside it in her bare feet. Jeans and a T-shirt under the dimmed light, she steps outside it and back as if to try and look at what's been offered with my eyes. Her back obliquely to me, she lifts off her cap, flicks it into a cane basket full of clothes in the corner. She undoes her hair and lifts fingers through it in practiced, precise gestures, gathers it again into a mad frothy bloom and in movements chef-professional doubles and ties the band at the root of another perfect ponytail. She wears a soft white T-shirt, tiny little holes at the shoulder seams, tucked lightly in her jeans and hanging doubled over the first two inches of her brash hips, and then her hands on them I'm made aware I am just standing here, stunned, by her hips and ass, the way she stands in bare feet, the color changing in the denim at her thighs, one single pale crease behind each knee, the frayed white roughness around the pockets, the dip and curve between her cheeks, curves that now seem to represent the exact opposite of the violence, the slash and burn of kanji, curves that to me, I feel with something epiphanic, belie all the importance of an ancient language in a moment's selfless lean.

A terrible moment, dumbstruck. Eight awful things to say occur to me; eight ways to mess this moment up. Head tilted, she examines the flaws in the food I cannot see.

"I . . . can't imagine how long this took you," I say.

"That's because we have different imaginations," she replies.

Outside, her wind chimes tone in the soft hot winds.

It's getting on toward eleven or eleven-thirty at least, and no mention has been made of trains. Marvin Gaye is playing on her little Muji stereo—*Too Busy Thinking About My Baby*—as she drinks her apple Chu-Hai and me my plastic tumbler of Delica Maison and we pick through the food she's prepared. She tells me to take the folded futon and she sits cross-legged by the little blue fridgefreezer. On top of it there are a couple of little wooden bowls of junk, girl stuff like change and hairties and clips, matchbooks from Trouble Peach and Belgo and Fonda De La Madrugada. An empty smoothie cup from Baskin-Robbins and a framed photograph in extreme close-up of a very slim dark-haired guy, all sunglasses and cheekbones, smiling not too confidently. Beside this, another photograph of her mother, the mix of Filipina in her revealed only through the khaki contours under and around her eyes, like something painted on the deep almost bluish blackness of her face. And although her mother is grinning kind of mischievously, in Ariel this has become a stroke of bruisedness, overemphasized when she is tired or sad. I eat some maguro and salmon, leave the ika and the tako because it seems neither of us likes things with tentacles. I light a cigarette almost immediately I'm remotely full, down another glass of wine, fill it again.

"So how does it feel to be back," she finally says, using her hashi to break up the tofu—the only thing she eats—on her plate.

"Good, I guess. Things to, you know, do. *Work* to do."

"You do . . . work?" she laughs.

"I work," I say. "Hold on. I think I asked that exact same question to Anton."

"You've seen him, then."

"I talked to him a few days ago. I learned he's importing . . . stuff."

She smiles again. "I know. I see him now and then."

"Oh, and I guess I caught up with Jacques a little bit. Who hasn't changed."

"Uh-huh. That ain't true. Everyone's changed."

"Who else? I don't know. I haven't seen Michael. I hear his sister's here as well . . ."

I trail off because she gets up and disappears with her can round the corner into the kitchen. A second later she's back, opens the refrigerator, crouching, looks inside.

"You want that other apple Chu-Hai."

"No," I say. "You go for it."

"How about Brigit? I haven't seen Brigit for three months or something."

"I haven't seen her. I don't even really know her that well," I say. "I hear she's breaking up with Drew. Jacques told me this. But it's like, breaking up with someone here is more of an accommodation problem than anything."

"That ain't true," she says, shaking her head exaggeratedly as she sits down again. Then, leaning over to me, her eyes a little bloodshot, though I guess mine might be too because we're drinking fast, "That ain't true, boy. Give me a drag on that cigarette."

I laugh, let her lean toward me a little longer till it's almost uncomfortable, almost a dare, then hand her the cigarette.

She holds it, sizes me up a moment. I lean back against the pebbled wallpaper, cool with the aircon, staring right back at her. She takes a drag, screws her face up. "You juice your cigarettes," she says, and hands it straight back.

"Uh-huh. Smoke your own then."

She turns and rummages through the plastic bags by the refrigerator.

"I lost them, that's why."

I throw her the Mild Sevens, and she takes one, lights it, exhales up to the light and leans back against the wall and sips her Chu-Hai. I reach for the bottle of Delica without leaning off the wall, grab it by the neck and pour another cup, lay the bottle in my lap.

"Anton," she says, "has like twenty Japanese girlfriends."

"Uh-huh."

"He has a diary. Appointments in his Palm Pilot."

"Let a player play."

She's silent. Then, "Still, it's way less complicated than gaijin." She makes a popping sound with her lips. "Cosa de gringos. What-a-fuckin-situ-ation."

I don't say anything, watching slightly my awareness fade with the alcohol, watching the way her lips moved, a tiny tremble, watching her leaning back, the fall of the old white cotton between her breasts, strangely distant now.

"I want to do things," she suddenly says, looking down at the can of Chu-Hai. "I'm gonna leave this place. I'm so sick of Tokyo. Go home, study Tagalog. I want to visit where my mother was born, you know, but with the language. I'm gonna study languages properly, and I want to study yoga."

"You can do yoga here," I say. "There are classes. And for languages."

"Tagalog? Here?" she smiles. "You don't know what it's like. Getting looked at on the trains. J guys saying things. Getting touched. You don't know what it's like." She sighs. "I get ... so professional at averting my eyes from them I don't even see them after a while. Until I get so I feel like I'm lost in the pose. In a cocoon here. That's the worst, you know. When you feel Japanese. I just want to study Tagalog somewhere real. With some money in my pocket. Not wanting to stay at home all day. Just feel like I'm getting better, you know? I never will. I get sick of ... feeling like everything here's a disaster, you know."

She sighs, and there's a long pause while she thinks. There's something about the way she's said this, like she's been waiting for someone to listen. I wonder how long she's spent alone out here.

"I remember Brigit," she says, "telling me how before they came to Japan on JET, she and her old boyfriend had talked about, like, experimenting, you know, as part of the experience."

She's aware I'm looking at her, and I'm aware I'm not trying to hide it, but there's something wrong here, like we both knew how this was going to work although we have not seen each other in more than a year. A sense of lines, a sense of saying things said before.

"She told me how they'd talked about this together, all excited, completely agreeing with each other, you know? They'd been together a year or something. They knew they were in love. Yet they talked about this for when they were going to travel. Other people. That sex is a ... that you want that kind of bodily confirmation of this new place. You want to see if culture shock can go that deep inside. You're daring it. Or if you can, like transform it from the inside out. Make your sex bigger than the world. Be someone new. Be ... *internationale.*"

She drinks some more of her can of apple Chu-Hai.

"They ... wanted to experiment as part of the experience. Not to let the love stop them from you know, seeing the world. Loving the world. But all they wanted really, then, was each other. You know? Just fantasies. You're excited all the time. Everything's sexual, everything's loaded. Your hackles are always up. That's what I think."

Her wind chimes tone again out the window, over Marvin Gaye.

"Then they get here and twenty-four hours and the whole thing explodes."

"She found Drew, though."

"You know," she says, lifting her chin, an imitation of a child's defiance, "everyone's more comfortable with J fucks. It keeps things simple. Everyone, even the dweebs, get theirs."

"Cosa de gringos," I say. "What about Michael. Who does he fuck?" It's her word, so I use it.

She snorts, drinks more of the Chu-Hai, runs the can across her forehead, and as she stands, she says, "New Zealand people just argue until they're exhausted." She puts her drink down on top of the refrigerator, too close to the edge. Then with her back to me she pulls off her T-shirt and she's braless underneath, and she disappears into the kitchen.

At the door to the bathroom, out of my sight, she says, "It's exhausting, Simon," and laughs.

Mercy Mercy Me turns into *Stop, Look, Listen, To Your Heart*.

I drop my cigarette butt in an old empty Chu-Hai can and on my way to the bathroom go to move the can on the refrigerator. In a wooden bowl, under another maple leaf postcard, on top of a pile of mixed Japanese and Canadian change, is a crumpled Canadian five-dollar note. Written in small, uneven writing, along the blank border: *I love fish tacos too. And you.*

Meredith
October 2000

The reason Meredith has bought a camera is threefold, but not so equally weighted.

She does want to film Tokyo. She has a kind of outsider's guilt; a tourist imperative. Not knowing what to do with the city, she has decided to film it. With no real interest in watching what she produces—more simply to give her a way to look. A problem is that she gets stared at on trains because she is white, because she is beautiful. She doesn't know where to put her eyes when they stare so she wears sunglasses a lot. Looking back, at the LCD display, will be a shield and a weapon. To watch someone examining you in liquid crystal is hard, no matter how beautiful they are, no matter how easily they lend themselves to a stare. People will look away, sigh, mutter, but most importantly they will try to ignore her when she films them. This was the first reason.

The second is closely related: simple boredom.

The third reason for the camera is what she was looking at. The stacks of digital videotapes on Michael's desk, minus the tape in her pocket she had used to select the camera.

On the desk was an unopened bottle of Smirnoff vodka, surrounded by loose sheets of old paper lined in kanji. There were stacks of hardback books, goldleaf kanji on the spines, the covers pebbled and maroon. On the spine of one, old, thick and ragged, the only English in the stack, two peeling stickers with faded type:

TOKYO WAR TRIALS
Transcript of Proceedings
Northcroft J.
Volume 89
1947
November 5th,
6th & 11th
Pages
32432–32773

She flicked a page. There were no barcodes; no information on publishing dates or reprints. The paper was thick, coarse and sandy. The type on the pages was fading. This book was an original.

Thumbtacked to the wall above the desk were three pages. On the first, a list of names and nationalities, written in purple ink:

Northcroft E.H.	N.Z.	M
Webb W.F.	Aus.	D
Higgins J.P.	U.S.A.	C
Radhabinod Pal	India	P
McDougall E.S.	Canada	B
Lord Patrick	U.K.	S?
Zarayanov I.M.	U.S.S.R.	S

Mei Ju-ao	China	S
Röling B.V.A.	Holland	A?
Bernard H.	France	J
Jaranilla D.	Philippines	A

She recognized the first name, the dead New Zealand judge from the old book, from that memorial. The rest a mystery.

On the second in purple ink again, a long list of maybe thirty Japanese names. On this list, only one had a letter beside:

Matsui, Iwane   K

On the third page, this time in black ink, in fine, tiny handwriting:

Potentialem: a found poem 7/4/99
defeated annihilated disarmed lined up stripped starved beaten assaulted decapitated disemboweled carved roasted boiled fried in oil impaled hung by tongues on hooks nailed thrown buried alive raped gang-raped fucked slaughtered slain seized dragged sodomized nailed alive to walls eaten by German shepherds castrated forced to rape wives daughters mothers sons grandmothers grandfathers sisters brothers nephews nieces babies bayoneted ripped apart shot machine gunned forced into poses photographed bought sold stolen plagiarized copied edited doctored distorted compiled collaged auctioned proliferated practiced feasted fattened coaxed trusted convinced believed motivated disposed discarded piled burned charred camouflaged looted defiled beheaded stabbed picked registered counted led screamed plunged burst scarred distorted swung spurted sprayed spattered washed gushed coursed trickled foamed witnessed ignored undressed hurt held shaped herded marched ordered dehydrated eviscerated tied experienced happened clawed hacked gouged out pricked pushed ripped committed accompanied jumped doused soaked fired frozen flung bombarded jerked tormented poured saturated consumed disbelieved believed choked suffocated pried slashed savaged kicked violated thrust meted rammed clasped dropped diseased doubted sliced ravished entered penetrated resisted ruptured stained swollen blistered burned devastated protested ordered suicided suffered crawled tried endured resisted

raped raped raped raped raped raped raped raped raped raped
raped raped raped raped raped raped raped raped raped raped
raped raped raped raped raped raped raped raped raped raped
raped raped raped raped raped raped raped raped raped raped
raped raped raped raped raped raped raped raped raped raped
raped raped raped raped raped raped raped raped raped raped
raped raped raped raped raped raped raped raped raped raped
raped raped raped raped raped raped raped raped raped raped
raped raped raped raped raped raped raped raped raped raped
raped raped raped raped raped raped raped raped raped raped
raped raped raped raped raped raped raped raped raped raped
raped raped raped raped raped raped raped raped raped raped
raped raped raped raped raped raped raped raped raped raped
raped raped raped raped raped raped raped raped raped raped
raped raped raped raped raped raped raped raped raped raped
raped raped raped raped raped raped raped raped raped raped
raped raped raped raped raped raped raped raped raped raped
raped raped raped raped raped raped raped raped raped raped
raped raped raped raped raped raped raped raped raped raped
raped raped raped raped raped raped raped raped raped raped
raped raped raped raped raped raped raped raped raped raped
raped raped raped raped raped raped raped raped raped raped
raped raped raped raped raped raped raped raped raped raped
raped raped a raped rape raped for raped every raped thousand raped
lives raped fall raped through raped this raped flood raped and raped
drink raped it raped deep raped then raped try raped and raped
breathe raped and raped every raped time raped you raped cry raped
you raped lie

Meredith was remembering a boy she slept with at Otago for a little while, a boy who through the winter had thumbtacked a massive banner to his chill bedroom wall with the word "EXCITE" spray-painted on it in giant glittering blue letters. An impulsive guitarist with four earrings, a boy named Nick, second name Tin, who sometimes wore makeup, and told her, "Every morning when I wake up, I want to look at that word, and I want to feel it." Certain aspects of Nick had reminded her of Michael. Looking at the page of black handwriting on the wall her brother might have written she thought of a boy named Tin who had grinned like a shark and owned an MG and made her aloo mattar every Friday, a pea and potato curry, which she first heard as "Hallo Mudda," and then always as, "A Low Matter," and wrote it off as his private joke, something to do with potatoes and Dutchness and dikes, because of the potatoes, and the way he pronounced it, and where else would a name like Tin come from? But he made it every Friday night for the weeks she slept with him in second year, authentic, and delicious, with popped black mustard seeds and fenugreek. Because cooking was the only thing this boy really demonstrated much care for getting right after he dropped out. He left for Korea, ostensibly to teach little children English but really just to get out and travel, that year, which was the autumn of 1999, the year she dropped out too.

The page was neatly divided in half by the patterns of the words. Meredith stared closely, and tried to ascertain if the writing was the same as on the first; if she recognized it. But it had been written so mechanically: the word "raped" written again and again, too precisely, each word occupying the exact same space as the last, and though the paper was unlined each row of words the exact same distance from the row of words above it. The exact same heaviness of ink. No sense of the writer growing tired or losing momentum. No growing raggedness of writing. No change in the size of the letters; no variation in the cursive links between letters. She tried to picture him sitting at this table; caring about this enough to finish it. Or caring enough to structure this thing to fit a single page that might be tacked to a wall. She couldn't tell if it was his writing and didn't want to look too long at the thing; black and squat like a cockroach on the smooth beige wall, a thing that seemed as if it could move quickly, fat, shockingly fast. So she didn't notice the last embedded line, didn't quite calculate the conscientiousness, the care.

She still tried to reconcile this thing with her brother, and found it hard.

"What the hell are you doing, Mikey," she whispered, half to herself, half to the wall.

She riffled her fingers through the loose pages on the desk. There were photos, too: a black and white shot of a long bridge spanning a sandy river, connecting two clusters of settlement. Without color the water and the land the same shade of gray. Typewritten beneath it: NONTEXTUAL EXHIBIT PX 201. Maybe forty or fifty other photos. Uniformed Chinese and Japanese men, some of their faces circled; scrawled kanji beneath. Severed heads with closed eyes on gray earth stained black; smiling soldiers holding swords. A young soldier proudly displaying a new tattoo on his bicep. A single pressed dry flower in among the stiff old photographic paper. A newer photo, color, taken out in the living room. A group of young kids, all in their twenties, ten or fifteen of them, standing against the west wall. Jacques in the middle next to an Indian boy, flashing V-signs, imitating Japanese kids in photos. She turned the photo over. Purple ink: *Jacques, Anton, Pras, Brigit, Drew, Catherine, Ariel, Shannon. 7 July 2000. Date of the Marco Polo Bridge Incident.* Among the stack of old hardback books, a smaller one with no brown pages to be seen, but pitted bronze bars instead. Where a right hand's thumb would rest could it be opened, held in palms and read, a miniature keyhole, burred and scraped to silver at the rim by a key.

And beside the books, lying under pages of kanji right next to the vodka bottle, she found a piece of the blade of a narrow sword. It was heavy, and broken jaggedly at one end. The metal at the break was gray and dull, but on the planes of the blade it shone in ripples; the wave pattern of only a few swordmakers' hammers. And next to the blade were the stacks of videotapes, maybe thirty in all, small and black like decks of cards.

Hence the camera: the first real clue to Michael may be what he had been filming.

There was a knock at the door, and she jumped.

She opened it to the maid with a silver trolley. The maid stayed out in the hallway and said, "Excuse me" in Japanese and bowed shyly. Meredith sighed, said thank you in English and wheeled it inside. An opened bottle of chardonnay, a porcelain bowl of popcorn, an ashtray and a single wine glass all on a silver tray, which she carried into the bedroom and placed on the floor at the foot of the bed. Next, she wheeled in the big Sony Trinitron, against the wall opposite the bed. Leaving the new bags of old clothes on the coffee table, she unpacked the camera and connected it to the television, the cables long enough for her to sit with her back to the bed's end and the camera beside her, eating popcorn and drinking wine from the bottle, watching the tapes, and later, maybe, David Duchovny for relief.

The first tape, the most obvious choice, was the tape she took into Shinjuku. Written on the spine label—in purple ink again, this time—simply, *FILM 1.*

Simon
October 20, 2000

Her aircon flicks off, self-timed, in the middle of the night.

I get up off the futon in the semidarkness, and carefully step over the dishes and plates piled by the step into the kitchen. Inside the bathroom I turn the light on for a second but it hurts, actually pains me, and I turn it straight off. I'm so thirsty, the aircon and alcohol have totally dehydrated me, but my stomach feels too small and I'm too nauseous to even think of drinking water. In the digital light from the clock in the kitchen I can see my body in the bathroom mirror, and already I look thinner, my arms less muscled but my stomach more so. I want to see that deeper line between thigh and stomach. That beautiful slant too soft and cool to be called any-thing but . . . what? That shadowed contour of pelvic muscle and stomach. I want it revealed. I use the bathroom. Sip a little water, wash it through my mouth and spit, brush my teeth with a finger and some foamy green toothpaste that's gritty to get rid of the chlorine taste, and then I pull the door gently closed to not wake her, and in the darkness of the tiny bath-room—a shub, a sink and toilet mounted on an angle, all in a space not much larger than a desk—flush.

I watch my shadow in the mirror, and inspect its angles. I consider being sick. I consider the burning tang in my mouth all night long. And her in the morning in this foreign place. The possibility; the probability of a kiss. I consider leaving right now, standing naked in the dark. Getting out now. And as the mirror recedes a kind of panic comes over me, a terrible freezing shiver that I'm trapped, my clothes scattered all through the sheets and plastic bags and her clothes in there, a foreign mess of gray shapes in the gray light of the streetlamp through the curtains, unsolvable. I have to sit down on the edge of the shub as the panic attack gains force, my heart banging fast in my chest that I somehow feel in slow motion. I can't leave, because I don't know the way back to the station. Money runs out. I didn't pay enough attention, didn't note which bus, what number it was, what stop we got off at, where that stop is in relation to here, the 7-11, any kind of landmark at all. Something all cold coming over me, in the heat out here, saliva flooding my mouth as if I might really be sick but that would be the worst, sober, or half-sober, a clenching, frozen salivated feel-ing, the conviction that I'm trapped, this is what really being trapped and helpless feels like, merciless, silent and speechless, I depend on her and she's lying to me, and a further nauseous leap of logic somehow imposed: that this is happening somewhere else, and that this has happened before, and that I'm missing things, or misreading things, in my absence something vital happened, now I'm only going through motions, things fitting too neatly, coming too easily, my response the only variable in a system that doesn't need me. I see as the panic attack rolls me frozen like a choppy wave under a waiting surfer, both a violent shaking infinitely detailed frenzy and a silent patient swell, I see as my eyes become accustomed to the darkness, flicking around the bathroom, a thin line of gray light under the door beginning to illuminate a hallucination of detail in here, foreign things, a C-shaped piece of waterproof carpet slotted around the base of the toilet, a miniature white Panasonic hairdryer with a Hello Kitty decal hanging by a flexible rubber clip on its handle from the empty towel rail, toiletries on the cistern, a tube of orange facemask with its name I can't read in hiragana, Nivea skin cream the only one in English, a small pink sponge, a pink razor, why is everything in pink, a Print Club sticker on the bathroom mirror that when I lean closer, trying to distract myself from the speed of my heart, which seems impossible, a battering that slows every movement I make down and makes every movement somehow absurd and exaggerated like I'm acting my existence in all these movements alone, and I lean closer, my eyes stronger, my head pounding, and in the tiny photo is her, Brigit, Michael, Catherine, an Indian boy I don't know, and behind it in the mirror is a dark oval in the darkness, as the cistern fills to the brim.

That must be me.

The next morning.

We're both dehydrated, hungover, and walking to the Softbox to rent some *X-Files*. In the drunk sex of the night before, we lost the bottles of VOLVIC water, all mixed in with the clothes and bags, coating the parquet completely, so the night was parched for both of us. This morning I lay on the futon, after three sleepless, breathless hours with no aircon, and watched Ariel sit naked on the floor and cover her entire body with skin moisturizer. This morning I made eggs and tomato on thick white Japanese toast for breakfast, and she said, "This is too perfect," shaking her head as though I was tricking her, or as if she didn't somehow deserve this. This morning I moved behind her as she washed the few dishes there were from breakfast, and I put my hands on her ass and my chest to her back, and she slipped sideways, away from me. This morning, a term Anton once used to use occurred to me. A term I've used in relation to others; a term I don't think I ever thought would be used in relation to me. A term I don't want to occur to me here, with her, because this is what I wanted.

The term is "Sportfuck."

Because my sunglasses, too, are lost in the minor chaos of that room, she has loaned me an old pair of Renaulds that belonged to her mother, and that may be incredibly expensive and appropriate for the wife of a diplomat, but look ridiculous on me, square and large, silver tabs above the lenses. But it's too bright and I've had too little sleep to refuse, so we're on our way through Hachioji in the morning, to the Softbox in the wrong sunglasses to rent *X-Files,* and even this, too, has some tinge of familiarity to it, as if I had dreamed or imagined this scene, and this is some attempt, by me, or this place, to color it in, fill in the gaps, convince me of something I'm growing more and more doubtful of.

And even when she's tired and dehydrated she is truly gorgeous, the one thing I can say and believe with complete conviction. As we walk beside a canal walled in with sloping concrete slabs and past an abandoned bicycle in a lonely clump of rushes the sun finds ten more colors in her hair and makes her skin almost vibrate, shine in a way that absorbs light, and in the daze of too little sleep and too much cheap red wine I can be both sick and high on the fact of her beauty; a step behind her in the wrong sunglasses and a crumpled linen shirt I am in her thrall.

"Ariel."

"Uh-huh."

"You speak French."

"Oui, un peu."

"Hold on a moment."

Beside the canal, we sit down on a massive shard of broken concrete sprouting rods of steel like the ligaments of an arm in the sun. I see the hills near Hachioji for the first time, forested mounds rising sharp and lime-green hazy from the edge of the urburban horizon of pylons and tawny buildings. Everything strange out here for being low; three and four stories and sprawled, violating some rule or agreement I had with Japan.

"Those are the first real hills I've seen here," I say. "Like, with trees."

"We've hiked those," she says, only half here. "It's a national park."

"Hey."

"Hey what."

"Jacques said something to me and I didn't ask him what."

She's relieved.

"I don't know much, you know."

"It was about Michael. I said something, asked him what he was doing, and he said, 'un grand guignol.' Like gee-nyol."

"A guignol is like a puppet. A marionette. But it's a character. The guignol is a character played by a puppet." She loves to know things. I let her talk, let her show off a little. She loves to be respected, so I will. I light a cigarette and let her talk because it's nice in the sun to let her be smart, let some other subject ease the tension. "He's a trickster. He makes you laugh. But you don't know if he's foolish or wise. Or if he's lying to you. Or if it matters."

"So a grand guignol is a like really grand version then."

"That's . . . maybe. Originally. But the grand guignol is something different. Did you juice that yet?"

"I don't have any fluids in my body," I say.

And she laughs for the first time today.

"Give it here," she says, "let's go."

I give her the cigarette and we leave the canal, take a dirty side street between two little fields of absurdly small, withered lettuces, a mess of wire, cracked and green skyhigh above us.

"How far is Softbox? Where the hell are we?"

"You're totally lost aren't you." She hands me back the cigarette. "It's a kind of play. A particularly bloody kind of play. Very violent and sexual. In Paris, at this one particular playhouse. Till twenty years after the war, when people'd lost their taste for it. And then the riots. Almost everyone dies, in extravagant ways."

"Like what ways."

"Eyes gouged, tongues cut out, you know."

"So what did he mean?"

"You know, Michael, Jacques, Anton. They've got things going on here. Drug stuff. Film stuff. Academic stuff. Art stuff."

"Stuff."

"You know."

I don't, and the cigarette's making me more nauseous so I give it to her, but it seems she doesn't feel too well either. She flicks it away into one of the parched little fields and behind her sunglasses her eyes could be anywhere.

"He hated it here. Michael. He actually hated it. You know what I said about New Zealanders arguing all the time? He was once a little like that. Maybe when you knew him. But he actually asked real questions. He was interested, you know? He was one of very few who ever actually listened. Here for a while everyone asks stuff and nods and tries and tells you about their life. You know, about their old jobs, their families and their pets, politics, music. Film or authors or painters or whatever they're into. We tell each other these stories without connection to anything here, anything that's real now. They're just the symptoms of a homesickness we didn't learn to live with yet. The only one the story is for is the teller. Any listener's just an excuse. But he listened, you know? To all kinds of fucked-up people as well. That anorexic from Toronto who said she was a vegan. Everybody knew. He didn't patronize people, or humor them. He wasn't trying to be the good guy. He just took time. And you could tell."

"You could tell."

"Yeah. You know why?"

"Why."

"He remembered every single little thing you told him."

"This doesn't sound so much like the guy I knew."

"Somehow, I don't think his . . . honor was at stake then."

I don't even make a face at this.

"He was so single-minded it was a little scary, you know? But here where all that's left of your old life is what you remember—someone who listens to that shit's just a saint. I trusted him."

"Did you . . . two. Are you."

"Oh Simon." She doesn't take this with a smile. But she doesn't stop, either. "All that stuff he's done, you know? All the awards. But he can be cruel."

"It was media theory, and history essays. The one I remember was called, 'Son et Lumière: Media Atrocity after Dien Bien Phu.' He showed a short film at lunch-hour, with all these exhibits, cartoons and stuff, and even though none of those guys even knew where like French Indochina was before that, people went along. There was some kind of vibe attached to him. At school he didn't turn up to classes and he didn't turn up for the prizegivings. It was a joke. We had a kind of free reign in seventh form."

"'Sound and Vision.' And you chauffeured him, right? You with your Trans-Am. What did you see?"

"I saw him reading. I saw him writing. I saw him drink half a bottle of Smirnoff and climb out the sunroof on the motorway round the Kapiti Coast." I sigh. What does she want to hear? "I felt him hug me. He did his real stuff alone, I guess."

"He studied war."

"He studied military atrocity. Any other subject and a kid like that would've had it beaten out of him before senior year."

"There's something so . . . fucked up . . . about people who look at terrible things and are kind."

I don't say anything.

But she laughs. "When he came back from Nanjing, he insisted Jacques go. He insisted. He paid for him, you know? Jacques was a kitchenhand. To see Mufu Mountain, cos he knew for damn sure he would love it. Paid for him to see some of China, to see this pretty thing."

"Ariel, he's just young, still. He's selfish, he's self-absorbed. A ticket to China's less than fifty thousand yen."

"I know. He's cruel. A mean, cruel brilliant guy who managed to arrange Brigit and Drew visas. Could have got himself deported."

"And them, Ariel. Do you really think it's such a sweet thing to do something that could get your friends deported? Or like, imprisoned?"

"It was their choice," she says.

"Was it? You're defending him."

"You're attacking him."

"He was my friend," I say.

"He was mine too."

She's shaking her head, and we walk in the sun down the long straight road for a few quiet minutes.

"Do you know this little J boy he's hanging with?" I finally ask.

She visibly flinches.

"What?" I say.

"Ko's . . . gone, now."

"Right, 'Ko.' Gone where?"

"You don't know, Simon. You don't know things that have happened."

"Tell me, then. Man, everyone's been so freaked out since I got back."

"Asia takes its revenge for our invasions. It does, Simon. Watch out. You only find out too late."

What can I say? This is not going how I wanted it to go, though certain things are becoming clearer.

"Michael went back to China in July and we haven't heard from him since," she says. "Some of us are worried."

"Why?"

"Because when he left he was down to a hundred and six pounds and acting really happy."

"He was thin."

"You don't know thin."

"In Japan, you get fat, or you get thin. Everyone knows this."

She thinks for a moment.

"I am a lazy hole through which the horror flows," she says at last. "I wish I were a fountain."

"What . . . is that . . . supposed to mean."

"A fountain."

"Uh-huh."

"Remember him, Simon."

"Come on."

"His words. Himself."

"He's self-obsessed."

"I always see him as some sad eye, turning the colors of what it sees. They say he's addicted to drugs. That he might be HIV-positive, now. People say he was arrested in Beijing once, for protesting with students. Like, who else do you actually personally know who people really argue about?"

I wait a long, long time, sweating out alcohol, greasy on my hand when I wipe my face. When I think back on those times, exile in New Zealand, there is one particular moment of him, and his family, that I always remember, that seemed to define some fundamental thing about them, but I can never quite explain what.

Parking the Trans-Am my father bought me outside their house on Bolton Street, an old expensive steep street near the motorway and the cemetery and the Botanical Gardens. Leaving it in second gear, the hill is so bad. Maybe it was a Friday or a holiday, but I was going to take him with me on a roadtrip all the way to Auckland. Seeing Meredith through the side window watching TV, lying on the floor looking like she'd sunk into the shag carpet, knees bent, her feet in white bobby socks hooked together, bobbing. A cushion from an armchair under her elbows. I stood in the porch, and banged on the front door with the leadlight windows, through which I could see the banister of the staircase, dark, rosy mahogany of the wall behind, strange shapes of light falling over it all from the huge stained-glass window above the stairs. Michael's mother's voice, calling out, "Meredith! Door!" Looking down at the little park bench where M & M apparently had to wait when they would lock themselves out. Saying hi, and running up the stairs. Hüsker Dü getting excited by the racket and galloping up after me. Andy nowhere to be seen. Andy always equaled "absent." Banging on Michael's door and barging in, tripping over the clumsy dog. Michael sitting at his desk, reading a huge old book. Looking at me and smiling with something that wasn't quite a squint, as if he had a headache. Hüsker Dü dropping his big sad head in Michael's lap, and Michael petting him, very slowly, staring down at his drooping tongue, or his teeth. Like he was examining him. A look on his face I can't really describe. Like horror, or something. Like strain. At that time, he was my best friend. We were sixteen or seventeen, I guess.

"Un grand guignol, then," I sigh. "I don't know." A pause. "Do you get tired of language problems?" I ask her. "I do."

"You don't know how tired," she says, and I've finally made her laugh again, just a little, even if in a dry, empty way.

We get on better when I act as if I could take or leave her. Is something wrong with me, or her, or us, in this? What am I trying to do? Another fool for Ariel's beauty, is what I guess I'm pleased to be.

The Softbox is only one floor, but that floor's bigger than the Tsutaya in Shibuya, which, however, goes up six more. I let her choose the videos, episodes from season six I think I've seen before, at home, but she hasn't, and it's something almost everyone has in common here, a near-blanket response to homesickness and the impenetrability of Japanese TV: *Buffy, ER, X-Files.* She knows the attendant here too, and they converse very briefly in Japanese, and she won't let me help pay, and we leave.

Ariel produces a caplet of hash oil from inside an empty minidisc case filed on her bookshelf. We tidy the room and open the front and veranda doors to air the apartment out, futilely in the humidity. I fold the futon and blankets into a messy flattened Z. Then she shuts the doors, closes the curtains, sets the thermostat on the aircon. The tape we have is tape six,

episodes fifteen and sixteen. The TV and stereo are to the right of the sliding doors, in the corner of the room, and along the same wall is where she
always rests her futon, so I do too, and we sit low, side by side, she to my
left and higher than me, my head and her head and shoulders resting
against the wall. The softness of the makeshift sofa means our hips and
thighs are touching as she leans over to me to fastforward the piracy warnings. She's seen the first episode already on a tape sent from home. Fastforward, in silence. Then as the credits roll—typed up, on a black screen:
Alpha, then *File No. 616;* and the same again in Japanese—she pulls a cigarette from a pack on the floor—she's found her Indian Spirits—and splits
the caplet in two. She dips a piece of guitar string in the smaller half and
smears a line of the oil thickly down the length of the cigarette. She looks
up to the screen and stares for a moment over me. Reads, *"Zetsumetsushu."*
She carefully cleans the oil off the string on the tip of the cigarette. *"The
first zing,"* she whispers, absorbed, closes the caplet, returns it and the guitar string to the MD case. *Presented in Dolby Sound Where Available.*

She lights the cigarette. It hisses and burns more reluctantly than usual.
I watch her lips in the lighter's light, mauve-tan and finely lined, a little dry
and full, and her closed eyes like in Michael's photograph as the cigarette
is passed to me, her concentration, her held breath, her lips shaped into a
kiss.

I take the cigarette from her and the episode begins.

We watch a ship approaching on a darkened ocean. Letters flick up as
if typed in the bottom left of the screen:

FREIGHTER T'IEN KOU
PACIFIC OCEAN
9:17 PM

The translation types up above it in two rows.

Next shot, in the freighter's hold, two young Chinese boys, one confident, one wary, approach a large metal crate sitting apart from the rest.
They speak in Chinese and yellow subtitles appear at the bottom of the
screen; the kanji equivalents now vertical and white on the right:

"Come on, Fong. Don't be scared," the confident one says.

"Maybe it's a tiger."

The confident one slides back a peephole, shines his torch inside. Shot
of low red glowing eyes.

There's a growl, the eyes leap.

Crash.

Fong falls to the ground, terrified. The crate shudders and rocks absurdly, then abruptly stops.

The other Chinese steps forward daringly, and slaps, then kicks the box.

I hand her back the cigarette, and speaking to the screen—she's too close to turn and look her in the eye as she watches the screen over me—I say, "I asked you because you're part-Canadian, right, you speak some French. But if the guignol thing is actually French, how do you know about it?"

I hear the cigarette hiss dully, as the Chinese boys peer into the box, a pause, her exhale.

"Jacques," in a low, husky whisper. "Look, Simon. They look like you. Sexy little Chinese boys."

"Jacques told you?"

"Jacques." She coughs.

Unreadable expressions on the Chinese boys' faces as they peer inside the box.

Now there's a shot of the T'ien Kou tied up at the docks somewhere American. A senior sailor and two Customs officers descend the stairs into the hold. Two men are missing, the sailor tells them. The cage and hold were locked in Hong Kong. They find a man crouching, peering at blood leaking from the crate. Introduces himself, he's Detweiler; inside the crate is an animal that belongs to him. It needs care. The sailor opens the crate's lid; shot through the opened gap to the faces of the sailor, Detweiler, the officers.

Inside, the bitten bloodied bodies of those two Chinese crew.

The credits roll and the hash comes on, a tired wave, a slop on the beach, a poor relative of my panic attack. I sink a little lower on the futon, my feet further out on the floor than hers.

FBI HEADQUARTERS
7:10 PM

Mulder and Scully in an office, and I'm starting to have trouble keeping my eyes open. The episode runs on as I start to doze off for real, and it's all about these two merchant marines found in a crate locked from the outside, dead from bite wounds.

She's sceptical, he's wry—"Bad dog"—and cut to an attack on a customs officer in Bellflower, California, by a truly awful-looking husky wolf-type dog, with big gums and red eyes and growling, then screams.

Back to the docks, and I can barely pay attention to the slow parts without action or dialogue, and there's an officer from U.S. Fish and Wildlife and Mulder being "kooky" and suddenly the wolfish-looking Detweiler again, and I'm somehow slightly saddened by my boredom, my tiredness, the predictability of this episode, it's a Wan Shang Dhole, a supposedly extinct Chinese dog with mythic qualities that Detweiler caught in China. Mulder conveniently knows a lot about this dog, but suddenly there's a report of the attack on the Customs officer in Bellflower, and it's all beginning to blur together for me, and in the quiet moments my eyes almost close. Ariel has not made a sound since the episode began. We're watching in silence. My neck is getting cricked, but I'm too weary to move, I've seen too far ahead already, and I realize that I no longer care, that this no longer works, that these tapes used to do something, have some soothing qualities—of distraction, humor you don't have to dumb down to communicate, the comforts of sarcasm—that now have somehow faded. I am restless and totally exhausted at the same time.

A different U.S. Fish and Wildlife guy finds the Customs officer's hand by a dumpster, and as he carries his torch and noosed pole through the dark buildings and staircases, I start wondering about wildness in man-made places, questionable or indefinable motives, tenuous holds on the sanity of space, how what's wild can make what is old new, thoughts that seem not quite mine, my eyes so tired now, blood throbbing and sore, itching, and as my body relaxes I feel Ariel relax too, for perhaps the first time, my shoulder to her side, joined from neck to knee, and is it because of the hash or is it because I'm falling asleep I don't know and can't care, and the Fish and Wildlife guy sees the silhouette of a man through the dry ice in the basement of this building and calls out, "Hey, hello sir. Maybe you've seen a dog I'm looking for. Sir? Can you hear me?" and it all seems to mean much more than it must and as in the dry ice the silhouette of a man warps to a beast and the Fish and Wildlife guy cries out, and tries to run, and as the Chinese dog savages him, I fall asleep.

It's night in a Tokyo park on the cusp of summer and fall. Typically, there's gravel instead of grass, huge trees, swings, a few young J boys and girls

talking and making out on scattered park benches. The darkness comes
down strongly just outside this park where there are unlit buildings, old,
but their architecture indefinable, neither Western nor J nor anything I
know combined. I am walking briskly through the park, knowing I'm
being hunted by Alsatians. So what I'm looking for is somewhere to hide.
Although the park is designed for elementary school kids and none of the
swingsets or jungle gyms are high enough or steep enough to escape a big
dog, there are, inexplicably, ladders here and there, mounted vertically in
the ground. But I try to climb one and it's not firm, it sways, and sinks
skewedly, leaning further off to one side. The higher I climb the more I
exaggerate the lean. The dogs are just beyond the circle of trees, running,
patient, knowing somehow these ladders are useless. The J boys and girls
aren't bothered. I'm thinking sure, but these dogs were my friends, I love
dogs, why do they hate me, why do they want me. I come to another ladder and can tell it's useless too, protruding up out of the gravel on a slight
but pregnant lean. It's all, of course, silent. A woman's voice, not Scully.
You admire it, don't you. A man's voice. *I admire its ability to survive.* Softly,
softly, cushioned in my ear, nothing more than a child's whisper, *alien.*
Telling me a long time ago, she's an only child, her mother scolding her,
for as they sit and watch TV, Ariel shouts at the characters, exhorts them
to *stop,* to *go,* to *yes,* to *no, oh no.* Her mother says, Ariel, don't. You scare
me. I make for the edge of the darkened park, a place I seem to fear to go,
with a determined stride. At this the dogs suddenly break from the tree-
line, coming for me, not red-eyed, just dark cantering shapes appearing
independently, staggered through the trees. At the edge of the park there's
a final ladder, leaned, this time, against a shambling house. Around the
base of the ladder are littered pieces of broken white dinner plates. I
snatch one up, and climb the ladder—so slowly, though, my legs are thick
and terribly stiff and unused to this—and halfway up, I turn awkwardly,
the ladder behind me, to try and fight off the first two dogs. Not to fight,
but to kill the dogs, it is clear. I hold the half-plate high above my head in
two hands, fingers clamped around the rim to use the jagged broken edge
as a weapon as the two dogs with silent speed are half up the ladder in the
darkness before me, satisfied with nothing but my face, my eyes and
cheeks and tongue, and I half-step backward up another rung, raise the
plate high and then hack down into the beautiful, tawny-furred brow of
the first Alsatian, its too-near brown eyes that belong to . . . Hüsker Dü, I
realize, Michael's dog, I hack down hard again into its sad and pretty skull,

above the warm, brown familiar eyes, torn, hacking away, backing away, looking for brains or higher ground.

She tenses when I wake.

The first thought, the first realization past my glad viciousness the only thing that works, the necessity of power, is that she had relaxed, finally, beside me. That somehow she is intimidated by me, that I read her wrong. That I should be kind to her, and in this way get what I want from her.

"Oh I . . . had a dream," I mutter, my voice hoarse from the hash.

"You were jerking," she whispers softly. "Your feet moved."

I snuggle closer to her, and there's a click and a hum as the aircon comes on again.

"A bad dream," I say, and I lift my left hand and place it on her thigh beside me.

She doesn't move.

We stay like this. On screen I'm almost shaking.

She lays her hand on mine, and moves it between her legs. I cup her gently, stunned and dazed for moments, the hard denim of the fly, the line of the seam down my palm and fingers. She parts a little and I start to grow hard, and start, too, to massage her, tensing and relaxing my hand against her, the cool, lifeless denim here, the soft it follows into a warmer fall.

She's not breathing, her mouth close above my ear, her lips moving in my hair, then she exhales in a plosive gentle sigh I feel hot and shivery on my scalp.

This is what I do for minutes more, leaned almost away from her to reach down left-handed, trying not to look at the television, the red-eyed dog or Mulder's bemused faces—just my hand and warmer denim, her breath, my half-hardness pressing through my trousers.

Then she shifts beside me, her right shoulder presses over mine, and my hand slips from out between her legs and she moves down beside me, her hair against my cheek taut and springy as I turn to her to kiss, but she's unbuckling her belt, pushing off a tiny white bobby sock with a white-socked toe, then unzipping her jeans, pushing them down intently, and pinkcream satin panties underneath and the softness and ivory smoothness of her thighs almost shining next to that satin is almost too shocking—I stop, with just my belt undone, and up on one elbow have to lay my hand inside and feel her, have to touch that contour of her leg, shocked at its softness, the play of a ribbonlike muscle under my fingers as she shifts to let me. With my left arm jammed beneath me I try to undo my fly but leave it as she turns to kiss, her eyes closed as in that photo again and her lips shaped to kiss are just open, the colors of her lips too much, and we kiss and I gently place my hand over her again, and then up onto her stomach, under the hem of her T-shirt, I don't know why, just to feel her, but she takes my hand again and pushes me back down. I cup her harder this time, and she makes a sound in our kiss, our tongue tips touching, playing, and I hook her panties with my thumb and drag them down and she lifts up and reaches down and helps and when they're gone lays back and lets her legs relax against mine, back against the futon, wider, and I cup the crispness of her pubic hair, shocked again like a virgin by it, and the hot wetness makes a line down my hand like the denim and she makes a different sound because I am too rough.

She pulls back from the kiss, eyes closed, she whispers, her breath on my lips, tells me, and I'm glad, "long...smooth strokes," and this time this is what I do.

Gently, fingertip alone sometimes, stunned that someone so strong, so beautiful could be so sensitive she can hardly bear to be touched up there, I am careful.

After a while of this she relaxes more, her legs open wider, and she reaches over to me. I unzip myself and she takes me in her hand as I heel my trousers off.

As she gets closer to coming she whispers, "Oh you feel so good," right by my cheek and soon she stops stroking me, and clenches her hand, a ring on her finger pinching me that I ignore, silent, for her. Her eyes never open once, her cheeks redden, and she shivers all over when she comes, shivers in three separate moments and I close my eyes then, to not be cold, to not watch her coming, to simply feel her shiver, the subtlety and surprise of her, her soft abrupt squeeze and a hot wetness come on fingers.

But I don't.

I watch her, and I do it all so coldly, almost slowly.

We lie like this a little while.

The wind chimes tone again out there, and she stirs. I look over at the television to see the credits rising up the screen and kanji appearing on the side. Outside it's grown dark and I'm still half-hard beside her, my hand still in her thighs.

She stirs again, and then she moves, sits up. She peels off her T-shirt and in just her bra she stands without looking at me and disappears into the bathroom.

I take my hard-on in my wet hand and masturbate back to hardness. Try not to look at the television, judge the static there from the flickers on the wooden floor.

The flush from the bathroom, the click and squeak as the door opens.

As she steps into the dimmed room and undoes her bra with astonishing speed and familiarity, flicks it casually into the corner, I'm smacked like with a hammer by a wave of déjà vu, impossible to define or explain, an astonishing wave of recognition, or memory, or connection like the sight of the dog's eyes and as she stands over me, steps astride me, takes me in her hand and feeds my cock inside her slowly I'm rock hard despite or because of my acceptance that I'm living in loops like in another's dream, that here we all dream the same, and they are true, that she does not love me, the sensation of her is stronger for my giving up to it, and as I thrust into her she undoes the buttons of my shirt and places her hand flat on my own heart, her breasts a gentle sway between her strong arms and I'm absolutely consciously aware that I am giving up something, and becoming something, and though I do not do it gladly I do it with all my strength.

Meredith
October 2000

Sitting in the bedroom the way she always does to watch movies—on the floor, back to a bed, snacks at hand—Meredith took a long drink of the wine from the bottle. She lit a cigarette in the beige room and, hearing a thick metallic banging deep inside the hotel, but choosing for now to ignore it, she pressed play on the new camera.

The screen flickered once. Static appeared and ran for several seconds. Then the picture suddenly came clear. It was handheld, late afternoon by the light, somewhere busy.

In the corner of the screen in green digital, the date 05/29/00, and the time, 19:03. The first shot opens with a close-up of a promotional poster for a film. The gold lettering at the top of the poster read, *THE DIARIES OF JOHN RABE,* and beneath that, smaller, in white, cursive this time: *"The Oskar Schindler of China"—Iris Chang.* On the poster an airbrushed picture—the Japanese-style airbrushed or painted version of the original—of Jon Voight as Rabe, with a swastika armband on his left arm, slung protectively around the shoulders of Maggie Cheung, dressed as a Chinese nurse. Arrayed behind them were smaller scenes of burning houses, plumes of smoke, soldiers marching, a mass grave, and behind the two central figures, a bleeding rising sun.

Above the credits, more white cursive: *THE IMPORTANT, SHOCKING, MOVING TRUE STORY OF THE NAZI HERO OF THE NANKING MAS-SACRE.* Beneath this, in katakana and English: SPECIAL PREVIEW SCREENING.

Zooming out to reveal a young Japanese girl staring up at the poster, hands hanging limply at her sides, head slightly cocked. She seemed distracted; her eyes focused somewhere before the poster.

The cameraman said, in a French accent, "She is not looking at the poster. But she is not looking at me. Though she knows I am standing right here. Looking at her. Filming her."

When he says "here," the sound is something like an effort; someone used to successfully not saying "eah."

"This girl is looking . . . you know . . . at the idea of being looked at. At how she looks, to me, looking. This is very common in the girls in this city, I think."

It is Jacques.

She's not seen him in nine or more months, but his voice is instantly familiar.

Jacques, who taught some poor Japanese secretaries awful English for weeks after he arrived.

Who she met the first time she had come to Japan. Jacques, pottering around the world, so aimless she adored him and worried for him. Who she met at her gaijin house when Jacques was working long hours at a French restaurant, *Le Toile,* and who brought her home double-baked, left-over chou à la crème, the pastry all brown, glazed and flaking, the custard cream only good for the one night he'd bring them to her. He'd get home exhausted, and lie on her futon (at the gaijin house, to avoid sharing the penthouse) telling her stories about the "fascist chefs" (pronounced "fah-

seest") who would literally kick the help in the ass, including him (she'd
make immense efforts not to picture this: his surprised face, his jump), and
anecdotes of how the Japanese treated him when he was in uniform, compared to when he was out in the street. And the things he was always *going*
to do. She'd nibble a chou à la crème, watch his shaven head and his gray
eyes so earnest and foreign she couldn't not love him, and lend him yen,
and think about how soon she was going to leave him. Jacques who wrote
long letters to his little sisters, who had names she loved, too: *Geneviève.*
Sandrine. Whose father, he had told her, had damaged his hearing in the
Congo the year Jacques was born. That he had paid his fare to Tokyo with
money his mother (*Laure,* like a sigh) had loaned him. And when she
found out what French men were doing in the Congo in 1976 she didn't
press him for any more information on his family than all he ever volun-
teered. Who hissed when he came, a low sound through his teeth like a
"tss."

Jacques, who told her he was making a film. And who she couldn't tell
she only liked men who were good liars. Jacques, who looked like a star,
and thought like a housewife and was good for her for a while. And she
wondered what he was doing for money now. And she thought, he's still
not touching J girls, then, and the thought was, for a moment, only a little
calculating.

The camera panned past the Japanese girl to reveal she was part of a
long queue of people, unmoving; only distinguishable from the crowd as a
queue because, unlike the hundreds of others moving beyond them in the
shot, the line was not moving. The group also made more distinct by the
greater ratio of Westerners to Japanese. Maybe a third, waiting in a line of
forty. In the background, loud tinny music played with a recorded voice,
repeating prices of shoes on sale in brash, distorted Japanese. The constant
mumble and hum of the crowd. Their clothes said summer.

"Are you shooting?" asked a voice out of shot, only just audible, the
accent unidentifiable.

"Yes, shooting now," Jacques said. "And am a little too fucking hot,
also."

Pan left to find at the very end of the queue a recessed doorway with a
raised entrance. On the door there were torn notices and spraypaint.
Standing in the doorway holding sheafs of paper were Michael and a
Japanese boy Meredith didn't recognize. They were both slim and pale,
their hair shaved very short. The Japanese boy was maybe seventeen or

eighteen and wore a khaki-green military T-shirt with MARINE written on the chest. A silver ring in his left ear. Michael's T-shirt had a stencil, too: BUNDESWEHR. They were both wearing fatigue trousers. The Japanese boy looked distracted. He was staring at the queue, his eyes bloodshot and tired. Michael's head was bowed; looking at the papers in his hands.

Meredith tapped her cigarette on the silver tray and took another gulp of the wine. She exhaled in pleasure, breathing up to the ceiling as the first little buzz came on.

"Cheers, baby," she said to herself, and was suddenly shocked at the sound of her own voice, her fun compromised by hearing the sound of her own accent. She reached down and paused the video. In the silence that followed she looked round the large bedroom, listening hard. The hard metallic banging sound she had heard before was still there, but not coming from inside the hotel, she realized. It rattled rapidly, and subsided. Knocking hard, then falling off. She could hear it and feel it too, insistently vibrating through the floor, in her calves and thighs. But she realized then that it was coming from outside, through the wall of curtained windows.

When she turned back to the screen, Michael was looking up at the camera and grinning. She stared at the paused smile and tried to think of the last time since school she had ever seen him grinning and could not locate the memory.

She pressed play, and the hollow whistle and scrape of wind on the camera's mic echoed, and his voice filled the room.

"Okay. I thought I'd start this with a couple interesting things," he said to the camera. "First, it turns out that more NZ males are eighty-sixed and subsequently blackballed from Tokyo clubs than any other nationality. They're known—renowned, actually—for being large and sexually aggressive. Where they come from this is tolerated. The other thing is that the Nationalists' Jeeps and vans are now military green and they're wearing khaki fatigues as opposed to the regulation black and they have been seen in Shibuya today. We're in Shibuya by the way. Outside . . ."

"Cinema Rise," Jacques said from behind the camera.

"Cinema Rise. We don't know if they know about the showing of this film, if it has anything at all to do with it. We're staying cool."

He smiled. The Japanese boy didn't. Michael looked down at his papers and then to the boy.

"Okay," he said softly to him.

The Japanese boy sighed. He looked up at the queue and then to the camera and then back to the sidewalk. The camera zoomed in on his tired-looking face. He smiled briefly down at the ground, shyly, as if thinking how he might appear, and his eyes flicked up to the camera once.

In a low voice, only barely audible above the crowd, he said in perfect American-accented English, "My name is Ko Ishikawa and I'm sixteen." He looked up at the camera again, as if for affirmation, and the shot nodded. He looked back down to the ground. "I am currently . . . taking a break . . . from completing a Master's in Public History at NYU in the States. I was born and raised in Tokyo, and I completed my undergraduate degree at Keio University here. I am an only child and am . . . currently . . . estranged from my parents."

His mouth worked something between a wince and a smile at this last. The grin settled in a thin, serious line. He turned slightly to Michael and mumbled something. A brief moment and he lifted a lit cigarette to his lips and inhaled hard, then breathed out toward the ground.

When he lifted his eyes to the camera again they were deeply black.

Staring into the camera, he said, "Once peoples find themselves both capable and motivated in lying for a cause the concept of truth is immediately anachronism. Superfluous." Meredith blinked. "The concept of justice as moral force is displaced by jurisprudence. The combative legal process which at its least polysemic and least ambiguous and most effective is dismissed by history as the kangaroo court. At Rabaul Australians were trying Japanese military personnel for conducting kangaroo courts in the war, courts that were in fact legal under Japanese military law. And these trials themselves had to be sped up on American and international—political—imperatives. Kangaroo courts for kangaroo courts. At its most encompassing, at its most multicultural. . . . "

He paused, and inhaled deeply from the cigarette again. Meredith noticed he pronounced multi as "mull-tie." Forehead crinkled, she stared at the boy.

"When it is most *true* to the components it is comprised of, the combative system becomes this battle of propagandas. Essentially . . . lying for the cause. Death and massacre and gangrape become just . . . factors in the dispositions of power between parties. That are most generally nation-states. The . . . appeal to moralities outside the jurisprudence is no longer acceptable legally to us because this means . . . the selection of a morality and so the exclusion of all other moralities. This is a fascism. So in the twentieth and twenty-first centuries the appeal is tacitly made to . . . poli-

tics. The rape and death of...a child...is systematized...made an exhibit
...a massacre as a disposition of power...and legal retribution whichever
way...is just another disposition....This is the martial male apocalypse.
...This is the logical end of...of...both patriarchy and multiculturalism
and international law....The futility of the particular..."

He dragged on his cigarette. He glanced up at the camera again.

"I hold that the logical outcome of international law is...a maelstrom
no single enculturated human can fathom, and I'll cite the endless IMTFE
...completely forgotten for these reasons...as...the inevitable legal
wrangle when...external moralities...*have* to be brought to bear on cultures clashing...and that those external moralities are determined on...
and always will be...*political* grounds...and that what any court must do
...in these situations...is single out...is compromise...is *scapegoat*..."

He dragged hard on his cigarette again, and gestured violently to the
ground with it.

"And I hold, too, that the revered Mishima's...militarism was totally
linked with his misogyny and effeteness...and essential...*cruelty,* and that
turning to nationalism in search of identity is both fundamental...and...
fucking...*weak....*"

He broke off, shaking, staring down. He glanced quickly up at
Michael, then back to the sidewalk.

"Alright," Michael said to the boy. He looked up to the camera.

"Il a seize ans," Jacques murmured, not loud enough for the pair to
hear.

"And one more thing," the boy said, looking up again. "In interviews,
years after the massacre, soldiers were quoted as saying...that the Chinese
women who were forced into becoming prostitutes for the Imperial Army
were referred to, and thought of, as 'public toilets.' The consequences...of
this...for what a cock is...and what an erection is...for what having these
things is...and for what heterosexual sex can ever be...are something law
and history...can't explain...to a man. Can't explain how it is possible to
ever...have...the blindness...to have the ignorance...and the temerity
...the fucking *gall*...to be proud...of being...a *man.*"

He turned to Michael and whispered something.

Michael looked at the ground and nodded.

The Japanese boy spat.

Meredith stared at the image of the boy on the screen. The twilight in
Shibuya caught the curve of his jaw under his ear, a fine shadow, a blur of

darkness, as he frowned down. She took a big gulp of the wine, and stubbed her cigarette out. The banging sound seemed to be growing louder. It sounded like *buhbuhbuhbuhbuh. Buhbuhbuhbuhbuh.* Meredith relaxed further against the end of the bed as the alcohol came on. Almost okay now to wonder idly about the kinds of people Michael always seemed drawn to; to wonder idly without feeling too much pressure to think of how to find this Ko boy without being able to read a phonebook.

Simon
October 20

After the sex she rises off me and turns off the aircon, slides open the veranda door and disappears.

I wait a few moments alone, and then I stand and walk to the door. My cock still wet from her, dripping my cum onto the floor.

Has this all happened before?

Out on the veranda she's sitting naked and beautiful on a deckchair in the darkness, smoking a cigarette and crying and staring out through the black trees.

I stand at the door like that: not moving, staring out at the black trees too.

Meredith
October 2000

On screen Michael was now looking a little shyly up at the camera. The camera nodded to him, and he leafed through some of the pages in his hands. Then, "Alright. So, a little context for what's going on here. The UN war crimes trials for Yugoslavia and Rwanda have created some renewed interest in the debate over the idea of international law's jurisdiction over sovereign nations and the concept of crimes against peace as an indictable offense. The founding documents for this concept were the judgments at Nuremberg and the International Military Tribunal for the Far East, which was held here in Tokyo, in the same building, actually, where Mishima died, and anyway, is largely unknown and misunderstood. Many Serbs are actually claiming similar things to what Ko believes. That the convictions are never more than, maybe not so much the slapping of a wrist, as the cutting off of one single hand, in retaliation—political retaliation—for crimes, ex post facto declared *as* crimes in the case of the IMTFE, crimes that the parties or the countries they represent handing down those judgments have been guilty of for literally centuries. Colonialism, empire building, extermination, genocide and war on the basis of race, color and religion. And that the cutting off of a hand is largely symbolic. The scapegoat. Lord Wright was the first ever chairman of the UN War Crimes Commission and he said it best: 'All that can be done is to make examples.' Nothing is holy. Examples to who? If this was the actual agenda of the IMTFE, and if the actual results prove anything, then the Tribunal is not an example-maker, it's a propitiation that gained all its flavor from the public's boredom. If three hundred thousand civilian lives in a month and a half are that cheap, what are you worth?"

"Come on," Jacques said.

"I'm asking you."

"I'm not answering. Move on."

"We have to do this, Jacques," Michael said. "Anyway, I think it's well-known that Khrushchev faked the Tanaka Memorial and that what the General had in mind, and what the army had in mind, and, according to Bergamini, Hirohito too, was nothing more or less quote, immoral than a Napoleonic, Roman or British Empire. An Asian empire from Manchuria to Papua New Guinea. Stability in the region. Japan like a baby held in the arms of the colonies. It's the execution—the means, not the ends—that I've been . . . thinking about. And the subsequent lights those means can be cast in."

Michael looked intently at the camera.

"Did you know Hirohito was an amateur mycologist, Jacques?"

"No. Continue."

"The film showing today is the . . . story if we can call it that . . . of John Rabe. The Nazi doctor who was based in Nanking in the thirties. Who administered the International Safety Zone and saved thousands of Chinese lives by sheltering them under the swastika and threat of international exposure while the soldiers pillaged the city. Nanking was a beautiful city, nestled in a fold of the Yangtze, maybe sixteen square miles completely walled, with gigantic gates the size of air balloons, named Water, Radiant Flower, Great Peace, Tranquility. There were the hospitals, international factories, the universities, and the great tomb of Sun Yat-sen outside the walls on Purple Mountain. In the early thirties after Mukden and Marco Polo the Imperial Army was ranging through Manchuria fairly independently, while here the civilian politicians were being lied to and sidestepped and repeatedly assassinated if they protested or tried to intervene. During Mukden, the General and War Minister Minami lied his way past the Prime Minister who escaped with his life, unlike the men before or after him. Anyway, the invasion of China for real began in thirty-seven. After Shanghai was taken the Chinese soldiers retreated up the Yangtze to Nanking, and Rabe set up the safety zone in the city to protect civilians from the invasion and the subsequent alleged massacre.

"This film is based on his diaries, Iris Chang's book, and the stories of the people he saved. The West is lapping it all up, the same way it lapped up *Devils at the Doorstep,* Chang's *Rape of Nanking,* all the controversies in the eighties over the lacunae in children's textbooks with regard to the Rape and all the other atrocities outlined in the IMTFE evidence. What Roger Rosenblatt called America's omnivorous appetite for all things World War Two. The taste for war, anyhow.

"The Japanese are not. Lapping it up. Their kids aside, I mean. The fact that this film is even being shown here is something of a testament to the fact that some Japanese want to—and do—apologize and make reparations, some want to deny, but most, especially our age bracket, really don't have a clue what happened. Most of our generation in the West don't either.

"What we have here is a film, quote, *based,* on the diaries. Representation cannot exist without a project. Culture is a straitjacket and the very ground you stand on. True multiculturalism is always war. This is Fish. This is the quote, 'debate,' I got from university in the name of an education. I would have preferred a list of facts, quite honestly. But the metaphor for this is what Ko was talking about: the combative legal process. Where the judgment is always partisan and usually American. That's why Ko abandoned his M.A. and came back. Because of the necessary appeal to an external morality in Anglo-American jurisprudence, especially in the IMTFE, whose charter was written by its own judges with MacArthur's hand guiding the pen. A morality which was not Chinese nor

Japanese...but brought to bear on them anyway. Okay, but Chang's project was memorial, indictment, a looking back. Chang who claimed the book was written with George Santayana's immortal warning in mind: that those who cannot remember the past are condemned to repeat it. But living here where all things meet we know nothing is immortal. Chang, the 'Chinese-American,' as like, panicked Japanese 'official' scholars, totally aware how long she spent on the *New York Times* bestseller list are always pointing out. As if, although raised and educated in America, being born Chinese explains her completely. As if that dams up her fury. Which it may do. A lot of these revisionist Japanese projects are being very openly touted as a looking-forward, creating relationships, bygones be bygones. It's not about Ishihara and Morita and saying no to the West anymore. Though ironically, Ishihara famously denied Nanking too. It's about cementing relationships with new US administrations. Histories are currencies. They fluctuate in relation to one another. Their relationships to other histories make a country weak or strong. The drive for preeminence is the same: to gain the place to stand where there is leverage. There is no true here, anymore, no memory; just weak or strong. Truth makes for more moral war. What's the difference between the strategy of exaggeration and propaganda and simplification in the cause of alerting the public to an event, whether recent or historic, and the same strategies in the cause of denial and downplaying to suppress what is perceived as hysteria and xenophobia? They're the same thing. They use the same techniques. The blurs in evidential citings, the shaky sources that only lead to more shaky sources and eventually get lost in time."

Ko looked up at this. "It's funny, but the denials often seem more pedantically academically rigorous." The camera zoomed in on him. "It's not really funny."

"This film takes it a step further. Representation of a representation. I mean how trustworthy are diaries as a form of historical record? This film is so far from the event itself that it's safe. This, incidentally, is also the logical fraudulent end of Emerson's prediction of stories—novels—giving way to diaries and autobiographies. The idea of truth becomes a special guest star. I loathe the historical novel. It's a decadent, corrupt genre that makes claims it cannot fulfill from behind a veil of chronological color. But this is taken one more step. The diaries become films, propagandizing a man's bravery. I have a copy here of the script for this film's trailer, that's been showing in mostly arthouse theatres all over the world for a few

weeks now. They got Corey Bartlett on board for the voice-over. Heir to
the baritone throne of trailer voice-overs. Check out this copy: 'Four years
before Pearl Harbor . . . deep in the heart of China . . . another battle raged.
. . . ' You can hear the pregnant pauses. 'As the Japanese invasion sped up
the Yangtze . . . an ancient city prepared for the worst. . . . One man knew
what was coming . . . and for a forbidden love . . . would face the might of
the Imperial Army . . . and the Third Reich. . . . To save the people and the
woman he loved. . . . The wrong man in the wrong place at the wrong time
. . . will try and make a difference to thousands. . . . While time runs out for
a city . . . a people . . . and an age. Jon Voight. Maggie Cheung. Universal
Pictures presents. A Martin Hammacher film.' Cue titles.

"Bartlett is a genius, but Rabe never *had* a mistress for Christ's sake.
They're already proclaiming this film a 'document.' We know the project
is not a search for truth, not a portrait of a man, not a condemnation of a
massacre, not an artistic examination of what real meanings of 'massacre,'
'gangrape,' 'slaughter,' 'torture' might be or have been. It's about titillation. The West loves the disaster and the horror. Hands off when it's real
and not financially beneficial to intervene, but in film, on a page and it's
art, with truth as a moral justification. It's a safe thrill to look at death.
Especially if it's Asian. The Rape of Nanking is a porn web-ring."

"Come *on*," Jacques said.

"Alright," Michael said. "What we have is a single photograph. The
Chinese claim three hundred thousand lives and the Japanese hotly refute
it. There are various claims on various bases from the dissenting Japanese.
All essentially saying far, far less than that, and mostly soldiers, not civilians, and either no rapes, or very few rapes, immediately punished. So one
photograph is as good a place to start as any. It all comes down to this. We
have three copies. Three sources. All different; all linked, all used in major
works on this issue. Chang's copy from *The Rape of Nanking*. The copy
used by the Japanese Professor of History from Keio University, Professor
Matsudaira, that he showed at the Foreign Correspondent's Club in Tokyo
in 1999. And the Chinese Nationalists' copy shown in their book *A Record
of Japanese Atrocities*. Two years ago the Nanking Museum was displaying
it there, also. This is it. Chang's copy."

He held up a small black and white photograph to the camera. The
camera shakily moved toward it, zoomed fluidly in and held it there, all
grays, with a single pink and nailed fingertip at a corner.

The photo shows a section of a bridge, made from rough-hewn, uneven lengths of timber. Behind the bridge, the sky is white, and the branching of a tree is starkly outlined. On the bridge there are maybe fifteen people. Their clothes—all but one—are difficult to distinguish, but the first one is certainly a woman, maybe late teens, early twenties, in a thick dress, tight around her abdomen, long to her ankles. She is tall and turned looking down to the river, in midstep. At her stomach she is either clasping her hands or holding a handkerchief in two hands. Her hair is cut in a bob. To her right is a small girl whose hair is cut the same. To her left is what appears to be a young boy. Other figures behind her on the bridge are wearing long garments, similar to hers, but the quality of the photo has blurred their details. There are six or seven heads, most of them hooded, or wearing some kind of bonnet. Some whose faces are visible look toward the camera. Because of the photo's quality and their long garments, it is hard to distinguish exactly what they are wearing. One may be carrying a baby, or just a bundle of clothes. The starkness of the sky, the bare tree, the thick clothing; it's winter.

The only seemingly unambiguous point of reference is the single figure in the center of the bridge. He is a soldier, Japanese, carrying a rifle on his shoulder. There is space around him on the bridge while the others walk in groups. His height and bearing suggest that the others on the bridge are mostly female, or children. Behind the young woman, there is a silhouette, long, thin, parallel with the soldier's rifle. It may be there is a second soldier carrying a rifle also. It was hard for her to tell.

Meredith saw a bridge being crossed; a single Japanese soldier, armed with a rifle; a group of people crossing with him, but not close to him. Outside: *buhbuhbuhbuhbuh, buhbuhbuhbuhbuh.* She saw the silhouette of the second gun and shifted uncomfortably against the end of the bed.

The camera lingered on the black and white photo for several seconds, then it was gone, suddenly replaced by a blur of shapeless colors as the lens struggled to adjust to a long shot of the queue.

Michael's voice: "Okay. Let's find someone."

Shakily, the shot followed Michael's back out onto the street and into the crowds.

Alongside the queue, passing the shoulders in T-shirts and haltertops and tanktops. Mostly black or black hair dyed brown, but every fourth or fifth head was taller, and the foreigners seemed big and heavy and pale in the collage, their clothes ill-fitting, shabbier. There were necklaces and headphones, bag straps on thin shoulders. Meredith counted four Louis

Vuitton handbags. She checked the green digital date in the corner of the screen again: 05/29/00. The new Stephen Sprouse designs hadn't yet made it to Japan, so the relentless chocolate and fawn; the interlacing logos. She felt relieved, a little lighthearted, just for a second. The camera panned back over the queue, and the differences became clear. The Japanese looked away; spoke to each other, looked at the ground. The boyfriends stood a little straighter beside their girlfriends. One girl nearest Jacques on the fringe of the queue lifted a timid V-sign, but lost her courage and began to giggle, clutching her friend's arm, burying her face in a bare slim shoulder. But the foreigners stared back. A tall white boy in a Tokyo Giants cap back against the theatre wall sneered at the camera. Jacques zoomed in on him and he lifted a middle finger. Zoom out, pan past to a red-haired woman with a Japanese girl who sneered too, waved sarcastically.

"Jacques," Michael said.

Back, and an untidy gathering of focus. He was standing by a Japanese girl in a white linen shirt. Meredith saw the Louis Vuitton strap on her shoulder and groaned aloud. The girl was smiling shyly, eyes flicking up to the camera, down to the ground, up to Michael's T-shirt.

"Okay," Michael said. "Hello, there."

She giggled, bowed slightly, mumbled, "Hello."

"My name is Thomas, and we're students at Keio University here in Tokyo. We're wondering if we could take a little of your time while you're stuck here in this queue to ask you some questions."

She giggled again, looked at the camera, and didn't answer.

Michael said, "Can we ask questions?" exaggerating the upward lilt on the question.

"Okay," she said.

"What is your name?"

"My name is Hiromi," she said.

"Where are you from?"

A pause.

"From," she repeated.

"Where is your hometown?"

Another, longish pause as she composes her sentence.

"My hometown is Tokyo."

"Why are you coming to see this film?"

She looked at the camera, smiling helplessly, then at Michael, then imploringly back to someone in the queue.

From beside the camera, a voice said, "Eigo hanase imasu ka?"

It's Ko. The girl looked up at this, and her helpless smile turned dry.

"Chotto," she said, and made a gesture of size with her thumb and forefinger.

"Forget it," Ko said. "She doesn't speak enough."

"Arigato gozaimasu," Michael said, patted her on the shoulder. She bowed, giggling again, muttering, "Sumimasen," and retreated, still bowing, into the queue.

"Try a foreigner," Ko said.

Michael walked back along the queue, and the camera followed, panning across Japanese heads. Suddenly, the camera paused, let Michael leave the shot, and moved back to one Japanese girl who was staring straight, unembarrassed, back at Jacques. She had heavily made-up eyes and wore a black T-shirt with the sleeves ripped off, DRAGON ASH written on the front in English, her hair cut short and ragged.

"Ay," Jacques said. "Michael. Here we go."

Michael came back into shot.

"Sumimasen," he said to the girl. "Eigo hanase imasu ka?"

"I'm English," the girl said.

"Do you mind if I ask you some questions?" Michael.

"What would they be about?" she said.

"About you, Japan, and this film. We're working on a Master's project for Keio University, and we're collecting some data on especially young foreigners living in Tokyo."

"Okay," the girl said.

"What's your name?"

"Shannon."

"How long have you been in Tokyo, what are you doing here, and how long are you planning to stay?"

"Aren't you going to ask the question the Japanese always ask?"

"What do they always ask?"

"'Why do you come to Japan?' It's always 'why,' like one step away from 'why the hell.'"

"So?"

"It's pretty obvious from my face, isn't it? My mother's Japanese. Why am I staying would be a better question."

"How did you hear about this preview?"

"I saw it advertised in the *Tokyo Classified*."

"Do you know what the film is about?"

"It's about the invasion of China in 1937."

"Do you know who John Rabe is?"

"I've read *The Rape of Nanking*. I know who he was. He was a hero. A humanitarian hero. And he made being a hero more complex because he was a dedicated Nazi, too."

"Okay."

"I can see your point in this. You're trying to demonstrate how little most foreigners know about this country, what's going on, right? How they just come here for sex or money. Well you're right. Ninety percent of the Canadians and Americans and English and Australians come here and teach English or conduct wedding ceremonies or whatever crap that's around for the cash. Or the guys organize like, round-robins of J girls. Who cares."

"What do you do?" Michael said, looking interested now.

She looked at him, assessing him. "I absorb."

"You absorb."

"Uh-huh."

"Okay. And British."

"Uh-huh."

He looked at the girl frankly for a second. Ko moved into shot beside him, watching his reaction. Michael looked distracted, as if he were adding something, shuffling appointments, sifting priorities. She stared back at him. Then he smiled.

"Well. You might just be perfect then. I'm going to show you a photo. Then he,"—he indicated Ko—"is going to read you five different possible captions for this photo. And then all I want you to do is choose one caption, only one, and tell us why you chose it. Okay?"

She looked at him, and up at Ko, and the camera. "Serious?"

"Serious," he said.

A pause.

"Alright."

He passed her the photograph. She held it and stared down silently. The camera zoomed in on her face as she studied it.

Then out again to Ko, stepping forward and turning his back to the camera. Zooming in over his shoulder to the typewritten pieces of card as he reads them aloud.

On the first:

> Caption 1
> "As the Japanese moved across China, they rounded up thousands of women. Many of them were gang raped or forced into military prostitution (Politburo of Military Committee, Taipei)."
> From The Rape of Nanking, *by Iris Chang. Basic Books, New York, 1997.*

On the second:

> Caption 2
> "This photo has [originally] appeared in the *Asahi Graph,* a weekly photo journal, published in Japan on November 10, 1937, about one month before Nanking battle ... taken by Correspondent Kumasaki in the province of Paoshan in the vicinity of Shanghai, on October 14, 1937. ... The very picture is captioned with 'A group of women and children from the Rising Sun Village returning from the fields, guarded [from their own Chinese soldiers] by our soldiers.'"
> From The Alleged "Nanking Massacre": Japan's rebuttal to China's forged *claims, by Tadao Takemoto and Yasuo Ohara, bilingual in Japanese and English. Meisei-sha, Inc., Tokyo, 2000. (All sic)*

The third:

> Caption 3
> "The book where [this photo] originally appeared is *Facts of Atrocity of the Japanese Army,* published in 1938 by the 'Politburo of Military Committee, the KMT.' [Kuomintang, China] But, in the book, the Politburo of Military Committee has used this photo and already twisted the meaning and added to it the explanation saying: 'These women of a farming village of Jiangnan were taken to the Japanese Army headquarters one after another, and were raped and murdered.'"
> From The Alleged "Nanking Massacre"

Fourth:

> Caption 4
> Gist of the caption provided for this photo in the Chinese text, *Records of the Japanese Atrocities,* published by 'the Politburo of the Nationalist government of Military Committee in 1938' (all sic) and translated and quoted by Professor Matsudaira at the Foreign Correspondent's Club, Tokyo:

"Group after group of women and girls from farming families in the Jiangnan District was led away to Japanese Army Headquarters, where they were humiliated, gang-raped, and shot to death."

Matsudaira's subsequent comment as recorded on the site: "The book was published in 1938, only a year after the original appeared in *Asahi Graph* [in an article entitled, A Wartime Refuge: The Rising Sun Flag Village in Jiangnan]. The Politburo, which was the propaganda arm of the Nationalists, was already busy using a photo from the Japanese press to concoct what they called proof of Japanese Army atrocities."

Matsudaira claimed the soldiers were protecting the civilians from the atrocities of their own soldiers, and that the photo in Chang's *The Rape of Nanking* was manipulated to change the atmosphere of the photo from bucolic to beastly. He claims the photo was trimmed to remove the little child and older women walking behind and the cotton cart at the end of the procession; and that the images were blurred to eradicate peaceful expressions of the villagers, including the smile on the boy. He provides a blow-up from the photo, showing the girl with her hands clasped, the boy smiling, and the soldier, also, smiling. The details are indeed much clearer than in the photo in Chang's book. They even seem clearer than Matsudaira's own original, lifted, he claims, from the original *Asahi Graph*.

And the last, the latter part of which was handwritten:

Caption 5

"Asian Confucianism... upheld female purity as a virtue greater than life and perpetuated the belief that any woman who could live through such a degrading experience and not commit suicide was an affront to society."

The Rape of Nanking, p. 53.

I look down to a river carrying their sin and mine to the Yangtze,
to the sea.
But see the bright white sky reflected,
silence; such patience and
I do not earn my bride price,
a single *jin* of coarse grain
in times of famine, so they say.
I do not go home again.
I do not pluck cotton with my mother and
I am not twenty, the cotton blush-warm

in my fingers, in a future, in forgiveness.
No, the soldiers walk with sin, and like the winter
all inside me, all mine now, and I—
—I am lost, inside
the image of
the river's white.

There was silence but for the clatter of the crowd, the squawking of the recorded voice calling out prices.

"So." Michael.

"So, I choose...caption five," the girl said.

"Why do you choose it?"

"It's simpler. After the rest...it's a poem. Poetry is...easier, I guess. Truer to a feeling in the picture. To that girl who's crossing that bridge."

"Uh-huh. But what does it mean?"

"It doesn't mean. It feels. Caption five is about passion. And it's shorter, the way a caption should be."

"So what happened to the girl in the photograph then? Who was she?"

"It doesn't matter now. She isn't real. She's a blurred image in a photograph. I'm real. What I feel matters."

"You're sure of that."

"Yes."

"What you feel matters."

"Yes."

"How does it matter? Who does it matter to?"

"It matters to me."

"Uh-huh. What if I told you I know her name."

"Whose name?"

"The name of the girl in the picture. The one speaking in caption five. In what you called a poem. That she was born in 1917 and is twenty years old in the picture. And the girl beside her is her twelve-year-old sister. That there is another sister aged fourteen. That their mother died from tuberculosis a few months earlier and they left their village with their father and came to this place. This limbo between sanctuary and murder. Where they've been abandoned by this photo. Scraped off by history. And now you."

"They're just other aspects of a poem. Techniques. Methods to convince me of its honesty, its importance. To move me. A name is the feeling of reality; a genuine voice, with real pain. You know, a dilemma, a crisis. Doomed beauty. A detail to be convinced by. To enthrall me. What's your name again, by the way?"

"It's poignant."

"Poignant?"

"Caption five."

"Yeah, it's poignant. Fleeting poignancy, which the Japanese supposedly love so much. You know, a single firework at Hana-bi; a single photograph from history. I especially like the tiny sag in the bridge there, just behind the soldier. The bridge seems so solid, even that sag looks historic, like it has some ancient story behind it."

"Details enthrall you."

"Sure."

"What if I told you I know this woman's entire history, then. That I know of people who missed her. Who subsequently died, but missed her for a time. That I know she missed them. That I know from diaries she didn't like her little sister to use her hairbrush."

"You'd enthrall me more. You're playing the game."

"There can only ever be a story."

"There can only be a story."

"I want to ask what about her though."

"What about who?"

Michael didn't answer.

"Do you see what I mean? Besides. It's strong. It's convinced of something, even if I don't know what that is. The poetry makes me feel your reality more powerfully. In the first caption, the statement's strong, sure. In the second, the detail is good. Convincing. The third one kind of rebuts the first. So that makes you question both. Or examine them closer."

"You just forget about the photo, right?"

"Maybe. Maybe. I'm not going to fall for that, though. Like the fourth, even if it were true, is too convoluted and difficult. This is the point you're trying to make, right? It gets too messy to figure out? There's no gut reaction to something that's arguing and not stating. The English in captions two and three is really bad, as well."

"Presentation matters."

"Translation matters. And presentation matters, yeah."

"Translation and presentation matters."

"Yeah."

"And your feelings matter."

"Yes."

"Okay," Michael said. "Thanks. British citizen, right?"

"Yes."

"We're having a little party tonight. Shinjuku Prince. Penthouse. And you should be there."

Shannon smiled—"I'll see you a bit later, maybe..."—and the camera followed her back into the crowd. Nothing was said for a few moments.

Meredith lay back against the bed. Initial discomfort had given way to scepticism. She could see Michael's point, but at the same time she could see him forever trying to tell, to preach, to make people care about things he never seemed to ask himself why they should care. Michael was someone who would find romance in playing a game he could not win. She thought of herself, slightly tipsily, as someone far more pragmatic and balanced; less prone to illusion.

The problem was that for her, those who found romance—even in error—became somehow romantic.

"Hey, Ko. Why were the images blurred?" Michael's voice off screen said.

The Japanese boy looked up to the person who spoke. He flicked through the pages, looking for the quote. He looked up to the speaker, then to the camera. "According to Matsudaira?"

"Yeah," the voice said.

He looked back down to the pages and read.

"'To eradicate peaceful expressions of the villagers, including the smile on the boy.'"

"But according to Chang, you might suggest the images were blurred to achieve the exact opposite. To *create* peaceful expressions. To create a smile."

"This is opeless," Jacques muttered and panned to Michael.

Michael said, "Not only that, but poorly scripted, if at all, ad hoc, jury-rigged..."

Ko laughed out loud at this.

"Not particularly attractively filmed, dense beyond absorption, plotless. Done on impulse with no real care taken for overarching structure, or even any real, you know, point—"

"Some of this film is attractive, I think," Jacques said. "Ko is attractive."

Meredith looked up sharply.

"—any kind of possibly interpretable conclusion refuted by its own content, but accepting of this, which I like..."

"What exactly do you want of it?" Jacques asked.

"And ultimately demonstrating what it represents," Michael finished.

"And what is that?" Jacques asked.

"If you don't stand for something, you're just a collection of shadows."

"What do you mean? These people are not shadows."

"You've got to remember that these people are not representative. These are sympathizers. But in both senses. As in, they're sympathetic, but they're not activists. They're using this currency for now. But without currency you're no one. Prey to those who have. And currency without a project, in the absence of nation or religion—nothing of consequence can be made. Without guilt, fear, desire or conviction, all that briefly remains is personality. 'Undiminished personality'; what Stephen Dedalus saw that bore Shakespeare up when he could or would not be taught by his own wisdoms. The undiminished personality of a ghost. But we're not Shakespeare. We make no plays. For this girl's disappearance into propaganda we should have a way to act. To either burn this theatre, attack Chinese on the street, attack Japanese on the street—"

"These are not advisable ideas. How many Chinese do you see round here anyway?"

"—or immolate ourselves in protest of the fact that three hundred thousand people can die or one girl can die and it can have no consequences but more death and misunderstanding. But we won't."

"What kind of understanding can there be, man? And what if we don't care? It was fifty years ago. We are not Japanese or Chinese. It doesn't concern us."

"Exactly. We are nothing here. We use the yen for as long as it suits us, then we stroll away."

"Are we finished?"

"Turn it off, then." Michael said, angry now, to the camera. "Turn it off."

"You are high, man. You are out of it."

"No, Jacques. I have become the perfect example of all that's wrong with us. Cultural tourists, soulless dilettantes. And I intend to do something about it."

"You're funny, man. You are so articulate when you are writing. All those essays and articles I hear are so beautiful and good. But when you speak you are always sounding like you're agonized and confused."

"If you're not confused, you're not trying hard enough."

"What do you want to say then? What are you thinking?"

"I want to say that I can't believe the Chinese and I can't believe the Japanese. I want to say that I can't have any kind of belief in an international court's ability to mete out a justice that is over and above, more moral and more central to something, more core to being human, more ...true...than Chinese and Japanese versions of events. 'All that can be done is to make examples.' This, in a legal system based on precedent. I say that I have nowhere to stand so now I believe nothing and so have nothing to say."

"Uh-huh. I am sceptical of this."

"I want to say that nation and religion are the original moorings and that now—and then—they lapse. Jacques. Difference between unmoored and unhinged."

He's laughing.

There's a pause as Jacques thinks.

"I can't tell a difference. Unless this is another cursed idiom."

"And that in this moment where they lapse I can no longer retreat but I can no longer tell you where I stand and so I am directly responsible either for the torture and murder of three hundred thousand people and the mass rape of thousands of women or I am responsible for nothing at all. Which is worse? Jacques? Which is worse?"

"This is not your battle," Jacques said.

"It is everyone's. At night I have a vision of a horse burning, smoking clouds of smoke that rises and turns into spiders. Inside it I can't see. It's all dark. This is my nightmare."

"Michael?"

"What is the photo of, Jacques?"

"It's a girl on a bridge."

"Who's that in the photo?"

"A girl on a bridge."

"What's the photo of?"

"Everybody knows, it's a *girl*...on a fucking *bridge.*"

"Which caption will you choose then, Jacques?"

"You know what your problem is, Michael?" Jacques said.

"Just some girl in a photo, yeah."

"You're like an artist with no art form. You have no place to go."

The camera watched Michael, peering into the lens.

He was pale, hunted-looking. But something in his eyes, in his smile, looked a little like triumph.

The shot panned to the Japanese boy.

He had the same look, the same small grin. In the cock of his head and a sneer, the same sense of a thing hard-fought lost; accepted. Or something a little like a strange pride.

He mouthed a word to Jacques.

It looks like

surrender

the shot cut off abruptly, and static followed.

Meredith stared at the screen.

"Oh god," she whispered, just barely, to herself. Her head buzzed and hummed lightly. The static of the television sizzled and hissed. Light through the thin curtains was growing steadily fainter, the walls and floor of the room a gray hue now; something colorless, somehow surreal and artificial after half a bottle of wine.

Meredith sat there, contemplating the screen. There were a thousand possible options now. More than thirty more of the tapes. The papers to wade through. All the kanji she didn't know. All maybe just as old and unhelpful as this. And what even was this stuff? Raw material for some project. What's happened to him? Why was he so thin? Was he really at university here? But Jacques, no way. So why him on camera? Who was the boy, Ko? He must have had money back then. Maybe he was traveling again. Who dreams of burning horses?

She climbed a little unsteadily to her feet, and shuffled barefoot through the thick carpet to the closet; the four large mirrored panels that took up the entire east wall of the bedroom. She drew the far right door across. The same XEROX boxes full of paper as when she arrived. Posters in cardboard tubes leaned beside them. The YSL shirt and the suit on hangers above the boxes. Behind the suit, a page taped to the wall, in the now ubiquitous purple ink:

Records of rule and misrule, of the rise and fall of dynasties.
Let he who studies history examine these faithful chronicles,
Till he understands ancient and modern things as if before his eyes.
The Three Character Classic

More old books on the top shelf. She leaned inside. Behind the next door were her own clothes, shoes and suitcase. Beyond them, the closet was empty.

She turned and leaned against the door. On the television the static shimmered and seethed. She looked around the bedroom, and sighed.

"*Fuck* this," she muttered. "I don't understand you."

She sat down on the bed and picked up the phone. It was immediately answered.

"Good afternoon. How may we help you?"

"Hi. This is the penthouse."

"Yes, mahm."

"I was wondering if you could tell me what date Michael Edwards checked out?"

"Just one moment."

A pause and clatter of keys.

"I'm sorry, we have no record of Mister Edwards checking out."

"Do you keep records of guest correspondence? Phone calls?"

"Any external phone calls are billed to the suite account. I'm afraid no records of correspondence are keeped. Kept, excuse me."

"How about how many phone calls have been made out of here in the last couple of months?"

"Just one moment."

The keyboard clattered again. A pause.

"The last external phone call made from the suite was last year. The eight of August, which was a Thursday. Mobile phones work very well inside the hotel though, you should be aware. Because it is so thin."

"*Last* year?"

"Yes, mahm."

"Thanks. Thank you."

The metallic banging, knocking sound had returned. Insistent, and thick. Growing faster, one beat more emphasized and authoritative than the rest now: *Bubububuh, bubububuh.* What was it? The sound of construction?

She sat on the edge of the bed.

"*Fuck* this," she muttered again. Then, "Oh, you idiot. Mikey. Why do you do this to yourself. I'll find you. But you can wait a little longer."

She stood, poured wine into the glass. From the suitcase in the closet

she pulled out her minidisc player and headphones and put the headphones on and the player in her pocket. She lifted the new North Face
jacket off the bed, put it on, dropped her keitai into a pocket. She pressed
play on the minidisc's remote control, pulled the curtains, pushed open
the sliding doors onto the east balcony.

She stepped out onto the cold concrete, wincing, balling her toes, into
the gathering twilight of a November afternoon.

Before the music started, she realized the knocking sound she had figured as trains entering Shinjuku station couldn't be. This high the only
sound they made was a slithering hiss like the static of the television.

And then the first sad chords of *Purple Rain* as she stared out over the
city.

Inside the room the television flickers.

The dark is running into the room quickly, staining the carpet deep
brown-black. The flickers play on the ceiling, mostly. And in the glass of
the wine bottle, one-half empty on the tray. Outside there is the sound of
a cell phone's melody, which continues for six or seven loops. A muffled
voice.

Inside the other rooms there is near–pitch blackness; a dim but lighter
charcoal-gray near the windows. Enter the living room from the corridor
and it is vast. To the right is a long wall, broken only by the door to the
kitchen, almost always closed, and beyond this the door to the bathroom.
Between them the giant mirror leaned at a steep angle against the wall
reflects the charcoal-gray of the curtained windows and a piece of the
wall. To the left, the east side of the wedge-thin Prince, the main room
opens out. Close by is a desk and chair. Surrounded by yards of carpet.
Before the large, double-glazed window in the east wall is the space the
television normally rests, an unscuffed, dented rectangle of darker carpet.
The south wall holds a large sideboard, in front of which there is a leather
sofa, two armchairs, a long, low coffee table. The television's light comes
through the doorway at the end of the south wall, diagonally opposite
the bathroom's door. It casts shudders of low silver light, shadows of
proud tufts of carpet shooting out; receding; thrusting; submerging again
into the darkness. A shadow moves on the wall into the bedroom, and the
bed is most of the room, a great hump of gray-white duvet; a nightstand

and the headboard against the south wall. On the east side uneven curtains to the balcony where someone is speaking. At the end of the bed a tray with a bowl of popcorn, untouched; a dirtied ashtray; the bottle of wine. Near this, the Sony video camera rests crookedly on the carpet; wires, crimped in sections like parentheses from bundling, running toward the television.

On the camera a tiny green triangle glows.

From the television the flickers are uneven now because the steady shimmer of static has been replaced by footage.

It's a party.

Filmed by someone fairly tall, the shot taking in heads and shoulders. There are wine glasses and cigarettes, held by young people, in their early twenties and late teens. In the shot now is a dark-skinned Indian boy, leaning down to the shoulder of a girl with creamy coffee skin, aqua eyes. She's sipping wine, looking past this boy into the camera, smirking at what he is whispering, at the way he's been caught in whatever he's confiding. There is very loud music; too many voices to discern more than snatches of phrases, single words. The room lights up when the camera catches a light, or a white T-shirt. All the young people are dressed lightly: T-shirts, linen shirts, haltertops. A girl in a bikini, talking with two topless boys. The date in the corner of the screen reads in green digital: 05/30/00, and the time: 03:01. The camera retreats into a corner, to take in the entire room. There are more than fifty people. Standing in groups talking. Some are lying on the long beige sofa; a couple kissing. Leaning over the two a shirtless boy is pointing close to their faces, saying something, making fun of them. The television by the window is momentarily visible through the shifting bodies, playing a tape of fire. Someone laughs loudly near the camera, and shouts

Tell him to take a number.

The shot turns left, through a blur of colors, and focuses in on a small Japanese girl with very short hair, standing by a closed door. She's already watching the camera, and she blows a kiss off her palm. The camera rocks back, the shot momentarily of a beige ceiling, as if the blown kiss had impact. Back down and around, moving slowly through the crowd now. Up to, and then past, a white linen shoulder, very short hair and an ear, and then suddenly too close for focus.

The camera is nuzzling this person. It struggles for focus, a rapid blur, the music more muffled. Suddenly a brown hairy knee. The camera is hanging at his side, but still there are voices.

We need margaritas man. We need tequila. Immediate tequila.

Charge it, charge it, charge it.

Anton was sick. Where's Ko.

He's around.

Michael, Michael. What the things are called. Spiky English beasts. I think of spinehog.

No, no. Porcuspine, man.

Porcuspine.

The camera lifts again and gray eyes bloodshot and smiling appear, close up.

Say it.

The voice repeats it and there is laughter all around from the listening and the gray eyes don't care. Pulling back because someone moves in front of the camera, the struggle for focus again, and another close-shaven head appears in front of the gray-eyed boy, kissing him.

Moving past the two now, a circle of five young girls sharing a joint. One of them is Japanese, and she has a T-shirt on that reads DRAGON ASH. One of them, the curly-haired girl with the aqua eyes from before, stepping toward the camera, and smoke as she exhales into the lens and they burst into laughter as the one with the camera coughs, shakes. Their voices are excited, accents exaggerated, husky with smoke.

Put a fucking shirt on.

It's not sexy.

It's unfair.

Your nipples are too close together, Mikey.

Brigit likes her nipples wide.

Brigit likes her boys wide.

Don't, don't. Give me that, Ari-el.

Don't don't give you that? Okay baby you don't get nuttin. And put your shirt on Mikey. There are too many hormones in this room, baby. Too many whore moans, baby, I'm tellin you.

It's the aqua-eyed girl, smirking again on screen. The camera lingers, the only one privy to her joke, and she knows. Zooms in on her eyes and forehead. She's a full head shorter than the camera.

Something is passed between them.

The moment lingers, then away, around the edges of the circle, toward the couch. Then up past the couch and in the corner there's a tall blond girl, dancing by herself, in a tiny white tanktop, a purple taffeta skirt to her knees. She has long arms, moving fluidly above her head, twining together, the fingertips of her left tracing her right forearm. She is murmuring the words of the song to herself, eyes half-closed, and the shot shakily zooms to three-quarter, but she sees the camera; watches it expressionlessly, then she turns away, her eyes closing to the music.

Where is you, I wonder the camera's voice whispers.

In the bedroom, the images from the party on the television light up the end of the double bed, making complex shadows on the gray-white rumples of the duvet. From the television the murmurs and high-frequency buzz of the music and voices are a tinny static, but loud enough that the voice outside on the balcony is inaudible; impossible to tell if it is still speaking. It has grown so dark the curtains are lit only by the television, no light at all from outside.

On the screen the camera pans away from the blond girl, back over the crowd of the young, many dancing now, to the small short-haired Japanese girl who blew the kiss, standing at the doorway. She's been waiting for the cameraman to return, and she beckons hard, her eyes wide; excited, or agitated. The camera moves through bodies, toward her, and she gestures with her thumb to the door just ajar behind her now.

Hurry. Mouthed.

Toward her, pushing past shoulders gently, glimpse of itself in the odd casement of the leaned mirror, a black clutter moving between reflected heads, cut off now, a male left hand appearing to protect the camera.

Then there, blurring close-up to her face, eyes wide.

What, what.

He is. Waiting. Go in, shut the door. See him.

The door swings wide, whether by her hand or his, impossible to tell.

It's a kitchen, yes, by the tile, the cupboards, shakily, an oven, rows of wine and beer and spirit bottles, some opened, some not, glasses and tumblers, bowls of salad, fine wire cages from champagne bottles, twisted and relaxed, a tower of white china plates, empty plastic baggies, trays, loose cutlery, a microwave, a faucet running into the sink, the water a trembling

tapered stem inside the sink beneath, further down, the cabinet's beige,
and down

Hey, no

    to see that at the far end of the kitchen kneeling on the beige tiles
is a naked Japanese boy silver glints an earring and a thin silver blade in his
right hand resting on an olive hairless knee, staring with black eyes at the
camera and the door shuts behind and makes the music go dull, the girl's
voice is urgent

Nande?

    the boy watching the camera hard, his thin chest sweat-
ing and working, his hands fists on his thighs and one with a thin short
sword, the silver wavy like a stroke of finely whipped chrome cream and
he's kind of panting almost, his genitals shaking hanging rosycolored
between his thighs and the music louder for a moment and then gone in
the slam of a door and the boy looks down sharply and moves the knife
inside his leg and with two hands grips and saws hard up and down and
blood abruptly jumps down his thighs and falls to the ground and he
screams and saws again once and the camera does not falter once though
the scream merges with the girl's the camera doesn't shake or shift or
move away even when the boy lifts up a bloody bundle grinning white and
pale and collapses forward cracking his forehead on the floor his red knee
slipping out in the blooming rose of blood and the prints of his heels two
pink spots on his buttocks and his nose breaking a soft sound in a quick
second between the sounds the girl is making who is screaming too.

III

Deus Ex Yasuhiko

Yasu
March 2000

Yasu's lost it.

And doesn't know how to find it.

He's searched through his living room; plundered the mess. Overturning piles of clothes, shaking shirts thoroughly. He's checked the pockets of every pair of shorts and jeans he owns. And he owns a few. He's rooted through his meager collection of CDs, looking for that one that lies aslant. He's upended every pile of books. He's shifted things enough to pull the wardrobe door ajar; nothing inside but the safe, more clothes, books, some CDs and DVDs. He's even picked through the kitchen's trash. He'd been in Tokyo all afternoon, and suddenly, thinking this is unusual, why no calls? or at least, why not? he checked his pockets, patting them abruptly in a panicky flagellating spasm. In the middle of a sidewalk he held up street traffic, a resolute, distracted stone in the flow of a stream, his backpack slung in front, rummaging through MDs, wallet, loose, screwed pages, empty baggies, right down to the pen caps and sweet wrappers, the flakes of tobacco and dust bunnies, fingertips dredging through the jetsam of a long-faithful bag's tides.

But nothing.

Now he's home, and the search has its own momentum. There are plenty of other options open to him; he could even do these things in person. But it feels wrong, and shifts the balances of power in his relationships. He prefers anonymity; not secrecy, but distance. The lonely often do not wish to be reminded of the depth and mystery of other lives. The author of experience feels their impact too deeply to feel it often. It's growing darker, and though every light in the small apartment is on, he has a Maglite in his teeth as he plumbs the depths of the nest of wires behind his old, soon-to-be-replaced audiovisual equipment.

Nothing.

But the search really has taken on a life of its own, independent from any real urgency it should demand. Just to find the damn thing, is the thing. Sometimes sneezing in the dust he's stirred, sweating, skin itchy and welty, a small cut on his thumb. His knees cracking as he bends and lifts his futon for another look. Outside on the veranda, fluffed, well-shaken bedding lies in a loose pile.

"Dammit," Yasu hisses hoarsely past the torch.

Under his futon the tatami is still bare, but then, somehow spurred by the sound of his own exasperation, one corner of the futon hanging in his grasp, Yasu realizes.

"Of course."

The terrarium.

He'd left it in the terrarium last night, checking up. It's been a month since Heaven On Earth had tried to weasel their way back into his good graces and get him back supplying, and losing close to forty percent for their brokerage. He had originally used them to get some good exposure, to make his name a little more widely known in certain circles, and to make some quick cash. He worked hard, prior to offering them samples. One part of him felt they'd certainly take interest once a few of his choicest children had been tested, so he went into high gear, production-wise. Extraneous equipment was shifted out of his bedroom; radical hygiene protocols drawn up and followed scrupulously. Extra terrariums were purchased, solemnly heat-treated and installed in the newly purchased shelving system. Humidifier filters were scrubbed down or replaced. Literally *sacks* of brown rice flour were bought, and spore prints—F-II's and F-III's, technically not hybrids but new race strains, mutants he'd cultivated as part of the project he was working on when he was expelled from Saitama U.—were reverently removed from the safe in the wardrobe, their tiny Perspex envelopes milky with age and regret.

He'd gotten his act together. Tidied up the terrarium and readied it for stepped-up, "semi-industrial" production.

"Semi-industrial," he'd mutter quietly, proud, as he mixed the flour and water, as he scrubbed, as he inoculated jars after lengthy, brutal heat-treatments, as he sealed the small terrariums and flicked on the minihumidifiers. Sometimes the imperial "We" was called for.

"Yup. We're semi-industrial."

The other part of him, though, felt foolish, childish—absurd and blindly bold. As if he were finger painting pictures to take to a gallery. The irony, though, was that the conflict of pride and doubt over the borders of his ability, and ability to work hard, had the same result: he worked hard, and well. There was rigor, and focus. And in the hard work his doubt became displaced, by necessity, by the mass of the task.

Yasu didn't know the Afghan wisdom—and would have never thought it applied to him at all if he did (which, unknown to him, fixed further its materiality, and consonance)—that he who demands obedience because he is khan is not khan; that he who agonizes, wonders if he is fit to be khan, is khan.

Yasu agonized silently, and alone.

After the grueling preparations, the silent, sterile, pumice-scraped and naked inoculations after which his entire body shook with tension, there then came the weeks of waiting for first pins. In this time Yasu kept occupied. He followed his cleaning protocols. He wiped drip trays. He emptied the ceiling bowl with withering punctuality. He monitored hyphae with a candle so as not to shock the fruit with torchlight. He read from his father's *Kojiki* late into the night. He watched endless *Melrose*, and contributed long episode commentaries to respected chat rooms. He laid down the free-growth trays using some organic Chinese cornflour he'd found in Omiya. He smoked only outside, not so much suspicious as superstitious about his airlock.

And only when he'd harvested, desiccated thoroughly with big bowls and Tokyu Hands' best, most ridiculously expensive desiccant, only when he'd bagged and stored the first batch of shrooms while the next batch fruited and another batch pinned, did he feel he had the necessary protocols in place, the funds and audacity to offer the boys samples.

He did, and the boys, after days of recovery time, were all over it.

Yasu sold all three batches and was exhorted to maybe drop the "semi-".

He peels back the outer layer of the airlock, naked, and seals himself inside. After a brief scouring, he sidles awkwardly into the next chamber and seals that too. The plastic immediately starts to mist with his breath, and he tries to keep his exhalations shallow. Another brief scouring, the stiff brush returned to its plastic pocket, his skin red and glowing, he steps through the last sheet, taping it behind him. The coolness and moisture envelope him and soothe his inflamed and raw cheeks and thighs.

This is new Yasu now.

Capable Yasu. Slim, loved, professional Yasu. Industrial Yasu.

"Now where are you," he whispers slowly. As he turns his head, the Maglite in his teeth sends a mottled spot around the walls and equipment. Although they manipulated him, although he knew they made fun of his weight behind his back (he'd heard the term once, paused, horror-struck on the concrete stairs to Heaven On Earth: "The pet carp's coming for his feed"), although he eventually found his shrooms (Yasu can tell his own shrooms by sight; an unheard-of gift, regarded with overt suspicion and covert total stunned disbelief by Manabu and Hiro) in a foreigner's baggie that was marked with HOE's house brand, and returned to the shop and silently removed all his bags from their fluoro-lit display case by sight alone, picking them precisely from the bags of Hawaiian, Dutch and Mexican shrooms, Manabu and Hiro gaping, trying to scoff, muttering vague remonstrances with regard to his mistake and the impossibility of his being able to know, that the reason there were no Yasu-branded shrooms on display is they just walked out the door, man, they just *flew* out, despite all this, Yasu regards the whole experience as valuable. He learned to function at a level of industry he'd not thought possible. He learned that loneliness is purity. He learned he was good enough to be stolen from. And he'd started to think seriously on what to do about the beginnings of his own client list.

He checks the desk, and makes a face when he sees there's nothing there, and an approving grunt at dustlessness. He removes the Maglite from his teeth, and plays it down the shelving.

Still nothing.

"Goddammit," he mutters.

He checks inside the open fridge, even.

Yasu puts the Maglite back between his teeth and leans both hands on the desk, deep in thought. His belly wobbles and hangs ignored above the naked, vulnerable cluster of his genitals. He watches the spot of light play on the plastic-covered wall just above the desk's edge.

And sees something move.

Stock-still now, watching the spot.

Maybe just the light refracting through the plastic, makes some strange effect on the wall behind.

He shifts the spot minutely to the right.

The thing shifts again. A tiny black movement, a shadow spot scuttle, immediately gone.

"Izanami?" Yasu whispers, past the Maglite. There is no other sound after his word, that past the torch sounds like, "Iya-a-ee?"

But he knows, too small for fat matriarchal Izanami.

He waits. Then shifts the light infinitesimally back to the left. And another minuscule black flitter, this time beneath the torch's spot, right above the desk's edge.

"Unnh," Yasu murmurs, and hands on the desk he slowly crouches into a squatting position, knees crackling, belly hanging, genitals now dangling comically.

Under the desk a strange odor rises from the trays of substrate, fumey and metallic. He plays his light across the surface of the cornflour. It's all blue with strange mycelium, coated utterly, furry as a kitten. In the far corner, little luminous blue miracles cluster, perfect. He pans the light upward, traces the leg of the desk. The polythene behind is alive with transparent baby spiders, a multitude, a million millions, pin-prickly black-eyed and swarming from the light. Up to the web, and Izanami's deflated burst corpse dangling. Back to the polythene, the seething spiders shift and flurry.

He pauses, staring, amazed.

And the spiders pause too, as one.

He stares.

His eyes track down to the tray, to the crop of perfect new blue mushrooms shiny with strange resin, quiet as idols on the substrate, then up again to the polythene beyond them.

After a few moments, paused like this, the spiders shift again, and in the blue metallic odor, Yasu stares across the substrate at the awestruck face of Yasu, in a mirror there that's made up all of tiny spiders.

Catherine
March 2001

"There is no cuckold but calamity," Feste says.

He means there is no way to be forever true to the thing that has hurt you or broken you. It is a curious thing for the Fool to say, because if you read the play closely, you can see that Feste is sad, too. Something terrible has happened to him outside the five acts of the play, sometime in the past, that affects everything he sees, and says, and does. It informs the jokes he makes and it shapes the way he responds to the so-called sadness or romantic melancholy of the main characters of William Shakespeare's *Twelfth Night*. It is very interesting, because I believe that what the Fool believes sets him apart from those he follows, mocks, and judges, shapes and guides and comments upon, is kind of the same or a similar thing that hurts all the main characters, too. What could I call it? It is a thing that informs everything you see after it has happened, at least for a long time. It is a "calamity" that does something to your expectations of the world. It is to do with age, and damage, and a sense of the world as fractured, and shifting, and benign in a terrible way.

So it is so strange to hear Feste say that "there is no cuckold but calamity" when I think that he is married to a calamity invisible in the play that, despite his maturity, and lightheartedness, his opinions, and friendliness, shapes everything about the way he sees the world

806 + 264 = 1070
1/5th done
_____

Simon
November 2000

So on the Chuo back into Tokyo I see three white bombers flying low in over Hachioji, and I see the weather change.

The colors of the houses shift not as if into shade, but as if the colors die a little, subside; trashy little houses right along the railway lines, the iron and wood clogged with the substances electric trains throw off, ferrite and carbon, grow even duller, till the suburban landscape, a model of itself, a tourist attraction, a photograph, turns pure monochrome.

Drinking Kirin whisky from a hipflask on the almost empty inbound, sleepless and strung out, my hand bruised stiff, I watch a trumpet player at the other end of the bright orange velour seats opposite practicing on an imaginary instrument, his eyes closed, leaned back, jazz in his head, his fingers tracing trails like smoke rings from his mouth.

"Anton. What time is it?"

"Seven or eight, man. Are you coming out?"

"I'm coming out. Where are you?"

"Belgo."

"Shibuya?"

"You know it."

"See you soon."

The mezzanine at Belgo is almost too small for Anton, the tiny stairs so narrow it's kind of a joke to think of him humping up here. It's all black and supposedly Belgian and in a gigantic windowed double-door refrigerator they have over a thousand beers from all around the world and none of them cost any less than ¥800 each, but this is not really a problem because almost the most costly things of the last two days were the train trips out and back.

He's still violently bald (he has a Headblade, he tells me, when I rub his head in greeting: "Totally boss. It has fingergrips") and he's hunched in the corner table like a pale gargoyle in a big boxy pitch-black suit, pipes and air-ducting inches above his bright white head, sitting with two young Japanese girls, one he introduces as "Run Run" and the other as "Mary-Beth, an American, an analyst at Morgan Stanley Tokyo." The scar on the top of his head is a near-semicircle of puckered white flesh, shadowed in the low lights like the imprint of a jagged blunt bite; it looks ridged and dark and lumpy, like the spinal cord of a curled fetus sleeping under his scalp. Anton shaves his head because no hair grows on the scar, and it's too wide to hide. He was in an Amsterdam streetfight, and he gets sunburned easily.

He introduces me by saying, "This is Simon Chang, an American, who is the manager of a restaurant in Long Beach."

I don't say anything and I must look bad, the disheveled, crumpled linen shirt and creased trousers, too little sleep, same clothes for two days, reeking of whisky, sweating it out though it's turned so quickly cold.

"You missed the worst damn summer ever, Simon," he says, leaning over the table to me. The two girls sip lemon sours and don't speak to each other. "I was carrying around two or three shirts every day. Yves Saint Laurent for the subway, Issey Miyake in the morning, different YSL in the pm and Imitation of Christ or something fun for dinner. Nuts, but fashion not fahrenheit, you know . . ."

"It seems like it's over," I say. Anton nods in slow, deep nods, looking in my no doubt bloodshot eyes for any trace of humor or sarcasm.

I scratch around for something funny to say to break the ice, try and connect with Anton again, who is talking to Mary-Beth, who was brought up in Wisconsin or somewhere but speaks fluent J and seems fond of him, and I think of saying something to Run Run but she's leaned back in her little chair, looking down out over the balcony, silver makeup around her eyes, a truly tiny sequined bright red dress.

I can't think of anything to say, to Anton or to either of the girls, so I mutter, "drink," and stand carefully, bent over, and descend the stairs backward like a ladder. Down at the bar I take some matches to match Ariel's and some promo leaflets in kanji just to make the point to the barman that I speak J and choose to speak English, and that I'm basically not taking any crap right now and order, "Just something American," not caring if I sound harassed or absurd, and he semi-bows quickly and indicates the mezzanine and says, eyes tentatively meeting mine, "Please," and I leave a thousand-yen note on the bar and head back up the steps and I'm basically ready for anything.

Anton and Mary-Beth are talking about cruelty to animals.

"Chimpanzees *make* and *use* tools," Mary-Beth says in this fat, corn-fed Midwest accent, all hick r's and singsong drawl, bizarre in someone so thin and J in a trouser-suit. "They strip leaves and shoots from branches with their lips and teeth, and then they go on and dip them in a termite's nest, pull 'em out and lick off their dinner. And we go ahead and send them into space. Test their reactions to zero-gravity."

"Sure, but—" Anton starts.

"And what *I* think about," Mary-Beth says, "is if in space no one can hear you—a human—*scream,* what does a little chimp, little Han, who is way beyond using tools, who can *sign,* who the poor thing—"—counting off on her fingers—"—gets wheeled in on a gurney with his paws all strapped down, and shoved in a *rock*et, what does Han hear up there in space, alone, in a rocket? You know?"

"Are you retarded," I mutter quietly enough so only Anton hears, but he doesn't react too much, or maybe a faint grin.

"And if a real human screams in space, can the chimpanzee hear it? Or hear him*self* scream?"

Anton leans over and looks at Run Run, then at Mary-Beth. I smile.

"Uh, well, yes, I would say," he nods, deadpan. "They are . . . sensitive creatures."

"No, I don't mean—"

"Yes, I know what you mean," he says, "but I think your record of cruelty to chimpanzees is nothing by ours."

"Oh," I say.

The barman appears and murmurs "Sumimasen" by my ear, places a bottle of Bud on the table, lifts off the inverted glass that's resting on it, opens the bottle carefully, replaces our ashtray, murmurs "Sumimasen" again and leaves. The tables in here are cheap black Formica, the chairs chrome and black vinyl. The walls are smoky black brick and the entire mezzanine looks as if it's made from old stained railway sleepers.

"We," Anton says, "were responsible for the very first infection of a chimp with HIV. In 1982. Dutch HIV chimps were flown under quarantine to the States to found research colonies. My country founded this science. We were very good at it. Very efficient. Cages with walls which contract to trap the animal so it can be injected with anaesthetic, shaved, and liver samples taken."

Mary-Beth doesn't say anything. Run Run takes a Salem delicately from the pack on the table and lights it with a Harley Davidson Zippo. She smokes with the elbow of one arm cupped in the palm of the other. I still can't tell if she understands any of this.

Suddenly, loud techno bursts out over the speakers, and we all jump. It's turned down quickly, and a muttered "Sumimasen" comes from the man at the bar, and good-humored chuckles from people up here around us on the mezzanine. All but us. It's hot up here this close to the ceiling and I can barely breathe though outside the temperature is dropping fast, the fall coming on like a storm. It's only maybe seven o'clock so to actually think of walking just a couple of blocks past Hachiko to Marui and buying a nice jacket on impulse, out of pure need and vast opportunity, seems to calm me, have some feeling of homeliness attached to it. Anton's head almost glows. One thing can be said about him for sure: in Tokyo the people you meet fresh off the boat always seem to feel a need to justify their nation, to forestall what they see as imminent, inevitable criticism. English always denying classism; Canadians with border anxiety.

I can't and don't deny anything, and no one does here after a couple of months. Even stories about home get forgotten because the only way to share anything here is to share what's here. And Anton's truly Dutch, or was, at least: a total pragmatist.

"In the colonies they wind the roof back to show them the sky," he says. "But you know, that chimp from '82 is still healthy. There are two hundred HIV chimps in the world, and only one has developed full-blown AIDS."

Run Run is now looking speculatively over at me through the smoke she's just barely exhaling over the table.

"So we're in total collusion," Mary-Beth says.

"I have seen footage," Anton says, and despite his enthusiasm, this does seem to mean something to him, and I wonder if something about my presence has turned the conversation this way, and what, and why, "of caged chimpanzees crying. Behind the bars, their eyes flick back and forth very fast. When they cry they sound a little like cats keening. Is keening— is that the right word?"

He looks at me.

"Yeah," I say.

"But those chimpanzees might've or probably *would*'ve gotten culled if it weren't for AIDS though now don't you think?" Mary-Beth says. "What I mean to say is HIV probably saved them. They do that. Cull lab animals that are a drain on resources."

"Their eyes flick side to side, and up and down," Anton says. "With the bars so close, I think, it's difficult to get focus on the outside and the inside. So their eyes seem to . . . spasm, or something."

I pour the Bud into the glass with my stiff hand and do it too fast and messily, and it bubbles and froths, and foams up inside the glass as fast as something in a test tube reacting, and when it froths over the lip of the glass I have to lean down and suck it in, to stop it spilling on the tiny table and into our laps, and when I do I knock the half-full bottle with my elbow and start it rocking on the table, clicking on the Formica, teetering in a semicircle.

There's a second there, waiting, as we all stare at the swaying bottle in the middle of the table, rocking back and forth, half around in little abrupt circles. I'm stopped right there, my lips at the rim of the glass, ready for any anarchy, almost willing the bottle to sway and fall, bounce, explode off the table and the ashtray, beer and glass splinters everywhere, into our laps and our shirts and our dresses and suits. The bottle rolls and rocks and sways and pauses so that I almost feel it at the end of a miniature pirouette, rolling around on the ridged rim, audibly, a brown and red and white bomb, wobbling, fused, ready.

It over balances, falls and Anton lunges forward, and as he leans there, looking at me, I drink the beer I have.

I drain the glass, staring him in the eyes as I do, drinking the glass dry, daring him, and he waits there holding the bottle while I finish the whole glass and finally place it back on the table, and my eyes are watering, staring right at him.

There's a moment of silence.

The beer all up inside me, Anton, fist full of the bottle, Mary-Beth eyes wide, Run Run bemused in a bored kind of way, she'd wished it fell.

Mary-Beth finally says, "Whoops."

There's another beat of silence.

"Okay," Anton says.

"Braggadocio," I say, and laugh. "Alsatians. Cancer. You fucks."

"I sinku he looks a lot, very, you know quite is it . . . photogenic or somesing like zat," Run Run says, smiling at me through her smoke, the first thing I've heard her say.

The homeless are curled wrapped in ragged blankets in alcoves under the old bridge of the Shibuya station tracks, and the streets are full to bursting. Mary-Beth and Run Run are ahead of me and Anton's beside me, trying to rap, tripping as he tries not to step on their heels.

He mutters something like, "Microphone checker, twenty-four seven session, most radical, total, fat, phenomenal head wrecker . . ." looking at me for a reaction, a smile, some encouragement, anything.

I manage what unfortunately feels like a weak sick grin.

It's dark and so cold and getting colder, and I shout, "Hey, hey, Marui," over the roar of the traffic, and when Mary-Beth turns quickly I point over across the Hachiko intersection, up Jingu-dori maybe, and I wonder for a tiny second, where is Jacques right now? I'm cold but getting drunker, so you know, it's okay, isn't it?

Anton subsides.

"Before you ask, I met them both at the Swedish embassy party on the weekend." He has to shout it in my ear. "What do you think?"

"I don't know," I say. "What do—"

He can't hear me, and shouts, "Run Run likes you, I think, huh?"

"I'M COLD," I shout. "I NEED CLOTHES."

He nods, and Mary-Beth turns at the phone boxes outside Hachiko which is simply berserk like I've never seen it before, never seen so many people, and in the cold they're all moving in streams, no one hanging around, streams that have their own internal structure and logic but only in relation to those coming in the opposite direction, and no matter how much I may suddenly hate it, want to fight my way into the queue coming in this direction where there seem to be gaps and inviting holes, it's totally impossible to even fight that far; small steps, black-haired heads all up in your face, total frustration, trips and stumbles, shuffles, this is life.

Mary-Beth looks irritated, and says, "We're gonna do some karaoke, right? Nomihodai somewhere. I feel like singing. And I *gotta* sit down somewheres." She turns without waiting for an answer, and then the lights change and we're instantly drawn out onto the intersection, seething, rising steam of breath lit by walls of television, and Anton's shuffling beside me trying to keep up, and we're—or at least *I* am—dizzy and chilled and sick.

"Give me a cigarette," I say in his ear too loudly.

He does, and leans to me, "You wanna do karaoke. Cheap alcohol and I think you're in, huh?"

"Sure, I'm just cold," I mutter through the cigarette, and a woman beside me tries to lean away as I light it and I sway a little focusing on the cigarette end, trying at the same time to see where people's heads rise where the sidewalk begins so I don't trip up on the curb.

"Just think: earthquake," Anton says. Then, "Karaoke, yes!" he shouts and Mary-Beth nods sidelong without really turning, and Run Run just keeps on walking quietly beside her in the tiny red dress without any kind of reaction to the cold, and I suddenly think that she is actually pretty sexy, that it's a total Japan cliché, but she does, literally and completely—her skin, the proportions of her body, of her face, her high, childlike forehead, her delicate cheekbones, how her eyes are spaced wide and kind of blank and laughing at the same time—Run Run looks like a perfect beautiful specially made doll. There's even glitter in her hair, too, and I like the way the crowds don't faze her at all, and how we seem so gawky and mis-shapen beside her, I mean, of course Anton, but even Mary-Beth and I; we walk wrong and I suddenly see our stiffness and frustration and even the looks on our faces for what it is.

We just want to be different.

And with this, at last, I relax. Like a mantra, I murmur inside, absorb. Just be what it wants you to be. Marui, karaoke, nomihodai, be drunk, be bad, be sly, pay cash, this is it, get what you want and get better later, noth-

ing more is being asked of me right here, right now, and saying it to myself
with a hipflask of whisky inside I check out Run Run again, and think,
basically, yeah, sure.

Anton walks into a waist-high iron pole set in the sidewalk outside the
Häagen-Dazs. He crumples, and gets held up by a laughing embarrassed
little J girl he almost envelopes and crushes, and next to us is a kebab caravan and two Western guys playing Hacky Sack outside Tower. I can walk
quite slowly now, and smoke like Run Run does, elbow in hand to keep
the lit end up and clear of flammable puffy North Face jackets. Taxis and
traffic and not a soul over twenty-five, same old same old, and bent, releas-
ing the J girl, Anton turns his face to my feet and says, seemingly completely serious, "It tries to take away . . . your dignity."

"Are you alright, Ant?" I say.

"Don't call me Ant. Hmmm. Oh . . . God," he says with a sigh as he
straightens, doesn't like it and bends back down again, hands on his mas-
sively long thighs. He's looking past me to the road, at a guy sitting on a
blue Vespa by the kebab caravan, and this guy is old and Western, maybe a
debauched thirty-five, and plump and balding and wearing bright orange
PVC trousers and a sleeveless pink puff jacket, and he has, I swear, pink
inflatable waterwings on his arms, and then Anton's saying, "There is nothing . . . more pathetic . . . than the Canadian fags who overstay—" and I'm
laughing, "—and get fat on kara-age and more and more pathetic and
teach English until they are too old to do anything worthwhile—"

"Hey, Anton—"

"Waterwings!"

The old guy says, in an English accent, "I can hear you."

"Anton," I say. "Cool it." I'm watching the guy's reaction but all he does
is pull on his orange helmet, and Run Run and Mary-Beth have turned to
watch, and Anton just won't stop:

"The only consolation for Japan is the fags don't father any more useless international bastards—"

"Jesus," I mutter.

Run Run doesn't seem to understand or maybe doesn't care, but Mary-
Beth's expressing tipsy faux-shock, wide eyes and agape, just once, and
Anton stays bent and then he moans, "This land wants . . . debridement.

Oh, god," with his hands in his crotch where the post has hit him somewhere worse than I thought, so he doesn't even see the old fag give him
two fingers.

"You're balder than *I* am, you great big ugly lunk," the old fag says, and
he's totally English, lunk sounds like loonk, and where Anton dredged up
Canada I don't know, but the old guy doesn't say much more because
Anton's scar is pretty obvious bent over like this, and he just starts up his
Vespa and buzzes off intently into the incredible traffic in his waterwings.

"He's not as ugly as you, you old goose!" Mary-Beth shouts after him,
"You're just *so* jealous!"

And ah, I'm thinking, so. Anton and Mary-Beth. And I wonder, where
is Sonja. And I check out Run Run and find she's checking me out right
back.

"They try and take...your dignity away—" Anton mutters again to the
pavement, bent double but still almost as tall as some of the J girls who
pass, smiling, covering up their giggles with their hands, admiring him, or
are they?

"Who does?" I say, and smile at Run Run.

The Marui Young escalator, fourth floor, going up, clothes shopping.

"Kireidayo," Anton tells me is how to say "you're beautiful" in Japanese.

"Ki-re-i-da-yo. How about...'you smell nice'?"

"Um. Iinoi."

"Inoi. Is that it? But, is that like, nice?"

"Ii-noi. Longer. Say it nicely; it will be nice," he says. The girls are five
escalator steps and ten J ahead and can't hear us talking.

"How's nuts. Better?"

"I am indestructible. Or, I will be with nomihodai."

"I won't be long, man. I just need a jacket. Relax."

"Tonight we drink Echo Karaoke dry," he says. Then, muttered, "I
think I'm swelling up."

"Yup."

"Tonight we disappear."

"Yup."

"Tonight we go deep, to find the very essences of things."

"Uh-huh. How about, 'you have a nice body.' 'A beautiful body.'"

Run Run and Mary-Beth get off on the jewelry floor and we turn onto the next escalator.

"Kirei...nakara...dadane. Tonight, we are free. To lose and find ourselves."

"Get a grip. 'Can...I have a kiss.' 'Please may I kiss you.'"

"Kisu...shitemoii? Something. Just use your ways, man. Use your ways. Tonight we...oh. That's..."

He's looking past me with big blue bloodshot eyes, his tie knot askew, at the reflection of us and all the young well-dressed Japanese around us going up in the mirror above the down escalator, but then he turns past me, going down, and I catch a glimpse, see in the mirror something different, in amongst all the Japanese going down there is an anomaly, all brown extra-curly hair, the back of her small head, and then I see her, going down on her own on the fourth-floor escalator.

Looking right up at us.

Anton waves slowly.

"Hell-o?"

She doesn't react, just stares for a long hard moment, and then she turns back and starts pushing down the escalator.

"Ari-el," Anton calls, and she disappears from view and we arrive at the sixth floor and turn onto the next escalator, funneled there basically, life lived in queues, falling up through Marui Young like we're powerless.

"Funny how you always seem to seek out the foreigners in a crowd," Anton says. "But that goes away for a while." He says this kind of wistfully. Then, "I mean, after a while."

"Hey. What else are we gonna do tonight, Anton," I say. "Like; edify me."

"Tonight we are going to drink unlimited and only slightly watered-down Japanese beer until we forget our own names. Tonight we are going to become pure foreign white energy." He sighs. "Wow. I wonder what happened to her neck. Did you see that bruise." He checks up the escalator. "Tonight, I am going to sing until I or someone nearby is sick."

Chaos, obscure and opaque, a hiss and fizzing when we arrive at the first floor of menswear, where there's a man-sized polystyrene statue of a Buddha, waiting in lotus, painted bronze gone green and wearing, neatly knotted around the folds in his great big neck, a Guy Laroche tie.

There's a sale bin and a pile of T-shirts as big as a man, and a mannequin on the corner wearing a complete sickly yellow snakeskin suit—with snakeskin shirt—that has a price tag of ¥200,000. The brands here all or mostly foreign: Untitled, Melrose, Men's Bigi, Nice Claup. Anton and I walk slowly through the racks and booths on this, the first of three floors of menswear, not counting Marui City or Marui Men. Some Levi rip-offs, but with pre-bandied legs, are new and have a rack all to themselves—more than thirty pairs of jeans surreally cut, for thin, bowed J boy legs. When I was here last I remember a rumor going around that the Ministry of Education was dosing preschoolers' lunchtime milk cartons with hormones to rid J girls of "radish-legs" and make a new generation Western, tall and slim. I remember seeing who browsed these racks, or more particularly, who served behind these counters, and I believed.

Jeans, belts, T-shirts, muscle shirts, string ties, Jean-Paul Gaultier bracelets made of tartan and silver that cost a salaryman's monthly paycheck, shiny leather trousers that are totally middle-class in Tokyo, necklaces, beanies, caps, bags, wallets, key cases, a slim black Prada MD player case that costs two and a half thousand US dollars. Snakeskin is in, and part of me sighs, and part of me says, well, why not? Just because it's atrocious?

I'm in Nice Claup when Run Run comes in. She stands near, not too closely, looking at a rack of corduroy jackets I'm looking at too. I glance at her, and back to the jackets.

"Hmm," she says, and nods as if to encourage me.

"Uh," I say, and point. "Kore?" With a lilt. This?

She dips her head a little, and smiles a little slyly, just playing at the gesture. "Mm, kawaii desu," she murmurs, a sarcastic husky highness.

"Uh, chotto kawaii," I say, thinking, never has my Japanese been so good. A *little* cute. And I guess I'm greedy or I guess it just feels right and almost funny, but after all, *she* came and found *me*: "Kirei?" I say.

Beautiful?

"Uhn?" she says like a question. What else have I got? Numbers?

"San man yen?"

"So, ka?" To the jackets.

Take a chance, just use my ways.

"Kirei da *yo*," I say, with a big emphasis on the *yo*, knowing simultaneously it's a total bluff, but that also somehow *yo* is, in some nonverbal universe, *you*, or just, Christ, get the idea.

And she laughs, a single sound like a scrape of fabric, no more than a breath released, just once. But no move to shield her mouth; no flinch or check for who overheard.

"So, ka?" So coolly, nodding.

Essentially, oh yes? Who is this girl?

"Um," I say. "Kore?" Point to one of the jackets.

"Uhn," Run Run nods, and laughs that single mocking piece of static again. "*Ko*-re."

Since when was condescension sexy? Since I became unsure if it was even happening or not, and since when it didn't seem to matter. Grab the jacket, head for the counter.

"Kore," I say to the Nice Claup clerk, with all the confidence in the world.

And it's enough. The clerk looks like he's about thirteen years old, and he is absolutely beautiful, slim, tobacco-colored skin, and he gives me a smile, scans the jacket, and on his T-shirt printed over an icon on his slim chest is: WHAT IS A HAPPY SCHOOL LIFE? HAPPY TIME SPEND TOGETHER WITH FRIENDS ON THE SAME WAVELENGTH. ARE YOU INTERESTED IN STUDYING?

Has Ariel gone by now?

Back there, Run Run waits for me.

Go go go.

Outside Echo Karaoke, it's somewhere in Shibuya, three bikers in full Nazi regalia, uniforms, helmets, boots and medals, one with an Iron Cross that looks camp as a cravat, pass by, their Harleys roaring. But it's funny, they don't seem ominous or dangerous to watch because they have nice faces under their sunglasses, clean and young, and even though they rev their hogs they're trapped in traffic and they look, well, rich. I guess you're supposed to hate and fear the well-dressed Nazis the most, but rich, upper-middle-class, expensively dressed Nazi impersonators stuck behind buses? Huge Harleys creeping along slowly in the thin streets of Shibuya. I laugh out loud.

Mary-Beth says, "It's so bad. They don't even know what they're wearing. It isn't in the curriculum."

I say, "It's comedy. The Japanese admire the Germans. The more they try and be frightening the less they are. Everything—" I cough here, phlegm suddenly in my throat, "—is so . . . safe here . . ."

Mary-Beth says, "Okay?" but she's turned and looking past me down the street, hugging herself in the cold, her eyes glittering, tipsy and excited. As soon as Anton catches up we're going in for nomihodai, unlimited beer or greasy watered-down spirits delivered up to us in a room like a darkened cell, with benches round the walls, a low table and ashtrays, a big-ass TV. She's excited because she's going to sing, and because I am going to sing, I am calm.

I cough again.

Run Run shows a little concern, just a minute raise of her perfect, nearly transparent eyebrows. They seem as thin and fine as the down on a girl's spine: this unearthly delicacy, this quiet precise beauty makes me feel messy and hungry. It's going to be around ¥4000 each for two or three hours of nomihodai karaoke. Something I find very sweet and reassuring is that even with astronomical incomes people from all over the world here can walk for hours in the freezing cold for a song and a seat in a box full of beer. And it's only seven or eight, and there are five or more hours before the trains stop so what it's like is: drink quick, have fun quick and you may not have to commit to the entire night out and a tripling or quadrupling of your bill for the evening. It's not ever like we want to get this over with. It's simply like we're in a hurry. And I suppose that as quickly as I want fun, I want some peace, too.

"How would you get a bruise like that?" Anton says on the thin steep steps up to our room.

"How would who?" Mary-Beth says.

"We saw this girl we know," Anton says. *"Man."*

"Who knows?" Mary-Beth says.

"Do you mean," Anton asks, "who knows how you would get a bruise like that, or who knows *her.*"

The clerk opens the thick soundproofed door, one of at least twenty in a long thin corridor in the heart of the fifth floor of Echo.

"We should have scored some shrooms," I say.

"We still can," Anton says, and grins brilliantly, and then he snarls.

"Nama biiru, yotsu," Mary-Beth says to the clerk, holding up four fingers. "Hayaku, kudasai."

We file in, Anton, Mary-Beth, me, Run Run. The clerk changes aluminum ashtrays and turns on the big TV in the corner, and the room is just as I had imagined or remembered it: windowless, the size of a West-ern queen-size bed. There are vinyl-cushioned benches on three sides, a low table in the center, the smell of dried beer. Two microphones and leads at the ends of the benches, a framed picture of a pavilion in Kyoto hanging on one wall. We could be anywhere in the world.

"What does 'hayaku' mean?" I ask no one in particular.

Anton jumps up on one of the benches, bent to avoid the ceiling, and snarls again.

"Itu meansu—" Run Run says, and she smiles at me, shyly for the first time, and I smile back, "—quikuly."

We sit like this, in a U facing the television: Anton closest to it, then Mary-Beth beside him, Run Run at the end of the room and me beside her. The beer has arrived, the harried clerk explaining to Mary-Beth with J and sign language that consists of four fingers followed by two crossed ones that their limit is three pitchers of beer at any one time. But it's okay because they're pretty huge, two liters at least. Mary-Beth orders a pitcher of gin and tonic which is a bad idea and two packs of Mild Sevens are ordered by Anton.

It's dark in here after he turns the lights down; all that's left is the blue menu on the television. Anton is hunched, flicking through a laminated folder of songs.

"Smapsmap. Find me some Smapsmap," Mary-Beth says into the microphone and it's set to echo and her voice is hollow and shimmering in the room, and I'm pouring drinks in plastic tumblers and there are three cigarettes burning in two ashtrays and all of us, Run Run included, drink so fast it's like it's water.

"I'm hungry," Anton declares to the folder. "Can we order food."

"Eatingting," Mary-Beth says hollowly through the speakers, "is cheat-ingting."

"Can I order *you*," Anton mutters, and laughs at himself.

Mary-Beth checks us, Run Run and I, very quickly, and what does she see? Me pouring drinks in cups very carefully with my head back to keep the smoke from a burning cigarette in my lips out of my eyes, and Run Run peering past me at the menu on the TV.

What doesn't she see? Run Run's hand on the bench, fingertips just touching my leg.

"Say, Takadanobaba twice, Mary-Beth," I say, slurred through the cigarette.

"Takatadanokatabababatwiceice."

"*Spell* it, goddammit," Anton shouts at the folder.

I finish the pouring and lean down the bench and grab the other microphone.

"Run Run Run. Kireinakanaradaradadaranene."

Anton cracks up, and Run Run starts to laugh too and chokes a little on her beer.

"Whatwhat?"

"Run Run Run has two beautiful bodies," Anton says, and checks his shambolic tie for dribbles. "It's good for your pronunciation, Simon, you dilettante." Then, "One four two seven," he says to Mary-Beth. "Smap, *Lionheart*. You've got the remote control."

"Okaykay."

"You first, then me, then Run Run—" Anton says.

"Iie, iie," Run Run says, acting shy again now. "No, Ahnton, no."

"It is compulsory," Anton says, "and first, big drinks, and then Simon."

The beer is so watery it's easy to drink the whole cup, and the others do too, and then, "Come on, Mary-BethBeth," I say not into the microphone, and stub out my cigarette, and when Run Run puts her hand back down on the bench, I carefully trace lines up each of her slim fingers with the tips of my own.

The song starts and Mary-Beth starts to sing and it's so awful, the song, her singing, both, but her Japanese is pretty good, and she occasionally gets a scan quite nicely and obviously knows this music, I have to admit, but even so, I have to check my keitai halfway through, and I have two new skymails.

The first: Ariel2.

LFT JCKT. DNT CALL DNT TRY DONT COME NEAR ME.

The second from my father:

WHERE ARE YOU?

I look up to no one in the room, and I grin brilliantly. On TV there are some J girls on a beach in bikinis, a beachball, and another ball bounces over the words, hovering there with a little sexy shimmy when a word gets held for, like, longer than usual.

And by the end of Mary-Beth's song Anton's sitting by me with his folder, and "Kimigahoshii" is, he tells me, how to say "I want you."

"How do you know all this," I whisper in his ear.

He reaches inside his suit jacket and shows me—literally—a little black notebook, and then he drops it back inside again.

"I have this J love phrasebook. It's one of our products. It's for the entire arc of a relationship here."

"It's pretty . . . fake, dude."

"No, man. It's what's the word."

"What? Pragmatic?"

"No."

"Like what? It's . . . realpolitik?"

"No. It is . . . when in Rome, do as the Romans."

"Uh-huh. When in Rome, do the Romans."

"But just a little faster."

"Uh-huh."

"Which by the way if you ever get to hear the phrase, 'motto hayaku.'"

"'More quickly.' You're a total creep, Anton."

"I'm a total Roman, Simon." He smiles.

"Anton!" Mary-Beth calls over the microphone.

Anton picks up the second mic, and murmurs, "Yeeees?"

"One more for me? Can I?"

"Take my turn."

"Cheers, matemate," Mary-Beth says in a hollow, echoing English accent. "I want Hitomi, *There Is*."

Anton flicks through the folder, and I swill back a little more beer, thinking, I want to sing; thinking, this all feels very familiar; thinking, we should order more beer ASAP; thinking, it turns me on to think of having sex in Japanese, how it could be both so much more and less real. I lean back against the wall, and my hand is still caressing hers.

"Hmm. Um, so what does that mean, Mary-Beth?" Anton says quite casually into the mic. "'Cheers, mate.'"

And with this, a very strange feeling starts to come over me; that moment I've had and heard about a thousand times.

A moment of clarity.

The warm hum of my drunkenness seems to hiss away and almost audibly pop. My eyes suddenly and abruptly become accustomed to the dark. I seem to say, in an entire sentence, in an audible internal voice that is cool and dry and very certain and, in itself, actually, and oddly, familiar, I seem to hear myself say *this has all happened before.*

"Sometimes, Anton," Mary-Beth says, "in northern parts of England with certain accents, people even say, 'chesmay' ..."

"Hold on, but I still don't understand it," Anton says.

"When they're *really* lazy."

I watch Anton for his reaction.

He laughs loudly into the mic, but still not quite sure.

This has all happened before.

I look closely at Mary-Beth, and in the suddenly cold banal dim, her suit and hair a little mussed but her eyes bright despite her growing drunkenness, she peers at the TV.

"So, what's the code?" she says.

I turn and look closely at Run Run.

She glances at me, then sips from her cup.

And so I decide to test something.

"Oh, *bullshit*," I say loudly to the room.

Very loudly, full of feeling, the words clear, delineated, precisely spoken, "bullshit" emphasized as it would be if it were very much venomously meant. But I don't mean it. I am repeating something I have said before. Something that was posed and affected the first time I said it. Slightly amazed that no one seems to sense this but me, but also that no one here was there then, except maybe Anton, at the Buddha Trickbar for Christmas, just blocks from here. Almost a year ago. But it wasn't him that didn't understand... was it? It was... Dwayne? Dwayne from New York?

So, of course, the next step, the test: will they laugh? Laugh like they did last year? This incredible sense I am almost actually controlling—*manipulating*—their reactions; that I can generate them because I've seen them before. It was Dwayne, and it was Shannon, or Chantelle, a Japanese-English magazine editor, for *J-Select,* or *Tokyo Classified. Wasn't* it? He didn't understand, and she did tiredly lie to him; past culture shock and frustration and almost into despair, lost in her own sarcasm, wondering internally if sarcasm even exists if you alone are privy to it. I partially saved her sanity that night, and we went on to White, and in the toilets there was a code, a San Kyu, a gratuity, her laughing face close to mine, there was her smile, her breath in my eyelashes and her hand moving in my lap. Dwayne laughed loudly too, but still didn't get it. Does any kind of complete lack of comprehension even really matter if you can laugh it off? This entire realization in a nanosecond, and I take a small mouthful of beer, and I spit it, spray it over the table to the bench where Anton sat before, in an absurd and phony gesture, and too late, far too late to express any kind of amazement or incredulity, far too affected and like *televisual* to be taken remotely seriously, or *sincerely*. I mean, I actually *spoke* before I *spluttered,* and this supposedly in *surprise,* in some kind of exasperated *amazement.*

This is what I do: I hiss, "Oh, *bullshit,*" and then I take a mouthful of beer and spit all over our table.

And Mary-Beth turns to me, her face so beautifully full of clear-eyed wonder, and near-delight: she knows she's been busted, and she's so *glad*. I stare back and my doubt and my astonished scepticism at this totally physical déjà vu is misinterpreted by her as amused scepticism of *her lie,* and get this: like Chanel, or Shona, or whatever, she's *pleased.*

She laughs, shy like a little girl, and settles, physically relaxes for the first time.

I see, since I've met her, some tension that's been here all night, some Tokyo adultness, self-reliance easing in her, staring gratefully, with *delight,* right in my eyes. Because we are sick of belief in each other's international lies, aren't we? *Are* we?

Anton laughs loudly, great Dutch guffaws, and I knew he would. But he's unsure what has happened here. To him I have merely made her laugh; brought something out in her he hasn't seen before.

"Um, four two five seven, Mary-Beth," he says, and then he checks me. Thinking I am moving in on his analyst from Morgan Stanley who supposedly comes (originally? possibly? in *pieces?*) from Wisconsin.

I finish the rest of my beer, clap the cup down on the table, take a gigantic drag on my cigarette, hold it in while I stub it out, exhale hugely, and declare, "We need more beer, Anton," then turn to Run Run, and what I seriously say is, "Run Run, kimigahoshii," looking right into her eyes, and knowing what I see there is interpretable as nothingness, but simultaneously as acceptance, I lean forward and gently, delicately kiss her on the lips, and she lets me, and she kisses me back, and this, too, both is and is not something new.

And like the racks in Tower and HMV here is the English section of the karaoke catalogue alphabetized by first names. When my turn comes the plastic page is open to D.

"One four nine three," I tell Anton.

Run Run's hand is on my thigh. Anton and Mary-Beth are kissing as the first "oriental" chords of *China Girl* chime in this dark little room in Echo Karaoke. And at this, Anton turns from Mary-Beth, they both turn, thrilled and surprised at the recognition, the joke, the flashback, the echo, the *repeat,* and Anton scrambles for the other mic and knocks over a cup that spills beer and foam over the table and onto the floor like a thousand times before, and no one cares, and laughter is heard over this "Asian" riff just before the drums kick in, and Anton gets to the mic just in time to sing, high and breathy, *uh uh uh oh-oh...little China girl.*

Times two, and then my time has come.

I could escape this feeling, I sing, and sing it low and husky like Bowie does it, deep and true to his odd scans. *With my China girl.*

I feel a wreck without my...little China girl.

And there's the ubiquitous surprise on these faces across from me, they never do expect it, but they do recede in this moment, and I do and don't feel Run Run's hand tighten on my leg, and *I hear her heart beating,* I sing, and give the next word astonishment and that extra half-beat that is all Bowie, a man who's never sung a line on autopilot in his life, *loud as thunder...saw they stars crashing...*

The bass is fat and the drums ride it on, it's all so perfect, and I'm leaned back against this wall with, of course, no need to read the words, but one tiny check to see this karaoke gets the line right, so often do they misprint and tell it that the stars are *slowly.*

I'm a mess without my...little China girl... and Anton's stood up to dance and Mary-Beth's bobbing her head and swaying and watching me sing now, and this is sung to Run Run, to whom I do not look, but of whom I'm thinking, and picturing her stomach as I sing, white and cream and perfect, the stomach of a doll, and cool, her utter physical perfection and purity like she's made of ivory and glass, the contours of something real and unreal, a petal of porcelain, she *is* and I *Wake up in the* morning Bowie goes high and I do too, like a surprise and a sad delight, a breath, a disappointment, *where's my...little China girl* and closer to the mic so I can hear my exhalations for words that are all immortal and emphatic and cliché, *I-hear-her-heart's-beating...loud as thun-der* and I know, and know that karaoke machines don't, that Bowie's second verse adds himself in just one breath, *I,* is a sigh, *saw they stars...crashing* and oh, here we go.

I'm feeling tragic like I'm—high inhale—*Marlon Brando-uh* the scan is hard here, a single syncopation, off the beat, the trick is to hold the first not the last syllable of the name, and on the TV, a glance, I see they transcribe this as "a-tragic," and I turn away.

When I look at my . . .

And I close my eyes as Run Run runs her hand inside my cheap new jacket and onto my chest, I feel as if my heart might burst with the power inside this little song, this little moment, knowing what's to come, his control, his structured feeling simply and always astonishes me, because he takes it down—and I do too—a quaver here on *China girl* and then it's gasping high and breathless, doubting and sure, *I could pretend that nothing . . . really meant too much, when I look at my . . .* and it's high inside my head, this sound that drifts like a car off an elevated freeway into bass, the drums, a flicker of restrained guitar that's like the violet twilight on the news TV where I once saw this thing.

And I sit up here, eyes firmly closed, give my diaphragm some room, there's a crash down by the television I ignore, that's part of the song, that's Anton doing what he does, and *I stumble into town,* I sing, *just like a sacred cow,* give it everything, and oh, *visions of swastikas in my head* rise like flags on poles proud to howl *Plans for everyone . . .* and so lost, and frightened, and sure that all the wrong things are true that *it's in the white . . . of my eyes . . .*

And down now, and listening closely for and to the change, the subtlety and surprise in her, to get this right I find myself thinking of Ariel over me, my hand on her heart too, and hers, and up, whispering, confiding that

my little China girl
you shouldn't mess with me
I'll ruin everything you are
I have
You know, I'll give you television
She was so lonely
I'll give you eyes of blue
My hand up to her neck and a panic attack I'd say, get off me I said, what is it she said, *get off me*
I'll give you a man who wants to rule the world . . .
To get that pain off me
I break off and open my eyes.

They're all watching me. Run Run not touching me. But smiling, like

I'm hers, like she's proud. Anton standing, towering, white, with a waste-basket on his head by the TV. And the guitar still quivering, the scent of spice in my nose, the other mic in his hand. Mary-Beth stunned and star-ing at me across the beer-shining table.

And when I get excited Anton says in deep and flat Dutch tones.

My little China girl... says

And Run Run mouths to me, coming closer, face to mine, her finger on my lips, *Oh baby, just you shut your mouth.*

She says, shh

And as the song runs down, she whispers, *shh,* and the others take the chorus over, and she says, *shh,* and she kisses me again over the guitar solo, long and hard and drunk and passionately close. And as the song runs down, I swear, the others applaud.

Anton sings another song. Mary-Beth, oh god, sings another song, then starts on the oily gin and tonic that arrives with more cigarettes and two more pitchers of beer. Another cup gets spilled on the table and the floor, and Anton slips in it when he tries to stand and dance, and he sits back down, surprised. He's still wearing the wastebasket on his head, and sings his song with the mic held up to the mesh. I stop kissing Run Run when she starts to whisper garbled things in Jinglish to me, things I just don't understand, things she says and then laughs at with her glittered eyes closed. When Mary-Beth is singing Anton gets his phrasebook out again and shouts out to the room through the wastebasket's mesh:

"Hanaretakunai, everybody!"

Run Run laughs and says, slurring, "I not want leave you too, Ahnton."

I guess I just sit here and drink from the G&T that tastes like greasy carbonated water. Mary-Beth's song finishes, and she drops the mic on the wet table, and suddenly she looks exaggeratedly worried. Inside, some deep and sober kernel has just become aware she's really drunk, she's in some danger.

"Zuttoishoniitai," Anton says.

Run Run leans heavily against me, and mutters in my ear, "Ahnton want stay witsu you, forever." And I lean past her to stub my cigarette out and she falls behind me, between my back and the wall, and giggles, lying there with her eyes closed, and instead of helping her up I pour another G&T and move along to let her lie on the bench beside me. Anton takes the wastebasket off his head and leans over to Mary-Beth who is rummaging in a little handbag with one eye closed, and he whispers in her ear. She shakes her head. Slowly and unsteadily, she pushes one hand into his big chest, pushing him away.

And he laughs deeply, and turns a page of the phrasebook, and shouts over some tinny, flashy J pop, "Sawatte! Kante! *Sawanaide!*"

I'm sitting here and he's looking at me for a response, a laugh, a sly grin, anything, but I just widen my eyes, shrug, drink some more. What?

"Touch me!" he shouts over the table, over the music. "Sawatte! *Bite* me! Kante! Sawa*naide! Don't* touch me!" He literally bellows with laughter, and I guess I kind of laugh too, and check out Run Run, who's lying beside me with her feet up on the bench now, but her eyes are open just a little and she's smiling over at Anton and notices me looking and smiles blearily up at me and she puts her slim pale hand on my thigh again.

The karaoke is on random or something, and it changes automatically to a new song with a darker video and the room gets dimmer. Mary-Beth stands woozily up, still looking in her purse.

"What's up?" Anton shouts.

"I have to make the trains," she says. "I have to."

"Make them what?" Anton says.

And she lifts out a small wristwatch from the handbag and checks the time, and she says, "Shit! Oh, shit, I've gotta—" and kind of stumbles past Anton and puts her hand down on the wet table for balance, and there are wet spots all down the legs of her trousers, and at the door, she calls out "Bye-bye," like a J girl and there's a kind of shocking glimpse of banal and blindingly lit corridor and then it's gone again.

Anton slides around the bench toward us.

"Will she be alright?" I shout.

"Daijobu," Anton says, and Run Run laughs a little and looks up at me and moves her hand on my thigh a little higher.

"Here," Anton says, and leans over and takes off one of her tiny little pumps. Run Run murmurs, "Daijobuyo," and looks down to him and then she lifts her other foot for him. He takes off her other pump and starts to massage her bare feet.

"San kyu, Ahnton," she murmurs, and I put my hand on her head, and stroke her hair, and finish the rest of the G&T.

"Don't you get cold," Anton says.

"Mmm?" she says.

"Don't you get cold," he says again, differently.

He moves up to her calves, massaging them in his big hands, her legs so small they're like someone's wrists. He looks up to me and widens his eyes. Run Run murmurs, and sighs, and she moves her hand higher up my thigh, and when she does this my first reaction is to reach over to the table and pour another G&T but I do it too fast and the cup falls over spilling more liquid onto the table and the floor so then I just take the pitcher and drink from the spout. Anton is rubbing her knees quite gently, his fists so big he can enclose them completely, and she fumbles at my zipper and I'm just sitting here, letting her, my heart thumping but unaroused and too drunk, or something, and he starts to push the little red sequined dress up her thighs a little, but she's lying on it. She turns and rolls onto her stomach and as he gets the dress up to her waist I see she has the slimmest hips like a boy's, tiny little white panties smaller than a folded handkerchief. Anton lifts her up onto her knees with one hand.

"Kimigahoshii," he says in a deep mock-J male voice over her back. I look up at him over her. He laughs. And he gets up onto his knees on the bench behind her and on the karaoke the song changes again. He pulls out his shirt and starts to unbuckle his belt. She has me in her mouth but I'm soft and her mouth feels cold, the only real sensation her breath in the hair. Anton pulls her panties down with a thumb, and pulls himself out of his boxer shorts, semi-hard, with his other hand. I take a last long swig of the G&T and drop the empty pitcher on the floor where it clatters and splashes. She murmurs into my lap. He fumbles, trying to put himself into her. Staring down with a very serious expression, and suddenly she makes a squeak, her whole body jumps, and she lifts her head abruptly and reaches out behind her with one hand, but touches nothing. Her dress is all rucked up above her buttocks, and she says something high and desperate that sounds like, "*sashiku—*"

Anton thrusts roughly into her, two or three times, then stops. He reaches into the breast pocket of his suit jacket, pulls out the phrasebook and begins flicking pages.

Then he looks up, triumphant. "Softer! *Mottoyasashiku!*"

He flicks another page.

"*Mottofukaku,*" he growls and pushes hard into her and she makes a sound again, but doesn't try to stop him.

The karaoke changes songs again.

"*Mottohayaku.*"

Run Run says what sounds like, "Itai. Itaiwane," and makes a sort of low soft keening sound over my lap.

"It hurts." Anton says after a moment. Then, "Say it. Sawanaide. Say it."

I slide out from under her and zip myself up.

She slumps onto the bench. The floor is really slippery, and the music is too loud, and I wonder if I can make the trains. Maybe, but the subway is definitely out. It's definitely time to go and I'm wondering if we've left anything in here, my vision kind of blurry, feeling dizzy and sick and drunker now than I did when I was sitting down.

"Simon," Anton says when I'm looking around for my wallet. "Simon."

"What."

"Look. Look, man," he says.

I turn around, and see that he's pushed her dress up way further. And that there's a tattoo. From the narrow pale small of her back right up under her bra strap, over her shoulder blades but not onto her arms, in yellow and black and blue, there is a tattoo of a prancing snarling tiger. She murmurs something with her forehead on the vinyl, and makes that keening sound again.

"Jesus," Anton says.

"Let's go," I say. "Let's go, Anton."

He pulls out of her and tucks himself in and she slowly folds down on the bench.

"Shit. Jesus," Anton says. He looks around and then wipes his hand on the bench and grabs his cigarettes, his lighter.

At the door I tuck the wallet in my back pocket. Anton pushes past me, slipping on the wet floor, opens it a crack and looks out.

Then, "Hey, wait a second," he says, and takes out the phrasebook again. He flicks a page, then another, and then he finds what he's looking for.

"Zannen dakedo boku tachiawa," he reads into the dark room. "Nakatsu tandayo." He looks up at me. "'I'm sorry it didn't work out,'" he explains, and then he grins and then he snorts like I don't understand.

He disappears into the corridor. In the strip of light from the fluorescents I can see her left hand is lying in the spilled beer on the floor, and some of the tattoo is a dark smear upon her back. She lifts her head. Her eyes are very black and unfocused and I can't tell if she sees me or not. She's still making that sound, that could be made of words, or not. Anton's no longer here to translate.

"Come *on*," he says from the corridor.

I close the door behind me.

Anton and I are standing in the street outside a subway exit near some homeless guys. We're all waiting for the subway to open and it's still dark. They're just waiting to get warm, but we're waiting to go home. We've both got our headphones on, listening to music. Anton is eating an apple from the 7-11, and although the music is loud in my ears, all I can really hear is the convenience store jingle, repeating a high J girl chorus.

Sebun—ere-bun. Iiki-bu-n.

It's at 4:40 a.m. that the doors finally rattle up and the homeless stir like the wind has changed.

I look at Anton, and he mouths

Time to go home

I don't nod or say anything.

He shrugs.

What is he listening to on his headphones?

I don't know.

He finishes his apple and throws the core far away down the empty street toward Hachiko, his arm held high for a moment that makes his gesture ironic, then dropped like in disgust. The core bounces, and sprays little white chips, and then seems to disappear, and then we go down in the subway.

And on the train Anton tells me (and it's kind of irritating, and I'm tired, and I'm glad to leave him, soon, at Omotesando) about how he once had a pet squid, named Engelbert. He kept it in an aquarium like the empty one in my apartment. He tells me how she was fond of peanuts, which he'd feed to her with hashi, twice a day. And I don't even say that the aquarium in my apartment doesn't even seem to have a lid to hypothetically be lifted for any hypothetical fish to hypothetically get fed. Then as I exit the train at Omotesando, Anton shouts, "Hey. Missin' ya, Simon! Missin' ya already." I stop on the empty platform and stare at him in the train, our eyes meeting yet in no way connecting. "Missin' ya . . . in a heterosexual way," he says, as if, and I guess it's true, I will forgive him in some ultimate sense of the word. I feel as if somehow I am failing at something I don't even have to look at; that may not even be real. I feel cold and high and tired and glad of sleep. I feel myself folding in and around my own experience, finding glee in places that by all accounts are wrong. Not what Anton does, or likes. But the possibility of him. His mellow malignance. I feel a thousand lies making a new world. I feel refreshed, somehow. I think of Ariel. I think of being sorry. Telling her I'm sorry. Doing the wrong thing and being sorry. Trying again. Nothing being necessarily morally finite. Nothing being... *out of the question.*

That these concepts exist here, mean even more than home where they are all used up. I feel as if I could be and embody these things and somehow get realer, get better. I feel more real.

I feel free.

Yasu
March 2000

Under the desk, Yasu crouches under his face made of blackeyed spiders, and carefully and delicately plucks a little miracle from the cornflour.

The luminous blue resin on the cap smears his fingers shinily, and he drops it in his palm.

After a little while, he's sitting naked in the center of his darkened room, shroom in his palm, blue and shining, sticky, too. He seems to stare at the transparent spiders swarming, but his eyes are black and fixed, remembering, like the eightball hemorrhages of a gunshot victim.

Method Acting

You could see on another of the tapes, Film 18 or 19, possibly forgotten, misunderstood, ignored or just lost, a piece that shows the dark-haired boy sitting candlelit in this same hotel room, slowly rubbing a hand across his almost-shaven head, talking to the cameraman's feet in what seems a pose, an imitation, a parody of Brando's final rambles to a kneeling Sheen in Coppola's Vietnam film, a parody that has a distasteful mocking quality but also, as it progresses, something genuine when you realize the boy's in fact pretty strung out and the tears that come at the end of the plaintive speech are real and that maybe he's using the framework of the parody to express something that's quite real and meaningful to him and probably just can't find a way to express it without trying to poke fun at the same time, the first line, "I saw an insect with a halo on my windowsill," delivered with that tired, resigned but matter-of-fact air that implies the speaker knows the lines are not really worth delivering to this audience, that their minds are already made up and any speech will edify only the speaker and thus is a total waste of time for him and them, and yet can't seem to stop himself, speaking slowly perhaps just for the pleasure of hearing words in the darkness, even if their shapes are borrowed, because a momentum, a flow might gather, that could be what's just behind the sarcastic premise, a truth might just out if only he could use this place to start and not shut up, and not fall into that essentially bitter and self-mocking project of mimicking something you really obviously admire—his second line, with pregnant, semi-sighed gaps between the words: "I was outside smoking"—this is where he seems to get interested, because, well, maybe it's true and irrefutable, a fact and a setting, metaphorically bereft, aflorid, followed closely by, "I glanced down to the sill, where the light from the half-open curtains made a strange geometrical shape there. The insect crawled toward me, from nowhere, into the light," and the hand drops from the head here, as if the act's maybe getting dropped too and he's found a way into a place he can say just what it is he wants to try and say, to us, to the camera, to whoever's in the room—there's smoke floating in the dim red light around him; are these people stoned?—or just to himself, a start given him by way of this lapidary scene, etched on the imaginations of two generations of certain hungry young men, and the final circumstances are fleshed out by way of his line that's not really delivered Kurtz-like but really more semi-astonished, quietly pleased, almost delighted by the memory, maybe, "And caught in its antennae, floating above its tiny twisting head, was a halo—a *halo*—made of dust"—it's apparent he's actually listening to himself now, lost in the imagined or remembered scene, and this is where the audience also, which is really the camera, and us, forgets it's filming in the same way the boy forgets he's a) copying, and b) speaking, so actually in a way he's not really listening to himself and not really listening to or looking for closeness in tone or body language to that Brando scene that is in fact a kind of imagined hybrid, an amalgamation of what appears in the film as a recorded broadcast, played by Harrison Ford to Sheen and the Colonel and the ominous, brilliantly cast rodential

CIA man, as evidence Kurtz has very obviously gone insane—Obviously, Sheen's Willard replies, in a semi-solicitous way that's all baffled hangover and delivered so deadpan its earnestness undercuts the possible sarcasm— such a long pause—so finely there's a definite parallel with this filmed situation here where you really can no longer tell exactly how much truth is being told, how much sincere emotion you're receiving, and if it really matters in the end, or if all that does matter is what this person does or does not do, regardless of what they say or how they say it; Willard, the implicated Alice—but a recorded piece of monologue nonetheless that was cut from three weeks of Brando and Sheen improvising, Brando basically bitter at the business by this point—"He's like a force of his own. He don't give a shit," Coppola said at the time, both intensely frustrated and quite awed—but nevertheless, in the midst of his self-importance and self-disgust and self-obsession delivering lines that were totally heart-stopping and self-forgetting, so in more than one way there's something new going on here, in that scenes are being grafted together, from both the beginning and the end of the film, and the boy slightly happy, slightly amused to hear this thing come from his mouth that doesn't try for Kurtz's bleak, paradoxical metaphor of the snail crawling on the straight razor or any kind of allegorical or philosophical truth or really anything deep at all, just aims instead at representing something he saw, and felt for, and that, it seems, he wants to share:

"When it reached the light, the insect stopped. It paused for a moment, and then it walked backward out of the light. And I realized I'd never seen an insect walk backward. Maybe I'd seen a spider flinch, halt, even cower. But never walk backward, as if by choice, away, out of light. Retreating as far as it could, out of that light, to the frame above the window's sill, along the frame, back into the frame. A perfect, vertical halo of dust still within the light until it disappeared; a zero, arrayed within the antennae, quivering, tentative, absurd, perfect.

"And I thought, what could I do? What could I do with such a vision of an angel insect, fleeing from the light?"

He stares down into a middle distance that could be more smoke, or that angel's dusty halo. A slight, distracted gesture with the fingers of one hand as if under the chin of a child. In the film Brando asks if his methods are unsound. His hand clenched.

The boy says, "Nail it. To. The god-damn wall."

Yasu
Late March 2000

Late, late night, Yasu stands in the heart of a Shibuya emptied out by the last trains (resigned to a cold night's sleep in the park and the risk of municipal eviction) right outside the small, raised door to Heaven On Earth, a door made of riveted metal plate with a raised lower lip like a submarine's, pocked with the rivets like the polythene in his terrarium. He is muttering quietly and intensely to himself. Something that sounds like "Zen, zen. Zenzen. Zen." There are more rivets per square inch around the mail slot in the very center of the door, into which Yasu is squeezing an envelope with a little thumb-sized bulge in the very center. What he might mean by what he's muttering is a mystery. Already the paper of the envelope is dark and soft in a spreading patch around the lump, obscuring the kanji of his signature, and the damp patch is getting darker and softer and almost blue-tinged— though that could be the neon light from the nearby Dydo drinks dispenser—as Yasu pulls the edges of the envelope taut, trying to squeeze it just a little flatter without his fingertips touching the paper that's soaking up the bright blue resin quicker than he'd bargained on.

Merdy
November 2000

What gigantic project required so many hours of film? What huge undertaking were these tapes and pictures and handwritten pages the remains of, like the debris of a trading post in the Congolese jungle, the remnants of an impossible commerce left behind, the ruthless, debauched and passionate Europeans all gone, and behind, clues of their enterprise and its demise left for the jungle to subsume, or a bland hero, a Marlowe or a Willard or an Alice, to piece together, to forget, to alter, or be altered by?

Old packing cases with peeling rusted metal straps; punctured empty cans of diesel fuel. A rainswollen log book detailing an animal attack and a looming completion date. Ant-ridden unsent love letters, and a shrunken human head on a stick. Windows broken in the manager's cabin; one hinge wrenched from the doorjamb, the flimsy door ajar and bloodstains alive with midges on the threshold.

Too many movies; too many mystery stories. Too many neat narratives of clue and quest and gaunt discovery. The real ominousness was missing. In its place the barely audible hiss of aircon, the powdery scent of freshly steam-cleaned carpet, the paper sash across the toilet seat, the loamy-colored shine of bathroom slate. A single dead bluebottle on the windowsill. Real mysteries are silent, and steam-cleaned. Real mysteries are only ever interpreted. Real mysteries remain so: their cogency as mystery at all in question.

Although there was all kinds of evidence in that room, it still didn't *feel* like anyone had been here, like any kind of life—simple, scholarly, orgiastic or insane—had been lived here, so this naturally made it hard to act as if there had. It made it hard—despite what still remained unexamined and untouched under the bed since that night more than a month ago—not to accept this as a generic place, a stage worn with uncountable feet, the stacks of paper and books and videotapes as permanent and shin-barking as a coffee table or a prompt box; to not make this place—through her own clues, her own human mystery and mess, her own forensic path lain of breadcrumbs, chestnut hairs and drifts of perfume, postcards and phone calls—her own.

So the next day, having finally talked to someone—Simon, and Jacques—and despite the irony that she's arranged a dinner—with the two boys, to sound them for information—Merdy is in Don Quixote, buying groceries. Filling up a two-tiered trolley with cans of spaghetti sauce, bottled water, Montana chardonnay, pasta, pantyhose, some minidiscs, instant udon, tubs of white and scarlet kimchi'i, spinach, yogurt, a kilo of rice.

Her phone doesn't ring; the mystery does not deepen, or coalesce; the traffic is really no more horrific than before. His absence is not filled or accepted or regretted or even forgotten, just looked past, like sometimes, say in the middle of a good movie, you realize you've decided you're going to the dentist tomorrow and in the possibility made probable the toothache disappears for minutes on end.

Outside Takashimaya she stops and stares at a window display of Japanese armor, two bags of shopping in regular plastic supermarket bags at her side. Bags the same the first world over. The same ragged holes in the same folded handles for the same chrome spokes to suspend from the same chrome checkout frames. Handles that wizen down to sharp white strings with the heavy groceries of any country. She'll get some fresh bread from La Maison. Some days can be just days here. Sometimes just a little decision takes you not back, because back is a place and time and who you were in that place, but at least closer, in a different shape and style, to a familiar way of looking. Sometimes a decision helps you look at the future the way you looked at the future from somewhere good, somewhere the boundaries of which—not physical, not moral, not spiritual, but more like *powerful*—you'd define as home. Purpose is power, and purpose is continuity. Purpose is the chrome bar that suspends each day's difference, folded intricately into what's gone and what's next. Always ready to be opened and filled, really used. Days are bags of your life. Purpose is direction; that which holds days together. Food is continuity, too. This is just a day, and today, after a month in Tokyo and the gentle decision to start looking properly, she's decided to start cooking properly, too.

Simon
December 2000

So Michael and Dennis Hopper in gorilla suits—on my mind on the way to buy drugs for the Christmas party I'm planning. The only person I have spoken to in a week is Ariel. And because I know for damn sure no one else will get it done, I am organizing a Christmas party for every foreign person I know in Tokyo. I'm on the Hanzomon to Shibuya, with a TGIF napkin in my pocket scrawled on by Jacques a week ago in bleeding smudged blue ink, a map to the supposedly amazing and reasonably priced shroom house Heaven On Earth that according to this map is not more than two blocks from Hachiko. Christmas is always a time I get kind of panicky, and drink too much and wind up doing stupid, regrettable things.

I have a seat into Shibuya and shades are on, headphones are on, Bowie's *Station to Station* warming up and sound-tracking this, which is my version of fun, now, in Tokyo. In the last week I have come to accept that I am one of those people who will have a truly awful, visceral, self-shaking dream and then forget it and spend the entire following day inexplicably traumatized, itching, irritable, tired and generally freaked out without having any clue why. Until some moment happens, late in the day, after the first drink, often—as if, perhaps, I need to tell my psychic defenses to chill—and then the dream presents itself in emotional techni-color, suddenly fully remembered and as real as a memory, as real as déjà vu. When you're always alone, dreams, good or bad, are company.

The situation was this: on the platform at Omotesando maybe ten minutes ago, staring sunglassed across the tracks at a massive billboard for facial reconstructive surgery, I was avoiding giving the impression I could see the little J boy, maybe seven years old, turned from holding his mom's hand and staring back at me. This tiny boy with thick glossy black hair forming a coarse frill around a blue military-style cap with a thin shiny plastic bill. The rest of his school uniform was absurdly, almost *sickeningly* cute: the navy blue serge, the three shining silver buttons on the coat, the intricate badge on the cap, even *epaulettes* for Christ sakes. Something fetishistic about it, something so contrived and intricate as to make a per-son wonder who imagines their child so dressed, so intricately made up.

He's gone now; as we pull into Shibuya he and his young, kind of sexy mother (who is a total MILF—at school in Wellington we had long debates about whose mother was a fox, whose mother was a MILF—a Mother I'd Like to Fuck; never, *never* once had the balls to suggest Elise to Michael, though she was, I guess) are standing in the doors waiting for the train to stop, the little boy looking like a tiny dwarven admiral, his hand pressed to the stainless steel of the right-hand door, lifting it off, examining the clouded chrome of perspiration in the shape of his little palm and fin-gers shrink and disappear like some kind of regression in his age—small, smaller, child, baby, embryo, gone—then replacing his hand immediately as the shape disappears as if to keep himself alive. He places his hand; removes it; watches; puts it back again.

He turns up to his mother and says something, and she bows to reply, half by necessity, half, I can tell, from love. The Japanese are so indulgent of their children.

He was sitting beside me as the hum of feedback and the rattle of the *Station to Station* train in my headphones began to replace the rattle and knock, the rich real sound that is like tiktik*tukka*tiktiktik*tukka,* and his MILF was just past him, and this tiny little bright boy tapped the thigh of my left leg with the three middle fingers of his right hand, his pinkie lifted in the same way I simply know it would be on a little boy-sized cup of sake.

It scared the living daylights out of me.

Train compression—I mean the full-body press—is the only time a per-son gets touched in Tokyo. You hear that couples stop having sex, especially in summer. I know foreigners who pay tens of thousands of yen a day for massages, not because they really need them, but just to be touched. I know foreigners who have told me—confessions here are free—about their daylong masturbation sessions; men and women; just trying to come back to their bodies, trying to situate some self inside their sensations. Just to be touched. Foreigners crying in tiny rooms all over this little country.

He tapped me on the knee as Bowie sang the first line and I full-body jumped, whipped around to see, bigass headphones and Armani shades staring down from a looming obscured face at this tiny little boy in his military marine uniform.

I think I said—maybe really loudly—"Oh!"

And then, kind of pathetically, but maybe also kind of in a benign, fatherly way, I pulled my headphones down around my neck, lifted the sunglasses up and said, not in a very fatherly, benign way, I admit, but my heart was truly banging: "What?"

And then he said something in Chinese.

I blanked out. It was the first thing I'd heard in Chinese in maybe six months.

I was suddenly very confused. The boy was Japanese. The boy was examining my face very carefully, and smiling; his eyes on mine but making little reconnaissance glances to my mouth, my lips, my ears, my hair.

His mother leaned over his little lap, and bobbed her head and smiled sympathetically and apologetically at the same time; the look in her face like a humble missionary, a timid fierceness like she had devoted her whole self to this prodigious child, and the solicitous mode was for his benefit, not mine. She was even sexier because of this.

"I don't uh," I said.

I have spoken to just one person in a week.

"Ah!" said the mother, rising and surprised.

"Oh!" said the boy, flat and seriously.

I heard the mother say, "Ei-go wa . . ." something, something; a rapid fluid rattle of high-pitched Japanese directed down at him. His eyes never left my face; her eyes never touched my face.

She finished speaking.

He stared in my eyes and I stared back in his and wondered what he saw; wondered in turn what I saw, too.

His forehead furrowed a little, and then he said, "Where do you go?"

I smiled. I said, "Shibuya."

"Oh!" said the boy, nodding vigorously. He considered this. The announcement, *"Mamonaku, Shibuya, Shibuya desu,"* called in comforting, sincere tones over the loudspeaker, husky as if to a confidante. His MILF leaned forward again and said, "Thank you." She bowed, smiling still, and then, for the first time since I have been in Japan, this trip or the first, standing up or sitting down, I bowed too.

Then they were gone.

Last night's nightmare for this day's daydream was this: Michael and I were lying side by side on the double bed in his little upstairs room at the Bolton Street house. We were probably sixteen and I was sipping a Sodastream cola and he was asleep, unmoving, lying curled away from me, his hands limply clasped before his face. I was watching a movie on the TV on the sea chest at the foot of the bed. In the movie Dennis Hopper, two guys and a girl were walking on the Wellington waterfront toward the camera, in black suits with thin black ties, the girl too—what Michael said William Burroughs used to call "Banker's Drag." Hopper was ahead, some kind of leader. The dream stuttered, started again. The three were still walking, still approaching, but Hopper had jumped ahead in the frame, very close to the camera, and now he was wearing a gorilla suit. The dream stuttered again, as if shocked itself, but this time it was for a good reason, a narrative-based reason, because in the dream I had drifted off to sleep in the middle of the movie. I knew this because it was dark now, and when I turned to look for Michael he was gone, the bedclothes were rumpled and creased and gray in the darkness, and my one-third-full bottle of cola was capped on the nightstand on the side of the bed where he lay. It was the same feeling in the dream as in life, when you wake in the dark selflessly; as without self as a baby, absorbing the action of your surroundings, composing your responses to what happens, which at a point intersect to form yourself.

At the foot of the bed was a man in a gorilla suit and it was Michael.

The terror was the unexplainable malice of this; the self composed of the terror of the very first response. A self composed of terror. While I slept he dressed this way.

I scream.

He knows me, thinks about me, came back for me. He is intimidating: tall and dark and hard.

In the wings, just beyond him in the dim room is Elise, his mother, supporting him in everything he does. I hear children laughing; echoes in the house.

I lift my heavy leg to kick him, ready to really and truly fuck his shit up, break a nose with my heel; ready in my terror to grind his face, his teeth and lips and eyes with my boot.

My foot gets grabbed and held.

This is my dream, and the day's edge was made by it, but I did not even remember it until the encounter on the train. That I woke with my ankle aching like it remembers this thing really having happened. And I have become increasingly convinced—though at a distance; as if this is just a book I'm reading, or a long movie that composes a second level to my life here in Tokyo, that no one knows about—that things are repeating themselves. It is a price of freedom, I think, and a consequence of some of my choices. This is why I am attempting to replicate last year's Japanese Christmas. A hint of what real possibility is. It's like an experiment; an intriguing, private, vitally important and yet not entirely unpleasant experiment in déjà vu.

Doing inept things or being inept in public has this effect of reminding me of—forcing me to call up—all the inept stuff I've ever done in the past. I shouldn't do this recycling of my mistakes because I know very well it contributes to the making of more, but nevertheless what I am thinking about as I descend the steps inside Hachiko, taller than everyone and noting how every single J person is looking down at their feet more so they don't stand on their neighbor than so they don't trip, is spilling a G&T on giant jowlish lumps of fat on Zhou Guy's back at the Xin Jie restaurant launch in Century City. I guess I was fifteen, and there were a lot of ice sculptures and a rickshaw from the valet parking with a real-looking coolie that most (but not Zhou Guy) declined. There was a tiger in a cage at the doors to the lobby that smelled strongly of ammonia and there were maybe thirty waiters and waitresses all around my age and all brought out from China especially for this launch. This was back when my father was still opening *Chinese* restaurants. And there were important people, I knew, because my father was wearing his contact lenses, which he hates, and he was waiting in the lobby with his hands clasped, standing just in front and to the side of a mime who was pretending to be a monk, praying and chanting with a basket for alms at his feet, but as I knew, he actually *was,* the mime, chanting for alms, that is: his contract stipulated they were tips. Waiters carried around token thimbles of Chinese wine and flutes of champagne and there were oysters for success everywhere and seaweed for wealth and lotus root and dried bean curd for wealth, too, and I spent most of my time in the kitchens talking to a kitchenhand who was on the dish steamer, this gigantic machine like a sheet-metal press that boiled glasses clean, because if I came too far inside the kitchen the chef would scream at me, son or no son, totally with my father's consent, and if I went out into the lobby I would end up speaking to someone, and I knew my father really didn't want me out there, anyway. And although I had to wear a tux and although I wasn't allowed to speak to any guests the G&T was, I suppose, flowing.

Outside the koban outside Hachiko, in the exact same spot I met Jacques, just eight weeks but like about forty degrees ago, I light up a cigarette and check his mapkin.

On the front is this:

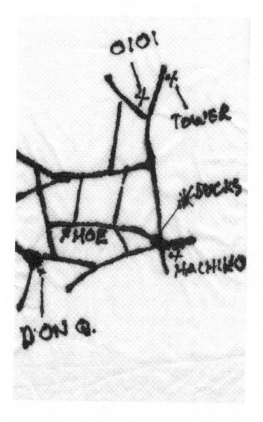

I have noted Jacques has at last figured out that Don Quixote is not some kind of Spanish mule, and on the back is this:

I head across the intersection with the crowd, over toward the four-storey "*BUCKS" and into the maze, with a sort of sinking feeling, knowing how simple this map looks, yet with these crowds and knowing how much is crammed in here and how near to impossible it will be to find one "metal door" beside one of how many thousand "drink machines" in amongst all these tiny blocks and tiny shops and tiny alleys papered in inscrutable bills and usually not even marked on the maps, and all with my only reward an excruciating conversation in Jinglish with some dealer dude—some *legalized* dealer dude—named Manabu, like he's a goddamed ewok.

Zhou Guy had bodyguards, a fair indication of who he was, and he was so grotesquely fat he actually availed himself of the rickshaw to lug him the twenty carpeted yards from the valets into the lobby. Other fair indications were my father's bowing, and the gift he gave Zhou Guy that was passed straight to his bodyguard without being examined, and my father's gestures with the open hand and the sweeping motion combined with the bow and overall patheticness in general.

I was standing just outside the kitchen doors with Ming, an incredibly hot young waitress originally from a town named—literally—Klang, who'd been in LA since she was nine, which looked like maybe a couple of months ago. She was waiting for the maître d' to seat guests before she took orders for wine and I was telling her who people were, half-bored, half-flirting, which is usually effective, but wasn't, in this case.

"Massive fat dude in purple and sweat is Zhou Guy. Total gangster, totally scary dude."

"Yes, he scary."

A typical exchange, but she was probably either sleeping with him, or one of his gimps, or had aspirations in that direction.

The swing doors opened; I intercepted a G&T, my father caught my eye and flicked a glance back in the kitchens—meaning, get the fuck out of the lobby—then turned to murmur to the Xin Jie maître d' and examine his tortoiseshell clipboard. Everything had to go so smoothly. The maître d' came straight over and as he passed me, muttered, "Simon. Here," like I was a dog; something he had picked up off my father—the "here" thing; the first-name thing—and I rolled my eyes at the inscrutable Ming and followed.

"Your father asks you to stay out of sight."

"I ask *you* to stay out of my face."

"Mr. Chang—"

"Kiss my ass."

This was where I was at with the senior staff.

And as the lobby filled up with the guests, and more and more oysters and raw fish of a thousand kinds and trains of booze passed me by in the kitchen thoroughfare and out there, I stood like an idiot, chugging intercepted G&T's and only once smoking surreptitiously.

Then later I guess I was kind of drunk, but not that bad—it was just so damn crowded, and I was holding my glass high, dying for a cigarette, sidling through the crowd, grinning slyly and I thought kind of winningly

at Chinatown luminaries as if I knew them and they knew me, which I
suppose they did, and like I was part of my father's world until I definitely
stood on someone's foot and I looked down to see, got jostled or jostled
someone, and spilled the drink.

And the thing about Zhou Guy is that he isn't *masculinely* fat. It's not
like he has a big Western joggling belly and thick legs. And the thing about
being femininely fat is that you're fat every which way, including your
back, and your *neck* for Christ sakes. So I mean if it wasn't that he happened to have such a gigantic, round fat *back* (I mean how many people
are there with clinically obese *backs?* Backs that have *jowls?*) that protruded
out into, like, other people's space, the spilled drink wouldn't have ended
up all down this huge expanse of tight purple silk over his planet-sized and
-shaped back, and, as attested to by the pitstains *he already had,* wet purple
silk darkens pretty flamboyantly, and Zhou Guy jerked and one of his
bodyguards turned quick and grabbed my arm, the arm with the dreg-
filled glass, and I knew I'd done something radically dumb but it was also a
total accident, and but the kicker, I guess, was that it took a moment for
the ice-cold G&T to soak through, and as Zhou Guy turned as well he
suddenly half-shrieked, viciously *squeaked,* and the bodyguard holding my
arm wrenched me away from him, out of the crowd, and I dropped the
glass and then he slapped me across the face and I lost my balance and
staggered backward into the intricate ice sculpture of Kannon, god of
mercy and wisdom, snapped off the lower three of her left side's four fragile arms and sat down in the drip tray.

It was Chinese New Year, and two months later I began my schooling a
month late in Wellington, New Zealand.

I am not falling to pieces; I am in pieces. It's not so bad.

Since I have been in-country something has been wrong all along; now,
it isn't so. The sensation of invasion—the boy into my song and my trip to
find these drugs—is right and true, and I can accept my ineptness in dealing with him. By arranging this party—in the preparations and in this
busyness—I am at home, part of this city: I am this city. I know how I
appear to people who appear calm, who work at appearing or even, in
fact, maybe truly are calm here, to people who are together, focused, who
speak the language and are sure of many things. I know I appear frantic,
impassioned, goofy, excitable, skittish, *uncool.* They say *yes* and they say *no,*

and I do too, but there is a sense of randomness to me. But at least I can now say that this expression I seem to have little or no control over is true and un-self-conscious; where I am and where I'm at, and a far more sincere and open thing than any J wishful zen silent emotional control I read in the commuters around me. I am foreign here; I am ugly and I have rights: one of them is the right to blow out. I am going to spend anywhere between twenty and forty thousand yen on magic mushrooms weeks ahead of time just to have them, prepare them to hand them out at just the right moment—immediately after dinner, just when the expectation of fun is on the very border of thoughts of trains; just when everything is possible, and for even those who refuse to indulge the fascination of watching those who do will be, at least at first, irresistible—handed out in tiny perfect aluminum and beribboned Christian Dior gift boxes, right there with honey to wash them down on the table next to the twenty- or thirty-foot-high golden Buddha at the Shibuya Buddha Trickbar—seating: twenty or more. From there to karaoke—Echo—and then, Meredith's permission pending, to the Prince, where there will be waiting cases of champagne and Chinese wine and sake and Christmas cake and buckets of KFC spicy chicken wings for a little Xmas J joke (maybe, actually, only one bucket). I am going to get invitations printed, or even made out of some weird substance like ceramics or lacquerware or even candle wax. I am going to hire a DJ and the party will have a name, something that encompasses the entire evening. At every opportunity I am going to trust my own sense of déjà vu. I'm sure Meredith will say yes to the Prince, but I'll have to try and be friendly to her at this dinner tomorrow night; try and help her find Michael before Christmas and get him back here for this party. That would be nice, and that will make the party bigger and better and avoid weirdness when the inevitable questions arise, since the rooms are his. Buddha Trickbar; Echo Karaoke; taxis; the Prince all night long and a champagne breakfast on Boxing Day. And gifts. Personalized gifts for everyone. Or if not personalized gifts, which would take a lot of research and work besides, then cards, maybe. It could be black tie. I could hire a barman so the girls could have real lemon sours and not have to make the shift to Chu-Hai. Ariel doesn't drink champagne. I have to think about decoration: massive posters both to cure the blandness of those rooms and to remind us of home. David Duchovny and Gillian Armstrong, The Nightmare Before Christmas and The Grinch Who Stole Christmas, Dr. Seuss version. Something massive of Prince for Meredith. Rammstein for Jacques could be just a little minor-interest, but maybe, still, a gift, a T-shirt, or jewelry. Fritz Lang's *Metropolis*. *Nosferatu, Blade Runner, Alien, Blow-Up. E.R.* and *Apocalypse Now.* I know a place in Shimokitazawa where I can get massive film posters but they will still have to be framed. Tim Curry as the clown in *It,* Bowie from *Diamond Dogs* or *The Man Who Fell To Earth.* Nothing of Dennis Hopper—or yet maybe, should I? In the spirit of repetition, déjà vu and dreams meaning something. I'll paper those walls in famous Western faces so huge they'll seem abstract; the names of the films in roman letters the size of gaijin.

I could have the party filmed; set up webcams in the corners of the rooms, a roving handycam, too, and edit it all later—send it out in gift boxes to the guests a week afterward, release it to the American Short Shorts Film Festival where it will tour Japan: Tokyo, Sapporo, Nagoya, Okinawa, Matsumoto, then to Singapore, then the world. Jacques will help, but we will need a name for the whole event, film and all: something singular and at first almost affectless and so bereft of connotation it will conjure mystery and later only the event itself. Something both foreign and familiar; one-word and punchy, enigmatic, slightly surreal yet not evasive—something coded for us and us alone. Something possibly Jinglish yet not goofy; something layered and unlame.

A guest list: Ariel, Meredith, Jacques, Michael, Catherine. Brigit that Canadian girl who is into organizing events, and if controllable maybe can help. Drew the *Tokyo Classified* guy. Anton, Sonja, maybe Mary-Beth but then again, maybe not. Pras, this Indian chef Jacques is planning to introduce me to, for my father. And that J English girl from the last Christmas party. Shona? Shania? What nationalities would be there? Filipino, New Zealand, French, American, Canadian, Indian, Dutch, Russian, English, Australian and me. We could have no Japanese, or maybe that would be lame.

We could have *everyone.*

Heaven On Earth has been gutted, but not by fire. I do eventually find it, realizing only after walking right by the place two or three times. Plastic decals of glittering mushrooms stuck onto semipornographic manga bills finally lead me down a side street and hard right: an alcove there, up three steps and there is the Dydo drinks machine, the window filled with dirty yellowing plastic copies of canned coffee and Fanta and narrow cans of

Coke, some of them tipped and leaning, as if an earthquake has knocked them loose, and there is the metal door beside it, half open.

The door is elevated from the ground, a kind of nautical-looking raised section at the bottom, and it's covered in rivets and would maybe look designer and expensive if it weren't so dirty and papered in old illegible peeling posters. Something about the rivets and the metal reminds me of Ariel's apartment door, but I put a lid on that shit straightaway, and check out the promotional leaflets jammed in the letter slot, filling it completely, drooping out swollen into a mass of gray paper pulp. More are scattered inside the door, all over the landing at the base of a steep narrow set of stairs. There is an empty and crushed Lark cigarette packet and a McDonald's cup lying on its side spilling twisted butts and ash.

5f says my mapkin, so I climb the concrete stairs, my feet scraping loudly on coarse grit and bits of broken glass. At the third-floor landing a small fire has been built from trash, leaving the shape of a blackened fir tree burnt up the concrete wall.

5f: there's a blacked-out window that faced out on the street and the stairs continuing up are impassable, full of ancient dead computers; dead gray monitors and dirty beige keyboards with lost keys like missing teeth, dented CPUs with gouged-out disc drives piled high as a man. The only door on the landing is to my left, and it's open, and though on the door in scuffed violet linked roman letters is written, Heaven On Earth, the place is history. The floor and the walls are more bare whitish concrete, and the blue fluorescent tubes that wound around the skirting are all completely smashed and thin phosphor-powdered shards of glass like eggshell litter the floor between the empty metal caps. At the counter in the far right corner of the small shop the display cases are smashed and not just emptied but stripped—if they were ever more than bare concrete that's all they are now. Wires protrude from a recessed gap for a cash register. This is Shibuya, and this, though it may not be the eighties anymore, is prime real estate. A roll of register tickertape is spewed and twisted all over the floor behind the counter, mixed in with hundreds of little plastic baggies and blank white labels. It smells like chemicals; a kind of steely stink like burnt plastic, but there is no evidence of fire anywhere. A blue neon sign up on the otherwise bare pitted concrete wall behind the counter is smashed and dead. The odor is sour and stings in my nostrils.

It's then I see that the dead neon sign faces, on the opposite wall, huge kanji spray-painted in almost transparent blue and close to glowing in the fetid darkness—like a warning or a curse—and they seem somehow very familiar; and they look like this:

死彫れい吸

A sudden scratching noise behind me, like a foot draped in the tickertape scratching across the gritty concrete behind the counter; someone waiting, shifting restlessly.

There's nothing there; the dead room is empty; Heaven On Earth is history.

Jacques
December 1, 2000

Last night I had a very strange dream about Prince, the little singer, and guitarist.

It was a sexy and naked dream, and I woke very slowly, with a big uncomfortable hard-on. And a small bit of unease, too. Because (Thank God) the autumn is here and the heat has gone I am reading again: Tim O'Brien's Vietnam novel, Going After Cacciato. Because another thing that is giving me worry in Japan (amongst many things now, it sometimes feels to me) is the strong feeling that my English is running away one word at a time on little fast and directionless legs to be lost in my dark, foggy ignorance. Now I have decided to drink less, so the light of my memory stays shiny and I retain all the vocabulary I learn. Instead, of course, I use cigarettes and coffee, and hash, sometimes coke, expensive E, and good mushrooms from Mr. Y, the Emperor of Toadstools. But the funny problem now is that with all these former I can't sleep at all and with the mushrooms I sleep well but my dreams become very strange and supple and vivid. This is what gives me more unease and agitation, because dreams are very important, even more when you are far from your home.

My sleeps are like suitcases, full of dreams.

I miss my sisters.

I miss Geneviève and Sandrine.

I write them letters that are long and full of only the good things that happen. Letters on paper that take weeks to get to France. I tell them about the foods of Japan, about pink and soft and fatty toro tuna, how it melts on your tongue. A fish that dissolves and gives a taste so gentle it is like the taste is just a memory of itself. I write them letters about the cool people I meet, about the free concerts and the Frisbee-throwing in Yoyogi Park. I write about Georgiou, a Greek guy with expensive dreadlocks I met, who told me of his father who measures journeys by the number of cigarettes he smokes along the way. How far is it to the beach? Almost a pack!

I think it important to write only and passionately about what you love when you write in your home. I believe that the words cast spells on the rooms in which they are read or written. Look: they make mirrors that reflect the other side of your apartment—and a desert or a lamppost. The words and thoughts you write or read hover and feed the dreams of the sleepers sleeping who slumber and breathe them. Plants of the rooms hear them and react. I see them. They turn to them like the sun; flourish, rejoice. Wilt, decay, or mutate.

Write the words of a bitter sad letter and they will haunt you, live in your bedchamber, descend from the rafters dusty, nightly, squat on you and your lover's face.

Because of this, I wonder about Michael and the things he studies. At how he gave me the Vietnam book. About how he will be. Michael the Warboy.

I miss my sisters and I miss being in love. I miss the feeling of waking from a sexy but nasty dream like this morning and turning to someone nice and having early-in-the-morning sex to replace the nastiness of the dream. To be comforted; to be loved. Everything moves so fast here that there is not time ever for early-in-the-morning sex. Everyone has places and appointments they must go to. Everyone must be on time like the Japanese. If you are late for an appointment with a Japanese person—oh, the terrible shame. They will treat you as if you must be awful, untrustworthy. If you are foreign, you must be untrustworthy.

I miss my sisters.

Even more now Simon is back, for some funny reason. I should be content because now I have a pal and sometimes he is a lover. Or was. I love to use this word. I love to say it clear and high, because it makes me feel so free. There are no complications when I say this. No politics and no hidden meanings, for a brief moment:

He is my lover.

What else could it mean?

Is, was.

But to me, not to him. I know he gets frustrated with me. I see it in his eyes when he gets bored and restless and then he makes me crazy. I do stupid things to make him concentrate on me, like I could want to make him hate me. At TGI Friday's last week he bought a big US steak and I only bought a breads selection. All he did was eat his steak and drink his wine and did not even look up at me. So I got so quietly mad as to remind him of his job here. I said things about his Papa because I know how much of a sore place Simon Sr. is.

"So is your Papa going to have steak and other Western-type foods at his Asian restaurant then?" I asked.

Simon looked down at his steak and stopped eating for a moment, and I am filled with bright power.

Ah-hah, I thought. At last, I thought. I have fired-for-effect. I have fragged his heart, affirmative. I have given him a tunnel wound like those in GI boys in Vietcong tunnels. High into the chest and going steeply down inside.

"Because we haven't been at a Japanese restaurant properly for quite a while, really, Simon," I said, quite quietly.

Simon stared down at his steak for a long minute. And then he muttered, "Dude. What you know about my father is this." A shape between fingertips of nothingness. "So I suggest you keep your nose all the fuck out of it."

And there it is. Papa Two Niner. Dinner is Killed In Action.

What can I say. Cruelty makes me quiet but also a little content. A firm thing to lean against is someone who does not love you back. A strong wall of doubt, and bricks. You can always find out who you are and who you aren't, just this way.

Long-lost Meredith loves Prince, the young brown Master.

Maybe this is why I dreamed of him, knowing she is back and we meet again in a night or two for dinner. This is funny, because usually I dream about people directly. In my last year in Japan my dreams have changed. I dream about other people and am never myself in my own dreams. After Ko, Michael went to Korea, and then it's the rumor he stayed in China for a while. That he became *débauché*. Sometime after those times I had a terrible, electric scaring dream of him, Michael, how troubled yet gleeful he sometimes seemed.

In my dream he was sick.

He had a brain-sickness that made him pale and sweating. In order to get well he had to eat coins. The coins had to go through his system. He had to cut himself on his thigh, on the inside, high up, to let them out.

The only character for me in this dream was strange, for I could taste the coins that had to go through Michael. The brassy, red, electric taste that was in my mouth when I awoke.

This is the quality of dream I have often now. Haunting and surreal but somehow hurtfully true in a way I can't explain. I cannot entirely call Japan or these many shrooms I do now the causes of these new dreams, or the return of so many people back to Tokyo. It is easy to say it is the combination, for combined things have power.

In my dream of Prince last night for once I was in the dream. I was making love with him in a small white bed. His body was small and hard and the hairs on his chest were tight and wiry. He was very dark. His sex was aggressive. He climbed over me, and licked me. He turned away and held his cheeks open to show me. I lay on my back and was so hard it hurt. There was a strange quality in the combination of my lying back passively and his prance and dance over my body; my sad watching of his color and contour; his dark shapes and secrets moving almost frantically over me. Something was sad about his sexual experience, how clever he was at loving. I lay, pale, and watched.

And I realize he was me.

Simon–Jacques–Meredith
December 1, 2000

So I'm inside and Jacques is waiting out there in the courtyard full of little statues, just outside the door. I can see the dude is there, just outside the sushi bar's doors, waiting for the maître d' to notice him or even a waiter. Because of the little green curtain I can only see him from the waist down, but I know it's him because I recognize his trainers and the dude is wearing what for all intents and purposes looks like a *skirt*.

This is it, the final straw. I make a decision. That the guy's become more a liability than a contact can warrant. I'll freely admit the catalyst is this skirt. It's khaki and kind of expensive army surplus. I can see through the windows in the door that it has cargo pockets and zips, a drawcord around the hem with a large red plastic toggle, but this does not alter the fact that the dude has now taken to wearing a fucking *skirt*.

I'm in a booth at the back of this restaurant, the name of which I couldn't read the kanji, but the decor is like a Muji nightmare, like some high-level J-Ikea merger. Everything—the booths, the tables, the bar—is done in light pine. The chefs are behind the counter that's lined with this chrome and glass refrigerated cabinet full of hundreds of different fish.

I've seen five or six different chefs so far, but they're all Japanese; no sign of this Indian guy, Pras-something, Jacques has told me about.

And he's inside now, gesticulating gently at a little J mama in a white apron. She doesn't seem too fazed at the fact he's wearing a black V-neck sweater, blue trainers and a skirt.

They're not communicating too well. She's staring at his hands and he's looking up at the sky for help with his Japanese phrases.

I sigh.

"Jacques," I call out loudly. The three men in suits in the next booth look up at this. *"Jacques."*

He looks up too, and smiles.

He makes his way toward me, not too campily, thank god—guys in the booths next to us have noticed him, and two of the chefs are staring at him, and these guys are more polite than J girls. He's smiling so fucking sweetly I feel like an asshole, and look back down at my menu.

He sits down opposite me.

"Fire for effect, Simon," he says, after a moment. "Let me help us go to work."

I sigh.

A much longer moment passes.

I say, "Take your hand off my knee, please."

The noren curtain hangs down only one-third of the sushinoya's glass and blond pine sliding doors. It is dark green and divided into long strips at the base, like the fingers of phone numbers to be ripped from the bottom of a homemade MISSING poster.

Each of the three central fingers of cloth has cream stylized kanji lettered down it in a speckled, fading cursive imitating the calligraphist's brush. On the first finger is the kanji for Yuisei, "superior," followed by "no," in hiragana, the syllabic script possessive marker, then "ya," in kanji again: "bar." On the second finger is the restaurant's address: 4SF Hommura Bldg. 2-13-5 Sanban-cho, Ichigaya, Chiyoda-ku, Tokyo. On the third, a double-bordered cream circle inside which a fierce bandanna-sheathed sushi chef glowers fanatically offstage.

The doors to the sushi store are at the foot of a deep atrium, the walls lined in a gray tile that blends effortlessly with the twilight overcast sky that is a hexagonal shape far above. Narrow stairs rise three stories up to street level; the busy four-lane intersection at the end of Yasukuni-dori, outside Ichigaya station, only five stops and as many minutes from Shinjuku station and the Prince Hotel.

Down here the twilight is older, traffic sounds are radically muted and it's even more chill. The pine and the warm dark green and the soft yellow light in the squares of glass in the sushi store's door—even factoring in translation problems and the usual embarrassments—look homely and comforting. The yellow light plays out in misshapen trapezoids a few feet over the atrium's floor—which is glossily tiled, too—but the shapes of yellow tile don't quite fully reach the first of the small statues that are scattered around the base of the stairs, every foot or so in the small courtyard, that resembles nothing less than the bottom of an empty well full of tiny frozen figures.

Of course, there are the ubiquitous Rodin miniatures. First and most obviously, *The Thinker.*

NOVA, the near-hegemonic chain of English schools, one at almost every station like McDonald's, has appropriated the very European, muscularly frowning man, head thought-heavy on his fist, thighs bulging. It has achieved a kind of delicate, cross-cultural amalgam of ego-soothing. One of the Frenchman's originals is a permanent exhibit in the Tokyo National Museum of Western Art, along with *The Gates of Hell, The Kiss,* the early *Age of Bronze,* his electric, super-natural *John the Baptist.*

But there are others here in the courtyard.

A faun in a dress coat and top hat stares apprehensively into the tile. A sandstone Blakean dragon raging; a woman coiled in its tail with her arm high, her hand's back to her brow, mimicking in despair and horror the gesture that the *Age*'s young man seems—only seems: Rodin actually removed the javelin at the last moment—to make in ecstasy.

There is a foot-high Amita Buddha, a model of the forty-foot Buddha down in Kamakura, whose one hundred and twenty-one bronze tons have survived tsunami. Alongside, a unicorn prances on a pedestal.

And in a corner just outside the kind light of the sushinoya's doors, Meredith stands ponytailed and smoking, looking down at a winged, angelic cherub, slumped on a stone globe with its hands in its lap, and the sudden concrete connection with home has given her a small smile, and, in just a few moments, the strength (just a *few* moments, she says to herself, and almost audibly groans, both at the ordeal to come and her inability not to procrastinate) to go inside and face dinner with both Jacques *and* Simon.

At the first minute I hear Simon hiss my name in the sushinoya I know his mood is of the shitty kind, and he has embarrassment of me.

"*Jacques,*" he hisses, with urgency, and looks all round himself like a little boy in some trouble.

I give the sushi-mama a nice bow and walk toward his booth and see that, first thing: Meredith has not come yet; and second thing: he has this big embarrassment of me.

He looks up at me and, Pow! large immediate smile from me. This is met with, Fizzle . . . Simon looking away inside his embarrassment, at salarymen at the tables, at chefs who are behind the bar. He looks for their reaction to me, not his own. Then he looks down at his menu, and makes the false study of it.

I know that Pras will be in the back, washing dishes with his slim and clever hands, and I know that Simon would never find someone with the high usefulness of him. This is how I will gain the upper hand of my situation. And even if now it is too late to really frag someone's heart, once they have grown tired and embarrassed in the public area, at the smallest point of this, our parting, I can give him Pras, the good sushi chef, and make Simon able to help Pras, and even himself.

I sit down at his booth. His is the sulky face. Mine is the shiny smile.

"Fire for effect," I say, with brightness. "Let us go to work."

I pat his leg in a manly style, but he takes away offense and asks me not to touch him.

Meredith sucks the last millimeter of her cigarette and drops it on the tile of the atrium. She leans down and pats the sad cherub's head, then turns toward the sushinoya's door.

Far above her the traffic surges as the lights change and as she parts the pendent flaps of the stenciled green noren, extra yellow trapezoids of light bloom around her silhouette, dim and dancing, picking out more tiny gray statues deeper in the darkness of the courtyard. A Pan, an Eiffel Tower, a lion rampant. A pilot in a flying helmet and goggles, feet wide and arms akimbo. Miniature marines erect a furled blank flag against a strong wind, on a patch of ground no larger than themselves. A caterpillar sits gray-eyed, smoking a hookah on a gray mushroom. A tiny girl in a dress does nothing.

As she pulls the low glass door open and the trapezoids give way to a solid block of light, the figures—the dwarfed icons of a dozen different realities—seem to shift eerily; turn, curious, toward the bent figure moving in the doorway. The first flake of this first December day's snow spins through the darkness above them, down through the atrium's triple-storied depth, to land and almost instantly dissolve into a coin-sized spot of darkness by the left cloven hoof of the worried-looking faun.

Merdy steps through the door and into the light.

"His name is—wait for me—Pras. Shortened for Prashabadad something. He is an Indian by birth but a traveler. His father was a journalist and his mother started her own restaurant in Ebisu. They came here when he was quite young, so all his school was international here in Tokyo. He is, I think, twenty-four or -five. I did photography for *Eating Out* here last year. Pras is the only one with good English in this sushinoya."

"..."

"Sorry about hand on the knee, then."

"Is he any good?"

"After high school, sushi chef training for five years. Very unpopular with his mother, but his father is alcoholic and doesn't give two shakes. So five years of training, the last two years here. But still they keep him in the back where he must wash rice every morning, starting early, four and five a.m., finishing late doing cleanup. Though he is an achieved sushi chef, he still gets a kick on the ass like an apprentice, and the shitty money, you know. Such is the restaurant trade for foreigners. And worse for other Asians. He is good and underused and so a little bitter. His bad moods are quite bad. But yes, he has prepared for me, and is very good."

"..."

"This was my twice-entendre that you missed. Hey?"

"Don't, Jacques."

"If you worked in a place like this, you would get your ass kicked too, I think."

"   ."
"Simon?"
"Uh-huh."
"You're extra-terse and uncommunicative today."
"Uh-huh."
"Is it because of Meredith."
"The Backdoor. Backhanded, Backslider, Baxterhausen. No, man. I don't care."
"Simon?"
"What, Jacques."
"What does she know about us?"
"Bauhaus, Bobsled, Bantamweight."
"   ."
"Bitchslap bistro, Backdoor blues."
"Simon?"
"There is no 'us,' Jacques."

She stands in the doorway in the sudden warmth. From behind the bar to her left, which crooks and extends the length of the dark wooden pathway in front of her, a chef in pure white calls out, "Irasshaimase!" without looking up from his work. Spurred, three other chefs along the bar call out, too. Different pitches; different timbres; varying contractions of the greeting. "I"—pause—"ra"—pause—"shai," with emphasis. All the wood is blondish pine and the effect is almost overwhelming after the darkness outside. Lining the counter, chrome and glass cabinets contain trays of fish flesh and condiments: dollops of Bavarian cream-colored scallops; sheets of toasty nori; dominoes of crimson tuna, pink tuna, oily and expensive toro tuna, marbled almost white. Small aluminum pans of sprouts; large plastic bins of sushi rice.

The chefs make a concise and complex sign language, hands dipping precisely and independently into different trays for letters, deftly jerking like Rubik's Cube experts, abruptly producing onto a tiny plate the word: a small and perfect thumb of rice, capped with a moist and shining tablet of fish.

Their fingers stay smooth and unwrinkled, despite the constant dips into the bowls of water on the counter. The rice will stick to dry fingers but a dash of vinegar in the water keeps their skin silky.

The rest of the bar is boothed seating, spreading away to her right on raised, pine floors, lighter in color than the bar's immediate pathway. Patrons' shoes shine and line the wooden curb like large and careful cockroaches, and across the low wooden walls that divide the booths Meredith sees the heads and shoulders of this bar's patrons: all men, upper-echelon, suited, a hundred different permutations of hair product and problems. She looks briefly for Simon or Jacques, but some seated, who face her way, have noticed the dark foreign girl and stare.

She looks down and left, and at the bar more suited men sit on tall stools. Coat hooks and trench coats densely line the walls behind them. And a tiny woman in a perfect white apron appears from beyond the last man and shuffles rapidly toward her.

"Irasshaimase," she says, and smiles shyly, and it sounds, from her, in the final upward lilt, like a question.

The lady is inside the sushinoya door and has seen us.

She gives the cool shoulder to the sushi-mama, and now is the big tension, for Simon, for me, for both of us. The tension makes my English difficult for me. There is no looking at me from Simon; no looking at him from me.

She looks very tall and strange and much more womanly than I remember. And very, very pretty.

Am I pleased to see her? I cannot give a very quick or clever answer to this question.

She sits down with a carefulness and self-conscience, to take away her shoes.

Sitting on the wooden curb Meredith slowly undoes the laces of her Timberland boots. The boys are two booths in and she can feel, if not their eyes, then certainly their attention. And not only of them, but of the other men sitting cross-legged at the low tables in the booths near her. In a low conversation very close behind her, amid the clipped, clattering music of Japanese she hears the word *gaijin* muttered, and a guffaw. Her heart beats quite loudly and she knows she's near the point where nervousness comes out as anger. At the position she's in, at the certain knowledge they've been talking about her, at the fact that she's the last to arrive. And at all the men in this place, and that if there were women here, it might not give her a context in which to place her body language, but would at least give her somewhere comfortably to look.

It occurs to her that the removal of shoes could be akin to low doors in teepees. The visitor made vulnerable on entry; bent, preoccupied and fundamentally assessed.

She stands in socks and towers over the group of three men sitting on flat, square cushions in the booth behind her. The two older men don't acknowledge her. One sips from his small porcelain thimble of sake. The younger man opposite them has a four-button suit, a fat-knotted tie and streaks of brown in his hair, and he lets his eyes slip sideways, but he's almost trapped in a perpetual half-bow anyway, so when his apologetic dip comes she can't catch his eye or the attention of the older men, so, somehow energized by what is neither victory nor capitulation, she walks past the two booths between them and Jacques and Simon—both booths full, all men, none of whom look up to meet her eyes, because the positions have not reversed, she realizes, more like what cannot be assimilated is ignored—and so, in a kind of weird power the invisible have, she towers over their squatted mutterings and reaches the two foreign boys, and Jacques is looking up with a big bright smile that's just a little nervous, too, and Simon is semi-sneering as per usual, looking up sideways at her like she's a bright light in a dark room, a gesture of his she knows is the closest he comes to the demonstration of relief or simple pleasure in seeing someone once again.

When she reaches them the early little victory of sorts has purged most of the nervousness and she says brightly, "Hello, boys," and proceeds to take her keitai out of the back pocket of her jeans, place it carefully on the table across from Simon's phone, unzip her new North Face jacket and sit down cross-legged on the cushion, beside Jacques, who looks down at the table, but still smiling, though the smile is just a little strained, and diagonally opposite Simon.

Who yawns.

The girl is so self-conscious I almost laugh out loud.

Jacques is trying not to look but I just stare at her taking extra time to get her boots off, pretending to ignore the sniggering dudes in the first booth, pretending to strut down here, pretending to be confident, pretending she doesn't care, isn't nervous, is not freaked the fuck out at the thought of sitting down with us.

But when she says, "Hello, boys," it's weird, because her accent has changed and I can hear Michael in her, and see him too, in the dark eyes, the dark hair, and I can see the past too, though it doesn't feel at all fresh or real. She looks and sounds like someone from a movie I watched a long time ago, who has grown up, seen things, got hard.

I've got to admit it.

She looks pretty hot.

"You know," Simon, sitting over the table from us—at long last—says, "ever since like the first day I got back here, I've been seeing deformed people. It's starting to freak me out."

There has been the large, uncomfortable quietness from the time she sat down. His statement is a big surprise and so a big relief. Why is this a relief? Maybe because it is something outside of us and only a matter of him.

"Like what's going on? Armless people, burned tourists. These appallingly damaged salarymen. Retarded children, paralyzed people in wheelchairs on the banister elevators in stations. Every day I see someone. What's going on?"

No one answers his question.

"You know the Israeli girls? The hot Israeli girls who sell the watches and bracelets and rings and all that crap from out those suitcases on trestles on the sidewalk?"

"They have generations underneath, for the lights at night," I say. Meredith gives me the smile and looks down at our table. Pow! Relief. I smile at Simon. "Hey?"

"Right. Well."

Quietness.

"Well, what, then," I say.

"Well. I saw one with a fucking eye-patch."

He is shaking his head.

"An eye-patch?" Meredith says.

"An eye-patch," he says.

"Israeli girl in eye-patch," I say.

"What's up with that? Does anyone else see these people? Is it like just me? If so, is something wrong with me?"

"Do you really want an answer to that?" Meredith says and smiles straight at him for the first time.

He looks up into the air, not at her, and makes the shoulders and two-hands gesture of, not you or me can help me out of this problem.

"Maybe it's a fetish you have," she says quietly. "You're unconsciously seeking out damaged people." I laugh loudly. Simon snorts.

I say, "No, maybe he is just a caring and loving, social-problem concerned person. He wonders about insurance, and welfare."

He says, "Are you like being sarcastic, Jacques. Because people can never totally tell with you."

"Ah-hah." I look out of the tops of my eyes at him with the play of a *minette*. "I am the mystery to you. This is a fateful confession. You cannot figure me out."

"It ain't too difficult, man." He sneers at the table. "It ain't too difficult."

"I am more mystery than you think," I say. "And what you don't know must come back and hurt you."

A quietness falls again.

Simon shakes his head and looks away through the restaurant with the extra amount of I Don't Care. Meredith leans back against the little booth wall. I play around with my coaster. Simon lights a cigarette. It gives us all the spur to consecutively light cigarettes, with little pauses to not seem as if we are all copying each other or nervous at all.

When we have all lit, Meredith laughs her pretty little laugh at the pantomime.

And another quietness falls.

I wait for quite a long time before I say, "I have thought fetish meant only for feet, so I am corrected."

Simon groans, and she laughs again.

My statement is not true, but I am trying in my own way to counterpoint his bravado and all that is unspoken. To break our ice that we are stuck in, calling to each other. I remember something Ko used to like saying, in a knowing smile, smug yet sad, before he hurt himself with the antique *yoroidoshi*.

Whom do you really trust here?

After her "Hello, boys," things get a little quiet and quickly uncomfortable. Jacques seems happy to see her, if a little tense, and Simon simply doesn't seem to have changed at all. And despite her annoyance that sometimes borders on near-repulsion for the boy, she has to admit that it's he—though he does so in his usual self-obsessed and frustrating way—it's he who puts himself out there for all the tension between them to center on.

He drops some typical, "The Japanese are all like *this* today," comment, something about following handicapped Japanese, and she can't resist making some smart retort, the first thing that comes to mind. And stupidly, she makes her quip vaguely sexual, and instantly curses herself for the total failure at aplomb, her transparent crudeness. All the kudos of her uncontrived entrance evaporates.

These things never happen under pressure. Or only occasionally.

She tries to think of something serious, something she can hold on to and pull herself out of being fifteen and absurdly vulnerable. She flicks through her bank of sexual encounters, boyfriends and relationships long and short (two long; too few short), and hard decisions (never enough to help), to collate some references for someone who's very experienced and very much over it.

It never works.

He and Jacques are jousting, with more familiarity than she remembers. Simon won't look at him directly. He mutters his replies to the table, and away into the restaurant. Jacques doesn't seem so cute and earnest as he once did to her, and with his last riposte their conversation dies.

Simon shakes his head and pulls out a Seven Stars from his pack on the table, and instantly she's dying for one, too. Pure appreciation for Japanese smoking laws washes over her, and she lights a Marlboro gratefully. A moment later, Jacques reaches down beside her, and she shifts in the tight booth to give him some room. She laughs out loud when he produces the pack of cigarettes from a pocket in what appears to be some kind of army surplus sarong.

He lights up. Three cigarettes smoulder quietly. Jacques makes some quip and she relaxes a little. Then, the serious thing presents itself, the way to bypass all this bullshit.

But before she asks them about Michael, she finds herself evading again, and asking, "Well, shall we order something or what?"

"A good idea," Jacques says. "Let us go to work."

"I need a drink," Simon says. "Now-ish."

"Well, I'm hungry too," she says. "Let's order everything at once."

Jacques laughs. "Everything at once. 'Let us have everything at once' can be our order."

On the low pine table, they unfold their menus.

Meredith sighs, in something that's part horror, part resignation.

The menu is completely in Japanese.

There are boxes, lined vertically with kanji alongside. Inside they're filled with rows of kanji and hiragana combined. The entire menu is in Japanese, even the prices because the only kanji she recognizes with any kind of immediacy is the character for yen.

The fanatical sushi chef in the top right corner of the menu seems to be less glowering than gloating, now. She stares at the laminated cardboard, a codebook for another nation.

In the periphery of her vision, Jacques is leaning intently over his own menu, examining each row carefully. She flicks her eyes over to Simon, and in the tiny shift in aspect of his dark, leaning head she realizes he was quietly assessing her reaction too. A quick calculation is made: Jacques can hold his own; Simon is either as lost as she is, or wanting to know just how lost she is.

And the next quick thought is: no way is she going to ask for anybody's help.

As her eyes scan the characters without seeing, she is plundering her memory of Japanese phrases, determined not to lose face.

Some phrase for deferring choice, or for a set menu. Or for sushi of the day. Was there such a thing? She half-felt, half-saw Jacques, leaning, drag on his cigarette, exhale from his nostrils a puddle of smoke onto the menu. And Simon, leaning back away from the table, against the wall of the booth, closing his menu gently.

Do you ask for a set menu? Or for the waiter to choose for you? There was a phrase, she just knew it, a concept—a trump card to be played when faced with a menu devoid of illustrations. A Get Out Of Jail Free card to use when you cannot simply point at a photograph to order your food.

Jacques, deep in thought, running a finger along a row of kanji, cigarette clamped in his mouth. Simon across the tiny table, one arm up on the booth's wall, staring across the restaurant.

Dammit.

"Simon," Jacques says. "Hey."

"Mmm," Simon says, staring away.

"Do you want to make the choice? For the sampling?"

Simon snorts, and doesn't turn back to the table.

What was the phrase? What was the concept she couldn't frame, let

alone remember the words of? Let the waiter choose, or the chef choose.
Was it the chef, or the waiter?

"Simon?" Jacques says.

"I want a drink."

The chef. It was the chef. The phrase was to let the chef choose.
Omoko. Something. Or the waiter?

"Just a drink," Jacques says.

"Just a drink, man. That's all I want."

She stares at the menu, trying to think. She sees Jacques turn to her, a
little bewildered. *Omakase. Omakase shimasu.*

Thank god. She remembers. The amount you want to spend, then
omakase shimasu. ¥4000 *omakase shimasu. Shi-sen-yen.* It doesn't sound quite
right. *Shi* means death, so say *yon,* instead. *Yon-sen-yen, omakase shimasu.*
Four thousand yen. You decide.

"Meredith? Have you a decision?"

"Let's go *omakase,* Jacques," she says coolly.

"Uh-huh." He nods, and looks up, confused, to Simon, then back down
to his menu. "A good idea. Yes. We can go omakase and let Pras decide."
He checks Simon. "For Pras to decide for us, then you can ascertain him,
hey? His goodness of choice, and skill."

"Whatever, man," Simon says. "The important thing right now is my
thirst."

Jacques stares, a little baffled, something close to hurt on his face. She
looks from one to the other. Jacques turns back to her. "Simon is going
to recruit a friend of mine for his father's business. We are giving him
the testing. He is a hand here, but a good chef. In the back. Pras, is his
name."

"Oh."

"Shut up, Jacques," Simon snaps.

"What?" Jacques, bewildered. "Why?"

"Just don't . . . like . . . spell everything out all the time, man." He taps
the menu. "Order from this fucking Indian and let's get on with this. Get
me a goddam drink."

He sighs, and looks away over the restaurant again.

In silence Jacques stares at him, then turns to Meredith.

"So," she says. "How did you meet this guy."

He thinks about it for a while.

"Um. I guess, it was after I leave the Jujo gaijin house," he says. "After I met you." A small smile. "It was last year, I guess. A party, somewhere. He knows of Ariel, somehow, I think."

Jacques looks thoughtful. Simon starts to fumble in his pockets for his cigarettes.

"It was your brother introduced him to me, actually," Jacques suddenly says, and he breaks out in a big, surprised grin. "Yes, yes. Your big brother."

I'm sitting here wondering if like radical baldness could be considered a deformity. Enough to be added to the list. I'm not saying much, just letting these two tiptoe round each other, internally reliving their sordid affairs.

Or if not baldness, then at least combovers. Which they call barcodes here. Because there's so many of them. There are at least five guys beside this booth with totally blatant barcodes, all sitting at one table. Together. Does it become a fashion? Is deformity fashionable? Can you imitate someone else's barcode? Are there different kinds? Are there some combovers that are totally out this year? Like completely unacceptable in combover circles? I want to know if there is a subculture of barcode fashion I was hitherto unapprised of. Can combovers have circles?

I want to know if a deformity is something that happens to you, something that's done to you, or something you do to yourself. I want to know why ugliness and self-sacrifice—or at least hard work—go together. I want to know where men get the idea that baldness is not the end of the line. I want to know what it takes to get someone to order me a drink, because like Meredith, though she hid it pretty well, I cannot read the goddam menu.

I give the beckoning to the sushi-mama, who is standing over at the chef's bar, awaiting. I call out, "Sumimasen!" in good J style. Maybe my style is just the little overfeminine; too much of the enthusiasm and charisma, too little of the manly Simon I Don't Care.

But I Don't Care, hey?

She shuffles in the slipper-thongs toward our booth and us three just a little uncomfortable people. She crouches down by the end of our table and the attached order clipboard and invites us to order from her.

"Please."

"What will you have to drink?" I ask the table. "It's sushinoya, so sake, and beer for chasing sake's tail would be appropriate, huh?"

"Loads of," Simon mutters.

"Sure," Meredith says.

In what is okay Japanese language, that the sushi-mama smiles at the clipboard with response to, I ask for three Asahi Dry beers and a carafe of sake. She nods, and nods, and writes briskly on her clipboard.

In my determination not to appear touristy, I ask for what kinds of the sake she recommends us.

And in a little sympathy, she speaks with slowness and simplicity for me. I translate to the table.

"Um. She says they have two good sakes she recommends us today. The first is *shirataki*, which is very clear and light and shiny sake. *Shirataki* meaning 'white fall' sake. And the other is *otokoyama* sake, which is a deeper, strong and dense sake. *Otokoyama* meaning . . . um . . . male mountain."

I make no single sign of amusement or anything campy whatsoever. "Which do you want, do we think."

There is a silence from the two.

"Clear fall, or male mountain."

"Whichever's strongest," Simon mutters.

"I haven't had sake for quite a while, Jacques," Meredith says, in the sheepy tone. "I might not be able to have much."

"Both," Simon says. "Get both. What's J for 'both,' Jacques?"

"Um."

I think for a moment.

"*Ryoho*, I think. Yes."

"*Ryoho*, please," Simon says with a little more perkiness to the sushi-mama, who is already nodding. "*Ryoho*, baby."

"Two sakes," I say. "*Shirataki* and *otokoyama*. Money is not an object. Buvons à temps, quand on est mort c'est pour longtemps."

The sushi-mama has a little smile to her pad and is writing.

Simon goes back to the sulky face.

"What does that mean, Jacques," Meredith says. "You enigma."

"Just let us drink now when we can, for when we die it is forever," I say.

"That," Simon says, "is by no means bullshit."

"Food, Jacques," Meredith says. "Food."

So then, with some difficulty, I begin to explain to the mama our request.

My grammar is a problem. Mine is the grammar of a trout in salty water. I am unsure how to substitute "Pras" for "you" in the appropriate sentence. The one in which I ask her to decide.

To add further problems, I suddenly think of how maybe that the staff do not call him Pras at all. And that my knowledge of Indian naming traditions is very thin, and my knowledge of, in particular, the name of Pras himself is likewise very limited. My good mood at my competitive language usage begins a quick fade. Is Prashabadad his correct name? Does this sit in the front or the back of his entire name? Do the Indian race have two, three or four names, like the Balinese dishwasher at my old restaurant Le Toile? Hamdad Bin Said Abdulaziz. Do the Indians do so likewise?

Uh-oh.

I settle to ask the mama, crouched at our table in a polite way, holding the clipboard of our order.

"Excuse me," I say. "Do you know this sushinoya's Pras? Indian Pras? Apprentice. Hand. In the back."

I start well, but settle for the gestures and Jinglish when I cannot think of the correct kind of word for "back" in Japanese. I glance to Simon, a sharpness of pain for his gentle long *senaka*, a body jolt. *Senaka*, which is his tan human back.

But she is surprised, and relaxes a tiny bit. Restaurant working affinities are strange and strangely deep after a time. The new worker must bide his time and his kicks in the ass, but after that time and knowledge, the bonds are strong.

"Purasu, is it?" she says. She half-laughs, at the sense of sharing the old joke. Pras in J is the same as Plus. She gestures with her hand holding the pencil, to wash her face with darkness.

"Yes, yes," I say. "Purasu, the Indian apprentice and hand. Back." I have to say it again.

"Yes, yes. I understand," she says, with a little impatience.

"Minus, is it," I say, and guess their nickname for him. "Mainasu."

She smiles with friendliness and nods.

"Yes. India's Minus."

It's a funny way that the conversation is so crooked and raw, yet I feel the impression the other two have. I feel extremely competitive.

"He is my friend," I say.

Then, a thought.

"How much, guys? How much yen do we spend here?"

A brief pause. Meredith lightly shrugs. Simon looks interesting for the first time.

"Aim high, dude," he says, and grins.

I give him a secret grin too. "Fire for effect?"

"Kick-*ass*."

To the sushi-mama, I try to say, "Let Purasu decide our choice. With freedom."

What I really say is, "Purasu wa, kare ni osusume wa nani ka? Kiite kureimasen ka?"

In English, this might be, As for Pras, what are his favorite foods? Ask him, could you?

"Takai wa, taihen daijobu."

As for expensive, it's very much okay.

This is a little showing off, and possibly rude. She smiles and nods and excuses herself. Simon calls out loudly, "Thank you very much," in funny-accented Japanese.

"Here we go," I say.

"Cool," Simon says.

Then Meredith makes the mood a little funny again.

"Do either of you guys know where Michael is?"

And so when she finally asks the right question, the answer is surprisingly simple, and yet not so.

"Why don't you just call him," Simon says.

"Yes, why don't you just call him," Jacques says. "I have his numbers."

The table of Japanese salarymen behind her erupts into laughter.

She's startled, and glances behind her: a plump Japanese man, nearly fifty, his suit disheveled, his face red and sweating, a crazed grin, a long, thin line of hair hanging between his bloodshot, staring eyes. He is shaking his arms violently over the table at her, a single mad slug of rice stuck to his flushed cheek. He quivers his wrists, splayed fingers stretching white and scarlet-splotched.

He shrieks at her, past her, in thick, drunken, slurred English, "Aru you afuraido? *Aru you afuraido?*"

His table erupts again.

"What a plague she means to take the death of her brother thus."

She turns back quickly, shaken.

"What did you say?"

No answer.

"What did you *say?*"

Simon sneers down at his menu. He flicks his eyes to Jacques, then to the loud salarymen.

She hears a loud sharp smack behind her, and turns again, ducking, frightened. The drunk man is holding both hands protectively over his head and the laughter rises again, a shrieking foreign ugly cackle, the man beside him with his hand held high threatens a further blow. Some social threshold crossed, he flinches and spurts a shrill gulp of Japanese. The man beside him grimaces, threatens; the drunk man relents and lowers his hands. His neighbor strikes him hard again. There is a harsh clap; his hair flies and the laughing is crazed and hard and right up close to her.

She turns back shaken.

"Drinks approaching," Jacques says, looking past her.

"What the fuck did you say to me, Simon," she says.

He sighs, tilts his head to the side and flicks his menu end for end.

"I just *said* . . . what a drag. Always being late for your brother's bus. Jesus. Relax."

He eyes her contemptuously.

Dudes are going crazy next to us, getting quickly fucked up on the lethal sake that's coming our way.

Sake's the best drink for bingeing. It starts strong and makes you just that little bit wary. There's a snap to it that's unlike any other alcohol. More mellow and less acidic than gin or vodka, and cleaner than wine or dark spirits. The snap eases quick, and then the shit doesn't taste or kick until you wake up on the street somewhere.

And the great thing about Japan is your pockets will still be full when you do.

"Just call him up," I tell Meredith. I make some crack, and she hasn't changed at all. Whatever he does, her world shifts to accommodate him.

"Just call him up."

Our sake is served up to us on a lacquery tray. We have two of the creamy porcelain carafes, as small as round beer bottles. In a space in their undersides, a tiny candle rests and burns to warm the sake for winter drinking.

We are given two small creamy cups for each of us, placed carefully by the mama, who ignores the loudmouth men behind me with good care.

"As for the beer...," I say quietly, in reminder.

"Yes. Just a moment, yes?" she says. The testy sushi-mama. They are better than a stereotype.

"So. You have his number, then," Meredith says, with shaking. She is pale, shocked by the loudmouthery and shouted rudeness of the drunk men. So close to her; it shocked.

"I have, I think, three numbers," I say. "Yes, three. Different numbers for three keitais. He has a three-G, a Palm Pilot and an old large amusing phone, too."

Simon sniggers with this.

"Yours is large and funny, too," I say.

"It's functional, paid-up and on the verge of being replaced, dude," he says. "Don't give me any shit about the phone. It's an old friend."

"An old friend that will be replaced, huh."

"Doesn't pay to get sentimental about your technology here, man."

"Or your friends," Meredith says.

He pours us one of the sakes into one of our cups.

"Let's just have a drink, and then we can call the dude up on each of his phones," he says. "Relax."

He is cheerful now, with the sake.

"Okay?"

"Okay," I say.

"Okay," white Meredith says, after a pause.

The first drink of heated sake is a shock; a breathless whack like falling flat on your back. But unlike hard spirits, it doesn't give her that second biting flash in the back of her throat. The taste of sake always seems to her the taste of waiting: for the shock that never comes. Sake is a tease; its real power in accumulation.

But almost instantly, the lights and pine take on a richness and depth, a luminous warm gloss that's in the air and inside her. Harsh detail recedes; smiles become primary, depthless and pleasant.

She sighs, and tastes the hot foreign breath of the sake again.

"Oh," Simon says, "yeah." He reaches across the table and takes the second carafe. He pours the second thimble.

"It's nice, huh," Jacques says. "Nice winter drink."

"One more," Simon says.

She picks up the second thimble. Inside the sake is thicker than water. She sniffs, and the scent carries the alcoholic jolt that never quite delivers, always demands more.

She downs the second thimble in one.

"Huh?" Simon nods, grinning. "Huh?"

"Yup," she says. "It's good."

And then the small woman in the blinding white apron returns.

This time, she's carrying two trays.

On the tray balanced on her left forearm and palm are three tall, narrow handles of beer, a solid fourth of foam brimming at the rim. On the right is a large elliptical plate. It's filled with thin, steaming brown liquid, dotted with shining spots of transparent oil. And alarmingly, the fluid surrounds and leaks from the long huge head of a fish.

Its skin is crumpled and mahogany, eyes shrunken and rumpled in their sockets. Its mouth is just ajar, cooked open, and rows of teeth like a kitten's are more brown in withered, roasted gums. It's steaming, ugly, leaking and smells delicious.

The woman bends and deftly places the trays on the table around the sake vessels. From the tray with the beer she takes three rolled and steaming towels and three disposable hashi in paper envelopes and places them on the table in front of Meredith and the two boys. Then she crouches at the end of their table, and as she writes on the small clipboard, she murmurs to Jacques.

Meredith takes the hot towel, unrolls it and wipes her hands as Jacques listens closely, nodding.

"What in the hell is it, man," Simon says, leaning over toward the steaming brown head. "It's like, *Alien Resurrection*."

"How do you eat it," Meredith says.

"*Do* you eat it," Simon says.

Jacques thinks. "Um, she says Pras' first choice for us is this. *Kama*. Whole, roasted jaw of the tuna fish. Good for winter. And beginning sushi meal. He is coming out soon, when they give his break."

Simon doesn't reply.

The woman finishes writing and shuffles to another table. Meredith watches her crouch and murmur to a suited man. She is kind to him; nodding and maternal, in a way she wasn't to them.

She turns back to the boys.

"Before we eat, I want to call Michael," she says. "Please. I need to know where he is. Now."

Simon is poking at the tunafish's black and blistered eye with a chopstick. He sips his beer, and pokes again.

"You very much want to know," Jacques says.

"Please."

"Give her the numbers," Simon says. "Get it over with."

"If we must then," Jacques says.

He takes his phone out from a pocket in the sarong. The phone is slim and silver and Panasonic. As he flips to his directory the phone's screen and keys light green in his hand.

She picks up her own phone.

Simon picks up his.

"Give us a number each," Simon says. "We'll all call him."

"But if we all call him simultaneous at the one time, though," Jacques says.

"What, then," she says.

"He may suspect an emergency or something, from home, or an earthquake in Tokyo, or who knows."

"Whatever it takes," she says. "I don't care."

"Saturation bombing," he mutters, eyes reflecting green squares. "Cover all the bases."

"Boredom attrition," Simon mutters.

"So. Meredith first." He reads out the list of numbers; a 090 Japanese keitai number. She keys it into her phone, and as she enters Michael's name into her directory for the second ever time, she misses the number Jacques reads to Simon.

"Alright," Simon says, phone to his ear, his cheek lit mauve by his screen. "Here we go."

Meredith presses the small kidney-shaped button, marked with a mint-green floating handset. She lifts the blue glowing screen to her ear.

"Aru yu afuraido, Meredisu?" Simon says in a grotesque Japanese accent and grins widely. He drinks from his sake, then his beer, and waits, watching the men behind her.

She hears a faint hum, and three clicks. Jacques is pouring more sake carefully from the carafe held with his right hand, into the thimble in his left, his tiny phone wedged between his head and collarbone.

It connects.

The ring tone is tripartite; fuzzily rippled. She tries to remember her brother's voice. She tries to graft a memory of his voice onto the context of this ring tone. Smear it with static and distance; sterilize it with technology so the graft might take.

Ring tone.

How did Michael answer the phone? It's something she's never consciously tried to frame in a phrase, a simile, even a memory. Did he sound bored and cool? Was he funny? Did he say his name? Who does he expect calls from now? Who does he hold long expensive international calls with? Or short local calls about missing home and what's grotesque on Japanese TV. Does he laugh with them?

Ring tone.

Simon swigs his sake; pours another, one-handed. Sake splashes on the table.

"Be careful of the candle," she whispers. Her gesture to the carafe is raised eyebrows and a nod. He dips his head. "Whoops." Straightens the tiny candle in the porcelain cave.

"I get no answer," Jacques says. He takes his phone left-handed, stretches out his neck.

"Wait," she says.

Ring tone; the suspended time of the threshold. She feels strangely alright. A little more direction, a firming of a path.

Can she remember him saying simply, "What," in a grumpy mutter? Or was there a memory of a low, stoned, "Good *evening.*" What will his accent sound like now?

"Bullshit," Simon says. He drops his phone from his ear and catches it in the same hand. He presses END.

"Simon, no," she says over the tone.

"He ain't there, baby."

"You don't know—"

"He's gone."

"Well leave a goddam message then. Don't be such a prick."

"Listen Meredith," Simon says. "Eighteen tones, no answer, and no answering service means no one home and that same no one wanting to stay that way." He drops his phone on the table.

"I, too," Jacques says. "No answer, no service."

"He's gone."

"Strange to have no service. That is an intentional feature. With design."

The ring tone rings on. But like the lost toy in the wardrobe you find when and only when you give up and start to hunt for the next-best toy, if she keeps talking, she knows he will suddenly answer, in the middle of her own sentence, in the middle of a lost, wandering thought.

But she can't think of anything to say, and she isn't thinking about anything other than this plan of not thinking itself. Does this count as a different thought?

Jacques hangs up, drops his phone on the table too.

Is she thinking about Jacques now, so he will answer, whisper, hello *baby*, think she's some J girl and be surprised and pleased and embarrassed she's not?

Now she's messed up, thinking wrong, thinking all about this ringing, relentless, distant, floating, placeless, international sound.

Five more tones, then.

Five more tones, then.

Three more.

Three more tones.

She hangs up.

"Too bad," Simon says. "Let's eat this thing."

It's not, I reiterate, *not* that I'm not interested in maybe hooking up with Michael again. But how I look at it is this: if the dude wants to get lost here, he can, and should be able to do so without basically getting hunted down. Three phones and no answering service means the guy needs phones for international use, and for his *own* use. I.e. for mutually exclusive babes, and not to get called up every couple of days by sisters and bored motherfuckers looking for parties, or fathers who are basically just checking up to make sure you're just still out of the country and not coming back to cause trouble for their business with like public drunkenness on the premises and one drug bust and only halfhearted demands for food and bar tabs all over the state, fathers who are more than happy to bullshit you about a job and a future to keep you out of their ridiculous hair.

I don't want to meet this Indian.

The sushi-mama arrives with a specially large tray while the tunafish is still very whole and not touched or eaten much of by us, who are more interested in the sake, it seems. She lays down a small plate of *yanaka* each, lengths of the root of ginger, with mellow miso paste for dipping, and easing of the ginger fire. Then there are three small smoky glass bowls, in which she calls to me are *ankimo*. The liver of a deep fish in *ponzu* sauce, with onion and kelp. The *ponzu* is a citrus sauce, bright and tart in flavor, dark and mysterious in color. The *anko* liver is a soft and pinkish plod in the bottom of the sauce. She tells me this is *chinmi*—very delicacy, a restaurant's special dish for special customers only.

"Purasu wa doko ni arimasu ka?" I say, my J slipping further with the sake. As for Pras, where is he?

"Chotto mate, chotto mate," she nods and nods.

Just a moment, just a moment, she is getting just a little snippy.

"Nama biiru, mo mitsu. Sake, mo yotsu, onegai shimasu," I say. Three more beers. Four more carafes of sake. Please. Fire for effect, for Simon. Aim high. Kick-ass. Indulge his despair.

Meredith is quietness and tense contemplation, Simon is relaxed and drinking faster and faster, leaned against the pine wall, and I am tasting a piece of the gingerroot carefully when all our keitais go off at once.

She stares down at her blinking phone, humming and buzzing, blue screen pulsing, moving on the table between the trays and plates and glasses.

Beside her, Jacques laughs abruptly at the three phones shuddering. Then he stops.

"Whoa," Simon says. "Timing."

She picks up her phone, moving in pulses in her fingers. On the little screen, from the directory entry she'd made just five minutes ago, the name and the miss-key in innocuous blue digital:

MICHADL.

The background merges from gray to blue, the name inversely. Before she can touch the talk button, the phone goes suddenly silent and still. Jacques' phone and Simon's phone follow, seconds later.

"What," Simon says. He hasn't moved. "Was it him? Did he just hang up?"

"I don't...know," she says. The sudden strange adrenaline in her; the mutter and laughter of the restaurant around her. Jacques picks up his phone.

"What an *asshole*," Simon says, and laughs. "You do *not* want to hook up with him, Merdy. Dude is on his own wavelength."

"What's . . . happening," she says. "I'm going to call him back."

"No," Jacques says. "No."

"Why not?" she snaps. "What exactly do you know, Jacques? You know where he is, right? This is a dumb joke, right?"

"No," Jacques murmurs. "Look, no joke."

"What, then?"

He taps the screen of his phone.

"Skymail."

"What?"

"Bullshit," Simon says.

"Uh-huh. Skymail. To all of us."

She holds the screen up close, and sees, blinking in the top right of her new bilingual keitai's screen, a miniature mauve paper dart.

She presses the toggle key; toggles down to SKYMAIL, to READ, to NEW MESSAGE, and hiragana spools down her keitai's screen.

The kanji for yen.

The points of the compass. Book, big, sushi.

Sukiyaki, rice paddy, expensive. Big or fat.

Telephone, on a particularly alert day.

New: half of Shinjuku. Bridge. And language.

The numerals one through four. Person. Big person. Big J person. In north Shinjuku, stands in a rice paddy, or on a bridge over a rice paddy, and orders a J book on expensive sushi over his phone.

In whatever tense.

Given a couple of hours and the inclination I could *maybe* guess.

But this is hiragana, and it is totally full—this skymail takes up all of one screen and all of half the next. One hundred and fifty characters, with no spaces between. Jacques would be able to read this in Japanese, because even I can read a little hiragana; but what it might actually *mean*—in kanji, let alone in *English*, what the characters actually *signify*—is a totally different story.

"You know he must have had this ready to reply so fast," I say.

"What do you mean?" Meredith says quietly, staring at her phone.

"The size of this," I say. "In Japanese. How long would it take to type a thing like this into your phone. Think about it."

"Yes," says Jacques.

"So what are you saying?" Meredith says.

"He was waiting for someone to call," I say, realizing it only when I say it.

"He was waiting for us to call," Simon says.

And it is strange—and what is my sensation? Is it a pleasantness to see some plan spring into action? To see a flytrap's gentle speed? To see a long-brooded strategy burst a strong and fleshless hand from pounded earth of a grave? When I was a young teenager I saw the grave of Jim Morrison at the great cemetery of Père Lachaise, where Oscar Wilde is buried. My father took me for safety from the junkies. No wonderful poet but the perfect actor in the play of his times. A soul at a cusp. A statue of his head and shoulders, younger, before the brandy made him fat and slow. On the stone face were graffiti, *Angelo 3/3/85* on his left cheekbone; *Fabio* follows him, *3-5-85* under the right stone eye. *Gera loves Tim* on a curve slant near his mouth. *Beppe 3/3/75*. *Ferdy* all down his broken nose. My father took me because he was a child of sixties, a beatnik, a fan, and because he knew the new film would change everything. My father, with his soft and careful voice, and a silver glint inside each ear. The bust was taken after the film was shown. The graffiti cleaned and security patrols to stop the heroin began. A hole in his lip, and his lost blank accepting expression made strong by a convention in sculpture you do not see in classics: the pupil and iris of the eyes were a concave, a hollow in his eyes. Some lover, some fanatic had colored in these holes in his eyes, inked in the stone. For what reason? Realism? or a wasted quick idea from nowhere? *Rebecca & Andrea.* The stink of urine. The stone mane of his hair.

No, it is more than strangeness, this feeling. It is more than just a pleasantness. It is life, it is memories become real, it is the corpse hand from the turf, the beak through the eggshell and bloody pearl of womby fluid. No matter what is the malice or the extent, in the boredom of Tokyo I like that it is art, it is truth, it is purity, it is energy, it is meaning in our message on a face, but more than anything I like that it is excitement.

"Hmm. Do you think so?" I murmur. I stare at the message glowing. I flick from first to second screens and back again. "Waiting?"

"Totally," Simon says. "Do the math. How long would it take to make a coherent message in English this long, let alone J? How long did we sit here? Two, three minutes?" He gulps extra sake, excited, too.

Meredith sits in quietness, watches her screen.

"'Sa, ku, sha, mi, sho,'" she says. "I can read it. I don't understand it, but I can read it." She looks to me, hopefulness. "Jacques, can you read it? I mean, at least if it's coherent? Not just nonsense or something?"

"Maybe," I softly say. "I understand some of the objects. 'Island,' perhaps. 'Island Dutch'? The grammar is a little funny maybe, but it seems to mean something, I think."

She turns back to her own screen, and a sigh, she makes a crumpling with her whole body.

"Hey," I say. I put my arm around her. "Hey. It's okay."

"Why would he do this?" She is near tears. "Why would he not call. Why would he send this shit."

"You're worried about what your father will say?"

She jerks, moves apart from me.

"I'm worried about *him*."

"'Ga, ra, to, i, ko, ki,' something, 'no, so,' some shit." Simon is strong in competitivity, but not in his big round slurring r's, his goofy drawly US vowels. "Why don't you just call him back then. Dude is obviously right on top of all his phones."

"Yes," Meredith says sharply. "Yes. You're right." She looks sideways, as if overhearing something, and sits up. She thimbles sake for a shot, and toggles her keitai to press the dial.

I light a cigarette, sniff mildly, lean back in the booth. "What of the poor *kama*," I murmur, signify the cooling fish in the center of the table.

No one hears my question, both dialing. Now I can say, in this moment, the beginning of something very special, that I no longer feel connected to this growing drunker boy across me, dialing at his phone. Now I can say, go, okay, let me see *un grand guignol* at play. Instead of a lover in the balcony beside me, give me bigger and just as flitting thrills on the stage. Give me a wider romance. A spectacle. I will no longer wait.

"Jacques," Meredith says sharply. "What's this." She holds her phone to me. I take it and listen. What I hear is the chirpy recorded J girl voice saying that the denwa bango is no more a service.

"It has been cut off," I say. "And so quickly."

"Jacques," Simon says, and leans over with his phone. "Listen."

The message is the same. I shake my head sadly.

"Disconnected. No service."

"What—the *hell*—is going *on*," Simon only a little slurs or funny emphasis reveals his growing drunkenness.

"Cut his phone off straight away," Meredith thinks out loud. "We call, he sends this, he cuts his phone off. Can you arrange a phone to star sixty-nine with a skymail? *Automatically?*"

Simon burps.

"I don't know," I say. "I'm not sure."

"Well we need to get this translated then," she says, sitting upright. She looks me hard in the eyes. It is easy for me to look back. "And you aren't going to be quite good enough, Jacques."

"I know," I say.

She smiles. She is excited too. Her eyes are alive, not colored hollows.

"Well, who then. We need someone we can trust."

"True," I say. "I wonder where Pras is."

"Oh Jesus *Christ*, look at *this*," Simon hisses, and we both turn to him and see his stare over to the sushinoya's doorway, where there are two young girls in overcoats lightly touched at the shoulders with snow, laughing very silly with their show of shyness, hands across their mouths. One of the overcoats is light-lighter blue; the other bright fire-engine red.

Always the adept at symbolism, she thinks. It makes sense he would begin this way. A straw in the flood from who knows where out there, but a direction, now, to swim. She thinks, with a kind of private fatalist glee, I'll play this game. I'll surf this beach. For perhaps the first time since arriving back, a kind of clarity descends. Purpose; power. Direction. Something to give oneself up to. This is what I am here for. This is what I'm here to do. No foreigner's Japanese will be enough, either. To do this properly she'll need a native. And someone who won't patronize or evade or hide behind a posed politeness. She needs someone who can and will really help. Someone with a stake.

Her first thought is her mother.

"Oh," Jacques says beside her. "Here he is, the man itself."

She's been staring lost in thought at the two giggling girls, helping each other remove their coats, and noting the men who glance, and shake their heads in resigned, familiar disgust and turn back to their beer and sushi, somehow satisfied. Noting how Simon's attitude, unhidden, is a species of theirs. Though she knows he would not agree. Lust as disgust, she thinks, and then also, hard on this thought, the uselessness, or more the futility, of moralizing against an entire culture. Railing against the monolith. Is this all going to change?

But those girls are in her; she is of them. How much so, she wonders. How much of her is what she sees in them; and is her gut reaction just as real and false as what provokes it?

But this has happened before, she knows, and will again. Questions and decisions based on a flash of culture shock. She knows the decision too; and its inevitable result. It is always a kind of nightmare. The end of daring. Stasis, self-control.

"Who?" she says.

"Here is Pras," Jacques says, and he is twisted in his seat, looking behind her. He's smiling. She turns, and an Indian boy, in blinding white trousers and shirt, a fresh apron but no hat, is flicking off his sandals at the wooden curb. In that beautifully practiced, negligent manner.

He approaches in socks, and smiles a handsome, close-lipped smile, pleased and arrogant, like maybe it's an effort not to laugh, his fleshy chin held just high as in a dare. At the end of their table he falls easily to his knees, J style, pauses a moment watching Jacques, who waits, and the Indian boy carefully composes a serious face.

"Um," he begins, but stops, and almost laughs. Jacques starts slightly, overcomes something. "Uh, we . . . were in the jungle," the boy says, in some placeless international accent, no vowel committed too broadly far or narrow, no consonant given any more than its due. A bracelet glints at his left wrist.

"Oh, no," Jacques says, and smiling down at the table, intones, "Nous 'tions dans la jungle."

"There were too many of us," Pras says.

"Uh, um . . . nous 'tions trop nombreux."

Jacques is translating him, she realizes, this is some boy thing. She relaxes, glances over at Simon. He idly stirs through the remaining Seven Stars in his pack with his fingertip, ignoring but listening.

"We had access to too many uh, too much money."

"Nous avions trop beaucoup, euh, trop d'argent."

Even the falter precisely mimicked.

"Too much equipment."

"Trop d'équipment."

"And little by little, we went insane."

"Et peu on est devenue fous."

With a final smile that seems simultaneously part of this little skit, yet brought on by it, Jacques looks from sceptical Simon to her, and back to Pras, with an expression, wry yet pleased, that says, this is what we always do, and, however silly, I've missed it. Meredith smiles, and with the sake coming on stronger now, she relaxes, pleased, content.

"You shitty cook," Jacques says.

"*Bakayaro*. Crappy kitchenhand," Pras says, and they both laugh loudly, and she joins in and even Simon too, for one second, in a tiny involuntary burst, in that helpless abrupt way no matter if you've missed the joke.

The girls over at the door burst out in giggles too, as if in echo. Pras nods toward them, looks at Jacques.

"You know what the old men that come in say about the young girls now?" he says.

"What, then."

"*'Hashi ga korogatte mo okashi.'* They will find amusement at chopsticks rolling."

He laughs, but she wonders if she sees a tiredness in the cook's dark eyes, if he's trying just a little too hard.

"Simon, this is Pras. Pras, Simon Chang, who is American, of the new LA restaurant, Shinsekai," Jacques says. "'New World.'" And with this totally melodramatic gesture, palm up, wrist bent like an actor—a *camp* actor—indicates me.

"Yup, it's a pleasure," I say.

"Nice to meet you, Simon," Pras says, his head bent, a struggle between deference and pride, or like he's been bowing far too long. The dude is a cook. It's just absurd.

"And this is Meredith Edwards," Jacques continues. "Michael's sister. From New Zealand."

"Hello," she says.

"Hi, hello," the Indian says. "I've heard a lot about you."

"Oh?"

"Uh-oh," I say, and laugh, maybe a bit loudly, because neither Meredith nor Jacques joins in, and Pras is obviously torn because he thinks I'm going to get him work, he wants a job in the States and a green card so bad he can taste it, and just widens his slightly bloodshot eyes a little, checking out this scene, maybe just a little embarrassed at his and Jacques' little recital.

"How is the work today going?" Jacques, the peacemaker, asks him.

"It's okay," Pras says. "It's reasonably quiet tonight. Weekdays are quieter."

"How long have you been here?" Meredith asks.

Pras looks from her to me, to Jacques. Then back to me, and makes some kind of leap of faith.

"Well. Almost two years now," he says. "I have worked for three years before this at a smaller, more family-oriented sushiya down in Hamamatsu. Then I came up to Tokyo to work here at Yuisei." He smiles. "I'm sure you know about Edomae-zushi. Tokyo is the birthplace of nigirizushi. Tokyo is old Edo. Originally the sushi rice was only there to prevent spoilage of the fish. They were packed together, and as the rice fermented, it produced an acid which pickled the fish. This became traditional for curing, while the rice was always discarded. This was soon seen as a waste, so new techniques for rapid maturing eventually culminated in a man named Matsumoto Yoshiichi, a doctor to the Tokugawas, based right here in Edo, adding vinegar to the sushi rice, for flavor and faster maturation. Then suddenly, it was 1824, Hanaya Yohei conceived of raw fish and the fingers of vinegared rice, together, straightaway, made in front of you. And nigirizushi was born. Right here. It was invented in Ryogoku, six stops away from here on the Sobu line."

Pras is totally serious, telling us what we need to know. Jacques, nodding along with this. It's almost a pity. The Sobu. I'm trying not to laugh. The endless local, all the way out to Hachioji.

"The history, the real traditions are all here. My thinking was that if you're going to learn a craft, you should learn the craft from the pioneers, and the innovators. In a place that confers a kind of responsibility upon you. A tradition exists here that I feel I have to live up to, work inside. An ongoing conversation."

"Actually, she's just *making* conversation," I say. "She's not with me."

He's bewildered for a moment.

"Oh, I only meant...tonight," Meredith says, unsure. "How long you had been...here. I'm not anything to do with...the restaurant...or anything...." She trails off.

"Merdy is...um, you're just trying to track Michael down," Jacques says, and turns to her. "Right?"

"Oh. Right," Pras, really embarrassed, says. "Michael. Sure. Sorry." Just a little stiffly.

I lean over and grab a full pitcher, drag it through the plates of untouched food toward me.

"Well, I've been here since five. This morning," he says.

"Oh," Meredith says.

I catch Pras glance at Jacques, looking for some assistance here.

"Mm-hmm," Pras says. "Fairly long days."

I lift the pitcher, gulping down ice-cold Asahi, loads of excess foam almost going up my nose, the beer sinking in the narrow glass in sharp, abrupt descents. Where did those girls sit down? I look out over the restaurant and have to stifle a burp.

"Well, I see you . . . haven't eaten too much yet," he says, looking over the table, and half a slightly amazed laugh escapes. "The *kama* is very good. It's a specialty of Mori-san. The head chef here."

"Have a drink, Pras," I say. "Relax. You know, we're not really foody people. Ironic, isn't it? We're boozy people, hey, Jacques?"

"Yes?" Jacques says.

"I'm just looking for your agreement," I say. "It wasn't, like, a question."

"Oh."

Pras is starting to look more than just a little disconcerted.

"I, uh, can't really try anything to drink, I'm afraid," he says. "I'm on a break. It's not really done to even be out here." He laughs a little shyly. "I also had to change."

"And you chose *that?*" I say.

He reaches into his shirt pocket, puts on a pair of glasses. "Yeah, uh, that's right."

Everyone is waiting for me.

"Meredith," I say, "has a test for you. Don't you, Meredith?"

She's looking at me with a kind of amazed disgust, but it's just as easy to let this as anything slide out of your awareness.

"You know," I say, "your Japanese has gotta be tip-top, for this work."

"Right," Pras says. He knows I'm drunk, but feels he's on safer ground now, a little relieved. "Well, I have san-kyu on the Proficiency exam, and I will probably go for ni-kyu in the next round, if I'm still in Japan. Of course I could do it . . . elsewhere, as well."

The hint does not escape me.

"What does this say, then, san-kyu boy." I throw him my keitai. It's pathetic to see someone so Japanized here. Pathetic to see the confinement, the courtesy, the self-imposed restriction on his gestures, the worry, essentially the *fear.* Kneeling there, he catches the phone like I've thrown a dead animal at him.

"The skymail's in hiragana," I say. "It's a message from Michael."

Momentarily freaked out, he glances at the message, and says, "Right, well, my reading comprehension is a little slower than my speaking, and my uh, listening comprehension."

"Sure," I say. "But just try for us"—I smile over at Meredith—"for Bacteria and her fuck-up brother."

"You're pathetic," she hisses at me. "You pathetic, drunk loser."

"Whoa," I say. "Like, 'back' the fuck off, Meredith."

She starts to get up, Jacques, shaking his head at me. Pras holding my phone, dressed all in white, with no idea what he's walked in on.

"Wait, wait," Jacques says. "Hold on one moment. Calm down. Please, Meredith."

She stands, picks up her jacket, jams her keitai in a pocket, from the other pulls out her wallet and throws some bills down on the table.

"Meredith," Jacques says.

People around us are starting to take notice of what's happening. Look at poor old Pras, sixteen or more hours of work, up on one leg now.

"Simon," Jacques says, leaning over, to put his hand on mine.

"Huh?" I say. "What? *Jacques?* Is there—a major *problem?*"

"Why?" Jacques says.

Meredith leaves without saying another word.

"Why the fuck not?" I say, laughing. "Good-bye."

She is a storm, a rage, dropping money, floating notes down upon the table. Pras is amazement, shock after calm and business back behind the bar. She, at the end of the booths, pulls on boots, unlaced, and does not look back to us. She stalks down the sushinoya, pulls the sliding door and gone—into falling snow.

"Why?" I say. "Simon?"

Why cruelty. Why rudeness is worse. Brutishness. There are sniggers and murmurs from the loudmouth men behind. Simon leaned head, stare to me, all contempt and—"Why not?"

"You don't care," I say.

"No," he laughs. "I don't care. How does that feel?"

"I should go," Pras says. "I'm sorry, Jacques, I should get back." He turns to leaning Simon, who is shaking slowly, head full of bloodshot eyes across the table and grin, to me. "I'll leave my contact details here," he says—a meishi, business card by the order board—"if you were interested in speaking again, at a . . . a better time."

"Wait," Simon says. "Wait on a goddam minute."

"Stop it," I say.

"I really have to get back," Pras says, to me.

"Show me one thing," Simon says, his voice thick with hating. "Show me one thing. I'll talk to my father. I'll talk to *Dad*." Pras waiting for a moment, and I am divided—Meredith—Simon—Pras and work—myself. "Read a line of it," Simon says. "One line of this and I'll talk to him." His gesture to the phone, his slumped in the booth, all anger.

Pras waits, and checks me—for suggestion, for sanction, I don't know either.

I shrug him onward.

"Try, then," I say. "It may help us all."

Pras peering then at the screen, looking for a meaning or a clue, a hole-way or a door.

"It . . . says . . ." Pausing, unsure.

To Simon, I say: "I am going after her to catch her. This is no good."

"Let her sulk," he says. "Let her have her hissy fit. *What*—the *fuck*—does it *say*. *Pras?*"

"I'm going," I say. "Now. Here is money." Pras is peering, glance once to me but look still is the diverting mystery. I pull yen from the big pocket, drop it on her notes.

"Who cares?" Simon says by Pras to me.

The people in the booths watch us disintegrate with slight slyness, sideways, over drinks and whispers, turning fast away, and listening. I stand. Grasp my phone and save the message, put it away.

The sushi-mama—my hardly friend—who knows how she sees such a mess?—down at the line of boots.

"*O-kanjo,*" I say—the bill, with no please, I'm rude—and cross my fingers in an X for the sign. I point down to the mess of money.

"If it ain't enough, I'll be in touch," Simon sneers. "*Jacques.*"

"I bet that you will," I say. "It is enough."

"I think I know what it says." Pras, small wonder looking up. "The first line."

"What then?" I say.

The sushi-mama coming.

"The first line says, 'We are like statues among them. We are like statues. Among them.'"

Traffic floods eight lanes of Yasukuni-dori, and in the chill and lightly
falling snow, she sees across the moat the lit letters of the British Council,
demure among the kanji.

Alone now, stiffened and sobered by the cold, armed with plans and a
future, she waits for the signal to change. Yards behind her, the snow falls
three stories deeper, into the hollow courtyard.

I sit alone, finish every drink on the table as I wait for the change. What in
the hell does ichimanhachisengohyakuniju yen mean to me?

Nothing.

Leaving Simon, leaving Pras, my inside promise to telephone, to make a
mend.

I slide the pine sushi door open to a burst of chill and snow-gray flutter
falling from the sky. In the tiny courtyard, the little sculptures gather wet
transparent crusts, on heads and helmets, mushroom and pipe and dress
and dragon's tail.

She is gone.

Flick my keitai to her number as I slip on the stair tiles, upward to the
sky and the hiss of the taxis.

It rings two moments and she answers.

"Hello?" Meredith says on the down escalator to the Namboku line.

"Me. It is me here."

"Don't say anything. It doesn't matter. I'll do it alone."

"I do know someone. Someone who is closer. With knowledge. A professor at Rikkyo University. A husband of Catherine Barnes."

"It doesn't matter, I know someone too."

"*Entre nous.* Simon, he is crazy. He does like this sometimes, when he's
crazy."

"You go ahead and forgive him, Jacques," she says.

There is a crackle and a buzz, and she checks her phone.

At the foot of the escalator, the kanji for no signal, in a little box, right
there.

I am on top of the stair, her phone voice is quickly gone. Light fluttering through gray falling snow, nothing lying on the ground.

"Yu," I say to no person, to the steam from my own breath.

I stand here for long enough to coldness, going deep. I light my cigarette and think, Where now? Walk over to the highway, enter the auto-opening door of the first orange taxi I discover? Go back down the slippery stair to the bar to help, or make apologize for Pras?

Go home?

There is a loud crack from deep in the earth.

And again, and scattered clattering following after. Coming from the well that makes the sushi bar's accessway. I turn back, and to the railing. I look down through darkness for the source, three stories down, and there is dark and tile, there is the noren curtain of the sushi bar pulled back, making light out into the courtyard, and there is a moving figure, raging mid so many smaller moveless ones, there is Simon using statues to smash statues in the snow.

Catherine
March 2001

Here is my argument for Feste's hypocrisy. This is why I believe he is cruel and kind outwardly because only of an event in his past—is it a bad decision or a death or a love gone bad?—that seems to make him selfish and manipulative, and shows that deeply he believes that his own calamity is deeper and more deeply felt and so more real than those of the other in the play.

(Keep in mind that in a way he is the moral winner of this play.)

(also remember that the calamity is the more deeply felt and more deeply significant because it is barely mentioned and only ever hinted to)

(hinted at)

Feste's first line is a fatalistic joke, like that of someone too hurt and tired to care: *Let her hang me.* It is a joke, but we choose our jokes for a reason.

Feste is cruel. All though right through the planning of the Malvolio trick Feste says nothing, he is present but silent, in the background. He never exits. Later, he take a very active role in the trick, getting Malvolio in the dark house and convincing him he has gone crazy. Why? Just because Malvolio called him "a barren rascal"? he does not just comment, he gets involved, he wants Malvolio to think he is mad and not only that but he is very good at making him think so. Why do we do cruel things? Because we feel the world is cruel, because we see cruelty, because cruelty has been done to us. Because we are familiar with cruelty. Feste is familiar with cruelty.

When Feste meets with Sir Andrew and Sir Toby, Sir Andrew comments on his funny fooling last night, and then he says a very curious thing, the one key thing we should always keep in mind through out reading the whole play.

Andrew says, "'Twas very good, i'faith. I sent thee sixpence for thy leman, hadst it?"

"Leman" means sweet heart (reference).

Feste answers in nonsense that he "did impetticoat thy gratillity" whatever that means and then mentions Malvolio and that his Lady has a white hand. Is he just fooling or is he evading? Feste has a love that he cannot bear to mention, and that the author, William Shakespeare, cannot bear to mention either, except in clues, and in Feste's cryptic blurting words of spirit and nonsense whenever she is mentioned. Because right next he sings a song so movingly:

O mistress mine! Where are you roaming?
O, stay and hear: your true love's coming,
That can sing both high and low.
Isn't that Feste?
What is love? 'Tis not hereafter;
Present mirth hath present laughter,
What's to come is still unsure.

Later he chooses a song with the line *I am slain by a fair cruel maid.* Although he asks for it, Orsino calls the song nostalgic and silly, and to this Feste says things to him with venom and hatred.

ORSINO: I'll pay thy pleasure then.

FESTE: Truly, sir, and pleasure will be paid, one time or another.

And later Viola says, I warrant thou art a merry fellow, and car'st for nothing. Not so, sir, Feste says, I do care for something; but in my conscience, sir, I do not care for you.

The one no one thinks can love is deeply in love, and deeply hurt, too. And in his hurt he wants to hurt, in turn.

806 + 264 + 578 = 1648 words.
 O god.

Meredith
December 2000

Two days later Meredith received, in a tiny red lacquer box with a ribbon, an invitation to a party at her own house.

It was a statue of a little girl in a dress, with the head broken off. Stamped into her thin stone chest were three kanji and some hiragana:

死彫れい吸

Followed by, MEREDITH EDWARDS—DECEMBER 25TH—BUD-DHA TRICKBAR SHIBUYA—7PM. Simon had included a letter, and in a strange mix of apology and gall, had asked her if they could celebrate Christmas at the Prince penthouse after the Trickbar dinner.

Meredith thought it over, and, a little intrigued, sent him a skymail that she thought combined just the right amount of forgiveness and aplomb.

It said, FINE.

Yasu
2000

The other associated irony was that as Yasu grew better, in the last year of his short, sad life, in those last few months before he went out into the world, as his techniques—his innovation and his rigor—bore this literal, pure fruit, and as he began to operate at levels of efficiency, intuition and accomplishment that often left him bewildered (as if someone had sneaked

into the terrarium, composed a substrate, imagined a hybrid and its potential with supreme, Godlike elegance, and left it for him to find, baffled and
chastened), the irony was that the doubt didn't leave him, and did, in fact,
grow proportionately with his achievement. Not given to metaphor, Yasu
knew, but would not—could not—ever have thought to apply Archimedes'
principle—in bath conceived—to himself. A waterborne body is subject to
an upward force equal to the weight of the water it displaces.

Yasu's silent, private achievement gained weight and inertia and
moment, but, as if to maintain the equilibrium of loneliness required to
generate this achievement, his self-doubt, social ineptitude—his primal
shyness—gained a similar mass.

The upshot was that though he made things that could make an old
kendo master sit in a corner and cry, Yasu remained a silent child; eyes on
the concrete, deep and heavy backpack all full of hell.

Boys are attracted to militarism because it is a pride that matches their
ambition and self-loathing and disgust.

You see, Yasu thought of himself as the kind of boy girls love to hate.

Thus his communications with others were reduced primarily to awkward transactions with foreigners on the web, followed by even more awkward transactions with foreigners in the world.

But as to the former, for example, one email in April (where at least
something got shared):

Subject: Re: Japan Cap Question
Date: Sun, 04 Apr 2000 23:50:52
To: <tanabeyasuhiko@yahoo.co.jp>
Attachments: 0 Printer Friendly Version
(Delete (Previous (Next (Close (Reply (Reply All (Forward

Hey Yasuhiko
    Glad to get your email and to know there are other needle-phreaks
way over there in Japan! We had a little trouble understanding some
parts of your email, but I'll try to address all your carefully bulleted
points anyhow. First of all, glad to hear you're using brown rice flour
and water with a dry vermiculite layer on top, PF-Tek-style. We
couldn't quite make sense of your request about identifying your possible *Psilocybe* species, and at first took it to mean you actually
wanted us to somehow attach you a list of all *Psilocybe* species, with
their psilocybin and psilocin yields (!!!!!!!) The godlike Guzman's new

article has now suggested there are over 200,000 species of Mexican fungi alone, of which we only know three and a half percent. And that's just Mexico man. Not intending to be assholes here, maybe we just misunderstood. And as for Japan (if that's what you were getting at by, "help me against a the new mystery cap, a seriously modern of Japan,") we don't have a clue. Here's a list of some recent figures for the genera *Psilocybe, Inocybe, Gymnopilus, Pluteus, Panaeolus* and *Conocybe* with alkaloid percentages after cold desiccation. It's been hypothesized in a couple of journals now (Repke et al. said it first) that baeocystin may be playing a central role in the biosynthesis of psilocybin, and may in fact be a primary precursor. This is useful for reading the figures below. It's also a mild respiratory inhibitor and can cause fevers in children, so don't let any asthmatic kids near yr stuff, know what I'm saying? Back to yr questions. Uh, the correct English designation for psilocin is 4-hydroxy-N, N-dimethyltryptamine, and for serotonin, 5-hydroxytryptamine. It's kind of important you get the spelling right and everything, man. Also, in your email you said some stuff we couldn't make a lot of sense from: "The baffling dream's mirror; the baffling mirror's dream" "moving in a looking-glass, sadly, and its reflection, commenting back," for egs. With "blue time," and "old time," and, our favorite:

> At an exciting point, I could see through my certain complex experience by a choice, all laidly smooth for my vision and dream to scanning. Which experience (family, father's careful words, or the trial, or very simple like lunchtime or walking in the street) is I choose to place in every order I want them, leaping free the place, the time or something like that, I could not be sure I was safe where I was, or where I was, even so. Time was like a wrapping paper around me, and the cap showed me this. I could unwrap and wrap again with folds of my own choice. So I don't know what is true.

This is now printed and pinned to the lab noticeboard, and we "assumed" you were referring to the pretty radical temporal distortion that's possible at explosive dosages, and uh, though we're totally nodding in knowing but and also just a little titillated sympathy there, we'd recommend you get some serious posology done first, if at all possible, before you embark on some kind of extreme high-dose long-term Leary-Jungian self-experimentation. About the blueing of the shrooms—this is alkaloidal rusting: usually a sign of age and alkaloid breakdown, or bruising in a high-psilocin shroom, so that's real weird you'd get that so early in an untouched flush, and so resinous and potent. A blue mycelium is—at least to us—unheard of. We're extremely interested, especially if you think you can recreate the substrate and the seed. You said you'd used some PF-Tek spore syringes and race strains in the past but that (I gotta quote this too) "now the superception is completed, I am acceptable of University honor with the end of my project's life-cycle, the new growth and glorious blue change." We were wondering if you could kinda be a little clearer on that point there, and even if you don't tell us exactly what your amazing race strain is—sure, we understand, authorship and due credit and locus standi and all—but maybe you could tell us if you've isolated it, and if so, are you investigating it?

Keep us up to date man, we're fascinated.

Last points.

We had no idea the shroom was legal in Japan so we're writing this email on the way to the airport, wringing hands in anticipation. Here follows a list of the above-mentioned species and alkaloid percentages, and a list Our Man In Tampa (OMIT) sent in of some Japanese *Psilocybe* variants which might be helpful (or not, and which obviously we can't vouch for the factualness of).

Good luck for your research into the experience you tried to describe, and don't go that far too often, or at least not alone, would be my advice. Once a week for a major psychedelic event, is always my rule.

Last point, on dedication and high hopes.

We had a friend in Wisconsin who was into some end-of-the-pier research up in his parents' cabin in the moist hills of Three Lakes all alone. This guy identified four new US *Panaeolus* species in the space of a few months. Then he set the cabin up much as you described your terrarium, to farm these *Panaeolus* in which he told us he'd found psilocybin and psilocin percentages so high he sometimes mistook them for his students' GPAs. He sold his car and hiked in with just a backpack, fourteen miles each way, up old logging tracks, that is, and if you never hiked an old logging track in the wet, it's true to say you've never truly suffered. Not just the one time, either. Multiple times to set up a farm for this new alkaloid-dripping *Panaeolus*. Hiking in wearing old holey tights and military surplus and not shaving for months and living on

popcorn and tinned salmon mousse and Gatorade. This is a guy with
standing in the legit mycological community, teaching freshmen, close to
finishing his doctorate. A guy with real potential. A friend.

Then he appears out of the woods nine months later, with bags of
this like almost totally benign *Panaeolus*.

We found a little 5-hydroxy-L-tryptophan, some accumulated serotonin, urea, and that was it.

Alls I'm saying is, don't go mad in your room for nine months and
then walk out expecting to change the world with a big bag of nasty
cardboard-tasting stirfry.

Best,

the boys at *High Life*

Psilocybe semilanceata indole alkaloids in dried fruit bodies (%) Psilocybin: 0.91–1.12 Baeocystin: 0.15–0.21

Psilocybe cubensis the Matriarch: quicker fruiting than *P. semilanceata* (3–4 wks vs. 3–4 mnths) no baeocystin, high high high psilocybin, quick, potent, cheap, low maintenance and high yield, as rice to
the Japanese, so *P. cubensis* to the needle-phreak but uh, you know
this, right. . . . ?

Psilocybe bohemica Psilocybin: 0.21–1.34 Psilocin: very little Baeocystin: 0.008–0.03 also 0.15–0.21% psilocybin found in the mycelium
for *P. bohemica* so you know, if you just can't wait and you don't mind
that furry taste sensation. . . . Found wild in Czechoslovakia, Austria,
Germany, and along with *P. serbica* below sometimes grouped as *P.
cyanescens* here (States)

Psilocybe serbica

Gymnopilus spectabilis reports of hallucinogenic exp.s here and in
Japan so ear to the ground cos the literature is gaping with lacunae

Gymnopilus purpuratus Psilocybin: 0.21–0.33 Psilocin: 0.20–0.31
Baeocystin: 0.03–0.05 Drying showed some falls in alkaloid %'s vs. wet
shrooms, which goes against conventional wisdom but what can you do

Pluteus saticinus Exciting rumors of 0.2–1% psilocybin (!!!!!!!), no
psilocin and plenty of precursor. A comer, maybe, for inquisitive
Czechs with lots of deadwood round the yard.

OMIT's list of putatively Japanese *Psilocybes* and others:

Psilocybe coprophila (Like, grows on shit)

Psilocybe subcoprophila (Grows near shit)

Psilocybe subcaerulipes Hongo

Psilocybe subaeruginascens (*HL* editor's note: rumors that somehow evaded OMIT are that this well-known shroom might be toxic,
even lethal: *caveat emptor!*)

Psilocybe argentipes Yokoyama

Psilocybe shiboreisu azurescens

Inocybe fastigiata (poss. non-hallucinogen but can and will cause
perspiration/probs w/ breathing)

Psilocybe venenata

Psilocybe montana

(Plus thousands of other undocumented hallucinogenic shrooms on
top of those documented only in Japanese or Chinese and unknown to
the West.)

High Life's Cooking Tips #31 in a Continuing Series:

As we all know, sometimes the shroom can be pretty distasteful. So
as a continuing series *High Life's* cooks are working on recipes to ease
discomfort for needle-phreaks with squirmy stomachs. Remember that
cooking shrooms is not the same as cold desiccation where there is
minimal loss of potency. Heat causes some of the psilocybin to break
down and sometimes a 25% to 50% loss of efficiency. Although, if
you're lucky enough to have a strain of shrooms that is like, whoa
nelly! this can be a helpful method to calm down a dose for safe and
happy trips. But if your shrooms are regular joes and you can't face
that nasty taste

Try this:

Mushroom Juice

Multiple spoonfuls of a frozen juice concentrate (we recommend
Dole orange-pineapple-banana) in a blender with shrooms, some ice
cubes, a 500 mg vitamin C tablet for tartness, a little water and blend
on high. Let it sit for a few minutes, then enjoy.

Two or three minutes in a microwave though can calm a mad
shroom down (especially if it's desiccated and really potent) enough
for a mellow trip. You'll have to experiment!

---

http://oped@highlife.../imap4.asp?action=showmessage&folder30&
rndno=784/04/00

And as to awkward transactions in the world, it was midday on May
Day—a Monday—that Yasu stood, munching on a teriyaki chicken burger
from McDonald's, at the edge of the wide expanse of the plaza on the
west side of Ikebukuro station, waiting to meet, for the first time, a fellow
he knew only by the emailed initials "M.E."

The plaza seems a void in the stippled landscape of Ikebukuro, or
"Pond-Bag" as foreigners know it in unsympathetic translation. It's a built-
up area, but an upstart; a lower-class and vulgar rival of Shibuya, or Shinjuku, which in turn compete, without the benefit of history, with the
glorious antique commerce of the Ginza—the site of Tokyo's first electric
streetlights. Ikebukuro, especially the west side, starts earnestly enough,
with Seibu and Parco department stores straddling the second most complex station in the city, but past the plaza, just a block from the banks and
fast food, the striptease and pachinko and cheap rip-offs of Wu-Wear,
Levis, Champion and Tommy Hilfiger proliferate, fronted by scarred touts
from Nigeria, Senegal and Ethiopia, visaless swaggerers who stand splay-
footed in the streets, and whose only double-sided conversations of any
duration are with one another. In Roppongi, the Nigerians whisper, *"Topless bar, topless bar."*

On the west side the touts are more often the weathered, old Japanese
men, one inch from utter homeless destitution and municipal eviction to
the suburbs, standing for hours blankly on the bright street corners southwest of the station. Their cigarettes hang from their mouths and once in a
while drop tubes of ash that disintegrate and drift down the great billboards
that hang from straps over their shoulders, proclaiming from chest to shin
all kinds of picture, position and price. Even the sushi bars here are down-at-
heel; the revolving tuna opaque and leathered and dull as a tongue.

But in the plaza, nestled between the glass of the Metropolitan Art
Space and the clutter of Ikebukuro station, it's not so bad. The plaza's
bricks form concentric circles of gray and taupe and ecru, under a milkwhite sky, surrounding to the south in cornflower blue an intricate circle
of fountains. Break-dancers practice, watching their bodies reflected in the
windows of the Art Space. Even the weather of May is waiting: the poise
before the pounce of June monsoons. Surrounding the brick space loom
buildings and billboards, Yen Shop, Doutor, Tokyo-Mitsubishi, KFC, izakayas, more banks, McDonald's, giant beautiful blond-haired girls smoking Salem cigarettes, like an audience in a dress circle, patiently surveying
the polished brick of the plaza, half-smiling down beneath gigantic fragile
floodlights.

The west side lacks the vitality of the east, and maybe that's the plaza's fault. Maybe it's too large, too empty, something merely to cross on the way to something else that's no longer worth the effort. Not when entertainment is as dense as the twelve huge floors of the station buildings alone. But maybe the peacefulness and emptiness is the point. Either way, it's a useful place for meetings, especially for wary types who survey their approaches, who prefer to stand in trees on the fringes of all situations, and delicately negotiate their entrances, as quiet and watchful and distant as a black and white woman with a Salem cigarette eight stories high.

Yasu stood and waited quietly, under the trees at the north end of the plaza, eating his teriyaki chicken burger—no drink, no fries; he's too damn fat, too shy—on May Day, 2000. Today, he was going back to Rikkyo, his first university, for the first time in five years, and he was taking a foreign stranger along, who went by the internet sobriquet of "M.E."

Because the point of his email to *High Life* had really been all but missed. *High Life,* a covert, loosely connected and mostly US coven of doctoral students, crop analysts, research assistants and viticulturalists, had already had a website shut down in the States and now served out of China, where political and pornographic material may get firewalled into oblivion but where this kind of coded and intricate designer drug manufacture survives; hardcore hallucinogenophilia, stripped clean of the breathless Shaman worship and fact-stretching Aztec frieze interpretation and general earnest mystic fast-and-loose playing with historical fact some of your average mushroom sites get bogged down in, stripped clean of any pictures at all in fact, even color, even headings in different point size; the site in fact presented in pages so relentlessly either amateur or intellectually impenetrable it seemed thus somehow banal and benign; bland and white and aesthetically indifferent, pages of tiny frail alienatingly Courier-fonted English multihyphened chemical nomenclature taking up the bulk of entire huge and jerkily justified paragraphs, all to create an effect so utterly opaque and obscure and so very-special-interest-only-seeming (just a very small step away from "very-troubled-fetishist-only") that the site managed to escape interpretation by the administration's dour and Spartan net regulators as at all subversive or dangerous or arousing, and just a month after its US demise promptly resurfaced with a dot-org-dot-cn on the end, and stayed there. But the point of the email had been that that day in March Yasu had plucked one little sample cap and had then seemed to sit like stone for a full working afternoon and long into the quiet night, in the hum and the dim of his terrarium, eventually swarmed over his entire body by transparent tripping spiders, on merely *the resin* secreted from that little one, simply a shiny blue stickiness of alkaloidal rust, smeared upon his palm.

And, by the time he had eventually stirred, hours later, and showered slowly, dazed and cosmically sad and oddly euphoric, picking tiny crumpled spider-corpses from his hair, undisgusted—*fascinated,* even—and had at last returned to the terrarium, by this time the odor under the desk had soured and turned steely. The silverblue of the strange furry mycelium had gone. It had turned thin and dusty as bread mold; and the miracles themselves: black and withered and lifeless as if burned. Touched with the eraser-end of a tentative pencil, the clusters crumbled like ash. The substrate underneath was black and lined with cracks and fissures, scorched earth, utterly drained of moisture.

And scattered everywhere, hanging in the spiderweb around Izanami's deflated corpse, on the trays, the floor and the desk, the tiny clenched white blackeyed fists of a massacre of spiders.

And he was bewildered.

So Yasu turned first (real evidence of his bewilderment) to Manabu and Hiro at Heaven On Earth, then to the internet and *High Life,* and, that failing, the city of Tokyo.

He began to advertise obliquely in *Tokyo Classified,* as he set about trying to iterate the circumstances and parameters of his breakthrough.

And it wasn't very long before he had a reply.

Enter Michael James Edwards—or exit, really, from the doors of the Yamanote line, platform five at Ikebukuro, four stops from Shinjuku and the Prince. Wearing gray gabardine Armani slacks and a bright red long-sleeved T-shirt with a black star on the chest. He stepped carefully past the queued ranks of lunchtime crowds waiting to replace him on the train, and made straight for underground, clear-eyed, moving with a purpose. Short-haired and slim, intense but with a distracted, somehow gentle air, he moved for others; didn't wait for the Japanese to move for him.

Yasu finished his burger and dropped the wrapper in the trash can he stood beside. His ad had been strangely worded, nearly impenetrable. Unsure, he'd placed it in consecutive weeks under different sections: *Selling: General; Collectors; At Your Service: Health; Personal: Friends and Interests; Join The Club: Arts, Leisure and Environmental; Join The Club: International.* The compulsion to subtlety had sprung, ironically, from years of solitude, paranoia and imagined conversations, and though from the advertisement it was difficult to derive any clear meaning, Yasu had cursed himself, just a moment too late, at his mailbox, for poor English, for brashness, for folly.

Where the advertisement needed to go, he didn't know—solitary reckless idealists have little knowledge of things like real estate, insurance or marketing. Though the means were hazy to him, the end he wanted was clear.

Cash.

Previously, the trickle of yen from Heaven On Earth had kept him in his parents' house, kept his landlord quiet, kept him supplied and rudimentarily fed. It was never much, but Yasu had no context within which to place his income, no real idea of the extent to which he was being abused. To work, and to study, to do what he does best uninterrupted, with fast food and Mild Sevens, held a continuity with life under his parents' care, and represented a state of ignorant yet productive amniotic bliss. He was working, he was cooked for, he didn't need to contemplate too much the disgrace that had brought him to this pass. But Manabu and Hiro learned the flip side to ascetic pride and self-sufficiency: they could starve him, abuse and manipulate him—but when they tried to usurp authorship, there was never any going back.

But no longer any money either. Your average young foreigner on the hunt for legal shrooms would usually consult the commercial ads in *T.C.*— *Head Shop Booty* in Roppongi, Shimokitazawa and Shibuya; *Zippy!*, *Whoopee!*, *Bo Peep* and *Freak Brothers*—not the classifieds. Or rely on rumor, word-of-mouth, crudely drawn maps, the generosity of new friends or sheer streetwalking luck. So Yasu's advertisements caught the attention of just one young foreigner, who saw proofs a day before issues hit the stands and the internet, courtesy of an Australian staff writer named Drew, and who was himself immersed deeply enough in Jinglish and the technical patois of psychedelia to penetrate Yasu's inadvertent mystifications.

So, via email, they got to talking.

Michael's previous connection—a promising young Chinese ex-surfer who'd lost most of a leg to frostbite, surfing in the snow the vicious icy waves off Otaru Beach in Hokkaido (a hundred and fifty or so miles from Russia, and pack ice) *sans* full-body wetsuit and goggles on a dare—the man they knew as Mao, though brilliant (a man who built his own prosthetic limbs, lived in conditions too appalling to describe, knew the dialogue to *Platoon* by heart and named his race strains after Brat Pack actors: he had a Charles Sheen, an Emilio Estevez, a Keifer Sutherland, a relentless Judd Nelson, a weak, low-yield Ally Sheedy, for girls), was temporarily put on hold.

As Michael dropped his ¥190 ticket into the JR gates and the plastic flaps opened to admit him to Tokyo's second maddest station where nine subway, land and private lines converge, Yasu stood under the trees at the north edge of the west side plaza, and blinked behind his glasses.

Then he did something for perhaps the fourteenth or fifteenth time that day.

He crouched slowly, to the backpack at his feet, and gingerly unzipped it. Inside, visible through the opening, gray marl fabric, and screenprinted black letters: KEEP BA. He unwrapped a corner of the fabric, to reveal gauze. He detached a piece of medical adhesive tape and lifted a triangular flap of the gauze. Underneath, the lid of a small transparent plastic lunchbox, sealed again in medical vacuum-pack. The three mushrooms, fruited the previous evening, plucked by forceps just that morning, sat blurry, blue and still and undecayed or aged as yet. Yasu tightly rewrapped the gauze and fabric, and checked other items. Keitai, a dispenser box of disposable surgical gloves, an anti-allergenic paper facemask, a complete change of clothes, a Kinko's printout of his last reply from "M.E."

He wasn't to know he'd have enough money for a Mac G-4 laptop in under a week.

He rezipped the bag, stood and shuffled forward slightly so it rested between his shoes. In May the air is body temperature and an overcast sky is the color of fat. Yet he was sweating, nervous as a chess player three moves from checkmate. Giant Tokyo crows in the trees above him croaked and shuffled heavily in the bare branches, horny claws scraping on the bark. Everything he feared, everything he desired, was coming to a point: an end to loneliness, to rejection and obscurity. Finally that fearful chance to show Rikkyo, Saitama, Maeda, even the mama at Tomozushi exactly how far he'd come, exactly what he was worth. The chance the long-time-down find so easy to blow through unpreparedness. To talk with someone who might appreciate his labors. Who says the frog in the well knows not the great ocean? There are oceans in kind and degree. Out there in a tiny bark, he'd been tossed by waves of which he'd like at last to tell.

But why did it have to be a foreigner?

Yasu lit a Mild Seven with his father's Zippo.

Michael chose the Southwest exit from Ikebukuro station so he could walk outside in the open air before he met the mushroom grower.

Passing through crowds underneath huge department stores, Parco and Seibu, which, in 1970, the year of his suicide by *seppuku,* had a window display of arcane items related to the author—*Mishimalia.* Michael was thinking of pretty words for terrible things, and of Sugamo prison, where the Class A war criminals were housed during the trials and before the executions; less than two hundred yards and two minutes away. The building where Tojo prepared for death. Where Okawa Shumei, the civilian intellectual and propagandist, practiced his madness and the choreography of its first manifestation on the stage at Ichigaya: sitting in the dock, he leaned forward and slapped Tojo on his tan bald pate with the rolled-up charges brought against him, and had to be restrained before he did it again. Where old Matsui, the patsy Butcher of Nanking, chose dying a Japanese over any juridical version of truth. The night of his execution: *I sincerely appreciate the infinite grace of the Throne. It happens that I have come to be sacrificed for the Nanking Incident.* It was he who led the doomed men in the final banzai, and of the first group to be hanged he was the last pronounced dead. The building long since gone, the Sunshine 60 Building of Sunshine City now rises sixty floors near where the indicted slept on straw. Michael thought of *arquebus,* or *harquebus.* Tempura, tobacco, and this gun and tripod introduced around 1560 by the Christian Portuguese. *Falconet.* Another kind of cannon.

Surprisingly, perhaps, Michael does little in the way of hallucinogens, though his knowledge is near-encyclopedic. Some early forays at age thirteen and fourteen had prompted a rapid schedule of research and reading, and the realization that in his home country there would always be a ceiling on the quality of medium for this kind of experience. He had learned enough from gang acid, shrooms and microdots to see both the potential and its debasement. Michael had been the kind of boy to see horizons and possibilities for exploration where others saw recreation. But someone who was now used to the kind of work that can quickly reveal an end to one's own awareness, one's own abilities. Someone who was accustomed to seeing his own shape in the world too clearly. Someone who now characterized his own perception as a kind of rut. Volcano vents of superheated gases over which Inoue's minions held the martyrs. *Solfataras.* He already knows that this Tanabe Yasuhiko is of a different breed than Mao, and is glad. For all the tragedy and farce of his situation, Mao is a cowboy, a part-timer. Michael can be harsh, he knows. But since the amputation,

Mao had never attempted getting back on any kind of board, be it snow or surf. There is something broken in him, past his sarcastic humor and grubby T-shirts, that hurts to be around. And money alone seems to make no difference to him. The time has passed for hobbyists. Michael thought of Minnie Vautrin, another Christian missionary. The "Living Goddess" of Nanking. Who, like Rabe, saved so many in the International Safety Zone. Four years after, she suicides like Sylvia Plath, her good deeds insufficient to shield her from the moaning of the old Nanking wind, to wall off the abyss in which she looked. She was fifty-five. Michael was feeling restless and confident about this new grower. He's considering the nickname Hirohito, though this will be a private moniker, to avoid offense. *Anatsurushi*. What the pit for apostasy was named. Shusaku Endo wrote that the apostate Provincial Ferreira was scarred behind the ear. But suspended upside down in the shit-filled pit, the martyrs were bled from the temple. *Korobase*. To apostatize. Recant. *Fosse*. The pit. To be *fossed*. Suspended in. Tied tightly, ankle to neck, to squeeze the blood from nose and mouth and ears and eyes and modest temple vent. One arm free to signal *korobase*. *Sanguinary*. Mizuno Kawachi-no-kami said that in convincing the Christians to recant, all else exhausted, the measures to adopt be *sanguinary*. In his dream of war, every night Michael sees the burning horse. *Ossuary*. A charnel-house. A bone-urn. His head aches. But he's never been to Rikkyo University before, and he's looking forward to seeing the old buildings. *Effigy*. The pretty, offhand sound of *effigy*.

Yasu finished the cigarette and threw the butt a little less than a foot in front of him. He stepped forward and ground it out with his shoe. Then he stepped back, his backpack never breaking contact with his other ankle. Sometimes, on the train into Tokyo, he curls his arm through both the backpack's straps, so he can fall asleep carefree. This was not the same thing. Hands in his pockets, he played with the Zippo as he stared out over the park. With the pad of his thumb, he fingered the design embossed on the casing. Lupin Sansei, some kind of 1970's Franco-Japanese criminal in a pointy hat. A cult manga character from before his time, that held no particular meaning for him. The colors of the embossment faded from the figure's raised edges to its center of burnished metal, over Lupin Sansei's heart, worn away by his and his father's hands and trouser pockets. The thing was an antique, precious in a casual way, as loved and living parents taken for granted. A rock-solid piece of his world, at once completely familiar in every way; the grain of the steel, the darkened burnish at the seam of case and lid, the ancient carbon crust inside, the fine shine of each corner, the single flake of blue paint in the shape of Australia all that remained of Lupin Sansei's hat. And also, like parents living or dead, familiarly mysterious. Who was he before he came to Yasu? What more or less could he mean to a fan of the comic? The Zippo is precious to Yasu in the way of something the loss of which had never in its remotest form occurred to him. He loses his keitai all the time. He absently lights cigarettes with Lupin Sansei as he tries to remember the last time he saw his phone. Yasu's the kind of person who has never ever worn sunglasses.

Past the fountains, he watched couples walking together; young boys in dark trousers and white turtlenecks, with young girls in jeans with cuffs turned up once halfway to their knees. Pairs of office girls in smocks crossing the plaza and giggling behind their hands. Two salarymen smoking, half in the plaza, half on the sidewalk, on a break from an office across the road, as if afraid to commit to the plaza when all they have time for is a smoke. They laughed loudly, but tensely. Over on the station side of the street, a cluster of salarymen still in charcoal winter trench coats bowed elaborately as their group split in two. No one seemed alone. The fountains seemed to hiccup, then surge higher, a purer white than the sky. The hiss and clotted frothing merged with the sound of traffic. The Salem lady, deep in pensive thought, smiled down at the plaza, and at the two groups of salarymen backing away from each other now, who were passed by a young boy, crossing onto the street to give them room. He appeared again from behind the fountains, heading directly toward Yasu. And at this, Yasu thought, oh no, is it someone from university, or even worse, from school. Or maybe he is just coming over here to use the bathrooms beyond the trees. But the boy was looking straight at him, and Yasu had to look away, shuffle his feet just a little, thumb the lighter's cap just open, thumb it closed again. Perhaps it was the trash can. Corner of his eye, a glance. He's not full-blooded Japanese, Yasu could tell now as he approached. Not committed to Asia round his eyes. Too feminine the waxen color of his skin. Maybe he was mad, or *bosozoku*, a yakuza prospect looking for a fight. But not dressed like this.

The boy stopped.

"Sumimasen," he said.

"Hai," Yasu said coolly, over to the fountains.

"Tanabe Yasuhiko, desu ka?"

Oh no, it must be university.

"Hai," in an utterly disinterested tone.

"Hajimemashite." The boy bowed. "Watashi wa Maikeru Eduwadusu desu. Emu-ii desu. Yoroshiku onegai shimasu."

M.E. spoke and was at least half Japanese.

Yasu bowed quickly and deeply, perplexed and thoroughly embarrassed, so quickly he almost fell over. He tipped, and as he put a foot forward to balance, felt the stranger's hand on his shoulder, and in a curious compromise leaned there, as—sharply; too sharply—he reached a protective hand to the bag at his feet.

They made a strange yet strangely comfortable pair, walking quietly together across the broad expanse of taupe-bricked plaza. So oddly matched in mind and gait and all else physical. Apart from something palpable between them. They walked on, the awkward, overwrought Japanese introductions smoothly left behind. As they crossed in front of the Art Space and its endless escalator up, the crows in Yasu's tree took fright and flight, a noisy scrabble and clutter and then the thuds of their wings, but who could know what frightens crows so big?

Six months later, Michael's younger sister would cross the same plaza in the same direction, unknowingly retracing his steps but with a Tourist Information Center map in her hand, heading toward the old university's grounds that begin just a quarter mile away.

Yasu didn't hold his backpack's straps protectively as he walked; it's okay to have his hands by his thighs, but just a little odd for those hands to never move. He always seems deep in a perplexing problem when he walks in public, his face blank and his eyes fixed somewhere between himself and whatever it is he faces. Slightly bent at the hip, and arms straight and rigid at his sides, his jeans hanging loose at the knees, his black faux-leather belt white and flaking around the buckle holes. But every five or six steps Yasu seemed to poke his chin a little forward, as if cresting an incremental rise on the larger slope of what worried him. Odd in a Japanese: it would usually be body language for subservient acknowledgment in conversation with an elder. But in Yasu, this showed how relaxed he was. Because the boy walking beside him seemed so lost in his own thoughts, and thus so artless and open as to seem, paradoxically, thought-less, Yasu felt no need to explain or discuss or even mention the circumstances of their meeting. Yet his memory didn't offer up the recognition that the last person with whom he felt this way—this quiet, alert, at ease—was his dad.

In this part of Ikebukuro, the commercial rapidly gives way to the suburban. As they briefly waited, then crossed the expressway at the traffic lights, hotels and banks merged into private homes and small businesses of two and three stories, sandwiched tightly together. Each house with the air of a building holding its breath. That white glare of sky, that no-temperature. Seasons shift quickly at this latitude.

Pretty words For terrible things *Shoftin* plural of *Shofet*; the verb: *Shafat* Hebrew for *Judges;* judge; to be judged Old Jephthah chapters eleven and twelve the bandit exiled son of a whore and Gilead who was patriarch of the house of Ephraim and the land which bore his name Jephthah *Shofet* of Israel for six years *And Jephthah judged Israel six years* And in true Old Testament style history repeats itself cyclically over a period of four hundred and some years Again the Jews of Israel turn to false idols *Baal* and *Astarte* Yahweh withdraws his shielding hand and delivers the people of God unto their enemies Repent and beg for mercy o ye faithless Unto them a *Shofet* comes and delivers them from evil In the Anglican liturgy of his father's church Michael remembered a little five-year-old's Gordian knot: the Lord's Prayer "Forgive us our sins but deliver us from evil" "But" is crossed out and in black and spidery fountain pen there is "and" How many times all that could be seen or read was that correction How much is lost in the grammar or was it the translation Inoue of Chikugo was called the *Torquemada* of Japan Found that apostasy gained more political points than pointless bloody martyrdom *Of how many* The wily magistrate master of the pit and rhetoric After the sulphurous hot spas at *Unzen* two lay Portuguese ladies mangled and sent back to *Macao* Were they made ugly *It is noe abiding for us in Japon* To judge to *Shafat* the blur in meaning in the Hebrew between juridical judge and ruler: one who wields government Charismatics the spirit of Yahweh came upon them in times of need of the people of Israel Gifted them with extreme and temporary powers to wield in time of crisis Jephthah called back into the familial fold as the Ammonites made war Promises were made to him as to the Pied Piper another wise Fool in exaggerated motley His delegation to the Ammonites skillfully worded rhetorically sound *persuasive But the*

King of the Ammonites would not heed the message which Jephthah had sent him The boy beside him lost in thought the same or similar age as he An odd intensity What's that other pretty word that means a broken hiding thing? He is harsh he knows *Hikikomori* J boys who live in their rooms with online gaming foreign porn and Playstation cigarettes and any alcohol but sake *Turtle* living in their shells Sad and angry twenty-somethings stuttering endless recession suppressed suicide statistics stabbings in the stations Ststststststststabbings in the ststststststststations The Chuo line is the suicide line so-called To wait and grow late on a halted train while they clean is something to grow numb to Memories of this place but a year ago a corpse-polluted river drunk deep from every day helpless to desist But this one works This one's mother doesn't pass him dinner every night through a hole in the rice paper doors This one's parents are dead Then is he *otaku*? Just a nerd They say that they sleep, they sleep and sleep until they feel their eyes begin to rot They say they only want to sleep Living in their shells so many but come some must be lovers here and there a genius a fine singer a games theorist maybe mediocre a good soldier *In time of need the charismatic will rise* Merciless Jephthah made a promise to Yahweh The first out his door if he returned from battle would be a sacrifice For two months after his victory he let his beloved daughter bewail her virginity in the mountains And then he smote her down Even now the Jewish women remember her in ritual But four days only for there is work to be done He can remember Merdy asking him to sit in her room as she tidied Just to keep her company she said He sat by Hüsker Dü at the foot of the wall by the cupboard and watched her Beloved Behind the head of the bed there is a spider and big brother can wrap it in a tissue for her because she doesn't want it dead To the window shaken out over the valley and the fire escape He would do anything for her then Anything Hüsker Dü sneezed in the dust and they laughed until he licked them into protest Nothing funnier than the look on his face The surprise His old sad head Go lick Michael Merdy said Go lick him instead *A lady sir though it was said she much resembled me was yet of many accounted beautiful* What happened? He lost his love or was it not strong enough or was it made impossible when German shepherds learned to like to eat civilians He doesn't recognize them He can't translate their voices Can't understand them in his new language He does not love them now List these off like your three times table races that you at six once drawled in

seven seconds You know you feel you know them like your family They
are your poor dead family now

Northcroft EH representing NZ
Webb WF representing Aus
Higgins JP representing USA
Radhabinod Pal representing India
McDougall ES representing Canada
Lord Patrick representing UK
Zarayanov IM representing USSR
Mei Ju-ao representing China
Röling BVA representing Holland
Bernard H representing France
Jaranilla D representing Philippines

Old Erima Harvey Northcroft who once during the Bayly trial in
Dunedin flew all the way to Auckland in a Puss Moth of all things, to consult with Hanlon KC who'd retired sick Northcroft at whose memorial
service you made of yourself a willing fool Northcroft who you once
admired more than any of your young country's men Northcroft who you
as a twelve-year-old thought your dad was like Can you look at that old
idealism with "tender contempt" like gentle Dennis Potter with his trembling fag in his crippled fingers his "tubes of delight" before he died?
Northcroft of Wellington New Zealand with his Homburgs and striped
suits The angler who left for the Hakone lakes when he wouldn't buck the
quorum Who had a house at Nikko where he loved the red autumnal
maples And oh There's the old buildings of Rikkyo as old as your young
country and see the ivy crawl the brick like lustrous emerald spiders A
flooded river a poisoned ear of corn a black hole in time in memory in
motivation An end to colonialism An end to humanism Judged by the so-
called masters of both An hundred thousand point biological emotional
spiritual dead end Forgotten *Those who cannot remember the past are condemned to repeat it* The cliché is the only scripture The Ephraimites made
war on Jephthah's Gilead from jealousy Peter's third denial of Christ: they
said to him: Surely thou also art one of them; for thy speech betrayeth
thee Whose words are these? *Scheveningen* The victorious Dutch made
those fleeing Germans speak Say the word Peter *Scheveningen* If they
couldn't combine guttural and sibilant Of equal weight is every little word
because *thy speech betrayeth thee* Matsui entered Nanking after he missed

the invasion bedridden with his tuberculosis They cleaned a street and the little Buddhist rode through the triple archway of the Mountain Gate and suspected something had happened His narrow-white-raced chestnut was upstaged by the uninvited Colonel Hashimoto's thoroughbred bay behind The brash man who sunk the *Panay* Michael has a military postcard of the parade where Hashimoto is pointedly drawn closer just a millimeter higher than in the photograph of the real event The fictions reveal deeper realities For his reprimands Matsui Iwane the other good man of Nanking is shipped off to Shanghai One or two or three hundred thousand more die Retire again Iwane back to Japan to Atami he builds his shrine from Yangtze clay and ten years pass with four million more and then you hang and stay hanged *O my lady will hang thee for thy absence* Little man Little Butcher It is this simple to "make examples" It is this simple to shake all foundation away Everything is ready The horse see the horse no thoroughbred a race is a stripe upon a brow a fine chestnut ablaze The burning screaming horse We are moths in this driving ashen snow We clutch tight to her belly we ask only for a sheltered spot to air our wings To sleep She smokes clouds of spiders who search for us and I will find a place for you *Take the fat on your sword as condiment to the feast of death* Young man There is that desire in him to be Dionysian To truly be Nietzschean To affirm and be *über* To embody To embrace and to affirm If only to channel But why? To purge, always But why? To seek relief Those who cannot remember the past *A charnel-house A bone-urn* Are condemned This burning horse The chestnut unicorn runs from the river charging past all full of agonized energy and mindless intent There is no taming of a burning horse And to seek relief is *weak* The prettiest word of all: *Art thou an Ephraimite? If he said Nay; Then said they unto him Say Shibboleth: and he said Sibboleth: for he could not frame to pronounce it right Then they took him and slew him at the fords of Jordan: and there fell of the Ephraimites and there fell of the Ephraimites and there fell of the Ephraimites Sibbolet:* the word means ear of corn or stream in flood Modern commentators prefer the latter on the ground that on this view the selection of the word is naturally accounted for as the slaughter took place *at the fords of Jordan* the horse aflame has terrible eyes and the head of a man and its horn is a sword

Michael asked Yasu, gently, "What—" but broke off, his voice grown harsh with lack of use. He coughed, and tried again. "Excuse me. What time are we to meet your professor?"

But, his forehead furrowed, and accidentally, his eyes gone gray, he'd asked the question in English.

They were standing, Japanese and New Zealand exiles, willed or otherwise, on a path.

The path was lined by overlapping half-hoops of wire designed to keep students off the fringes of the gardens. The administration building of the old campus of Rikkyo University sat like an emerald-colored ogre before them. The two-storey building was long and squat, with two towers in the raised central section, bearded utterly with the ivy, rising either side of, at top, the bared face of a clock, and at middle, old leadlight windows looking out, and at the bottom the shadowed, ivy-overhung grotto of the inner courtyard where the path led. All brick and emerald and woodenly white, the building showed its more than one hundred and twenty-five years. The windows on the ground floor were just a foot above the grass, as if the building had subsided, the windows peeking through the thick, spreading leaves that had mortised them like sunken sockets awaiting eyes. Rikkyo University—St. Paul's—stared out blindly past the two boys.

Yasu blinked behind his glasses and looked down at the brick path.

"Ah," he said.

Michael looked up and smiled to reassure him, not yet realizing his mistake.

"Ah," Yasu said, and thought hard. "Two . . . o'clock . . . p.m."

"Oh," Michael said. "I'm sorry. Sumimasen. Ei-go daijobu desu ka?" Is English okay?

Yasu concentrated hard, and glanced once up at the stranger. He made a shape of an inch of space between his thumb and forefinger, and hitched his backpack up with a roll of his shoulder.

"Just a little."

"So desu," Michael said, and nodded.

"Ah," Yasu said, and began to blush. He indicated the shadowed path leading into Rikkyo under the clocktower with an open upturned hand, and said, "Please."

Inside the courtyard, three worn and weary stone steps, hollowed like slept-on pillows, led up to an intricate mahogany and glass revolving door and on into a maroon-carpeted lobby. The two boys shared a sector of the door, then Yasu led the way, tense but not hesitant, toward a glassed-in receptionist who was bent to a task. Michael waited in the center of the lobby. He was reminded of his father's old house, the connection suggesting a symmetry something more than coincidental; something traceable through the probabilities of certain nationalities taking root in certain places, building monuments, scripting laws.

The receptionist looked up and Yasu whispered rapid Japanese bent to the window's intercom. Michael waited politely. He studied the giant scaly palimpsest of an immense noticeboard, thickly feathered with thumbtacked messages, hung by thick string, like his father's prized Millet, from the polished wooden walls. The lobby had the settled silence of truly old buildings. Not so much a waiting as a sense of having seen more than any single person could attest. The silence of responsibility, of forgotten fame.

A silence at last broken shyly by the receptionist, whose voice came crackly and desiccated as she indicated a half-open door opposite.

Yasu bowed and murmured his thanks and turned to Michael staring at the giant board papered in kanji. Momentarily struck, again. He realized he'd have to compose yet another sentence through his tension.

"Ah," he said. "We . . . wait."

"Nihon-go daijobu desu," Michael immediately replied. Japanese is okay.

"But I must . . ." Yasu smiled, "increase English." He indicated the door ajar in exactly the same way as the receptionist. "Please."

Michael led the way into a room for meetings and waiting for meetings. Inside, Yasu placed his backpack gingerly between his feet as they sat. Shortly afterward, the receptionist closed the door behind them. A water cooler and a green tea machine, a gaudy golden clock ticking loudly inside a sealed cylinder of glass, a low black lacquer table with an ashtray and two wide, low leather sofas on which Michael and Yasu sat facing one another, postures similarly erect, because on sofas so low the only other option would surely be an unseemly slouch.

There was more than five minutes of silence before Yasu finally spoke.

"Michael-san. Appointment is made," he said. "I . . . cannot to . . . laboratory. Professor Maeda-san will meet here. Us. One hour early."

He blushed. "Professor" sounded like *pu-ro-feh-sa*.

"Okay," Michael said.

"Michael-san, I want to explain . . . mushroom feeling. My experience."

He looked briefly up, then down again.

"But English . . . is difficult."

"No, no," Michael said quietly. "Your English is very good."

He watched Yasu shake his head reflected in the lacquered coffee table, the ashtray passing back and forth over his face.

"Where did you learn to speak English? Here at Rikkyo?"

Yasu composed the face of an insoluble problem and didn't answer.

Michael waited, and then said, "Why can't you go to your professor's laboratory?"

Yasu exhaled through his nose, and blinked.

Thought very hard again, and in his concentration relaxed enough to say, "The story explains—"—he held up a finger—"Number one. My English. Number two—"—barely a flinch or a wince—"My expel from Saitama University; and not permission to the laboratories here; and so, Maeda-san, his kindness today. Number three. The story explains my mushroom experience in the best."

He looked up, his face open.

"Do you understand?"

"Is it the feeling," Michael said.

"Hai, so desu," Yasu said, a sharp and sure nod. "Three things, in the best. As we wait."

"Your story."

"So."

"Please," said Michael, in Japanese.

The story Yasu told, haltingly and stilted at first, but soon settling into a steady rhythm of fractured English and Jinglish and often outright Japanese as his self-consciousness subsided, was this:

Though his parents were never remotely Christian, they were, as modern Japanese, typically religiously tolerant. So when Yasu, at just sixteen years of age, was offered the Jason Llewellyn Burgess Fellowship in Natural Biology at Rikkyo—a four-year scholarship arranged by the chemistry grad school and funded by a turn-of-the-century act of tactical philanthropy by the Missouri-born, part-Episcopalian, part-Darwinist travel writer Burgess, a fellowship intended to provide a healthy empiricist foil to Rikkyo's "education of the spirit"—his parents were thrilled and financially relieved and unperturbed. So Yasu, at sixteen, had begun his one-hour daily commutes down to Tokyo and the degree that he would theoretically complete at the age not long after your average student left high school. Burgess Fellowship students were hero-worshipped by half the campus, and made pariah by the other. The upshot of all this for young Yasu was that it had been an intense and lonely first three years: commuting in with the chain-smoking construction workers, working twelve hours a day in the Rikkyo labs, commuting home with the drunken, often vomiting salarymen for another couple of hours' study, dinner at his low desk and six or seven hours' sleep before he rose to do it again. (Yasu, not a person to play up achievements, much less difficulties, conveyed all this in terms both understated and deadpan.)

But difficulties there were. And these pressures and challenges were only made bearable for young Yasu by the supervisor of the Burgess Fellowship, Junichiro Maeda, a tenured professor of sixty-three, an ex-Fellow himself, a specialist in biofilms who'd spent five years at Dartmouth in less than easy circumstances after the war, who held a Master's in French lexicology along with his Ph.D. Old Maeda, who had once met and talked all things French with Shusaku Endo himself, was mentor, counselor, go-between with parents worried at the harassed states of their sons, friend and teacher for Fellowship students. Yasu respected and loved the man nearly like his own father.

And for three years at Rikkyo Yasu excelled at all his tasks bar English—a significant deficit at a university founded under the name "St. Paul's."

So when Jonathan Dubuc, an eighteen-year-old fresh off the boat from Montreal, was admitted to Rikkyo in 1994 after the three-part, cripplingly difficult entrance exams had been passed, and the equally crippling nonrefundable application, admission, tuition and laboratory fees had been paid, it was Maeda-san who suggested the buddy arrangement with Yasu, who could ease Dubuc into school and Tokyo and Japanese food and the hours required to absorb the punishing number of kanji required to study chemistry in Japanese. The sagacious Maeda foreseeing this buddy system as also having the effect of preventing Yasu sliding into paranoia and a lifelong aversion to the English language.

Yasu agreed, more out of deference to Maeda's (retrospectively bad) judgment than any particular desire for an English-speaking Canadian pal.

Dubuc agreed too, because, at this point, having lied about his proficiency test (he'd claimed the prerequisite Level 1: Advanced: 2,000 kanji, a vocab of 10,000 words and more than 900 hours' study—the fact was that Dubuc, a better forger than he was or ever would be a language scholar, had altered his certificate with Adobe Photoshop) to get away from Montreal and his Catholic bishop and super-strict and son-beating dad who had nonetheless financed the first of four years at Rikkyo (with allowance), and Dubuc at this point having been only one week in Tokyo (Maeda and the professors at his orientation putting his quietness and constant nodding down to nerves and an endearing enthusiasm for all things Japanese, including deference to one's superiors), the young Canadian agreed to be buddied because he was both sleeping very little and doing anything he could understand of all he was being told.

But that didn't last long.

And nothing at all about Jonathan Dubuc seemed to quite add up or feel destined to last very long. The first clue was the accommodation he had chosen. Dubuc had set himself up at Kimi Ryokan, a budget inn for tourists, just a few blocks from Rikkyo on Ikebukuro's west side. Perhaps it might not have seemed too odd, and was in fact interpreted by some students as typically opaque unexplainable gaijin quirkiness and/or impressive wealth. Because a single room at the Kimi cost around ¥4,500 a night, so per month his rent worked out at roughly *double* that of a standard gaijin house. Impressive for a student.

But this—although, of course, no one ever raised the matter—could have been explained away.

Another clue was Dubuc's violent reluctance to talk with any of the other foreigners at the university. From more than 13,000 students, there were more than a hundred from all around the globe. Dubuc avoided them; including the two Toronto geographers—Baka John and Hilary— who clung together as those with common nationality always did.

So then there was class. For the first few weeks, sometimes up to five hours a day, six days a week, he sat in lectures silently scribbling in a new Muji folder, never looking up, never offering a word, never offering an easement for a lecturer to call upon him. Yasu sat beside him in only two classes per week, as a favor, and never once heard him speak. But Dubuc took copious notes, carefully shielded by an elbow, and the instant the ninety minutes were up and it was polite to leave, he'd clap his folder shut and meet Yasu outside, where he'd smoke duty-free Gitanes until next class so furiously there was no opportunity for conversation.

But oddly, they did share a kind of camaraderie. Yasu, who didn't (and still doesn't really) understand the concept of an uncomfortable silence, was simply there, feeling worthwhile, a buddy. Thus, with Yasu pretty much tending to take people as they came, gradually Dubuc began to draw a meager sort of succor from his silent presence.

But cracks began to show.

Vague rumors began to circulate in the Chemistry Department some weeks before midterms. Rumors that Dubuc had been spotted entering and leaving in different states of disrepair some less than salubrious nightspots in West Ikebukuro. That he'd been seen haggling haggardly with an old man wearing a billboard strung around his neck that was pasted with a gigantic photograph of a smiling naked young J girl obscuring the face of an anonymous black-haired head with her ass. That someone reported someone else had seen him wading in the fountains of the plaza late at night reciting a Latin catechism in just a pair of stained white Speedos. That he had four or five Japanese girlfriends, one of whom was a high school student, another of whom was actually a Korean dancer from the infamous Light in Roppongi who for money slept with foreigners of any race. That he was a ghost. That he dealt drugs.

Yasu, not oblivious but ever reticent, continued his mycology: briefly, into certain psychotropic alkaloidal properties' hypothetical structural similarities to Parkinson's-inhibiting dopamine. He'd by this time set up two or three small terraria at home along the lines of Maeda's large terraria the university had imported from the Sudetenland.

And things more or less came to a head one morning when, between a first-year bio lecture and a tutorial for foreigners on Japanology to which Yasu wasn't planning to accompany him, between furious puffs on a dizzyingly strong Seven Stars (having rapidly exhausted his forty packs of Gitanes in those first few weeks), Dubuc invited Yasu to an early lunch in very formal stilted Japanese.

Yasu, more than a little shocked, said, "But... what about the tutorial?"

Bloodshot-eyed and furtive, Dubuc simply repeated the carefully rehearsed invitation, honorifics and all.

Put this way, and really the first time in his life someone had addressed him in such flattering and respectful language, Yasu just couldn't refuse.

But still, his first real suspicion that something might well be wrong in the alien world of Dubuc didn't come until their food arrived at the seedy little izakaya that Dubuc had quickly and unerringly led him to. Yasu ordered some yakitori and green tea; Dubuc ordered a large draught beer with impressively dismissive familiarity, then tapped a finger randomly on the menu with what Yasu wasn't sure was either extremely classy or somewhat worrying indifference.

Dubuc lit yet another cigarette and sat in erect silence, one epileptically tapping foot aside, until his beer arrived. He downed half the glass in one prolonged, un-self-conscious swill. Naive Yasu remained unconvinced of any kind of trauma in the world of Dubuc. The Canadian downed the rest of his Asahi, and croaked out "Sumimasen!" to the waitress through a burp.

He ordered another.

Yasu waited. Prepared to put lunchtime binge drinking down on his expanding list of cultural differences. He'd heard about the English, after all.

But the moment of epiphany came—that Dubuc might just be lost, desperate, freaking rapidly out—when, by a waitress who showed some equivocal familiarity with the boy (a sidelong glance; a nasal sigh), their lunch was served.

Dubuc had randomly ordered Sapporo-style *nabe*.

Nabe Sapporo-style arrives on the table as a box of matches and a miniature hotplate on three stilts mounted over a small sterno. The hotplate is piled with raw beef and cabbage, the idea being that the diner supervises the cooking of his own dinner, stirring and turning the meat with his hashi to cook it evenly. And although the meat—pinkish, fatty, in gristly blobs as big as fingers—was piled high on the flat little hotplate, and there was no bowl or broth as per regular *nabe,* Sapporo-style usually works very well. Somehow, the amount of meat is calculated precisely that it cooks in its own juices without overflowing the hotplate's little rim, steaming the cabbage above, and usually without requiring any more than a minimum of attention.

Yasu knew that something was up with the young Canadian when he didn't light the sterno and, with a minimum of attention, began (with the fingers of one hand; Seven Stars still burning in the fingers of the other) to wolf the meat down raw.

Over the shining table, Michael looked carefully at Yasu.

Yasu looked straight back.

"I do not need money," Michael said.

Yasu watched him quietly for a moment.

The golden clock ticked loudly.

"I did not mean a parallel," Yasu said. "I see you do not need much."

Dubuc did, however. Need money. Whatever his antics and decline, from a streak of vicious self-preservation inside him like a vein of tin in rock had been forged the shaky shape of an idea as sharp as it was potentially brittle. Dubuc, through various Shibuya explorations and experiments and new friends who didn't go to universities, had learned a fair degree of the state of play of the mushroom trade on the street. Particularly, the current dearth of supply. Generally, the vague and malleable legal language. That psilocybin, the active hallucinogen, was illegal, but the mushrooms themselves, technically, were not. That nevertheless, to stay on the slippery side of the law, the mushrooms are putatively "not for human consumption." That they are "offered" in sketchy promotional slash disclamatory literature as intended merely for "informational purposes"; "contributing to research in fields such as culture, anthropology and the arts." That the clientele varied wildly between the worryingly naive and the worryingly discerning. That markups were skyhigh and demand inelastic as all hell.

Dubuc was more than prepared to play on Japanese courtesy as much as he was on the undisguised qualities in young Yasu of altruism, loyalty to Maeda's buddy system as loyalty to the man himself, pity, cultural ignorance.

"In Canada this is what we would do for a friend."

He was a liar, and cruel, but desperate.

Yasu warned him that it would surely be three or four weeks at least before he could get some reasonably demure *P. cubensis* up to a saleable state.

Dubuc said I will be forever grateful.

Yasu believed people who could frame such words believed and meant and stood hard by them.

So he did as he was asked by the boy he thought of as his first real buddy, uncapitalized, and a foreigner at that. If a friend is in a scrape, different rules apply. At least in Canada. Yasu was learning about the world. Shaping personal creeds; shifting his definitions of self.

And Dubuc, somewhat shakily back on his feet, Rikkyo and Kimi Ryokan long since abandoned for the four-and-a-half-mat room and drug habits of a Korean exotic dancer in Hiro-o, was only busted for cocaine possession in a recession-generated club crackdown a year later when Yasu himself had graduated, lost his parents and begun the lonely doctorate at Saitama University. And Dubuc confessed as he'd never done in his ostensibly Catholic life when smiling armed policemen quietly told him in broken English all about Japan's drug laws and terms of sentence and showed him the exact conditions of Japanese custodial cells, intimating the awful states of the actual jails, and though his memory was by now nothing if not well ventilated, the trail quickly and concisely led back to Rikkyo in Ikebukuro, and thence to Saitama and hardworking orphaned Yasu, and though nothing could be proven from Dubuc's often confused, often self-contradictory testimony, and nothing was strictly illegal in Yasu's increasingly chaotic house, there was more than enough ill-feeling, rumor and loss of face at Saitama U. for a rapid hearing and a summary expulsion, a hearing at which Yasu couldn't more than once lift his head to meet the eyes behind the spectacles of his old mentor Maeda, sitting in the little orange-freckled one-piece extruded plastic tutorial chair in the very back—the perpetually banal settings for these kinds of cuspate moments—and the letter Maeda sent him a week later explained in shaky calligraphy that he was sorry but although Yasu was technically an alumnus due to events and Rikkyo regulations Yasu was never to darken the revolving door of Rikkyo admin nor those self-closing lab doors of Maeda ever again.

And did ask a question, never answered.

"Did you do this thing?"

Yasu, triply abandoned, triply orphaned.

April 1995.

But what is that fluttered, falling feeling after the mortal blow? *That,* Yasu told Michael, was the closest he could come to describing the sensation of that merely osmotic trip. The little miracle's resinous blue rust upon his palm. The entire trauma relived in one black afternoon more than a month ago and faded only now. The smell of a bitter disappointed silence from the empty urns of parental ash. The tasty black smell of burning hair as the sun went down. Maeda's glass-black eyes. The crick in a long-bowed neck. What an empty house feels like after a guilty verdict.

As the night came on, loss, loss, and again, loss.

"And you have never been back since then?"

"No."

"And you have not seen Maeda-san since then?"

"No."

They stared across the table at one another.

"And you have asked to meet again with Maeda-san for me."

"For me, also. Yes. To find compositions of this blue cap. He has equipment, to discover. Indole...arukaroido...."

He trailed off.

"And he agreed."

"Yes." Yasu's shoulders drooped.

"Thank you, Tanabe-san," Michael said. "This was brave of you."

"No," Yasu said to the shining coffee table. "I think this was just the kindness of the professor."

There was a gentle knock at the door.

Yasu leapt to his feet so quickly his heels caught beneath the base of the sofa. He abruptly sat back down. Before he could rise again, blushing and flustered, a voice murmured, "Shitsurei shimasu."

The receptionist appeared with a tray in one hand laden with cups and a small jug. She had brought coffee.

Yasu remained seated. He breathed deeply as she placed the tray on the table. She quietly said, just a moment, Maeda-san will soon be here.

The golden clock ticked loudly. Twenty to two. The door clicked shut behind her.

Michael leaned across the table and passed Yasu a cigarette. He lit with a shaking Lupin Sansei and laid it on the table and they both sat and watched the steam, a pale relative of their cigarettes' smoke, rise from the untouched coffee.

It would be more than six months later that Meredith Julia Edwards—wrinkled T.I.C. map of Metro Tokyo in gloved hand—would pass through the revolving doors just a few feet away, out of the bitter winds of pre-Christmas Ikebukuro and into the timeless warmth, wood and shagpile of Rikkyo admin. Like Michael, she too was reminded of home. Of their own home, but also of ceremonies, parties, memorials, the homes of family friends. An entire childhood of judicial privilege spent running on maroon carpet; small sweaty handprints left to fade from three-quarter mahogany walls. And like Michael, too, her attention was drawn to the immense noticeboard opposite the revolving doors, leaning like a pregnant dare to earthquakes.

The thing was a giant cipher: thousands of coded messages tacked to and through one another; asking for things, offering things, reminding, predicting, alerting, buying, selling, imploring.

Meredith's head had begun to work like monolingual foreigners' always do, a survival instinct to shore up the banks of a psyche: the giant flood of printed message is mercilessly and bluntly attenuated; the world radically foreshortened in a sleight of eye. All kanji, hiragana and katakana were eliminated in a muscular flash until only roman letters remained. A slightly more conscious effort was required to sift from French, Spanish, Italian, romanized Japanese.

After some time in Japan, you may find yourself struggling to elicit words. Obvious things, on the tip of your tongue: what's that special kind of table, where you read your books?

It's a damn desk, you curse yourself.

Meredith was at the point where the sifting mechanism was a valuable skill, no circumscription.

And what she sifted from the scaled mass of the board were just three messages.

The first was a tiny yellow Christmas card, edged with holly and bells, depicting kneeling children praying to a yellow star, the card otherwise littered with hiragana, and kanji with hiragana transliterations in superscript to help Rikkyo's foreigners along. Meredith didn't really even see them. But in black ink inside a shaky speech bubble, the message:

LOVE HAS COME!

This was all Meredith saw.

The second message, long out-of-date for her, placed centrally, and substantially overlapped, read

BILL GATES
Honorary Doctorate in Humanities
Tucker Hall, Ikebukuro Campus
Rikkyo University
Fri. June 16th 2000
12:10–12:30 Degree Conferral Ceremony
12:30–1:30 Commemorative Lecture
Rikkyo University is honored to award a doctorate to Bill Gates,

who is an embodiment of the American tradition of innovation and
the social tradition of helping others to achieve their potential.

Meredith was becoming aware of the odd linkages in Japan; connections
with depth but no resonance; ironies halved; parody reduced, denied of
that which is parodied. And she wondered whose social tradition they
were referring to, there.

The third message she could read was larger than most, and had a
color photo. It was almost a poster. The page was faded; bruised and
curled and melancholy.

MISSING PERSON

The text on the poster was red and black, a combination of Japanese and
English. Although due to point size it seemed there was far less of the latter. As if in English there was less of this person. Left of center, the color
photo showed an old, small, bespectacled and smiling Japanese man with a
narrow gentle face, framed by a densely packed bookshelf.

Junichiro Maeda (68)

Other, smaller messages overlapped it. They were tacked onto it, and
through it. Texts for sale. Furniture, with crude drawings and metric
measurements. Software and hardware. Baseball caps and soccer gear.
Rooms wanted and rooms vacant. Video, DVD, TV, CD-ROM, CD. Washing machines, toaster ovens, rice cookers, tutors. The man's face was being
elided slowly from the board by more particular concerns. The poster of
the missing man was experiencing time, attrition; enacting what it uttered.
A strange, lost beauty, like a tessellated transparency of crushed ice: the
man's face a footprint in the thawing snow of public memory. In Japan,
Meredith's mind worked a little more like her brother's. But the man in
the picture was Japanese, so—cruelly—her emotion was second-order, distanced. She couldn't see this disappearing notice of a disappearance in
firm connection with her plight.

The English words on the poster:

The missing person, a Japanese, was last seen on May 1, 2000, at
approximately 3.00 pm in Nishi-Ikebukuro, Toshima-ku, Tokyo. He is

175 cm tall and is described as having gray hair and dark brown eyes. Please refer any information to the Azabu Police Station at 03 (3479) 0110 ext. 401 or 402.

Why distanced? Why, for someone who was here in search of a missing brother, someone who as a teenager defined herself as someone who cares, who cleaned beaches and decided she wanted to work, someday, for the World Health Organization, who was half-Japanese by blood if not so much by appearance, did a friendly-looking old Japanese gone missing not elicit more reaction?

Three days ago, the day after the night at the sushi bar, Meredith had made a number of calls from the hotel, the first of which was home, her mother.

Meredith is someone who trusts her brother.

And together—though nothing is yet so permanent for her as him: she could still go back; she knows he never will—they had disappointed their parents badly by not finishing university. She had, after all and as a kind of proxy, gone to Otago University in 1998, to stay at Knox Hall in her first year and to study Law. And on the strength of high school habits more than a firm sense of where she wanted to go she had passed everything, pulling grades that in her parents' expectations ran the gamut of mediocrity from an A- in Statistics of all things to just a B minus in Law—not enough to gain entrance to law school. A year of curfews and institutional food and serious medical students who said they wanted to "do something with procedures" coming on to her, and then she spent the silent and frustrating summer at home as a librarian at a law firm named Russell McVeagh for some disposable income. And then, after a dream she had on Christmas Eve where she had driven out to Lyall Bay alone in a fast car (could it have been a TransAm?) to meet her father, a dream in which she knew she had a briefcase and she knew she had spoken coolly, convincingly and at length in court that day, she made the decision that eased things considerably at home—the difficult choice; the high road and the hard option. She would repeat the twelve points of Law and continue with a light workload of second-year papers.

So it's with ambivalent feelings that Meredith views universities.

First year quickly seemed like just another kind of high school once she began second year. Key memories: a Leith Street flat with two med students, Emma and Dan. How many Dans did she meet in Dunedin?

Both Emma and Dan had come on to her within months. Emma had nick-named her "my dark star." A party she attended across the road where boys played Superbottle for hours, throwing every bottle they could find in the three-flat complex—thousands—against the stucco of the complex closest to the Leith. She remembered the shock, the excitement, and then the dull repetition of it; a boredom to fight boredoms. The callousness; the pile of green and brown glass spread so thickly in the empty carparks. Only one Superbottle: Seagar's Gin; it survived the stucco and fell into the mounds of glass, and then the cheering. A boy sitting naked in an arm-chair on the balcony urinating idly on himself. But the next day the boys were up before lunch sweeping, and she found herself fond of them in an odd, repulsed kind of way, and she wished for things: thick carpet in her room to lie on; that it could ever be warm enough only one time to do that; just to wear a T-shirt. She worked at Law, and went to lectures. She bought different-colored pens to organize her notes. She wanted to be as smart and sure as Michael, and because she wasn't sure, she worked hard at Law. She went to the library in the evenings and thought of him to motivate herself. To dare herself.

Another key memory, though: in the dead bony heart of Dunedin win-ter, a party in a flat on Dundas Street. The north footpath iced over for three solid months. The boys and some of the girls were bonging keg beer. There was a plastic bucket for spillage and froth and the beer that came from people's mouths and noses. The bong was radical: a yard long, a funnel the size of a lampshade, the tube as wide as a vacuum cleaner's hose. Written on the side in black Vivid: MOAB: the Mother Of All Bongs. Boys tried to persuade her to bong but no way. Meredith had a minor and unspoken reputation for being proud. Boys dropped cigarette butts to dis-integrate in the foul spillage bucket. She met the boy named Nicholas Tin, a twenty-something guitarist doing profs for Law who had dreadlocks and a Volkswagen with a portrait of Johnny Marr on the bonnet and the words "The Draize Train" spray-painted in gigantic black letters on its flanks—one side written backward, so they would match—who arrived at this party in jeans, pink moccasins and just a thin pink large-lapelled shirt in this near-freezing weather. He was older and he was confident and he was brash, and she was quiet and sober. Boys spat in the spillage bucket, blew foam from emptied kegs in the spillage bucket. The liquid inside was gray-brown, the foam around the edges a yellow spume flecked with cigarette ash. Then they poured the spillage bucket into the bong and called a girl in from the kitchen named Sarah, who was a second year at Teacher's College and a little drunk, and they said it's your turn and they held it up for her and told her how to do it. Boys made signs for quiet. One girl left the room. One boy pointed at a cigarette butt floating in the tube. Boys tried not to laugh. Some of them were wearing polythene ponchos over their clothes, but Sarah was wearing a white cashmere turtleneck. Meredith remembers getting up to leave too late, and she remembers the girl Sarah dragging the tube away from her mouth too late, coughing, after the hydrostatic pressure had really kicked in, and the gritty liquid drooling from her mouth and nose and spurting from the tube onto her face and into her hair and onto her white cashmere turtleneck. Meredith left, then, past the laughing, cringing boys, and Nick followed her. Outside he made her laugh, once, after a while. And when the boys came outside to burn the flat's fence in a bonfire they walked away up the hill together, this boy seemingly immune to the cold, and he pointed at the house on top of the Dundas hill, opposite Studholme, and told her there was a ghost of a girl who had been raped and murdered by her flatmate there, strangled, and beaten to death in a waterbed with the butt of a rifle, who wandered around the house and the castle behind and plaited her hair into homemade cornrows in the mist, and although all Meredith wanted was to lie on thick warm carpet and listen to old sad Prince that sounded like no way could music like that be written anywhere cold, there was something about this particular boy in his thin pink shirt in this weather. She said, come back to the house for hot cocoa, the first time in Dunedin she'd really been that daring.

And he played guitar and was immune to the cold and she began to miss some lectures, and then, in July, Michael appeared on her doorstep in an Armani suit like an alien among the students. She was glad Nick wasn't there that day, and they went for a walk together by the Leith and she told him whoever said dreams told the truth was a liar, and he nodded, and they watched a boy in a wetsuit sitting slumped in an inflatable inner tube caught in the backwash of a weir and cradling a bottle of peach schnapps in his lap get rescued by the Fire Department, and with Michael there life seemed to gain a density it hadn't had and she felt sad for herself and the dirty cold streets and the ugly library and the beer cans crumpled in the gutters and the students sleeping till midday. How even such a bitter winter could be tepid. Where boys trick girls into drinking grime. She realized she felt generally lost and alone and unreal, and Michael told her he was going back to Japan and that he thought university wasn't everything. That it was better to do anything else than to enroll and study what you do not love or respect. No matter what. They bought bagels and coffee at Ruby in the Dust and went to a film, and in the queue for snacks people looked at them when they got excited and recited lines from the episode of *The Muppets* with Steve Martin, daring each other's memories; that catechistic call and response, the dares, the memorial one-upmanship—but the aim benevolent: never to win but just keep the game going—and people looked at them like they envied the closeness of that dark foreign-seeming couple; how what they had seemed something fine. He slept in a sleeping bag on her floor and she didn't take Nick's call and the next day Michael took a taxi to the airport and that was the last time she saw him.

So here she is, in a Japanese university. After a winter decision to see Japan. Another winter, but real; another university. Remembering another life in overtired, early-morning, crisp and foreign detail. She doesn't have Michael's confidence. It still took a couple of months and Nick leaving for Korea before she could bring herself to make the phone call home and break the news she was quitting. Late 1999. There's always a sting in these places for those who haven't beaten them in one sense or another.

Meredith spoke to her mother three days ago. About translation.

"So how are you getting on, dear. I have been worrying about you," her mother said.

"Mum, I'm fine. I haven't seen him yet. Neither have his friends. He's not staying at the hotel. The Prince is empty."

"That's what he does. He travels a lot."

"Yes, but there are things here, Mum. Documents. Videotapes and photographs. Things he was working on. Some of his clothes."

"Are you eating properly? Do you need anything? Money?"

"No, no. But he's been working here. But now he's gone."

"He travels too much."

"Mum."

"Andrew and I haven't heard from him."

"How is Dad."

"Fine."

"Mum. He sent me something by skymail. A long message in Japanese that I don't understand."

"Well, that's ... good?"

"But I can't read it. It's strange. I've tried to get it translated by friends, but it's difficult."

"What are you going to do?"

"Well, I'm going to transcribe it and send it to you. I don't know anyone I can really trust here. To do this properly."

"Oh, Meredith. It's been a long time."

"What do you mean?"

"It might be difficult for me."

"Mum. This is all we have. No one, literally no one knows where he is. And this is only days old."

"Why do you think he wrote it in Japanese?"

"I'm not even sure they're his own words. I don't know what it is."

"Are you eating properly, Meredith? Enough red meat? It will be cold there now."

"Mum?"

"Meredith, what your brother reads and studies is his own business. What he chooses to look at is his own business. He is adult now. And we have always given him that right. I couldn't possibly . . . look at the things he does, or believe what he believes. I can support him and love him, but I cannot join with him in this, or agree with what he thinks. I know that I do not believe anything good can come of this endless turning back that he insists upon."

"Mum. It's all we have."

"That's not all we have. I haven't used the language in . . . twenty-six years. I would hamper your cause."

"But Mum. It's Michael."

"Really, Meredith."

She waited a long time, considering and discarding angles. In all her arguments, her mother seemed to recede when her point was made. Minutes passed, in a silence in which Meredith thought, and her mother waited.

But it was her mother who spoke first.

"You know, Meredith. I think New Zealanders have more kinds of silence than the Japanese."

To her surprise, a little horror, and a creeping sense of gladness, Meredith found she was hanging up.

The next call she made was to Jacques' keitai.

"Meredith! What are you doing?" His voice mellow and husky and dropped an octave from its normal pitch.

"Cutting ties. What about you?"

"I . . . am riding upon the monorail. Why do you call me again, Meredith."

"What? Why? To the airport?"

"Out to the airport, and then all the way back again. Twice so far on today. Like your calls. I like the canals and the fishermen. Now then again, I get off at a station and smoke a joint in the bathroom. I had one watching the horse-racing track at Oikeibajomae just soon. It's resting for me. No one in Japan can recognize the smell on me, you know?"

"Jacques, are you okay? Hey, I didn't call you again."

"I guess so. I guess I am a little stoned."

"Jacques, you told me you knew someone to get this message translated. After the sushi."

"'We are like statues among them.'"

"What?"

"That is the first line, so Pras says. Yes, I know someone. Someone better than Pras and me. And I, I mean, really. I know someone who is better than Pras and I." He laughed without feeling. A pause. "That sounds a little bit kind of ominous."

"Who is it, Jacques? Are you sure you're okay?"

"Let me get it right. His name is Yu Hayakawa. He is the youngest professor of comparison literature at Rikkyo University. Yu Hayakawa. And Meredith, if I am you, be kind of careful."

"Why?"

"He is Michael's girlfriend's husband."

She'd come to Rikkyo to find him.

Sitting opposite one another smoking cigarettes, a fundamental difference between Yasuhiko Tanabe and Michael Edwards was their sense of the relationship of aesthetics—encompassing here science and history, as metonymic systems to grid out oceans of experience, like a Go board does the game—to the experience itself. Out in the bark like Nietzsche's tragedians, Yasu watched the waves that tossed him, and tried to understand them; even tried to sail. Out there in the bark, yet more like the tragedians, Michael sat quietly, lost, in the contemplation of the redeeming vision, which to him was inextricable from the slop and roll and gurgling roar of time around and depthless under; was in fact informed by it: an aesthetic shaped by, yet transcending, circumstance. A dream with particular consonance and amoral authority on moral grounds; self-prophesying, inescapable.

Michael's dream was history from the craquelure, the insane hirsute haggard hand of history rising through aesthetic indifference gathering human difference in rotting rude fingers, holding up in one blinding flash eleven judges to the pristine empty sky. About four hundred years in the remaking, and almost half his short life, mad and emphatic. He knows more about what's in that bag than Yasu does.

Yet in the moments when the dream of a dream subsides, when the mind pushed to its limits finally tires, when emotions scorned for their predictability are entertained through sheer exhaustion, for Michael there's one last person who comes to mind, one last person who shakes his resolve. And so, aware of this, and as the proud pay favors with equal and greater favors, Michael began to tell Yasu a story of his own. A story that seemed to hold a truth about and encompass facts of his own life in a way his own life didn't.

There was an American girl, born with long Indiana arms and absurdly curly blond hair to a young single woman of Mormon parentage in the little town of Santa Claus, Indiana—population 1,203, near the Kentucky border—in the late 1970s; Mormon grandparents who saw to it the girl was secretly put up for adoption on certain lists in Indianapolis before she was even born. The little girl was taken from Santa Claus Land and the woods and the meadows and the horses before they could even become memories, and placed with an upscale New York couple who had argued about—mother for; father successfully against—telling the little girl she was adopted. So she grew up in Greenwich Village, an apartment equidistant from the UN buildings where her father was an environmental consultant and the Columbia University campus where her mother was a professor, specializing in Faulkner but occasionally mopping up some freshman Shakespeare. She grew up tall and she grew up Indiana strong, and she never learned to say y'all even as a joke, and she grew up with an atavistic yearning for meadows that came to her in dreams of horses, and that in its lack of expression became a very un–New York reserve; a quietness and melancholic nostalgia for something that wasn't in her memories, but in her muscles and skin. And when she finished high school she enrolled at Columbia, in Japanese and some English lit, including her mother's Shakespeare course. Then in 1998 her father was offered a position at the US embassy in Akasaka, Tokyo, as an observer and adviser on leaks in the canvas polymer undersheets of landfills on the Kanto plains, ruptures that were causing alarming dioxin readings and a groundswell of outrage in lower-lying villages. Her mother, whom she had almost forced to to fail her in the Shakespeare class, refused to give up Columbia even for a sabbatical. And because she'd discovered her natural aptitude for languages, and because as part of the embassy staff her father could get accommodation for family members that was all location, mostly Western, comparatively spacious and what's just next to gratis, and because she was restless for reasons she couldn't articulate, she chose to go with him. To Japan.

So there was an American girl there in the maelstrom of Tokyo money whose looks and her father made her a kind of star. There were dinners and parties and after-parties, an excited kind of alcoholism seemingly vital just to offset the stress and adrenaline, a suspension of time as anyone previously knew it. Old hands would see the wired faces and think, fresh off the boat. She met people from all over the world, ambassadors, producers, filmmakers, journalists, consultants to the International Telecommunication Union, assistants to ambassadors, secretaries to those assistants, hundreds of people passing through the crossroads of Tokyo. She traveled by absurdly priced domestic flights to Hokkaido, Nagoya, Kobe, Kyushu. That year she was too busy to think of needing anything to do. She was twenty-two. And then her father was offered a higher-paying position in the private sector as a consultant to a mining company in Irian Jaya, owned by a corporation known as the Chang Group, who—as her parents' separation became something they referred to as such—were being sued over poisoned rivers by a consortium of local villages represented pro bono by environmental lawyers on behalf of a well-financed Washington PAC. She argued with her father—it was a bullshit political assignment— and he left for Irian Jaya, and she stayed. And as her Japanese got better the money ran out. She didn't have a four-year degree and she wasn't good enough at lying to try and bluff her way into a job teaching English. She was too proud and too far away to ask for help from either of her parents. In the winter of early '99, she turned to hostessing to pay for the gaijin house in Setagaya-ku and the reduced circumstances she'd fallen into. The mama-san wore heavy makeup and black taffeta and was cruel and all business. On her first night she was given a photocopied sheet of rules in English, the comedy of which was lost and darkened in its pettiness and fascism.

Never wear pants.
Never pour you're drink first.

Always light the customers cigarette first and pour his whisky when it gets to half.

Do'nt talk to other girls, always talk to the customer.

You should'nt wear black.

Black was the mama-san's province. The girls changed clothes in a shared converted closet with one mirror, no seats, and in the washroom there was another rule taped to the wall:

Please check clean it here. Its you're own room and bring you're own tissue please! Affectionately, Mama.

She worked with an African girl who'd come to Tokyo on a scholarship, whose host family had moved on to England, who had found it too difficult to study in Japanese. She would remember the African girl forever sitting on the arm of a leather sofa unsmiling, her cigarette's smoke curling in the disturbed air where her customer's hand jerked, miming a milking motion at her breast. There was an Irish girl who didn't have a degree and couldn't teach English either. The Filipina-Canadian girl named Ariel, who turned up for two Friday nights and never returned. A blond Russian who spoke no English, wore a silver gown with a sash and a split, who had a gigantic bald Dutch boyfriend who snapped at her in a language that sounded like angry rustling because a blond was competition. A New Zealander who taught English and was there just for the extra money.

She hated whisky and that was all they ever drank. They were shy yet lewd and the conversation she tried to make was made of codes for her benefit alone: she talked about certain bars; bars she'd been to with embassy staff. About the pizza restaurant under Salsa Caribe, the restaurant where she'd met a beautiful rich DuPont girl and actually liked her. Better than demeaning herself using Japanese honorifics, she asked in English inane questions and in English earned rude answers.

"How long have you been at your company?"

"You have . . . small breast. *She* has bigger breast."

Because the men were free. The hourly rate was a mere ¥1500, but there was a bonus system. If she secured a customer's business card she could call him during the week to say hello and ask when he would visit again. If he came again and if he asked for her, she would get the bonus, and that was how the real money was to be made. She began to paint her toenails in her spare time with laborious, obsessive care, using different-colored cotton wool to keep each toe apart, but matching on each foot; a rainbow of tufts, mirrored at a point between her perfectly painted big toes.

RedWhiteBluePinkPinkBlueWhiteRed.

She began to pluck the hairs on her legs with tweezers as maintenance between waxings. She began to cause too much pain and take too much time over the process. She began to find too much calm there. The men knew the bonus system, and kept the cards to themselves. She couldn't bring herself to try harder.

So when the New Zealand girl told her about a job opportunity, that there were dancers wanted at Flood in Roppongi, it may have been a bad choice, but even for the same money just not to talk, just to dance sounded like something so sweet and so free.

Flood seemed all made of glass, chlorinated water running down in sheets and rivulets, lit through by halogen lamps. The whole club fluttered and rippled. She was interviewed in the afternoon as busboys wiped tables and vacuumed with Siemens A.G. machines strapped to their backs. The interview was conducted mostly in Japanese by two men in their thirties. They did not ask to see her passport or visa, which showed just a month of legal residence remaining. They asked her to strip down to the bikini she had ready underneath, and they asked her to dance to music muffled by the vacuum cleaners. She laid her suit carefully on a barstool and danced at four p.m. to a song called *Sweet Like Chocolate.* And one of her most vivid memories of this would be that to wear the new bikini she had waxed the highest centimeter of her triangle, and that there the cotton bikini was tight and hot and chafed the sensitive skin. She was employed at roughly double what she had been making as a hostess and she was changing fast.

There were songs, and then there were the things she vividly remembered, that made up her life. Prince, *Diamonds and Pearls* and waiting at Harajuku station for the first trains as the sky lightened. Wearing heels in the freezing dawn, chain-smoking, reading a leaflet about a short film festival by the sad milky light of a Dydo drink dispenser. New Order, *True Faith* and standing under Almond Café in the summer night when it was too hot to even try and sleep. Standing on the corner with other girls from Flood and saying little, and hearing for the first time that some of these girls were sleeping with Japanese men for a lot of extra money. Suede, remixed, *Everything Will Flow.* And hearing as part of the same conversation about the J guy who was stupefying foreign girls at his apartment and videotaping them and how some girls just disappeared. And equating the two, in a kind of final horror and retribution, and wondering if whatever drug he used allowed the girls to dream, and if so, of what. After two months, being invited to dance in a VIP room at Light, which was owned by the same faceless people who owned Flood, where she danced for older men in expensive suits who brought their own Japanese girls with them. How although she was never asked to do anything more, she felt like some kind of dumbshow; a prelude to a real event, a deeper, darker, later VIP room where anything could happen and that waited for her, clicking like a beetle. She learned only small pieces of information about her clients, all from other girls. That one man whose skin was so clean and caramel it seemed to glow was a director of Mitsui Fire and Marine. The girl who walked with him was so tall and slender and silent and had such poise and mute elegance she felt shy of her size for the first time in her life, shy of her muscled arms and rounded hips, shy that there seemed so much American substance to her body. And she found out later that the slender girl was a slave; that the director had bought her when she was thirteen. That she was now sixteen, and had trained herself to hold a can of beer completely inside her anus, because that was what the director wanted.

Tom Waits.

DJ Shadow.

Jane's Addiction. *Jane Says.*

Drunk and disheveled GIs in Yomiuri Giants baseball caps shouting at her and the other girls on the corner. How she thought of the director's quiet, polite voice, his cufflinks.

Stone Roses. *Fool's Gold.*

Gaps you walk between slow as you can, then leap without looking. The expiration of her visa. Dreams of horses; dreams of woods. One night when a desperate young Russian demanded she get in his car and she refused. Two weeks later the story about the Russian gangster's girls getting mutilated in retaliation for some slight, and he himself dismembered by a surgeon and drowned in a tarpit with no limbs to flail. She never knew if there was a connection, but she knew there was an edge. She bought new bikinis to let that line of hair grow back. It grew back coarser and harder than the rest of her triangle, and she could feel the difference, the clean delineation. Every night before she slept she touched it lightly, then touched beneath where it was soft.

There was a second gentle knock at the door.

This time there was no doubt and no mistake. The two young men stubbed out their cigarettes, rose and turned. The door opened, and in came Maeda, white lab coat, glasses, a brief smile for the foreigner.

Yasu stepped around the end of the sofa and bowed as deeply as he could. In Japanese, Maeda said, "No, no—" but it was too late, as Yasu went to his knees, palms of his hands flat to the carpet, and kowtowed— Michael in shocked understanding, stood awkwardly Western—and Yasu muttered, his forehead to the carpet, sharply, "*Sumimasen; sumimasen.*"

He was sorry; he was sorry. Ready to be forgiven; he needed forgiveness.

It was much too much; too late, too fraught. Yasu on his knees. Maeda turned to Michael, seemed to size him up in an instant. Then he turned back to the kowtowed boy at his feet, and Maeda said, "Tanabe-san."

"Yes!" Yasu shouted into the carpet.

"Please rise," Maeda said. "Perhaps this is a difficult situation for your friend to understand, and we must try to be sympathetic."

"Yes!" Yasu shouted again. He slowly and clumsily labored to his feet. He stood head bent low.

"Now please let us sit down together, Tanabe-chan," the old professor said, and smiled politely. "I always say these kinds of potentially jarring occasions, are so much more easily absorbed with the knees bent."

He turned to Michael, who had noted the affectionate suffix, and he nodded, indicated the sofa and said in English, "Please."

So they sat down upon the sofas, Maeda posture perfect alongside Yasu, opposite Michael. Yasu's face was red and flushed and downcast; he sniffed and clasped his hands between and beneath his knees, slumped, staring into some glazed distance of remembered shame. Ever the pose of those who curse themselves; of those gone beyond. Maeda's face showed concern, serious yet wry, a deliberate pose of a paradoxically lighthearted gravitas, Michael saw, to ease the tension without further loss of face for anyone. Michael saw in him immediately that special kind of diplomat who reserved his skills for moments when others were in need.

Michael introduced himself in Japanese. He finished, politely asking for the professor's favor.

In English, Maeda said, "It is a pleasure to meet you. And as I am aware you know of me, I must confess I know of you."

Yasu sniffed.

"Really?" Michael said. "I'm flattered."

"Do you know of the so-called vanity search? This is where a man enters his own name into an internet search engine in a moment of boredom to discover the extent of his own fame in cyberspace. After Yasu-chan's email, I conducted such a search with your name. This led me to ask some questions around campus, this and others."

Yasu sniffed again, differently, at "Yasu-chan."

"Oh?"

"Yes. And I was led in many strange and interesting directions. You are indeed internationally well-known, for one so young and now investigating a field with meager legitimate academic patronage."

Maeda watched Michael closely for a reaction; in his age not wary of eye contact.

Michael waited several seconds before answering.

"Indeed, Maeda-san," he said slowly and carefully, "the internet does provide a forum for the discussion of many . . . new, young, perhaps risky, perhaps . . . diaphanous fields of study."

Maeda watched eyes that stared right back, testing the boy's syntax and diction against the essays he'd read, probing seriousness, consistency and sincerity, matching face and clothes and stance, politics, mind and *matériel*.

The golden clock ticked loudly, and Yasu's sniffs subsided, his head beginning to rise as he absorbed the quiet.

Maeda smiled at last. "'Diaphanous.' Ha!" He clapped his thigh. "Excellent!"

Yasu looked wide-eyed from Michael to Maeda's knee.

"And now, Mister Edwards," Maeda said abruptly. "I am afraid I must leave you after this very brief meeting, as Yasu-chan and I will go down to the laboratory and examine this discovery he has written about to me. Perhaps I will send Kyoko in with some further refreshments."

"That sounds fine," said Michael.

They rose together, and Maeda turned to Yasu still sitting on the sofa.

"Shall we go to the laboratory, Yasu-chan?" he said in Japanese.

Yasu took a breath, then shut his mouth. He glanced once at Michael, then, to Maeda's chest, "The laboratory."

"Yes. I have many changes there to show you, and I am interested to learn your thoughts. And I am fascinated at what you have to show me, and all you have been working on during our long separation."

Yasu stood shakily and held his backpack to his chest.

"Please," said Maeda, and indicated the door.

Yasu shuffled, and Maeda turned at last back to Michael. "Excuse me, Mister Edwards. I hope to talk again with you soon, perhaps in more depth."

"Of course, Maeda-san," Michael said. "It has been a pleasure. Thank you for your assistance." He bowed. "Oh, and Maeda-san?"

"Yes?"

"I wonder if you know of a young professor of comparative literature here at Rikkyo. A man by the name of Hayakawa Yu."

"Of course," Maeda said. "You know Hayakawa?"

"As Endo might put it," Michael said.

Maeda smiled.

Together, they said, deadpan, *"Belles-lettres enfant terrible."*

Maeda smiled again. And this time, he bowed.

"You respect this respected man?" said Michael.

"He is known throughout the world."

"Forgive me. He is a farce, a pick-and-mix historian, a genre-jumper, a long, loud guffaw."

"Institution is not a thing to be bucked by those part-timers." Maeda grinned as if he knew everything. "We work for our violations, generate our own shock value. Our pride in our history is its own check and balance. To be a man what is else?"

"Very well," Michael said. "Yes, that is okay. Good-bye."

And then the two Japanese were gone.

Michael sat alone in the waiting room. It didn't matter that he was alone. He continued.

Tim Somebody, a boy he'd never met, was a half-Indonesian, half-Italian-American busboy at the club Light, and on the night Michael met this beautiful Indiana girl for the first time, to everyone but her, Tim was sick.

To her, Tim was probably staring at himself reflected in a juddering window on the Keisei line out to Narita and his plane to Italy. It was because of this busboy, Tim Somebody, she and Michael came to meet. One of Tim's daily tasks at Light in summer had been the emptying of the opaque plastic jerry cans that filled with runoff from the four leaking air conditioners scattered around the club. For her, there was something to do with fidelity in the absence of the sound of drips falling in a plastic jerry can. One of the four leaking air conditioners was in the girls' changing rooms, and the plip-ping sound in the jerry can represented a sense of loss, precariousness, recession; a general anxiety felt personally, that this business (and her Japan) was both cobbled together and winding down. The can sat in the farthest corner from the curtained door of the changing room, connected by a pipe to the Panasonic outlet on the wall above; the old plastic's white gone cracked and ivory, framed by a border of cream pebbled wallpaper that had not been so fully yellowed by whatever substance the air had leached into the rest of the stained walls. But as the working night dragged on, with the sound's diminishing came a kind of relaxation, a forgetting, an immersion in the task that seemed to be what shut out the relentless plipping sound. But later, after she'd quit the job she no longer needed, she began to wonder if it was in fact—that almost meditative state that came on around eleven p.m., a trance of efficiency in dance, cigarette, change, dance—*caused* by the overflow's approach on the brim; caused by the increasing subtlety in the sound of plips of drops falling into the swelling truly foul gray liquid, higher in frequency and pitch, receding as the waters rose, creeping closer with infi-nite care, and god knows what was in there, dioxins, carcinogens, heavy metals, freon, but near the end it got so quiet it was like that overflow wasn't even happening at all.

Or it could have been that at about eleven-thirty give or take, Tim would pound on the outside of the flimsy wall, a gesture of politeness made redundant as he simultaneously stuck his head through the curtain, and shouted,

"Look! On payday each inbox pokes out!"

to whoops, calls, ironic cheers and murmurs from the girls, mutters, and sometimes nothing at all. Because once Tim became comfortable with anyone, his earnestness dropped away and he communicated only in haiku.

Over a Scottish girl named Bianca's naked shoulder he murmured, "Wakabayashi-san calls, and waves his hand. A tardy and forgetful smack addict packs his bags."

Bianca eyed him in the mirror and fixed an earring, clip-on.

"Sean the bastard got fired."

"So desu."

"*Excellent.*"

Tim spread gossip, told rumors and lies, and passed on management secrets, always in haiku.

"Advertisement in *TC*: join disgruntled dancer lawsuit. In the manager's office they ask me: 'What do you know?'"

Often they were just general semi-facts and semi-anecdotes and pieces of semi-advice on Tokyo.

"When you see the weathered homeless man in the top hat on Roppongi Crossing, effluent in his beard: walk on by."

"Peopling their medical trials the Prozac import company pays citizens to admit they're depressed. Mental illness."

"Summer comes to my apartment. Lying on my back I press the soles of my bare feet against those of the man next door. Between us only a cool wall."

Tim made haiku about haiku, that often in their form managed to contradict what they asserted.

"Halfway up the stairs I stop in horror. When does profound simplicity become simplistic profundity, I ask myself. But I continue up the stairs."

"This thing does not imply that thing. This thing is only this. Salaryman vomit frozen on the midnight station platform."

He was largely ignored like those who in their consistency get taken for granted: only haiku specific to someone in particular got a response, and the rest were left floating in the changing room like bad but useless news. No one ever said, "Well what are you gonna do?" No one ever said, "Who cares?" Tim told it all, grinning slyly yet absently, lost in his own remaking of the world, picking his way across a floor draped with clothes to the corner of the room and the now near-silent jerry can of ominously silvergray water. Little things did get noticed, like the way he carefully held his hand over the can's open spout as he lugged the thing quietly from the garment-strewn room, and maybe in his sudden quiet he was absently composing a line for the busboys' room where the second leaky aircon was, something about a palm of a hand rotted through with radioactivity, something about an air-conditioned Jesus, stigmata of dioxin, a freon crucifixion. Something that broke the rules; was only half-funny; was relentless. Or maybe he was just trying dutifully not to spill any on their stuff.

In terms of composition, his haiku weren't strictly true to form. In terms of execution and delivery they offered no conclusions or respite, barely even a gathering of circumstance. His mind moved like he was taking Polaroids of his life; and once taken they were discarded; and he coped. People like Tim get taken for granted until eventually they're relied upon.

But that day in particular she knew he was going. That morning Tim had called her on her keitai at the gaijin house and he had asked her, lucidly, in sometimes multiclaused sentences, if she would empty the changing room's jerry can of aircon fluid sometime around eleven-thirty. He was calling in sick, he said, and the occupants of faulty-airconned rooms had to shift for themselves. But the truth was, he told her, that he was flying out to Italy that night, where she knew his mother lived (and she somehow knew, by a tone in his voice she'd never heard in her six months at Light, that for whatever reason he'd told and would only tell her). And she also somehow knew that this odd boy wasn't going to be coming back.

He signed off:

"But a spring dream! How vexing that I could not go mad!"

She didn't say anything, and waited.

"That's Raizan," he said. "Sixteen somety-something. You know. Around then. Hey, I'll see you, Cathy."

He hung up.

And so it was that in murderous 103°F heat, at just after 11:35 p.m., she was lugging the full jerry can two-handed, step by step down the cramped and silty iron stairs that fell steeply down to the alley behind Light. She wore a halter top and skimpy shorts, and as the jury-rigged cap of gray duct tape peeled away from the nozzle of the can her progress was slowed even further as she placed the thing step by gentle step down the stairs in the sticky night, to make damn sure that the evil stuff that brimmed over every sticky night—stuff that the more there was the less it drew attention to itself, the slyer it got, the less you noticed it and the happier you were in your ignorance—to make sure that evil stuff didn't splash on all that exposed tan Indiana skin.

It has come to this, was the thought that occurred to her, heading down the narrow, radically cambered alley for Roppongi-dori and a grate in the gutter out on the street. Not that this situation was any kind of rock bottom or even terrifically distasteful. The thing was more that the complexity of the circumstances was so totally original and unprecedented and yet at the same time so completely unsurprising that there paradoxically *was* a surprise of sorts: it has come down to this; the realization of this total lack of surprise, intrigue, sadness, even anger was itself only a dull, muffled, seemingly meaningless knock.

People passed by the end of the alley, on this side heading left, on the other, right. She steeled herself for rude comments in two or more languages, hoisted the jerry can in one hand, her other held out for balance, like someone old-fashioned on a bicycle indicating left, and she got as far as the near edge of the crowded sidewalk before abruptly halting and putting the can back down.

No one was going to make room for her to carry this stuff across; the sidewalk was too thick with people. She'd have to wait for a light change to create a gap.

"Would you like a hand with that?"

A young-looking foreign boy in a wifebeater with a notebook and a cigarette and a hipflask of Ice vodka tucked in his jeans pocket, waiting on the sidewalk at the corner of the alley, in accentless English.

"I'm fine, thank you," she muttered without meeting his eyes. And she waited; for a gap; for him to insist; for him to at the very least try again.

She could sense him looking at the can and then her face as she stared out over the street. She could sense him understand that she was still really looking at him, still really waiting for his next move and calculating how she'd have to counter it.

"Alright, then," he said.

He turned back to his notebook and took a drag on his cigarette.

The lights changed, the traffic surged and purred, she heaved the can across the sidewalk, trying to reveal a mere minimum of effort, and as she crouched and let the foul silver liquid pour down the drain, she turned her head from the rising sick sulphur-yellow odors of the sewers, and she felt the eyes of passersby on her, but not his.

When the can was empty but for a metallic silt visible through the cloudy plastic, she stood in the end of the alley, proud and un-shy in her gym shorts and halter top, and looked out on the teeming street with this seemingly oblivious young man almost right beside her.

Somewhere nearby a car alarm went off. Harleys passed on the street, their riders dressed like SS officers. Every car seemed to be a taxi, somehow aging this scene by fifteen years, their black and orange boxiness uniformly retro and incongruous. An African tout in an expensive suit passed by, turned, returned and approached the young man. He leaned in beside him and murmured slyly in his ear. The boy smiled and said something longish in Japanese. The tout smiled, then laughed, almost in delight, and turned and walked away without another word.

The car alarm subsided, then went off again almost immediately.

She didn't show it, but she was wondering.

He lit another cigarette and turned a page in the notebook. The car alarm subsided again.

"What did you say to him?" she suddenly said.

He looked up.

The car alarm went off again.

"Goddammit, just get the idea," she muttered out to the street.

The car alarm stopped again.

She looked directly at the boy.

"I told him Senegal beat Eritrea, two–nil, and they're into Group C in the African Cup of Nations. It's football. He's a Senegalese."

"How did you know he's a Senegalese?"

"I—" he paused. "Well, I guessed, actually."

"You guessed."

"I guessed. A good guess."

"Can I bum a cigarette," she said, and it was only about ten minutes later she would be asked by a boy, for the first and possibly only time in her life, what time she finished work. And it had got to the point in Japan where she would have lied or evaded or just turned and walked away if it hadn't been for Tim's leaving, the jerry can, the silver leaking from an old Panasonic air conditioner and that look on his face of something like surprise when he found himself asking.

So, surprised, she told him

One: take a group of ten or more and tie them all together with the signal corps telephone wire that you found on the road, as tightly as you can, because, Two: when you herd them and push them into the hole in the ground—a foxhole, a drained goldfish pond, a shell crater will do—the wire will undoubtedly become, to a certain extent, loose, and Three: throw one grenade each in with them. No more. More would be a waste of resources. Four: back quickly away before the explosions and the blood and matter and spattered pieces of their bodies attach themselves to your uniforms. Show no fear, show no disgust, and remember training when they made you eat your rice ration cross-legged beneath a dead and gutted man hung from a rafter above you (and you did), as, afterward, you bayonet any of the things left alive in the soupy hole (thick steam rising gently in the winter air) one by one to save bullets; miss any twitching limbless gasping Chinese pig and you will be beaten and humiliated until you'd like to die

He closed his eyes once, and opened them again.

He remembers a night going shopping together in Shinjuku. They walked into Marui Young on Shinjuku-dori, took separate routes around a huge high circular display of wallets that rose two stories past the mezzanine to the ceiling, and they met again in front of a small Miu Miu collection. She picked up a small handbag of blueberry simulated snakeskin, that knew and quietly flaunted its artificiality. He remembered this as if he were watching two people from afar; as if he could not see through his own eyes in his memories.

"That's so cool," she said, and wandered off. He took it immediately to the assistant, and as it was being elaborately gift-wrapped she noticed what he was doing and came to stand beside him. He remembers noticing then for the first time that she is exactly the same height as him, and slipped closer to his own eyes for a tiny, fleeting moment. "No, Michael..." she murmured, pleased, and on the Marui Young speakers a Prince cover played, and he thought wildly for a moment of Meredith, a memory like a stated meaningless fact, and leaned and whispered, quietly, as though someone in this store might overhear, might understand, a little secret for her alone, a little reminder of how something might be done "at home"; "*I wanna be your lover,*" he whispered, and she made a smile that turned into the shape of a kiss as she suppressed a laugh. Facts revealed themselves. Later when she wrote to him about sex, about touching herself, she called it *self loving.* With no hyphen. It hurt to read the letters from when she was so open with him. *Time for an I remember...I remember holding on to your wrists during sex. I can see the silver bracelet on that inch of flesh before the jean jacket. Your hands long and slender like mine, but somehow bonier, more graceful. After sex my head was on your chest, your arm around my shoulders. I could feel your silver necklace against my forehead. To be naked and entwined again, I can hardly imagine that pleasure. I could hear your heart—sometimes steady, sometimes frantic, more rarely relaxed...* Bergamini claimed the contest between Noda and Mukai to be the first to decapitate one hundred Chinese was reported in the December 7 English-language version of the *Japan Advertiser.* They wouldn't reach Nanking until the twelfth; on Sunday the fifth Mukai had eighty-nine Chinese heads; Noda, seventy-eight. *On the trains—I look all around me and only see uniforms, suits, black-orange-brown Asian hair, platform shoes, blank or pained faces. Why can't I see my lover's face among them?* Iris Chang ran with Bergamini in *The Rape of Nanking,* but in the bilingual *Alleged "Nanking Massacre"* Takemoto and

Ohara claim that for the trial of Noda and Mukai by the Kuomintang the only evidence proffered was the original article in Japanese, written by Asami Kazuo, published in the *Tokyo NichiNichi*, on December 13, with the interview elucidating the Murder Race dated December 12. *Facts* revealed themselves. In the Chinese court the death penalty was served on both on the basis of a newspaper article, and pretty words form important sentences: collections of nouns, verbs, proper names, pidgin, Pinyin or Wade-Giles; indictments, counts, "moral wrongs," "atrocities"; piles of barely burned bodies bloating the local dogs incongruously. The poor phrasing of a sentence is more important than the life it professes to memorialize; things fall to fragments; decay is the historical process. . . . *A surprise glimpse would sustain me for weeks. No hope for a mistaken apparition in this crowd of lazy eyes. My heart fades, unfed. My face goes blank, pained.* Witness: Suzuki Akira claimed Asami said the article was not by any means what he had witnessed, and was a mere interview, the race hearsay, and that Noda and Mukai were executed without a single piece of direct or indirect proof. (Via Takemoto and Ohara, laboriously, the translation horribly comical. *Someone, somewhere, is applauding.*) And further, that although Asami claimed the interview was conducted at Purple Mountain, neither Mukai nor Noda's units were stationed anywhere near Purple Mountain.

Mukai, 106. Noda, 105.

The target was raised to 150. Mukai reportedly (by who? where?—*he can't remember*) damaged his blade cutting a Chinese, through his helmet, completely in half. *I'll write a proper letter on the train to Hakone (tomorrow!). I'm finding it hard to be strong. I want comfort, to relax and rely on someone, not to be responsible.* Chang cites Bergamini, and yet reminds us that his *Japan's Imperial Conspiracy* was criticized for supposedly fantastical quotes and a lack of referencing. Takemoto and Ohara citing revisionists and Webster's in a translation so pompous and laboring; its form so contrived (and yet aptly, given the IMTFE? The precedent they set? He closes his eyes, noticing he can hear his eyelids, a blink is just a click—thinks suddenly of *cannonading*: the Imperial British practice for mutinous sepoys; strap them to the cannon's mouth and blow their bodies to pieces; the Indians knew a dismembered body made a restless ghost, and so, obviously, did the British—what happens to the ghost of a man sliced completely in half?— *Anyway it can't be done*—does it fall to *him* to ascertain that?—is that *laughter* he can hear?) the form of their book so contrived to somehow conform to the American Criminal Procedure Act, and placing the burden of proof on some proposed historical "prosecution." Not what do you believe; what do you *feel*? What do you believe enough to *be*? Is it Stephen D. he hears, his plaintive plea? *I have amended my life have I not?* What *does* happen to the ghost of a man dismembered? The same fate as the sense of a sentence dismembered? How many ghosts, then, in the old city? Is a ghost just a man turned into nonsense? Is it Marc Bloch he hears, historian and resistance fighter, who died at fifty-eight in a German torture cell? *Let us not say that the true historian is a stranger to emotion* (Ha! He stirs in the silent waiting room, bent over and examining his laces): *he has that, at all events. . . . Are we so sure of ourselves and of our age as to divide the company of our forefathers into the just and the damned?* No, no, he thinks, we are not. Do we apply the legal process to the materials of history? No, no, he thinks, of course we should not. Yet it is Takemoto and Ohara's bilingual book that sits for sale in quiet piles under glass, ¥1900, in the foyer of the Yushukan Museum of treasures and articles of dead soldiers, whose spirits repose in Yasukuni Shrine less than one hundred yards away.

Amakusa Shiro: *Tenchi dokon banbutsu ittai, issai shujo fusen kisen.*

"All things on earth originate from the same roots, all human beings without regard to rank."

Thus all are judged alike.

His dreams are sometimes filled with the stink of turpentine, vague clownish figures with knives and painted eyes performing acrobatic feats. What will he do? What *can* he do? *Heads should be cut off like this.* Why does he fail as a historian? *After sex my head was on your chest.* Why apostatize and recant, now, or at least pathetically *want* to? Because he's *fossed*: is he? tied and bound, upside down in the shit-filled pit, one arm maybe free to signal *korobase*, head full of bitter blood, ripe to be cut. Because now he knows so deeply that with every atrocity *nothing so terrible could not have happened*. Michael breathes shallowly, and yet reaches to the table for his pack of cigarettes.

He can see the beautiful Indiana girl, riding through Shinjuku all night in the back of an orange taxi, murmuring good J directions to an impassive white-gloved driver, her hair tied up in a bun.

There is so much of me that is attracted to you. And yet I want you to leave. I want to leave you. I don't want love. I want to be selfish, to think only of myself, to be alone. No boys or "men" coming or going for once. And yet. I want every moment I can get with you, to talk, to touch, to explore. To see more of you and more of me. What is this energy between us. And yet. I fear your boredom and hate you for it. Every time I feel your doubt, your question, I want to claw open your flesh, starting with the slits on that arm and show you pain, wake you up.

I am a rose.

Time passes.

This is how it slips away. He can remember her leaning against him as they stared at themselves in the huge mirror in the rooms of the Prince. Her face beside him, her back to his chest, watching his own hands, one on her breast and the other on the ivory planes of her stomach, barely recognizing the open smile on his own face. He can remember every hint she left him, every allusion to her lie: *Can you understand why I said that? Please still trust me.* She arched her back into him and they lost their balance a little, and she laughed. *I know, but I have done terrible things.* It seemed too laughable, almost pathetic that she could do anything *terrible* by any definition he observed. Time passes and he knows well how the pain of the memory of her leaning against him as they examined themselves in the mirror—oh how he hates mirrors—how the pain of that memory will become the memory of that pain—a pure marvel; he *knows* how it will feel—the memory of the pain will be an image of an image of itself, growing more distorted with every contemplation, each detail expanding with commensurate degradation, each pixel bloating with the fat of time, until the thing itself is only suggested, no more than a vague approximation of a reminder of itself, and God help those who tell of it for telling is the catalyst of utter oily oblivion. Time is blanding, he knows this, and being old is knowing this.

You don't . . . you shouldn't trust me.

I feel the same way.

That you cannot see divinity in us in this time saddens but doesn't surprise me. Just because you don't love me the way you think you should doesn't mean you don't love me with all you have. Desires depend on levels of consciousness.

He knew she had stopped dancing full-time because one night she asked to dance for him. It was much harder than he ever thought it could be; the way it so obviously made her happy. Eyes closed, arms twirling above her head, then down, fingers grazing across her underwear, he thought then he felt how it must be for her; the shock of finding oneself watched when the music fades is waking from a dream to a pitiless city. He may have been right, but it didn't matter, and as for any dancer, it was eclipsed, it was lived with; the promise of a dreamed future sustains. Sex afterward was angry, lonely, suffocated; a violation, turning cruel. They would not see each other for days, and meet in love hotels, which were a foreigners' joke, but fun, fleeting; some drama was suspended and it felt easy to be dirty in a kind way. Or was it to be kind in a dirty way. Mister Donuts for breakfast, and they parted for days, and emails they sent back and forth:

Her: *I am capable of horrible lies.*

Him: *I dreamed of a spider on my tongue last night, biting.*

Her: *"God sits on the tongue of man. It is not an insignificant thing."*

His work on atrocity "progressed." She sent him fragments of thoughts and quotes composed late at night—the time on her emails reads 0:32 a.m., 3:14 a.m.

With humility one is aware; with shyness one is only afraid. My favorite quote in the world is a simple one by Eleanor Roosevelt: "You must do the one thing you think you cannot."

He didn't yet know why she wrote so late, but he knew it wasn't because she was working—she went home to New York for three weeks while he was in Shanghai. When he returned he had a postcard waiting for him. The message read: *Went to get gas for Mom's car a couple of days ago. As I was paying, the lady said, "That's a nice little purse there. Where'd you get it?"*

I paused. "Um, thanks. Tokyo."

Tokyo!

When she came back, two days before she told him she had been married to a Japanese man for four months, she asked him a question; what was behind it he had ceased the struggle to understand.

Would you break my heart if I asked you to?

He closed his eyes once again, and opened them again.

He knows he is someone who sometimes has to struggle to control his thinking. He knows this and accepts this and it comes with the territory.

He often has difficulty sleeping, and often dreams too intensely to rest when he does. Near-anorexic, ha, and he supposes he drinks pretty heavily, but determined it's all he'll allow himself: to wall up and subdivide his thoughts; to prevent leakage and bleeding. Tells himself he is working hard enough; he is strong enough; and drinks to keep the bad apart from the good. Like scents in a family house: perfume; petrol; paint; shampoo. They mix and merge into a feeling, and if you don't want that feeling, if you want to control your longing it must be broken down into its constituents; reduced, analyzed and defined. Reduce; divide; control. But what, surely, can reduction do for your *work*? Sodastream gas, and rich raspberry syrup—Gross mixing it with chilled water for Hüsker Dü's water bowl, for the old dog's birthday, to make the kids laugh. (Remembers an experiment here, with Meredith, age ten: what could be gassed in a Sodastream? Always began with the accidental decant of syrup before the water was carbonated. He poured off a little and tried to gas the red water. It distributed itself liberally in a splattered spray over the white school shirt, the outside and inside of the Sodastream, the side of the fridge where the family photos were magnetized, the counter, the kitchen floor. Same result for milk, regular or low fat. Same with half-bottles of Hawke's Bay Chardonnay, claret and Chablis. Same for precarbonated beverages, too. Beer, Coke, Schweppes lemonade and tonic. The viscosity of mayonnaise and three different jars of wholegrain mustard combined— Coleman's; Barker's; Village Green; he *does* remember—didn't lend itself to carbonation either. Eleven and fearlessly curious, then, and Meredith nine and thrilled. All together over the floor and the bench and down the drawers and cabinets and shirt, because there was no point cleaning up between each when more experiments were likely to join the mix, was there? Meredith screaming in delight each time he pressed that button; hands over her eyes behind the island; her dark hair falling forward, shielding her too; she couldn't watch; she couldn't.) That phrase, "what could be gassed in a Sodastream." And Go-Dog dog food twist-tied in a fleshy plastic bag; and schoolbag leather; chlorine, ordure *à la* Hüsker Dü, a slightly darker little pile on the terracotta tiles by the pool, steaming in the morning before school; and calamine lotion, breathless eucalyptus Vicks, Frador fumes like medical brandy for his braces' ulcers, as orange-amber as the packaging, Meredith's polish for her old school shoes, what was it? *Waproo*, it was, for her *Nomads*, white and oil-creamy, and those endless fucking frail pages old and read till nearly scentless and senseless but there's a hint, or is it just the paper on the pebbled covers so ancient and maroon it flakes up and cracks like dried old blood? Favorite color: indigo that don't know it's blue. Favorite place: two of them: the first: the Bridal Veil over Lake Tekapo: the clouds spill down a great gully in the mountains in a helpless carefree massacre, when the weather is settled, ironically; and when it isn't: abandonment; a sense of poise and pose; a delicious *we're waiting for you,* and the sky left like a gaping mouth, hopelessly arc-ing blue overhead from one jagged nicotine-stained line of broken teeth to the other, the world beneath its howl too high for human hearing. Johnson and Johnson's Baby Powder; the white Dettol antiseptic cream in the crumpled tin tube flaking paint at the seams like the steel of a crashed car, smeared on his cigarette burns. The Palmer's Vitamin E Cocoa Butter Formula: "this was supposed to be very good for stretch marks" his mother once said with a quiet smile, and it was equally useless for the wide puckered pink razor scars crisscrossed like messy swastikas exploded over both his upper arms; and the smell with that old ache of the pain not forgotten and the guilt (it smelled like oily, somehow medical chocolate, melted fattily in a pan) bled together, instant and perpetual nausea, his cursing of his weakness. Just to keep things separate that he needs to be separate; that's his goal; and he asks himself how strong is he, if it's so hard. Memories sometimes seem obsolete, mere strings of words, functional, narratable, conversational things: windows that he looks through from a place of extremity, compromise, doctored photographs, atrocity, lauded lies—his future. His memories have become manipulable, speakable, pale. Those mountains: in summer-brown, shrunk like corpses' hide on the bones of spurs, shrunk like the hides of the dead myxomatosis-riddled rabbits, the sideswiped and flyblown sheep, the dusty broken-feathered puff of a fantail, hit and run from, left in the old MacKenzie Country air till aeolian harps are dried from their entrails and a rare music wrung from their ribs in the oxygen deep and blank, with a live birdsong so singular it seems to destroy that air, demand preeminence over the void, shatter the deafness, make of itself one and one only song—no; the birdsong is all, the harps are for few only, as is that romantic howl, those who would wish to have a trace of an imagination left: no, they sink, those corpses, like they all do, spread and settle and sink into the dried fecal earth that persists, persists. No no and no. There is no connection, none yet acted or pretended that might, in time, be real. There is the past and a past no longer viable; a past turned into ideas. Under his shirt his ribs, too, have proudly appeared, and he sat in the waiting room as quietly as he could and worked on this new thing, her story, that of a mother staying some-

where, a father going somewhere, and a child falling and falling in
between. He worked hard at remembering her, telling of her, purging her,
with the kind of energy that pain gifts; each tiny fact and feeling she'd ever
whispered or let slip to him, each moment they'd stood together, watching
themselves embraced in the great casement of that mirror. Just a girl; concentrate on the living. The second favorite place: those rooms used out of
simple familiarity as he paid his way almost entirely with scholarships and
royalties now. Rooms used with her, filled with the scent of her and her
things, her cane box of toiletries and the aged pages' beige and yellowed
superfine. Each little or large decision she'd made even when his mind was
well made up; each commitment to a moment; a moment of them; each
further fall toward them being together. Being good together. He worked
hard at imagining her moving through her Japanese world alone, then, no
husband, and he liked it there, with dreams that were lush and green, and
daily grinds and lost moments dancing, simple and clear in their compromise, for there briefly in her world there was no pregnant young Chinese
woman strewn over a snow-lined gutter, raped more than once, her stomach split open like a tamarillo from vagina to sternum, strangled as a joke
with her unborn child's umbilical cord wrapped around her neck, or
maybe it's supposed to be a scarf; the dead infant a cold gray stone at her
cheek with a cigarette butt crookedly protruding from its blueish lips. She
had her knowledges and horrors too, but there was something in the way
she walked and smiled almost sadly that said she would ask and ask again,
and in the asking never settle. There was something in imagining her and
remembering her that made him lift his head. Seeing her negotiate the
route from club to tiny room with pride and with determination that was
both so fallible and resilient. The way she lifted her head that first time, as
if to say, to dare: "Look at *me*." As if pride, flair, *style* redeemed something.
In a way she did remind him of his sister and the presence she'd been
through the beginning of all this. A warm dark glow in his sky above a
scene where a horse doused in burning kerosene ran insane with blistered,
marble-white eyes away from the river, back through the jammed cars and
piled corpses in the Water Gate, bucking off its pain, kicking off its skin
that the fire ate with transparent blue flickers through which the redness
was refracted, tripping hooves pounding dead Chinese bodies into bloody
jelly. The normality and yet the particularity and stubbornness of her anxi-
eties; the simple benevolence of her cares and indifferences; the wideness
and the selfishness of her agonies—*I have done terrible things*—and her so

palpable youth. But this girl's dark sun pulsed darkly over him, he could feel her moving, he came to a moment when what distinguished him, the horse and her was sable, inky, starless, shifting as a heat distortion. Bodies everywhere, a head knocking on a rock. In the winter, when she lay away from the heater in her room at the Setagaya gaijin house, her hair was cold, and he cradled her head in his hand to make it warm again, and so thin her skull beneath; an earthbone, a miracle. Her father did die in Irian Jaya of a heart attack, and she did mourn so silently, and how terrifying it was to hold her when she cried without a sound, just a pure sadness salty cool and wet pouring from her that he took onto his own cheeks, this bewildering sensation, pretty tickling tears so cold and light while he felt her heart buck in her breast. Oh god, and nothing could or should be said, and she said nothing. But cried in his arms so silently and went home to a professor of literature as he studied more murder till she came again. Each remembered scene was a miracle; each imagined one the same. He couldn't cry because to cry was nothing but to lie; to purge and find relief; relieve himself; pass water over graves. There are things that must be utterly denied. He cuts himself to get it out and go straight to hell, boy, for that. Yasuhiko burst in the door, his anti-allergenic mask a mute white paper convex maw over his mouth and nose. We have to get out he hissed in Japanese, we have to get out now. A Peynet postcard too, of a suited man embracing the woman in his lap, suspended in a vined loveseat beneath a balloon that was a fish, against a cobalt sky that was calm and bluely brooding. In the background was a city spread over islands. They smiled bluely, too; *Le poisson dirigeable*, it read. With three times the s. Her message read: *I bought this in Hakone when I dreamed of us being together. We still are, but in a way this is best for us both. I am sorry. Thank you Michael for having the strength to say what was in your heart.* A loveheart; that same so strong. What did he say? What *did* he say? Where is the backpack he said, where is the *pack*. In a ferry on the flooded river, with a weeping grandfather who impotently fucks the corpse of his son's daughter, dabs his flaccid penis in her bloody twelve-year-old thighs and moans, his wife an old woman with a gun to her head will die anyway, be chewed on by a dog like Hüsker Dü, and swim halfway to the sea by the light of burning China. He opened them he breathed it Yasu said, the scent he didn't believe the danger I had told him. When they made love he tore into her hair with his teeth, and the blond strands wound around his incisors. She scratched the slits on his arms wide open. He woke with her hair in his teeth. There are atrocities in love and there are no words for these acts

committed. But where are they Michael said. They'll all be ash by morning Yasu said they'll all be ash by morning we have to get out *now*. That
blood on the sheets in the morning was black and he touched the harder
line of her triangle lightly with his fingertips and she tensed, then he
touched beneath where it was soft. And knew in a curled, betrayed part of
himself that to be true he would betray her too, would leave her strung
out or uncaring. And he told her so, in a bed pure he could never make or
ever leave. This is all he will ever give of himself to her. The rest is numbness, pain and confusion. And in the lobby the receptionist had a tray of
yet more coffee and was baffled by Yasu's mask and agitation, an envelope
in his hand. Michael floats through it, sees the hospital at Treblinka where
behind the red-crossed fence, relief. Cynicism. The like of which the world
has not seen before, old Samuel Willenberg said, still amazed. There waits
an excavated mass grave and a man with a gun. *Cynicism*. Asia has seen it
all before. Matsui's air-dropped pamphlets of early December promised
safety too. Out in front of the university Michael gently took it from him
as they made their way from the scene of a crime. Matsui too sick to see
what came but somehow as he toured, oh, he knew. *Afford convincing proof
Japanese army behaved and continuing behave in fashion reminiscent Attila his
(sic) Huns stop.* And inside the envelope was a photograph, Maeda's last act
of forgiveness: young Yasu, his mama and serious bifocaled papa, and
Maeda wearing glasses too, but smiling to the camera in an office, each of
their hands touching a piece of the border of the kanji-littered certificate
of a scholarship, and a Print Club sticker of a cartoon speech bubble is
attached to the photograph, indicating Maeda's mouth, and written in
Japanese is

ブ　卒
ラ　業
ボ　生
｜　！

Bravo, graduate student! To Yasuhiko's cold black eyes—overestimating the
mask, he'd breathed its age in deep, was half inside his trip—in the back of
a taxi to the hotel, Michael began to whisper, and he began to whisper
back:

—*Do you know the substrate of your dream now?* —*Chinese corn fed with their bodies.* —*Whose?* —*My parents'.* —*How many judges were there at Ichigaya, Yasu-chan?* —*Eleven.* —*How many magistrates at Sakaide in 1642?* —*Eleven, and the interpreters. And the executioners, for Man.* —*What day was the capital taken?* —*Showa twelve, twelve. Twelve o'clock.* —*Western time.* — *Twelve December 1937. The twelfth year of Showa. It was perfectly timed and perfectly executed.* —*Did you see the burning horse, there?* —*No.* —*What is your shibboleth?* —*I . . . don't . . . know.* His cold black eyes were crying. —*What does it feed on?* —*I know . . . it feeds on history.* He couldn't look up. —*Did you see a burning horse by the Water Gate? A horse with the head of a man?* —*No. No, Michael.* —*Who do you love?* —*I can't love anyone.* —*What did Prince Asaka's soldiers sop their overfucked cocks with?* —*Sake. They poured sake on themselves.* —*How do you know this?* —*I don't know, I don't know.* —*Where do hot coals go?* —*Soft, oh, Chinese mouths.* —*What do you learn from the dream?* —*What I am responsible for. Secrets. The ability to respond.* —*What's your name?* —*Stop it.* —*Who am I?* —*You are a judge. A terrible, heartless judge.* — *Who is Ko Ishikawa?* —*He was going to be your Matsui, your prince. But he cannot be. He would not be.* —*Was he guilty?* He couldn't answer. —*Did he deserve to die?* He couldn't answer. —*What redeems war?* —*Individual flair.* —*If an individual mind is the universe, what then is a genocide? What does the indefinite enact upon the definite? How do you eat that which only eats? How do you know answers to these questions?* —*The answers know me.* —*What is history? Is history a disease?* —*History is now.* His head raised, eyes gone sable. —*What, then, is immunity?* —*I . . . there isn't. There is none.* —*Is defeat an answer?* —*It is as much a defeat as victory.*

And he knew he'd found it; he was sure. *Le Japon Theatre Du Grand Guignol* shook itself awake like a military dog. Bloch: *In other words, the scholar, the historian, is urged to efface himself before the facts.* Very well then, this is the end of the occupation. Because *burned houses make bad billets.* At Rikkyo reception, six months later, Meredith used her carefully prepared phrase: Which way to the office of Hayakawa Yu? "The entry of the Imperial Army into a foreign capital is a great event in our history . . . attracting the attention of the world. Therefore let no unit enter the city in a disorderly fashion," said Matsui from his sickbed.

Blackeyed Yasu patted down his pockets, desperately.

He'd left Lupin Sansei in the university.

IV

The Dark House

On the Study of Military History
Now

Just when you think the last spider is dead—that is the beginning. That is
the moment you sense that something has evaded you; there is a crucial
something you've forgotten. You lift the corner of the rug and there they
swarm. You tear back the rug to reveal this missed horror, and right to the
edges the swarm of spiders shifts like static; a rectangle of audible dry-
legged undulation. But you do summon up all your courage and disgust,
and stamp and stamp and stamp, until all are dead, a minor massacre of
blood and greenish guts and yellow hirsute skin, fewer than fright had
made you fear.

But it's then you realize: spiders come from somewhere. Obsession
becomes practical necessity; roots must be ripped up or you merely fight a
delaying action. You take an afternoon to tear up the floorboards, and
there beneath, in the crawl space, there is nothing but web. Dusty
draperies, sagging from right angles of pillar and joist, hung with nondescript and desiccated husks. You think they're all gone. But look closer:
what you took for a yellow smear on the foundation of your house—
builder's chalk, an electrician's semiotic—no, it's fat and legged, too; a
close round abdomen clung tight to the rough timber. Murder it, quickly,
with the sole of your boot; don't look back, never test your disgust and
fear with autopsy. There are a few others, and it's quickly over.

Rest, now.

Look around as night falls and as your eyes become accustomed. You
did brave the dark corners of the hiatus, did purge what seethes under
where you live, this dark house. Check what floorboards remain above
your head, and they too are clean and webless, this place now dry and
infertile. Past each post you slowly pan and think of your first blindness
with a shudder. What if you had carelessly leaned against that yellow
monstrosity, or peering around the pillar had placed a smooth and sensi-

tive palm in a gentle cupping of his fanged and hairy spiderness? Up and down each post in relief and satisfaction. Was it mere paranoia; rigor ratcheted a notch too high?

Your gaze comes to the fertile loam beneath.

When you dig a hole all you get is dirty, deep and strong. Down through the fecund dirt occasionally you transfix a webbed and dusty empty tunnel. Their size is of concern but you do not hesitate or wait, nor even think of borrowing their trajectories for a small respite. No, you trust your muscles—which hypertrophy and grow to fit you for this work. You're *strong;* you really are. But strong enough? *Keep going.* One tiny upward glance to those dark spots in your descent where webbed rags hang from your tunnel's violation. Nothing stirs there and one glance is all you will allow yourself, and indeed, is hard enough with your method and position—you dive into this earth; carving your way so literally with tooth and nail.

And this is the reason why when you at last break through your fall is so immediate and utter. You drop so free, and there was no way to save yourself so late. And these new muscles do weigh you down, make the fall so much faster. Plummeting, at first you feel the light brush and flutter as windblown ash upon your cheeks and chest and back, and that's familiar. It's when the numbing bites take your attention, the invasion of nostril, ear and mouth, anus, tender armpit, blinking eye, every other awful possibility, you realize that your termless fall to fire is ever through an unplumbed oubliette (and we all know that means "forget") of a seething smoke of spiders, ever, ever.

Yasu

June 2000

It was his own idea to test it on his own little girl. Since the discovery he's not spoken to a soul, not left his house since the semivengeful trip to Shibuya and *HOE,* down to eating only Pizza-La that he gets delivered and asks to be left upon this veranda—this veranda where he stands by half a scallop shell for the yen he leaves in turn for the delivery boy, yen paid to him in turn by the foreigner for this: his final triumph that's left him more silent and even more alone than ever before.

Hello!

Doesn't hear me.

Where is she. Gone back inside now, again? But the sliding door does not close.

Come on. He's been waiting for this opportunity a week, and today alone some hours. ("Sweeping the veranda"; knowing she's home. And a little conspicuously, too, sweeping before imminent monsoon.)

Hello!

Are you sick today. How are you feeling. You have gotten so big in such a short time, ne? Soon you'll be at junior high. Will the monsoon begin today? Not sure. Is your. How would.

Something like that. Careful, though.

Hello!

Maybe, *Yes, I know the yard needs cleaning. Yes, very badly. Tend to look out on that yard and feel a great weight like a quilted jacket, slow me to a stop. But that is not to say I do not watch the corruption of my father's garden with great, almost fanatical interest, as if something were being revealed slow-motion, as if some fundamental truth lies in decay. Truth lies in decay.*

Ha ha.

Brittle beep of his watch alarm as he waits under her balcony.

Drops the broom, jumps briskly up the veranda and inside the living room in a wobbling sidelong shimmy through the reluctant gap in private sliding door. Don't slip—just skip; onto futon, off. In the kitchen, his feet slide in spreading mounds of manga, odd odors of the rubbish rise. Miso soup is made of dashi dissolved and boiled in water. Just before serving, miso paste is stirred in a soupçon, and gently returned to the broth. It is held beneath a simmer for just a few minutes, then served. Three ready-made single-serving plastic sachets of miso, with embedded seaweed, and perhaps even dashi, sit ready by the gas hob. But the dashi that boils in the pot was in his cupboard, and had been since his parents were alive, but he supposes more can hardly hurt when a strong not to say dominating flavor is on the menu. The only things left in his parents' cupboards seem to be in sachets; freeze-dried like his life. A shroom plucked early, not vivid but demurely blue inside a sealed plastic tub, sits far enough from the heated pot. Undecayed, as yet. A deliberately premature draft, but still: forceps laid crossways on top.

Is the dashi stock and water boiling over? Is it time to dissolve the lobes of miso in the small decanted dash? Is time then running quickly out, and, revealed, a cusp emergent, which distinguishes between *finishing this* and *backing out:* two slippery slopes tending far from one another? Unless you're used to losing, don't you always go on?

The answers are: yes, yes, yes, definitely, *yes.*

He turns the gas down to 2.

The watch alarm meant *ready.*

What was that sound? A sliding door, or footsteps?

Back out. (Not off.)

Ha ha.

Odd how someone so silent and serious skips so jigglingly over his junk and MDs. He leaves a sweaty palmprint on the slid veranda door. Not odd, just someone unaccustomed to gestured excitement. The plump boy peers up. The palmprint dissolves like a tidal pool in a fastforward sun and outside the monsoons stir themselves.

That's good for all kinds of reasons: noise and lateness of potential interruption, difficulty and general disgruntlement. *Diversion.*

If only balcony floors were slats, this would be much easier. Is she there? Soon the rain will be wall-to-wall. Moisture charges the air. Feel it swelling not just from above but from below as well, like the earth's sexual yearning to touch these clouds any way it can; and will try: skewed stalagmites of splattered puddles jumping vainly at the sky like salmon at a weir. Rain coming up; the world in reverse. Stalactites stick tight to the ceiling; stalagmites might someday reach the sky. *Stalaktos:* dripping; *stalagma:* drop. There'll be a million million points of white noise in this garden, alone. Monsoon roars like a gray lion, with a curious gaiety.

Hello?

"Oh! Hello."

Don't you think it will pour down soon. Are you watching the lightning.

"Yes."

Still there, looking cloudward above balcony.

Are you sick today? Or is there no school.

"Yes, I am. I have the flu. I am feverish. Very feverish."

I'm sorry. Is your mama home to look after you?

"Mama is shopping in Omiya."

Oh.

"I've seen foreigners come to your house. They come up the path. A few times, lately."

Yes, I have many foreign friends. *He is sarcastic. He is showing off!*

"Hmph."

First, he is a New Zealand, and the second, a France.

"Hmph."

They are friendly. We Japanese are shy, too shy, but they are friendly. Rich, and friendly.

"I think they are handsome."

Yes.

"They are pale like ghosts."

Yes.

It builds and builds, and crackles far off over the rooftops, one hundred and eighty degrees of sporadic forked lightning, pure arc-white fractals shivering out at the horizon: one there—one there—one here under purple bruised sacs like internal organs, clouds heavy like meat, like lungs or like brains sending shocks to the earth, a world migraine, a vast plan. The country will join the sky and the sea, all indistinct in suspended water. Difference without distinction. The dripping and the drop linked, steadfast. The bonsai hunch like disappointments and burned-out ambitions; they may be obliterated. To this now he is finally indifferent. No sound of thunder; just flash and shiver, splitting through all this waiting.

A perfect, perfect day.

You know what is very good for a fever?

"Rest, and liquids."

Yes.

"Feed the cold and starve the fever, Mama says."

Yes. Well, how about soup, ne? Soup is not really feeding. It is good for equilibrium. For a stable temperature.

"Soup."

Miso soup, with a little mushroom.

"I can't be bothered."

I have made a pot of soup, just now. I could ladle off a bowl, with a couple of matsutake, for you, if you like. *He's so sly.* For nutrition, and equilibrium; your fever.

"You mean 'the take.'" *No, he doesn't.* "And I have my own soup bowl. A Morning Musume bowl."

Oh, you like Morning Musume?

"They are my best band."

If you would like to pass it down, I will ladle you a bowl. You can watch the storm with hot soup to drink.

"Your yard is quite messy."

Ha ha. Yes. It weighs on my thoughts.

"Not enough to clean it up."

No, you are right. You're clever, for ten.

Nodding, nodding, knowing how to wait. Who would think he'd be so good at this. So ready. Who would pick the flare of ego. Who'd have thought such claws on someone who creeps sideways through his life, head down into the current like *kawa-ebi,* a river prawn.

He's so clever.

What's your name, little girl?

"I have lived here all the time and you don't know my name yet?"

Do you know mine?

No answer.

What is your name, little girl?

"It is Tomoko."

My name is Tanabe Yasuhiko. Miso soup chef extraordinaire. You are nearly as old as some of those girls of Morning Musume.

"Hmph."

How do you like the Shingo-mama song, "Oha"?

She's *surprised.* It is ever detail that captures. "We sing it in the morning at school. 'Good morning,' to the teacher. It's a joke."

I have a Shingo-mama autographed CD.

"No!"

Yes. I can prove it to you. But I can't risk bringing it out in this rain.

"But it's not raining yet. I like rain."

Do you like soup? And mushrooms? Come down the steps at back and I can show you. We can sing along to "Oha."

"It's only a song for children. I'm too old. I'm ten."

Then only I will sing. The soup will help your fever.

"I do have a fever."

Come down the steps at back, I will meet you there. But only I will sing, and you will hear how fine it is, my voice, my song.

The first few drops of the monsoons begin to fall and a blanket comes down all over Saitama and half of northeast Asia, and as bad things born of dreams come true in solitude start their bloom and flare, drip and drop, atmosphere and ocean and distinction merge and blend.

Jacques
December 12, 2000

It's a melancholy truth: when Jacques is sad he likes to get high and ride trains all day. Alone. He'd waited around at the hotel room for almost an hour, made coffee in the spotless kitchen and smoked some cigarettes, stared out the window down to the Shinjuku station train lines. And Michael hadn't come back. The first time he'd seen him in literally months, and he just hates it when his mood ruins what could have been nice. Out at Y's not much had been said. Too messy to go inside, they'd stood on the veranda and given Y their respective knots of cash, and taken their respective bags of shrooms, though Michael's, he'd noticed, had been packed inside a sexy little white leather Inéd satchel that he'd admired absently. Y was terse and overpolite as usual, ashamed of his house but, you know, never enough to clean up.

"Meredith is here, looking all over for you," Jacques had said.

"Soon," was what Michael had said. "Don't tell her you saw me. I'll see her soon."

"I like your suit, big guy," Jacques said, and Michael had laughed and looked at him strangely, but when you're sad you maybe pick up on things like that, but somehow just don't have the flair to do or say anything about it. So they walked through Ageo to the station, boarded the Takasaki, both of them in sunglasses for this was a glaring beautiful blue-white winter day of little temperature and awesome light. Omiya was the place the next words were said. Twenty minutes away.

"You take the Saikyo, I'll take the Keihin–Tohoku and the subway, and we'll see who gets to the Prince first," Michael said. "Hey?"

"I shall win," Jacques said.

"Maybe."

"You are going to see Meredith at the Prince? She has been staying there."

"Maybe."

He watched Michael check the timetable over the ticket gates, and the crowds rolled around them in the great arena of Omiya station, so many thousands of scarves. Two foreigners, both overfamiliar with this place but in completely different ways, paused in the middle of the stream.

Jacques stared through his sunglasses looking for Michael's eyes behind his. Where did he look? What did the Warboy see?

"Hey, Michael?"

"Yeah?" He turned.

"You okay, and everything?"

Black glass watched. Then Michael smiled, and said, "Come here." They hugged. Then they stood awkwardly for a moment, and Jacques felt himself too wrapped up in his own business to really feel this.

Michael checked the timetable again.

"Coming soon," he said.

"Only in theatres," Jacques said, and then he was gone.

Underneath the Zegna jacket, the scarf and the Helmut Lang turtleneck, only Jacques knows he is wearing his new J girl hippu-hoppu T-shirt that reads in Japanese: I MAKE BOYS CRY. He's sitting in the monorail—post–lunch hour rush, he's got a seat—because he's started this day this way, and he's going to ride trains all day. The Haneda monorail winds out of Hamamatsucho station over the trash islands of Tennozu Isle, over Shuto Expressway No. 1 near where a *kogyaru* girl driving in platforms had lost control of a car named a Cynus and killed herself and two others in a four-car pileup the week before. Along the canals, elevated, there are only two perspectives: the very near, and the very far. The head above the seat in front, the chrome prison bars of the luggage racks above, and the trees around the bankrupt Daiei superstore on Oi Central Port Park, the bridges over the canal, the petrol shining in gentle rainbow stains in the little geometrical shapes of water that appear abruptly beneath the train after the giant buildings of JAPEX on the Isle. Then the racetrack at Oikeibajomae to his right, and the five-storey stables, the dirty end of the glamour looking out all plastic buckets and dung-stained straw onto the concrete voids, charged with iron and electricity, pierced by the pillars that hold the monorail so high.

Then it's over real water, after Ryutsu-Center and the baseball diamond where occasionally can be seen the Self-Defense Forces in kendo practice, as the canal begins to widen and is subject to tides more palpably: there or not, spiky, amputated posts from out of nowhere right in the middle of the river, and sometimes around them seagulls walk on water. The monorail clings to the edge of it, past and over a little rocky corner by a carpark where a bashed boat relaxes slimed-green on the stones, and old fishermen in waders don't talk to one another. Showajima, then Seibijo and the spare monorail train on the alternate track down on his right, and on his left the first few planes on another trash island, and the Air Traffic Control College where fresh out of high school the kids go to study six days a week and live in dormitories with no aircon. He knew a British boy who was living with a Japanese boy who had waited three years for an interview to be a steward with All Nippon Airways, and there were so many like him the interview only lasted three minutes and then the dream was over and he had to think of something else to do. Then it's Tenkubashi, Shinseibijo, then the airport proper, and then it's back again. And if you get tired of the detail, on one side the denseness of the city stretches away in a gray ragged stroke leaching up into the blue, on the other it's all trees and stadium lights like black flowers from the horizon and almost-sea and acres and acres of brilliant winter sky.

But who can see it when they're this brand of sad. Things mix and fragment; lost in a thought or a memory for minutes he sees nothing till the train jolts from the platform in the wrong direction and he realizes he has reached the end of the line. Or not a thought in his head as it banks beautifully out of Hamamatsucho, over the edge of Hama Rikyu garden, and around the corner of a skyscraper so close he could wave to that office lady were she looking up from her computer; were he so inclined.

Jacques waited at that hotel for a long time, and then he knew Michael wasn't coming back and he grabbed the little microwaved mushroom and slammed the oven door and headed down and to the station. What a joke. Experienced, he'd got to Hamamatsucho in less than fifteen minutes. Chuo, Yamanote: time those changes right. Who cares. The skills are just your muscles after a year. You don't take pride in what you take for granted. It is Jacques' twenty-fourth birthday on the twenty-sixth of December, and no one in this city knows. Though most people here accept that, that no one knows, and tell others the date and just pretty much get over it, he hasn't told anyone.

That isn't why he's sad.

As they always do, at the Oikeibajo stables the train doors shut in three increments: the first assertive, the second sure, the third tentative; somehow elderly. He puts his feet up on the seat in front of him, and leans back, his neck cushioned by the soft knot of his scarf on the vinyl antimacassar. His gloved hands are in his pockets, warming up, and by his left hand there

is the hard square of his MD player, and in his right he squeezes the little
blue shroom moist in its baggie, and looking down, at a stablehand leading a big chestnut horse out a stable door and round into a straw-littered
alley between the buildings, he catches a glimpse of its gigantic cock casually gushing a far-off but incredibly still visible white flood of urine down
onto the asphalt like poured and spattering milk.

Fingering the shroom, like the Tour de France sceptics angrily shout,
he murmurs *"Dopé, dopé,"* idly to himself. And smiles. And then stops.

What was that phrase in German? *Was du verlachst wirst du noch diener.*
What you laugh at, still will you serve. He'd rather serve than laugh. At
the gentle temple of a hot tissue-skinned cock, softer skin than his cheek
where he'd always brush it across, because lips and tongues are made for
that sort of thing, for sucking and licking, but cheeks are for love and
polite pecks, and the juxtaposition turned him on. But only if he'd shaved.
He'd heard some boy say knowingly that pythons have claws beneath their
scales. But what a lame metaphor. Things are taken and left much easier
than that. The knocking of the monorail as it starts off again and he closes
his eyes. And soon he gets idly kind of hard. Warm and tired and sad and
hard. A diener is something in English, too, right. Yes, a morgue attendant.
Yes? Is it? Or deiner. Is it. Who cares, he gives up on the thought, and tries
to vividly, vividly remember the burning shy hot spot of the touch of a
cock to his cheek. Blood and life, and trains and sex and sleepiness. Then
onto his tongue, a full rosy white—or, like Simon's, rosy-brown—mute
tube inside his mouth, fat and hot and fit to burst. The quietness of his
stomach to his forehead, a gasp far away above is all he hears and may as
well not be there. To lie with a hard Simon-thigh under hand. As he had a
hundred times. This is Jacques' lazy sad Tokyo day, now; two years spent
in the fingers of this old city, and he feels so, so sexual every other day but
with barely the energy to do anything about it.

He's kind of flush with cash, too.

Paid on the tenth for a casual blagged translation job for Japan Tobacco
exactly two weeks ago, just before the terrible dinner. Sniffling with a cold,
he had been led by the guard at the gate into a building that resembled and
smelled more like a hospital than anything. Two very nice Japanese, a boy
and a girl in matching beige JT overalls, led him into a meeting room, and
there they didn't even remotely suspect he wasn't a native speaker, and he
helped them to translate a document on measures to reduce tobacco dust
buildup around machines on the factory floor. Because it turned out

tobacco dust was the key thing that attracted tobacco beetles, which in turn got "processed," causing—Jacques could remember his exact rephrasing of their notes—"in 1998, thirty-nine incident of customer exposure to beetle." Eyes closed, he smiles to himself and remembers asking if he could smoke, and there was a little pause while they searched for English, and then one or both of them said, "Of course." He had kind of hoped they'd offer him some free JT products but no luck. And sniffling, spacing out in the hot room in the well-guarded heart of Japan Tobacco, trying to focus on the English words, he offered the two quiet employees a cigarette, and they both said no thank you I don't smoke and he didn't even laugh.

An extra ¥80,000 and one bad dinner and two weeks later I MAKE BOYS CRY. He guesses he's glad, but not really.

Beside him on the seat is O'Brien's *Going After Cacciato,* and there's a girl sitting on the other side of the train on a seat that faces inward. *"Texte intégral,"* Michael had said when he'd given him the book, the night after the night after the party at the Prince, and Ko's *automutiler.* The girl on the other side is wearing amazing boots. Mauve snakeskin to the knee, zipped long on the sides, mahogany heels so high the arches are like overpasses. *Kick-ass,* Simon would say. Jacques' forehead itches in a short thin line heading straight back from his shaven widow's peak. He remembers going to a Rammstein gig with Simon just before he left. How Simon in his desperation then was all sexual energy and frantic emotional openness. At his little cold gaijin house in Mejiro they dyed their hair using some J product with untranslatable instructions. They sat by his little heater waiting for this dye to dry, picking the hard black drops from each other's naked shivering shoulders. Then at the gig Simon was drunk and Jacques was high and Simon pretended not to be a little freaked by the giant strap-on dildo of the singer that shot sparks out all over the audience in a melodramatic fountain, and even cheered a little at the feigned fellatio performed on the guitarist, and all the campness he's found Americans don't usually get in German metal Simon seemed to open himself up to just a little. And then in the heat and the sweat of the gig, moisture dripping from the ceiling of the Akasaka Blitz, the dye they didn't understand and hadn't washed out as they should have—but together—began to seep from their hair and run down their faces and necks and ears and into their eyes, and those crazy J just loved it, and touched them, Jacques and Simon, stealing the stains and smearing it on their own faces like a Dionysian orgy. And Simon went a little crazy in a good way for once, and they smeared it on each other, tore off their ¥6000 Rammstein tour T-shirts and to cheering all around them smeared the leaking dye all over each other's bodies, and the banging electronic bass like a migraine over it all, dancing and kissing and groping each other madly in the cheering crowd who wiped the dye from their bodies on themselves. And then outside into the winter never so cold as shirtless, torsos and faces smeared black they staggered home because no taxi would stop for them. That's what Jacques misses: in love and being *can go very crazy*. For Jacques, *eau de vie*. Sex is the source. His forehead itches, and the girl in boots is asleep and dreaming, her eyelids flitting and twitching, struggling to match the things she's seen. She has a purple T-shirt under her fur coat, with ONE THING THAT MAKES BEAGLES SUPERIOR IS OUR NATURAL HUMILITY printed on the chest. Pure craziness in love, glee in Glizy, abandon in Bendon, revel in Revlon. Fire for effect. The monorail lurches from Tennozu Isle for the second time in this direction. A man strides long as the train's floor leaves him behind. Jacques didn't understand the call signs in *Cacciato* for a while, and took "Orphan Indigo Papa" quite literally; such a sad English phrase.

Down to his left there is the unused baseball diamond that verges on the canal. There are men in khaki with wooden swords practicing kendo. Their movements miniature, abrupt and sharp; the *clack* of contact only in his head. Six white Jeeps are parked by the dugout. But the last one is a darker khaki than the uniforms.

Jacques takes his right gloved hand from his pocket and sees the shroom's a little squashed in the baggie, and the condensation's mixed with the blue coating to make drips of blue on the plastic, and a little fat solid V of blue moisture in the bottom corner of the bag. Have a joint or eat a shroom is the biggest question he's going to ask himself today, because he has a tunnel wound. Like O'Brien's Nam GIs, on all fours, in The Shit, shot: high into the chest and going steeply down inside. Today, my main man, we do what the hell we marijuana. Or? You only microwave a shroom to mitigate the dose. Why would he do that? The little adhesive label has blackened in a semicircle, partially obscuring the purple inked message. What remains is AT ME. Some of the drips have squeezed from the ziplock and onto his glove.

He remembers trying valiantly to study Japanese in the time he was in love. *Japanese For Busy People;* trying to neaten up his grammar with a basic textbook. Working briefly hard at Lesson 14, page 103: "Yesterday's

Enjoyable Kabuki." But Appendix L was "Parts of the Face and Body." He flicked to page 204, and found himself drawing little sketches in the margins. *Ago.* Chin, jaw. *Kami;* his hair. A homonym for spirit or ancestor. *Onaka;* stomach. *Ashi;* his foot, or leg. *Oshiri;* buttock. Just the one? So he drew only one, obliquely, catching the light on the downside of the muscle, falling into shade. *Sebone;* his spine. Pronouncing the words slowly and succulently as he drew, savoring them in Japanese, gave him the same feeling English enunciation once had done. It was the body foreign and angelic, newly shaped; defined differently and curved in emphasis. He had spent a long time flicking his pen nib to get the density and curl of pubic hair just right. Foot, or leg. It made the words bodily again; distinguishing and distancing until he really saw. *Koshi;* hip. Who doesn't love his *koshi* when you're up to your neck in it? And his long tan Chinese American back that gets a long tan Japanese word. *Senaka. Se* is for the small; *na,* for widening and the modest flare; *ka,* for the K and geometric bloom of his shoulders, and for the beautiful fragile collarbones sheltering the shallow hollows that begin the crest of his chest, the hollows in the lee. The wind at his back was breath, hands sliding up his *sebone* and spreading over, deep inside him as his head was bowed: *Se—na—ka—a—a—a.*

His innermost rind, relict of a love, drying on Jacques' body in the night.

Matsuge; his eyelash, look, widowed on your pillow in the morning.

Oh.

Jacques abruptly tears the bag open, and with a little shudder at the bitter ashy taste and just a single chew he eats the mushroom. Chomping only after it's gone to get that ashen liquid off his teeth. And another shudder; tears in his eyes. The monorail glides into Seibijo and the Traffic Control College; one stop from Tenkubashi, then Shinseibijo, then Haneda Airport, and then let's do it all over again.

After *domo*—the equivalent of "hey," "thanks," or sometimes just some kind of polite grunt of acknowledgment—the first casual J phrase he ever learned was typical of the crowd he always moved quickly into, out of and back on his own again. He hates cliquey fags. *Epon nuite.* Jerk it off. He's never had to use it, because gay J boys here most often get so enamored of him he has to gently fend them off.

Kudasai.

Oh, *please.*

The doors judder shut, and the monorail glides on again.

There are no sanctuaries in memory but there is sanctuary in movement. As if imitating the winter mid-afternoon sky, the bright blue drops in the baggie darken slightly with exposure to the air. He folds the baggie into his pocket again. He could eat the shroom quite casually in the train for a couple of reasons. The first that the car is almost empty, but for him, the girl in the T-shirt and fur coat and boots, and one salaryman asleep too, at the far end. The second that shrooms are legalized here, though the possible technicalities of public consumption are obscure to him. The third, though, is that for foreigners it just often seems for good reason that there are no rules here. Though you will pay through the nose for your apartment and your employer must agree to be your guarantor, once you've got money you are quite free to do and be what you want in your jail of Japan.

The night after the night after the party, and Ko, and his *blessures volontaires,* back in June, Michael and Jacques had met at the Starbucks in East Ikebukuro. Both sleepless, harried, and white. Jacques' abiding memories of that night would be a pool of blood on the kitchen slate bigger than the boy, and being taller than the paramedics who wore orange plastic helmets. As if this, their height, their absurd helmets, their Japaneseness meant they couldn't be trusted. One of them had a cupped two-handsful of a bloody bundle, bent over it like a boy with a newborn bird, and Ariel, Anton, Shannon, what of the rest? The party huddled in the living room or left, and Ko's face was disconnected from everything that seemed to fade away; he smiled from an acrylic stretcher, pale as a page. His eyes like colored hollows filled with ebon ink; a maroon glisten, that was spatial with something like peace. Almost all Jacques could ask Michael—co-Warboy with Ko, war scholar, *Japonais atrocité spécialiste,* the exemplary man (or was that *Ko?*)—in Starbucks, passionless, drained and uninflected, was *why.* And they sat in silence in the air-conditioned murmur upstairs until Michael finally began to talk. And it wasn't long before Jacques began to shake his head and murmur, *non, non.* And at last placed his hand over Michael's whispering mouth. Into Haneda Airport station now and outside there is a hint of a suggestion of twilight, just a whitening at the hem of the sky, and a pixel or two of violet bleeding into the faded blue above. And in silence for further static-filled moments as Jacques struggles to bring anything he knows or remembers to bear. The doors smoothly open, and two women with wheeled and frame-handled suitcases board in beautiful caramel cashmere overcoats, one nougat and the other honey, and Jacques sits up a little straighter and lifts his feet from the seat. But they head toward the doors to the next car, to align their seats with their final station's exit.

The doors judder shut and the train glides out, his back to the direction they're heading in, now.

Jacques had finally told Michael of *Un Grand Guignol*. How he saw it was all about location, a certain notion of realism and primitive catharsis. Played out as it was in a chapel that was all that remained of a convent destroyed in the Revolution, 20 bis rue Chaptal in Montmartre. It was tiny and close-up and began at the beginning of the twentieth century. How it was said the most famous *Guignol* actress had been a woman named Maxa, who in her time at the theatre had been murdered, all told, more than ten thousand times, and raped more than three thousand times. One woman. *Tranche de mort*. It was all Jacques could come up with to answer what he'd been told. Slice of death was the aesthetic, and his was an aesthetic defense. Minimalist plots and 2-D characters and one-act durations, multiple plays to a bill, each culminating in cathartic moments of hyperviolence that caused audience members to faint and vomit at stage properties looted from the offal bins of the butchers of Montmartre. And of course it was a smash hit and a favorite of Paris society for decades. In balconies obscured by trellis-work dukes and princes and heads of industry made love to their mistresses, titillated by the horror. Even World War One couldn't tarnish the *Guignol*'s shine. Audiences watched and vomited and hyperventilated and staggered into the alleys fainting and returned again and again. Jacques didn't know if the attraction was about the distinction between their lives and the theatre, the manifestation of a dream, a terrorism of the imagination, or if it was the refraction of certain brutal daily realities in turn-of-the-century Paris. Condensed and shown with a high consideration for grim and utter physical realism. He guessed he was naive, that Tokyo had softened him. He supposed he believed that certain sights dealt shocks to the head that were curable only in the craziness of love. And that without love some crave more horror, and some crave only sleep. Jacques had told Michael about *Un Grand Guignol* to try and illustrate a point. *La terreur n'est pas française.* Fear is not a French emotion, to quote the poet. But revulsion still remains. But Jacques found himself too battered to say it with feeling. Michael was quiet a while, then, staring into red velvet of a Starbucks couch, said, But Rimbaud also asks us, *un homme qui veut se mutiler est bien damné, n'est-ce pas?* Jacques nodded with the recognition; the comprehension. A man who would mutilate himself is well damned, isn't he? Michael said, Ko knew it was futile, yet he did it. Do you know what the biggest horror is? It's a test. It's his own private shibboleth for us, to see how we'd react. To see what we would do. And there are so many different sets of rules here that no one trusts their own; thus no one will react. I think it's the strongest statement he could make. To see if he is truly banging his head against a brick wall. I guess I think he was amazing. And if he is damned then as he tells me, he and I were damned a long time ago. *Il a seize ans,* said Jacques. *Tout pourtant m'est permis,* said Michael. And yet everything is permitted me. Here it is different; and he deserves our respect. Ko was a genius, and they breed and cull them young here. Damnation shifts by nation.

The train slides into Shinseibijo and the sleeping girl in the boots stirs. Jacques realizes she's been going back and forth with him for at least two cycles now. That perhaps his little hobby is shared. But now she stirs, and sits upright with the sudden bleary panic of the passenger who's gone too far, and ducks for a line of sight beneath the window's rim, looking for a station sign out on the Shinseibijo platform.

The doors clump open, and she checks the seats either side of her, too dazed to remember if she had bags or not, and she rises unsteadily high on her hugely heeled feet and clomps across the car floor and out onto the platform. Two men in suits let her pass and step inside. They check the car, glancing past the foreigner, and take the inward-facing seat she left. The PA plays the recording. *Shinseibijo. Shinseibijo desu.* A tone rings to warn that the doors will close soon, and Jacques stares back down along the length of the thin, open-air platform to the narrow concrete cord of the monorail track curving away through the void beyond the train. A man in military khaki appears at the top of the steps at the middle of the platform, out of breath and carrying a heavy-looking leather attaché case. He pauses, for a moment indecisive as to whether he'll run for this particular train and risk defeat or wait around ten minutes for the next. The tones ring again, but the doors don't move. He has urgent business so he makes his decision; Jacques wonders if he's with the kendo training men near Oikeibajomae, if there's water between the two that forces him to take the train just these few stops. He decides, and abruptly makes a run for the door to the car from which Jacques watches. Sitting facing backward, Jacques watches the split in his uniform's jacket part at his crotch in a well-tailored flexing khaki lambda as the man lopes directly toward him, holding his cap on hard with one hand, the other lifting the attaché case out toward the car almost comically like an offering or a baton in a relay race. He almost makes it. He's ready to jump inside like the late always do, and once inside, panting, like a fastforward button released they'll pause, and then walk as casually as they can to the next carriage, eyes averted from everything but the door and the seat they'll take where their indignity wasn't observed. But of course he's too late, the first phase of the door cycle starts, that violent double guillotine, one-third of the tantalizing gap. He's almost there, could get a shoulder in, and push the rubber-edged windowed panels open again just enough, or gain the grace of the driver, who'll call a scratchy amplified *"Go chui, kudasai!"*—Caution please!—but retract those doors just a vital second. Or he'll risk putting a foot in the door of Jacques' car, so dangerous, who really knows the strength of these doors when they're in their final phase. What if they're so strong, and with the platform's end just ten hopped yards away, a barely man-width gap between the railing and the train, then a broken ankle and a dangle and twenty dropped yards to the road. The second door phase gentler now.

Clu-clump.

The driver's seen him.

"Go chui, kudasai!"

And the tones ring again. The man's eyes are wide with desperation to make this train; Jacques sits up straight with a sudden excitement and a sharp unexpected burst of adrenaline. What will happen? The man runs straight toward the foreigner, attaché case up in the air, as if to say, a vital message for you! Almost there, and the doors start the final gentle phase, and Jacques is safe inside, it's too late for the soldier's shoulder, he'll just carom off the metal, he won't risk a foot, all his weight is forward, no one's stupid enough to use their fingertips—he jams the attaché case between the doors and they clump closed and squeeze. Almost immediately the monorail begins to glide from the station. The soldier pulls at the case. Realizing it's too late. A terrible mistake has been made. There's something bulky in the inner half that's caught in the doors like a barb. Jacques can see in the car's fluorescent lights the inner half-a-case suspended in midair, so utterly incongruous in a moving train to see a door so violated. Halfway in, halfway up. Not even comical, for Jacques; just odd. And through the angle of the window's glass distortion, the look of the moment just prior to bewilderment on the soldier's face, walking beside the moving train, tugging at the protruding end of his case. Inside like an odd reflection minus him, the soldier's suspended case pivots and jerks. His watery face jumps something nearer to horror as the train accelerates quickly; he's starting to jog, he sees the chrome railings of the platform's end coming up, and Jacques sees his refracted shock completely ebb, the shake of his head as he simply stops and lets the attaché case go, marooned half up, half in the monorail doors, gliding faster and faster from him, abandoned in khaki on the concrete staring.

Jacques gives him a little wave as he turns and fades.

From the west, clouds unfurl from the horizon like spools of white videotape set rolling on some frictionless plane, curling into Tokyo regenerating as they discard themselves. Jacques stares for a while at the case suspended in the doors. He briefly checks out the two salarymen who had glanced at the awful mistake then looked away again. Twenty seconds pass, and the monorail pulls into Tenkubashi. They rise to their feet and move to the doors. As the train slows to a halt they take a hold of the chrome pillars either side, and when the doors open and the attaché case thuds to the floor in the exit the man on the left nudges it sideways with a casual instep, and they disembark.

Jacques shivers, and saliva fills his mouth in an oily geyser of nausea, the ashen oil still greasy on his teeth. Doors close, on to Ryutsu Center and Oikeibajomae and he decides. Too nasty a taste to ignore, he'll go down in Seibijo station, minimalist though some of these monorail stations are, to hunt down a canned coffee vending machine or at the very least the cold tap in the bathrooms. Before Seibijo he stands, and at the doors he stares down at the attaché case's bruised leather, and its brass clasp on a triangular flap like an envelope. The train pulls in. *Seibijo. Seibijo desu.* He checks the car quickly but there's no one home, and the glass in the doors to the next so dirty and security-wired it might as well be opaque. The doors shudder open and he bends and then he steps out on the platform with the attaché case under his arm.

The monorail crawls on.

He drops a ¥100 coin in a machine by the platform steps and removes a can of Georgia Café Au Lait, drinks it up on the platform and then at the bottom of the steps he sees his first execution on the sidewalk opposite the ticket gates. It's an old man sweeping outside an abandoned tollbooth office, its anodized windows freckled with stone-thrown holes. His broom is made of twigs and the soldiers are the ones from the baseball diamond, carrying their *boken*, wooden practice swords, gently arc-ed, with rounded handles merging into the triple planes of the spines of the polished pine blades. They are passing by the old man when a soldier in the middle cleanly breaks the handle of the broom in two with his *boken*. The soldiers stop. They begin to sympathize, saying ah, sumimasen, sumimasen, gomen nasai, in serious sincere tones, ringing around the old man. Jacques stands in the ticket gate, left hand clutching the attaché case, his ticket in the fingers of his right hand, paused over the ticket slot to exit. In shadow, unseen and unnoticed, paused here, watching. The old man is bowing, his hands scrabbling with pieces of the broken broom, gathering the twigs that are molting from the split handle. He backs away dragging the twigs until his buttocks touch the aluminum of the tollbooth and in the goldly anodized reflective windows Jacques can see the soldiers' faces, spread among the holes in the glass, and beyond them can see a darkness that is the place he stands, and some of their faces are blank and expressionless, some are animated, speaking faux-seriously, apologizing for the soldier's mistake. One points with the tip of a well-weighted *boken* at a twig the old man has missed. The old man reaches for it and the soldier next to him with a two-handed grip casually flicks his *boken* down. There's the sound of a heavy stick hitting fingers, a second's silent pause, and then the old man shrieks. He seems to flinch all over, seems to shrink from his own dimensions, assume a mass diminished. He holds his broken hand to his chest like an expression of something heartfelt. This is how I feel, he seems to say. A different soldier prods him in the stomach with the thick pine tip of his sword. Immediately opposite, the soldier who broke his hand steps forward in a perfect wide-foot stance and two-handed slices diagonally down with a cry, and the sword strikes the old man's head and the sound is not a clean thock, but clotted, deadened by contact with his ear. Jacques' train ticket is suddenly sucked into the gates because his hand must have slowly drifted downward and the tiny belt inside the gates whirs and subsides and the plastic doors clunk open. He doesn't move, just watches two of the soldiers use clean, precise strokes to destroy the old man's arms and knees, and then the soldier who struck first is let forward to beat him to death with blows of the *boken* to his old thin skull, drops of blood flying back from the wooden sword on the upstroke, the soldiers parting, no-sound of his crushed upward face receiving the strikes.

There's some sensor in the ticket gates that knows Jacques hasn't moved, so the gates stay open. He watches the soldiers walk away, not looking back, not noticing this paralyzed French boy in the ticket gates of Seibijo station.

Sitting down on the end seat of the bank of plastic chairs up on Seibijo platform, Jacques sips his ¥100 heated can of Café Au Lait, contemplating the borrowed attaché case in his lap. The ashen taste in his mouth, diluted a little by the sugary warm coffee, had done a decent job of dissuading him from smoking a cigarette. The clouds furling in from the west over the almost-indigo are dampening the day's winter light down quickly, and it probably won't be long before the streetlights, and maybe, if he's lucky, if it's a racing night, the stadium lights at the racetrack come on. He turns the attaché case end for end on his lap, and sips his coffee. Traffic passes on Shuto Expressway, across the canal tributary that runs alongside the road beneath him under the monorail tracks. Idly, with one hand, he turns the case end for end once more.

And his keitai begins to vibrate, moaning in his pocket.

On the little screen reads, MEREDITH.

It turns out she's had a change of heart, and just as Michael had told him that day in Starbucks, using almost the same words Michael had told him she would, she asks Jacques for the contact he knows.

"His name is Yu Hayakawa," Jacques says. "He is the youngest professor of comparison literature at Rikkyo University, and Meredith, if I would be you, be kind of careful."

"Why?" she says.

"He is Michael's girlfriend's husband."

She doesn't really want to talk to him, too caught up in this scheme where the play plays the players and not the other way round. Jacques sips his sugary milky coffee, and washes it in his cheeks, sucking it back through his teeth in noisy ruminative squeaks and pops. Thinking, my sisters would like Meredith. He turns the case one more half-turn until the clasp and flap are by his belt buckle, where he will open it and see what's inside. The line on his forehead itches incredibly. Would Geneviève like the fact that though he's not in fact lying to Meredith, he's certainly doing more than not telling the whole truth? Would Geneviève think he was guilty? Of spectatorial acquiescence; a tourist's bland passivity? Of believing more in Michael's conviction than his philosophy? He always thinks of earnest Geneviève when faced with a moral dilemma. When they were little, Jacques and Geneviève and Sandrine would sit inside the darkened wardrobe in Sandrine's room, and they would pretend they were going down to Narnia. Though in the story, Lucy, Edmund and eventually the others go *through*, in Sandrine's wardrobe, to Geneviève's whispers, they would always go *down*. *Now we're going down to Narnia*, she'd say. *Shhhh, now we're going down to Narnia. Down and down and down, shhh.* And he and Sandrine, with Geneviève as God, would sit in the dark in collapsing cardboard boxes full of painted blocks, and believe until it was true. Jacques presses the little brass button of the clasp, and lifts the flap of the attaché case, and drops his can of Café Au Lait with a dull clang on the platform, and into the pool of lukewarm coffee that spreads in the shape of a wide brown keyhole into the concrete some of the swarming spiders that spill from the case into his lap in a writhing clustered flood *fall* and quickly drown but some walk lightly off on the meniscus.

He gets halfway down the steep steps inside the station sipping his can of coffee when his keitai shivers and moans in his pocket. It's Meredith. And Jacques remembers what Michael had told him, how she would come looking, how she would be seeking a translator. And Michael likes to start shit, he supposes, because he wants to send Meredith to Yu, tall quiet Catherine's husband. Mustached smug Yu. So Jacques does it, whatever, his loyalty today is to loss. He finishes the call inside the white corridor before the final steps down to the Seibijo gates, drops the phone back in his pocket. He hitches up under his arm the lost attaché case that he's going to hand in to the stationmaster at the office by the gates, if there's even a stationmaster at these tiny minimalist stations, and as he descends the final set of stairs he fumbles in his pocket for his ticket and can't find it, so he pulls off his glove with his teeth as he comes to the foot of the stairs and the body of the old man is still there across the street, hunched unnaturally, his neck broken, skin of his bared legs not bloody but mottled oddly with the blows, and the ticket gates are closed and Jacques has no ticket in his pocket.

The soldiers walk away, not looking back. The old man's blood runs in a thin rivulet straight to the curb and down into the gutter where it pools in a narrow trench, another gutter in the gutter. From here it looks black like a thick smooth split in the concrete, and the old man's body is a collapse freeze-framed, a photograph, partway through the fall.

In the darkened reflection in the anodized windows of the tollbooth, Jacques watches himself as he climbs over the gates and then steps sideways, until he's a darker shadow against an aluminum pillar lined with a slot for the station doors to slide down. His reflection above the body is pocked with blacker holes. On the pillar next to his shape is a white rectangle. He turns and sees that taped to the pillar is a MISSING PERSON poster. The hostess, Lucy Jane Blackman. She has blond hair tied in pigtails and half a grin. Twenty-one years old. The missing person, a British, was last seen. His forehead itches terribly now, and there is no stationmaster here, no office even. Nauseous, he scrabbles in the pocket of the Zegna jacket, and pulls out the buds of his minidisc earphones. He checks his breast pockets for MDs, and finds DJ Honda, Rammstein, Duran Duran's *Seven and the Ragged Tiger,* Wham's greatest hits, *The Final.* It's a Muji MD and he pulls it out of its sleeve and loads it in. He toggles the switch to *Play Mode,* to *Shuffle,* presses *Play,* and >>I, once, enough that anything might happen.

Baritone George Michael says, *You do the jitterbug.*

Jacques steps out of the darkness to *Wake Me Up Before You Go-Go,* watching himself in the pocked gold windows go left and under the monorail tracks, attaché case under his arm, ears dotted black like his deaf father's dotted silver, circling around he disappears from the reflection as he avoids the tollbooth and the heap of bloody clothes.

The loud music is like silence, and Jacques follows the dirty asphalt road under the monorail tracks. With the tide at neap the tributary is filled to the concrete walls of the canal on his left. On his right is a chain-link fence the length of an anonymous commercial building like a giant aluminum kanji-littered box. He's breathless, his heart in his head. *You put the boom boom into my heart. You send my soul sky high when your loving starts.* The stolen case in his hand that's sweating, and what he feels is a downward spiraling anxiousness, a twisting of himself, and he's heading along the chain-link fence that's edged with all kinds of jetsam and debris like cans and onigiri wrappers and a spewed glistening mound of audiotape, fluttering looped pennants espaliered by an old wind along the foot of the barrier. He's walking back toward the city in shock, noticing everything visual in hyperreal glitter and delineation, each object framed partially by another, shifting as he passes. A gigantic warehouse after this one looms along the fence and just as slowly and abruptly cedes its power to the next warehouse like a compère cedes the stage; the building bows out whitely in fractured angled retrograde. *Yeah yeah it goes a bang bang bang till my feet do the same.* He breathes in shallow gasps, glancing down the lanes between the great structures, checking for further signs of life, anything, anyone, and when he glances down the fence protruding is the white fender quarter-mooned black by the partial tire of a Jeep. It's a twist on his face, a squint like a *no* but fatalistic *yes* and he sees that yes he's come this far and that this is the entrance to the baseball park he'd seen before. In his time on the monorail they have shifted the Jeeps and there are only three now, this first white and the two behind a yellow-stained khaki. They are parked in single file between the looming wall of the last warehouse fenced closely by a ninety-degree turn of the chain-link, from which corner he sees the back of the dugout's bricked wall beside the last Jeep after a brief gap and another smaller warehouse on the corner of the fenced drive opposite him. There's human movement there, through that gap, and he turns down the drive close to the fence and he can see the white of the water of the main canal terminating this drive, far from the illusion of shelter the monorail tracks provide *but somethin's buggin me, somethin ain't right, my best friend told me what you did last night.* The music's loud, loud and silver in his ears, stereo-imaged by the good bud earphones like it's broadcast from the physical center of his skull and going out and through his ears and into the world, and the thin line of irritation at his shaven widow's peak itches so incredibly, and it's lucky he reaches up to scratch right now because when he walks straight through the drifting spiderweb it wraps and sticks across his hand and not his eyes. He makes a sound, half a grunt, half an exhalation, like *uh,* that's inaudible to himself as the chorus calls, cries in giddy delight—*wake me up before you go-go!*—and he flails at his face and at the clinging tickly minute tentacling on his cheeks and ears and shaven sensitive scalp and swipes at the back of his hand to get the stuff *off me hanging on like a yo-yo* but there's no spider there and still he stops and scratches madly, shuddering, running his hands hard over his skull, turning to unwind out of this winding sheet of drifting web as if it won't adhere, eyes focused in some impossible near-distance for that escaped and mindless scuttling *thing,* and though he finds no such on himself, not in the collar of the turtleneck nor on the coarse velvet of his scalp, he throttles himself briefly with both hands for better guts and spiderblood on a neck than a live and frantic angry *thing* intently crawling there, and though he finds nothing he sees indeed in turning comically about that the chain-link fence beside him is not riddled but unriddled with web and quiet clustered waiting bodies, the metal frames delicately and completely filled and filigreed by holes in holes in holes and in the windless indigo air the spiders one at least to every chain-linked cell have their filament legs spread wide in a hairy tracery of found and poised and silent horror.

Jacques steps shakily back from the spiderweb and between the fenders of the last two Jeeps to *I don't wanna miss it when you hit that hiiiiiigh* and turns the opposite direction and he's seeing through the chain-linked gap between the dugout and the corner warehouse through a faint and waiting haze of populated web humans passing by out on that baseball diamond. There is no wind, yet an old wind has brought a glistening ribbon of the audiotape in a long loop down the road with him, and he steps on it unknowingly as he walks up, then with his step drags the loop up and around his ankle. There's a graveled gap of a yard or so between the dugout's brick and the small warehouse, and through the web-riddled chain-link Jacques is looking at the khaki backs of at least fifty soldiers in caps and wound puttees and some in hooded greatcoats belted at the waist. Most of them have their hands in their pockets, and most of them have their heads bent slightly as if in Christian prayer. They shuffle occasionally, some of them, shift from foot to foot. One lights a cigarette, passes it to the man beside him, lights another for himself. Then they part and from out of the dugout appear three more soldiers with rifles hung at their shoulders, hands holding the bound wrists of a single prisoner each. They lead them across the muddied earth of the diamond through a loose aisle left by the soldiers, who seem alert and watchful in their expressions, yet somehow slow and purposeless. So many with their hands in pockets. At the end of the aisle they form is a rough gouge in the earth, a sloping-shouldered trench chest-deep; one side sheer, the other more sedate as if the diggers had lost interest or motivation and left an easy way out. The three soldiers lead the three prisoners carefully down the slope, steadying them on the thick clay clods. They lead the young men to the steep side of the trench, and there they all stop, as if all these players have momentarily forgotten their lines, all at once accusing himself in the mild serious unpanicked knowledge that this is just a rehearsal; they can try again. There's music playing in Jacques' ears but the song is winding down and the singer sings *don't leave me hanging on like a yo yo yo yo yo...*

Take me dancin...

A boom boom boom boom...

Oh!

They awake. The first two soldiers push the Chinese to the ground. They pull their bayonets from scabbards at their belts and lock them to their rifles with practiced twists. The first steps up. The man at his feet hands bound is fetal, pulling his uppermost knee to his chest like a frightened beaten child, offering only his boots and his buttocks and the small of his back, *oshiri, sebone, senakaaa* the most primal expression, offering that both most and least vulnerable to love and attack. His mouth moving open and shut, watching for the soldier's bayonet, writhing on the yellow clods. With the bayonet fixed the soldier's rifle is very long, and the soldier checks his stance, his feet spread wide, knees bent and weight centered. The prisoner kicks at nothing with the sole of a boot, frantically as a tickled dog, his eyes shut tight then open, flinching, face contorting like a smacked child. The soldier stabs him lightly once in the underside of his raised thigh and Jacques sees but does not hear him scream, and his leg judders down in a defensive shudder, seems to spasm, and his chest sidelong is exposed. The soldier is watching him intently as a fisherman with a billy club watching a flapping snapper on a boat deck, looking for this opportunity, and conscious of his weight and balance, with just his arms, shoulders squared, his left arm straightens, right drives, he bayonets the manchild in the chest.

The dead man dies, curling round his pierced heart.

One or two of the watching shuffle, shift hands in their pockets. A man in a greatcoat turns and walks away. And Jacques' song fades out totally and at last he breathes.

A plane rushes overhead or maybe it's the monorail, then between songs no analogue hiss but pristine digital clean quiet obtains. There's something on his face, but now he feels no need to find out what. They do the same to the other two, by turns in the quiet and the screams.

It's now Jacques realizes suddenly that the man in the greatcoat who left has passed in front of a young soldier, near the back of the crowd, and that the young soldier is actually staring at him through the fence by which he stands. He pulls the earphone buds from his ears. The soldier stares at him, and then down at the attaché case under his arm. He seems to realize something, and hitches up his rifle and shoulders his way carefully through the soldiers toward the dugout. The wind is rising, but even so, the earphone buds draped around Jacques' neck make an audible tinny sound, all treble, hissing the drums and saxophone solo of *Careless Whisper.*

And Jacques just waits, because he has nowhere else to go.

From behind the dugout appears a short, thick officer with wide shoulders, polished brown boots, a badge on his cap, a moustache. He looks briefly through the fence and sees the young foreigner. The young soldier follows behind him as he approaches.

Jacques breathes deeply, intently, concentrating. Noting how the soldiers at the rear of the crowd are turning to see, staring at him like no Japanese on the street has ever done. George Michael murmurs *I feel so unsure, as I take your hand and lead you to the dance floor...*

The officer stands in front of him, staring him right in the eye, another first for Jacques, never stared at thus outside the kitchens of *Le Toile.*

And so he shrugs. What?

The officer's eyes widen, and he stares at Jacques. A long moment passes as he assesses the foreigner. Then, he shrugs back, mouth pouting in contempt and imitation. He turns back to the soldier and says something to him. The soldier stares at the ground and says nothing as the officer laughs. He turns back.

Nodding an aggressive, slanted nod, eyes wide, his voice high and strained and scornfully mannered, he says, "Nani wo shiteimasu *ka?*"

Jacques translates. *What are you doing?*

The automatic mechanism of reply and deferral—he supplies the most obvious answer.

"Ano, miteiru," he says quietly. *Uh, watching.*

"*Miteiru?*" the officer says in sneering incredulity. "Honto? *Miteiru,* ka?" The soldier sniffs, and Jacques hears crackles in the distance, thunder, gunshots, and it's then he decides to get himself gone.

"Sumimasen," he says; "gomen nasai," and he bows and begins to back away, but before he can the officer says, "Chotto mate, chotto mate. Nihon-go hanasemasu ka?"

This is familiar.

"Chotto hanasemasu," Jacques says, nodding, his body language all J before this man. *I speak a little.*

"*Na-ni* . . . wo shiteimasu ka?" the officer asks, more seriously. *What are you doing?*

Jacques' heart beating very fast, the music tinny on his shoulders, an ashen taste in his mouth and the scent of sour smoke in the air.

"Chotto, chotto," he mutters.

"Weru ah yu furom," the officer says in thickly accented English.

It's a familiar question, and Jacques replies automatically.

"Furansu, shushin desu."

"So, ka? Dahntonu, Robespie. Dokokujin desu ka?" The officer smiles, and thinks a moment. "Cahntrimahn, yesu?"

Danton, Jacques realizes. Robespierre. The merciless Jacobins.

"Hai, hai, sumimasen," Jacques says carefully.

"*Jama de aru,*" the officer suddenly growls, tongue rolling the penultimate consonant.

You are in the way, Jacques translates, knowing it's too late for apologies, nods further, never having been spoken to thus by a Japanese, with such pride and contempt, he's almost bowing, something he's only ever done sarcastically.

"Sono naka ni nani ga haitteimasu ka?"

Jacques looks up; facial cues give meaning. The officer nods impatiently at the case under his arm.

He looks down at the case and back up to the officer. The soldier behind is a little interested now, past his uncertainty and fear, privy to some possibly serious, international event.

What's in there?

"Uh . . . ," Jacques searches for Japanese. Finally, all he can summon is "Ano, kumo, desu."

It's spider.

"*Kumo,* ka?"

The officer turns, grinning, half to the bewildered soldier, and says, "Kumo, ne. Doseiai no gaijin, Suzuki," and laughs. "*Kichigai.*"

Jacques has heard these words before. He's seen a J-only gay bashing outside Maniac Love. The same tone, the threatening sardonic growl, the same turn to a crew for support. Gay gaijin. Crazy. *Homo no doseiai. Cho yaba shitto.*

Very bad shit.

"Koko ni oide," the officer snaps, and points away past the dugout. "Suzuki, *ikinasai.*" He sharply slaps the soldier's back, and the scared-looking boy runs down the fenceline.

And here Jacques suddenly finds a clear, coherent thought. This is ridiculous. The rifle bouncing on the boy's back is exactly the same as the antique Michael had stored under his bed at the Prince. He turns unsteadily down the fence for where he can get away.

Koko ni oide means *come here.*

Thinking: looters. Thinking: is everyone okay. Call his mother, call his sisters. Thinking: under martial law the first thing they do is round up all the foreigners. All his stuff toppled from the shelves. How the cupboard doors bang and bang like in some maddened wind. The monorail cord twisting and flexing, oh that good J engineering, how was it that he'd not felt a thing? Between six and seven, surely, and oh what have they learned since Kobe, and are they prepared. Will keitai cells be down and thank god again he's not in the city, or in the suburbs, there'll be fires, there'll be agonies, there'll be so many deaths. More than can be borne; *oh my god the subways.* The *train lines,* the *rivers.* The engineering is incredible, he'd not felt a thing, so blithe, lost in his head as the city flexed and shook itself, the Kanto planes shivering volcanically down to the sea . . .

He decides: down to the river. Away from built-up areas, the river will be safe, tsunami don't affect rivers. But it's tidal, though. He knows it's tidal. Any wave will wash up, taking the bridges, sweeping the junks and the flat-bottomed ferries into their moorings, spewing the diesel and flotsam over the decks, into the hatches and down into the engine rooms to bear up more filthy oil out and into the mouths and nostrils, to paint rainbow the wide eyes of the old drowned fishermen carried down in their waders, the river flooding, upward against the current, everything going backward, Honshu bucking like a frantic horse, and the fires coming after, telling us, again, *you are not wanted here.* When you see the wave it's too late. But *everywhere's* built up. *When you see the wave:* That's for beaches, not for rivers. The canal's wide here, split in two. It'll be okay. He decides again. Jacques heads for the river.

Meredith
December 2000

"Hayakawa Yu-sensei no jimusho ni ikitai desu," Meredith said in her carefully prepared Japanese to the young male receptionist.

I want to go to the office of Hayakawa Yu.

The young boy in his suit stared right up in her eyes and blinked once, then snapped back to the desk in remembered politeness. Meredith let all her ambiguities sink in: her odd dark eyes, her indefinite skin, her height and smooth black Japanese hair. The boy stared down at his desk, deciphering her poorly pronounced question and marshalling ideas for a non-verbal response. On new ground under her own steam Meredith was bold, even in her accent, a badge of who she has become: maybe monolingual, but a foreigner with a place to go.

The young receptionist opened a drawer by his thigh and drew from a photocopied pile a map of the campus. He placed it on the shining mahogany counter and she looked down at nondescript boxes marked by indecipherable kanji. He frowned at the map, rose slightly from his chair and circled with a red felt-tip pen two sparse characters; one like a director's chair, the other a collapsing temple gate. A *torii*, Meredith suddenly thought.

He looked up.

"Reception," he said, and Meredith heard, *deception*.

"Here," he said, and touched the counter.

"Hai," Meredith smiled with a touch of indulgent sarcasm she enjoyed, and only half-hoped wasn't too rude. She's not *this* slow.

He drew a red line through a putative lobby to a pair of small boxes, and Meredith was a little surprised to find herself reading the kana, and saying aloud, "Erebeta." She smiled again at the man. "Desu ka?"

"Hai," the receptionist said, a little irritated at her now. "Sankai?"

"Third floor."

"So."

He placed another map from the drawer over the first, and she saw in the copying either the original had shifted or the copy paper had been loaded with a slight skew; the long rectangle of the third floor was chopped at the corner by the paper's edge, and gave the impression the paper, not the copied design, was awry. A long red line from corresponding boxes down a corridor, then right.

"Go storaito," the receptionist said to the paper, and she realized he was trying on a little sarcasm too; the ubiquitous phrase lifted from nearly useless years of high school English.

"Go raito."

The line finished. He carefully drew a red circle over the corner office cut up by the copier.

"Hayakawa-san no jimusho desu."

"Arigato gozaimasu," Meredith pronounced, and bowed elaborately. The boy was forced to reply in awkward and exaggerated kind.

As the doors closed she looked up at the roof of the elevator with the trace of a smile.

"That is right," Yu Hayakawa said to her in his small, intact office, smiling mustachioed over his desk.

Meredith heard, *zat is light*.

"'We are like statues among them' is indeed this first line. Just a moment, please."

He bent down to the sheet of paper on which Meredith had, after two deteriorating efforts, achieved a passable transcription. The secret, she had finally found, was to ensure that each character, no matter how much they differed in appearance, occupy the same amount of paper.

"And the second line reads, 'As statues they remain.' Just a moment please."

Meredith realized he had stock English phrases he used to simulate casual conversation. When she'd knocked at the anonymous door in the anonymous corridor, a muttered, indecipherable sound was enough to convince her to open it confidently wide. She was changing. The room was small, maybe four tatami mats in size, but entirely Western in design. Bookshelves on both major walls, floor to ceiling, leading to a great mottled window under which Yu Hayakawa sat at a mahogany desk, empty but for a silver laptop with a bitten white apple embossed on the closed cover. He was smiling as she entered, and he smiled wider as he took her in, bemusement revealed only in the slightest tilt of his head. He was younger than she thought. He had moussed hair, a tweed jacket with yellow flecks and a deep blue Lacoste polo shirt beneath. He had a neat moustache, Dolce & Gabbana eyeglasses, intelligent, reticent eyes that observed her with confident perplexity. He had waited for her to speak, and she'd been careful. A friend of Catherine Barnes' had given her his name. A friend met at an embassy party. Oh, really. Which embassy, with a studied, flat rise in pitch that signified his question. The Swedish embassy. Oh, really. It was a conversational tool, his Oh, really; an equivalent to the Japanese *so desu ka?* He smiled a lot, and she was suddenly thinking of the kind of woman that married this man and cheated on him with her brother. And she somehow couldn't connect this face before her with rage, with disappointment, with bitterness. The man seemed unflappable; not in possession of a private life, let alone with that tall blond woman she'd met only once. She suddenly thought of him in bed with that somehow tragic-seeming woman, her long body moving over him; his moustache. Oh, *really*. She felt the sudden real possibility she might Get The Giggles.

Yu Hayakawa rose from his chair and moved precisely to the bookshelf on his right. Meredith studiously examined the old windows rippling the winter into long blurred pixels, and felt his attention never leave her as he removed a large book from a higher shelf and returned to his desk.

As he flicked pages quickly, right to left with an intermittent delicate dab of his index fingertip to lower lip, she was glad to see he wasn't smiling at the book. A set of golf clubs nestled in the corner behind him.

Who was this man?

He turned the book in a circle on his desk and tapped a black and white painting with the same forefinger.

"This first line is Xavier," he said, and smiled at her, and smiled down at the page.

"Oh?" Meredith said, and heard herself mimicking the pitch. *Oh, really?* And had to try hard not to finish the phrase, to be oh so obvious.

"He was the *bateren*. A very old Japanese word for 'padre.' Most famous Jesuit missionary in Japan from 1549 until 1552. 'We are like statues among them,' he wrote, famously, of the *bateren* among the Japanese. Thus, it is a quote, and this next line here is some other's work. 'As statues they remain.'"

In the picture, a crisply bearded man with soft Italianate eyes crossed long-fingered hands at his chest and contemplated a crucified Christ who rose from him into cherub-clustered clouds. His lips were pursed and full; the lashes of his eyes thick and feminine, yet spaced widely as a man's. The center of the crucifix bisected the H of the letters *IHS*, silhouetted by a second sun beneath the first that shot rays from behind the crux. The crucifix terminated at the base at what appeared to be Xavier's flaming heart; he touched it gently with the three inner fingers of his right hand.

He looked to her something like a sad and rabbinical Dracula, cape and all, full lips pursed over giveaway incisors.

At the bottom of the picture ten or twelve messy-seeming, spilled archaic kanji seemed to show mere hints of design compared with the heavily seriffed capitals above: S.P. FRACISCUSXAVERIVSSOCIEATISV.

"This painting is a Japanese artist's work, and there was some problem with the translation," he said. "This should read *Societatis Jesu,* not *Societatisu.* This Francis Xavier," Yu, smiling, "was father of Jesuit missionary work in Japan."

Meredith's keitai moved in her breast pocket.

And before she was to learn all manner of things of what and how far back and how entwined with both his and her present her brother's work had gotten, from a little fragment of a play translated by a professor of literature cuckolded by a failed historian two-thirds his age, Meredith took this phone call.

"Oh. Excuse me," she said. Hayakawa blinked, and she took the phone from her pocket. "May I take this in here?"

"Mmm, *dozo,*" he said. "Please." If he was at all put out, he didn't show it. The name on the screen read JACQUES.

"Hallo Jacques."

There was static, clicks and feedback.

"Jacques?"

"Ooh is it?" came his voice, distorted and delivered piecemeal through the noise.

"It's Meredith," she said, and rose from her seat to stand by the door. Hayakawa politely turned back to the book and her sheet of paper. "I can hardly *hear* you."

There came a roaring like a *shussss,* and she held the phone from her ear.

"Jacques?"

"Don't be afuraido . . ." his voice came again, pixilated senselessly, trailing off.

"Where are you?"

"Cela s'est passé," he said, suddenly coming clearer. "Oh! *Non . . .*"

"I can't hear you. Speak English, Jacques. Can you call back or something?"

There came more noise, static and crackle.

"...non, non, non. Que je dorme! *Ptits cris,* que je dorme." The white noise rose again, popping and fizzing. Suddenly, she was cut off. She examined the screen. It read 0:00:32, ticking on for six more seconds before coming to a halt at CALL DURATION.

She turned back to the professor. He raised his eyebrows politely.

"A bad connection?"

"Yes, a friend of mine forgetting I don't speak French. I'm sorry."

"Oh, really? French?"

"Yes..." she looked down at the phone, then back to the young, healthy-looking professor, shaking her head slightly, "Do you...?"

"Oh no, no. A little, only."

She said, "Very strange. He said something was passé."

"Oh. Something was over; in the past."

"It sounded like, say la say passé."

"'That is all in the past.'"

"Oh. How about, 'que je dorme'?"

"'Let me sleep.'" He smiled.

She smiled too, disliking him intensely. "Sorry for the interruption."

"No, no." He shook his head, then gestured to the transcription. "But this is very interesting."

And so over the next three or four hours one week immediately prior to the big Christmas party Simon Chang was arranging for every foreigner he knew in Tokyo, Meredith learned of the four-hundred-year-old story of a witch named after a thorn, who vaporized from history eleven plump Dutch merchants with a mushroom, a witch whose older brother walked on water, and who—the brother—at age seventeen in December 1637, led thirty-seven thousand Christian men, women and children to a Jacquerie and their deaths and had his head jammed on a stick in Nagasaki for his trouble and his passion.

It's said the tides of the Seto Inland Sea move so fast it's hopeless to search for those missing presumed drowned either as flotsam or as jetsam on the rocky seashore, so the missing in the Seto usually stay so: lost, in process, swept along with the shallow stirred alluvium of the seabed, past the innumerable islands between Honshu and Shikoku, under the six bridges of the Seto Ohashi, keelhauled round the blasted granite capes only to be snared and viciously manhandled in the great whirlpools that form in the plughole of the Naruto Straits, and then, ragged, harried and pale, the missing are spat out into the ocean, to float and rot head-high and boot-low over the Philippine Basin, as pacific as the heavy depths of the ocean that has claimed them.

So when the eleven Dutch merchants and the English pilot who had brought them to Japan went missing from the second of their artificial islands of exile, Mejima, near Sakaide on Shikoku, in 1641, just their first year there, the local authorities went looking for culprits, not victims.

Their craggy Dutch names are lost with their bodies and the peculiar note and flourish of each man's idleness; and even the island of their exile is subject to speculation now. It's said, too, that when the Shogun Tokugawa Iemitsu was beseeched by the local Nagasaki and Sakaide businessmen constrained to pay for the artificial islands, three years before the Portuguese *bateren* were finally purged for good, their ships burned or turned back and the word was made law that only those mercantile and Protestant Dutch (also variously called "pestilent," "piratical," "freebooting," "meretricious" and, of course, "heathen") might stay—and later only on that pair of manmade islands, freestone piled offshore in Nagasaki Bay, and off Sakaide in the Seto—it's said that when the formidable Iemitsu was beseeched to name the shapes these freestone manmade islands might be—he at once snapped open his fan, drew it down beneath his left eye, and glowering, deigned to remain speechless.

The businessmen fled, and at once, in 1636, before Shimabara, the catalyst of the final purge of all European foreigners bar the Dutch, the construction began of Deshima in Nagasaki harbor, an island in the shape of the blade of an open fan—557 feet wide near the shore, and 706 falcate feet facing out to the ocean—and of Mejima in the jactitating tidal Seto, shaped as Iemitsu's watchful almond eye 313 feet wide, peering sidelong into the brutal currents such that diluvial silt might not gather on any transomed edge (and thus provide the Dutch exiles there more Japanese soil on which to wallow in their idleness) but instead might sweep around the lashless eye and pour from the eastward terminal point like wept tears of sand into the Pacific.

Lost in the Seto, 1641: Peter Trippelvitz, the *operhoofd*, the fatalist Chief Factor of Mejima, and Willem Wiersema his second in command; the red-bearded bearlike *pakhuismeester*, Niels de Wilde, warehouse custodian and occasional carpenter; the *doctoor* Jacob Baars; and Koenraad de Graaf, his

rakish *ondermeester,* the medical assistant who demanded a different whore
every three days, the bare minimum period decreed for the Dutch by the
Japanese administration, who controlled, basically, everything; and *assis-
tents* Matthiu Maassen and Filip van den Berg, the latter famous then
among the local municipality for on their first day declaiming to the interpreters in broken plaintive Japanese, "I have no sense of humor." The
schrijvers, or secretaries: the reputedly asinine Thomas Assenberg, and
Willem "The Other" Schermer Voest; the gentle, precisely sideburned and
lanky Sander Waagmeester; Joost de Groot, the portly syphilitic
boekhouder or accountant; and the thespian-minded Colin Edwards, the
intrepid English pilot of the ship that brought them to Japan, who via
Shogunal vicissitudes found himself confined to the little island of Mejima
as well. All disappeared into the ocean, before their very first VOC ship
could arrive and unload some cargo for trade, reify their mission and vali-
date their leisure; all disappeared into a rabbit-hole in time.

Deshima, the fan, meant "fore island," or "the island that juts out." It
lay in front of Nagasaki township, separated from the shore by a small
stone bridge like the fan's handle, guarded night and day. It was a pun,
also, on "te"—the kanji was not for "hand," but for "exit," "outflow,"
"going out" or "one's turn to appear on stage." And the verb form, "shi-
mau": to finish, to close, to put an end to, put away. *Mejima* meant Eye
island, with a nod to *mejiri*—"outside the corner of the eye"—watched
only as it was by if not devoted then at least beholden barons in Sakaide in
Shikoku, to which it was connected by a stone bridge at the western end
like a tear duct; and much closer, though unknown, as it was, to Kyoto, the
old capital, but most importantly to the pun, just up the coast lay Mikawa,
Ieyasu's home fief, and Edo—Tokyo—from where the Tokugawas now
reigned. Iemitsu did in fact carry on his grandfather's work by encourag-
ing foreign trade, however restricted and clandestine and tucked in the
Seto, to benefit and be controlled by his seat alone: while the silk of the
Portuguese ships burned and the barons went without (yet stayed carefully conspicuous in their praise of Iemitsu's bitter resolve), the goods destined for Mejima were destined solely for the Shogun and his court. Thus
the vigorous action of the fan—the great display of sovereign power in
pushing off the foreigner—shielded the wink of the eye—the covert maintenance of a trade intended to completely exclude the powerful Kyushu
barons and benefit the House of Tokugawa, its court and environs alone.

And the Dutch were compelled to rent these islands, too: 5,500 Dutch taels per annum for the Fan, or almost 500 pounds of silver; and 6,000 taels for the Eye. Massive sums, more than the cost of the artificial land outright. And any Hollanders who died during their stay upon these two islands would find a grave in the sea; now by decree, none would ever find one in Japanese earth, no matter how contrived that earth might be.

"Um, what's all this about," said Meredith, after fifteen minutes or so. "If you just tell me what the poem means, I'll take off."

"Well, it is never as simple as this," said Hayakawa. "Please."

Now somewhat earlier than the building of the artificial islands, after the battle of Sekigahara when Tokugawa Ieyasu, Iemitsu's grandfather, united the Empire by sharp arbitrament of the sword, entirely reshaping Japan after his own image by banishing and promoting barons afterward according to where allegiances had lain, Portuguese missionaries were, despite the frequent Dutch pirating of their annual "Great Ship" from Macao full of supplies and gifts and their goods for trade, making a go of it in what Endo called "this swamp of Japan." There had been no general sanctioned persecution for almost twenty years under Ieyasu—since the Martyr's Mount at Nagasaki in 1597 no European missionary was put to death by the Shogun for his religion. But much to Portuguese and Spanish chagrin, Ieyasu, knowing full well the soul of trade was competition, was cultivating foreigners of all nationalities and religious bents. Back in Europe, Philip II of Spain and Portugal had closed Lisbon to the Dutch in 1594, in prosecution of the Eighty Years War, and with news of rich pickings and instructions to smite at will all merchants of the Spanish flag, the hungry and intrepid Dutch headed east, in ships, it seemed almost invariably, piloted by mad dog Englishmen. A few returned rich, and in 1602 the States-General amalgamated all rival companies into the Dutch East India Company or VOC, and sent them Japanward with united purpose. At midnight on Candlemas Day of that same year, one of these Englishmen, who would later pilot the Dutch ship *de Nuk* in 1640 with Trippelvitz, Wiersema and De Groot et al. on board, Colin Edwards, a boy of ten, son of a two-bit actor working in Properties to keep body and soul together, helped strike the set at the Middle Temple in London of the inaugural production of a new play, William Shakespeare's *Twelfth Night*.

"How do you know that?" said Meredith. "How does that fit into this?"

"Wait," said Hayakawa. "Just a moment, please."

But the real clincher for Ieyasu with regard to Christianity in his fairly peaceful kingdom was in the year 1612. The Christian baron of Arima had bribed the secretary to the Chief of Ieyasu's Council of State (a Christian too) to retrieve for him by policy some territory he'd lost in strife some years before. The secretary agreed, forged a privilege, then, blaming anti-Christian elements, forged its revocation and pocketed the money. Puzzled at the sudden *volte-face,* Arima gravely approached the court of Ieyasu for a little more info as to his shift in dictate, and thus both men were exposed for their intrigues. Arima's head got promptly rolled and the secretary burned alive. Ieyasu, already seething at all things Christian, grew even more enraged at the rosary-fondling and bended knees of the Christians at the secretary's funeral, and to top it all off, Ieyasu was learning via private spies of the Christian proclivity for heretic-burning, empire-building and heretic-monarch-excommunication back in Europe, plus of his own sixth son Tadateru's involvement, however peripheral, in a conspiracy with the baron Daté Masamune to rig a covert contract with Philip II of Spain for private gold-mining rights.

Furious, Jodo Buddhist Ieyasu resolved to take action, via the expulsion Edict of 1614, *alea iacta est.*

"What about the missionaries?" said Meredith. "Their story's a little different, right. You know they were commending his soul to heaven. He was burned to death by heathens. They were praying for his eternal soul."

"He was a thief and liar," said Hayakawa, smiling.

"I'm sure you understand that's just one way of looking at it."

"It is the Japanese way of looking at it."

And now to this little fragment of a play: around that time there was that *ronin* Masuda Jinbei, whose three eldest sons died untimely, who lived in Oyano on Amakusa Island, an area ruled by the cruel and avaricious baron Terazawa Katataka. This *ronin* Jinbei had remaining a fourth son, Shiro, an elder daughter named Fuku, and a younger daughter named Man. Man was Jinbei's last child, and, insofar as she was a somewhat useless girl in those times of bitter poverty, might well have fallen prey to *mabiki,* or thinning-out, were it not for the loss of Jinbei's other sons—birth was taxed by the shallow-pocketed Terazawa, then, and friends and relatives deferred their congratulations until well assured the child would be let live. Masuda Shiro went on to become that Amakusa Shiro, who at seventeen or thereabouts would lead the *Shimabara no ran,* the Christian peasant uprising against the Shogun. Man would live, and go on to become little more than a footnote to a folktale version of history, lost in bloody politics.

Shiro was born in 1622, around the time of the Great Martyrdom of fifty-one at Nishi-zaka, Nagasaki, the same place where the twenty-six Jesuits had died back in 1597; Man was born in 1624, one year after Iemitsu's accession to Shogun and the beginning of the revised and systematized persecution of the Spanish *Kirishitan.* From a young age both showed themselves prodigal. Later, tales of the young Shiro would have him walk upon the water, heal by laying on of hands, call a pigeon from the æther and have it lay an egg upon his palm, from which he drew forth paintings of Christ and pages of the Christian Bible. At four years old, Shiro recited the entire Chinese Confucian Keisho. At five years old, Shiro's calligraphy made adults blush and stride soberly home to practice. At seventeen he was leading them to battle, massacre and glory. He was charismatic, forceful, impassioned, pious, and above all, beautiful.

What of Man?

In those days, especially in mountainous Kyushu, poverty was extreme and the arable land meager and infertile, and yet still the barons set their taxes disproportionate, especially Terazawa and that Matsukura Nagato-no-Kami of nearby Shimabara, who spent his time intriguing at Edo court, and demanded of the peasants on pain of death *koku* of rice that could not be grown. While in Kyoto and Edo the courts dined extravagantly on eastern produce bought with the tithes of these sorely pressed barons, the peasants who indirectly laid their tables ate the roots of ferns, wild acorns, radish leaves; they boiled barley in place of rice, and drank hot water in place of tea. This young Man, wild-haired and dirty-faced, scuffed unsandaled through her village, pus-filled wounds on her lips and chin, translucent lunes of seared skin dangling from her cheeks in rags, for she would not sip her boiling water but messily bolt it down in one. Her mouth was daily scalded blister-white. The villagers avoided Man; her *ronin* father, old Jinbei, once faithful retainer to the great Christian warlord

Konishi Yukinaga in the Korean campaigns, lay drunk in the ditch outside an inn; it was only Shiro, her prodigal brother, who ignored her growls and moans and applied a poultice of pounded seaweed to her seared gums, smoothing her bedraggled hair to calm her, stop her spitting it from her ravaged mouth.

In those days thieves were executed by beheading in the commoners' execution ground. Passing samurai might deign to test the style of their strokes and the mettle of their blades by hacking at the mangled headless bodies as they lay upon the earth. This Man—the kanji for her name meant *briar,* or *thorn,* or phonetically, with the feminine suffix, as the slang Manko, *cunt*—would shuffle to the grounds and lie down beside a mutilated thief as if a lover, and growl as a dog at any passing idle samurai who chanced to unsheathe their blades. Disgusted and unsettled, shaking their heads the samurai would leave the girl wriggling on the blood-soaked ground, urinating helplessly in her rags as she clutched the heat-bloated body of a headless thief, pulled his arms around her in a stiff and black-fingered embrace and smiled up at the samurai through her mangled, ruptured lips, blowing them bloody kisses.

She was nine or ten.

And in those days, too, though there were many Christian peasants in Amakusa and Shimabara, there would increasingly come the call for a persecution of smaller or greater size, the victims' Christianity often a mere excuse for a baron's sadistic whim or a conspicuous toadying to the Shogun. Then would come *mino odori*—the straw dance. A victim was bound, wrapped tight in a raincoat made of straw and thereupon set ablaze. The "dance" of an agonized leap and roll upon the ground to fight a fire worn was laughed at by the magistrates and their retainers. But what did not cause amusement was shuffling mad-haired Man, writhing in imitation of the *odori,* just ten years old, waving her arms about, beating out imagined flames and scratching at her thighs, shrieking and wriggling on the ground in mimicked throes of a death by fire. The magistrates called for her to be dragged away, their recreation soured by the insane display, and as their man took hold of Man, the dirty writhing little girl, masturbating feverishly now, was heard to giggle, snarl, "Listen to my triumph, father; it is any ringing in your ears!"

Further perturbed, the magistrates would retire, murmuring one to another *shikata ga nai:* nothing can be done; too sickened by her madness to bother with further bloody pursuits.

Man, who conversed with running water, who humped upon the dry ground. Man who collected slaps and curses as if seashells; who with a dirty claw reached and lifted the kimono of strolling samurai to see what was beneath, but somehow never lost her cackling head. Toothless Man, whose blisters never healed, whose hair was never cleaned, whose beautiful half brother would lead an army; Man who flung ordure, rolled in ordure, who was said to eat of ordure. Who mirrored some deeper extremity of her time, in some protest of the viscera. Man the hard girl, briar, thorn, monad, cunt, bitch, the witch, her father Jinbei said, gum-blistered, would prance outside the Jesuit mission where her brother's head last was spiked, growling black-eyed up at the crucifix in some gone ballet, in the belly of an ancient purple gun.

It was Man who poisoned the Dutch.

One night, though, Jinbei chanced to meet with another *ronin* of Konishi Yukinaga, and the two became flown with tales of old glory. They demanded whores, flasks of sake and elaborate pickles to be brought to them at a local izakaya. They drank and declaimed upon the uselessness of Christianity, and bitterly mourned their fallen state, and in their cups ordered delicacies for which their pockets could never provide.

The master of the inn at closing demanded payment. Full of sake, blasphemy, fatalistic insolence and impotent fury, Jinbei exhorted the master to take from him his bewitched and useless daughter, and use her, sell her, whore her, what he would. The innkeeper, long accustomed to poor and masterless samurai full of religious conflict in these parts, and seeing some small chance of compensation for dishes and damaged tables, accepted.

So it was that this innkeeper's wife came first to batter senseless, then paint and pamper little Man; wrench the brambles from her hair and cut it back, shave her eyebrows, make her face and strip her rags for an old kimono. At that time the blackening of teeth was considered feminine and beautiful. Despairing of the toothless girl's market value as a whore, the innkeeper's wife took several pieces of blackened ember from the kitchen fire with her tongs, shaped them shrewdly with a butcher's knife and eased them in her blistered gums.

Her years of self-abuse and the residual heat of the coals rendered the wounds near-bloodless; the ruse was sufficient. She was sold the next day to the Chinese master of a passing spice junk headed back to Nagasaki. The innkeeper's wife felt no shame at her misrepresentation: keeping slaves was viewed as a despicable business by the local Japanese.

And this Chinese captain only discovered his error en route, when he came to feed and water his small cargo of slaves. Pretty young Man, rouge caked thickly over the holes in her lips, slurped the sailors' boiling gruel in one, and spat out steaming charcoal teeth into her empty bowl.

A pragmatic man, seeing some opportunity for return on his investment, however meager, the captain called for Spanish smoked paprika, cayenne pepper and a cream of ground rice. He screwed Man's missing teeth back into their corresponding wounds, powdered over her face with flour, mixed his ingredients with a little of his own spittle, and rouged again her ruined mouth with the burning paste. He sold her as a pouting whore the next day in Maruyama, the red-light district of Nagasaki township.

It is said that from this day until she found her brother's head, Man smiled but never spoke, neither in grunts nor in shrieks, nor in tongues to rushing streams.

1636. At twelve years old, Man is a second-tier prostitute in the shipping town of Nagasaki, working in a brothel that in times gone by catered to sailors English, Portuguese, Dutch, Chinese, Spanish and Formosan. But Tokugawa Iemitsu's architecture of a foreigner-free Japan moved inexorably onward, apparently throwing off concerns with trade and exotic goods, clocks and silk and telescopes, crushing Christians as it coalesced. The persecution became sophisticated, self-aware, and began to concern itself with methodology. It saw how martyrs bred martyrs and admiration, and adjusted its techniques with practical cunning. The Jesuits, Franciscans, Dominicans, Augustinians and all their Japanese neophytes no longer met with glorious crucifixions and the merciful sword: no longer was this a mere purge; now they met with torture and interrogation, existential intimidation and the bitter persuasion of fallen peers. *Anatsurushi—fossed*—bound upside down and suspended by the ankles in a six-foot pit filled with dog feces, blood pounded in brains declared Christian, oozed from their mouths, their noses, ears; spurted from their vented temples. Neophyte families were turned to set fire to one another, women raped by beggars and ruffians, parents' eyes were gouged, their children tortured hard by, and they with tears of blood called *for an end to their sufferings that had no period but their lives.* Portuguese priests were dipped in searing sulphur springs and questioned mildly; a bathos that spun a hideous futility, some vast image out of *Anus Mundi*. Apostasy, not martyrdom: make the *kirishitan* betray itself. The Spanish religion met with an odd symmetry: they were the heretics here, and they met with the same brutal and gratuitous fate any Buddhist mission might have found in Catholic Europe.

From Satow's translation of the *Kirisuto-ki*:

To find fault with a nation for being determined to maintain its political integrity and independence is at once unreasonable and unjust; to accord our meed of respect to the Christian missionaries in their devotion to what they conceived to be their duty would, on the other hand, be ungenerous. This persecution was a duel to the death between Christian priests determined to carry out the command of the founder of their religion, and of the Japanese equally resolute to preserve the independence of their country.

"Reasonable if a little disingenuous, ne?" said Hayakawa. "My feeling is the Jesuits love as much gore as the Japanese did, I think. To bring them closer to God. I am reminded that Michelangelo advised Jacopa da Pontormo, when working for the Spaniards, to be sure and show 'much blood and nails.'"

"Do you know my brother?" said Meredith.

Man watched dogs spurt floods of urine in the street, eyeing her with wary concentration. Man watched the construction of Deshima, and heard rumors of the same of Mejima. She watched the toil of the coolies piling freestone in the harbor, the anchoring of the thirteen posts that would ring the island with kanji-ed signs forbidding vessels to draw near. Man cleaned for the other prostitutes; swept tatami and carried lacquered trays of tea. Man watched Christians burned, crucified, decapitated, imprisoned, forced to apostatize and paraded as pathetic, fallen and typical. Man heard the rumors of those who had trod and spat upon the *fumi-e* of the Madonna before the magistrate, and those who balked and lost their heads. What she thought or felt, no one knew. She spoke to no one, and no one knew her past. She was but a silent beautiful young whore with scars under her rouge, who after given her first dental inspection by the mama of the brothel was left to menial tasks.

Man: serving, close-mouthed smiling, sweeping.

One night a drunken Dutchman rampaged into the brothel brandishing a harquebus, took a swipe at one girl and overturned a flower arrangement, all the while cursing the Japanese as bloody-minded backbiters whose subtlety and officiousness unmanned him. It was little Man who approached the great and red-faced sweating man with his straggly auburn beard all full of rice and pickle rinds. She stared up into his bloodshot aqua Hollander eyes until his bluster ceased, then led the nearly legless man behind the paper doors. There she gently steadied him, sunk softly to her knees and took him in her toothless mouth.

Thirty minutes passed, and the Dutchman emerged, and pronounced in slurred and pidgin Japanese, *"Funbetgamaxij guinaredom."*

Although I appear to know, I do not know.

He presented the mama with the horn of a unicorn imported from "Europe" and fifty *momme*—nearly two hundred grams of silver—for the services of Man, and another fifty *momme* for all the trouble he'd caused.

Man was promoted—her scars became her badge of rank, and her specialty was foreigners.

And so months passed, too, before the news came. There had been an insignificant incident in nearby Shimabara, an area taxed to distraction by that same baron mentioned earlier, the Edo *poseur,* Matsukura Nagato-no-Kami. A vainglorious high-flown governor under his command had placed claim upon a farmer's daughter in lieu of unpaid debts. The anguished farmer could accept her fate as hostage, but hearing she had been rendered nude and branded about with red-hot irons, became enraged, and with friends put down the governor and thirty of his satellites. With the prospect of this man's prosecution and punishment—after the slavery of their children, the unpaid work conscription in the salt mines, the absurd taxes that extended to childbirth and the chattels of their very homes—window taxes; door taxes—this man's act of revenge became the minor event that catalyzed the greatest suffering of the persecution, the *Shimabara no ran.*

"History is so ugly," Meredith said, thinking of her brother's photograph of a missing Chinese girl. "It always seems to me like high camp, or the worst, chillingest, most emptiest feeling of waste."

"History is not real," Hayakawa said. "Think of it as you would a party political broadcast."

Still 1637. The mama sends Man, whore to English, Dutch, Spanish and Portuguese, to the Chinese herbalist's store near the wave-washed foundations of Deshima to procure *kudzu* root, the herb *suan zaoren* to constrain perspiration, monkey's head and *maitake* mushrooms for healthy tea, and a little *chishao* for a new girl's dysmenorrhea. Man walks quietly through the streets, shuffling in geta and kimono, a basket hanging from one crooked arm. At the herbalist's store the Chinese are taking mid-afternoon victuals; she is served by a slim store boy the color of tobacco, a beautiful Japanese just a little older than her.

"Madam," he says politely. "May I help you?"

She watches him, and waits.

"Man?" says the boy.

She nods as she has been taught: head inclined, the slightest bend of knee. But a squeeze of her misshapen lips makes the gesture sarcastic.

"My, how you've changed," says the boy. "How have we all."

Man stares beyond him into the storehouse, then back, over his ragged clothes.

"I am studying in my spare time to be a medical doctor. I am trying to learn from the English medical men, but in these times..." He shakes his head, smiling brilliantly.

Man examines his teeth. She examines the contour of his cheekbones, the attitude of his neck, as if to fathom his will.

"I wonder if you still dance," he says. "Or if now you see mimesis is an infantile reaction."

Man smiles at this, and her lips move cryptically, the pocked upper labia pulled up and inward by the ruptured lateral band.

"Christ is not of our age, therefore we are an experiment in the ingestion of a *modus operandi*, not a string of historical events. Man, you look so beautiful, but so old for one so naive."

Tears had quickly sprung up.

She reaches out, and with the soft pads of her tiny fine fingers drags the tears down his face till they become mere streaks of luminescence, that quickly evaporate in the last of the Kyushu summer heat.

"You're pregnant," he says.

She doesn't respond.

"Is it a foreigner? Man," he says. "If it is a foreigner, you and the child may be deported, or worse."

Man points to a tied bundle of *maitake* medicinal shrooms on the counter, and places a coin alongside.

"I am returning home, Man. There are precipitous events. Please, come back to Amakusa with me."

Man snarls, suddenly, her jagged lips jumping spastically, a concertina of craters splitting, crevasses breaking in the rouge, seared gums pink and white inside, a rocaille of shards of broken white enamel and flesh in flux.

The slim boy does not react.

The Chinese apothecary emerges from the dim storehouse.

"Hallo! Beautiful young woman," he cries in broken Japanese. He sees Man's money alongside the bags. "Ah, look, here we have Yokoyama and Hongo and Sarunomiso mushrooms for you. These, as my boy will tell you, are very great and refined entertainments! They will show your clients hills and fireflies, barbarian lands full of magical acts and perverse and beautiful women to save your tired girls their troubles!" He pulls out bags of even more demure-looking mushrooms from underneath the counter. "Here we have Seishinwasa—stars and loops—and Dora-musuko—the lazy son. If your client is too drunk for performance, simply make him a little mushroom tea and leave him to grand erotic dreams where he can love gymnastically! You? Shah! Relax and count your money!" He watches Man for reaction; a smile, anything. Finding no response, he changes tack. Conspiratorially, he asides: "Or even take them with friends, and you may quickly enter a consensual hallucination such as our Christian friends abide within. But the consequences: so much slighter!" He claps the boy on the back and laughs as dust rises in the shop. "I don't understand the country of Japan who leaves such a brilliant boy doing the low-grade job as this." He breathes *kyara* incense and betel on close-mouthed Man. "What a waste of genius to leave him like this!"

"We are one with Christ," says the boy to Man. "We do not mimic, but we mirror. Come home," he says, and as she turns once at the door, leaving the herbalist's store, he points to the abandoned Jesuit college opposite the muddy piles of Deshima, and says, "You shall see me again."

Two months later, October 1637, on the eve of the great insurrection, five *ronin* addressed the religiously vulnerable villagers of the port of Kuchi-no-Tsu in southernmost tax-scarred Shimabara as follows:

"*Hankan*, the 'Mirror of the Future,' as prophesied by Saint Francis Xavier, was left to us by a banished Father of Kamitsura. The prophecy of the mirror reads:

"Hereafter when five into five years have passed—'"

Hayakawa looked up from his book. "Variously interpreted as fifty-five, or five by five equals twenty-five," he said. "Oh, and by the way, Kuchi-no-Tsu is level four of *Samurai Sho-down IV*, if you are playing as Amakusa Shiro. Have I explained this synchronicity to you?"

"Please, Mr. Hayakawa," said Meredith.

"'—a remarkable youth will appear in Japan. He, without study will acquire all knowledge.'" Hayakawa interrupted himself again. "I made a note here, in regard to Shakespeare's play," he said. "Maria, the servant, says to Toby and Sir Andrew Aguecheek, of Malvolio, that he is 'an affectioned ass that cons state without book and utters it by great swathes.' Act two, scene three."

"What is it with *Twelfth Night*," said Meredith. "This is twice now. I'm getting a little tired of the evasions. If you could just tell me what this story *means* and why it was sent to *me*."

"'This will certainly come to pass. Then the clouds will be bright along the East and West. A wisteria flower will blossom from a dead tree. All men will wear the sign of the cross upon their heads, and white flags will flutter on the sea, on rivers, mountains and plains. Then the time of honoring Jesus will arrive, &c.' We now learn from this book that the time referred to is this present year. Many clouds are bright in the East and West. Also a red wisteria has blossomed on a cherry tree in the garden of Oye Genyemon. He who without study understands all sciences is a youth called Shiro, eldest son of Jinbei of Amakusa—one who, though young, is without an equal in understanding and learning. The time has then already come."

Hayakawa then said, late in the first day, "You are reminded by me of our so-called national perversity for nostalgia? The national obsession with the samurai drama all over the television? Playing on sets placed on stands by the ashtrays of embattled employees of the great corporations? You have heard the expression, '*Natsukashii ne?*' This is our exclamation for present-day reflections on past times or merely things that may or may not have happened, in tones of delicious mourning and fatalistic pangs of heart throbbing."

"I think you might mean propensity."

"And, it should be said, the Japanese historians are prone to a flight of fancy in the thrall of the *nostaruji*. It is instructive to note that Amakusa Shiro now appears as an evil and effeminate wizard with cheekbones, long nails and a great shock of witchy hair in what I mentioned, Neo-Geo's cabinet and Playstation and MAME game, *Samurai Sho-down IV.* He is much reviled, with great if confused affection."

"People always feel nostalgic when they somehow or other can't do or get what they want. I think it's a kind of frustration."

"Even the common academic identification of *nostaruji* as false and deluded is a cliché, to my way of thinking. Nostalgia is merely a certain kind of imaginative history-making for the common man in a nihilist void. It is a creation, yes. It is unsophisticated, perhaps. Is the emotion it renders then unreal, or somehow delusory? Even thus, we cannot say this thing should not exist unless we are Marxists or feminists or any other -ists. I am an aesthetician. I have faith in the imagination and its possibilities. Thus I am free of the tyranny of any possible occluded real. In this way, I elude and defeat the historian. *I cuckold him.*"

"What about the author, though?"

"Ah. There I am beholden."

"Quite literally, really."

"Hmm."

"You do know my brother, Mr. Hayakawa, don't you?"

Shiro soon returned to Amakusa—all vitality and charisma—to lead the incipient rebellion.

Meanwhile Man's mama held up an unsoiled sanitary napkin from the dirty laundry and looked Man in the eye. For the first time, Man could not look back.

Arima fell to *ronin* and farmers in mid-December, the nobility dead or shut up in their castles. The archipelago of Amakusa, from which Shimabara may be reached by walking the seabed at low tide, fell days later. The armies joined and Shiro assumed command.

Man left the brothel wearing the ragged kimono the wife of the innkeeper had dressed her in, the horn of a unicorn tucked in her sleeve and a mere five *momme* in her hand, and headed for a local izakaya favored by the Dutch. There she approached a low table full of rough sailors taking miso soup and *sembe.* Standing behind and over one red-bearded bearlike man, she

dropped the napkin in his soup where it first messily splashed and then rapidly and effectively absorbed the liquid remaining. This de Wilde reared up
roaring, demanding fire and reprisal, and what with she in her ragged dress,
and he in his rage and embryonic drunkenness, he made no recognition, and
punched her sharply to the ground. He called furiously to the innkeeper for
an explanation, suddenly ashamed he had struck a girl so slight.

She gathered herself, and bowed and smiled as the innkeeper ushered
her out, de Wilde standing splashed with soup and a faint remembrance,
and she headed for the waterfront to earn herself some traveling money.

And there Man plied her trade as the *Shimabara no ran* played itself out in
the wings, with no audience, no disinterested observer, no noncombatant.
A few hundred miles from Nagasaki the land was turning on itself.

Masuda Shiro had taken a new name. The *ronin* and farmers under his
command flew the silk flag of golden crucifix and chalice, worshipped by
angels. Lovvad Seiosactissim Sacramento—Worship the Supreme Holy
Authority. Masuda Shiro was now Amakusa Shiro Tokisada. Amakusa was
his place of birth; Shiro meant "fourth son," and was a homonym for
"white"; and Tokisada was capable of several meanings, depending on the
kanji combinations:

関断 —meant war cry and judgment, or severance.

時貞 —meant the time of chastity, constancy and standing upright.

斎断 —meant the refusal or dismissal of food.

信貞 —meant truth and righteousness.

From Nagasaki the progress of the battle was clear. Throughout the
closing days of December 1637, Man watched messy drunken parades of
marching soldiers and samurai pass through the city. Standing at the road-
side, she was approached by men who fell from formation seemingly
without even a pretense of secrecy, who took her for brief sojourns in
alleyways, breathed sake, dropped coins and fell back into file as if they
were the soldiers of a long and fearsome occupation, where civilian acquiescence to the power they wielded was a tired and tiresome fait accompli.

Her pickings were slim when days later these same soldiers returned in clumps and stragglers, burned and bruised and mutilated, glazed of eye and silent, staring at the road before their feet.

Fresh soldiers came from Saga, northern Hizen and Kumamoto, and Man's travel fund grew. The sojourns grew briefer and more frantic, as the soldiers familiar with rumors of the conflict grew free with their money.

After one desperate and impotent moment, one soldier pressed a bundle into Man's hands. "Take it all," he said. He laughed shrilly. "I am silver-polishing. Understand?" He sighed, straightened his robes and disappeared. Inside the small bag he'd given her was a brush, inkstone and inksticks, and far too much money.

Soon into the new year Nagasaki streets began to fill up with the wounded. Man wandered the docks: sailors still had libido: Shiro's farmers had only fishing junks to go to war. She found a man, with a bandaged, sharply tapering stump between his elbow and where his left hand should have been, lying against a stack of shoyu barrels and staring palefaced out at Nagasaki harbor. She stood over him until the man said, "Sit, or leave me. But do not loom."

Man knelt, and in silence the soldier and the prostitute watched the sea. Nagasaki harbor is sheltered on three sides by steeply canted mountains. The harbor itself is renowned for its calm and safety. Nearby, the waters quietly tapped at the unfinished foundations of Deshima like patient fingertips on a table.

Man reached into her robe and produced the bag, brush, inkstone and stick. She ground a little of the ink into a rusty puddle on the dock, and then, on the white cane of the barrel beside the soldier, began to paint a face. The soldier watched, eyes glazed. Man tapped her lips with the brush. Mute. The face took shape. The soldier realized.

"The hungry white demon."

Man nodded.

"They are insane. The women fight. They throw stones. The children fight."

Man nodded.

"They have nothing to lose. If they die this way they live forever." Man laid her hand on his lap, and he reached and clutched it, pulling it into his robe. "Nabeshima and Kuroda have them besieged in Harajo castle. The land around is burned to its bones. There is no food, so now we wait and let winter finish them on this earth."

Man nodded and smiled at the amputee, her hand moving in his lap.

"But the baron is bringing the Dutch and their cannon from Hirado, to shell them from the water. Those cowardly money-grubbers, hairy barbarians who bicker with the *bateren* over scraps. Base, craven men, now they will bomb the Christians just to keep their trade alive. Oh!"

The sharpened end of the paintbrush slid into the man's groin, and in his semi-aroused and weakened state he bled quietly to death in minutes, staring blindly into Man's maw and gently tapping at her knee with his narrow stump, as if to say, "Excuse me, excuse me."

On February 23rd, the Dutchman Koeckebacker, the chief factor at Hirado, arrived in Nagasaki harbor in the *de Rijp* (the "Hoarfrost"), of twenty guns. There Man watched four Dutchmen from the township assist in loading the ship with extra powder and shot, then board and depart. One, of course, was the red-bearded, burly de Wilde.

Koeckebacker would later write in the Hirado *dagregister,* "The houses are merely made of straw and matting, the parapets of the lower works of defense being made of clay and the uppermost fortress being surrounded by a good high wall, built with heavy stones. . . . It was evident that it was not much use to fire guns from the batteries of the Imperial army, nor from our batteries."

Nevertheless, the *de Rijp* lobbed 426 Dutch shot into Harajo. On March 12th, they were thanked, and withdrew, silently sailing straight back to Hirado, taking de Wilde with them. On April 4th, 3,000 of Shiro's men fell on the camps of Nabeshima, Kuroda and Terazawa, in search of ammunition and food. They found nothing. 100,000 Shogunate troops surrounded Harajo, and on April 12th the castle finally fell. 37,000 emaciated men, women and children were massacred incontinently. Only 105 prisoners were taken. Archaeologists have probed the ground around the castle, and found a solid sedimentary layer, ten to twenty inches deep, of bone, bullets and burned earth. Shiro's head was spiked outside Harajo for five or six days, but there was nothing and no one left to witness and be warned. Shiro's pretty head was thus removed to Nagasaki and gibbeted in front of the Jesuit college near the gates of Deshima. Soon after, and for four more years, Man slips from our view.

"Thus, a vein of bone and bullets and burned earth, and texts, are what I might say are two sides of the coin of history. Yes, I am familiar with your brother's work. In a sense we are fairly bitter rivals, in academe."

"Yes," said Meredith. "I do see."

"For how we differ is in the difference between *simulation*, and *emulation*. Do you know this difference?"

"..."

"The note Mr. Edwards' last work finished on was that of all historical knowledge is simulation. That is, as imitation or counterfeit, a resembling without authenticity, a pretense. This is familiar, but the extent and the passion with which this thesis was argued was his, perhaps, most singular attribute. His voice, for one so young, was, if naive, refreshingly vital, and informed."

"You...respect him?"

"Of course. But as to where we differ. Mr. Edwards, I think, could never live with the fact that historical knowledge, all texts, approach the status of *emulation*. They *equal* or *excel* what they once may have referred to. They imitate and rival so zealously that they replace. Let me give you the example I have referred to, *Samurai Sho-down IV.*"

"You're giving me an interpretation of this Japanese skymail."

Hayakawa lifted open his laptop and touched the spacebar. He turned the computer to Meredith. The opening titles appeared: *NEO-GEO, Max 330 Mega, Pro-Gear spec, SNK.*

"In terms of the play, your brother is a little like Malvolio. 'Dost thou think, because thou art virtuous, there shall be no more cakes and ale?' Theory, to some people, is cakes and ale. And what Mr. Edwards does not realize or will not countenance is that there might be no moral condemnation for a man who lives on cakes and ale."

"Cakes and ale are cakes and ale. The metaphor's a little loaded, or biased, to say the least."

"Yes, yes. This is the game *Samurai Sho-down IV: Amakusa's Revenge.* Or, *Amakusa Kourin*, in the Japanese, meaning 'ascendancy,' or 'advent.' A little like 'second coming.' Amakusa Shiro appears in this game both as the final villain to be destroyed at Harajo castle, on a specifically mentioned Shimabara peninsula—Harajo completely surrounded by dead, burned wasteland—an ultimate villain who is an evil effeminate wizard filled with passion and malice and superpowers, but also he appears as a character, an actor in the drama who, if play goes well, *may battle himself* at the final level."

"Oh."

Hayakawa tapped at the keyboard, and the credits meter climbed. Meredith watched the man, how elevated he had become.

"Occasionally throughout the game, Amakusa Shiro—as the final villain—will descend upon a mid-level bout and cast a spell where characters' damage to one another is multiplied. This, paradoxically, can happen when Amakusa himself—the character—is playing. Thus he may haunt himself, causing heightened damage to both him and those he competes against. But the key metaphor is here: this game appeared in the cabinet version in popular arcades in 1996, and has now been retired. But now, in an amazing democratization, legions of young have conspired to create software that emulates the hardware of those great companies' machines on personal computers, and will play the disc images of the games that were software to those machines. This is called emulation, and right now the most notorious is MAME: the Multi-Arcade Machine Emulator. Both emulators and disc images are free on the net, to those who will find them. The writers ask their students merely to donate sums to charity. The new history is disseminated in color; interactive, simplified and bloodless. Hardware becomes software. The simulation becomes emulation; the imperfect but extant copy eclipses the earnest simulation that imagines some missing reality. In the game Amakusa Shiro is a spirit, a vital personalized force whom the player can occupy and learn, or fight cleverly against. *In Amakusa*, he is merely the lonely statue of a boy pointing to a sky crowded with lies."

"Which is the one my brother believes in."

"My idea is he believes in the second one."

"It wasn't a question."

"This is the defining metaphor: all we can hope for, in a sick, self-conscious age, in the way of something most democratic, accessible and least problematically authentic, is perfectly executed effigy, and emulation. Thus, you see, this poetry is now anonymous."

"But you yourself, you've shown me you know things that should not be forgotten."

"There are parallels and little intersection, in my experience of knowledge. History is a game of cards, an intellectual exercise. Here was the source of the differences in our work."

Meredith stared at him, making a gigantic effort not to speak. Did he really and truly not know about Catherine?

Finally, she said, "So you can play these games now, on your laptop, sitting at your desk, with unlimited credits. You can finish a game in one session, I bet. Just sit there pumping in money with a key on your keyboard.

Do you remember the tough Maori kids with the cigarette lighters up their sleeves, rubbing them across the buttons to make their Olympians run faster? And how they rubbed holes in their sweatshirts and hooked their thumbs through, to pull their sleeves over their hands? The white kids lost to them because they didn't smoke. Do you remember things like that? When you're in here minus anyone with you and what you might come to know of them?"

"I am saying that even this, your passion, is a nostalgia of sorts; and that your memory, perhaps is strong and passionate, but it is still a posture adopted toward the absent, just a one of sadness, and pride, and a kind of resentment of those prepared to discard the pretense."

"What about bone and bullets and burned earth?"

"No more or less an archaeological text, to be wielded by politicians, than mass graves will be in, say, Serbia, for instance. No real use, anymore, in themselves. The archaeologists' writings *themselves,* of course, the *words* 'bullets' and 'burned earth,' and the ways they are deployed, are an entirely different matter."

"What would you make of, say, the rape of Nanking?"

"An immense exercise in comparative historiographies. A textual disaster area."

"You're not human."

"I am thoroughly, contemporarily human."

Thus in late, late 1640, the *de Nuk* slunk into a Nagasaki harbor much changed. Peter Trippelvitz, then a VOC officer and captain of the ship, stood beside Colin Edwards, at the wheel of the sturdy Dutch merchantman. As they watched the Japanese guard boats issuing in throngs from the docks, the Dutchman noticed a large book bound in plain calf upon the wheelstand.

"You had best cast your Gospels overboard, sir," said Trippelvitz in glum English. "They may cost you your head."

"They will have much a do to chop off my head for *that,*" said Edwards, nodding without looking at the book. "It is Mr. William Shakespeare's Comedies, Histories and Tragedies and cost me one pound. There is the one only available text of his *Twelfth Night,* my favorite play. I shall have much a do to hold my hands that I would not cut off one or two of their heads if they would deny me of *that.*"

Though justifiably wary, Trippelvitz might have been considerably more so had he known of recent events—though how, possibly? The *de Nuk* had been at sea when the post-Shimabara Edict forbidding any subject of the Spanish king to set foot in Japan was issued and, this time, strictly enforced. The *de Nuk* had been at sea near the Moluccas when the Macaoese ship, carrying four envoys, the four most respected Portuguese in the colony, had arrived in this same harbor four or five months ago in an attempt to placate the Japanese, convince them of absolutely zero Portuguese involvement with Shiro and the farmers, and that their trade (on which the survival of Macao depended) was cleanly extricable from their religion. The *de Nuk* had been at sea when the Macao ship was stripped of rudders and sail, guns and ammunition, her crew taken ashore and imprisoned on Deshima while contact was made with Edo. The *de Nuk* had been at sea when Edo's verdict was returned in record time, and sixty-one men were summarily executed on Martyr's Mount, their ship burned and just thirteen able seamen left to carry the news back whence they came. "Let them think no more of us; just as if we were no longer in the world," read the message of the Governor of Nagasaki. The *de Nuk* had been innocently at sea when Hirado *operhoofd* François Caron made the offer of a Dutch ship to get these thirteen survivors home, an offer smartly rejected by the proud and traumatized Catholics, who made their way back to Macao, with the news that there was serious business meant, in little more than a ridiculous dinghy.

So Trippelvitz, Wiersema, *doctoor* Baars, de Graaf, Maassen, van den Berg and Assenberg, Schermer Voest, Waagmeester and de Groot, and Colin Edwards, along with twelve other Dutchmen and thirty East Indian and African slaves, had much to come to terms with in the following months. Managing to convince the authorities of their inarguable, hard-fought-for (and fervently lukewarm Protestant) Dutchness, and after humiliating, bruising searches, they were shepherded up the coast to the Dutch factory at Hirado, where the capable Caron took them in and counseled a very low Dutch profile for the months to come. It set the tone for the whole tour of duty of the Hollanders of Mejima: surrounded by a mountain of spices, sugar, pilchards, beef and pork, pickled fruits, coconuts, treacle, liquorice and dried sea bream, the Dutch waited quietly in paranoia and sickly tension for what would become of their and their United Provinces' livelihood, and, not least, their lives.

In May of forty-one the fearsome ex-Inquisitor Inoue Chikugo, now an Edo minister, arrived in Hirado with a military retinue, clandestinely intent on inciting an incident to precipitate the flicking off of these last clinging foreigners. Caron's policy of appeasement and diplomacy rankled with the prouder Dutch—especially one fierce de Wilde—but few knew how close they came to massacre. Inoue found but one cause for indignation: dates inscribed on the eaves of a new Dutch warehouse after the method of the Christian calendar. Caron immediately ordered the building destroyed and catastrophe was held at a twisted arm's length. As a compromise sent down from a conflicted Edo cabinet, the Dutch were ordered to betake themselves, their ships and merchandise down to Nagasaki, and the Hirado factory—a Dutch appanage for thirty-two years—was to be closed forever.

The ships left fully loaded; the bewildered *de Nuk* crew, fresh off the boat, got right back on (de Groot grown yet more portly from his last twelve sedentary months of travel, and a shipboard diet consisting almost solely of rock-hard radically aged Edam, crumbly old North Holland, pickled mangoes and strong Dutch gin; his bookkeeping and his East Indian slave, Alan, both beginning to suffer from the rages of his incipient but metastasizing syphilis, which was not least of his reasons for getting far from his wife back in Gouda, and was, of course, his little secret).

May 21st: the Dutch get a shock: Nagasaki, a far more natural and sheltered harbor than Hirado, had at first seemed a very tempting compromise. They were not to know they would no longer set foot on Izanagi's spear-dripped land, but on land decanted therefrom: the ships were temporarily berthed and unloaded of all the *matériel* they carried on the northwest side of the Deshima fan, studiously designed with a lowered platform for lading. Hundreds of officious Japanese officials and mediocre interpreters, backed up by scarred Shogunate troops, made the situation and their future in Japan quite clear: artificial islands, on pain of death, were it.

After four days of reluctant settling-in, a special Shogun emissary clad in purple finery, backed up with apparatchiks, interpreters and a squad of elite troops in intimidatingly rich garb, arrived at the Deshima guardhouse. Maximiliaen Le Maire, successor to Caron as *operhoofd,* protested to no avail. Ten members of the crew of *de Nuk,* plus Colin Edwards, Niels de Wilde and ten slaves demanded by Trippelvitz, were sequestered along with the cargo of their ship, stores and, to Le Maire's disgust, the pick of the Hirado warehouse goods. The men were loaded, baffled, onto the heavily laden *de Nuk,* and set sail outnumbered ten-to-one by two-sworded soldiers, in the midst of a flotilla of heavily armed Imperial junks, round the cape of Kagoshima and up into the Seto Sea.

Within a week these special men were again unloading their threemaster, rocking at its moorings in the shifting tides, on the northwest corner of Iemitsu's eye: Mejima. The island was waiting; already equipped with houses, sheds and warehouses faithfully designed—Christian dates aside—after the fashion of the sturdy buildings back in Hirado. Filip van den Berg, at the end of his tether (and meaning something else entirely), shouted out in Japanese to the interpreters and inquisitive Sakaide villagers gathered across the water to watch the spectacle of the disembarking Dutch, "I have no sense of humor!"

Laughter carried back to him. Japan, and their fate, was sealed.

"An interesting aside, Miss Edwards. In these years I am speaking of, Man's disappearance, 1638 to 1641, we see the foundations laid too of the *kakure kirishitan.* They are the secret Christians of Kyushu and Shikoku. Despite the pogroms, many persisted in their religion. They disguised their Madonnas as Kannon, holding their sacred infant in six of her eight arms. They recited their own coded catechisms in secret meetings and buried their martyred in graves disguised as Shinto shrines. Over the years of isolation and with no religious guidance their religion changed into an entirely new system, comprising an orthodox Roman Catholicism blended with Pure Land Cult Buddhism, obscure folk medicine and local earth cult. It was a blend that would have had the practitioners well burned as heretics in both Japan and Spain if discovered. Witches, magic mushrooms, guided visions, possession by demons, and the sacrifice of animals and humans in flesh and effigy were embraced. Some of the extraordinary abilities assigned to Amakusa Shiro are believed to have derived from the *kakure.* During this time it is believed Man was in Shikoku, and it is theoretically possible she is fashionably connected to the Shikoku entity *Fukumokizu,* or Mouthwound; a kind of *bakemono,* a bizarre ghost or earth apparition. In Shikoku, children still think you, the foreigner, is *bakemono. Fukumokizu* means "She Who Holds Wounds in Her Mouth," or "She Who Holds Wounds in Her Embrace"—she was a patron witch of those who mutilate themselves. Although of course, there may be some confusion here with Fuku, you remember, the elder sister of Shiro and Man, of whom nothing is known. But who can tell?"

"I don't think you mean 'fashionably,' really."

"And in the years of her disappearance, as we may refer from the poem, Man could well have realized that the Dutch foreigner de Wilde's first gift, the unicorn's horn, which the Japanese people believed gave powers of healing, fortitude and great memory, was, in fact, not any such a thing. De Wilde had given her the long, spirally twisted tooth-tusk of a narwhal, *Monodon monoceros*, a kind of small Arctic whale. Narwhal, accidentally, Miss Edwards, is Old Norse for 'corpse whale.' This false product was a common Dutch import to Japan. Traces of this seminal lie remain in modern kanji. This character—*tsuno*—means 'horn.' As a modifier it means 'corner,' 'section,' 'point' or, as many interpreters find a strange entry in their dictionaries, it also means 'narwhal.' When modifying the character for animal, beast or brute—*kemono*—the kanji together mean 'unicorn.' *Ikkakuju*. Beast, and horn, beast and point, or beast and banal narwhal, was Man's unicorn.

"But in the kanji for corner or point remains the trace of that Dutch falsehood like a folk tale or a faded tattoo. There are two excerpts here, from a *No* play named *Rei*, or *The Actors*, in English. It is an early Tokugawa play, in an old-fashioned way bridging the Zeami and Kan'ami traditions, allowing, within the one diegesis, both gods and mortals to cross between the real and spirit worlds, or, this and the next. The *ato shite*, or protagonist, relates to the *mae shite*, or deuteragonist, the story of a terrible battle, a peasant uprising. Don't leap to a conclusion, though. There is no specific mention of Shimabara. The death of the leader of the uprising is the point of flux between the natural and supernatural worlds; the second part of the drama where the *ato shite* reveals his true identity as the hero of his own story, the leader, and dances madly, and the *mae shite*, in order to pacify or placate the ghost of the tortured protagonist, recites scriptures which will bring about his rest. These excerpts are recited by the chorus in this short play, of which the text is hopelessly corrupt, and which has no known author."

He turned a page around on the table.

"I'm sorry for taking so much time with this background. Here is what you have asked. These are seeming appropriate kanji for your hiragana, my romaji, and a rough English translation. The first excerpt."

作者未詳
我我は、
像似通う中
諸氏。そういった
べし消え残る。
古雨脚洗眼。

Sakushamisho
Warewarewa,
kata nikayou naka
shoshi. souitta
beshi kienokoru.
koameoshi sengan.

Anonymous
"We are like statues among them."
As statues you shall remain,
An old rain washing your eyes.

"The second except reads:"

茨に眼島
蘭人がらんと以降
兜の袖は
紺碧死彫れい吸
瀬戸内海濯ぐ

Man ni Mejima
Ranjin garanto iko.
Kyonosode wa
Konbeki shiboreisu
Seto naikai susugu.

Man stands on Mejima / Thorns cover Mejima,
Deserted by the Hollanders hereafter.
The assassin's sleeves are azure
And patterned with ghosts; they smell of death.
Rinse them clean in the Seto Sea.

"Disappointed? But be especially interested in this first kanji of this second excerpt of *Rei!* Typically we would use the reading '*ibara*' here. However, for the sake of the dynamic rhythm required, to ensure a total of five morae, or syllabic sounds, the alternative reading is '*man.*' Now you see how this is all very fragile. Because without this consideration of rhythm, there is no Man. Only thorns, covering this tentative island, mentioned obscurely in this corrupt text. You see? For here, in *Rei,* is the second to last extant literal mention of the Mejima island of the Seto Sea in Japanese history, and we are subject to an argument that there is no such story of Man, and that the story of the Hollanders of Mejima was a fantasy of revengeful Japanese thoughts against the idle southern barbarians, or *Namban,* as they were known. The theory is that this play, which is extant only in pieces, was merely a fantasy, a fiction that indulged a desire in a strict era for a politically correct expression of anger, safely."

"Now, in the last key, we see the famous poet of Kyushu, Hakushu Kitahara, who died during the Great Pacific War in 1942, make one small mention in his first collection of poems, *Jashumon Hikyoku,* or 'Secret Music of the Heresy,' in 1909, two hundred and sixty years later. '*Namban no santo mejima o hata araki chinta no sake o,*' he writes. He is perhaps leaving us this tiny clue to something of the island he has discovered in his research of the period, the smallest of concessions in historical and textual guerilla war. Or there is merely the legitimate use of *san to mejima* as 'striped suits.' Is there or was there a Mejima? The documentary evidence is not extant, and only folk tales survive. *Ibara,* or *Man.* Thorn, or girl. Shall she be erased? As to the mention of the '*shiboreisu,*' in the second excerpt, it is comprised of the kanji for '*shi,*' which means, of course, death; '*bo,*' which means carving, or engraving; '*rei,*' which I have left as hiragana and so is not specific, but could mean either actor, or ghost; and finally, '*su,*' which here I have taken to meaning inhale or imbibe. I have thought perhaps it is a borrowing from the Hebrew, into Japanese, 'shibboleth'; '*shiboreisu.*' You see? Another clue! The horn of the unicorn, or a tooth of a corpse whale. Thorn, or girlchild. Definition or revelation. You can choose! You can always choose!"

Hayakawa suddenly lunged out over the desk, scattering papers, slamming his hand on the table. Meredith jumped back in her chair.

"What? Are you alright?"

"I'm sorry. I thought I saw a spider," said Hayakawa, sitting back.

"Kapot!" cried de Groot, too loudly in the dressing room.

"It's gin o'clock, I think," said Koenraad de Graaf. "And this play had better be finished by wench o'clock, or it shall be missing a principal, I'll tell you."

"Kapot," hissed de Groot again, viciously. "This play, this work, our beloved *operhoofd,* this pathetic island, this whole country and everyone in it. Pah!" He spat and let out a kind of shudder.

Sander Waagmeester passed by, smiling benignly, out of costume.

De Groot swore yet again.

"Who's he again?" murmured a mild and disinterested de Graaf.

"Uh! The nonentity plays a nonentity. He is *Fabian,* of course."

Trippelvitz and Colin Edwards strolled out of the chill twilight and into the giant double doors of the warehouse, emptied at the northern end to form a rudimentary stage.

"And here he comes again now. Gah! The so-called director and his absurd star. Blah!"

"Relax, Joost," said de Graaf. "Concentrate on dinner."

A ripple of placidity and calm ran down de Groot from eyes to jowls to belly to fists to feet. He sat down on a crate of soap, wax and lead pencils.

"Dinner. Yes."

"Gin o'clock." De Graaf sighed lasciviously. "Five past the hour now, I'd say."

Six months had passed for the Hollanders of Mejima, six months in complete isolation. To be sure there were Japanese in plenty, allocated to the island, hired out of Sakaide and paid out of Dutch pockets: cooks, scribes, messengers, servants, attendants, subordinate officials, platoons of interpreters useless as furniture. But in six months there had been no communication between Mejima *operhoofd* Trippelvitz and Deshima *operhoofd* Le Maire, or his successor in November, Jan van Elseracq, and it was the latter who came to make the prestigious and monotony-breaking trip to

Edo to flatter the Shogun, and it was Trippelvitz who knew it, resented it, and nursed his jealousy like a sick cat as only the fatalistic, cabin-fevered and brutally bored know how.

The Mejima Dutch had learned how to wait. The eleven men and their English pilot and their brand new warehouses bulging with goods squatted on Iemitsu's eye (could it be they were too close to be seen?) and amused themselves as best they could, policed as they were to Rhadamanthine extents by the paranoid and superstitious Shikoku locals. They waited for the magical day when the first VOC ship would silently sidle up to the isle, full of fresh new blood and freshly aged cheese, word of Europe, word of home, letters from family, work to do. Trippelvitz maintained the *dagregister* with the same terse daily entries, that multiplied down the pages until they formed a kind of optical illusion, wherein a picture of some kind might be seen—isn't it always a sailing ship?—were it to be stared upon for long enough. This too, was not to be.

"Nothing of note occurred."

Filip van den Berg lost countless games of cards and high-stakes draughts, and racked up enormous IOUs to every Dutchman on the island. Niels de Wilde built fantastically intricate and tsunami-proof four-poster beds for every Dutchman on the island, and medical assistant Koenraad de Graaf spent most of his days in his, accompanied by local prostitutes (disappointingly for de Graaf, only one at a time, but a fresh girl every three days, just as the law allowed).

On the gate of the Mejima guardhouse, mounted over the tear duct that led to the eye:

Whores only, but no other women shall be suffer'd to go in.

Bibles and religious literature, let alone observing a Sabbath, were strictly outlawed and the prohibition rigorously enforced. Left to the whimsy and wont of each man's own mind and the inertias of flimsy pre-occupation, on a petty yet cozy decanting from a godless archipelago, all meant for a certain lapse in Calvinist zeal.

Second-in-command Wiersema and *Doctoor* Jacob Baars spent three months compiling exhaustive botanical studies of Mejima grasses. They began together an intricately subdivided herb garden just outside the kitchen's windows, had a brief, passionate affair, and then a violent falling-out over the proportions allocated to chives and mint. In the three months following, up until the rehearsals for the Christmas Day production of *Twelfth Night*—director: Colin Edwards—they were yet to

exchange a word. Wiersema, tortured by religiosexual confusion and conflicted feelings for his wife back home, spent his time gambling with the
schrijvers Assenberg and "The Other" Schermer Voest, and briefly (and
lucratively on paper at least) with shambling young van den Berg. Archi-
tectural sketches and amateur paintings enjoyed a brief renaissance—*ban-
ketje, ontbijtje, fruytje* and *conversatie;* banquet, breakfast, fruit and
conversation paintings, all fashionable at the time—were begun and abandoned by all and sundry after bickering over limited paints led to sched-
ules and rosters and general frustration, and finally common woe
over—of all things—the absence of a decent cobalt blue sullied altogether
the fun. The Dutchmen waited for ships. There was a short-lived craze
for island tennis, with the requisite hurriedly seeded tournament and
feverish competition; this, too, faded away as ball after ball floated rapidly
away on the shifting inland sea. Sander Waagmeester's unflappable good-
will got everyone down. Vicious jokes about his sideburns circulated,
were expanded upon indecently, died and were buried. Conversation
began at first to be prefaced, then replaced, by sighs. Off Yokohama back
in June amidst a flotsam of storm-wrecked ship, arrayed in the shape of
an ankh on the waves, the Shogun's emissary's purple robes dipped and
jerked as Pacific fish nipped on his flesh. The Dutchmen waited for ships;
anybody's would do. Joost de Groot's rages grew more intense; Alan
roamed the island bruised and dazed, and the interpreters steered clear.
Matthiu Maassen began to sleepwalk, and would wake late at night wandering the overstocked warehouses, his fingers trailing over the crates of
leather, eyeglasses and ivory. A vegetarian, he would find bones in his
pockets, and stains on his shirts. He dreamed of waking in bed with
William of Orange, who turned to him with a look Maassen knew he
could only describe—if ever he would, which he wouldn't, not ever—as
"carnal satisfaction." Uncanny warts grew on his hands, and he began to
avoid food altogether. Colin Edwards meanwhile read and read, and penciled extensive pseudo-directorial marginalia around and about his
revered First Folio. *Doctoor* Baars developed an infected ingrown toenail
and performed a minor amputation sans anaesthetic out of sheer, brutal-
izing boredom, and fainted over his four-toed foot. Typical behavior of
the man in prison; typical too was that no one on the island made comment on his limp. Silence was like humidity; 90% and rising. Everyone
smoked incessantly. And still the ships did not come.

"Nothing of note occurred."

Until, that is, Colin Edwards proposed a Christmas party: gifts, dinner, drinks and a full and complete production of his favorite play, with—the consanguinity was delightful—the eleven Dutchmen for the eleven principals: Viola, Sebastian, Antonio, Orsino, Olivia, Sir Toby Belch (who else should play him but Joost de Groot?), Sir Andrew Aguecheek, Maria, Fabian, Malvolio and Feste. And various interpreters, servants and slaves were in no short supply for officers, sailors, musicians, lords and attendants. A good director is a dictator, and one who plans ahead; Edwards approached each man separately with a proposed part, a laboriously transcribed script with a small but helpful commentary in Dutch, and a spoonful of sugar to help the medicine go down.

The promise of a party to end all parties.

The locals were notified and extra cooks brought in. Edwards planned the evening with his actors in mind—that drunkenness might not perturb the production the play would precede Christmas dinner. Part of Warehouse No. 2 was cleared and the great double doors—closed and locked for six whole months—were opened to face the sea. Japanese tailors were put to work on costumes and curtains and the stores were looted for props. Rehearsals went on until it became clear to all that scripts must needs be carried. Edwards took the news with stoic and admirable aplomb. The Dutch began to learn, slowly and gradually, but with increasing vigor, to submerge their identities in their parts. A new calm and unspoken camaraderie began to settle over the tiny island. De Wilde spent many spare hours building rugged Protestant pews for their audience. "Nothing of note occurred," read the *dagregister*. The feast would be a combination of Dutch and Japanese cuisine, it was decided: bread—white *herenbrood*—was baked in great quantities, and cheese for trade unwrapped. Radish, cabbage, mushrooms and eggplant, huge live octopus, crab, *meibaru*, sea bass and herring were brought on from Sakaide. Crates of gin and barrels of sake were set aside—Trippelvitz studiously neglecting to record their requisition. Assistants and servants were trained as waiters and fitted out with suits. Some of the eleven Dutch were even seen poking and peering in the dim of the cluttered warehouses, perhaps on the hunt for gifts.

Christmas Day, 1641, dawned chill and clear, and for the entire morning not a soul was to be seen wandering the island, attending to chores, watering the gardens or taking up a hammock or veranda chair for a postprandial pipe. But there was livid activity in every Dutchman's bedroom. Voices carried from the windows, reciting the caramel English lines in softened yet imperative guttural Dutch tones. Pacing, tapping and rapid rocking of chairs. For the first time in six months no slightly bedraggled or red-faced geisha made her way from de Graaf's to the guardhouse. Lunch was taken in isolation, then finally around half past three in the afternoon the principals emerged and made their way to the dressing room.

The great tension there was alleviated by much joshing and jostling and verbal jousting, flicking of towels and swapping of insults in Shake-spearean patois. Though Wiersema and Baars were in the same curtained-off corner of warehouse, they managed, even without eye contact, to remain civil enough to pass makeup. Only big Joost de Groot kept himself to himself, the syphilitic bookkeeper squatting in the corner on his over-sized hams, glaring out seemingly right through his bushy eyebrows. The imperturbable Koenraad de Graaf took up next to him, and parried any bitter thrust with apathy and epigrams of languid desire. Yet even his foot tapped on the stone.

Outside the twilight swooned from cyan to violet to indigo in almost audible tones. De Wilde's pews, lined impeccably before the makeshift stage—just one freestone block above the grass—could have catered to an audience of one hundred. But at half past five with only half an hour before curtain, who should be there in the stalls?

Alan, two Jakarta slaves, a "Swart," or negro, purchased in Formosa, and six Japanese prostitutes.

But the show must go on.

The gaslamps about the warehouse doors were ignited and Edwards trem-bled in the wings. De Wilde's curtain rails held fast and the great drapes—sewn from finest Ming crimson silk—drew languorously back to reveal one *operhoofd* Trippelvitz as Orsino, with a script in his lap, reclined on a de Wildean chaise longue. The amateur tinkle of an imported harpsichord subsided.

"If music be the food of love . . ."—a sigh of depthless drugged ennui—"*play on.*"

It was a triumph.

How had Edwards known Trippelvitz's earnestness and utter igno-rance of satire would lend Orsino's egoism such a pathetic and affecting air? The naiveté was consummate, the heartfelt sigh supreme. A forty-five-year-old Japanese interpreter stammered his way through Valentine with appropriate—and barely acted—nervous deference.

Scene two: the baffled, haunted Maassen black-eyed with insomnia as a damaged, saddened, shipwrecked Viola lent a touch of mad Ophelia as he gestured to the Seto Sea just twenty feet away and whispered hoarsely, "What country, friends, is this?"

The resolution to dress up as his drowned twin brother and make a go of it in this strange land was met with an enthusiastic kind of consternation, coached into the Captain—a young fisherman named Tatsuya—by Mr. Edwards.

Next up: tension in director and principals high alike, the wildcard de Groot staggered on as Sir Toby. The first sounds from his twisted mouth: "Gah! What a plague means my niece to take the death of her brother thus? I'm sure care's an enemy to life." In the audience Alan flinched but couldn't tear his eyes away. De Groot rampaged and bellowed with venom and wit and the occasional belch, red-faced, purple-jowled, taking every inch of vicious delight in the cantankerous debauchee. Collective sighs in the wings were quickly followed by muted gasps, traded glances, then pure self-forgotten audiential rapture. Enter the asinine Assenberg as Sir Andrew Aguecheek. He tripped leaving the wings and fairly rolled onto stage. The prostitutes giggled behind raised hands (all but one). His honest bafflement at the words of the script and the witticisms made at his expense seemed to capture Andrew in amber as some international archetype abroad. Edwards drew furious notes in the margin. Young Filip van den Berg and Willem "The Other" Schermer Voest reprised their gambling tête-à-têtes with the tables subtly turned. Through the companionable fooling, a certain odd and appropriate knowingness surfaced in Filip's Feste, and Schermer Voest as Maria began to seem like the man in debt.

Enter limping *Doctoor* Jacob Baars as Olivia, wearing the mourning for her dead brother on his mutilated foot like a too-tight shoe, and van den Berg gently quizzes him. (Ever alert to anti-catholic spies and the threat of accidental martyrdom, Edwards had made a deletion in scene V, and "question" stands in for Feste's "catechize.")

And then a fraught moment: enter Willem Wiersema as Malvolio, to quarrel with his briefly beloved, Baars—never has Olivia's "O you are sick of self-love, Malvolio, and taste with a distempered appetite" held such compressed venom, regret, cold excommunication, and never has it been received with such beautifully petty heartsickness, tagged as hatred and hurled sidelong at the Fool. Next scene: Baars and Maassen, in a baffling hall of gender mirrors, wear their respective ages and regrets with flair; Matthiu's haunted, pale face briefly lighting up in the affected vital warmth of Viola's wit.

Enter the solid de Wilde as Antonio, trading gruff pledges for sad tales with libertine de Graaf as Sebastian. The bodyguard aspect of Antonio taking precedence over the homoerotic edge, of course, but de Graaf's mournful self-effacement coupled with an irrepressible rakish leer left the women in the audience (six minus one—she seems to sneer) in a smiling silence that spoke more than giggles.

Edwards in the wings took notes.

Toby de Groot, Andrew Assenberg and Feste van den Berg drink and sing as if their days are either numbered or innumerable. Malvolio Wiersema's plaintive face seems to wear their disgrace as private, personal pain. Maria Schermer Voest in ridiculous false breasts fills their cups then possesses the drunkards of a plan to cut Wiersema down to size. The audience, utterly baffled, watch as their masters caper and huddle, declaim and sing and fall about, struggling to reconcile this tradition with the somewhat more restrained and muted *No*.

And thus Wiersema strolls the box-tree, fantasizing aloud about Baars. De Groot's curses and swears as he eavesdrops leave Alan and the servants sweating in the chill Christmas evening. Assenberg falls over three times. Wiersema takes the bait of the dropped letter. Baars, offstage, hides inside Olivia as he watches the second in command recite his lines from a script that in this scene and only this—as letter—serves as prop. And manages to hate him. Sander Waagmeester delivers Fabian fittingly boring and banal, then strolls off stage with no apparent change in demeanor.

The play gains pace as the moon rises and glitters in a widening line over the sea to the stage like a spotlight.

Olivia Baars delivers his lines of love to Maassen, examining the pretty young man's high sharp cheekbones as if he'd like to lick them. Wiersema capers cross-gartered and in yellow stockings like a lovesick fool. Some in the audience laugh carefully. Some stare at the grass. De Groot and Waagmeester watch on and pass comment as Maassen and Andrew Assenberg attempt to start their duel, but big de Wilde, mistaking Maassen for de Graaf, steps in. Enraged, de Groot growls and shouts and wades in too.

Alan in the audience nods feelingly. Meanwhile de Graaf and the misled Baars agree to get married.

De Wilde, detained by Trippelvitz's soldiers, asks Maassen for loaned money back, still thinking him de Graaf. Maassen palely knows not whereof he speaks, but suspects perhaps Sebastian lives. De Groot goes after him and encounters Sebastian de Graaf, and picks a convincing fight. Filip van den Berg intones, "I would not be in some of your coats for two taels," and Edwards looks up sharply at the improv. One of the prostitutes rises from her pew and makes her way through the cooks and kitchen help now gathered at the back. She holds a small cloth bag with a drawstring in her gloved hand.

Baars dispenses more convincing love, to the more receptive de Graaf this time, and Wiersema summons up all his hurt and pain for a heart-breaking howling Malvolio, laid there in the hideous dark house. "Sayst thou that house is dark?" asks Feste van den Berg, dressed as a Buddhist *bonze*—all mention of the words "curate," "padre" and "parson" erased. "As hell, Sir Topas," Wiersema wails. "Why," says van den Berg, "it hath bay windows transparent as barricadoes, and the clerestories toward the south–north are as lustrous as ebony. And yet complainest thou of obstruction!" Wiersema cries, "I am not mad, Sir Topas. I say to you, this house is dark." Feste wags a chiding finger. "Madman thou errest. I say there is no darkness but ignorance, in which thou art more puzzled than the Egyptians in their fog." Wiersema whispers, broken, "I say this house is as dark as ignorance, though ignorance were as dark as hell."

Thinking of Olivia Baars' disfavor, the sport begins to sour for Toby de Groot. Final act: Trippelvitz sternly reprimands the notable saltwater pirate de Wilde in terms he'd never dare in life. Baars tells Trippelvitz where he stands romantically, in no ambiguous terms. *Operhoofd* T is appropriately and splutteringly angered. The complication rises to crisis level as those on stage surpass in number those in the audience. Baars thinks Maassen is in love with him. Captain Trippelvitz loves *Doctoor* Baars. Maassen loves Trippelvitz. Maassen is a man dressed as a woman dressed as a man, and is negotiating three names. De Groot viciously cuts the legs out from under the faithful Assenberg, his onetime prandial pal. De Graaf strides on stage and the rest fall about, for here are two Sebastians. High farce commences and is sustained. The girl from the audience emerges from the kitchens empty-handed and from the doorway watches the end of the play. De Graaf and Maassen rediscover each other, Trippelvitz, horny old toad, opts for Maassen with the merest foreshadowing, and Baars likewise de Graaf. Van den Berg chooses this moment to remind everyone of Wiersema, and the broken second in command makes his final appearance onstage.

The only true love affair ever on this little artificial eye-shaped island acts out its final moments in verse. The principals gathered, van den Berg intones, "And thus the whirligig of time brings in his revenges." The limping pragmatist Baars murmurs to tortured Wiersema, "Alas, poor fool, how have they baffled thee!" A fingertip touch to his stubbled tear-streaked cheek. Pious and guilt-ridden Wiersema, acting not at all, lets out a guttural cry masquerading as a suffocated snort of scorn; "I'll be revenged on the whole pack of you!" he says, more anguish than defiance, lets fall another tear, and turns away.

Colin Edwards in the wings shakes his head slowly and only a little shamefacedly, stunned at the genius of his casting.

Alone, center stage, van den Berg sings his foolish little song of good-bye. The curtain falls.

Over the darkened moonstruck Seto Sea the silence is almost complete; marred only by Alan, the only man in the nine-strong audience taught by Europeans to clap.

And so the sad coming-down after performance. The cold cream and the towels, the whispered congratulations, the cheroots and slowly packed pipes filling the dressing room with smoke, wafting over the tarpaulins and over the crates of goods. De Groot nodding curtly at the compliments, Trippelvitz dazed as a boy after his first wet dream. Costumes reverently folded like an amazing book closed slowly at its end. Exhaustion and adrenaline. Edwards moving slowly among the throng, murmuring sober endearments.

"Filip, o Filip, what can I say. The very model in motley."

"A minor triumph, *Doctoor* Baars."

"Matthiu, were I not already married to one far off, to be sure I would have much a do to forestall a rude and premature proposal."

"Tomas—the comic timing. A revelation."

"Mr. de Wilde, you were solid as your chaise longue."

"That slow burn of love was magnificently stoked, Mr. Schermer Voest."

"Sander; such restraint. I'm in awe."

"Koenraad. A dream, sir. A flaxen-haired dream in tights, you were."

And for Willem Wiersema's Malvolio, a tribute that naturally reserved a moment all its own. He sat at his mirror and wiped the tear-streaked makeup from his bristles, then rose, a broken, august, proud and anguished figure, and the dressing room broke out in spontaneous applause for their star. Wiersema's eyelids drooped, and he sketched a vague bow.

Baars stared.

"To dinner, sirs. Let us to dinner."

The men filed out of the warehouse in silence and made their way to the dining hall adjoining the kitchens. The Christmas banquet lay spread and waiting on the huge table. Alan, the Jakartans, the Formosan swart and five prostitutes lingered nervously in the background. Even de Graaf took no notice. In a great and immortal spirit of weary companionship, the men sat down to their mushroom and steaming blueish miso soup.

Silence reigns, but there are different versions of what happened next:

An obscure entry in the Deshima *dagregister*—the *Deshima dagregister*, that is—dated Christmas Day, 1641, on paper slightly differing in appearance and in slightly different handwriting and unsigned:

At last! Dec 25th, 1641, chill and clear. We all feel sure nothing will ever again be the same for us after this day. That we have learned much of something inexpressible in words. We all feel a new connection, to each other, and to our "hosts," and to our homeland, however tardy they may be. Tonight, tonight! Such excitement I have not felt since leaving home nigh on two years past. Tonight! I shall open, and I shall be there at the close. I shall lead them, and I shall be there in the wings when they need no leader. I am filled with immense confidence and thrilled anxiety. My stomach is acid and churns without cease. The question I cannot forestall asking myself, is the perennial amateur actor's: how does one be bored when one's mind is full of whirling fragments? How does one be piteously sad when one is thrilled—I say, at last, *thrilled*—so utterly? To the absolute core?

Boxing Day, 1641: the Deshima *dagregister*, among the invoices and memoirs, with no reference to the preceding purple prose, and in paper representing the bulk of the first hundred years of records, records: "Nothing of note occurred."

On the Japanese side of affairs, enigma reigns. Play aside, one resonant footnote in an Imperial councillor's diary has been linked in the most tentative of ways to a theory regarding the fate of the Mejima Dutchmen. Relating the story of a 1643 trial of a very young woman by Shikoku magistrates for an unspecified crime, the councillor, after suggesting the death penalty was more than appropriate and passion no mitigation of culpability for whatever it was she had allegedly done, suggests—in hindsight, correctly—that history would disperse the sordid events preceding the trial "like cut grass in the wind." His entry for the day concludes, somewhat elliptically, but with several pregnant ocular references,

> In actuality, it will be as if they had never been there. As if no proposals were made, no actions taken on no one's instigation, no vision had and thus no vision fulfilled. As if there were no buildings raised, and thus none to raze; as if once a door is closed, no conversation is overheard. The washed wound heals quickly. Thorns will indeed grow there, like scars on an eye, and with them folktales like blind spots in otherwise clear vision. But yet in time it will be as if there were no such fallacious stories of cries heard over the sea, of untouched meals, scattered clothes. The eye will heal, and compensate for what it has lost by extrapolation from what it retains. Or to put it another way, it will be as if the land takes back into his house an estranged cousin who has wandered far, doubting not his tale of a sleepless night, visions, insights and ghostly visitations, but in his present concern for his cousin's—and his own—future well-being, paying his tale no mind.
>
> To my mind it is perhaps a hard lesson, but the guilty are scraped from the chopping block of time to fester and mutate in the compost of myth and rumor and cautionary tale, to at last become the fetid, fecund mulch of history, from whither it is might that flowers and is recognized, not from whence it came, but for what it is.

Some in the superstitious Seto say that Trippelvitz saw his own death at a hot spring in Unzen—the screams, the smiling mouths and the steaming wooden ladles. That, leaving the main courses on the tables, he loaded the maddened men onto a raft hurriedly fashioned from warehouse doors and emptied barrels, piloted by Colin Edwards, freaking out, and in a scene reminiscent of *Le radeau de la Méduse* the twelve struck out on the midnight Seto in the moonlit dead of winter, each carrying his own personal mirror to keep a constant monitor of his identity. And that the flimsy craft did ride the tide moonward up the glittering spotlight of the moon's reflected glare into the heart of the black Naruto gyre and there was sucked into the heaving maelstrom to be spat out Hollanderless into the Pacific fifty fathoms below sea level, whereupon it rose like a sounding whale to burst from the surface and fly thirty feet in the air.

Another story runs that a fracas broke out after entrees were served, six months of tensions erupting, the Dutchmen suddenly turning on one another with their cutlery and in a fit of fevered barbarism lasting all through the night killing and consuming one another, the last left standing cleaning up and hurling himself into the forgiving and forgetting sea.

Another story runs that there never was a Mejima at all.

Nevertheless, it remains true that the Mejima *dagregister* eventually must have found its way to the other island of quarantined Dutchmen, and was subsumed into the mountain of state and corporate documentation there, its pages lifted and inserted into the Deshima *dagregister* at the appropriate dates, to create a near-seamless record (radiography and fiber analysis of the papers pending): "Nothing of note occurred" again and again in the flux of compressive and deciduous history: the two artificial islands must have been rolled into one, and casualties forgotten are casualties absorbed in the will to simplify and understand and thus wield, and in the diplomacy of a trade that consistently earned profits for the Dutch of more than fifty percent—indeed, in the calm decades that followed, VOC profits would skyrocket as high as seventy-five. In the early Meiji era, Deshima would be absorbed into the Nagasaki foreshore as the port, along with the nation, was expanded, modernized and prepped for major Western-style industry. In 1978 construction of the Seto–Ohashi bridge would begin, an immense structure that would island-hop in six discrete bridges from Honshu to Shikoku, ending a near-eternity of isolation for the island, and stretching five miles from Kurashiki—sister city to Christchurch, New Zealand—on Honshu, to Sakaide on Shikoku. Anchorages the size of carparks would be built, the foundations seventy-five yards deep and supported by roller-compacted concrete and slurry walls against the restless sea. Immense caissons would be towed by tugboat—six required against the tides—out into the sea, held in place by barges with GPS and auto-adjusting unidirectional propellers mounted on all four corners, then sunk down to the dredged and scoured granite floor, there to be filled with underwater concrete and form the foundations of the giant pillars of the bridges. In the first foundation on the foreshore of Sakaide, the first step across to far Kurashiki, engineers would discover a surprising amount of geologically incongruous freestone in a clam-shaped section three hundred feet wide. Surprising but hardly call for pause. It would be excavated, ground into metal for concrete and poured into the caissons of the next foundations of the next pillars of this, the most beautiful and the longest bridge, the Minami–Bisan Seto, of the eventual six of the awesome Seto–Ohashi. Thus, though in the texts it would be claimed with a vehemence the power of which most certainly lay in mere numbers that "nothing of note occurred," it is most certainly true that over just enough time the statement gains credence when "nothing of note" remains.

V

The Closing of the Embassies

Everyone
Christmas Day

The digital videotape shows the principals leave the mirror, one by one by one.

The first, a tall, black-suited man with a bald, scarred head steps from it, holding the hand of a blond woman in a silver gown with a sash and a split. They turn and back inside the kitchen door. Following them a young Japanese woman with hair cut short and ragged, tattoos on her upper arms, torn T-shirt and torn jeans seems to lead from the casement from behind a shirtless Indian boy, black-eyed. A coffeeskinned girl with curly hair, black-eyed too, holds the hand of an Asian boy, who holds in turn the hand of a slim, haggard European boy wearing military fatigues, who lets them lead him from the mirror and away where the others behind him went. A couple, next, who hold hands too; too slim, sick and beautiful, emerge from the mirror. And before them, a long- and dark-haired Eurasian girl steps out with her hand before her as if leaving the grasp of someone she loves, and the mirror image shimmers, seems to coalesce into a bronze and smiling face of a mask with something small and white at its forehead, like the head mirror of a surgeon.

But that is only ten.

There's a knock at the penthouse door.

But loud and pounding drum and bass are playing in the empty hotel rooms, and the sole occupant, chopping chili peppers in the kitchen, at first doesn't hear. It's evening high in the Shinjuku Prince and the sounds of the aircon—*hismistresshismistresshismistress*—and the sandy sighs of sheets of snow washing against the windows are drowned out by the music. The main room is empty but for the desk crusted with books and papers, piled on and around it so the whole thing appears as a ruined building subsiding into the beige carpet. But there are some other things of note: champagne flutes in rows on the coffee table, little aluminum Christian Dior gift boxes piled beside; a huge mirror by the kitchen door; a camera on a tripod by the balcony's sliding doors; four small cameras mounted in the high corners of the room like surround sound speakers; and a large television on a stereo, playing scratched black and white images of bombed-out buildings and bombers passing overhead against a milkwhite sky.

The knocking comes again, and a muted, shouted voice.

"*Simone.* Hey. Haro-oh. Let us in."

There are immense posters lining the walls of the main room like gigantic Easter Island idols: Jeremy Irons as Beverly Mantle in brick-red OR scrubs, goggles and surgical head mirror, from Cronenberg's *Dead Ringers.* Pensive Harrison Ford and vampish Sean Young with curious hair air-brushed on Scott's *Blade Runner.* Waldemar Swierzy's Polish promo poster for *Blow-Up—Powiekszenie:* face upraised Christ-like of a girl shattered into huge pixels of violet, flesh and shadow, rendered by a brush in orderly digital rows, each just off. Every pixel in the poster is big as a hand and close up it looks like nothing at all. A long landscape on the north wall above the large sideboard of an audience peering toward the kitchen in various states of concentration—one man looks to be weeping into his hands, he's so bored. *Paul Newman à l'Actor's Studio, 1955* and he's front and center, his chair is backward, tight white T-shirt, loafered foot up hanging by a heel on the folding chair's edge; he's all arrogance and attentiveness, poised cigarette hanging in the cradle of his dangling hand, looking for what he wants. There seems to be a kind of light on him and no one else. He's as big as he is, or was. Running around the walls from the bedroom door to the bathroom, the bathroom to the kitchen, round past the door to the corridor, around the desk and back to *Dead Ringers* beside the balcony are Lou Reed at the Rainbow Theatre, 1976; *The Nightmare Before Christmas, Metropolis,* a still of Rodin's *John the Baptist,* Gillian Armstrong's face painted silver on a *Details* cover six feet high; a photograph, blown up to immense size, taken at a farewell party for someone no one can remember, of Ariel, Anton, Michael, Jacques, Catherine, Brigit, some others, sitting around a table with pitchers of beer and Gitane cigarettes and no food, arms linked, in some Yurakucho izakaya more than a year ago. Liza Minnelli in *Cabaret,* Bowie peering through sound baffling in *The Man Who Fell To Earth* from the cover of *Station to Station.* The great tripartite woman of Jenny Saville's *Strategy (South Face/Front Face/North Face)* from the Manic Street Preachers'

The Holy Bible. Marlon Brando as Sebastian, aged twenty, a private photo from a production of *Twelfth Night* at the Long Island Sayville Summer Theatre. Bruce Springsteen, thirty-something, arrogant and tense, in a shadowed doorway in *Nebraska*. Giselle. Madonna. Kate Moss for Gucci. Each poster is oversized and framed, and each occupies the same amount of space, apart from the last, a narrow banner hanging vertically J style above the desk, that reads in pale blue kanji:

死彫れい吸

Murmured voices behind the door. Drum and bass and the chopping of chili in the kitchen.

Then the door simply opens and the big man, bald head ivory as a cue ball, wearing a huge beautiful black Giorgio Armani overcoat, the lapels pulled up around his ears, enters, and he simply says, "Well whoops, whatever. How was *I* to know."

Behind him is a tall blond woman in a silver Donna Karan gown under an open fur coat, who enters too, saying nothing.

"Simian!" the big man loudly says. "What the fah." He reaches inside his overcoat for a large cigar. "The place is rocking." Lit and puffing, he dances a little dance, a clumsy pass at a pirouette that comes to an end in front of the kitchen door.

"Simulation!" he shouts over the music, and inside the kitchen the Chinese American boy chopping chili on a butcher's block flinches and steps back, cleaver-holding hand to his heart like someone much older.

"Jesus," he says. "How'd you get in?"

The big man holds up a silver key. "Penthouse floor key is penthouse door key. Duh." He puffs a triumphant ball of thick smoke. "Are we gonna have some proper yuletide fun or what the hell am I doing here."

The Chinese boy gestures to the counters of the beige kitchen with the cleaver. On the butcher's block a heap of diced chili as big as a red fist. On the benches beside it there are tomatoes and capsicums and gnarled knobs of ginger, six or seven lettuces. Lemons and raspberries in punnets, bottles of tonic water and Classic Coke and CC Lemon. Crates of Krüg champagne, squat bottles of Suntory whisky, cases of Asahi Dry.

"There's still some work to do, dude."

"Why don't you have a barman, man. Catering. A waitress or something. Come *on*. I think we've had enough dinner. Eating is *cheating*."

"Hi, Sonja," the Chinese boy says past him. But she stands just inside the main room, smiles a little, doesn't answer, turns away.

"And I don't trust 'em to do it right, is why."

"You've found your niche. Your vocation and calling. You're gonna be a cook."

"What*ever.*"

"Daddy's boy makes good and takes over in the kitchens. The coup comes from within. The sous starts a coup."

"Let a player play."

Anton grins at Simon, staring straight at him, but he's lost interest. "Simon. Where *is* everyone. We took a taxi. They didn't *walk,* did they."

"Coming soon, man," Simon says more irritably now. "Or better be. I told everyone ten." He turns back to the chili.

"Only in theatres," Sonja murmurs to herself out in the main room. It sounds like *only in tearters.*

"What?" says Anton, low and hard, without turning.

"Take your coats off. Make yourself some drinks," says Simon and chops again at the head of another chili with the cleaver, the blade embossed with kanji.

"The magic words," says Anton. "The magic goddam words is what I mean to say." He takes a massive draw on the cigar and sighs out smoke, surveying the kitchen. "What do we got."

"What don't we got," murmurs the boy, professionally scooping out the pith and the seeds, using the blade of the cleaver held horizontal, sliding down the flattened half-tube of the chili.

On the digital videotape playing in the silent empty room is captured the hollow hiss of the wind and the sandy sighs of the snow on the security glass of the windows, but what the video is showing contradicts or only perhaps very abstractly complements the audio: the sighs and hisses sound track bluish flickering flames, photographed close-up. The blue is cartoonish, nearly violet like burning methylated spirit, and slightly out of synch, like the flames have been recolored. It's so very close one squat triangular sputter of flame fills the screen. Ghosting over the surface is a bright doorway framed in darkness; a doorway moving with darker human figures inside. But pulling back, the focus widening, more fat sputtering flames are revealed, dying, igniting, rising higher, sprouting yellow amber-frilled plumes. Flames flickering over a shape now, following a form; the screen's center filled with a white, bubbling collapsed orbicular crater, fringed with singed stumps. Tiny blue flames dash and expire and stay out for long moments; kindle quickly again. Slowly, the crater's crumpled whiteness expands into something semihemispheric, uncrumples into a sphere ringed about and hidden by wrinkled, blistered blackness and follicles sprouting higher scorched tree stumps. Tiny white blisters, bubbling, then translucent, suddenly coalesce from tattered spats of fine material, and shrink quickly, one after another, turning opaque and milky, subsiding into the larger orb. The convex surface like the earth's curvature from space that they vanish into punctuated now by a darker center on the lune, painted over gray. In the ghost doorway the figures move, many of them; their shadow arms reach and take things from shelves. The darker center of the orb is a pupil, depthless black of the void in a pupil. The camera is pulling back and a great curvature of seared pink surrounds the white, emerging from the black stump-strewn landscape, and reaches as the camera retreats, reaches for itself just outside the frame, and meets. The white orb is darkening quickly, to become at the very last instant, pupil expanding like an orgasm, deep chestnut brown coming on around, filled with tears condensing from wept falling steam, quickly, an eye. Finally it disappears behind a seared and twitching lid.

The camera pulls back much faster now, and flaring, quivering nostrils form in the foreground from dry blurred pigpink burn from crumpled black; the flayed long contours of the veined and iron muzzle rising, from black to pink, growing skin, chestnut hair, growing flame. And the eye is blinking, opening again to the burning, rolling in the socket revealing finer lunes of blood-crazed white, and the horse is breathing. The tiny flames licking bluely all over the brow and eyes and muzzle are momentarily dampened down in a redblack rivulet, sizzling and smoking, which creeps quickly back up above the blinking, rolling eye to what the camera now can show is the snapped and sunken blade of a sword embedded high into its forehead, the rippled waves of the gradated steel moving in the heat distortions, as if the blade is alive.

What happens next happens fast: the ghost figures through the doorway move minimally—one kissing another—over the broken blade in the burning horse's brow that suddenly, from an acute angle, gathers to itself in a snap a handle and a hand, which heaves, shifting the horse as if it is shaking its saddened head, and in the constant retreat of the camera is revealed a background now, mud and bloodied snow, brashly recolored, and the sword slides quickly from the horse's head and hand and arm and sword rise up sharply out of sight and the great creature seems to thrash at the loss; bucking behind the kissing ghosts in the door as it lies sidelong on a muddy, snow-streaked road, thrashing, a horse aflame in the gutter, chomping, neck twisting as if at a bad bridling, mane slowly growing, inhaling smoke; and retreating yet further until suddenly the horse slides a yard away down the gutter, leaps obscenely sideways to its feet and starts to gallop back away from the screen, burning, its eyes almost ringed with wild white quickly disappearing, dragging in a trail of fumeblack vapor, a man with a rifle steps into the frame and the burning horse disappears among two burning cars and softly rising snow and tramples crumpled shapes—one springs to life from under its hooves—vanishing into a darkness whirling with snow, inside which the ghost door moves with figures, inside a great arched stone gate that fills and defines the sky.

It's all silent, though it's clear there was a gunshot, the horse was screaming. But though the snow and fire were silent it's all sound-tracked by what's here and now: the sigh and the hiss through the teeth of the sleet, scratching across security glass outside the empty room. The camera is filming some old film on a television. The film reaches some beginning, and then it starts to play again.

They must have taken taxis from the Buddha Trickbar together, because everyone arrives at once: first through the penthouse door is Pras, followed close behind by a curly haired and coffeeskinned girl with striking aqua eyes, Ariel. The Indian boy in a pale linen Agnès B. three-piece suit; he's no sooner inside than he removes the jacket and he's shirtless under the high-buttoned vest, dark arms' full musculature shifting as he unties his scarf. Ariel is in a gold-embroidered fuchsia satin slip by Emanuel Ungaro, an overcoat over her arm, coffeeskin shining, mouth set, chewing on the insides of her cheeks, palpably—arrogantly—nervous. The music is loud and the two split, the boy wandering over to the desk, the girl hovering in the center of the room, feeling in the pockets of her overcoat for something, cigarettes, a keitai.

Next a ragged-haired Shannon steps into the room, sneers and says, "Wow, déjà vu," in an English accent. She immediately starts to take off a coat with designer rips and rough-sewn pictures of Johnny Rotten and the Queen of England on the breast. Underneath, a torn T-shirt and tapering torn Dior jeans, her arms are bare, and there is a tattoo from the base of her left deltoid to above her elbow of the face of a long-haired somber Renaissance Christ, lined beneath with white stripes of self-inflicted scars. Ariel stares a moment too long, before she lights the joint she's found and passes it to her, who, in turn, takes it too casually; overfamiliar with the act of uncomfortable courtesy acted out whenever she shows her scars, too aware of the spirit in which it is given.

"Ta."

And here is Meredith, resplendent, pale as a ghost in an Yves Saint Laurent black bustier dress, that makes a deeply cleaved heart at her breasts, in near-black lipstick, wet-looking hair combed hard back, muscles in her neck and shoulders and the hollows of her collarbones too sharply defined in the penthouse light. She's gotten very thin, but not as thin as the two who enter after her. Drew, who always struggled with the gear and now struggles with food of any kind, is rake thin, the once-Australian garbed in classic NY gear: black 501s and a black T-shirt with TRIUMPH in bright blue, a leather Armani Jeans jacket hanging loosely from coathanger shoulders. He's with Brigit, who's gone very J and seems to have lost weight in sympathy. Her jeans are rolled high, a bright floral Gap shirt visible under a caramel fur-lined suede coat, too much makeup, scarf too high, too tight, too precisely tied. And, at ten o'clock, inside—sunglasses.

Jacques walks quietly in, silent and haggard, his eyes rimmed with bruising, clad entirely in rough military surplus fatigues, half-full bottle of Jack Daniels in his hand. Behind him Catherine emerges from the corridor quietly, tall and still, in Prada beige drill jacket, dress trousers, Prada ribbed white T-shirt, a suede overcoat over her arm.

No one looks at anyone else, the music bangs and they spread slowly through the main room.

Simon stands in the kitchen doorway, wiping his chili-stained hands with a cloth. The music bashing and hammering away. Behind him Anton says, "Sumimasen!" in faux J girl izakaya-style—affected childishness, drawn out; like kids say "good morning" to a teacher—and Simon steps aside and Anton carries through a crate of champagne, over to the coffee table, and everyone in the room turns, and everybody seems to brighten.

"Simon!"

It's Ariel's voice and Simon almost visibly jumps, everything about him subtly firming and affirming.

But all he does is raise his eyebrows.

She takes a drag on the joint and passes it to Shannon again. Simon is wondering suddenly, tingling, why he could never remember that girl's name, and though when he looks straight into Ariel's soft, sad, hazel blue-green eyes in a no-bullshit self-involved face his only thought is the phrase *everything's gone curly* repeating itself again and again, he manages to keep on wiping his hands and lifts his eyebrows and murmurs only, "Yes?"

Ariel's starting to dance. She's bent at the knees just a little, swaying from side to side, a little grind, a shoulder forward and back.

Simon looks away, smiling. Thinking of the way boys always look at Ariel, J boys included, lust and a repulsion composed of amazement, bafflement, self-doubt and confusion. How knowing this doesn't make him any different. Over the others in the room, each in turn. Lets his eyes pan coolly over Jacques standing at the balcony curtains, holding one aside, staring out in the night in his military fatigues with the bottle of Jack Daniels hanging in his other hand.

Finally Ariel loudly sighs, but keeps on dancing.

Simon indulges her, quickly so she won't turn away again.

"Ye-es?"

"Chu-Hai? Anything? Anything but champagne?" She's dancing, looking not in his eyes just in his direction.

"Oh we might have some lemon sours out here, something like that."

"*Ohmigod,*" she says, a full-body near-collapse enacted, like a radical physical sigh of relief. "Brigit, Simon's made lemon sours," she calls out and Brigit, still in sunglasses, turns, calls back in ridiculous J facsimile, "*Oishii,* desu ne!" and heads over and Simon's ridiculously warm when Ariel uses his name, and as she passes by him into the kitchen she lays her hand on his upper arm very lightly, sidles sideways, whole body touching his for a very brief second.

Jacques turns from the window filled with the red aircraft warning lights of the Shinjuku highrises slightly dimmed and refracted into falling pixels on the glass by the drifting snow, and Simon meets his eyes at the same second and there's nothing there, and he turns away and Simon turns into the kitchen with the girls.

Pras is over near Jacques, kneeling by the big television and the stereo, looking through a stack of minidiscs and digital videotapes on the carpet.

He lifts up another Sony digital video camera from beside and behind the cabinet, puts it back down among all the cables. He turns on the television, and the live feed from the cameras in the corners of the room seems to be playing, from shifting angles, what is happening right now. He snorts, seeing what's on the screen, stands, and glances at Anton pouring champagne. Glances at Jacques, and then reaches down and takes the dangling bottle of Jack Daniels from his hand.

He takes a big drink.

"Uh, we are in the jungle," he says, perusing the room. He is visibly excited, yet acting calm; head still, his eyes moving rapidly.

Jacques doesn't say anything, takes a pack of cigarettes from the breast pocket of a sergeant's shirt.

There's a silence filled with music.

Pras says, "You know J girls go overseas and J guys here call them 'yellow cabs,' because anyone can get a ride, but foreign girls here are just the same. It's what it is is a combination of loneliness and extreme freedom. Hey?"

Jacques doesn't reply.

Pras says, "For like, boys, you know, you go out, and you don't go with the first boy that comes at you, you know, but the second, the second..."

No answer, no response at all. Pras looks at Jacques.

"You're gonna go with him."

Nearby, Anton calls out, "Champagne! Everyone!"

"We're no different, here."

He looks Jacques right in the eye, but he's staring at each huge poster in turn, panning around the room like a baby, with dead, new eyes.

"We're no different, right?" Pras says, looking at Jacques for a longer second, very open, then looking away again. "Right?"

Jacques doesn't reply.

"I know this fellow," Anton says to Shannon when he gives her a glass, "who is English, and who is the head Christian priest of Sendai, and who is, literally, twenty-seven, and a total, total atheist."

Shannon's brow furrows at this, and she takes the glass, takes a big drink, and says, "Uh-huh?"

"This fellow," he says, and he's leaning over her, a man almost twice her size and weight, "is a complete atheist from Hayward's Heath, who lives in

Shibuya somewhere, and takes the shinkansen up to Sendai once a month and conducts a Mass and about fifty-eight weddings in a weekend. He gets his photo taken fifty-something times, and then takes the shinkansen back down to Tokyo, where he is a part-time English teacher and atheist. He makes five hundred thousand yen a month for this priest job. For a weekend every month. I think he writes a newsletter too. I mean," he cocks his head sideways, checks Shannon's face, "he's bilingual."

"You import sex toys, right?" Shannon says. "Why are you telling me this?"

"I'm just, you know, I saw your tatt. This fellow's a total liar. A total, total liar and hypocrite and obvious fake, but somehow, it doesn't seem to matter."

"It matters," Shannon says. "I mean, I respect *him* far less than I respect *you,* and I don't respect *you* very much."

But then she's a little guardedly taken aback, because Anton checks her face again for exactly how serious she is, leaned down, big scarred white head almost sideways, and seeing she is completely so, he straightens; surprised and pleased he bursts out laughing, in loud un-self-conscious guffaws.

"No, no," after a while he finally manages to say. "Tell me what you *really* think!"

"Oh, I'm getting ready to," Shannon says.

Drew watches Brigit and Ariel as far as the kitchen door. Lights a cigarette and inhales deeply, does a mental inventory on what he's eaten tonight. Beer at meals he allows himself—a couple anyway—because he still drinks and the weight of beer helps when others are eating around him, helps when at these long and seemingly endless celebrations. He's always the first to light a cigarette when the meal is winding down, remains still littering his plate. But here someone always closely follows him and the J smoke with their meals all the time so it's never that obvious. So at the Trickbar he'd only had some spicy meaty tofu stew, and he'd prised each piece of tofu lightly from the plate, let the stew drip, and slowly chewed each one probably a lot longer than was really necessary. The meat stew stayed, and, true, he'd had one small bread roll, but he hadn't dipped it; wanted to, but didn't. And ordered a gin and tonic straightaway. The Catherine girl had kind of watched him, but that's okay, he doesn't see her enough for anything to be said. It's okay. The Simon boy's been cooking but he won't want or need to eat tonight. There's so much booze. He'll drink instead: lemon sours are good; light and astringent and effective, and the lemon's a good diuretic, and stops you retaining water. Brigit had told him that and she's the queen of lemon sours. They are the King and Queen of lemon sour, and they share everything that's light and astringent and effective, or should he say *all* they share is anything that's—

Drew has just two days left to finish an article on foreigners who've had legal problems with the landlords of their gaijin houses, but he only needs to interview people he knows so it will probably be mostly interviews and pretty much write itself. He's kind of weak, and standing very still because of it. He hears Brigit in the kitchen make a very J high-rising interrogative "eeeeeh?" but in his concentration he doesn't even feel let alone enact a flinch. There's a kind of warm black bloom just off to the side of his vision that he counters or exacerbates with a drag on his cigarette. It's not unpleasant. The beginnings of parties suck. The way he stands when he's very hungry—posture very correct, very erect, almost prissy—prompted a J secretary at *TC* to say to him one day, her eyes all full of desire for popularity and difference and marriage to a foreigner, "You are very Japanese." He was sipping tea, was that all it took? The Dutch guy gives him a glass of champagne. He wonders if Michael will be here tonight; he hasn't seen or heard from him in months, and anyone out of the loop that long is like, such old news, treated as if they've gone home, as if they're no longer real, not even dead, never even were. He doesn't talk much when he's this weak, and shouldn't really be this weak but truth be told even though he only ate the tofu and the one small sweetish bread roll that kind of looked a little sugar-glazed, the stew's sauce was spicy and greasy and thick and it would of looked stupid to scrape the tofu with his hashi because that's something girls do and the scent of the Dolce & Gabbana eau de toilette is rising off his clothes and making him a little queasy because truth be told he did induce in the bathrooms just after dinner waiting for the gin and tonic, and sipping the champagne and smoking and watching the Indian guy talking to Michael's friend dressed like a soldier and who looks a helluva lot like he last remembers Michael looking—

"Funny thing," Anton who's stood beside him looking down at the messy desk says. "But sometimes I dream about . . . well, home, but getting vaguer by the day."

It was kind of shocking to him when he did it the first time, guys just mostly do it from too much booze, but the feeling of inducing is actually like sticking two fingers down the throat of a really warm fresh fish and finding just one gill down there; it's actually kind of sexual feeling (in an anatomical way) and does kind of put you off doing any sexual stuff that's at all similar-feeling because then the feeling's like choking on something sharp and bitter—

"Which," Drew says.

It's something you really do get used to and is no big trauma or drama or even that uncomfortable after four or five times—

"What?" Anton says, confused.

Yeah, with the booze you're feeling pretty good, wide awake, sharp mind, sharply dressed, high as a kite, looking alright and maybe tonight will be good but probably not. Christmas dinner at home would be far, far worse. The future is a long and unfinishable article on something painful to study. And must be written in a language he is yet to learn. He wishes he had a degree. Some Canadian friend of Brigit's once came to stay with them in Shimo and kind of had some experience in this area and she heard through the plastic toilet door and got angry and said to him "You think all this is gonna change?" waving her hand in a vague way, and what he didn't say was that it wasn't "all this" he *wanted* to change, it's the feeling after, the violent hiccups and the bitter taste they bring back up, which is hard unless you feel thin enough, that feeling, because your flesh moves when you hiccup and you can't control the hiccups so you have to control the flesh.

"You, or the dream," Drew says, and sips his champagne. "Getting vaguer, you said."

In the kitchen Simon scoops the mound of chili on the blade of the cleaver, holding it together with the cup of his other hand, and drops it neatly in a clump into a white porcelain bowl. Behind him Ariel dances out of the kitchen with the fresh lemon sour. He turns his head just slightly, glances at the skin of her back revealed by the Ungaro dress, and down, thinking of the white faded crescents on a pair of jeans, then casually glances past her out into the main room. The music shifts note, a slightly longer pause than usual, a minidisc changing in the multiplayer, and in the gap he hears the voices, the penthouse door open, voices, the penthouse door shut, the music rise again, something bright and bass-heavy, something very party. He turns back to the butcher's block and grabs a bulb of ginger, starts to chip away at the bark.

From behind him, Brigit says, "Hate to see her leave. Love to watch her go."

He chops and chips, then turns a little. Brigit's sitting on the counter opposite, jeans cuffed up to her knees, legs crossed, leaning back semi-flamboyantly and sipping on her lemon sour. He turns back again, keeps chopping, thin slices of fine pared ginger. He's leaning forward against the cabinets and he's uncomfortably hard.

"Uh-huh?"

"Don't play *dumb*, boy. Don't play *dumb*—with—*me.*" She giggles, then swears. "Ah! Namenayo, ba-*ka.*" The *ka* drawn out and absurdly authentic-sounding, and Simon turns again and she's spilled her drink and she's dabbing at her suede coat with a dishcloth, head up, peering under her sunglasses like an old woman with bifocals.

"You are mad strange, girl," Simon murmurs, and drops the ginger in with the chili.

"You're a nice-looking young man, and she's a nice-looking young lady. What's the big problem?"

"No big problem. No nothing."

Silence from behind. But the dishcloth flutters down on the counter beside him. He lifts a corner carefully from the bowl of chili and ginger.

"Uh," she says. "If I have to teach anymore, I'm gonna puke."

"You're *teaching?*"

"I know, I know," she sighs. "But like, I was an events producer, working fifty or sixty hours a week for the same money I can make for twenty hours and a couple of judicious privates on the weekend. So why bother?"

"Because it's suicidally boring? Because you want to learn Japanese?"

"Who needs it? How dumb."

Anton enters with a flute of the Krüg and sets it down beside Simon.

"Simon," he says. "Some old guy is here. With a suitcase."

"*Old* guy."

"Old guy."

"Antonio!" Brigit says loudly. "Are you a sweetie and do you have a ciggy?"

"Ah," Anton says, and produces a pack of Seven Stars. "I am, I do."

"Ooh, strong ciggies. Mind if I indulge."

"You are welcome."

"Simon's in love with Ariel."

"Oh *bullshit*," Simon says and turns sharply around, then quiets and turns back to his task.

"*So* sad," Brigit says. "What does it take to get you to admit the truth, man?"

"The drop of a hat, *man*. You're purely crazy."

"I'd go for it," Anton says, gone very serious now. "I'd totally go for it. Why not?"

"Beats me," says Brigit. "She's *fine*."

Simon doesn't indulge them.

"Or is it because..." Anton trails off.

"You're talking a hole in my head," Simon mutters.

"*What*, Antonio," Brigit says, excited.

"Is it because, because, because..."

"What? *Okama*...what?"

"He's in love with someone else?"

"Oh—my—*god*. Who?"

"Okay, who," Simon says. "You're finally starting to interest me."

"In love with someone other than the lovely Ariel."

"Dude, nature abhors a vacuum," Simon says.

Anton's laughing in little exhales at this, like an *uh uh uh*, and Simon checks him, smiling, starting to laugh too, thinking Anton's laughing at what he said, but Anton keeps laughing, falsely, in his little exhalations, at Simon.

"In love with..."

"Yes!" Brigit's drumming her heels on the cabinet doors. "Who!"

"...a little J girl..."

Simon turns again to look at Anton, who doesn't look back, eyes up in some middle distance, looking for a solution.

"Anton."

"...who we double-teamed...in a little karaoke bar..."

Simon's not saying anything, testing response, tense, hand on the cleaver.

"Oh, oh," Brigit says, and stops drumming her heels.

"...just a couple of weeks ago...and who turned out to be some gangsta's babe . . . and we had to totally bust outta there . . . after like, seeing that she'd pissed herself, and having to pour beer everywhere to hide it and then giving each other the signal; you know, let's split, meet you at subway exit *four* . . ."

"Shut the fuck up," Simon says. "Not a chance."

"And that seems to remind me of something you said . . ."

"Anton."

" . . . when you were in love, when she had your dick in her mouth on the bench, right. 'Shut up, baby,' something like that. Real macho, is Simon."

Brigit jumps down to the floor. Past the Seven Star hanging in her lips she says, "Oh, stick it in the outrage file," and then she heads for the main room. "San kyu for za tabako," she says in a high J voice as she disappears.

Simon stares after her, at Anton. He's almost laughing with adrenaline. "You . . . *fucker.*"

"Whoa, put down the cleaver, man," Anton says. "You look like you're gonna hurt someone."

"There are limits, man. There are limits."

"Oh get a sense of humor. What limits?"

Simon shakes his head.

"If you've messed this up, you're gonna pay."

Anton raises his hands like claws and growls like a tiger.

The tape on the TV is playing backward.

Meredith's in the bedroom packing. Her visa's been expired for eight days now, nine when she goes through Immigration tomorrow to meet a flight booked for eight o'clock, and finds out what this will cost her. Her suitcase is open on the big bed, and in between sips of champagne she's laying out all the new things she's bought in her three months in Tokyo—jackets, dresses, skirts, shirts, perfume, MDs, CDs. Emptying the mirrored wardrobe, putting out on the floor and the bed everything she brought here and everything she bought here. The only thing that's not hers that she's taking back is a page with angled pieces of tape in the corners; the purple-inked reminder that he left himself:

Records of rule and of misrule, of the rise and fall of dynasties.
Let he who studies history examine these faithful chronicles,
Till he understands ancient and modern things as if before his eyes.

Who is Meredith now? Three months ago, reading that little reminder
he left himself, she'd seen behind it someone steeped in a knowledge and a
practice entirely foreign, someone inexplicable and familiar only in the
emotions she associated with him, emotions risen in her memories of
him—somewhere else, somewhere safe, somewhere where who he may
have been inside didn't matter. She glimpses something behind that little
stricture now, a dark shape, a bronze face. She glimpses, as she packs her
bags, ready and glad to go—and in this gladness there is a perverse enjoy-
ment of who she's become, of the strength and cool this person manifests—that coming here, she'd feared him. That she feared what she would
find in him in a place where everything is permitted. That she sensed he
wasn't a person who could or would transcend his environment, and so
she feared what she would find him doing, thinking, feeling. And that
reading that little stricture she had attributed to it, and the choice made to
place it there, behind the clothes they wear every day, a rigor, a seriousness, a puritanical drive, a kind of brutal total focus that wanted, or
expected or worse even demanded something that she knew she didn't
have. Reading that note three months ago her brother seemed distorted,
warped, seemed to care too much. Her brother seemed foreign.

Now things have changed.

And though the words that occur to Meredith when she ponders this
last clue, as she tears it from the wall and lays it in the bottom of the
empty suitcase, where the tape's adhesive, dotted with paint and clouded
with dust, still does indeed stick just a little, are words like *naiveté, simplification* and even *lie,* what she's really looking for is *irony.*

Catherine is sitting on the chair by the nightstand on the other side of
the bed, sipping champagne, smoking a cigarette, watching Meredith
pack. They listen to the sounds of the party; the music, the laughing, the
doors opening and closing. They don't talk; someone unspeakable
between them.

Simon comes to the door, looking kind of red in the face, looking kind
of drunk, kind of embarrassed, kind of excited.

"Um, Meredith. Your *father's* here," he says.

Andrew Edward Edwards stands in the doorway of the hotel rooms, and the four Japanese girls and the two Japanese boys, none of them older than twenty, who'd rode up in the elevator with him, the boys silent, the girls trying not to giggle, politely slip between him and the porter with the trolley and his luggage, and they go inside where some of the young foreigners seem to recognize them but who recognize *him* as little as he recognizes *them*, but who are, nevertheless, holding *a Christmas party.*

He stands there completely at a loss, a feeling totally foreign to him, checking faces, turned to briefly stare at him, for his daughter, for his son. He's momentarily distracted by a slim man at the balcony doors dressed in military gear, but that's not him and immediately he doesn't know why he thought it might have been. There are huge *posters* all over the walls, none of them remotely Christmasy. And finally he recognizes a face—Simon Chang—who peers out from the kitchen door then ducks back in. He turns to the porter, murmurs, "Domo, arigato, sumimasen," the sum total of his Japanese to date, holds out a thousand-yen note, and the porter blushes, and forgetting himself holds up his hands in an X for a brief second before remembering his training for foreigners, lets them drop, and says, "Thank you, sir," doesn't take his tip and backs out hurriedly. A tall thickset bald young man comes out of the kitchen, beaming over at him. Andrew suddenly gathers himself, tired and befuddled though he may be, after a twelve-hour flight, four brandies on the plane after he slept, which was after a parliamentary Christmas Eve thing last night, and the long N'EX in, the taxis, the snow and now *this,* and he's about to demand something or at least say something loudly but can't quite find the words, and most in the room have turned back to their conversations now, and the tall bald young man is making his way over to the coffee table under an absolutely huge poster of, of all people it looks like Paul Newman, and but is incredibly still beaming at him, the tall man, a smile like a conspiratorial lover when privacy is finally assured, sidling past a young couple but facing him, not turning away and beaming at him, and continues to do so as he leans a long way down to pour a glass of champagne that looks to be Krüg and then steps directly *over* the coffee table and makes a beeline straight toward him, beaming like his new best friend.

"Ah..." Andrew says.

"Anton de Jongste, Judge Edwards," the young man says. "And a very, very merry Christmas to you." The young man hands him the glass of Krüg, which Andrew automatically takes, then he reaches inside his jacket and produces a fairly handsome-looking cigar, and then a clipper. Andrew sighs, and sees that nothing particularly disastrous is going on, and that this is, in fact, another party, and that he probably should have expected something like this, but unwilling to suspend his indignation just yet, he waits for the young man to clip the cigar. Anton catches the end and a few stray fragments of the tobacco in his hand, and says, "Michael tells me you're partisan to a good Christmas cigar, sir. It's a Montecristo limitada."

Andrew examines the wrapper briefly; checks the room for his son or his daughter, then says, "Anton, was it?"

"Yes sir," the young man says, beaming, holding the cigar toward him with polite familiarity.

"My daughter is somewhere here, I take it?"

"She's just in the bedroom, sir. Celebrating Christmas with a nice glass of champagne."

"I see."

Andrew takes the cigar and the burning lighter in Anton's hand seems to materialize from nowhere.

"Weighing in . . . at one *million* pounds . . . It's Meredith's dad!" I say to everyone. The coke is really good, and I am the body and the soul tonight and if no one else is gonna have fun then I am gonna have some and then they will all just have to steadily catch up as they get jealous. I am no one's tonight so I can be everyone's. The Head feels very light and floaty and open which means my hangover could be a two-day thing, and could metastate into a mega-thing. *That* could be in the cards in this weather, so I will make the most of right this minute, because now at least I am free. Some people give a bit of a pseudo-roar at what I said, but The Judge is being a little bit stand-backish, but again, I can tell he likes a good champagne. I like the way he's dressed and damn if he doesn't look a little bit like Jeremy Irons though not in crimson OR scrubs. The Fag is almost underneath that one over there, The Indian and he not speaking. Don't see The Russian but not looking too hard tonight nowadumsayin? Yay girls joining in, moisties pleased to be here. This is a happening thing I'm starting to see. This is a kind of hip affair. Have I not spoken to *anyone*? Have I not served up drinks to *everyone*? The body and the soul and I am *energized*. Simon may be a transparent hypocritical dickhead but this is gonna be a good party if we can keep it here and I lied about the food. The bitch *can* cook. And I *do* dig the posters, macho gracias Simon Prankster, but the best one is the kanji hanging traditionally, Shiboreisu, the cosmetics manufacturer. I'm glad he's filming this; that one especially is the best joke of all of them; the most true to *my* Japan. A newish company, farmed out of some pharmaceuticals company, Taisho or Tanabe, targeted totally Shibuya/Harajuku, teen to preteen, primary colors, Day-Glo hair dyes, mousse and gel and wax and cool and violent names. It's brilliant and will be huge. Who's not having fun?

The Fag, I guess.

Who's here to make fun?

The Man. I am The Man.

The Man says to The Judge, "Are you a whisky man, sir?" (Heh heh.)

The Judge says, "Well, in fact I prefer a decent brandy, usually."

How would The Fag say it? *Bon viveur cavalier.* "I'll bet you don't bother with any nasty Chivas or Rémy Martin, either."

"Courvoisier," he says, still not sure of me. "I admit I do prefer Courvoisier." He looks at The Man and shaking his head, says, "Do you...?"

"Oh, no, no," says The Man. "Just an amateur. An appreciative amateur who's keen and ready to learn."

Sometimes I listen to myself and I double up inside. Sometimes I listen to myself and inside I turn a hunched somersault, writhe around and do a little bit of a wriggle, flip-flop, wince and throw my arms out wide for your applause. But all you see me do is smile my toothy smile, all you hear is exactly the right words with exactly the cute mispronunciyucktuations you want to hear me make, while I run a mile in a panting painted little figure-eight, shriek and gibber, dance around on every inch of my rubber insides.

I hate myself but I hate he who says I hate myself.

Because he is simple.

You see I love The Man, hate myself and love to play in my own disgust, sealed in a rubber bag of Him. Inside The Big White Man is the red gymnastic demon. The Man who Talks It Like He Walks It and Gets What He Wants. Talk Walk Get Want. Walk Talk Want Get Squirt Wriggle Puke Dribble Piss Plead Dance Dance Dance. Chant and wallow in my rubber bag, lie back and backstroke for a while in a pool bled of backed-up bile, sip a bit sideways and squirt it up like a backward whale spout, watch out, spurts too high, splatter blackly back down on my red face but some black bile lands on that meaty shelf up there and runs down and then the secret dribbles out, when bile drools from The Man's charming mouth. Ha *ha* ha *ha!* Hee hee! Ho ho! Are you like me? *Examine your behavior.* Tonight is gonna be a good night. Merry Xmas, Man. Why thank you Mr. Man, merry Xmas to you.

"Hello love," Andrew says.

"Oh, *Dad,*" Meredith says, and they both stand there and look at one another.

Andrew suddenly abashed somehow, says, "Oh love, you look beautiful."

"Oh Dad," Meredith says and looks down at herself. Andrew steps forward and touches her under her chin, lifts her head with two slim, gnarled fingers, and says, "Hey. Come here," and then he hugs her, wraps his long arms around her and Meredith sighs and lets herself give a little, crumples just a little against him. At another party maybe there might have been cheers, or groans, or murmurs even but here there are just a few turned heads; few here know who this man might be. Fewer care.

They hug for a full quiet minute and the party revolves around.

Andrew murmurs into her hair. Meredith sighs into his chest, color rising back into her face.

He leans back, looking down, neck rumpling brownly up under his narrow chin, and Meredith smiles up at this, the bizarre too-familiar detail in the midst of all foreign detail, that throws it into sharp relief; that seems to demand a choice.

"Merdy," he says, and shaking his head to say no, murmurs, "you haven't...?"

"No, Dad. No." She lets go of him.

He pulls her close again and when she says, "No one knows..." he says, "Alright. It's alright lovey. Don't you worry."

"I'm *sorry.*"

"Shhh," he says. "Come on now. He'll be found when he wants to be found. Just like always. Just like always."

"Is that why you've come?"

"That's right."

"But I fly back tomorrow. My visa."

"I know. That's why I'm here, too."

"You don't know what it's like here."

"It's alright. Let's get you a drink."

He places his palm under her forearm and he leads her to the kitchen where he spotted Simon Chang fleeing back to before.

Catherine loves the feeling of his eyes on her when she's looking away. She misses it; she used to love that beauty of the pure body connection. Talking to others at things like this, looking away. And then the music would start, any pounding bass and she would have to start to move, have to lift her arms above her head and let time fall away from her like scales in a slow and gradual jettison; have to remind herself that it was gone and ease its passing by a trace of her new muscle, remind her fingers of the contour of her arm from high up on her shoulder up the muscle and the modest dip of bicep and through the shallow valley of her elbow's upper flank and up through the fine hairs and bonelike contours of her forearm totally owned and up and up until as if even needing to be free of this her hand would drift from her wrist high up above her head, flit, turn like a bird stalling up in the wind, return to run with it behind. And she would sense more than see him tense, wherever he might be, and begin to move in the same way, mirroring her, and she could both be alone and deep inside the dip in the carved small of his waxen back, see and totally know its flex, though however clothed and far apart. He was the only one with whom she'd ever had that kind of link that ever turned into something real, and she knew it was the same for him. She used to find and keep a total high from knowing where his mind was as he watched or felt her dance, and from knowing where her own was at, though free of any need to do anything but this: move to beats made of static, feel him appreciate her at a level he couldn't control. For all the things she'd ever done to be free, she remembered. For all his torture, he felt it.

They'd never danced together.

The tape playing on the TV is still moving steadily backward.

When Pras takes off his vest and starts to dance shirtless, it's Anton, getting drunker, who shouts out, *I feel like an accidental tourist!*

You know it's a party when Pras gets naked Brigit shouts in Ariel's ear.

Someone says *The boy is too wide.*

They're all not so much dancing as pulsing, in a loose group in the main room watched over by a circle of Western idols and themselves blown-up, Michael among them staring down expressionlessly, red light off the TV's image from a camera momentarily trained on the *Dead Ringers* poster casting his face in bronze. Some still with champagne, Pras with a nobbled little bottle of Suntory shouts to no one *They weren't joking!* some with wine bottles, cigarettes dangling, a joint or two held studiously erect, all pulsing more than dancing, concentrating on the things they drink or smoke.

Simon leaves the bathroom, red in the face, and trips on the base of the mirror that teeters like a too-steep ladder and a J girl plants her hand on it and saves the day, and he gets waylaid by Andrew Edwards who takes him aside into the kitchen where he can hear him speak.

Jacques the only one sitting down now, curled up in the beige leather armchair, sergeant's stripes on his shoulders, army-issue boots on his feet, Jack Daniels almost finished cradled in his lap like a child. His dark eyes gone darker, bloodshot even in the dim as someone's turned the lights way down and what mostly lights the party is fractured flickers from the television screen playing shots alternating from the four cams in the corners, not the camera on the tripod, which got knocked over and is broken but the Sony camcorder Drew is holding in one hand, walking through the dim and filming, boys and girls here lit up only by images of themselves.

Sonja's swearing at a frightened J girl. Shannon's watching, amused.

In Jamaica Ariel shouts at Anton *they don't say appreciate but they say apprecialove cos there shouldn't be any hate, you know?*

Whoa, whoa Anton shouts back. *Really?*

And they don't call a library a library. They call it a truebrary cos it shouldn't have any lies.

That's crazy he says loudly. *Man that's so crazy!*

Simon inter pares! someone shouts.

Do you-all have any drugs Anton? she shouts. *I want drugs* and then she blushes and hides behind the lemon sour, sipping, laughing, shaking her head to get rid of it, still waiting for an answer.

Simon joins the group, moving, dancing, a cigarette in his lips unlit, watching Anton leaning down to Ariel, insinuates himself not quite between them.

Anton immediately leans and lights the cigarette, and Simon takes a drag and then takes it from his mouth when Ariel backs up against him, moving, a little grind leaned into his body, and he leans forward against her, not looking at Anton who is laughing, laughing and Simon is smelling her hair and when he leans back a little to take another drag from his cigarette one curly hair is caught and suspended from his lip, pulled uncurled, and the surprise on his face is enough, and Anton, laughing, doubles over, laughing.

Meredith passes by her dad, standing on the fringes of the dancing group, looking over Michael's desk. She draws the flat of her hand across his back from shoulder diagonally down and then away, just as if to say, *I'm still here.* He looks up, and turns his hung left-hand palm up behind him, and she touches it, tries again to take it in hers, just as if to say, *I'm here,* but he's let his hand drop again, thinking her gone; but then he sees this too, lifts his hand again.

They miss.

She's headed to the door, glass of champagne in her hand, because someone said, *There's someone here.*

Merdy he says over the beats. *What's, this is interesting* as he indicates the calligraphed banner. *I don't know* she says. *It's just Simon's name he's given this party, hold on* and she's heading for the penthouse door that is just ajar.

Outside in the bright white corridor is a youngish plump Japanese boy. He's wearing a backpack and is extraordinarily shocked to see her. He stares for just a second and then drops his eyes guiltily to her feet.

Haroh? Meredith says, almost laughing.

His head snaps up but not his eyes.

Then he bows and mutters something in Japanese.

Meredith says *hey* and she reaches out and touches him under the chin with two fingers. But even though he lifts his head again he cannot lift his eyes.

Mai namu oz on za dor the boy says as if he's saying *zero one two three four. Oh!* Meredith says *I didn't know we had names on the door.*

The boy looks panic-stricken as if he'd not expected an answer, any answer at all. A thing totally unbargained on, he bows, grips his backpack's straps and backs away, muttering *gomen nasai, gomen* and Meredith says, *Hey wait. Do you know… Who? Do you know Michael?*

The boy looks up, suddenly still.

Maikeru.

Hai says Meredith happily.

Hai and almost clicks his heels he's so attentive, and Meredith says *Come on in.*

Kamu on in the boy repeats, and Meredith's turned and going back inside leaving the door wide open so the boy stands a moment staring into the loud dim from the blinding light of the corridor, and then seems to make a huge decision, steps inside and shuts the door.

Inside, Jacques stares black-eyed from the armchair at the new arrival, and then back to the television where no one else has noticed that the tape is playing what's going on here backward.

Meredith, Merdy. I'm going for a little walk.

Are you okay Dad? I'm sorry about this.

It's just a little loud. I'll just take myself for a little walk around outside and tire myself out, you know, cut jetlag off at the pass.

Dad, please wrap up warm. It's so cold out there.

Do you remember Ariel leaning back shouts in Simon's ear *the balcony?*

A moment only and then *of course I remember.* Simon's heartbeat banging into her soft back, feeling breathless close to gasping, though he's not. *I remember.*

Do you . . . wanna go see she says a little quieter and Simon can't quite hear, so a sigh and she just takes his hand and turns and she leads him away from the dancing boys and girls toward the bedroom past and behind Jacques curled up, and Drew, filming, turns to tape them go, and Anton still laughing but alone now, laughing not so hard, turns back to his group of dancers, Shannon, Pras, a J boy and two J girls, Brigit and even Sonja and he sees her and he reaches out and takes her hand and lifts it up and then he lays it flat upon his scar and Sonja looks at him as if to ask him *What is it that you're telling me?* and on the TV the room lights up as the door opens and Andrew walks in taking off his coat and then a pan of blur and dim and kitchen door and mirror reflecting poster and curtained balcony and then Simon leading Ariel from the bedroom.

Shannon comes out of the kitchen whisky straight in hand just in time to see Simon and Ariel enter the darker darkness of the bedroom. She steps aside to let the rotund little J boy with the backpack go inside the kitchen and then her sharp eyes notice something weird happen on the TV. In a strange kind of mirroring effect the framed and lit two figures in the kitchen doorway are played in a weird parallel: the strip of illuminated carpet from the doorway runs straight across to the TV where it occurs again in miniature, running straight back to the image of her. But what was weird was the way the J boy entering the kitchen was played back as an exit on the screen, as if it were an ill-lit mirror. She stands there, and raises an arm but as the silhouetted figure on the screen drops its arm the shot pans away and she notices in the dim beside the TV Drew turn the camera to her. Behind her the J boy is opening cupboards and she sips her whisky and moves through the high and drunken dancing kids and over toward Drew and the TV; steps over the drunk French boy's empty bottle of Jack on the carpet and hunkers down in front of the TV beside Pras, who's seated leaning shirtless and sweating against the cool of the balcony doors' security glass. She opens the cabinet door to the stereo and video.

Beside her, Pras is staring and then slurring just a little he says *You look like a boy.*

Shannon opens the video door, blurred dim images of dancers blurring colors across her face, Drew looming up above her, and she murmurs, *I am a boy.*

Oh I thought so Pras says *I thought so.*

Shannon peers in at the buttons.

You're really hot for a girl Pras says, then, confused, *I mean, a boy.*

She presses *Input Select* and the screen goes blue and the room takes on a cast of indigo all over, and the change is enough for the dancers to call and cry and Shannon smiles a little and turns the volume on the stereo a couple of notches higher and the dancers call and cry again. Pras reaches out and runs his fingers down her shoulder, over her tattoo, ridged with scars beneath that it almost hides, and over the scars under the tattoo it doesn't.

She ignores him, shouts up to Drew, *What are you recording on?*

Huh? he shouts down and he's swaying a little.

What. Are you. Recording. On.

He checks the camera. *I think it's just one of those tapes laying around. No, it's live* he says. *It's live.*

Shannon presses play on the video recorder.

A scratched image of an arched stone gate in near-darkness fills the screen, grayed with falling snow and rising smoke.

Pras says, *I think you're really hot, whatever you are.*

Shannon can see her own Japanese face reflected in the darkened archway of the gate and just behind her, the dim shape of Jacques in the armchair, watching, and behind him the plump and lonely J boy busily emptying his backpack in the bright kitchen.

In the bedroom Simon and Ariel are kissing. She's leaned up against the curtained balcony door; he's against her. They stop a moment, breathing hard, and Ariel says

Do you remember?

I remember Simon says.

We could have only been more obvious if we'd dropped our underthings in the middle of the room and done it in front of the TV.

I know, I know he's laughing softly against her, hands on her hips.

It made me feel real. It made me feel again. I can't feel here.

Simon's hands are under her dress, lifting it up above her hips. She arches off the window to let it free.

Why did you . . . why did you hurt me? she says.

I don't . . . I don't know. You make me feel . . .

You make me feel. But you make me feel bad.

She's gasping lightly and he can't tell if she's crying or turned on.

You do too he says.

She cups his crotch with one sure hand and with her other she pushes his hand down her panties, and he cups her too.

They kiss long and slow and hard and then she hisses, hisses hard and pushes his hand away and when he leans against her she pushes him hard again, hand flat to his heart and between her teeth sucks air in hard and pushes him hard away from her, then cups her hands to herself and turns and says *Oh . . .*

Simon, standing, bewildered, says *What? What?*

Oh god it hurts it and she turns away from him and bends and Simon stands there stupid and then she says *the chili . . . that chili . . .*

In the living room the tape plays the old scratched recolored film of the horse running from the gate and Drew naturally turns and picks up the fallen tripod and removes the broken camera and attaches his camera and begins to film the tape and film all its reflections, too.

Jacques gets up from the armchair, gathers all the Christian Dior gift boxes in his hands and heads toward the kitchen.

Catherine's stopped dancing.

She's sipping a glass of champagne and checking her keitai, the screen's blue lighting up her face violet from beneath, shadows of her hair hanging, casting shadows like trailed tears on her face.

The skymail is from Yu, and reads

WH AR YOU?

She closes her phone and sips the champagne. Meredith standing by Michael's desk past the dancing group is watching her. Catherine puts the phone and the champagne flute down on the coffee table, beckons to her, and turns toward the bedroom.

She enters the familiar darkness of that room, passing Simon emerging red-faced from the bathroom.

And she waits, standing in the darkness where she's stood so many times, dressing in the middle of the night, watching herself in the mirrors of the wardrobe silhouetted against the charcoal light of curtained Tokyo.

Meredith is in the doorway.

She comes closer.

"Catherine?"

"I'm going to go now, Meredith."

There's a soft pause.

Meredith says, "I'm sorry he didn't come."

"That's alright, baby," Catherine says. "Maybe he doesn't want to be found."

"Maybe he'll be happier this way," Meredith says.

"Maybe so," Catherine says.

They stand and examine each other in the dim light.

"You know you two are so similar," Catherine says, crying softly. "So similar."

"No," Meredith says, and she steps forward and touches the girl's cheek.

"Your skin," Catherine says. "Your . . . eyes." She touches Meredith's cheek and they stand, looking over each other's faces in the half-light.

Meredith leans forward and kisses her on the lips.

The kiss lasts for long seconds as each girl examines, no longer the other, but herself.

Catherine smiles when it ends. "You kiss a little like him too."

Meredith smiles a little shyly, a little drunk, a little surprised.

"Good-bye, Meredith," Catherine says. "Good-bye, Michael."

"Good-bye," Meredith says.

She waits for a long time, standing there in the dark room after the girl leaves.

In the kitchen Jacques has found the bayonet from the rifle under Michael's bed, just lying in the cutlery drawer, and he shows Yasu how he can scrape the wet spongy skin from his forearm with the rolled edge of the blade.

In his nervousness, Yasu's forgotten his forceps, so he uses the bayonet to lift each blue shroom in their EAT ME bags and drop each one in its very own gift box.

When Andrew returns around three in the morning, wet with snow, he finds her suitcase packed, no one home, posters staring emptily down.

Stands over his son's desk reading spines of books of law and historical atrocity. He picks up a King James from the stack by the right desk leg, flicks to *James,* and places a purple ink pen inside to mark the passage for him should he ever return.

But if thou judge the law, thou art not a doer of the law, but a judge.

The room is silent, aircon momentarily off, a faint hiss from the television—no, it's the speakers with the volume turned high and nothing playing—and it goes well with the images on the TV, the static seethe of the blank tape.

My son, I'm here he whispers to the empty rooms.

Catherine
March 2001

I have finished my essay.

This will be the first part of something different for me. This will be a first try at looking at worlds differently. I'm sure of it.

It's very, very late. So late up here, and time so very much in flux that lateness is just this feeling deep inside me, some quality in the way I taste things. But my essay is finished, and though it is too short, it is early. I have spell-checked and saved. I have proofread the thing three times this long night. Outside the airplane window eerie silver-white is smeared all over the clouds, but I cannot see the moon. It is behind the plane. It has come to me as I've written that when I arrive at the place I'm going he may not be there, maybe never was there. It has come to me that all his many cruelties and kindnesses have not made me a better person, and have not made me see anything more that was new. Other than what was in him. This course was a sweet thing to do for a person, I think. A sweet thing to do for me. I have a feeling my essay is better, somehow, than I could ever have thought it might be. That simply in the attempt, the thing gained a life I was not responsible for.

My laptop is closed and dead in the overhead compartment. I can attach the essay to an email and send it anytime I want, now. My eyes are tired, but I am not sleepy. The Japanese man beside me has been asleep for over six hours. He has slept his way right into the Pacific. As I typed quietly. I want to take this tiredness wherever I go. I want to take it with me away from old Tokyo, toward the place where I will find he isn't there. It's an empty tiredness, that runs on into something sleep won't remedy. It would be nice to listen to some music now. Some clean, quiet jazz. A drummer who doesn't stray from the high-hat.

Why is it dark? I thought I saw the sun rise. Did I dream it? Why do I feel like Japan has beaten me?

In my lap is still the copy of *Twelfth Night*.

I flick through it, and pull the homemade card from the page he chose, where there is a passage marked.

> And what's her history?
> A blank, my lord. She never told her love,

But let concealment, like a worm i'the bud,
Feed on her damask cheek.

Why? He thinks I am his Viola, when really, I am his Fool. The card is just a folded piece of brown paper, like the paper from a deli sack. It has a photograph on the cover, and a brief message to me inside.

On the front of it is a fuzzy copy of a photo of a young, good-looking GI. His version, I guess, of that long-ago beautiful blue *Le Poissson Dirigeable* with the triple s.

The boy is wading waist-deep in a muddy river, carrying a heavy-looking rocket launcher and a rocket. The river, and the equipment, the tone of the photograph all say Vietnam to me. There are twisted wires in the rocket's base. The launcher is in two pieces, strapped together, and carried over his right shoulder. It looks scratched and well used. The teeth of the zip on the boy's vest are missing in long chunks, and the vest and his T-shirt beneath it are darkened up to the armpits. The hairs on his chest, visible above the T-shirt, are plastered to his tan skin. He'd been in deeper water before this photo was taken.

The look on this boy's face—he's staring right into the camera, his tired eyes nearing a squint; his small mouth slack and just open above the helmet's chin strap, worn just under his lip—the look on his face is something like a blank concern, a vague worry that something hasn't been done right.

"My boots are full of mud," he says to me.

Written on the front of his helmet in childish lettering: *Wilson;* and beneath that, with a space where the writer's pen failed on the seam of his fabric-covered helmet: *Roc kets.*

And inside the card, scrawled in purple ink, the usual cryptic message from Michael. Something desperate. Something unfinished:

Cathy,
    For the tall who feel small

I don't know what the message means, or the card, but I keep it with me, in the book on the page he chose.

I look at it often.

But this time, as I read again, a spider flits across the page.

It waits there. I could blow it off with a breath, but I don't.

I wonder how it got onto the plane.

Acknowledgments

I wish to thank Bill Manhire, Bill Reiss, Jack Shoemaker, Trish Hoard, Heather McLeod, John Thomas, Neil Cross, Steve Braunias, Nick Ascroft, Fergus Barrowman, Jackie Davis, Rachael King, Jennifer Levasseur, Gabe McDonnell, Paula Morris, Susan Pearce, Katie Robinson, Jo Thorpe, Erika Schroll, Andrea Smith, Andrea Spakowski, Deborah Sharkey, Ian Toews, Kenichi Kobayashi, Shinichi Kato, Charles DeWolf, Richard M. Wiley, Carl Patton, Russell Monds, Fiona Wright, Jim Sweeney for patience with rent, Dave "Records" Clark for films, Patrick Evans, The Smaills, The Shukers, and David Foster Wallace